READER'S DIGEST
SELECT EDITIONS

The condensations in this volume
are published with the consent of the authors
and the publishers © 2005 Reader's Digest.

www.readersdigest.co.uk

The Reader's Digest Association Limited
11 Westferry Circus Canary Wharf London E14 4HE

For information as to ownership of
copyright in the material of this book,
and acknowledgments, see last page.

Printed in Germany
ISBN 0 276 44101 X

SELECTED AND CONDENSED
BY READER'S DIGEST

THE READER'S DIGEST ASSOCIATION LIMITED, LONDON

CONTENTS

W ith more than 19 million copies of her novels in print, Tami Hoag is among today's top thriller writers. Her latest best seller, *Kill the Messenger*, is a gripping story set in the mean streets of Los Angeles. When young bike courier Jace Damon agrees to make one final delivery of the day, he gets caught up in a brutal murder. All too soon, events are spiralling out of his control. Not only is he being hunted by the killers, who know that he is a witness, but the police also consider him a prime suspect. As he struggles to avoid the law until he can clear his name, Jace also needs to protect his young brother, Tyler, and their friend and unofficial guardian, Madame Chen.

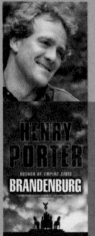

T he fall of the Berlin Wall on November 9, 1989, was one of the most exciting and important events in recent history. Inspired by the drama of that world-changing night, Henry Porter, who has been described as a worthy successor to John le Carré, has written a fascinating and compelling spy novel set in East Germany in the weeks leading up to that historic moment. Dr Rudi Rosenharte, a Dresden art historian and former spy, faces a stark choice when he is set up by British intelligence: to defect to the West, leaving his beloved family to the mercies of the infamous Stasi, the East German secret police, or return to his homeland to carry out a dangerous assignment.

DIGGER

MAX ANDERSON

327

When he was a small boy, Max Anderson was always digging for buried treasure in his grandfather's garden. And so it makes perfect sense that years later he should travel to Australia to spend a year prospecting for gold, and then write a book about his adventures. In Kookynie he rubbed shoulders with a host of unforgettable characters as he learned, the hard way, how to survive in the outback and how to live with the thrills—and crushing disappointments—that are a prospector's lot. There's much in these pages to enjoy, from insights into the history of gold prospecting, to Max's own lively revelations about the obsession that has shaped his life.

Pick up a novel by Robert Goddard and you probably won't be able to put it down until you know where the labyrinthine trail of clues is leading. *Sight Unseen* begins one hot July afternoon with a sudden abduction from the village of Avebury. Everything happens fast: there are few witnesses; the girl, Miranda Hall, is never seen again. The case turns cold until, twenty-three years on, the retired Detective Sharp gets an anonymous letter referring to his failure to find the truth, and composed, bizarrely, from the pages of a rare 18th-century book. Conundrums past and present eventually dovetail, with a startling revelation about a possible claim to the English throne.

SIGHT UNSEEN

ROBERT GODDARD

433

KILL THE
MESSENGER
TAMI HOAG

For Jace Damon,
life is a constant
struggle. By day he
lives on his nerves,
working as a cycle
courier; at night, when
he's not looking after his
younger brother, he's
studying for law exams.

He's just about holding things
together—but what he can't
afford is trouble. Which is
exactly what he gets when
a routine delivery involves
him in murder . . .

1

LA traffic. Rush hour.

Rush hour at four hours and counting. Every Angeleno busting it to get home before the heavens opened up like a bursting bladder and the rains came in a gush. The city had been pressed down beneath the weight of an anvil sky all day. Endless, ominous twilight in the concrete canyons between the downtown skyscrapers. The air heavy with expectation.

Legs pumping. Fingers tight on the handlebars. Eyes on the gap between a Jag and a FedEx truck. Quads burning. Calves like rocks. The taste of exhaust. Eyes stinging behind a pair of swimming goggles. A bag of blueprints in cardboard cylinders riding his back.

The two-way strapped to his thigh barked out bursts of static and the rock-crusted voice of Eta Fitzgerald, the base dispatcher. He didn't know her real name. They called her Eta because that was what they heard out of her all day, every day: *ETA? ETA sixteen? Base to Jace. ETA? What's your twenty, honey?*

He had three minutes to make it to the developer's office on the seventeenth floor of a building that was still blocks away. The guard locked the doors at six on the dot and had no sympathy for anyone standing on the street trying to get in. The guy would have turned his back on his own mother, if he had one, which Jace doubted. He looked like something that had sprouted up out of the ground. A human toadstool.

Shift his weight to the right. Cut around the Jag.

He caught the blast of the Jag's horn as he ran on his pedals to put a few inches between his back wheel and the car's front bumper. Just ahead of him the traffic light had turned yellow, but the FedEx truck was running the intersection. Coming up on the right of the truck, Jace reached out and caught hold above the wheel, letting the truck carry him through the intersection and down the block.

He was a master at riding the blind spot. If the person behind the wheel saw him and didn't want him there, a messenger could become a bug on a windshield in a hurry. The FedEx drivers were usually cool. Simpatico. Messenger to messenger.

The building was in sight. Jace checked over his shoulder, let go of the truck, and dipped right again, cutting across another lane. He angled to jump the kerb behind a Cadillac idling in a red zone. The car's passenger door swung open as the bike went airborne.

Jace turned the wheel hard right and twisted his hips left as the bike came down. The old lady getting out of the car screamed and fell back into the Cadillac. The bike's front tyre hit the sidewalk. Jace held his position as tight as a tick on the back of a dog.

He kept his eyes on his target. He could see the security jerk walking towards the front doors, keys in hand.

Panic. Not at threat of injury, but at threat of being locked out. If the package didn't make it, there would be hell to pay.

He dropped the bike, bolted for the door, tripped himself. Cardboard blueprint tubes shot out of his bag. He stumbled to his feet, trying to scoop up the tubes even as his momentum carried him forward. The security jerk stared at him through the glass, turned the key in the lock, and walked away.

'Hey!' Jace shouted. 'Hey, come on!'

The guard pretended not to hear him.

'Jackass!' Jace shouted. He would have kicked the door, but with his luck the thing would shatter and he'd be hauled off to jail. Not that he couldn't have used the rest and three squares a day. In Jace Damon's life, rest was not an option.

Juggling the cardboard tubes in one arm, Jace yanked his bike up and climbed back on. The entrance to the underground parking garage for the building was on the side street. The gate would be down, but as soon as a car rolled out, he could slip in.

He parked himself to the right of the garage entrance, back just far enough so as not to be noticed by anyone coming up the ramp. He had learned a long time ago to fly below the radar, to be invisible and furtive and resourceful. Survival skills of the street kid.

His radio made a sound like Velcro tearing free. 'Sixteen? You out there? Base to Jace. Base to Jace. Hey, Lone Ranger, where you at? I got Money chewing my ass.'

Money was Eta's word for a customer. The developer was on the phone screaming at her.

'I'm in the elevator,' Jace answered.

A green Chrysler nosed its way out of the garage. Jace shot the bike down the ramp and rode straight to the elevator, jumping off as the doors opened and well-dressed professionals stepped out.

People in suits and offices tended to look at bike messengers with suspicion. They were rebels, road warriors, fringe citizens in strange costumes invading the respectable world of business. Most of the messengers Jace knew had multiple tattoos and more piercings than a colander. They were walking billboards for life on the edge.

Jace made no such statements. He wore what he could get for little or nothing at Goodwill—baggy shorts and sweatshirts with the sleeves cut off, worn over tight bike shorts and a long-sleeved T-shirt. His hair stuck up in spikes through the openings in his helmet. The swimming goggles made him look like an alien.

He pulled the goggles down, rolled the bike into the elevator, and punched 17. He had run twenty-three packages that day and could feel the filth of the city clinging to him like a film.

When he finally got home and could take a shower, the day would come off him like a mud slide and he'd become a blond white kid again. He'd spend a couple of hours with his little brother, Tyler, then hit the books until he fell asleep on them. Too soon it would be five thirty, and another day would begin with him shovelling ice into the coolers at the fish market that they lived over in Chinatown.

My life sucks.

He allowed himself to acknowledge that fact only once in a while. What was the point? He didn't plan on staying where he was. He had a future. Tyler had a future—Jace had made sure of that. And their futures would be a thousand times better than anything life had given them so far. It was only a matter of time, focus and will.

The elevator dinged and the doors pulled open. The developer's office was down the hall on the left. Suite 1701. Major Development. Mr Major Development was standing at the desk, shouting into the phone. He stopped abruptly and slammed the receiver down as Jace walked in with the blue-print tubes.

'Well, it's about time!' Major shouted.

'Sorry,' Jace said, handing over the manifest.

Major snatched it away from him, scribbled a signature, and shoved it back at him. No thanks, no tip, no nothing.

Back out on the street, Jace radioed Eta to confirm delivery. He would make it back to the base office in fifteen and spend half an hour matching his delivery receipts with Eta's floaters—the notes she made assigning jobs to messengers. By seven fifteen he could be standing in the shower.

'Jace to Base. Got POD on Major Pain In The Ass.'

'Ten-four, angel. You'll go to heaven yet.'

'I don't believe in heaven.'

'Darlin', you got to believe in a better world than this.'

'Sure. It's called Malibu. I'm gonna get a house there when I'm rich.'

'And I'll come be your kept woman.'

Eta weighed more than 200 pounds, had three-inch purple fingernails, and a Medusa's head of braids.

'You'll have to get in line behind Claire Danes and Liv Tyler.'

'Honey, I'll eat them skinny white girls for lunch and pick my teeth with their bones.'

'Eta, you're scaring me.'

'That's good. How else can I tell you you got one more run?'

The groan came from the deepest part of his soul. 'No way.'

'Ain't no one else left. You're it, Lone Ranger.'

She gave him the address for both the pick-up and delivery and told him he could use the tip he'd get to buy her a diamond ring.

Jace sat on his bike under the security light beside the garage entrance and stared at the note he'd written with the names and addresses, and he thought of the only tip anyone had ever given him that was of any real value: it's better to be lucky than good.

As he folded the note, it began to rain.

THE TELEVISION was playing across the room as Lenny Lowell prepared the packet for pick-up. His office was an oasis of amber light in an otherwise dark strip of low-end storefronts—a yoga place, a nail salon frequented by hookers, a psychic. Down the block, the bail bonds/cheque-cashing place was open, and further down a 76 gas station lit up the night.

On the TV, a hot brunette was reporting on the latest crime of the century. Jury selection continued for the upcoming trial of actor Rob Cole, accused of the brutal murder of his wife, Tricia.

Lenny watched with one eye, listened with one ear. Only his jealousy was fully committed. Cole had retained the services of Martin Gorman, an attorney whose client list read like a Who's Who of Hollywood's most famous screw-ups. Lenny's client list read like a Who's Who of the Los Angeles Police Department's best-known dirtbags.

Not that Lenny hadn't done well for himself. The world was full of recidivists too flush for a public defender and too stupid to keep from getting caught. Lenny had a thriving practice. And his extracurricular activities of late had netted him a new Cadillac. Still, he had always coveted the spotlight claimed by lawyers like Martin Gorman. He had just never found a way to get there that didn't involve talent and social connections.

A photograph of Tricia Crowne-Cole filled the television screen. She wasn't especially attractive, kind of pudgy with brown hair too long for a woman her age. (She had to be fiftysomething, significantly older than Cole, provided that he was the fortysomething he claimed to be.) She wore glasses that made her look like a spinster librarian. You would've thought the daughter of a bazillionaire would have used some of that money to jazz herself up a little.

It was hard to imagine why anyone would want her dead. She'd devoted her life to overseeing her father's philanthropic trust. There wasn't a disease Norman Crowne wasn't trying to cure, a social cause he didn't champion or an art he didn't support—via Tricia.

It was impossible to imagine how anyone could have killed her so brutally, strangling her, then smashing her face in with a piece of sculpture. But Lenny knew full well what people were capable of.

Word around town was that Tricia, fed up with her husband's infidelities and endless dramas, had been about to dump Rob Cole off the gravy train. Cole had tanked his acting career with sulkiness, stupidity and a shallow store of talent. He had run through all his money and plenty of hers. A lot of it had gone up his nose.

The tailor-made Leonard Lowell client, Lenny lamented. But Rob Cole was Martin Gorman's headache. Lenny had other fish to fry.

The buzzer sounded, announcing the arrival of the messenger.

JACE COULD SEE Lenny coming out of the office and into the dark cubicle occupied in daylight hours by Lowell's secretary. Jace had been to Lowell's office many times. A lot of a messenger's runs were to or from lawyers—much to the displeasure of the messengers. Lawyers were notoriously cheap and impossible to please.

Jace kept to himself the fact that he intended to join the ranks of the loathed someday. Growing up the way he had, he had seen the law work against a lot of people—especially kids. He meant to turn it in his favour—turn his life around and hopefully some others' too. But he was taking only two college courses a semester, so most of his messenger cohorts would be dead or gone by the time he passed the bar.

Lowell pulled the door open, an unnaturally white smile splitting his long, horsey face. Jace could smell bourbon over his cologne.

'Hey, Lenny.' Jace pushed his way inside. 'It's raining, man.'

Lowell waved a big bony hand at him. 'Nah. It never rains in southern California. Unless you're some poor stiff like Rob Cole. Then you get a storm on your head.'

Jace glanced round the office. Next to a bowling trophy, two framed photographs sat on the desk—one of a racehorse in the winner's circle and one of a pretty young woman with long dark hair: Lenny's daughter, Abby. A law student, Lenny had told him.

'Gorman will get him off,' Jace said, picking up the bowling trophy to read the inscription: 2ND PLACE TEAM, HOLLYWOOD BOWL, 1974. It wasn't difficult to picture Lenny in one of those bowling shirts from the fifties, his hair greased back. 'Gorman is good.'

'It's better to be lucky than good, kid,' Lowell returned. 'Martin's betting against the house in a rigged game. Money talks. Remember that.'

'I would if I had any.' Jace put the trophy back.

'Here,' Lowell said, thrusting a twenty at him. 'For your trouble, kid. Don't let it shoot its mouth off all in one place.'

Jace wanted to hold it up to the light.

Lowell snorted. 'It's real.' He raised his glass in a toast to himself. 'To long life. Mine. You want a toot, kid?'

'No, thanks, I don't drink.'

'Designated driver?'

'Something like that.'

Designated adult, as long as he could remember, but he didn't tell

Leonard Lowell. He never told anyone anything about his life.

'Thanks, Lenny. I appreciate it.'

'I know you do, kid. Tell your mother she raised a good one.'

'I will.'

He wouldn't. His mother had been dead six years. He had mostly raised himself, and Tyler too.

Lowell handed him a five-by-seven-inch padded manila envelope. 'You've got the address?'

Jace repeated it from memory.

'Keep it dry,' Lowell said.

'Like my life depends on it.'

FAMOUS LAST WORDS, Jace would think later when he looked back on this night. But he didn't think anything as he slipped the package up under his T-shirt and tucked the shirt and package inside the waistband of his shorts.

He climbed on the bike and started to pedal. One last run.

He would leave his paperwork till morning. Go home, and crawl into that hot shower. He imagined Madame Chen's hot-and-sour soup and clean sheets on the futon and did his best to ignore the cold rain pelting his face.

His mind distracted, he rode on autopilot. Past the 76 station, take a right. Down two blocks, take a left. The side streets were empty, dark. Nobody hung around in this part of town at this time of evening for any good reason. He might have thought it was a strange destination for a package from a lawyer, except that the lawyer was Lenny, and Lenny's clients were low-end career criminals.

He checked address numbers as lighting allowed. The drop would be the first place on the right on the next block. Except that the first place on the right on the next block was a vacant lot.

Jace cruised past, checked the number on the next building, which was dark, save for the security light over the front door.

Apprehension scratched like a fingernail on the back of his neck. He swung around in the street and rode past the vacant lot again.

Headlights flashed on, blinding him for a second.

What the hell kind of drop was this? Drugs? A payoff? Whatever it was, Jace wasn't making it. He was pissed off. Pissed off and scared. Sent to a vacant lot in the dead of night. Screw Lenny Lowell. Jace stood on his pedals and started to go.

The car roared forwards and made straight for him.

For a split second Jace couldn't move. Then he was going, legs pumping like pistons, the bike's tyres slipping on the wet street. If he ran straight, the car would be on him like a cat on a mouse. He turned hard left. The bike's back end skated sideways. He stuck a foot down to keep from falling, pulled the bike back under himself. Then he was charging the car.

Heart in his throat, he twisted right, jumped the kerb back into the vacant lot, shooting past the car—big, dark, domestic. He heard the grind of metal on pavement as the car went off the kerb and bottomed out, then swung a wide, awkward, skidding turn.

Jace made for the alley as hard as he could go, praying it wouldn't dead-end. In the heart of downtown he was like a street rat that knew every crack in a wall that could offer a short cut, escape, shelter, a hiding place. Here he was vulnerable, a rabbit caught in the open. Prey.

The car was coming after him. The predator.

If he could get to the end of the alley before the car turned down it and spotlit him, he had a fifty-fifty shot at ditching it. But it was already too late. The high beams slapped at his back.

His luck was running out faster than the alley was. He couldn't outrun or ditch the car. To his left: buildings shoulder to shoulder. To his right: a chain-link fence crowned with razor wire.

Jace reached back with one hand and jerked his U-lock out of his messenger bag. The bumper kissed his back tyre. He nearly fell onto the hood of the car. Moving as close as he could against the fence, Jace touched his brakes, dropped alongside Predator's bumper.

He swung the heavy U-lock left-handed into the windshield. A spider-web of cracks exploded across the span of glass. The car swerved into him, drove him sideways into the fence. Jace grabbed the chain-link fence with both hands, hanging on hard as the bike was yanked from under him. The toe of his right shoe hung up in the pedal clip, and his body jerked wildly as the car pushed the bike forwards.

The fence bit into his fingers as the bike tried to drag him. It felt like his arms were tearing out of their sockets, like his foot was being wrenched off at the ankle; then suddenly he was free and falling.

He landed on his back, rolled and scrambled to his knees, his eyes on the car as his bike went under the back tyre and died a terrible death.

His only transportation. His livelihood. Gone.

Pain burned through his wrenched ankle as Jace pushed himself to his feet and ran for the buildings before the car could come to a complete stop. He was young; he was fast; he was highly motivated. He set his sights on a half wall blocking the space between two buildings. He would vault over the side and be gone. Bum ankle or no, he could outrun that car.

But he couldn't outrun a bullet.

The shot hit the Dumpster a foot to Jace's left.

Footfalls were coming hard behind him.

The second shot went wide right and hit another Dumpster.

Jace launched himself at the wall and was summarily yanked backwards as his pursuer grabbed hold of the messenger bag he wore strapped across his back.

He fell into the man, and momentum carried them both backwards, their feet tangling. Predator's body cushioned the fall as they went down. Jace scrambled to get his feet under him, to wriggle away. Predator hung tight to the messenger bag.

Jace swung an elbow back, connected hard with some part of the guy's face. A bone cracked loudly. Jace twisted out of the bag's strap and lunged towards the wall again.

Predator grabbed the back of Jace's rain slicker. The cheap poncho tore away like wet tissue. *Over the wall! Over the wall!*

He hit it running, scrambled up and over, rolling through muck and garbage as he landed. He got up, ran out of the alley, racing past the dark buildings, jumping shrubbery. Panting, dizzy, he turned left down the narrow corridor between two buildings. He stopped and fell against the concrete wall, wanting to puke.

Someone's trying to kill me. He was shaking violently, suddenly cold. Pain throbbed in his ankle. He sank down into a squat.

The two-way was still strapped to his thigh. He could try to call Base, but Eta was long gone, home to her kids by now. If he had a cellphone, he could call the cops. But he couldn't afford a cellphone, and he had no faith in the police. He had no real faith in anyone but himself. He never had.

Jace tried to listen for the sounds of pursuit. He tried to think what to do next. Best to stay where he was, out of sight with an escape route. Unless there were two of them, one on either end of the tunnel. He thought of Tyler, who would be wondering where he was.

Not that the kid was sitting alone somewhere, waiting. Tyler was never alone. A brainiac little white kid living in Chinatown and speaking fluent Mandarin stood out. People liked him and were bemused by him at the same time. The Chens treated him like some kind of golden child sent to them for good fortune.

Still, the only true family the Damon brothers had was each other. And that bond with Tyler was the strongest thing Jace had ever known. It was the motivation behind everything he did.

Gotta get out of here.

Footfalls slapped on pavement. Jace couldn't tell from where. The alley? The street? He made himself as small as he could.

A dark figure stopped at the end of the building and stood there, arms slightly out to his sides as he turned one way, then the other.

Jace pressed his hand against the envelope he had tucked inside his shirt. What the hell had Lenny got him into?

The dark figure turned and went back the way he had come. Jace waited until he decided Predator wasn't coming back. Then he crept along the wall and cautiously peered out. He could see a taillight, glowing like an evil red eye some distance down the alley. His bike lay crumpled on the ground somewhere behind the car. Jace hoped the frame wasn't shot. He could fix a lot of damage. If the frame was bent, that was something else.

Jace had inherited the thing, in a manner of speaking. Its previous owner, a guy who called himself King, had lost control dodging street traffic and ended up under the wheels of a garbage truck. The bike had survived. King had not. Messengers were a superstitious bunch. Nobody wanted a dead guy's bike if he died in the line. Jace didn't believe in superstition. He named the bike The Beast.

The car's engine revved, and the taillight disappeared from view. Predator was going home after a hard day of trying to kill people, Jace thought. Chills shook his body.

He went back to where his fallen mount lay, the rear wheel mangled beyond saving. But the frame was still intact. He'd caught a break. Two, considering he was still alive. He looked around for his bag, but it was gone. Taken as a trophy by Predator. Or maybe he thought he'd accomplished his true mission. Someone wanted whatever was in Lowell's packet, held tight against Jace's belly.

Whatever it was, Jace was going to find out. Lenny had a lot to answer for. Jace picked up the bike and started walking.

2

'**D**on't step on his brain,' Kev Parker warned. Kev Parker, forty-three, Detective 2, had been kicked down to one of the lesser divisions to finish out his career in disgrace and oblivion.

Renee Ruiz, his latest trainee, looked down at her stylish beige suede-and-leopard-print shoe. The spike heel was already stuck in a squishy gob that had splattered away from the body.

'Geez, Parker!' she squealed. 'Why didn't you tell me?'

'I just did.'

'I could have ruined my shoe!'

'Yeah? Well, your shoe is the least of your problems. And since you were standing behind a door when they handed out common sense, I'll tell you again: don't wear stiletto heels on the job. You're supposed to be a detective, not a hooker.'

Ruiz narrowed her eyes at him and spat a few words in Spanish.

Parker was unfazed. 'You learn that from your mother?' he asked, his attention going to the body on the floor of the office.

Detective trainee Ruiz stepped wide of the mess to try to get in Parker's face. 'You gotta treat me with respect, Parker.'

'I will,' he said, not even glancing at her. The dead body had his undivided attention. Massive trauma to the head. Whoever killed this guy enjoyed his work. 'When you deserve it,' he added.

Parker had been breaking in new detectives for four years. He didn't have a problem with women. He didn't have a problem with Hispanics. He had a problem with attitude. Parker had been working with Ruiz for a week and already he wanted to strangle her.

'Are you paying attention here?' he said impatiently. 'In case you hadn't noticed, we're at a homicide.'

Ruiz pouted. She was a knockout, with a body that would turn any man with a pulse into a drooling idiot.

'Where's your notebook?' Parker demanded. 'You have to write everything down. What time the call came, who told you what, what time you arrived at the crime scene, position of the body. Every damn thing in sight.

You leave something out and I can guarantee you some dirtbag defence attorney will get you on the stand and ask you about that one seemingly insignificant item, and he'll unravel the DA's case like a cheap sweater. The worst two words in the English language, babe: *reasonable doubt.*'

Ruiz came back with the attitude. 'You're lead. It's your case. Why don't you do the scut work, Parker?'

'I will,' Parker said. 'I'm sure as hell not trusting you to do it right. But you'll do it too, so when the next vic comes and you get the lead, you at least look like you know what you're doing.'

He looked around the room, cluttered with crap and crime-scene geeks. One of the uniforms who had answered the initial call stood by the front door. The other one—older, heavyset and balding—was on the other side of the room. Jimmy Chewalski. Jimmy was good people. Everyone called him Jimmy Chew.

Parker went over to Chewalski. 'Jimmy, where's the coroner's investigator?' he asked. No one could so much as check the dead body's pockets until the CI had finished his or her business.

'Could be a while,' Jimmy Chewalski said. 'She's helping out at a murder-suicide.'

'Nicholson?'

'Yeah.'

Parker looked at the body again. 'So what's the story here?'

Chew rolled his eyes. 'Well, Kev, we have here dead on the floor an un-lamented scum-sucking member of the bar.'

'Now, Jimmy, just because a man was soulless and amoral doesn't mean he deserved to be murdered,' Parker said.

'Excuse me? Who's in charge here?'

Parker turned to see a pretty twentysomething brunette in a smart trench coat standing three feet away, near the hall to the back door.

'That would be me. Detective Parker. And you are?'

Unsmiling, she looked directly at him with steady dark eyes, then at Officer Chewalski. 'Abby Lowell. The scum-sucking member of the bar lying dead on the floor is my father. Leonard Lowell.'

Jimmy Chew made a sound like he had been impaled with something. Parker took it on the chin with just a hint of a flinch around his eyes. He pulled his hat off and offered his hand to Abby Lowell. She looked at it like she figured he never washed.

'My condolences for your loss, Ms Lowell,' Parker said. 'I'm sorry you heard that.'

She arched a perfect brow. 'But not sorry you said it?'

'It wasn't personal. I'm sure it's no surprise to you how cops feel about defence attorneys.'

'It's not,' she said. Her withering gaze never wavered. She had yet to look at her father's body. 'I'm in law school myself. Just so you can get a head start coming up with new and different derogatory ways to describe me.'

'I can assure you, we treat every homicide the same, Ms Lowell. Regardless of who or what the victim was.'

'That doesn't instil much confidence, Detective.'

'There's not a homicide cop in this town better than me,' Parker said.

'Then why aren't you working with us, Parker?'

Bradley Kyle, Detective 2 with Robbery-Homicide—LAPD's glamour squad, bastion of hotshots. Parker knew this first-hand because he had once been one of them, and a more arrogant, hotshot jerk had never walked the halls of Parker Center. In those days, he had been fond of saying the building had been named for him. Stardom was his destiny. The memory bubbled up inside him now, burning and bitter.

Parker scowled at Kyle, moving towards him. 'What is this? A party? And how did your name get on the guest list, Bradley?'

Kyle ignored him and started looking around the crime scene. His partner, Moose Roddick, a big guy with no neck, a flat-top haircut and horn-rimmed glasses, spoke to no one as he made notes. Parker watched them for a moment, a bad feeling coiling in his gut. Robbery-Homicide didn't just show up at a murder out of curiosity. They worked the high-profile cases, like O.J., like Rob Cole, LA's celebrity killer *du jour*.

'Don't piss on my crime scene, Kyle,' Parker warned.

Kyle glanced at him. 'Who says it's yours?'

'My beat, my call, my murder,' Parker said.

Kyle ignored him and squatted down to look at the apparent murder weapon—an old bowling trophy, now encrusted in blood.

Kyle had been on his way up in Robbery-Homicide while Parker was being driven out. Kyle was at the top of his game now, eating up the spotlight every time he got the chance, which was often.

He was a good-looking guy, good face for television, a tan so perfect it had to have been airbrushed on him. He had an athletic build, but he was on the slight side and touchy about it. Parker, who was himself a hair under six feet, figured Kyle for five nine and not a fraction more.

Parker squatted down beside him. 'What are you doing here?' he asked quietly. 'What's Robbery-Homicide doing cruising the murder of a low-rent mouthpiece like Lenny Lowell?'

'We go where they send us. Isn't that right, Moosie?' Kyle tossed a look at his partner. Moose grunted and kept making notes.

'What are you saying?' Parker asked. 'Are you saying you're taking this? Why? It won't even make the paper.'

Kyle pretended not to have heard him, and stood up. Ruiz stood a scant few inches away from him in her ridiculous heels.

'Detective Kyle,' she purred in a hot phone-sex voice as she offered her hand. 'Detective Renee Ruiz. I want your job.'

Parker stood up and gave a dead-eye stare to his partner. '*Trainee* Ruiz, have you finished diagramming the crime scene?'

She huffed a petulant sigh at Parker, then tossed a sexy look at Kyle and walked away.

'Forget it, Kyle,' Parker said. 'She'd grind you up like lunch meat. Besides, she's too tall for you.'

'Excuse me, gentlemen.' Abby Lowell joined them. 'If I might intrude on your little game of who is the biggest jerk—' She offered her hand to Kyle, all business. 'Abby Lowell. The victim is—was—my father.'

'I'm sorry for your loss, Ms Lowell.'

'You're with Robbery-Homicide,' she said. 'I recognise you from the news.'

'Yes.' Kyle looked pleased.

Parker expected Abby Lowell to say, 'Thank God you're here.' Instead, she looked Kyle in the eye and said, 'Why are you here?'

Kyle gave her a poker face. 'Excuse me?'

'Come on, Detective. I've been around my father's business all my life. His clients should be way below your radar. What do you think happened here? Do you know something I don't?'

'A man was murdered. We're homicide cops. Do you know something *I* don't? What do *you* think happened here?'

Abby Lowell took in the mess as if seeing it for the first time: the files and paperwork everywhere, the overturned chair, maybe from a struggle, maybe from a ransacking after the murder.

Parker watched her carefully. She kept her arms crossed tight, holding herself, keeping her hands from shaking.

'I don't know,' she said softly. 'A disgruntled client? Maybe someone wanted something here Lenny didn't want to give up.'

Her gaze landed on a credenza at the far side of her father's desk. A cube-shaped black safe squatted in the cabinet, the door open. 'He kept cash in that safe.'

'Did you check the safe, Parker?' Kyle asked.

Parker turned to Jimmy Chew. 'Jimmy, did you look in that safe when you got here?'

'Why, yes, Detective Parker, I did,' Chew said with false formality. He didn't so much as glance at Kyle. 'When my partner and I arrived at nineteen hundred hours, we secured the scene and called in Homicide. While looking around the office, my partner observed the safe was open and that it appeared to contain only documents.'

'No cash?' Parker asked.

'No, sir. No money. Not in plain sight anyway.'

'I know there was money,' Abby Lowell said with an edge in her voice. 'He never had less than five thousand dollars in that safe.'

'Was your father having problems with any clients?' Kyle asked.

'He didn't talk to me about his clients, Detective Kyle. Even scum-sucking dirtbag attorneys have their ethics.'

'I didn't mean to imply otherwise, Ms Lowell. But we'll need to see his client records,' Kyle said.

'Sure. As soon as someone rewrites the Constitution,' Abby Lowell returned. 'That information is privileged.'

'A list of his clients, then.'

'I'm a student, not stupid. Unless a judge tells me I have to, you get nothing confidential out of this office.'

Colour began to creep upwards from Kyle's starched white collar. 'Do you want us to solve your father's murder, Ms Lowell?'

'Of course I want it solved,' she snapped. 'But I also know that I now have to look out for the best interest of his practice, Detective Kyle. This has to be done by the book.'

'You don't need to compromise yourself, Ms Lowell. Names and addresses aren't privileged,' Parker said calmly, pulling her attention away from Kyle. 'And it's not necessary for us to access your father's files. The criminal records of his clients are readily available. When was the last time you spoke with your father?'

He saw more value in trying to get Abby Lowell on his side than in bullying her into an adversarial position.

She rubbed a slightly trembling manicured hand across her forehead. 'I spoke with Lenny around six thirty. We were supposed to meet for dinner at Cicada. I got there early, had a drink, called him on my cellphone. He said he might be a little late.' She blinked the tears back. 'He said he was waiting for a bike messenger to pick something up.'

'Did he say what?'

'No.'

'Do you know what service he used?'

'Whichever was the fastest and the cheapest.'

Parker said, 'Do you know if the messenger ever arrived?'

'No. I told you, when I last spoke with Lenny, he was waiting.'

Parker glanced over at the safe, frowning. Bike messengers tended to be loners, living a hand-to-mouth existence. It wasn't a stretch to imagine one of them was hopped up on something.

So some down-on-his-luck junkie messenger shows up for a package, gets a look in Lowell's open safe, kills Lowell, takes the money, and vanishes into the night.

'Who called nine-one-one?' he asked, turning again to Chew.

'The ever-popular anonymous citizen.'

'Anything around here open or inhabited?'

'Not on a night like this. There's a Seventy-Six station and a bail-bonds place down the street, on the other side.'

Parker turned back to Abby Lowell. 'How were you notified of your father's death, Ms Lowell?'

She looked at him like she thought he might be pulling something on her. 'One of the officers called.'

Parker looked at Chew, who held up his hands in denial, then looked at Chew's partner, who shook his head.

'Someone called you. On your cellphone,' Parker said.

'Yes. Why?'

'What did the caller say to you?'

'That my father had been killed, and could I come to his office. Why?'

'May I see your cellphone?'

'I don't understand,' she said, pulling it out of a coat pocket.

'LAPD wouldn't tell you something like that over the phone, Ms Lowell,' Parker said.

Her eyes widened as the implication sank in. 'Are you telling me I was on the phone with my father's killer?'

'What time did you get the call?'

'Maybe twenty minutes ago. I was at the restaurant.'

'Do you have a call list on that thing?' Parker asked, nodding towards the phone she clutched in her hand.

'Yes.' She brought up the screen that listed calls received. 'I don't recognise the number.'

Parker held his hand out. 'May I?'

He checked the number, hit the button to call it back, then listened as it rang unanswered.

'Oh my God,' Lenny Lowell's daughter breathed. She pressed a hand to her lips and blinked away the gathering tears.

Parker turned back to Chew. 'I want to know if there was a single living being in proximity of this office between six thirty and seven fifteen.'

'Roger that, Boss.' Chew flipped Kyle's smirk back at him as he went to speak to his partner.

Parker went to the vic's desk. The Rolodex was closed. He flipped the cover up with a pen, then turned to a Latent Prints tech who was working nearby. 'Cynthia, I want every print you can lift off this thing.'

'Go ahead and cover the bases for us, Parker,' Kyle said tightly as he joined Parker behind the desk. 'But don't get too cosy. If the word comes down from the mountain, you're out.'

Parker stared at him; then a new voice called from the front door. 'Parker, please tell me your DB had a heart attack. I need a nice simple "natural causes" so I can go home. It's raining.'

Diane Nicholson, coroner's investigator for the County of Los Angeles, forty-two, and a long cool drink of gin to look at. She took no prisoners, an attitude that had earned her the fear and respect of cops all over the city. No one messed with a Nicholson crime scene.

She stepped just inside Lowell's private office and looked down at Lenny. 'Oh, damn.' She looked at Parker with flat eyes, then looked at Kyle and seemed offended at the sight of him.

'Parker is the detective of record,' she said. 'Until I hear differently from someone more important than you, Kyle, I talk to Parker.' She didn't wait for a response. She pulled on a pair of latex gloves and knelt down to begin her examination of the body.

Lenny Lowell's trouser pockets yielded forty-three cents, a Chiclet, and a laminated, dog-eared ticket from a horse race at Santa Anita.

'He carried it for luck.' The voice that had been so forceful earlier was now barely audible. Parker looked at Abby Lowell, watched her eyes fill again as she stared at the small piece of red card in Nicholson's hand. She didn't try to blink the tears back this time.

He touched her arm gently. 'Is there a friend you can stay with, Ms Lowell? I'll have an officer drive you. We'll set up a time for you to come into the station and talk more about your father.'

Abby Lowell jerked her arm away. 'Don't pretend concern for me, Detective,' she said bitterly. 'I'll drive myself home.'

No one said anything as she walked away and hurried down the hall and out through the back door.

Nicholson broke the silence, slipping Lenny Lowell's good-luck charm into an envelope in case it might turn out to be relevant. 'He should have cashed it in while he had the chance.'

JACE WORKED HIS WAY back to Lenny Lowell's neighbourhood, his heart racing every time a car crossed his field of vision. He had no way of knowing where Predator had gone.

It seemed to take forever to walk back to familiar territory. He tried to balance his bike up on its good front wheel and at the same time balance his own weight against it like a crutch. His wrenched ankle was throbbing.

He came to the 76 station from the alley, propped The Beast up against the back wall of the building, then peered towards the island of light surrounding the gas pumps. No one was buying gas.

His stomach rumbled and started to cramp. Lenny Lowell's twenty-dollar tip was in his pocket. He could buy himself a soda and a chocolate bar.

An overhang along the front of the booth offered shelter from the rain. A thin, dark guy in an orange turban sat inside behind the bulletproof glass. He started at Jace's sudden appearance, grabbed his microphone and said, 'The police are down the block.'

As if he had called them in anticipation of being robbed.

'I'm not robbing you. I just want a Snickers and a Mountain Dew,' Jace said. From the corner of his eye, he caught the watery red intermittent flash of a police strobe down the street, and his pulse kicked up a beat. 'What's going on down there?'

'A murder,' the clerk said. 'I listen to the scanner.'

Jace felt the blood rush out of his head. 'Who?'

'They call no names, only codes,' the clerk said. 'Codes and the address.' He repeated the address aloud.

Lenny Lowell's address.

Jace wondered if the attorney had been murdered before or after Predator had tried to turn him into roadkill. Could have gone either way, he thought, if what the killer was after was the package tucked inside the waistband of Jace's trousers.

An LAPD black-and-white crawled up the street. Jace quelled the urge to run. His hands were shaking as he removed his junk-food dinner from the pay tray. He stuffed the chocolate bar in his pocket, opened the soda.

The patrol car took a right at the corner. Jace watched them go as he chugged his Mountain Dew. Then he threw a 'See you' to the clerk and walked away as if he didn't have a care in the world.

Five blocks later, his knees were still shaking.

3

'What a creep.'

Parker walked into the bedroom, naked, with a glass of wine in each hand. He had hardly touched the hard stuff since about two months after he had been sent down from Robbery-Homicide. In those two months, he had downed enough booze to float a boat. Then he woke up one day and took up Tai chi instead.

'Was it something I said?'

The woman in bed didn't take her eyes off the television. Her face was sour with disgust. 'Rob Cole, that piece of dirt. I hope he gets the needle.'

'That's what I like about you, Diane. Overflowing with the milk of human kindness,' Parker said. He handed her a glass, set his on the night table and slipped between the covers.

He and Diane Nicholson had what they both considered to be the perfect relationship. They liked each other, were animals in bed, and neither had any interest in being anything other than friends.

Parker, because he didn't see the point in marriage. His parents had been engaged in a cold war for forty-five years. Most of the cops he knew had been divorced at least once. He himself had never had a romantic relationship that hadn't crashed and burned, primarily because of his job.

Diane had her own reasons, none of which she had ever confided in him. He knew she had been married to a Crowne Enterprises executive who had died of a heart attack a few years past. But when she spoke of him, which was hardly ever, she talked about him without emotion. Not the great love of her life.

Whoever had put her off the idea of everlasting love had come after the marriage. Parker had nosed around for an answer when they had first got involved, almost a year before. But no one knew who Diane had been seeing after her husband's death, only that she'd been seeing someone and things had ended badly.

Parker figured she was entitled to her secrets.

He liked having his secrets too. He had always figured the less anyone knew about him, the better. No one at LAPD needed to know who he saw or what he did with his time off the job.

Diane scoffed at his milk-of-human-kindness line. 'This guy deserves an acid bath.' She had worked the Cole murder scene more than a year ago.

They were watching CNN. It was late, but it always took a while to wind down after a murder. Uniforms had knocked on doors within viewing distance of Lowell's office, but the shops were empty for the night. Parker had locked down the scene, gone to the station to start his paperwork. From there he had gone to Diane's Craftsman bungalow on the west side.

The story running was about jury selection for Cole's forthcoming trial and a recap of the whole sickening mess—from the discovery of Tricia Crowne-Cole's body; the funeral with Norman Crowne sobbing on his daughter's closed casket, his son leaning over his shoulder; all the way back to her wedding to Rob Cole.

'I met him at a party once, you know,' she said.

'The memory is as vivid as if I had been there myself,' Parker remarked drily. Diane must have told him the story a hundred times since the murder. 'He hit on you.'

'With his wife standing not ten feet away,' she said with disgust.

Parker slid his arm around her. She sighed softly as she let her head fall against his shoulder.

Parker's attention was on the file footage of Cole being brought into Parker Center by a posse of Robbery-Homicide hotshots, Bradley Kyle among the pack. Cole, red-faced with anger; the Robbery-Homicide boys stone-faced in suits and ties, shades hiding their eyes. Everyone costumed and playing his part to the hilt.

'Why were Kyle and Moose there tonight?' Diane asked. 'You think the dead guy was connected to something big and juicy?'

'The Lenny Lowells of the world can't hook on to something big and juicy even if they trip and fall in it.'

'He tripped and fell in something. And it killed him. Something smelly enough for the Parker Center boys to come sniffing.'

'It's my case until my captain tells me it's not,' Parker said. 'Then I'll walk away.'

Diane laughed, a throaty, sexy sound. 'You liar. You wanted to run Bradley out of there like a tiger protecting its kill.'

'Well, I *do* hate the guy.'

'You're entitled. He's a prick. I hate the guy too,' she said. 'But that's all beside the point. I just don't get what RHD would want with the murder of a bottom-feeder like that lawyer.'

'I don't know,' Parker said. 'But I'll find out. Crack of dawn, I'm finding that bike messenger.'

THE CHINATOWN of LA was the first modern American Chinatown owned and planned by the Chinese themselves, home now to more than 15,000 people of Asian heritage. In recent years it has begun to attract artists and young professionals of all races, becoming a hip place to live.

Jace had moved himself and Tyler to Chinatown after their mother died. They had dumped their meagre possessions in a couple of laundry bags and jumped on a bus to a place no one would ever come looking for them.

Alicia Damon had died as a Jane Doe in Good Samaritan Hospital. Jace knew this because he had taken her to the emergency room himself. His mother had not given the admissions clerk her name or address. She had not allowed Jace to appear to be with her.

Alicia had trusted no one in any position of authority, her greatest fear being Children and Family Services, who had the power to take her sons away. What mail the Damons got came to a rented box, never to whatever crappy apartment they were living in at the time. They had no phone. Jace had been registered at school under the name John Jameson. They lived on what money Alicia could make at menial jobs that paid cash and on a monthly Social Security cheque made out to Allison Jennings.

They had no family friends. Jace had never met his father. When he was younger, he had asked why, but he had stopped asking by the time he was six, because it upset his mother so much.

He had an idea Tyler's dad might be a bartender from a dive his mother had worked at briefly. Twice he'd seen them kissing. Then suddenly the Damons moved to another part of the city. Some months later, Tyler was born. Jace never saw the bartender again.

Whenever Jace had asked for an explanation about the way they lived, Alicia would only reply: 'You can't be too careful.'

Jace had taken her at her word. After her death, he had made no claim on his mother's body, because people would ask questions. He had been just thirteen and knew without having to be told that Children and Family Services would swoop in like hawks, and he and Tyler would be put into foster care.

With stubby candles from the Catholic church three blocks from their apartment and wilted flowers from a Korean market, Jace and Tyler had made their own memorial to their mother. The centrepiece: a photograph of Alicia, taken in better times.

Jace had given a short eulogy; then he and Tyler had each named the qualities about their mother they had loved most. They had said their good-byes and put out the candles. Jace had held his little brother tight, and both of them had cried, Jace as silently as he could because he was all they had now, and he had to be strong.

The next day Jace had gone looking for another place for them to live. He had set his sights on Chinatown for a number of reasons. One, because he wanted Tyler to grow up in a place where he didn't have to worry some junkie would beat his head in for a nickel. Two, because the community was so eclectic, no one would think them out of place. And three, because he figured if he could get them in among the Chinese, he wouldn't have to worry someone would rat them out to Children and Family Services. The Chinese ran their community their own way, discouraging intrusion from the outside world. The difficulty would be in getting accepted.

Jace had gone up and down the streets looking for a menial job, being turned down again and again. He had been ready to give up, when Tyler had dragged him into a fish market to look at the live catfish in the tank in the front window. Typical Tyler, he had gone right up to the person who looked most likely to have answers and proceeded to ask half a million questions about the catfish—where had they come from, how old were they, what kind were they, were they boys or girls.

The person he had chosen to ask was a tiny Chinese woman with the bearing of a queen, nicely dressed, dark hair in a bun. She was fiftysomething, and looked as if she could have balanced a glass of champagne on her head and walked without spilling a drop.

She listened to Tyler's questions, then patiently answered each one. Tyler soaked up the information like a sponge. He looked up at the woman with wide-eyed wonder, and the woman's heart melted.

Tyler had that sort of effect on people. An old soul, Madame Chen called him. She had fed them dinner in the small restaurant next door, where everyone jumped to please her as she snapped at them in Chinese.

She had quizzed Jace about their background. He had been vague about most of it but had told her about their mother's death and that they had no relatives. He had admitted that they were afraid of being put into foster care, separated, possibly never to see each other again.

Madame Chen had weighed these matters as she sipped tea. She was silent for so long, Jace was certain she was going to tell them to get lost. But when she spoke, she said: 'Family is everything.'

The line reverberated now in Jace's head as he limped down the back alleys of Chinatown in the dead of night. In the best of times he felt detached from most of the world. He relied on no one, confided in no one, expected nothing from anyone. He had been raised not to trust.

But he liked the Chens and was deeply grateful to them.

He had managed to get back to Chinatown without arousing the suspicions of anyone. But tomorrow the cops would be making the rounds of the messenger agencies. He would become the centre of everyone's suspicions then. For all Jace knew, his would-be killer would be making those same rounds, trying to get to the package that was still pressed against his belly.

Whoever was looking would have a hard time finding him. The address he had put on his job application at Speed wasn't where he and Tyler lived.

He was paid in cash under the table—not an uncommon practice in the messenger game. Getting paid in cash meant none of his money went to the government; therefore, the government didn't know he existed.

No one could track him through utility bills, because he paid the Chens in cash for power and for the cable feed to the television in the apartment. Rent was traded for work shovelling ice for the cases in the fish market.

Even knowing how difficult it would be for anyone to find him, Jace felt nervous about going home. Despite the fact that he hadn't run into the cops or seen Predator's car again, he couldn't escape the feeling that someone was watching him. Or maybe it was just the onset of hypothermia making him shake as he opened the back door of the fish market and climbed the stairs to the tiny apartment.

Jace took a deep breath, exhaled and let himself into the apartment. The only light came from the television in the corner of the room, splashing colours over the two bodies on the futon: Tyler, sprawled, head and one arm hanging over the edge of the cushion; and the old man Tyler called Grandfather Chen, the ancient father of Madame Chen's deceased husband. Grandfather Chen sat upright on the futon, his head back, his mouth open.

Tyler didn't stir. Grandfather Chen jerked awake.

'It's OK. It's only me,' Jace whispered.

The old man scowled at Jace, scolding him in Chinese, a language Jace had not managed to master in six years of living in Chinatown. But he didn't have to understand Grandfather Chen to understand that it was very late and Tyler had been worried about him.

Jace held his hands up in surrender. 'I'm sorry.'

Grandfather Chen didn't even take a breath. Outraged, he held his thumb and pinkie up to the side of his head and pantomimed talking on the phone.

'I tried to call,' Jace said. He mimicked talking on the phone and made the busy signal.

Tyler woke then, rubbing his eyes. 'You're really late.'

'I'm sorry, buddy. I tried to call. The line was busy.'

'Grandfather Chen was on his computer, looking at Chinese girly sites.'

Jace cut a look of disapproval at the old man. 'I don't want you looking at porn sites,' Jace said to his brother.

Tyler rolled his eyes. 'They weren't naked or anything. He's shopping for a mail-order bride.'

'He's a hundred and twelve. What does he want with a mail-order bride?'

'He's ninety-seven,' Tyler corrected him. He looked up at the old man and rattled off something in Chinese. Grandfather Chen replied, and they both laughed.

The old man ruffled Tyler's hair fondly, then rocked himself off the futon. He was Jace's height, his posture straight as a rail, his body thin. He squinted at Jace's face, frowning. He pointed to the bruises and said something in a voice too soft for Tyler to hear. Concern, Jace thought. Worry. Grandfather Chen figured rightly that whatever had caused Jace to be so late wasn't anything good.

The old man said good night to Tyler and left.

Tyler turned on the table lamp and soberly studied his big brother. 'What happened to your face?'

'I had an accident,' he said. He lowered himself onto a stool and took his boots off. The ankle was throbbing.

'What kind of accident? I want to know exactly.'

'I fell. That's all,' Jace said, dodging Tyler's stare. 'Got doored by an old lady in a Cadillac, twisted my ankle and got some scrapes. Bent a wheel on The Beast and had to walk it home.'

'I thought you weren't coming back. Ever.'

Jace moved to the futon and sank down beside the boy. 'I'll always come back, pal. Just for you.'

'That's what Mom used to say too,' Tyler reminded Jace. 'And it wasn't true. Stuff happens that a person can't do anything about. It's karma.'

He recited from memory what he had read in the dictionary he studied every evening: 'Karma is the force generated by a person's actions to per-pet-u-ate transmigration, and in its ethical consequences to determine his destiny in his next existence.'

Jace wanted to say that there was no meaning in anything, and there was no 'next existence'. But he knew it was important to Tyler to believe in something, to search for logic in an illogical world.

He pulled the boy close and gave him a fierce hug. At ten, Tyler had reached the age where he was starting to think a real man didn't need hugs, and the fact that he still needed them was embarrassing. But he gave in to that need and pressed his ear against Jace's chest to listen to his heartbeat.

Jace held his brother close for a moment. In the morning he would have to explain some things, but he wouldn't do it now. Now all he wanted was a hot shower and some sleep.

After Tyler had gone to bed, Jace went into their tiny bathroom and squinted at himself in the mirror. He looked pretty bad. He carefully worked his way out of his wet sweatshirt and T-shirt. There was hardly a body part that wasn't aching.

Lenny Lowell's package was still tucked inside the waistband of his tight bike shorts. Jace pulled the padded envelope free, stared at it. In normal circumstances he would never open a client's package.

He picked at the envelope flap and tore it open.

Sandwiched between two pieces of cardboard was a waxy envelope of photographic negatives. Jace held a strip of them up to the light. Two people exchanging something or shaking hands.

Blackmail. And I'm in the middle of it.

With nowhere to turn. He didn't trust the cops. Even if he turned the negatives over to them, he would still be a target for Predator, who couldn't afford to wonder what Jace knew.

Jace had never felt he was a victim of anything. His mother had never allowed it, not for Jace, not for herself. Stuff happened, and he dealt with it and moved on. He had to look at this situation in the same way. There was always a way out, a way to move forward.

THE NEXT MORNING, Jace hobbled slowly down the stairs from the apartment in his socks, boots slung over his shoulder. He had slept maybe a total of an hour and a half.

Alicia had always told him not to waste valuable time panicking. Still, it was partly panic and pain that had kept his brain running like a hamster in a wheel those few precious hours he should have been sleeping. At four thirty he slipped out of bed, taking stock of what hurt most. The ankle felt thick and difficult to move.

At the bottom of the stairs he sat down and worked his boot on, clenching his jaw at the discomfort. He could hear the ice delivery truck idling outside the loading dock door. The first call of morning in Chinatown.

Jace found the noise and routine comforting. The rattle of a chain. The grinding of the motor that lifted the overhead door. The voice of Madame Chen's nephew, Chi, barking orders to cousin Boo Zhu.

Jace pulled in a deep breath of damp, fish-scented air and went to work. He said nothing about being injured. Chi, who ran the day-to-day business of the fish market, disliked Jace and disapproved of his aunt's decision to take the Damon brothers in. In six years he had not changed his mind.

Jace didn't care about Chi. He did his job and gave Chi no reason to complain about anything other than the fact that Jace didn't speak Chinese. Madame Chen had pointed out to Chi that bilingual skills were not a requirement for shovelling ice. Boo Zhu, who was twenty-seven and mentally handicapped, barely spoke any language at all and managed to get through his work without a problem.

The rain had become a thick, cold drizzle. Fifteen minutes into the job, Madame Chen appeared, a tiny figure in a trench coat, a huge umbrella in hand. She called to Jace to come into her office.

'My father-in-law tells me you are hurt,' she said, shutting the umbrella as she led the way into the cluttered space.

'I'm fine, Madame Chen.'

Frowning, she stared up at his face—wet, pale, scraped, bruised. 'Fine? You are not fine.'

'It was just an accident.'

'Are you in some kind of trouble?'

'Trouble? Why would you ask that? I've been hurt before.'

'I don't like answers that are not answers, JayCee.'

Jace looked away, fixing his gaze on a wall calendar. He thought about what to tell her. She deserved the truth, but he didn't want to involve the Chens in this mess. He didn't understand it himself yet. No one could trace him to this address, so there seemed no reason to alarm her.

'A truth does not take so long to tell,' she said firmly. 'Only a fiction requires so much thought.'

Jace sighed. 'I was making a delivery late yesterday, and someone almost ran me over. I took a bad fall.'

'And you called the police to report this, which is why you were so late in returning home,' she said, clearly not believing it.

Jace looked away again. Madame Chen was the only person besides his own mother he could not lie to successfully. He could fool and trick anyone else into believing anything. Because no one else cared enough about what he was telling them.

'I walked home,' he said. 'It took a long time because it was a long way and my bike is broken.'

'You don't call me?' she said, offended.

'I tried to call. The line was busy.'

'You have no respect,' she said, her hands on her hips. 'Six years I worry about you. You have no respect for me.'

'That's not true,' Jace protested. 'I respect you very much, Madame Chen. I don't want to worry you.'

'You are like my family, JayCee,' she said quietly.

Jace felt a burning at the backs of his eyes. 'I'm sorry,' he said.

'That you offended me, or that I consider you family?'

A crooked smile twisted his mouth. 'Both, I guess. I don't like to burden you.'

She shook her head. 'You were old in the womb. Not in the way of Tyler, but in the way of a man who has seen too much.'

It wasn't the first time she had made this particular comment. Jace never replied. There was no point in stating the obvious.

'I have to go, Madame Chen. I have to get the bike fixed.'

'How will you get where you are going? On a magic carpet?'

He didn't answer. She pulled a set of keys off a nail on the wall. 'Take my car. And don't tell me you can't. You will.'

'Yes, ma'am. Thank you.'

Madame Chen owned a two-year-old Mini Cooper, black with a cream-coloured top and a moonroof. Jace wedged The Beast into the car and crept out into the early traffic. The car gave him a disguise. Predator wouldn't be looking for a Mini Cooper.

The trick of the day would be getting in and out of the Speed offices without being seen by anyone watching the building. He needed to get to Eta before the cops did.

'Here.' Ruiz threw a single sheet of paper down on Parker's desk. Parker glanced at it. A list of messenger companies within a five-mile radius of Lenny Lowell's office. It had to have taken her all of three minutes to get it off Yahoo!

'You do realise "plays well with others" is a part of your evaluation, don't you?' he said as he got up and went to the coffee machine.

It was 6.43 a.m. He'd had roughly two hours' sleep.

Parker went back to his chair and sat down. 'You've got to learn to lock down that temper, doll,' he said seriously. 'I'm your immediate boss. You have to respect that whether you like it or not. You're always going to have a boss in this business, and a lot of them will make me look like a prize.'

He rose and dumped the coffee in the trash. Two slugs of it was enough to jump-start a truck engine. 'Fire in the belly is a good thing. But if you don't learn to control it, you won't last on this job. Anger clouds your judgment. You'll alienate people you need.'

'You're the voice of experience on that,' she said.

'Yeah,' Parker said quietly. 'You're learning from a master.' He felt a hundred years old, mostly spent running up mountains, cocky and sure of himself, then skidding down the other side face-first.

Parker shrugged into his charcoal Armani raincoat. A recent splurge courtesy of his other life. He flipped the collar up and reached for the old fedora he'd had since he made detective.

'Come on,' he said to Ruiz. 'We'll start on these messenger companies.'

'Can't we just do it on the phone?' she whined. 'It's raining.'

'You don't learn how to read people over the phone,' Parker snapped. She gave him the finger. Such a lady.

The first agency they tried had gone out of business. Six days ago, according to the bag lady camped in the empty office's doorway. Parker thanked her, gave her his card and twenty bucks.

'Why'd you do that?' Ruiz asked as they got back into the car and drove off.

'Who knows what she might see living here. If a couple of bucks makes her think more kindly about talking to cops . . .'

'I can't afford to hand out money to street people.'

'Right. That would put a dent in your shoe budget.'

'And you can afford to pass out money to whoever?'

Parker frowned. 'Twenty dollars? I'm not exactly going to have to give up eating red meat. Investing in a person like her is like putting a few on a long shot at the track. You didn't have snitches on that gang task force?'

'Not my job. I worked undercover. And don't talk to me about shoes. Those Tod's wingtips on your feet are six hundred dollars. I don't know any other cops wearing six-hundred-dollar shoes.'

'Except yourself.'

'That's different. Maybe I have a friend who likes to buy me nice things.'

'You have a friend?'

She didn't take the bait. 'Maybe you have a friend like that,' she said slyly. 'What about it? Are you some rich lady's toy boy? Is that where you got that Jag you drive on the weekends?'

'What do you know about my car?'

She shrugged and played coy. 'I've heard rumours.'

Parker glanced at her, then away as a traffic light ahead turned green. 'I don't think it's wise for a cop to accept expensive gifts. You never know. That special someone might be in a jam with the law one day. Maybe he asks for a big favour. Next thing you know, you've got some Internal Affairs parasite crawling up your ass.'

'If you haven't done anything wrong, you don't have anything to hide,' Ruiz commented.

'Everybody's got something to hide, sweetheart.'

'Yeah? What have you got to hide, Parker?'

'If I told you, I wouldn't be hiding it.'

They rode in silence, creeping along in the traffic until they arrived at the second agency—Reliable Couriers. A young guy told them Leonard Lowell was on their list of deadbeats who had racked up a bill, then refused to pay. They no longer did business with him.

'Do you have any idea what messenger company someone like Lowell would go to, with his bad track record?' Parker said.

'One of the small companies. Right Fast, Fly First, Speed Couriers.'

ETA FITZGERALD was a creature of habit. Every morning at quarter to six she dumped the last of her wake-up coffee in the sink, kissed her elderly mother on the cheek and hit the road.

She lived with her mother and four children in a nondescript house in a nice working-class neighbourhood. The Fitzgerald family had migrated to Los Angeles from New Orleans eight years earlier. Her husband, Roy, a jet mechanic, had taken a job with Delta and never missed a day's work in six years, until a platform collapsed while he was working on a 747 and he fell to his death.

At quarter to six it took Eta no time to get downtown. Her first stop was always Carl's Jr at Fifth and Flower, where she would sit down for more coffee and a greasy egg-and-sausage sandwich. More often than not, she saw some of her messengers there as they fuelled up for the day. Eta liked working at Speed. The messengers were strange and interesting characters. Eta was their mother hen.

Mojo raised a hand to acknowledge her. He was a wild-looking guy, that Mojo. The dreads, the dark black skin stretched over the tall, bony frame. He dressed in layers of rags, and when his eyes went wide, he looked crazy.

That was Mojo's gig, his thing that kept folks from looking too closely at him. Eta happened to know his real name was Maurice, and he read poetry and played saxophone open-mike nights at a jazz club in West LA.

She sipped her coffee and looked around for any of her other 'children'. Through the window she could see Preacher John pacing the sidewalk, already beginning his rant of the day. Mojo liked to play crazy; Preacher John was the real deal, but somehow he managed to get his deliveries made. The boss, Rocco, kept John on because he was a nephew or something.

Eta dumped her tray in the trash and went back out into the early morning gloom. She hefted herself into her minivan and reached to put the key in the ignition. The hand was over her mouth before she could even realise where it had come from.

'Don't scream.'

The hell I won't, she thought. Her eyes went to the rearview mirror. She wanted to see him, so she could tell the cops what he looked like before she beat his sorry face in.

'It's me.'

The tension rushed out of her in a gust of air.

'Boy, you done scared three lives out of me!' she snapped.

'I'm sorry,' Jace said. 'I knew you would react. If you screamed, you might have attracted somebody. Like a cop.'

Eta swivelled round, scowling at the boy in her back seat. He claimed he was twenty-one, but she didn't believe him.

'And just why don't you want cops looking at you?' she asked. 'What you been into, Lone Ranger?'

'Someone tried to make roadkill out of me last night. Did you see anything on the news about that lawyer Lenny Lowell?'

'I don't stay up for the news. Who's Lenny What?'

'Money,' Jace said. 'My last run. The lawyer.' He tossed a folded section of the *Times* on the passenger seat. 'Someone killed him last night. After I made the pick-up.'

Eta stared at him. This boy wouldn't kill someone.

'The cops are looking for me,' he said. 'I might have been the last person to see the guy alive, except for who killed him.'

'So you tell them what you know,' Eta said.

'No way I go to the cops. I was in that office last night. I touched things. My fingerprints are there. They get me in the box, match my prints . . . It's a slam dunk for them. No.'

'But, honey, someone tried to kill you,' Eta said reasonably.

Jace looked incredulous. 'And you think they'd believe me? Eta, you've got to help me out. The cops are going to show up at Speed sooner or later. They're going to ask a lot of questions.'

'You want me to lie to the police?' she asked, frowning.

He reached out and put his hand on her forearm. 'Just tell them you don't know anything about me.'

I don't *know anything about you,* she thought. In the couple of years she'd known him, he was still a mystery.

Eta sighed. 'What do you need? You need a place to stay?'

'No, thanks, Eta.' He glanced away, embarrassed. 'If you could advance me some cash . . . You know I'm good for it.'

'I got money in the safe at the office,' she said, starting the van. 'I'll park at the back door and bring the money out to you.'

'What if the cops are watching the place?'

'What do you take me for? Honey, I done forgot more about cops than you'll ever know. Lay down on the floor and stay there till I tell you something else.'

'You're the best, Eta.'

'You're damn straight I am,' she grumbled, pulling away from the kerb. 'I don't know what y'all would do without me.'

SPEED COURIERS. Stylish logo. A forties deco look. The guy who opened the door was tall and thin with the dark, shiny eyes of a zealot. 'All guests are welcome, all sinners redeemed.' He arched a brow in disapproval at Ruiz and the red lace bra playing peekaboo out of her black suit jacket.

Parker showed his badge. 'We need to speak with your dispatcher.'

Their doorman gestured towards a Plexiglas and drywall cubicle, where a large woman with a head of braids and a phone sandwiched between her shoulder and her ear was taking notes with one hand and reaching for a microphone with the other.

The woman's voice boomed over a speaker. 'John Remko! You got a pick-up. Take this manifest and get the hell out of here!'

Preacher John took the manifest and disappeared down the dark hall, a retreating spectre.

Parker stepped up to the window. The woman didn't look at him. She slapped her note up on a magnet board. The magnets each had a word printed on them—MOJO, JC, GEMMA, SLIDE. She secured the note to the board with PJOHN.

'You want a job, honey, fill out the yellow form. You got a job for us, fill out the top of the manifest,' she said. 'You want something else, you ain't gonna get it here.'

Parker slipped his shield into her line of sight. 'Detective Parker, Detective Ruiz. We need a few minutes, ma'am.'

The dispatcher faced Parker with an imperious glare. 'I got no time for you, Blue Eyes. A sharp-dressed man with a hat ain't nothin' but trouble.'

Parker swept his fedora off, grinned, and held his raincoat open. 'You like the suit? It's Canali.'

'I'll like it better from a distance. Ask what you gonna ask, honey. This ain't GQ magazine. I got me a real business to run.'

'Did you send a messenger to the office of Leonard Lowell, Esquire, for a pick-up last night around six thirty?'

She didn't blink. 'We close at six p.m.'

'Good for you,' Parker said. 'But that's not what I asked.'

'I send out a whole lotta messengers on a whole lotta runs.'

'Do you want us to interview each of them?' Parker asked politely. 'I can clear my calendar for the rest of the day. Of course, they'll have to come down to the station. What do you call those notes you put up on that board?'

'Floaters.'

'Every order goes on a floater. The floater goes on the board under the name of the messenger going on the run. Is that how it works?'

'You want my job?' she asked. 'You can have it.'

'I want you to answer a simple question, ma'am. That's all. You can answer me, or I can take all the floaters you wrote yesterday back to the station and go through them one by one.'

'You can get a damn warrant,' Eta barked.

Ruiz stuck her nose into the mix. 'We can make your life hard. Do you know the meaning of obstruction?'

'Sure I do,' Eta drawled. 'You ought to take a laxative for that, honey. There's a Sav-on Drugstore the next block up.'

Ruiz flushed red. The dispatcher sniffed her disdain.

Parker leaned on the counter. 'You haven't asked why we want to know if you dispatched a courier to this office. Why is that?'

'It don't concern me.'

'A man was murdered there last night. His daughter told us he was waiting for a bike messenger. The messenger might be able to tell us something that could be valuable to the case.'

Eta heaved a sigh. 'May the Lord have mercy on his soul.'

'You're making me suspicious,' Parker said casually. 'Being difficult like this. Makes me think you've got something to hide. We'll find out one way or the other,' Parker pointed out. 'Do you own this business, Ms . . .'

'Fitzgerald. No, I do not.'

'So you would have to answer to your boss, explain to him why he's losing a day's income, why his files are being confiscated.'

She stared at him. 'I know these kids,' she said. 'They march to their own drummer, but they ain't bad kids.'

'We just need to ask him some questions. If he didn't do anything wrong, he's got nothing to worry about.'

Eta Fitzgerald looked deflated. 'It was a late call,' she said.

'Where's the manifest?'

'The messenger's still got it. He didn't make it back to match up his paperwork. It was raining. I closed up and went home.'

'And is he working today?'

'He ain't been in yet.'

Parker pulled his notebook out. 'What's his name?'

'J.C.'

'What's J.C. stand for?'

'It stands for J.C.,' she said, perturbed. 'That's what we call him: J.C. Number Sixteen.'

'Where does he live?'

'I have no idea.'

'You have his phone number.'

'He calls on the two-way. I got no phone number for the boy.'

Ruiz spoke into her phone. 'Detective Renee Ruiz, LAPD. I need to speak with ADA Langfield regarding a warrant.'

'Maybe I got an address,' the dispatcher said grudgingly.

She went to a filing cabinet and dug through a drawer, pulling out what looked like an empty file folder.

'It's just one of those mailbox places,' she said, handing it over.

Parker said, 'Can you tell me what he looks like?'

'He looks like a blond-haired, blue-eyed white boy.'

'Thank you for your cooperation, Ms Fitzgerald.'

Eta Fitzgerald scowled at him and grabbed her ringing phone, dismissing him. Parker opened the folder, scanned the single sheet of paper—a job application—for pertinent info.

NAME: J. C. Damon

Parker closed the folder and handed it to Ruiz. Instead of turning for the front door, they went out by the back door. Parker looked at a couple of bikes chained to a gas meter. A dark blue minivan sat wedged into a parking space between a wall and a Dumpster. Eta Fitzgerald's car.

Parker took a peek inside the van through the windows. The usual. A football helmet, action figures and a black Barbie.

He started to move away from the van, then glanced back, something catching his eye. He frowned and went back into the building, Ruiz at his heels like a terrier.

Eta Fitzgerald, again juggling phone and radio mike, stared as they approached her window. 'What now?' she demanded.

'It's your car,' he said.

She turned ashen, cut the mike, and hung up the phone.

'It's your taillight,' Parker said. 'Busted out. You'll get pulled over for it on a day like this.'

Eta Fitzgerald's expression was one of sudden nausea.

'I just wanted to give you a heads-up,' Parker went on.

'Thank you, Detective,' she said softly. 'I appreciate that.'

Parker tipped his hat. 'We're here to serve.'

JACE WATCHED from across the alley, from inside a soggy cardboard box that had been left behind a furniture store. Crumbs of Styrofoam peanuts clung to him like fleas. Staying in in the back of Eta's minivan was too risky. He'd been a captive there, trapped, vulnerable. He needed space, a vantage point, escape routes. As soon as Eta had gone inside, he had slipped out of the van and gone across the alley.

Eta had promised to come back out with the money right away, but half a minute after she had gone inside, Preacher John had shown up. Then came Mojo. No Eta.

All she had to do was put the cash in an envelope and step out to put it in her van. There was no sign of Rocco, the boss.

Jace huddled back into his jacket and looked at the newspaper page he had tried to show her in the van. Lenny Lowell's violent passing had been buried in the depths of the *LA Times*. It said the lawyer had been found by his daughter, Abigail (a twenty-three-year-old law student), and that he had been bludgeoned to death in his office.

Abby Lowell. Maybe she'd seen Predator fleeing the scene. Maybe she knew who would want her father dead, and why. Maybe she knew who the people in the negatives were.

Speed's back door opened and two people came out. A man first: average build, expensive-looking raincoat, and a hat like a 1940s movie detective. Sam Spade. Philip Marlowe. With a petite woman in a black suit. Pissed off. Hispanic. Sam Spade ignored her.

Cops. At least the guy was, even though he was really too well dressed. Jace had a sixth sense for cops.

This one walked around Eta's van, slowly looking in the windows. A chill swept over Jace. Then they went back inside the building.

Jace shivered. Why would the cops be interested in Eta's van, unless someone had told them to be? She'd told him to go to the police. Maybe she had made the decision for him.

Jace told himself he'd been stupid going to her for help. But he'd seen a quick way to get a couple of hundred bucks. He didn't want to take money out of the box he kept hidden at the apartment. That money was for Tyler to live on, in case something happened.

Something *had* happened.

Time to go.

Using a delivery truck for cover, Jace crawled out of the box. He flipped up the collar of his coat and started down the alley.

A car turned in at the mouth of the alley, crawling towards him. A dark sedan. A cracked windshield.

Fear hit Jace in the belly and shot through his veins like mercury. Quick, toxic. He wanted to look, to put a face on his hunter. The car slowed as it neared him. Jace's chest tightened. He was on the driver's side. Could the guy put a face on him? He'd had his helmet on. And his goggles.

He glanced out the corner of his eye as the car came even.

A head like a square block of stone, small, mean eyes, beard, dark hair buzzed short. The guy had a piece of white tape across the bridge of his nose and a black mole on the back of his neck.

The sedan cruised past like a panther in the jungle, quiet, sleek, ominous. Jace kept walking, refusing the urge to look back.

The guy knew where Jace worked, of course. He had Jace's messenger bag. Next the guy would try to find out where Jace lived, just as the cops would. But none of them would be able to. The only address Speed had for him was the old P.O. box. And the only address the P.O. box people had on file was an old apartment he had lived in briefly with his mother.

But the sharks were in the water, moving, hunting.

Two cops and a killer.

Jace broke into a jog. He needed to find Abby Lowell.

'WHAT'S YOUR OPINION?' Parker asked, easing back into traffic.

'There's nothing to make much of,' Ruiz said.

Parker made the rude sound of a game-show buzzer. 'Wrong. First of all, we could have his prints on the job ap. We know his name, or an aka at least. We can kick up his sheet if he has one. He keeps to himself, gets paid in cash, mail goes to a box; no address, no phone. He operates like a crook.'

'What if he doesn't have a sheet?' Ruiz pointed out.

'If Latent can pull a clear print off the job ap, and if they can match it to a print on the murder weapon, we'll have that. And the dispatcher knows more than she's saying.'

'Yeah, but she's not saying it.'

'She's got a conscience; she doesn't like breaking rules. But she's protective of her messengers.'

'I think she's a bitch,' Ruiz grumbled.

'You can't take it personally. You have to learn not to throw the whole box at the head of every witness or perp you run into.'

From the corner of his eye, he could see her watching him.

'Geez,' he mumbled. 'I sound like a teacher.'

'You are a teacher. Allegedly.'

Parker didn't say anything. His mood had turned south. Most of the time he tried to focus on his goal in the department. He didn't think of himself as a teacher. He was waiting for the chance to make a comeback.

He could have quit. He didn't need the money or the hassle. The job he had on the side had paid off his debts, bought him his Jag and his wardrobe. But he was too stubborn to quit. And every time a case took hold of him, and he felt the old adrenaline rush, he was reminded that he loved what he did. He was old-fashioned enough to be proud that he carried a badge.

And every time a case took hold, and he felt that adrenaline rush, he was reminded that somewhere deep inside him he still believed this could be the case where he proved himself, redeemed himself, regained the respect of his peers and his enemies. But if this was the kind of case with the potential to turn his career around, Robbery-Homicide was sure to muscle in.

He turned the car into the parking lot of a little strip mall with a collection of food shops: Noah's Bagels, Jamba Juice, Starbucks. The driver picked the radio station; the passenger picked the restaurant. Ruiz picked Starbucks. Her order was always complicated, and if it didn't turn out to her liking, she made the barista do it over.

Parker went into Jamba Juice and got a fruit smoothie, then went into Starbucks and commandeered a table in the back and picked up a section of the *Times* a previous customer had abandoned.

There had to be something to the fact that Robbery-Homicide had come sniffing around his crime scene. They were front-page guys working front-page cases. Lenny Lowell had not made the front page.

'Watching your girlish figure?' Ruiz asked as she joined him.

Parker kept his attention on the newspaper. 'My body is a temple, baby. Come worship.'

He hadn't seen or spoken with anyone at the scene resembling a reporter, and he was the detective of record . . . but there it was, a few sentences stuck in a left-hand corner: ATTORNEY FOUND DEAD.

'Leonard Lowell, the victim of an apparent homicide, found by his daughter, Abigail Lowell (twenty-three, a law student), bludgeoned to death in his office . . .' Blah, blah, blah.

Parker called up his memory of Abby Lowell arriving on the scene the night before. She said she'd received a call from an LAPD officer notifying her of her father's death while she was waiting for him at Cicada.

It was too early to call the restaurant to check her alibi.

The byline on the story was 'Staff Reporter'.

'Ruiz.' Parker leaned across the table and snapped his fingers at her. 'Did you get a name for that phone number I gave you to check out? The number from Abby Lowell's cellphone call list?'

'Not yet.'

'Do it. Now.'

She started to object. Parker slid the paper across the table and tapped a finger on the piece. He got up from his chair, dug his phone out of his pocket, and went out through the side door into the cold.

'Kelly.' Andi Kelly, investigative reporter for the *LA Times*. A fireball in a small red-haired package. Tenacious, wry, and a lover of single malt Scotch.

'Andi. Kev Parker.'

There was silence. He pictured confusion, then recognition.

'Wow,' she said at last. 'I used to know a Kev Parker.'

'Back when I was good for a headline,' Parker remarked drily. 'Now you never call, you never write. I feel so used.'

'You changed your phone number and I don't know where you live. What happened? They didn't approve of your smoking, drinking, womanising, arrogant ways?'

'I repented, gave all that up, joined the priesthood.'

'Ah me. Where have all the icons gone?'

'This one crumbled a while ago.'

'Yeah,' Kelly said soberly. 'I read that in the papers.'

Nothing like a public flameout to win friends and influence people. The cocky, arrogant Robbery-Homicide hotshot Parker had been made the whipping boy by an equally cocky, arrogant defence attorney in a high-profile murder trial.

The DA's case had been good, not watertight, but solid. A mountain of circumstantial evidence gathered against a wealthy preppie UCLA med student accused of the brutal murder of a young female undergrad.

Parker was second lead in the investigation. He had a reputation for shooting his mouth off, for riding the edge of the rules, but he was a damn good detective. That was the truth he had held on to during the trial while the big-bucks defence team shredded his character with half-truths, irrelevant facts and outright lies. They had impugned his integrity, accused him of tampering with evidence. They couldn't prove any of it, but they didn't need to. People were always eager to believe the worst.

Anthony Giradello, the ADA set to make his career on the case, had seen Parker dragging down his ship and had done the cruel and certain thing any

ADA would have done: he took up his own whip and joined in the beating.

Giradello had done everything he could to distance his case from Parker, to downplay Parker's role in the investigation. Sure, Parker was an ass, but he was an *unimportant* ass who hadn't really had anything much to do with the investigation or the handling of evidence. The liberal LA press had joined in the feeding frenzy, always happy to eviscerate a cop doing his job.

Andi Kelly had been a single voice against the mob, pointing out that the defence was employing the shopworn but tried-and-true 'when all else fails, blame a cop' strategy. A gambling game devised to draw attention away from overwhelming forensic evidence, to plant a seed of doubt in the minds of the jury. One juror, and they would hang the jury.

They managed to convince all twelve. A murderer walked free.

The political fallout had been ugly. The DA's office had pressed for Parker to be fired, to continue to deflect the spotlight away from the fact that a killer had walked free. The chief of police, who loathed the DA and feared the police union, had refused to get rid of Parker, despite the fact that every brass badge in the department wanted him gone. He had been painted as a problem, a loose cannon, insubordinate. He was a black eye on a department that couldn't take another scandal.

The only interview Parker had granted during all of it was to Andi Kelly.

'So how you doing, Kev?' Kelly asked.

'Older, wiser, like everybody,' Parker said, pacing the sidewalk.

'Know anything going on in the Cole case?'

'You'd know more than I would. You're the one at the courthouse every day. I'm just a labourer now, you know.'

'Well, if you don't have a scoop, Parker, to hell with you.'

'That's harsh. Now that I'm down on my luck, eating out of garbage cans, can't you do an old friend a favour?'

'What do you want, Man-I-Haven't-Heard-From-In-Years?'

'It's nothing much,' Parker said. 'I'm working a homicide. Happened last night. There's a couple of lines in the *Times* this morning. I'm curious who wrote it. Can you find out?'

'Why?' Kelly was always keen for the scent of a story.

'It just struck me as odd,' Parker said casually. 'No one spoke to me. I was on the scene half the night, and I didn't see any reporter.'

'Some staff flunky picked it up off the scanner. Who's the vic?'

'Low-end defence attorney.'

'Why do you care it was in the paper if the guy's a nobody?' Kelly asked.

'They got a couple of details wrong.'

'So?'

Parker sighed. 'I don't remember you being such a pain in the ass.'

'Well, I always have been,' Kelly said. 'I have issues.'

'Honey, I can trump your issues any day of the week.'

'Now you're making me feel inferior.'

'Why did I call you?' Parker asked, exasperated.

'Because you want something.'

Parker considered and discarded the idea of telling Kelly about Robbery-Homicide's unofficial appearance at the scene.

'Listen, Andi, it's nothing I can put my finger on yet. I'm just getting a weird vibe here. Can you make a couple of calls?'

'And if this turns into something . . . ?'

'I'll buy you a bottle of Glenmorangie.'

'I'll get back to you.'

'Thanks.'

Parker stuck his phone in his pocket and went back into the coffeehouse.

'The number is a prepaid cellphone,' Ruiz said. 'Untraceable.'

'Every criminal's favourite toy,' Parker said. Every drug dealer and thug in the city carried one. The number was sold with the phone. No paperwork, no paper trail. 'Let's go.'

'Who were you talking to?' Ruiz asked back in the car.

'I called an old friend. I want to know who wrote that bit.'

'Because they got it wrong?'

'Because what if they didn't? If the daughter found him—'

'Then she's a suspect.'

'She has to be considered, anyway. You'll need to speak with the maitre d' at Cicada. When did she get there, when did she leave, did she speak to anyone, was she absent for any length of time.'

'But if she found the body, how did this reporter find out?'

'That's my question,' Parker said, starting the car. 'Chances are, it's just a screw-up. Some guy at the *Times* got a detail third-hand from one of the crime-scene geeks while they were sitting in a bar. Who knows? You can tell a reporter a story word for word, and they'll still get it wrong.'

'I guess you'd know about that,' Ruiz said.

Parker shot her a glance. 'Baby, I could write a book.'

5

According to the Pakistani clerk at the mailbox place—Box-4-U—Box 501 belonged to a woman named Allison Jennings, whom she did not know. The box had been rented to Ms Jennings in 1994. The rent was paid by a money order left in the box once a year.

The manager who had first rented Box 501 to Allison Jennings had stapled a copy of her Massachusetts driving licence to the rental form. The photo on the copy was nothing but black ink. Parker had the clerk make copies of both sheets, and he and Ruiz went back out onto the street.

As Parker put the car in gear and pulled away from the kerb, Ruiz called in the DL for Allison Jennings.

The address the woman had listed on her renter's form for Box-4-U was a red-brick building in a dicey downtown neighbourhood.

'You think this woman is still around here?' Ruiz asked.

Parker shrugged. 'Who knows? She filled out that form ten years ago. This Damon kid maybe bought the box off her or took it over. He's got to be around here someplace if he's using it.'

'Someplace' covered a lot of ground. Central Bureau policed four and a half square miles downtown, including Chinatown, Little Tokyo, the financial district, the jewellery and fashion districts, and the convention centre.

Parker pulled the car into the lot at the station and turned to his partner. 'First thing, take Damon's job ap to Latent. See if they can get a match with anything off the murder weapon. Then call Massachusetts. Then look for any local Allison Jenningses. And call the phone company for the local usage details on Speed Couriers.'

Ruiz looked perturbed. 'Anything else, Master?'

'Start going through the calls. Maybe this Damon kid doesn't have a phone, but maybe he does. And get the phone records for Lowell's office and for his home.'

'And what will you be doing while I'm doing all of this?'

'I'm going to talk to Abby Lowell. Find out how she got her name in the paper. She'll like talking to me more than she'd like talking to you.'

'What makes you so sure of that?'

He flashed her the famous Kev Parker grin. 'Because I'm me.'

With Ruiz out of his hair, Parker drove directly to Lenny Lowell's office. He wanted to walk through the crime scene without distractions. He found it centring to spend time in the place where a victim had died.

The neighbourhood was no more attractive in daylight than it had been at night in the rain. Less so, actually. In the stark light of a grey morning, the age and dinginess and tiredness of the place couldn't hide.

The little two-storey strip mall where Lowell's office was located looked to have been built in the late fifties. The better scum defence attorneys had offices in Beverly Hills, where the world was beautiful. This was the kind of place where the lower end of the food chain hung their shingles. Though it seemed to Parker that old Lenny had been doing pretty well for himself.

Lowell's Cadillac had been towed away to be checked for evidence. The car was new but had been vandalised. Lowell's home address was a condo in one of the new downtown hot spots. Pricey stuff for a guy whose clients used the revolving door at the bail bondsman's office.

Parker wondered why the killer smashed the Cadillac's windows if all he had wanted was to steal the money in the safe. Had the motive for the murder been revenge and the money a bonus? Or had the killer been after something he hadn't found in the office? If that was the case, this murder was a much more complicated affair. Besides the money in his safe, what could a guy like Lenny Lowell have that would be worth killing for?

Parker unsealed the crime-scene tape and let himself in through the back door. Lenny's office was a decent-sized space now awash in paper and finger-print dust residue and bits of tape marking evidence locations on the rug. Drawers had been pulled out of filing cabinets, out of the desk.

'You're disturbing a crime scene,' Parker said.

Abby Lowell, sitting behind her father's desk, started and gasped, and banged her knee trying to stand up and back away.

'Oh, my God, you scared me!' she scolded.

'I have to ask what you're doing here, Ms Lowell,' Parker said, taking a seat across the desk from her. The arm of the chair was speckled with blood. 'We seal crime scenes for a reason.'

'And do you make funeral arrangements?' she asked, gathering her com-posure around her again like the cashmere sweater she wore. 'Do you know where my father kept his life insurance policy? And what about his will? Can you help with that, Detective Parker?'

Parker shook his head. 'No, but if you had called me, I would have helped you look. I would have known what you touched and what you moved. I would have known if you had taken something other than your father's will or his life insurance policy.'

'Are you accusing me of something?' she asked.

'No. I'm just saying. That's how a crime scene works. The second your father ceased to breathe, I became his protector.'

'Too bad for my father you weren't here to protect him from being killed. And by "you" I mean the LAPD.'

'We can't predict when and where a crime is about to happen,' Parker said. 'You knew your father's habits; you knew his friends; you probably knew his enemies. Maybe you knew he was into something that could have got him killed.'

She looked incredulous. 'How insensitive can you be?'

'You wouldn't want to find out,' Parker said. 'You didn't seem all that sensitive yourself last night. Your father is posing for the big chalk outline. You seemed more upset that your dinner plans had been disturbed.'

'I'm not the hysterical type, and I do my crying in private. You don't know anything about my relationship with my father.'

'Fill me in, why don't you. Were you and your father close?'

She sighed and looked away.

'We were friends. Lenny wasn't much of a father. He cheated on my mother. He drank too much. His idea of quality time with me was to drag me along to the racecourse or to a bookie's, where he would promptly forget I existed. My parents divorced when I was nine years old.'

'But you forgave him?'

'We sort of found each other when I started college. Suddenly I was an adult. We could have a conversation. I wanted to become an attorney. He took an interest in me.'

She continued to look away, not wanting him to see her have an emotional reaction to her memories of her father. But it was there. That was some kind of steely control, Parker thought.

He supposed that was what a little girl learned to do while her father was handicapping the sixth race at Santa Anita. And what a little girl did when she was caught between warring parents, what she did when her father left, and when he reappeared in her life. She maintained control. She didn't let anything penetrate her armour.

'Did you know your father's friends?' Parker asked quietly. 'His ene-mies? Whether or not he was into something dangerous?'

'Lenny was always looking for an angle. Maybe he finally found one. I don't know. He didn't tell me.'

'Does he have any other family?' he asked.

'He has a brother in upstate New York. And three ex-wives. None of them would cross the street to spit on his corpse.'

'You're the only forgiving one in the bunch.'

She didn't comment. She got up and started a slow pace in front of the bookcases, arms crossed. Her profile had long, graceful, curving lines. Her skin was like porcelain, and hair spilled down behind her like a dark water-fall. She was model gorgeous in a sapphire sweater and matching skirt.

'Did you speak to anyone last night after you left, Ms Lowell?'

She leaned against the side of the desk. 'No. I went home.'

'You didn't call your mother? Tell her that her ex checked out?'

'My mother died five years ago. Cancer.'

'I'm sorry,' Parker said. 'You didn't call a friend?'

She sighed, impatient. 'What are you getting at, Detective? If you have a question, ask it. I have arrangements to make, and I have a class at eleven.'

Parker cocked a brow. 'A class? No day off to mourn?'

'My father is dead. I can't change that. He was murdered. I can't grasp that idea,' she said. 'I may seem cold to you, Detective Parker, but I'm deal-ing with this the only way that makes any sense to me—moving forward.'

'I've been a cop nearly twenty years, Ms Lowell,' Parker said, rising. 'I know survivors deal with grief in their own way.'

'Then why were you judging me?'

'I wasn't. I need to know the why of everything. For instance, I need to know why it said in the *Times* this morning that you discovered your father's body.'

Something flashed across her face. Surprise, maybe. 'I don't know. It isn't true,' she said defensively. 'I was at the restaurant when I got the call. And I don't know any reporters. I wouldn't talk to them if I did.' She put the strap of her bag over her shoulder. 'I have to go,' she said bluntly. 'I have a meeting with a funeral director.'

'I thought you had a class.'

The dark eyes snapped. 'The class is at one. I got it wrong, Detective. You know how to contact me if you need anything more.'

Parker let her go. She had the composure of a knife-thrower's assistant, he had to give her that. He wondered if there was anything more behind it than a lonely little girl protecting herself.

His gaze drifted across the desk. She'd left empty-handed, no sign of Lenny's life insurance policy or his will.

He went out to the car, got his Polaroid camera and went back in. He shot photographs of the desktop, the open filing cabinets, the floor around the desk. Then he carefully lifted a long black plastic envelope out of a half-opened desk drawer. In gold stamped letters across the front: CITY NATIONAL BANK. It was empty. The impression of a small key had been left in one frosted plastic pocket. Safe-deposit box.

THERE WERE TWELVE Lowells listed in the phone book. Three of them had first names beginning with the letter A: Alyce, Adam, and A. L. Lowell. A. L. Lowell was a good bet.

Jace put the restored Beast in the back of the Mini and headed west. He'd had to pay the guy at the bike shop an extra twenty bucks to get the repairs done right away, but he'd had no choice. He needed the bike for work.

His head was pounding, his ankle throbbing. He pulled into a 7-Eleven and bought a hot dog, a cheese burrito, a bottle of Gatorade, and some painkillers.

He ate in the car, careful not to spill anything, and tried to figure out what he would do if he found Abby Lowell at home. Knock on the door and say, 'Hi. I'm the guy the cops think killed your father'? No. He looked danger-ous or crazy or both with his face beat up. She'd probably take a look at him through the peephole and call 911. Who would he say he was? A reporter?

He liked that angle. If she didn't slam the door in his face, he might get to ask some questions and get some answers.

When he finished eating, he found Abby Lowell's neighbourhood. She lived in a two-storey rectangular stucco building with a few understated Spanish details on the façade. Built in the twenties or thirties, when people had style.

By the size of the place and the configuration of the windows, front and side, Jace figured there were four units, two up, two down. He parked the Mini around the corner and across the street, where he had a vantage point of the front entrance.

It was the middle of a cold, damp, gloomy day. With all the trees lining the streets and standing sentinel in the yards, the quality of light was as dim as the interior of a forest. Jace got out of the car and walked casually across the street to the building.

The tenants' names were each listed next to a call button on the wall beside the front door, but it didn't matter, because someone hadn't opened the door with enough force to make it latch when it closed again. Jace checked the apartment numbers and went in.

A central staircase led to the first floor, where there was one apartment on either side of the hall. Jace went to the neighbour's door first, to listen for anyone home. The only sound was some kind of bird squawking and clucking to itself.

Jace knocked softly on the door to the Lowell apartment. No one answered. He tried the knob, expecting it to be locked, but it turned easily. He checked over his shoulder, then went inside, wiped the knob with the sleeve of his sweater, and closed the door behind him.

The apartment looked like the neighbourhood had suffered an earthquake. Everything that had been on shelves or in cabinets was on the floor; chairs were overturned. Someone had slashed the upholstery on the couch and armchair. Someone had been looking for something. Jace wondered if that something was taped to his belly.

He made his way past the kitchen and down the hall. In the small bathroom someone had taken red lipstick and written on the mirrored medicine cabinet: NEXT YOU DIE.

'Holy crap,' he murmured. 'I'm living in a damn movie.'

The blow to his back was so unexpected that it took a second to register what was happening. His body hurtled forwards and his head bounced off the mirror. Stars of colour burst before his eyes. The assailant grabbed him by the hair and slammed his head against the medicine cabinet. Jace heard the glass crack, felt a shard slice his cheek. As his assailant let him fall, his chin hit the sink with the force of a hammer. Then he was on the floor.

Jace wasn't sure how long he lay there, drifting in and out.

You have to get up, J.C. You have to get out of here.

He couldn't seem to pass the message from his brain to his body. Slowly he brought himself to his hands and knees and saw the blood on the floor where his face had been. Head swimming, he grabbed the edge of the sink and pulled himself to his feet.

The reflection looking back at him in the broken mirror was from a horror show. His right cheekbone and eyebrow were swollen from being slammed into the medicine cabinet. His cheek was cut and bleeding, his nose was bleeding, and he'd chipped a tooth.

The apartment was quiet. Jace hoped that meant his attacker had gone. Still trembling, he washed his face, washed his hands, found a towel, dried himself, and wiped his blood out of the sink.

The apartment door opened and closed. Jace sat up straighter, straining to listen. Someone going out or someone coming in?

He could hear someone moving through the front rooms slowly, as if trying to take it all in, or trying to find something. He stepped behind the bathroom door and waited.

The shattered mirror gave a distorted, surreal reflection of the person stepping cautiously into the bathroom—an eye here, a nose there, a live Picasso painting.

Jace kicked the door shut and grabbed Abby Lowell, clamping his hand over her mouth to muffle her scream. She tried to jab him with her elbow, kicked backwards, connecting a boot heel to his shin. Jace tightened his arm around her, kept his palm over her mouth as she tried to bite him. She was strong and athletic and determined to get away. Jace shoved her forwards, trapping her up against the sink.

'Don't scream,' he ordered quietly. 'I'm not here to hurt you. I want to help. I knew your father. He was a good guy.'

She was watching him in the mirror, eyes round with fear and distrust.

'I came here to see you, to talk to you,' Jace explained. 'Someone had ransacked the place. He beat me up and left.'

Abby Lowell's attention had gone from him to the message on the glass: NEXT YOU DIE.

'I didn't put that there,' Jace said.

She had gone still in his arms. He loosened his hold.

'You won't scream?' he asked. 'Promise you won't scream.'

She nodded her head. Jace took his hand from her mouth.

'Who are you?' she asked, still watching him in the mirror.

'I knew your father. I did some work for him.'

'What kind of work?'

'That's not important.'

'It is to me,' she said. 'How do I know you didn't kill him? How do I know you didn't do this to my home?'

'And then beat myself into a stupor?' Jace said.

'Maybe Lenny did that to you before you killed him.'

'And I'm still bleeding? Maybe if I'm a haemophiliac.'

'How do I know you didn't kill him?' she said again. 'And now you're here to kill me.'

'Why would I want you dead? Why would anyone?'

'I don't know. One minute my life was normal, and the next my father is dead and I'm being questioned by detectives and having to make funeral arrangements, and now this,' she said, her eyes filling with tears. She pressed a hand to her mouth and tried to steel herself against the emotions threatening to overwhelm her.

'I know,' Jace said softly. 'I know.'

She twisted around to face him. They stood as close as lovers sharing a secret. 'Do you know what happened to him?'

'I know he was killed,' Jace said. 'I read in the paper you found his body.'

'That's not true. I don't know how that got in there.'

'So you didn't see anyone leaving the scene?'

'No. The police were there when I got there. Why would you want to know that? Do you have an idea who killed him?'

Jace shook his head, though in his memory the dark sedan slid past him. 'No. Do you?'

'I was told it was a robbery.'

'What about this place?' he asked. 'The perpetrator of a random crime kills your father, then robs you and leaves a death threat on your mirror? I'd say somebody was looking for something. Do you know what?'

'I can't imagine.' She watched him like a poker player.

'Was anything missing from Lenny's office?'

'Money. I don't know how much. He was waiting for a bike messenger last night. The police think the messenger did it. Killed Lenny, took the money and skipped town.'

'Doesn't look to me like the killer skipped town,' Jace said.

'Maybe this was just a thief.'

'And why would a common thief write that on your mirror?' he asked. '"Next you die." It would be a pretty amazing coincidence if the night after your dad was murdered, an unrelated serial killer just happened to single you out to be his next victim.'

Abby Lowell put her hands over her face. 'I need to sit down.'

Jace didn't stop her as she sat on the edge of the bathtub.

'If you know something about Lenny's death,' she said, 'you should go to the cops. Ask for Detective Parker. If you know something about why this unknown assailant broke into my apartment, you should go to the cops.'

Jace glanced away. 'I'm not interested in talking to cops.'

'Why don't you want to talk to the police?' she asked.

'I have my reasons.'

'Because you know something,' she said, standing. 'The only way you could know something is if you're involved.'

'I know someone tried to kill me last night,' Jace said as his anger bubbled up. 'I was doing something for your father, and someone tried to kill me. And on my way back to ask Lenny what he'd got me into, I found out he was dead. I think that gives me a right to be interested, don't you?'

'You're him, aren't you?' she said. 'You're the bike messenger.'

In a heartbeat she was running out of the bathroom door, yanking it shut behind her. Jace bolted after her, flinging the door back open.

She grabbed a portable phone on her way to the front door, then stumbled over books that had fallen to the floor in the ransacking.

Jace lunged at her, knocking her down, landing on top of her. She cried out for help and twisted beneath him.

'Stop fighting!' he growled. 'I don't want to hurt you!'

'What the hell's going on up there?' a male voice called from somewhere outside the apartment. Footsteps sounded in the hall.

'Miss Lowell? Are you all right?' The man shouted to someone else, 'Call nine one one!'

Jace pushed himself up off her and bolted for the door. An older man, with thinning hair and wild eyebrows, jumped back, startled. Jace shoved past him and ran down the stairs. He skidded around the base of the staircase and ran for the double doors and the courtyard beyond.

He hit the doors running. Burst outside. The courtyard had flowers and shrubs and a seven-foot stucco wall surrounding it.

He grabbed a wooden bench, dragged it to the wall. Stepped back, took a deep breath. Launched himself, grabbed the top of the wall. Hurled himself over. As he hit the ground on his feet pain exploded in his ankle.

Across the street, down the alley. Cut between houses. Double back to the Mini. He stuck his hand in his coat pocket and pulled out the keys. He yanked the door open, spilled into the driver's seat.

Now a siren sounded in the distance.

The engine turned over, and he threw the car into gear and started to spin a U-turn in the middle of the street. A horn blasting, tyres screeching. The nose of a minivan just clipped the Mini, knocking its tail sideways.

And then he was moving, headed east. He slowed his speed as soon as he dared and kept moving at a normal pace, like a normal human being in a normal situation. Behind the wheel he was shaking, his heart still racing.

He couldn't have screwed up any bigger than he had. And innocent as she pretended to be, Abby Lowell had to know something. Why else would some thug leave a death threat on her mirror? *Next You Die. Next*, as if Lenny had been a warning, or just the first on a list of things to do.

What now?

Now he was wanted for a murder and an assault, home invasion and vandalism. And for stealing out of Lenny's safe.

He wished he knew what he was up against—who he was up against. He could easily call to mind the blockheaded guy in the dark car. But calling up the memory of the attack in Abby Lowell's apartment, he came up blank.

What the hell is going on, and why do I have to be in it?

Luck of the draw. If he hadn't been late with the blueprints, he would have gone home that night, and Eta would have told Lowell they couldn't take his package. Lowell would have been a story buried in the paper. Jace wouldn't have paid any attention to it, just as the majority of Angelenos wouldn't have paid any attention to it.

Jace wondered if the people in the negatives taped to his belly might be famous. Some celebrity being blackmailed over deviant sexual behaviour. The kind of seedy story that made up the gritty side of LA.

He wanted to go home. He wanted to do something normal. He wanted to help Tyler with some project for school, watch television, make popcorn. Maybe he would do that, he thought. Mail Lenny's package to Abby, get a new job, start over again, pretend none of this had ever happened.

The two-way on the passenger seat gave a blast of static, then Eta's voice. 'Base to Sixteen. Where you at, baby?'

Jace reached over and touched the radio, fingered the call button, but he didn't push it. He didn't dare.

'Where you at, Lone Ranger? You gotta come on home to Mama, sugar. ASAP. I'm still holding money for you. You copy?'

'I'm in the twilight zone, Eta,' he murmured to himself.

6

'Abby Lowell's story checks out,' Ruiz announced to Parker as he approached the building from the parking lot. She stood outside the doors, smoking.

'You spoke with the maitre d' who was at Cicada last night?'

'Yes. He said she seemed impatient, checked her watch.'

'What about her waiter?'

She shook her head. 'They never seated her. The maitre d' showed her to the bar. The bartender said she had a vodka tonic. He saw her on her phone, but he didn't see her leave.'

Parker frowned, looking out at the gathering gloom as evening crept near. 'I want her phone records, home and cell.'

'You think she had something to do with it?' Ruiz asked.

'I caught her at her father's office this morning. She left with a key to a safe-deposit box at City National Bank. She went there directly after leaving and tried to get access to her father's box.'

'They didn't let her in?'

'She gave the manager her sob story, but she wasn't authorised to sign for the box. The manager told her to file a probate petition along with an affidavit and get a court order. Ms Lowell was not happy.'

'Did you get in the box?' Ruiz asked.

'We'll have a court order first thing tomorrow,' Parker said.

'I called Massachusetts,' Ruiz said as they went inside to the squad room. 'They ran the DL number we have for Allison Jennings. It came back to a woman living in Boston.'

'Did you get a phone number?'

'I did better than that,' Ruiz said smugly. 'I called her. She said she has no idea how her licence turned up here. Said she had her handbag stolen and lost her driving licence with it a long time ago.'

They went into the squad room. Parker hung up his raincoat and his hat and went directly to the coffee machine. He poured a cup, but the coffee tasted three times worse than it had in the morning. 'You were just a regular whirling dervish while I was out,' he said. 'I'm impressed.'

Ruiz leaned back against her desk. 'Latent has Damon's job ap. They haven't called back. And I got the local usage details for Speed, and for the victim—office and home.'

Parker squinted at her and asked, 'Who are you? And what have you done with Ms Ruiz?'

She gave him the finger and went on. 'The number off Abby Lowell's cellphone call list? Leonard Lowell called that number yesterday from his office at five twenty-two p.m. The call lasted one minute, twelve seconds.'

Parker frowned and thought about that. At five twenty-two Lenny Lowell had called an untraceable cellphone number. A little more than an hour later someone using that same cellphone had called Abby Lowell and told her that her father was dead.

How did that tie in with the bike messenger? It didn't. The lawyer had called the Speed office to arrange the pick-up.

Even if the phone belonged to Damon, it didn't make sense. Why would Lowell have called him directly, then set up the pick-up through Speed?

And then what? Damon shows up, kills Lowell, takes the package and the money from the safe, turns the office inside out looking for something, bashes in Lowell's car window on the way out, then calls a woman he doesn't know to tell her her father is dead?

'This isn't working for me,' Parker muttered, lowering himself into his chair. He yawned and rubbed his hands over his face. He needed a second wind. His shift might be over, but his day wasn't.

The first couple of days of a homicide investigation were crucial. Trails cooled fast; perps slithered away into holes.

'What?' Ruiz asked, perturbed. 'Looks pretty neat to me.'

'That's why I have the number two in my rank and you don't.' Parker shook his head. 'There's something wrong with this picture. A bike messenger is dispatched by chance. He gets in Lowell's office, sees money hanging out of the safe, kills Lowell, steals the money, beats it. Lowell didn't call him beforehand and say, "Hey, come steal my money and beat my head in."'

'And if it was a crime of opportunity,' he went on, 'the messenger doesn't take the time to look up Abby Lowell's cellphone number and call her to pretend he's a cop and tell her to go to her father's office. Why would he?'

The phone on Parker's desk rang. He snatched up the receiver. 'Parker.'

'Kev, Joan Spooner over at Latent. Got a possible match on those prints from the Lowell homicide. You can't hang your hat on it in a courtroom, but it's something you can play off of. I've got a thumb and a partial middle finger on the murder weapon and a partial thumb on the job ap.'

'And they match?'

'Between you and me, I think it's probably the same person.'

'I love you, Joanie,' Parker crooned, and hung up.

Ruiz leaned forwards. 'Hey, Romeo, what did she say?'

Parker stared into the distance, thinking. 'A probable match of a thumbprint on the murder weapon and on the job ap.'

'He's our guy.'

'Play devil's advocate. If you were Damon's attorney, how would you punch holes in that evidence?'

Ruiz sighed. 'I would say that we concede Damon was in Lowell's office. He touched a bowling trophy. So what?'

'Exactly. And where on the murder weapon are these prints located? To beat Lowell's head in, he held the trophy upside-down. The marble base did all the damage. Do we have photos back?'

'No.'

'Call SID now before they all go home like regular folks. You need to talk with the guy who lifted the prints off the murder weapon. And I need photos of the back of the desk.'

'My shift is over and I'm hungry,' Ruiz complained.

'There are no shifts working a homicide, babe.'

His phone rang again, and he grabbed it up. 'Parker.'

'Detective Parker?' The smoky voice was trembling a little. 'It's Abby Lowell. My apartment has been broken into. By that bike messenger. I thought you should know.'

'I'll be right there.'

He hung up the phone. 'Get those photos ASAP,' he ordered Ruiz as he shrugged into his raincoat. 'And get going on the phone records from Speed. We need to get a line on Damon. Abby Lowell says he broke into her apartment today.'

'And where are you going now?' Ruiz whined.

Parker put on his hat. 'To the damsel in distress.'

ABBY LOWELL lived outside the jurisdiction of Central Bureau. Parker flashed his badge to the uniforms standing in the foyer of the building. One of them nodded him past.

A pair of detectives from West Bureau, Hollywood Division, stood in Abby Lowell's living room. The living room had been tossed like a salad. A Latent Prints guy Parker knew was dusting.

'Some party,' Parker said. 'Mind if I join the fun?'

The older of the Hollywood cops, a square-headed guy with a marine buzz cut, curled his lip like a dog about to growl.

'What are you doing here, Parker? I thought they had you writing parking tickets.'

'Your victim called me in. Apparently, you failed to impress her with your commanding presence.'

'Crawl back in your hole, Parker. This is ours.'

Parker curled his own lip and took a step forwards. 'You think I want your lousy case? This is part of my homicide, ace.'

'The always charming Detective Parker.'

Abby Lowell stood in the archway leading to the private rooms of the apartment, leaning one shoulder against the wall. She was still dressed in the same sapphire outfit she'd had on that morning but had pulled on a grey cardigan. She was hugging the sweater around her. Her hair was mussed.

Parker went to her. 'You're all right?'

She smiled wryly. 'I'm better off than the last Lowell he ran into.'

'How long ago did this happen?'

'A couple of hours, I guess. I came home and the place looked like this. I went down the hall into the bathroom and he grabbed me.'

'Did he have a weapon?'

She shook her head.

'What'd he look like? Tall, short, black, white . . . ?'

'Blond. Young. White. He looked like he had been in a fight.'

'How did you know he was the bike messenger?'

'He wouldn't tell me who he was. But he said he knew my father, that he'd done some work for him, and I just knew it was him.'

'What did he want? Why would he come to you?'

'I don't know. I was sure he was going to kill me.' The dark eyes glistened with tears.

Parker watched her for a moment, then went down the hall into the bathroom. He stood and looked closely at the broken mirror and the inscription written on it in red lipstick: NEXT YOU DIE.

Why would the bike messenger want Abby Lowell dead if killing Lenny and stealing the money from the safe had been a crime of opportunity? He wouldn't. Whoever was behind the murder, behind this, had a more complicated motive. And as far as Parker was concerned, that ruled out Damon.

Abby appeared in the shattered glass, a multitude of tiny, fragmented images, as if she were inside a giant kaleidoscope.

'What's this guy looking for?' Parker asked her.

'I don't know.'

Parker cocked a brow. 'Really? Isn't it strange that shortly before he was murdered, Lenny made a phone call to his own killer? And that after your father was dead, the killer called you to tell you about it? I find that strange. Why would Lenny give his killer your cellphone number and address?'

She wasn't ready to cry now. She was getting pissed off.

'Maybe he got it out of Lenny's Rolodex.'

'But why terrorise you if you can't give him what he wants?'

'I shouldn't have to remind you, Detective, I'm the victim here.'

'Why didn't you tell me about the safe-deposit box?' he asked bluntly.

Her breath caught in her throat. She opened her mouth to answer, but nothing came out.

'What this killer is looking for—what he was looking for in your father's office, what he was looking for here—am I going to find it in that box when I open it tomorrow?'

'I don't know what you're talking about. I'm still looking for Lenny's will and life insurance. I thought they might be in the bank.'

'I'll let you know,' Parker said. 'I'm not hindered by probate. As soon as I have the court order, I get to find the prize in the Cracker Jack box.'

She took a deep breath and let it out. 'If you don't mind, Detective, I need to go lie down.'

'You should probably stay with a friend,' Parker suggested.

'I'm going to a hotel,' she said tightly.

Parker stood too close to her as he leaned towards the door. 'Sleep well, Ms Lowell,' he purred. 'Call me if you need me.'

'That's not likely.' She didn't blink, didn't flinch.

Parker edged past her and went back down the hall. Buzz Cut was on his cellphone. Parker approached the younger detective.

'Anybody see this guy get away?'

'One of the neighbours got a partial plate,' the kid said. 'A dark green or black Mini Cooper.'

'A Mini Cooper?' Parker said, taken aback. 'What the hell kind of a crook drives a Mini Cooper?'

The kid flipped a few pages in his notebook. 'He got clipped by a minivan when he pulled a U-turn in the middle of the street. Knocked out some of the plastic from the Mini's driver's-side taillight and scratched the paint.'

'Did the driver get a good look at him?'

'Not really. All she could say was young, white male.'

'You got a card?'

The young detective pulled a business card out of his pocket and handed it over. Joel Coen.

'Thanks, Joel,' Parker said, jotting the tag number down on the back of the card. 'If I get something, I won't forget you.'

He stuck the card in his pocket and went to the Latent Prints guy to tell him they were looking for a possible match to prints found at the Lowell homicide. He told him to talk to Joanie.

Buzz Cut was closing his phone as Parker made his exit.

Parker tipped his hat and said sarcastically, 'Thanks for the hospitality, Buzz. I'll call as soon as I've solved it for you.'

ETA HEAVED A SIGH as she locked the front door from the inside. The iron grates were already down. She had been trapped all day, daring to try only periodically to contact her Lone Ranger. Either he didn't have the radio with him, or he wouldn't answer because he was afraid of a trap.

She'd nearly had a heart attack when Parker had asked her about her van. But Jace hadn't been in it. Where he'd gone, she didn't know. She fretted that he might have thought she had brought the detectives in, if he'd seen them.

She worked her way towards the back. As she went to turn the lights out, the phone rang.

All she knew about Jace was that once she'd been shopping in Chinatown, and she'd seen him across the street with a boy about nine. She had watched them go into a fish market. When she had mentioned it to him the next Monday, he'd denied being there.

She wouldn't have answered the phone, but she thought it might be him. 'Speed Couriers,' she said.

'This is Detective Davis, ma'am. I need to ask a few questions.'

Eta scowled. 'Don't you people talk to each other? What am I paying taxes for? For y'all to go running around asking the same questions over and over like a bunch of damn morons?'

'No, ma'am. I'm sorry, ma'am. I just have a couple of questions about one of your messengers, J. Damon.'

'I know that. You got to get up to speed,' she said with annoyance. 'I got better things to do with my night than talk to you, honey. I'm hanging up.'

She slammed the receiver down, her gaze going to the radio. One last try. She keyed the mike. 'Base to Sixteen. Where you at, Lone Ranger? I'm still holding money for you. You copy?'

Silence. No static. No nothing.

Eta shut off the lights, pulled on her raincoat. It was late already. If Jace was going to call, he would have done it by now.

The alley was black as pitch. It had started to rain again. The light above the door had gone out like it did every time it rained. She dug her car keys out of her tote bag.

And then a light was in her face, blinding her.

'Detective Davis, ma'am,' he said.

This isn't right, Eta thought. If he'd been back here all along, why wouldn't he have just come inside? Why call on the telephone?

'I really need to get an address from you, ma'am.'

A strange feeling crawled over her. This wasn't right. She wanted to go. 'What address?' she asked, inching her way towards her van.

'Your messenger, Damon.'

'I don't know how many times I got to say this,' Eta complained. 'I don't have no address for the boy. I don't have no phone number. I don't know where he lives.'

Davis moved closer. 'How can you not know anything about him? You can't keep that up.'

'I can and I will. I can't tell you nothin' I don't know.'

Her escape ended at the side of her van. She clutched the keys.

'You want to do this the hard way?' he asked.

'I don't want to do this at all,' Eta said.

Davis lunged, the heavy torch hitting her shoulder, and flung himself on her back, trying to knock her down. The torch went flying. Eta's knees buckled and she fell, throwing him off. She tried to get up off the ground, but fell against the van. Davis threw himself at her, slamming her back against the vehicle. Something sharp was at her throat.

'Tell me,' he demanded, breath rasping in and out.

'I don't know,' Eta said. Her own voice was unrecognisable to her, shaking, frightened. She was crying. She thought of her kids.

'Where is he? Answer me and you go home to your family.'

She was trembling. She was going to die for keeping a secret she had no answer for. Eta gave him the only answer she could.

'I seen him in Chinatown.'

'Chinatown.'

She drew breath to answer him, but when she tried to speak, no words came out of her mouth, just strange wet sounds. Davis stepped back from her, picked up the torch, shined it on her. She lifted a hand to touch her throat and felt her life running out of her. Her hand was red with it.

Horrified, she wanted to scream, but she couldn't. She was drowning in her own blood. She fell hard to the wet, oily pavement.

7

Diane Nicholson sipped at a glass of mediocre champagne, bored. The Peninsula Beverly Hills Hotel was the epitome of class and wealth, two things required to attend a political fundraiser for the district attorney of Los Angeles. But very little in the political world impressed Diane. The glow had worn off long ago.

Her husband had spent a dozen years involved in city politics. Joseph's second great love. His job was his first, the love that made him a wealthy man. Diane had been ranked somewhere further down the list, after golfing and his boat. The last couple of years of the marriage, the most they saw of each other had been at events like this one. And even then, all she had been was an accessory on his arm, like a pair of diamond cuff links.

He had married her for her potential as a social asset. She had a good look, was well dressed, well informed, well spoken. But her career was an embarrassment to him, and Diane had refused to give it up. And the more strained their relationship became because of it, the harder she had hung on to it, afraid to let go of the one thing that was a sure thing, because her husband's love was not.

She allowed herself to be dragged to these events now because she enjoyed eavesdropping, and because appearing with someone warded off matchmakers. Also, she had agreed to come on the condition her date buy her dinner afterwards. Her date was Jeff Gauthier, forty-six, handsome, an attorney for the city of Los Angeles, chronic bachelor. He had been a friend for years and years.

She scanned the crowd. The usual suspects. District Attorney Steinman and his wife, the mayor and his wife, ADA Giradello and his ego, the assorted LA movers and shakers. Diane and Gauthier did the meet and greet. Gazes passed like ships in the night as everyone looked for the next important person to move on to.

And then that person walked into the room.

Norman Crowne was a man of average height and slight build, grey hair, and a beard precisely trimmed. Unassuming at first glance for a man who wielded the kind of power he did. He was followed by his son Phillip and a pair of bodyguards who looked like they had come straight from the Secret Service. The crowd parted before them as if they were royalty, and the senior Crowne went directly to the district attorney and offered his hand.

The son turned to Anthony Giradello and was greeted warmly. They were of an age, and both graduates of Stanford Law, but Phillip had been born a Crowne, with all the privileges that came with it, and held a cushy position in Crowne Enterprises. Giradello had been the son of fruit ranchers and had clawed his way up the ladder in the DA's office.

'One big happy family,' Diane murmured to Jeff as they moved through the crowd. 'That's blatant. The trial of his daughter's murderer is about to start, and Norman Crowne is all but laying money on the table for the DA in front of every media source in LA.'

Jeff shrugged. 'So? There's no conflict of interest. Giradello hardly needs to be bribed to go for the throat on this one. He wants to convict Rob Cole so badly, he can hardly stand it. He's not going to mess that up. To say nothing of using this trial to blot out the memory of that preppie murder your friend Parker screwed up for him.'

'Parker was a scapegoat. Giradello didn't do his homework. That trial was his first big lesson in "Money buys justice". This is his second,' Diane said. 'You don't think every average person in America isn't going to look at this picture on the morning shows tomorrow and say Norman Crowne is buying himself a conviction?'

'Well . . . I don't care, frankly,' Jeff said. 'And I don't see why you would, either. You'd have them stick Rob Cole's head on a pike. What's your problem with Norman Crowne's influence?'

'Nothing. I just don't want to see grounds for appeal.' Diane turned to get a better view of the Crowne clan, now joined by Tricia's daughter from her first marriage.

Caroline Crowne was just twenty-one, short and stubby, like her mother had been, though Caroline had done a lot more with herself than Tricia ever had. She was packaged in conservative designer labels, and her curly auburn hair was stylishly cut in a chin-length bob. Shortly after Tricia's murder, the tabloids had hinted at something sordid going on between Caroline and her stepfather, but the rumours had been squelched like a slug on the sidewalk.

What a list of headlines an affair between Caroline Crowne and Rob Cole would have generated. Poor old Tricia whacked to make way for a May-December romance between her daughter and her sleazy, rotten husband. Caroline had been nineteen when her mother died. Barely legal. It wasn't all that hard for Diane to imagine.

'One more and we're out of here,' Jeff said through his teeth as he smiled and raised his glass to someone off to his right.

'I can already taste the sea bass,' Diane said, letting him steer her towards the district attorney.

From the corner of her eye she saw a door swing open. Bradley Kyle and his partner came in looking like kids being sent to the principal's office. They were headed in the same direction that Jeff was taking her—towards the DA and the ADA, and Norman and Phillip Crowne.

Diane drifted a step in their direction as Giradello excused himself from Phillip Crowne and moved two steps towards the cops. Eavesdropping was the real reason she came to these things.

The conversation was terse; Giradello's face darkened; Bradley Kyle turned his hands palms up, like, What do you want me to do about it? Only the odd word escaped for the casual ear to catch: *do, what, can't, know.* Somebody was supposed to have done something but hadn't been able to.

Kyle and his partner had worked Tricia Crowne's murder. Not as leads, as second team. As the trial began, they would be called on to double-check, to pick at any tiny fibres that could become loose ends.

A trial as big as this one was a chess game, with layers and layers of strategy. The pieces were being jockeyed into position. Giradello was bringing his army into line. Somebody was supposed to have done something but hadn't been able to. She wondered what that something was.

A word, a curse, a growl, a name she didn't recognise . . . and one that she did.

RUIZ was long gone by the time Parker returned to the station. It would have been nice to go home himself, take a steam, have a glass of wine, order in some wonton soup and Mongolian beef from the restaurant down the street. He had a script to read. And sleep sounded like a good idea too.

But Parker wouldn't be going home soon. There were too many things he needed to know, and he needed to know them quickly. The oddities of the break-in at Abby Lowell's apartment—and with Abby Lowell herself— were rubbing against the grain. The hell she didn't know what her burglar was after. She was after it herself.

Lenny Lowell's death was no random act. And what would a bike messenger, assigned by the luck of the draw, have known about this mysterious something Lowell apparently possessed that was worth killing for?

A simple robbery didn't send a perp on to his victim's daughter to toss her apartment and threaten to kill her. Parker's instincts told him the words scrawled on Abby Lowell's bathroom mirror had an implied 'unless' to them. *Next you die . . . unless I get what I'm after.* Which implied the assailant believed Abby Lowell knew what he was after.

And how had the mirror been broken? The damage had been done after the message had been written on it. Abby Lowell hadn't had a mark on her, nor had she said anything about a struggle in the bathroom, the mirror getting broken, someone bleeding.

She said the guy told her he'd done some work for her father. What was that about? The Emily Post etiquette rules for murderers? *Hello, here's who I am, my references, my connection to you. So sorry, I'm going to kill you now.* What crap.

And the guy drives away in a Mini Cooper.

Parker ran the partial plate from the car through the DMV and waited impatiently. Ruiz was probably out salsa dancing with the sugar daddy who kept her supplied in Manolo Blahniks.

On impulse, he picked up the phone and dialled the number of an old friend who worked Homicide in South Central.

'Metheny,' a gravel-choked voice barked.

'Hey, Methuselah, you got it under control down there?'

'Kev Parker. I thought you died.'

'I kind of wished I had there for a while,' Parker admitted.

He had partnered with Dan Metheny a thousand years ago when Parker had been cutting a swath through the food chain to get to Robbery-Homicide. Metheny liked him anyway.

'You got any contacts working Latin gangs in your neck of the woods?' Parker asked.

'Yeah. Why?'

'I've got a trainee did some task-force work down your way. I'd like to find out how she was. Her name is Renee Ruiz.'

'I'll see what I can find out.'

They traded a few insults and hung up. Parker turned his attention to the results of his DMV search.

Of Mini Coopers registered in the Los Angeles area, seventeen were possible matches. Seven were listed as being green, five black. None of them were registered to Jace or J. C. Damon. None had been reported stolen.

The detectives at Abby Lowell's break-in would be looking for the car too. Parker couldn't let them go hunting first.

He dug a map out of his desk and began locating the addresses of the Mini Cooper owners. None were in the vicinity of the mailbox rented to Allison Jennings and passed on to J. C. Damon.

Parker found that one of the owners lived in the Miracle Mile area, not far from Abby Lowell's apartment. That car was registered to Punjhar, Rajhid, DDS. One was in Westwood, near UCLA. One was registered to a Chen, Lu, who lived in Chinatown.

Which car did Damon have access to? Where the hell did he live? Why was he so secretive about it? He didn't have a record. They had the partial prints from the murder weapon but not enough to get a hit running them through the system.

Maybe the kid was a career criminal. Or maybe he was hiding from someone. And if he hadn't killed Lenny Lowell, why would he search out Lenny's daughter? How would he know anything about this missing something everyone wanted so badly? And why had Robbery-Homicide shown up at that scene?

Parker rubbed his face. He needed fresh air, and he needed answers. He put his coat on and went outside in search of both.

Parker walked to his car and slipped behind the wheel. This one was the workhorse, a five-year-old Chrysler Sebring convertible. He drove it to work, drove it to crime scenes. Time off the job was for the green vintage Jag, his beautiful, sexy, secret lover. He smiled a little at that. Then the smile faded as he remembered Ruiz asking him about the car. She'd heard rumours, she'd said.

He dug his cellphone out of his coat pocket, dialled Andi Kelly, and opened with: 'What have you done for me lately, gorgeous?'

'You're a pushy s.o.b. I have priorities other than you, you know. Cocktail hour is at hand, and I have a date with a seventeen-year-old.'

'Still pounding down the Scotch, huh?'

'How do you know it isn't a young man?'

'Because seventeen isn't legal. So? Have anything for me?'

'My memory isn't so good before dinner,' she said. 'Meet me at Morton's in West Hollywood. You're buying.'

JACE PARKED Madame Chen's car in the narrow space behind her office. He wiped down the interior with wet paper napkins, trying to erase any sign he'd been there. Then he tried to decide what to do next.

Maybe he should go underground. That was what Alicia would have done. She would have packed them up and moved in the middle of the night. They would have popped up like toadstools in another part of town, with new names and no explanation why.

Jace had wondered why, many times. When he was Tyler's age, he had dreamed up all kinds of stories about his mother, always painting her as the heroine. As he had grown older, he had wondered all the time if Alicia had been evading the police. Why, he couldn't imagine. His mother had been a quiet, kind person. *Maybe she was like me,* he thought now, *in the wrong place at the wrong time.*

'Why don't you want to come into the light, JayCee?'

Madame Chen stood beneath the dim light over the office door.

'I have a lot on my mind,' Jace said.

'Your thoughts are heavy like stones.'

'I have to talk to you about something important,' he said.

She nodded and went back inside. Jace followed, head down. She motioned him to a hard wooden straight-backed chair beside her desk and kept her back to him as she made tea.

'I'm in a bad situation, Madame Chen,' Jace said.

'You are in trouble,' she corrected him, turning to face him. She couldn't hide her reaction. The colour left her face.

He had tried to clean up, but water didn't wash away cuts or bruises or swollen knobs of flesh.

She lowered herself to her chair. 'Tell me everything,' she said.

'You might hear some things about me,' he said. 'Bad things. I want you to know they aren't true.'

She arched a brow. 'You think so little of my loyalty that you would say this to me? You are like a son to me.'

If her son were living a secret life under aliases. If her son were wanted for murder. If her son had someone trying to kill him.

'The attorney I was delivering a package for last night was found murdered after I'd been in his office. The police are looking for me.'

'They are crazy! You would never kill a man!' she said emphatically. 'I will call my attorney. Everything will be fine.'

'It's not that simple, Madame Chen. They probably have my fingerprints from the office.' *And I was caught in the victim's daughter's ransacked apartment*, he added mentally.

'Why would the police think you would kill this man?'

'I don't know. Maybe he was robbed or something.'

She reached for the phone. 'Let me call the attorney—'

'No!' Jace reached across the desk and pushed the receiver back down with more force than he wished. Madame Chen looked at him as if she had never seen him before.

'I can't go to the police,' he said quietly, sinking back down. 'Please understand. If I go to the police, then it's all over. I'll go to jail. Even if I eventually get off, it takes months for cases to go to trial. What happens to Tyler? If Children and Family Services find out about Tyler, they take him. He goes to foster care—'

'I would never allow that to happen!' Madame Chen said angrily. 'Tyler belongs with us. His home is here.'

'That doesn't matter to them,' Jace said bitterly, his mother's warnings branded in his head.

'Let me talk to the attorney.'

'I'd rather leave him here with you. He'd be safer with you, but I'll take him if I have to. I don't want you in danger, or your father-in-law. I don't want Tyler in danger, but I can't leave him if I have to worry he won't be here when I come back.'

Neither of them said anything for a moment. Jace couldn't bring himself to look at this woman who had been kind enough to take the Damon brothers in, give them a home, treat Tyler like family. Treat *him* as family. He wished he hadn't told her. What a mess.

If he went to the police and they took him into custody, that news would make the papers. If reporters found Tyler and the Chens, Predator could find Tyler and the Chens.

If Jace got rid of the evidence or gave it to Abby Lowell, he had still seen the negatives. Predator wasn't going to leave a loose end that might come back and hang him.

'I'm so sorry I'm dragging you into this,' he said softly. 'I wish I didn't have to tell you, but I don't see a way round it. If someone comes here looking for me—if the police come—you deserve to know why. I owe you that.'

'If the police come,' Madame Chen said, 'I will say nothing.'

Jace looked up at her.

'I don't agree with what you are doing, JayCee, but my loyalty is to you. And I know you did not commit this crime.'

One of the few truly good people Jace had ever known in his life, and he was putting her in the position of having to lie for him. Possibly putting her in harm's way. All because he had answered one last call. A favour to Eta.

He could almost hear Lenny Lowell saying it: *No good deed goes unpunished, kid.*

TYLER KNEW EVERY INCH of the building. He was small for his age, which helped in his efforts to go unnoticed. When he wanted to be anonymous, he wore a faded black sweatshirt. It was soft with age and the sleeves were long enough to cover his hands, the hood so deep it swallowed his face.

Going unnoticed was a skill Tyler had honed from an early age. Jace always wanted to protect him from everything, shelter him like he was a baby or something. But Tyler wanted to know everything about everything. Knowledge was power.

He was just a little kid and too small to control his world by physical means, but he had an IQ of 168. He had taken all kinds of tests on the Internet. His brain was his strength.

He stayed back inside the hood now as he cracked open the door of the broom closet just down the hall from Madame Chen's office and spied Chi with his ear to the office door, trying to listen in. Tyler had never liked Chi. Grandfather Chen said Chi had swallowed the seeds of jealousy as a child and that the roots were now in every part of him.

Jace had been late coming home. Again. As soon as Jace had headed for Madame Chen's office, Tyler had grabbed his secret cloak of invisibility and scurried to get to the broom closet.

He knew something was wrong, and he knew it was worse than Jace just taking a fall from The Beast. He had known it the instant Jace had spoken to him the night before. Tyler had spent a lot of time observing people; he had developed an uncanny sense of whether a person was telling the truth. He knew Jace hadn't been, but Tyler had been too scared to call him on it.

But now, as he crouched in the closet that shared a wall with Madame Chen's office, he wondered if the truth wasn't just as bad. The police thought Jace had killed a guy! Tyler's mind raced, picturing what Jace was saying about going to jail and child services.

Tyler's stomach started to hurt at the idea of being forced to leave Madame Chen and Grandfather Chen. He tucked himself into a ball with his arms wrapped around his legs. It wouldn't do him any good to cry. He had to think. He had to try to gather as much information as he could and come up with some ideas of what to do, and how to help.

But he was still a little kid, and he'd never been so scared.

8

or a woman the size of a pixie, Andi Kelly's capacity for food seemed to defy the laws of nature. She ate like a wolf. Parker watched her with amazement. LA was a town where eating real food was frowned on for women. Half the women he knew would come to Morton's, order endive salad and a piece of shrimp, and go throw it all up afterwards.

But then, Andi Kelly didn't fit any particular mould. She said what she wanted to say, did what she wanted to do, wore what she wanted to wear. She greeted him like he was an old dear friend she'd seen just two days ago, sat down and started chatting.

Parker was too keyed up to eat much himself. The nervous tension that wound inside him during an investigation like this one—a case that intrigued him and challenged him—revved him up to a point where he didn't want to stop moving, not to eat, not to sleep. He wasn't quite to that point yet, but he knew all the signs. He could feel them now like the subtle foreshocks of an earthquake.

'So this kid, this reporter Caldrovics, says he got a tip on your murder,' Kelly informed him between bites of prime Angus beef.

Parker nursed a glass of cabernet. 'From who?'

'You're kidding, right? He won't tell me.'

'Beat it out of him,' Parker suggested, deadpan.

Kelly snarled and sliced another juicy chunk off her steak. 'I'll turn this little creep inside out if there's something in it for me.'

'You're not the only one who's after something in this,' Parker confessed quietly, his gaze scanning the territory. Tucked back in lush landscaping on Melrose in trendy West Hollywood, Morton's was a throwback to the days of old Hollywood glamour and was still a hangout for power players.

'Lowell's daughter is holding back,' he said. 'Someone tossed her place today, threatened to kill her. Assaulted her, she said.'

'Don't you know it's politically incorrect to doubt the victim?'

'My victim is Lenny Lowell. For all I know, the daughter had him whacked. She's looking for something besides her father's will, and she lied about it. Whoever tossed her place was looking for something, and she claimed not to know what. If she was at that murder scene before I got there, I need to know it. That's why I want an explanation from your little friend at the *Daily Planet*.'

Sitting back, Kelly gazed with satisfaction at her empty plate. 'The kid says he picked up the call on the scanner,' she said.

'If he caught it on the scanner, why didn't he come to the scene? He never talked to me.'

'Well, he claims he talked to someone who knew what was what and that he confirmed with the coroner's office.'

'Who at LAPD? Who at the coroner's office?'

'Hey, don't kill the messenger,' she said.

Parker sighed. 'So, I'm buying you a steak at Morton's so you can tell me all you have to give me is his name.'

'Actually, that's all you asked me to do. Think of it as goodwill that will pay off later,' Kelly suggested with a smile. Her eyes were an amazing shade of blue. Her hair was the colour of an Irish setter and looked like maybe she'd cut it herself with pinking shears. It stood up in a messy little spiky cap on her head. It suited her.

Parker shook his head, smiling. 'You're a trip, Andi.'

'To paradise,' she murmured dramatically.

Parker's pager vibrated at his waist. He unclipped it from his belt and squinted at the screen. Diane's cellphone number.

'Excuse me,' he said, standing up. 'I have to make a call to someone much more important than you.'

Kelly rolled her eyes. 'You just want to stick me with the tab.'

Parker ignored her and went outside to return the call.

Diane answered before the first ring had finished. 'Did I tear you away from a hot date?' she asked.

'Not exactly. Where are you?'

'The Peninsula. A fundraiser for the DA. I just overheard your name in a conversation.'

'Yeah? And then did they all spit on the ground?'

'It was Giradello,' she said. 'And Bradley Kyle.'

Parker said nothing. Everything seemed to freeze around him.

'I only caught a few words. I got the impression Kyle was supposed to have done something about something but hadn't.'

'And my name was in there somewhere?'

'First there was a name I didn't recognise. Yours came later.'

'The first name—do you remember what it was?'

'I think it started with a D. Desmond? Devon, maybe?'

Heat went through Parker like a flash fire. 'Damon.'

PARKER WENT BACK into Morton's, hailing the waiter. 'Let's go,' he said to Kelly. He handed his credit card to the waiter, then grabbed his coat.

Kelly stood up. 'What's the rush?'

The waiter hustled back with his credit card, and Parker hurriedly added a generous tip and scrawled his signature on the slip.

'I've got a dead low-end defence attorney nobody should care about but his nearest and dearest,' Parker said as they walked out of the door towards the valet parking stand. 'Why do you think Robbery-Homicide and Tony Giradello would have an interest?'

Parker could all but hear the wheels in Kelly's head whirring. 'They wouldn't,' she said. 'But they do?'

'A couple of Robbery-Homicide humps showed up at the crime scene last night. Kyle and his partner.'

'But they didn't take over the case?'

Parker shook his head. 'No. I called their bluff, and they backed down, and I don't get that at all. What the hell were they doing there if they weren't there to steal the case?'

Division detectives usually began the initial investigation. Then if the case was big enough or bad enough or glamorous enough, Robbery-Homicide would waltz onto the stage.

'And now I'm told those same Robbery-Homicide hotshots reported to Giradello in the middle of a fundraiser tonight.'

Kelly shrugged it off. 'They're preparing for the Cole trial.'

'Why would my name get mentioned in that conversation?'

'You didn't have anything to do with that homicide investigation?'

'No, nothing. The body was discovered by Tricia Cole's daughter, who called Norman Crowne. The Crowne brain trust called the chief directly. The chief sent Robbery-Homicide. The only common denominator between me and Bradley Kyle is Lenny Lowell,' Parker said, omitting the fact that the name of his chief suspect had come up in the same conversation.

It was one thing to dangle a carrot in front of Kelly; giving her the store was something else. But he liked Kelly and he owed her.

'But why would Giradello have any interest in your stiff?'

'That's the sixty-four-thousand-dollar question, Andi,' Parker said, digging his ticket out of his coat pocket and turning towards the valet. 'Why don't you ask someone who might know.'

Kelly handed her ticket over. 'And get back to you.'

'Symbiosis, my friend,' Parker said. 'In the meantime, we're going to go ask your little pal if Bradley Kyle is a friend of his.'

'He's not my child. How would I know where he is?'

'Where do the young monkeys hang out to drink and beat their chests these days?' Parker asked as Kelly's car pulled to the kerb behind his.

They each went to their respective driver's door.

'If you kill him,' Kelly said, 'I get the exclusive.'

A few minutes later, Kelly was leading him to a downtown bar that probably didn't look much different than it had in the thirties. Inside, she snagged a pair of stools at the bar that tucked them back from the crowd but allowed a view of the room and the front door.

Parker ordered a tonic and lime for himself. Kelly asked for the best Scotch in the place, then raised an eyebrow at Parker. 'You're still paying, right? I'm counting this as part of the date.'

'We're not on a date.'

'You want something from me, and you bought me dinner in hopes of getting it. How is that different from a date?'

Parker chuckled. 'You've still got it, Andi. You know, I'd kind of forgotten that. During that whole mess with the preppie murder, you were the only person who made me laugh.'

'I'm not quite sure how to take that.'

'As a compliment.'

'I don't see Caldrovics,' Kelly said. 'But that pack in the fourth booth down is the one he might run with. The obnoxiously young and hungry,' she said with disgust. 'I have jeans as old as they are.'

'You're not old,' Parker scoffed. 'If you're old, I'm old. I don't accept that.'

'Easy for you to say. A sexy guy is a sexy guy until he becomes incontinent and has to use an ear trumpet. A girl hits fortysomething in this town and she's culled from the herd.'

'You look great,' Parker said. 'You haven't aged a day. Your skin is luminous and you look fantastic in those trousers.'

She pretended to pout. 'You could score better on sincerity.'

'I'm out of practice. I'm a quiet homebody now,' he said.

'There he is,' Kelly said, nodding across the room. 'Caldrovics. He's coming from the back. Must have been in the men's room. Greasy hair, scruffy goatee, looks like a homeless person.'

'Got him,' Parker said, sliding off the barstool. He put some bills on the bar, then made his way across the room.

He put a hand on the kid's shoulder. 'Mr Caldrovics? I'd like to have a word with you, please.' Parker cupped his shield in his hand and flashed it discreetly to Caldrovics.

Before the rest of the table could become interested, Parker moved away from it, his hand at the base of the kid's neck.

'What's this about?' Caldrovics asked, dragging his feet.

'I'm sorry, I don't know your first name,' said Parker.

'Danny—'

'Can I call you Danny?' Parker asked, walking him out through the back door to an alley where a couple of staffers were smoking. 'I'm Detective Parker, Kev Parker. LAPD Central Division, Homicide.'

Caldrovics tried to put the brakes on. 'Where are we going?'

'Just over here,' Parker said, giving him a little shove as they passed a Dumpster, where they couldn't be seen.

The security light behind the building had the white of a full moon, and Parker could see the kid's every expression.

'I need to ask you a couple of questions, Danny,' Parker began. 'About that little bit you had in the paper this morning regarding the murder of Leonard Lowell, Esquire.'

Caldrovics took a step back towards the Dumpster.

'I'm the primary investigator on that case,' Parker said. 'That means everything comes through me. I'm a stickler for protocol.'

'That's not what I've heard,' Caldrovics muttered.

'Excuse me?' Parker took an aggressive step forwards.

'You can't harass me like this,' Caldrovics said. He was nervous but was trying not to show it.

'The fuse on my temper right now is the size of an eyelash. I've got a murder that smells like week-old oysters, and you've got information I need,' Parker said.

'I don't know who killed the guy!'

'You seem to know things the rest of us don't. How is that?'

'This is nuts.' Caldrovics tried to sidestep Parker. Parker shoved him back against the Dumpster.

'Hey!' Caldrovics snapped. 'That's assault!'

'That's resisting arrest.' Parker slammed him face-first against the steel container. 'Danny Caldrovics, you're under arrest.'

'For what?' Caldrovics demanded as Parker slapped on cuffs.

'What the hell is going on back here?' Andi Kelly rushed around the side of the Dumpster and skidded to a halt.

'Kelly?' Caldrovics looked at her, astonished.

'Butt out, Kelly,' Parker snapped. 'Your little pal here is under arrest. He's withholding information on a felony murder. That makes him an accessory after the fact, if not before.'

'You never heard of the Constitution, Parker?' Kelly said sarcastically. 'The First Amendment?'

'You people make me sick,' Parker said. 'You put the First Amendment on like a fashion accessory.'

Caldrovics looked at Kelly. 'Please, go call someone!'

'I don't have time for this, Kelly,' Parker barked. 'We're talking about a murderer who isn't finished killing people. He attacked the victim's daughter today, thanks to your buddy here, who obligingly put her name in the newspaper this morning!'

'What do you need to know from him, Parker?' Kelly asked.

'Who told him the daughter found the body?'

Kelly turned to Caldrovics. 'You didn't get it from him? If he's the lead on the case, why didn't you get it from him?'

'I don't have to explain myself to you, Kelly.'

Kelly stomped over and kicked him in the shin. 'Are you stupid? I'm trying to save your sorry ass.' She turned to walk away.

'Kelly! For God's sake!' Caldrovics called after her.

She turned around and spread her hands. 'You have information on a murder, Caldrovics. All he wants to know is who gave it to you. Why didn't you talk to Parker at the scene? He would have given you details.'

Finally Caldrovics said, 'I didn't go to the scene, all right? I caught it on the scanner. It was raining, man. Why should I go out in the rain and stand around just to have somebody tell me the guy on the floor with his head smashed open is dead?'

'And how did you know his head was smashed open?' Parker asked. 'That wasn't on the scanner. And why did you say the daughter found the body? Did you just make that up, Danny?'

Caldrovics sulked. 'I talked to a cop. What's the big deal?'

'It's a big deal,' Parker said, 'because you didn't talk to me. It's a big deal because, as far as I know, you didn't talk to anybody who was at the scene. It's a big deal because you put a piece of information in there that's news to me, and I want to know where it came from. What cop?'

'He's with Robbery-Homicide. Why wouldn't I believe what he told me?' Caldrovics said.

Parker felt like he'd been struck hard. 'Kyle.'

'Kyle who?' Caldrovics asked. 'The guy I talked to is Davis.'

'Who's Davis?' Parker asked. He turned to Kelly, who probably knew the personnel at Parker Center better than he did.

Kelly shrugged. 'I don't know any Davis.'

Parker looked at Caldrovics. 'How do you know this guy?'

'From around. I met him at a bar down the street maybe a week ago. Can you take these cuffs off?'

'He showed you ID?' Parker asked, unlocking the cuffs.

'Yeah. I asked him what's it like on the big team. He told me about a couple of cases he'd worked in the past.'

Parker's cellphone rang. He checked the caller ID. Ruiz. Parker felt a sense of dread prickle his skin.

'I just got called,' Ruiz said. 'I'm up, you know.'

'I'll meet you at the scene. What's the address?' Parker said.

'Speed Couriers.'

'DAMN,' PARKER SAID on a long sigh. He felt the strength and energy drain from him with his breath.

A spotlight from Chewalski's radio car illuminated the scene in white light, like the stage of some avant-garde performance artist. Eta Fitzgerald lay in a heap on the wet, cracked pavement behind the Speed office. Parker squatted down beside the body. Her throat had been slashed from ear to ear.

'That's a whole lotta woman,' Jimmy Chew said.

'Don't,' Parker said quietly. 'Don't. Not this time.'

'Geez, I'm sorry,' Chew said. 'She a friend?'

'No,' Parker said. 'But she could have been, in another time, another place.'

'She's got no ID on her. No purse. I'm sure her cash is running all over town by now. We found keys near the body. They fit the minivan. The van is registered to Evangeline Fitzgerald.'

'Eta,' Parker said. 'She called herself Eta. She was the dispatcher here. Ruiz and I spoke with her this morning.'

'That bike messenger, the one from last night, he worked here?'

'Yeah.'

'Guess he's our guy, huh? The lawyer. The dispatcher. What they got in common is him.'

Parker didn't say anything, but he didn't buy it. If Damon wanted to silence her, he would have killed her before she got to work, not as she was leaving. Why would the kid risk coming back here at all? And he supposedly had cash from Lenny Lowell's safe. What would he want with the contents of the woman's wallet?

Parker looked around. 'Where's Ruiz? This is her call.'

'She's not here yet. Probably taking extra time to sharpen her claws. You've got a real peach there, Kev.'

'I don't have to like them, Jimmy,' Parker said.

'Anything for the press, Detective?' Kelly asked from behind the yellow police tape.

Parker jammed his hands in his coat pockets and walked over. 'It's not my case.'

'And the detective in charge?'

'Isn't here yet. The vic was a dispatcher for Speed Couriers. Apparent robbery. Her purse is gone.'

'Kev?' Kelly was looking at him with concern.

'Lenny Lowell was waiting for a messenger last night. The messenger came from Speed Couriers. No one has seen him since.' That wasn't exactly true, but Kelly didn't need to hear every detail.

'This messenger is your suspect? For both murders?'

'He's a person of interest.'

A car roared down the alley and skidded to a halt behind Chewalski's radio car, stopping short of the rear bumper by three inches. The driver's door opened and Ruiz climbed out in head-to-toe skintight black leather.

'Where have you been?' Parker snapped. 'Moonlighting as a dominatrix? You called me half an hour ago.'

'Well, excuse me,' she answered. 'I don't live in some trendy downtown loft. I live in the Valley.'

Parker held up a hand. 'You're here now. Ruiz, this is Andi Kelly,' he said. 'She writes for the *Times*.'

Ruiz looked offended. 'What's she doing here?'

Kelly gave her a Valley girl sneer. 'Reporter, crime, story. Duh.'

'Ladies, no catfights at the murder scene,' Parker said. 'It's your case, Ruiz. It's up to you to decide what you want the press to know. I want you to run everything past me first. This murder could be related to my murder last night. We need to be on the same page. Do you know who the vic is?'

'The dispatcher.'

The coroner's investigator had arrived and was walking around Eta Fitzgerald's body, as if he couldn't decide where to start.

'It's your crime scene,' Parker said. 'Don't screw up, and try not to alienate more than three or four people.'

Ruiz flipped him off and walked away.

'Yikes,' Kelly said. 'Someone at Parker Center *really* hates you.'

'Honey, *everybody* at Parker Center really hates me.' He flipped up the collar of his coat and resettled his hat. 'I'll call you.'

He started towards the scene. The coroner's investigator was examining the victim's body for wounds, marks, bruises, lividity.

'How long has she been dead, Stan?' Parker asked him.

'Two or three hours.'

The man groaned, and strained to turn Eta Fitzgerald's body over. Her throat had been severed nearly to her spine.

Ruiz cringed and muttered, '*Madre de Dios.*'

Hardened as he was, this death rocked Parker more than average. Hours ago he'd heard wisecracks from this big, vibrant woman. Now there was no voice, only an anatomy lesson on the human throat.

'Have you got uniforms checking these other buildings?' Parker asked Ruiz. 'Someone might have seen something.'

She nodded.

'Who called it in?'

'I don't know.'

Parker turned to Chewalski. 'Jimmy?'

'One of our fine citizens,' the officer said, nodding for them to follow him across the alley.

A figure emerged from inside a large discarded cardboard box. As the figure unfolded, he became a tall, thin black man with matted grey hair and layers of ragged clothes. His aroma preceded him.

'Detectives, this is Obidia Jones.'

'I founded that poor woman!' Jones said, pointing across the alley. 'I woulda tried to recirculate her, but I couldn't turn her over. As you can see, she's pacidermical in size.'

'And you called the police?' Ruiz said, dubious.

'It don't cost nothing to call nine one one. I do it once in a while.'

'Did you see what happened, Mr Jones?' Ruiz asked.

'No, ma'am, I did not.'

'How did you find the dead woman, Mr Jones?' Parker said.

'I seen her laying right there after that car pulled away.'

'What car?'

'Big black car.'

'And did you happen to see who was driving that car?'

'Not this time.'

Ruiz rubbed her forehead. 'What does that mean?'

'Oh, I seen him before,' Jones said. 'He came by earlier. He look like a pit bull. Square head, beady-eyed. Undoubtedly of white-trash hermitage.'

'We'll want you to look at some pictures,' Parker said.

'At your station house? Whilst it's cold and wet out here?'

'If you don't mind.'

'I don't mind,' Jones said. 'Do you all get pizza in there?'

'Sure. One last thing, Mr Jones. Around the time of the murder, did you see anyone back here on a bicycle?'

'No, sir. All them bicycle boys was long gone before that.'

'What about a small, boxy black car?'

'No, sir. Big. Long and black as the grim reaper himself.'

The apartment was quiet and dark, the only illumination a white glow that came and went as rain-swollen clouds scudded across the moon. Jace prowled the small space.

Tyler had watched him closely but had asked no questions about the new cuts and bruises. The tension in the apartment had felt like static electricity building until their hair should have been standing on end. At ten, Tyler had gone off to bed without a word.

Jace packed quickly. A change of clothes and not much more stuffed into a backpack. He still didn't have a plan, but he couldn't stay here. Something would come to him; it always did.

He had what the killer wanted, and if it was worth killing for, then it had to be worth something to someone else too. Abby Lowell was the key. He didn't believe she didn't know what was going on.

He would have to lure her out somehow. Get her to meet him on neutral ground. He would tell her he had the negatives, ask her what they meant to her. Ask her what they were worth to her.

Jace wondered what she'd told the police. She'd mentioned a particular detective. What was his name? Parker. He wondered if that was the guy in the hat behind the Speed office. And he wondered what Parker had put together, what Eta had told him. He still didn't want to believe Eta had betrayed him.

'You're leaving, and you weren't even going to tell me.'

Tyler stood in the doorway wearing his Spider-Man pyjamas.

'I wouldn't leave without telling you,' Jace said.

'You told me you wouldn't leave at all.'

'I said I would always come back,' Jace corrected him.

Tyler was shaking his head, his eyes filling. 'You're leaving. You're not going to take me with you, and I don't get to say anything about it.'

'You can't go, Tyler. I have to clear up some problems.'

'We could too go,' Tyler argued. 'We could go someplace nobody knows us, just like when Mom died.'

'It's not that simple,' Jace said.

'Cause you're gonna go to jail?'

'What?' Jace didn't ask his brother if he'd been listening in on his conversation with Madame Chen. Obviously, he had. Tyler was notorious for knowing things he shouldn't have known.

'I'm not going to jail,' Jace said. 'I said that to scare Madame Chen. She wants me to go to the cops or talk to a lawyer. I don't want to do that.'

'So CFS doesn't put me in foster care.'

'That's right, pal.' Jace put his hands on his little brother's small shoulders. 'I won't risk you. We look out for each other, right?'

'Then you should let me help you,' Tyler insisted again. 'I'm way smarter than you are.'

Jace laughed wearily and mussed his brother's hair. 'If this were about geometry or science, I'd come straight to you, Ty. But it's not. This is a whole lot more serious.'

'Some man got killed,' Tyler said quietly.

'Yes.'

'What if you get killed too?'

'I won't let that happen,' Jace said, knowing it was an empty promise. Tyler knew it too.

A tear skittered down his brother's face. The expression in his eyes was far older than he was. A deep sadness, made all the more poignant by the weary resignation of past experience.

Jace pulled the boy close and held him tight, his own tears burning his eyes. 'I love you, little guy. I'll come back.'

'You promise?' Tyler asked, his voice muffled.

'I promise,' Jace whispered, his throat aching. Then Jace sighed and stood his brother back from him. 'I have to go, pal.'

'Wait,' Tyler said. He turned and ran into his room before Jace could say anything and came back seconds later with the pair of small two-way radios Jace had given him for Christmas.

'Take one,' he said.

Jace took the radio. 'I'll call you when I can.'

He put his army fatigue jacket on and slipped the radio into a pocket. Tyler walked with him to the door.

Jace expected Tyler to tell him to be careful, but he didn't. He didn't say goodbye. He didn't say anything. Jace touched his brother's hair one last time and went down the stairs.

Chinatown was silent now, the streets glistening like black ice under the streetlights. Jace climbed on The Beast and headed down the alley, turning towards downtown, where lights in the windows of tall buildings glowed like columns of stars.

And as Jace turned one corner, a Chrysler Sebring turned another just a few blocks away and slipped into its parking slot beside a former textile warehouse that had been converted into trendy lofts.

PARKER LET HIMSELF INTO his loft and dropped his keys on the narrow black walnut table in the slate-floored entry hall.

The soft glow of the small halogen lights spotlighting the art on his walls led him down the hall into the master bathroom. He turned on the steam shower and slipped out of his suit. The steam and pounding hot water soothed his muscles, warming away the chill.

The bedside lamps were turned on low—part of the elaborate electronic system a buddy had talked him into. Lights, music, room temperature—all were tied into a timed computer system so that he never came home to a cold, dark place.

The woman asleep in his bed was another matter. She had come of her own free will and made herself at home.

Parker sat down on the edge of the bed and looked at her, a little pleased, a little surprised, a little puzzled.

Diane blinked her eyes open and looked up at him. 'Surprise.'

'I am surprised,' Parker said, touching her hair. 'And to what do I owe the pleasure?'

'I needed to cleanse my palate of socialites. Decided I would find myself a hot metrosexual guy to hang out with.'

Parker smiled. 'Well, baby, I am the prince of metrosexual chic. I have a closet full of Armani. I can whip up a dinner for four with no frozen ingredients, and I can pick a good wine.'

'I knew I'd come to the right place.' She sat up and stretched. She was a strong, attractive woman, comfortable in her own body. 'Did you get called to something?' she asked.

'Yeah. Ruiz's first homicide as lead. It might be tied to the Lowell homicide last night.'

'Really?' She frowned a little. 'How so?'

'The vic is the dispatcher from the messenger service Lowell called at the end of the day. Somebody seems to be after something and is pretty pissed off not to be finding it.'

'Did Robbery-Homicide show up again?'

'No. Too busy off hobnobbing on your side of town, I guess,' Parker said. 'How long did they stay at the party?'

'Just what I told you. They exchanged a few words with Giradello and left. What did that name mean to you?'

'Damon is the bike messenger sent to Lowell's office last night.'

'I thought Lowell was a robbery.'

'I don't believe it,' Parker said. 'Maybe the perp stole the money out of Lowell's safe, but that wasn't what he went there for. Apparently, he thinks the bike messenger has whatever that is.'

'You don't think the bike messenger did it?'

'No. That doesn't track for me. I think the bike messenger is just the rabbit. I want the dog that's chasing him.'

Neither of them spoke for a moment.

'Lowell called a messenger to pick something up,' Diane murmured. 'The messenger left with the package—'

'We assume.'

'Someone killed Lowell and now has killed someone connected to the bike messenger. The bike messenger still has the package. The killer is after the package.'

'Smells like blackmail,' Parker said.

'Hmmm' was all Diane said, lost in thoughts of her own. She touched the curve between his neck and shoulder. 'Come to bed,' she said quietly. 'It's late. You can be the world's greatest detective again in the morning.'

MORNING WAS A SOFT, sweet dream on the horizon to the east of Los Angeles. The rain had cleared out, leaving the air washed fresh and the promise of Technicolor blue skies.

Under a freeway overpass at Fourth and Flower in downtown LA, Jace huddled inside a survival blanket, his army surplus coat arranged over the blanket to hide the silver stuff it was made of. He had dozed for a couple of hours, but he couldn't say he'd slept.

A block down, at Fifth and Flower, messengers would be showing up for coffee at Carl's Jr. He wanted to talk to Mojo, get the lowdown on what was going on at Speed, what Eta might have told the cops. Mojo was the messenger Jace came closest to trusting.

Jace strapped on his pack, climbed on The Beast, and started down the street towards Carl's Jr. There was no traffic. The city was just waking up.

He parked The Beast at the side of the restaurant and ran the risk of leaving it unlocked in favour of a quick getaway if he needed it. He couldn't go inside. Instead, he crossed Fifth and stood there on the corner, looking like a lot of guys on these downtown streets.

He'd been standing maybe ten minutes when he saw Mojo coming down Fifth. Jace started across the street as Mojo glided up onto the sidewalk at the alley entrance.

'Hey, Mojo,' he said.

Mojo stopped dead and stared at him. 'Lone Ranger,' he said at last. 'You look like the devil been chasing your tail and he caught you.'

'Yeah. Something like that.'

'Police came looking for you yesterday. Two sets of them.'

'What did Eta tell him?'

'She said she didn't know much about you,' he said. 'For someone nobody knows, you are a very popular man, J.C.'

'It's complicated.'

'No, I don't think so. You killed a man or you didn't.'

Jace looked him straight on. 'I didn't. Why would I do that?'

Mojo didn't blink. 'Money is generally the great motivator.'

'If I had money, I wouldn't be standing here. I need to talk to Eta, but I can't go to Speed, and I don't have her cell number.'

'They got no telephones where Eta is, mon,' Mojo said.

'What do you mean?'

'I came past Base on my way here. The alley is nothing but lines of yellow tape. A policeman was walking inside the lines. I said to him, "I work here, mon." He said to me, "Not today you don't, Rasta man."' His eyes went glassy with tears, and his voice thickened. "A lady had her throat cut here last night."

Jace backed away a step. Eta couldn't be dead. There was too much of her. Too much opinion, too much bluster, too much mouth. Guilt rolled over him for thinking she might have betrayed him to the police. She was dead. Her throat had been cut.

'Bad neighbourhood,' Mojo said. 'Bad things happen. Or maybe you know something we don't.'

Jace shook his head. 'No. I wish I did, but I don't.'

'Then how come you running?'

'Look, Mojo, I'm stuck in the middle of something I don't understand. I haven't done anything wrong.'

'But you're looking for help?' Mojo raised his brows. 'Is that why you're here talking to me? You wanted help from Eta, and now she's dead. That don't seem like a good deal.'

'I don't want anything from you,' Jace said. 'And I sure as hell didn't want what's happened.' He started towards The Beast.

Mojo got in front of him. 'Where you going?'

Jace pushed him back. 'I wouldn't want to make you an accessory after the fact, Mojo. Don't worry about me.'

'I'm not worried about you. I care about Eta. I'm thinking you should talk with the police.'

'I'll pass.' Jace pulled his helmet on and pushed off.

He sprinted ahead, wanting to distance himself from Mojo and from the guilt. And from the image in his head of Eta with her throat cut.

CHEN'S FISH MARKET was five minutes from Parker's loft. According to the DMV, one of the Mini Coopers that may have fled the scene of Abby Lowell's break-in lived here. Parker pulled up in front and went to the public entrance first, finding the place hadn't yet opened for business. But in the loading bay two men were shovelling shaved ice for the coolers.

Parker held up his badge. 'Excuse me. I'm looking for a Lu Chen.'

The men straightened immediately, one wide-eyed with fear, the other narrow-eyed with suspicion. The first had the round, doughy features of someone with Down syndrome.

'Lu Chen is my aunt,' the second man said.

'And you are?'

'Chi.'

'Is your aunt here?'

'I'll go see if she's in her office.'

'I'll come with you,' Parker said. The guy looked offended.

Parker boosted himself up onto the dock and dusted himself off, trying not to grimace at a streak of black dirt on the front of his Hugo Boss jacket. His sour-faced tour guide turned and led him through a small warehouse space, down a narrow hall to a door marked OFFICE.

Chi knocked. 'Aunt? A police detective is here to see you.'

The door opened, and a small, neat woman in a red blazer and black slacks stared out at them.

'Detective Parker, ma'am.' Parker offered his ID. 'I have a couple of questions for you.'

'In regards to what, may I ask?'

'Your car, ma'am. You own a 2002 Mini Cooper?'

'Yes.'

The nephew made a huff of disgust. Lu Chen looked at him. 'Please leave us, Chi. I know you have work to do.'

The nephew turned and walked away. She turned to Parker. 'Would you care for tea?'

'No, thank you. I just have a few questions. Is the car here? Do you mind if I have a look?'

'Not at all. What is this all about?' she asked, leading him from the cramped office out the back to the alley.

Parker walked around the car. 'When was the last time you drove it?'

She thought for a moment. 'Three days ago. I had a charity luncheon at Barneys in Beverly Hills.'

'Did anyone else take it out? Your nephew, maybe?'

'Not that I know. Chi has his own car.'

'Does anyone else have access to the keys?'

Now she began to look worried. 'They hang in my office. What is this about, Detective?'

'A car matching the description of yours was reported leaving the scene of a crime yesterday. A break-in and assault.'

'How dreadful. But I can assure you, my car was here.'

Parker pursed his lips. 'A witness copied part of the licence plate. It comes pretty close to yours.'

'As do many, I'm sure.'

She was a cool one, he had to give her that. He strolled to the rear of the car and tapped his notebook against the broken taillight. 'As the car was leaving the scene, it was struck by a minivan. The taillight was broken.'

'Such a coincidence. My car was struck while I was at my luncheon. I discovered the damage when I went to leave.'

'Did you report the incident to the police?'

'For what purpose?' she asked. 'To garner their sympathy?'

'To your insurance company, then?'

'File a claim for so little damage?'

Parker smiled and shook his head. 'You must be something on the tennis court, Ms Chen.'

'You may call me Madame Chen,' she said, her back ramrod straight. Parker doubted she topped five feet.

'My apologies.' Parker touched the scratch marks on the Mini Cooper's otherwise impeccable glossy paint. 'The minivan that struck the car leaving the crime scene was silver. The car that damaged your car was silver also.'

'Silver is a popular colour.'

'Interesting about paint colours,' Parker said. 'They're particular to make. Ford's silver paint, for instance, is not Toyota's silver paint is not BMW's silver paint. They're chemically unique.'

'How fascinating.'

'Do you know a J. C. Damon?' Parker asked.

She didn't react to the sudden change of subject. 'How would I know this person?' she asked.

'He's a bike messenger. Twentyish, blond, good-looking kid.'

'I have no need of a bicycle messenger.'

'J. C. Damon was the person driving the car that was leaving the scene of the crime.'

'Do I seem like the sort of person to consort with criminals, Detective?'

'No, ma'am. But again, you've managed not to answer my question.'

Parker tried to imagine what possible connection this dignified steel lotus blossom might have to a kid like Damon. There didn't seem to be any, and yet he would have bet money there was. This was the car. There were too many hits for them to be coincidence.

Parker leaned against the car, making himself comfortable. 'Between you and me, I'm not so sure this kid is a criminal. I think maybe he was in the wrong place at the wrong time, and now he's up to his neck in a serious mess and he doesn't know how to get out. Things like that happen.'

She glanced away from him for the first time in their conversation. 'I'm sure a young man in such a situation may find it difficult to trust, particularly the police.'

He reached into his pocket and pulled out a business card. 'If for any reason you might need to reach me, ma'am, feel free to call me anytime, day or night,' he said, handing the card to her. 'In the meantime, I'm going to have to impound your car.'

Anger sparked her to attention again. 'That is outrageous! I have told you my car has not left this spot in three days!'

'So you have,' Parker conceded. 'The thing is, I don't believe you. I should also tell you that if the results of the tests come back the way I believe they will, there is a chance you could be charged as an accessory. I wouldn't want to see that happen, Madame Chen. You strike me as a person who takes her responsibilities very seriously.'

'I'm glad you think so highly of me that you would treat me like a common criminal,' she snapped, and turned on her heel.

'I don't think you common in any way, Madame Chen.'

Unimpressed, she stormed off and disappeared into the building.

Parker sighed and looked around. The Chen family had a nice business going. Neat as a pin. Everything A-one. He had purchased prawns here once for a quiet dinner with Diane. Excellent quality.

He had left Diane asleep in his bed, putting an orange on his pillow and a note: *Breakfast in bed. I'll call you later. K.*

It had been nice to fall asleep with her in his arms and to wake up with her there. To do that more often seemed like a good idea. Not that he wanted something permanent. But as he became more settled in his life outside the job, and more content with the reconstructed Kev Parker, stability was becoming more attractive to him.

He called Dispatch to have a black-and-white sent to sit on the Mini Cooper until he could get his warrant.

The sensation of being watched crept over Parker's skin. His gaze swept the loading dock, the other side of the alley, and came to rest on a stack of wooden pallets sitting at the back of the next building.

Parker eased down the alley, the pallets in his peripheral vision. A small figure shifted position to keep him in sight, wedging between the pallets and the brick building.

Parker turned and looked straight at his little voyeur. A kid. Maybe eight or nine. Swallowed up in a faded black sweatshirt.

Quick as a rabbit, the kid zipped past Chen's lot, heading for the cover of a big blue Dumpster. Parker sprinted full-out after him.

'Kid! Stop! Police!' Parker shouted, sprinting back down the alley, his tie flipped over his shoulder.

The boy took a left into a parking lot wedged between a U of buildings. The cars were parked nose to tail, two deep and four wide. Parker walked behind the cars, his breath coming in huffs.

A glimpse of blond hair and blue jeans caught his eye as the boy dashed between a green Mazda and a white Saturn.

'I just want to ask you a couple of questions,' Parker said. He followed the scuttling sound back to the other side of the lot. He bent over and looked beneath a white BMW X5. Big blue eyes stared back at him.

'Kev Parker,' he said, holding his badge down for the kid to see. 'LAPD. And you are . . .'

'I have the right to remain silent.'

'You do, but you're not under arrest.'

'Anything I say can and will be used against me.'

'How old are you?' Parker asked.

The kid thought about that for a moment, weighing the pros and cons of answering. 'Ten,' he said at last.

'You live around here?'

'You can't make me talk to you. I know all about my rights against self-in-crim-i-nation as defined by the Fifth Amendment to the Constitution.'

'A legal scholar. What did you say your name was?'

'I didn't say. You really might as well not try to trick me,' the boy said. 'I watch cop shows all the time.'

'Ah, you're wise to us.'

'Plus, I'm probably a lot smarter than you are. I don't say that to make you feel bad or anything,' he said earnestly. 'It's just that I have an IQ of a hundred sixty-eight.'

'Come on, genius,' Parker said, offering his hand. 'My blood is rushing to my head. Come out from there before I have a stroke.'

The boy scuttled out from under the car like a crab, stood up, and tried in vain to dust himself off.

'I don't really consider myself to be a genius,' he confessed modestly. 'I just know a lot of stuff.'

'You're observant. You're smart. I'll bet you know a lot about what goes on around here,' Parker said.

The one-shoulder shrug. Eyes on the ground.

'You're below the radar,' Parker said. 'You can slip around, see things, hear things. Maybe you want to become a spy.'

'Not really. I just have an in-sa-tia-ble curiosity.'

'Nothing wrong with that,' Parker said. 'Do you know the Chens? From the fish market?'

Both shoulders.

'Do you know a guy by the name of J. C. Damon?'

The eyes went a little wider. 'Is he in trouble?'

'Kind of. I think he might have some information that could help me with a big investigation. I think he might have seen something.'

'Why won't he just come and tell you, if that's all?'

'Because he's scared. He's like you, running away from me because he thinks I'm the enemy. But I'm not.'

Parker could see the wheels turning in the kid's head.

'I'm not a bad guy,' Parker continued. 'You know, some people blame first and ask questions later. There could be cops like that out there looking for this guy Damon. It'd be a whole lot better for him if he came to me before they get to him.'

The kid swallowed hard. Blond hair, blue eyes, good-looking kid. Just the way Parker had described Damon to Madame Chen. This one had been right there at the back of Chen's, watching, listening.

Parker pulled out a business card and offered it to the kid. The boy snatched it, stuck the card in the pouch of the sweatshirt.

Just then the black-and-white radio car turned in at the alley and stopped. The uniform got out and called to him.

'Detective Parker?'

Parker started to raise a hand. The kid was off like a shot.

'Hey, Detective?' the uniform called from the parking lot. 'Anything I can do for you?'

'Yeah,' Parker said. 'Call Hugo Boss and send my apologies.'

RUIZ SAT at her desk with her head in her hand. She had put her aromatic witness in Parker's chair, at Parker's desk, willing to suffer the stench in the name of revenge.

Obidia Jones appeared to have had a fine night's sleep in a holding cell. A late dinner from Domino's, coffee and pastry from Starbucks for breakfast. He paged through the mug books as if he were reading a magazine.

'Personally, I prefer a heartier breakfast,' he said. 'Something substantiated to stick to a person's ribs.'

Ruiz rolled her eyes.

Parker came into the squad room, took three strides into the room and was knocked back by the smell. When he saw Mr Jones sitting in his chair, he turned a piercing look on Ruiz.

She smiled like a sly cat and said, '*Touché.*'

'I think I've got the car,' Parker said, ignoring her.

'Where was it?' Ruiz asked.

'Chinatown. Doesn't make any sense now, but it's going to. I love it when it all comes together,' he said.

Captain Fuentes came out of his office and crooked a finger. 'Kev? Can I see you in here?'

Parker followed him and closed the door behind him. 'I didn't do it. It's not mine. And I swear she was nineteen.'

Fuentes, who was a good guy and had an easy sense of humour, didn't laugh. He had soulful black eyes that seemed to carry the sorrows of the world when he was serious like this.

'You look like you're about to tell me I have six weeks to live,' Parker said to him.

'I got a call a little while ago. RHD is taking your homicide.'

Parker shook his head. The rage seemed to start boiling in his feet. This was worse than being told he had six weeks to live. The first case he'd had in years that smelt big. The kind of case a detective earned his reputation on— or rode back out of purgatory.

'No,' he said. 'Not Lowell.'

'There's nothing I can do, Kev.'

'Did they give any explanation?' In his mind's eye, he could picture the scene Diane had described to him over the phone. Bradley Kyle and his partner, Moose Roddick, and Tony Giradello with their heads together.

'Captain Florek told me they thought it might tie into something they already have. You know as well as I do, they don't need a reason. I'm sorry.'

Not now, Parker thought. Not when it was right there, beneath the surface. All he needed was to dig a little harder, a little longer.

'You can pretend we haven't had this conversation yet,' Parker said. 'I'm not here yet. My cellphone isn't working.'

'Kev, you're not going to close the case in the next three hours, are you?'

Parker said nothing.

'They want everything you've got,' Fuentes said. 'Pull the file together and take it over to Parker Center.'

'No. I won't go over there. If Kyle wants this case, he can come here and get it. I'm not going over there like some, some—'

Parker put a hand over his mouth and stopped himself before his control slipped any further. He took a deep breath and exhaled. Fuentes just looked at him with something close to pity in his eyes.

'You haven't seen me,' Parker said quietly. 'We haven't spoken.'

'I can't put them off for long.'

'I know.' Parker nodded. 'Whatever you can do. I appreciate it, Captain.'

'Get out of here,' Fuentes said, reaching for some paperwork. 'I haven't seen you. We haven't spoken.'

Parker stepped out of Fuentes's office, closing the door behind him.

Ruiz got out of her chair and came to him. 'You've got your court order for the bank,' she said. 'What's going on?'

'Robbery-Homicide is taking Lowell.'

'What are you going to do?' Ruiz asked.

Before Parker could formulate an answer, Obidia Jones let out a little yelp of excitement. 'That's him! That's your perpetuator!' he said, poking a gnarled finger at a photograph in the book before him.

'Who've you got there, Mr Jones?' Parker asked.

The old man pointed to a photograph revealing a head like a cinder block; small, mean eyes, five-o'clock shadow. Eddie Boyd Davis.

'Only he had a piece of tape across his nose,' Jones said.

'Mr Jones, you are a fine citizen,' Parker said.

Parker looked again at the face of the man who had murdered Eta Fitzgerald in cold blood, and he spoke to Ruiz in a low voice.

'Dig up everything you can find on this mutt. I want to know if he has any connection to Lenny Lowell. And if Bradley Kyle comes in here, you don't know anything and you haven't seen me.'

'Wishful thinking,' she muttered.

Parker went through a couple of desk drawers, took out a file, pulled some papers from a tray on top of his desk. He grabbed the binder that was the murder book on the Lowell case, containing reports and notes, sketches of the scene, Polaroids. He put it all in a plastic mail carton he kept under his desk for just this purpose.

'You haven't seen me walk out of here with that container,' he told Ruiz.

'Right,' she said, but there was a hesitation first.

'It's your case too,' Parker said. 'Lowell and Fitzgerald: if they take one, they take the other. Is that what you want?'

'It's Robbery-Homicide. We can't stop them.'

Parker gave her the hard stare. 'You sell me out to Bradley Kyle and you'll make an enemy you'll wish you didn't have.'

'I said all right,' she said grudgingly. 'Don't threaten me.'

She would sell him out to Kyle in a heartbeat, Parker thought, because Kyle could get her noticed by the right people in RHD.

He grabbed the plastic box and left the room and then the building. He had only a few hours to live. He couldn't waste a minute.

PARKER CALLED JOEL COEN from his car while driving to the City National Bank branch where Lowell's safe-deposit box lived. Coen was the young detective he'd met at the Abby Lowell break-in.

'Joel, Kev Parker. I've got something for you on the Lowell B and E, but you have to jump on it ASAP, got it?'

'What is it?'

'I've got your getaway car. It's sitting behind a fish market in Chinatown. Black Mini Cooper.'

'Geez, how'd you get that so fast?'

'I'm hyperactive. And when you get the car dusted for prints, make sure they go to Joanie at Latent. Tell her I sent you and that she's looking for a match with my homicide.'

'Got it.'

'And move fast, Joel. If Robbery-Homicide gets a sniff of this car, it's gone, and so's your case.'

'RHD? Why would they—'

'Don't ask. Beat it over to Chinatown.' He gave Coen the address and ended the call as the bank came into sight.

The manager checked the court order and escorted him to the location of the boxes. Lowell's was the largest size available. Parker put on a pair of latex gloves, took a breath and opened the lid.

Cool, green cash. Stacks of hundred-dollar bills. Parker piled them on the table. Twenty-five thousand dollars. And under the money, a small envelope containing a single photographic negative.

'That slimy s.o.b.,' Parker murmured. He didn't have to know who was in the photo to know what this was about. Blackmail.

Turning on one of his clients. That had to be it. Lowell had put someone between a rock and a hard place and squeezed. That explained the pricey condo, the new Cadillac, the cash.

Parker held the negative up to the light. Two people, shot from a distance. They might have been shaking hands or exchanging something. It was impossible to tell.

He put the negative back in the envelope. He asked the manager for a bank bag for the money, tagged it as evidence, and put everything in a brown paper grocery sack he had brought with him.

The elevator ride to the ground floor was silent. If the bank manager wondered what was going on, he didn't show it and he didn't ask. He had probably seen cops take stranger things than money out of clients' boxes.

The elevator doors opened, framing Abby Lowell sitting on a marble bench, waiting. She had a hell of a wardrobe for a law student. Camel tweed suit with a slim skirt. Maybe it paid to be the daughter of a blackmailer.

In one elegant move, she unfolded herself from the bench as Parker stepped out of the elevator. She looked directly at him, her expression calm but with an underlying quality of steel.

'Did you find my father's papers?'

'And good morning to you, Ms Lowell. Great suit.'

She didn't answer but fell neatly into step beside him as he started for the side door.

'Neither his will nor his insurance policy was in the box.'

'Then what do you have in that bag?'

'Evidence.'

'Evidence of what? My father was the victim.'

'I believe your father was blackmailing someone,' Parker said bluntly. 'I just took twenty-five thousand dollars out of his safe-deposit box.'

If she wasn't shocked, she was a fine actress, Parker thought. The brown eyes went wide; the colour left her cheeks.

He started across the parking lot, popping the trunk of his car with the remote. He didn't mention the negative, just to see if she would ask if he had found anything else in the box. She didn't.

'You're delusional if you think I'm a fool, Ms Lowell.' He put the paper sack in the trunk and shut the lid. 'Your father is murdered, and the killer calls you on your cellphone to tell you. He breaks into your apartment, tosses the place, threatens to kill you, but you claim you don't know what he's looking for. You're desperate to get into Lenny's safe-deposit box; then I find twenty-five K in the box and you claim to know nothing about it. Do you think I was dropped on my head as a child?'

She had no answer to that. She pressed an elegantly manicured hand to her lips. Her other arm banded across her stomach.

Comforting herself, Parker thought. It was probably something she'd learned to do as a child while sitting as an afterthought beside her father at the racecourse. Whatever else he thought about her, he felt sorry for the lonely girl she must have been.

'Who was he blackmailing?' Parker asked.

'I don't believe that he was,' she said without looking at him.

'Do you know a guy named Eddie Boyd Davis?'

She shook her head. She was fighting tears.

'If you know something,' he said, 'now's the time. Lenny's killer has you in his sights. A sack of money isn't worth dying for.'

'Don't I pay taxes for you to serve and protect me?'

'I can't fight what I don't know, Abby.'

'What don't you know?' she asked, impatient and frustrated. 'Why can't you find that bike messenger?'

'I don't think he had anything to do with it.'

'He attacked me!'

'If he killed your father for the money in the safe, why would he stick around to come and see you?' Parker asked.

'I don't know! Maybe he's just a psycho and he singled out Lenny and now me.'

'That only happens in the movies, doll,' Parker said. 'The kid got sent to your father's office by chance. I think he was in the wrong place at the wrong time.'

'Oh, I see,' she said curtly. 'He came into my home and attacked me, but he's just an innocent bystander? And I'm, what? The scheming femme fatale? Talk about fantasy.'

'The way I see it is this: Lenny was blackmailing somebody and he got killed for it. And yes, I think you're in it up to your pretty little chin,' Parker said.

She shook her head. 'I can't believe this is happening.'

'No? Well, you certainly seemed to take in stride the fact that someone beat your father's head in.'

She slapped him hard. Her lips flattened in a line of disgust. 'I am so through with you, Detective Parker.' She marched away. She was parked five cars down. A blue BMW convertible. New.

Parker watched her back out and drive away.

PARKER TURNED IN at the gates to the Paramount Studio lot and waved to the security guard.

'Good to see you, Mr Parker.'

'You too, Bill.'

'You here to see Mr Connors?'

'Not today. I need to see Chuck Ito. He's expecting me.'

The guard waved Parker through.

Chuck Ito's office was a building towards the back of the lot. He worked as a film editor, but his hobby was still photography.

'Look what the cat dragged in.' Ito's greeting was always the same in the five years that Parker had known him.

'My suit takes offence at that remark,' Parker said.

'So? It only speaks Italian. It doesn't know if I'm insulting it or not.'

Parker dropped into a chair and tossed the envelope from Lenny Lowell's safe-deposit box onto the desk.

Ito reached for it. 'What have you got for me, Kev? Something I'll get arrested for?' He plucked the negative out. 'Who's in it?'

'I'd tell you, but I'd have to kill you. I need this ASAP.'

'Go to the mall. They can do it in an hour.'

'This is evidence in a homicide.'

'Then why aren't you taking it to the LAPD lab?'

'You're kidding. I'd be lucky to get it back by Christmas.'

Parker couldn't tell Ito he wasn't supposed to have this piece of evidence. If he could get the thing developed, he could see who he was dealing with and have a bigger jump ahead of Robbery-Homicide. That was why he hadn't bagged and tagged the negative at the bank. He figured to get the thing developed, then seal it in the bag and no one would be the wiser.

'ASAP for me today is going to be more like late in the day.'

Parker got up. 'It's fine,' he said. 'Just don't tell anyone you have it. If you get caught with it, I don't know you.'

BLACKMAIL. Parker stirred the word around as he drove downtown. If Davis was one of the people in the photo, then that gave him a motive to kill Lowell. If the two of them had been in on something together, one might have turned on the other out of greed.

Whichever way it went, Davis was after the negative. That was why he had ransacked Lenny's office, busted the windows of his car. He would have done the same to Lowell's condo if not for the fact that it was in a secure building. It was probably Davis who had tossed Abby Lowell's place.

But there had to be more than one negative. Parker figured the one in the safe-deposit box would have been insurance. And Parker had a hunch that the person holding the other negatives was J. C. Damon. He wondered if the kid had any idea what he had.

Parker's phone rang. 'Parker.'

'Since you don't have any friends, I called one of mine.' Andi Kelly. 'There is no one named Davis in Robbery-Homicide.'

'I know.'

'How do you know?'

'I know it because a witness just identified Eddie Davis in a mug book.'

'He killed that woman last night?'

'Not my case,' Parker said. 'You'll have to talk to Ruiz.'

'She'll sell you out for a dime and give back change.'

'Well, there's definitely some truth in that,' Parker muttered, wondering if Ruiz wasn't even at that very moment selling him out to Bradley Kyle. 'Yes, I like Davis for the murder last night.'

'Why? What's his motive?'

'I'm still working on that. But it's a good bet that he went to Speed Couriers to get a line on the bike messenger.'

'Wasn't the messenger a "person of interest" last night?'

'He's still a person of interest. I just don't consider him to be a suspect. I need to talk to him before RHD barges in and blows everything. They're taking the Lowell case.'

'You're kidding. Why would they be interested?'

'That's what I'm trying to find out.'

'And you'll let me know when you do?'

'You're the only pal I've got in this, Andi,' Parker said seriously. 'I've got bogies all around me. The head of Robbery-Homicide told my captain they feel the Lowell murder might relate to something they have ongoing.'

Kelly was silent for long enough that Parker thought she might have lost the connection.

'And we're back to Kyle and partner talking with Tony Giradello, your name coming up in the conversation.'

'That's right,' Parker said. 'I'm looking at blackmail, Andi.'

'Who versus whom for what?'

'I don't know, but two people are already dead. And there's only one case Bradley Kyle has ongoing with stakes that high.'

'Tricia Crowne-Cole.'

10

Jace chained The Beast to a parking meter and went inside the bar. It was a dark, dank place with fishing nets and buoys and life jackets nailed to the walls. The place reeked of beer and cigarettes. Jace took a stool at the far end of the bar and ordered a burger and a soda.

The television that hung from the ceiling at the other end of the bar was tuned to Court TV. They were all over the Cole murder trial. A motion had been made by the defence to exclude any mention of Rob Cole's past—the drugs, the money, the women—on the grounds that that evidence was only going to prejudice the jury. Assistant District Attorney Giradello argued that Cole's past should be admitted into evidence to establish a pattern of behaviour. The judge ruled for the state. A serious blow to Martin Gorman's case. He was complaining about Norman Crowne trying to buy justice.

The burger arrived. Jace took a bite, still looking at the television. The ruling should have gone in favour of the defence, he thought. So Cole was a loser because of the drugs, the money and the women. So what? None of that pointed to him physically abusing his wife. Jace figured if Cole had ever laid a finger on Tricia, Norman Crowne would have come down on him like a ton of bricks.

But the ruling had gone for the prosecution, and if that was an indicator of how the rest of the trial would go, Martin Gorman had his work cut out for him.

Gorman was probably right. Norman Crowne held tremendous sway over Los Angeles politics, and his pockets were bottomless.

Jace thought back to the night he had picked up the package from Lenny. The television had been on with a report on the Cole case, and Lenny had said to him: *Martin's betting against the house in a rigged game. Money talks. Remember that.*

He wondered if Lenny knew those things because he had an inside track to information on the case. Lenny for sure had the inside dirt on someone. The people in the negatives Jace wore taped to his belly.

He polished off the burger, then slid off the stool and went outside to a pay phone. He plugged in a quarter and punched in Abby Lowell's number. She answered on the third ring.

'Ms Lowell. You know me from in your apartment.'

Silence. Then finally, 'Yes?'

'I have something I think you might want.'

'I don't know what you're talking about.'

'Let's not play games,' Jace said. 'I've got the negatives your dad was using to blackmail someone.'

'What makes you think I want them?' she asked.

'They're worth money to somebody. I'm giving you first crack.'

A long silence passed. Finally, she said, 'How much?'

'Ten thousand.'

'That's a lot of money.'

'No, it isn't. But I want out of this.' Jace waited.

'Where and when?'

'Meet me at Pershing Square at five fifteen. Come alone.'

Jace hung up the phone and stood, staring at nothing. He had just set the stage for himself to commit extortion.

If Abby Lowell was in on the blackmail, she would pay to get the negatives and buy his silence. If he played it right, Jace could take her money as payback for Eta's family and maybe as a little insurance for himself and Tyler. He could turn the cops on Abby; then the cops could get to Predator and that would be the end of it. He hoped. All he needed was a little luck.

Lenny Lowell's voice echoed in the back of his mind: *It's better to be lucky than good, kid.*

TYLER RAN STRAIGHT to the fish market after his escape from Detective Parker. He found Madame Chen in her office, crying.

'What's wrong?' he asked.

'I'm fine, little mouse. A moment of weakness only makes us see how strong we really are.'

'Jace left,' Tyler said.

'I know. I asked him not to go,' Madame Chen said. 'He thinks it is better his way. He wants to protect us.'

'I don't like his way. What if he never comes back?'

'He will come back for you.'

'Not if he gets killed or goes to jail or something,' Tyler said.

'This is true,' she said. 'But bad things can happen anywhere. We have no control of such things.'

Tyler looked at her for a moment. 'I'm scared,' he said finally.

'I know,' Madame Chen said. 'I am frightened too. We must all get through this together. Your brother is a good person. True and brave. He will do the right thing, and he will come home to us.'

'Yes, ma'am,' Tyler said.

A knock sounded at the office door, and Chi stuck his ugly head in. Madame Chen gave him her sternest look.

'Chi, never open a door until you are asked in.'

'I'm sorry, Aunt,' he said without remorse. 'There are more police detectives here to see you.'

The door swung fully open, and Chi was herded into the room by the two men behind him. One was very large and frightening, with a flat-top haircut. The other one looked like any businessman.

Tyler didn't like the look in that one's eyes. He wanted to scurry out of the office, but the big man blocked his exit.

'Mrs Chen—' the other one started.

'You may call me Madame Chen,' she said frostily.

'*Madame* Chen,' he tried again. 'I'm Detective Kyle, and this is Detective Roddick. We're with the LAPD Robbery-Homicide Division. We'd like to ask you about your car.'

'Another one about the car,' Chi commented.

Kyle turned to him. 'Another?'

Madame Chen snapped Chi a look. 'Chi, you may go.'

Chi left looking humiliated and angry. Once again, Tyler tried to slip out, and once again the big guy blocked him.

Detective Kyle turned towards him. 'And who are you?'

'I don't have to talk to you,' Tyler said. 'I'm just a kid.'

'He is my son,' Madame Chen announced. 'Adopted.'

The detectives looked at each other.

'Why did you come here, Detectives?' Madame Chen asked.

'We have reason to believe your car might have been used in the commission of a crime. We'd like to take a look.'

Madame Chen gave them a perturbed look. 'I see how my tax dollars are wasted. The detective here before you already looked at the car. I told him it had been damaged in a parking lot. He insisted on taking it anyway. Then more police came and towed it away.'

'What other detective came here first?' Kyle asked.

'Detective Parker,' she said. 'The car is gone.'

The muscles in Kyle's face flexed and tightened. 'Do you happen to know a young man named J. C. Damon?'

Madame Chen didn't blink. 'Why would I know this person?'

'Maybe you've seen him in the vicinity. Early twenties, blond hair, blue eyes. He works as a bike messenger.'

'I am a busy woman, in my office most of the time.'

None of what she was saying was exactly a lie, nor was it exactly the truth. Tyler stood by her side, as innocent as a lamb.

'Thank you for your time, ma'am,' Kyle said. 'We may call on you again once your car has been processed for evidence.'

He took one long look at Tyler, at the blue eyes and the blond hair. Tyler held his breath. The detectives started towards the door.

Chi's cousin Boo Zhu hurried from the warehouse to the edge of the loading dock. The bright sun made him squint like a mole.

'I know! I know!' he said excitedly. 'I know JayCee!' He looked proudly at Chi, who was standing on the dock trying to look as if he hadn't had a hand in Boo Zhu's announcement.

Kyle turned to Madame Chen, who was standing outside the doorway. She looked as pale as the white clapboard behind her.

'Who is this?' he asked.

'The son of a cousin,' Madame Chen said, crossing the small parking area. 'He is challenged, as you can see.'

Kyle looked up at him. 'You know J. C. Damon?'

Boo Zhu began to dance with all the grace of a bear.

'Boo Zhu likes to please,' said Madame Chen.

'Are you saying he doesn't know what he's talking about?'

'He knows that it will please you to say what he believes you want to hear.' She flashed a glare at Chi. 'He will tell you he knows the president if you ask him.'

Tyler darted back from the doorway. His heart was galloping so fast he thought he might faint.

'Ty R! Ty R!' Boo Zhu exclaimed.

'Tyler?' Kyle asked.

'Ty R, JayCee!'

Kyle turned to Chi. 'What about you? Do you know J.C.?'

Tyler's eyes filled with tears.

'If you don't already know this,' said Kyle, 'J. C. Damon is wanted for questioning in relation to a homicide. If you're protecting him, you're harbouring a criminal. If he used your car in the commission of a crime, you can be charged as an accessory.'

Chi stared for a moment at his aunt. When he spoke, he spoke in Chinese. 'You cannot risk yourself and the business, Aunt. Lying to the police is a serious offence.'

'You betray me, Chi. If you do this, I do not know you.'

'We can go downtown,' Kyle said. 'I can get an interpreter. If you're withholding information, you can be detained as material witnesses.'

Madame Chen turned on him. 'Do you think me a fool, Detective Kyle? I am an intelligent woman in two languages. You are a bully in only one. I am calling my attorney.'

'You can't stop your nephew from talking to us,' Kyle said. He turned again to Chi. 'Do you know J. C. Damon?'

Tyler held his breath.

'I defer to my aunt's wisdom,' Chi said humbly. 'It is her wish we consult with our attorney.'

Kyle turned once again to Boo Zhu. 'You know J. C. Damon?'

'Yes,' said Boo Zhu, but his smile of pride melted on his round face as he looked at Madame Chen. 'Ty R bother? Yes, ma'am?'

Kyle ignored Madame Chen. 'Tyler is J.C.'s brother?'

Boo Zhu looked at Madame Chen. 'Yes, ma'am. Yes?'

Kyle turned to his partner. 'Where's the kid?'

Like a shot, Tyler was down the hall and up the stairs. He ran into the apartment, grabbed his backpack, grabbed the walkie-talkie Jace had given him. He fled out of the apartment and up the last of the stairs, to the roof. He scrambled to the edge and started down the rusted fire escape, jumping the last five feet and hitting the ground with a thud. He pushed to his feet and crept along the back of the building, peering carefully around when he reached the corner. The lot and the loading dock were empty except for Boo Zhu. The cops had gone.

Sticking against the buildings, Tyler moved down the alley to the parking lot where Parker had caught him. He let his breath out, pulled his backpack off, and dug around for the walkie-talkie.

'Scout to Ranger. Scout to Ranger. Do you read me?'

Nothing. Tyler pressed the radio against his cheek. The safety he had felt with the Chens was gone. Just like that, his home, his only family, had been found out and threatened. The only other safety he had ever known was with his brother. Suddenly he had neither.

He had never felt so alone in his life.

Tyler wiped his nose on his sleeve and blinked back tears. He believed in his brother. He would try his best to do what Jace would do. No time for crying now. He had to clear his head to use his brain. There was no sense having an IQ of 168 if he wasn't going to use it when he needed it most.

PARKER PULLED THE CAR over into the patch of dirt that served as a parking lot for a tiny Mexican joint in a weedy, dusty, semi-industrial part of town near the Los Angeles River. Dan Metheny had eaten lunch at this place every day Parker worked with him.

Metheny sat at one of the picnic tables, a plate of fat and cholesterol in front of him. He watched Parker through silver-mirrored shades.

'Hey, GQ. You here to show us common folk how to dress?' Metheny had been on the job for about a hundred and twelve years, or so it seemed. A big, barrel-chested black (Metheny's own choice of words) man who ate too much red meat, drank too much bourbon, and smoked two packs a day.

'I *am* the common folk,' Parker said, taking the seat opposite. 'Robbery-Homicide just yanked my murder away from me, and I have a trainee who would sooner stab me in the back with a stiletto heel than look at me.'

'This chick Ruiz?' Metheny said.

'Yeah.'

'I asked a couple of guys I know working Latin gangs, and they never heard of her. I guess they could have forgot.'

Parker shook his head. 'This one they would have remembered.'

Metheny was silent for a moment, thinking, all the lines of his bulldog face bending downwards.

'Dude, I don't like this,' he said at last. 'You know Alex Navarro? Alex knows every damn thing that goes on with the Latin gangs. If he doesn't know this chick, she wasn't there.'

'So who the hell is she?' Parker asked. 'And why is she riding around with me?' Now he felt even more backed into a corner. Robbery-Homicide taking his case, Ruiz suddenly not who he thought she was.

'Flush her out and call her bluff, man.'

'Yeah.'

There was nothing else to do. Parker knew he couldn't trust Ruiz. He might as well find out why. Find out how many enemies he really had.

He was already questioning the timing of it all. Ruiz had come on just days before Lowell's murder, and now she was selling him out to Robbery-Homicide, and Robbery-Homicide was taking the case for themselves. But how could anyone have known Lenny Lowell was going to be murdered?

Metheny was watching him. 'There's no such thing as coincidence, man,' Metheny said. 'Not with Robbery-Homicide.'

'It doesn't make sense that Ruiz is connected to them.'

'Then what does make sense?' Metheny asked. 'Chip away everything this mess couldn't be, and you're left with the truth. If she's not some kind of RHD spy, what's left?'

A sick feeling trickled through Parker. He'd only ridden with Ruiz for a matter of days. She irritated him so badly, he hadn't paid attention to what she was all about besides being a pain in the ass. But she'd known about his Jag, and she'd known about his loft, and she had commented more than once on the price of his wardrobe.

'What's left?' Metheny asked.

The words were sour in Parker's mouth. 'Internal Affairs.'

11

'I got the info on Davis,' Ruiz said as Parker sat down at his desk. 'Besides a few minor drug charges, he's got a history of assaults, with two convictions. He's been out of prison for about two years. And his attorney of record for his last trial was Leonard Lowell.'

Parker nodded. 'Last known address?'

'He recently purchased a house in the Hollywood hills.'

'And if I go up there to check it out,' Parker said, 'will Bradley Kyle be there to greet me?' He stared at his partner.

Ruiz sighed and looked away. 'I'm not going to lie for you to Robbery-Homicide,' she said. 'I've got to consider my career.'

'And which career is that?'

She stared at him, appearing confused and frustrated.

'You want to work Homicide?' Parker asked, beginning to pace back and forth. 'Or is this just a field trip for you?'

A couple of detectives on the other side of the room had turned to watch the escalating argument. Ruiz's eyes darted towards them.

'Do you know Alex Navarro?' Parker asked her.

Silence.

'I'll take that as a no,' Parker said. 'Alex Navarro is The Man working Latin gangs.'

'Oh, yeah,' she stammered. 'I was too far down the food chain to have any contact with him.'

'Navarro can name every set of every gang in LA. Navarro has no recollection of Officer Renee Ruiz working with the Gang Unit.'

'So?' she challenged. 'What's the big deal?'

'You, Ms Ravenous Ambition. You never made a move on the boss of bosses of your undercover task force?'

'Are you calling me a whore?' she said.

'I'm calling you a rat! Who put you here?' Parker shouted.

'What's the matter with you? Why are you doing this?'

'Because I'm pissed off,' he said, getting in her face. To her credit, she didn't back down. 'I don't like being played. What did you give Bradley Kyle when he came in here?'

'Everything you didn't take with you,' she admitted.

'You told them about Davis and gave them his address?'

'I didn't have a choice.'

'You *always* have a choice, Ruiz.'

Fuentes stuck his head out of his office. 'What the hell is going on here? In my office. Both of you. Now.'

They went into Fuentes's office, Ruiz going to one side of the room, Parker staying near the door. He faced the captain and said, 'Where did she come from? Who assigned her here?'

'Don't be so paranoid,' Fuentes said.

'He's out of his freaking mind,' Ruiz said.

Parker threw his hands up. 'I know she didn't come out of the Latin gangs task force.'

'If you don't like the answers to your questions, stop asking them,' Fuentes said, a little too calmly. 'It is what it is, Kev.'

'Right. It is what it is,' he said, nodding. 'I know she's lying, therefore I can assume you're lying too.'

Fuentes didn't bother to object. 'She's your trainee. What difference does it make where she comes from?'

'It matters if that's not the reason she's here,' Parker said. 'What are you, Ruiz? A Robbery-Homicide mole? An Internal Affairs rat? Take your pick of rodents.'

Ruiz and Fuentes exchanged looks that said they clearly knew something Parker didn't. He turned to the door.

'Parker, where do you think you're going?' said Fuentes.

'I've got a job to do.'

'You're off Lowell,' Fuentes said. 'You have to hand everything over to Robbery-Homicide before they decide to charge you with obstruction.'

'They can do whatever they want,' Parker said. 'I don't know what their reasons are for taking this case, but I'm starting to put the pieces together, and I don't like what I'm coming up with.'

'You could lose your career over this, Kev,' Fuentes said.

'I don't care,' Parker said. 'You can take my job, but this case is mine, and I'm seeing it through, even if I have to do it as a private citizen.'

Fuentes sighed. 'I'm not your enemy, Kev,' he said. 'You have to know when to walk away from something.'

'I'm leaving,' Parker told them. 'If there's no job for me when I come back, *c'est la vie*. God knows, I don't do this for the money.'

'What *do* you do it for?' Ruiz asked pointedly.

'Is that what this is about?' Parker asked. 'How does Parker afford a Jag? How does Parker buy a loft in Chinatown?'

'How do you?' she asked, blunt and unapologetic. 'How do you afford your lifestyle on a detective's salary?'

'I don't,' he said. 'And the rest of that answer is no one's business. I've never been anything less than a damn fine cop. I come here every day, work my cases a hundred and ten percent, train little pissants like you. And you have the gall to investigate me because I don't buy my suits at JC Penney?'

'I'm not apologising to you for doing my job,' Ruiz said, getting in his face. 'In the last three years you've paid off two mortgages—yours and your parents'; you've purchased a loft in a luxury building in Chinatown; you've started wearing designer labels; you drive a Jaguar on your days off. You're not doing these things on what the LAPD pays you,' she said. 'How could you not think Internal Affairs would be interested in you?'

Parker felt his face getting hotter. 'Do you have one complaint against me? Do you have anything on file against me?'

'As a matter of fact, yes,' she said. 'We have you screwing up a murder trial where a wealthy defendant walked away without so much as a slap on the wrist. Your income seems to have increased every year since. Do you need a pencil to connect the dots?'

'This is unbelievable,' Parker muttered. 'IA has been watching me all this time. Giradello couldn't get rid of me outright, couldn't make me quit, so you people are slithering in the back door for him? I'd ask you why you didn't just call me in and grill me, but I know how IA works.'

'Would you have been any more cooperative than you're being now?' Fuentes asked.

'No. I haven't done anything wrong. I haven't done anything illegal. And what I do with my personal time is my business. I spent too many years with nothing but this job, and what did it get me?'

'If you hated it so much, why didn't you quit?' Ruiz asked.

'Did you even think about that before it came out of your mouth?' he asked, astonished. 'I don't hate the job. *I love the job!* Why would I stay if I hated it and someone else was providing me with a six-figure income?'

Ruiz just stared at him.

Parker looked at Fuentes, who couldn't quite meet his eyes. *Just doing his job*, Parker thought bitterly.

'I'm taking the rest of the day.'

No one tried to stop him as he walked out of the door.

THE HOUSE where Eddie Davis lived in the Hollywood hills looked like something a pornographer might rent to shoot X-rated movies. Seventies hip, a little run-down, trapezoidal windows, and teal-green vertical blinds. A solid gate led to the back yard, where Parker knew he would find a kidney-shaped pool, a hot tub and a bar. The Eddie Davis Swinging Bachelor Pad. Good to see he was investing his blackmail money wisely.

Parker sat in his car up the block, watching Davis's house for signs of life. There was no activity. No gardener. No cleaning woman. Eddie could have been sleeping off his last murder, Parker supposed, his anger stirring again for Eta and for her family.

He eased his car past Davis's driveway, parked, then walked up to the house. Through the dirty glass panes in the garage door he could see an assortment of older motorcycles and a brand-new red Kawasaki Ninja ZX12R sport bike. There was no black sedan.

He boosted himself up on a big terracotta planter full of dead plants to look over the gate into the back yard.

Kidney-shaped pool. Bar. Tacky hot tub.

'Hey! Who are you?'

Parker hopped down from the planter. Eddie Davis stared at him from the driver's side of a black Lincoln Town Car pulled to the kerb. He looked like he'd been tossed into the middle of a hockey brawl—a piece of white tape across his nose, one eye swollen.

'Steve,' Parker called, grinning. 'You Eddie? Rick sent me.'

'Rick who?'

'You know. Rick from that thing at the beach. He told me you maybe got a bike for sale. A Kawasaki road bike, maybe ninety-eight, ninety-nine?'

'Why were you looking over my fence?'

'I thought maybe you were back at the pool.'

Davis seemed to contemplate whether greed would outstrip caution.

Parker walked over, taking in the car, the licence plate, a parking sticker on the back window. He assessed Davis's body language as he got out of the car—tense, watchful. Parker had no doubt Davis was carrying a weapon.

'I don't know anybody named Rick,' Davis said. His left eye was swollen nearly shut and tearing.

'Rick Dreyer,' Parker said. 'Venice Beach. The guy with the tats all up and down his arms and legs. You know.'

The good eye narrowed. 'I know of him.'

Parker settled his hands at his waist. 'Whatever,' he said. 'Listen, Eddie, I've got a plane to catch, so . . .'

Davis pressed the button on the garage-door remote in his hand and the door started up. He tipped his head by way of invitation for Parker to go in. Parker turned, wanting Davis in full view. The guy wasn't tall, but he was built like a refrigerator.

'So what do you want for this baby?' Parker asked.

'Eight thousand.' Davis went two steps into the garage before he turned around. The sun hit him in the face and his eyes shut.

Parker pulled his gun out of the belt holster nestled at the small of his back and backhanded Davis across the face.

Davis's head snapped to his right, blood gushing from his already broken nose. He staggered back, falling on the concrete.

Parker leaned down, stuck the SIG-Sauer in his face.

'Eddie Davis, you're under arrest for the murder of Eta Fitzgerald. One word out of your mouth and I'll beat you to death. You would have the right to an attorney, but you killed him too. Roll over. On your face.'

Davis groaned, slowly turning onto his elbows and knees. Parker put a foot on his ass and shoved him down.

'What's going on in there?'

Parker glanced to the side. A shirtless older man sat at the kerb in a golf cart and Bermuda shorts.

'Police busi—'

Parker's breath went out of him in a sudden whoosh as something hit him hard across the back and ribs. He tripped over Davis's legs and went down.

Davis rolled out from under him and hit Parker twice as hard a second time across the back with the tailpipe he had got hold of. Parker fell forwards into a motorcycle. His gun was gone. He rolled and came up in a crouch. Davis took another vicious swing at him with the pipe but missed.

The old guy sat frozen in his cart, mouth agape.

Davis threw the pipe at Parker, got into the Town Car, and gunned the engine. The tyres squealed and the car leaped forwards.

Parker found the SIG and rushed back out and down the drive. Limping, cursing, he gritted his teeth and ran for his car.

He peeled away from the kerb and gunned the car down the hill. When he came around the curve, the road branched off into canyon side streets like streams on a river. Parker spotted no black Town Car going down any of them. Davis was gone.

He pulled to the side and called Hollywood Bureau, giving them a description of the car and of Eddie Davis, telling them that he was armed and extremely dangerous.

Now Davis knew the cops were on to him. Maybe he would try to run. But he didn't have the negatives, and he was obviously willing to risk anything to get them.

The negatives were the key to luring him into a trap. Davis had no way of knowing Parker had the single negative Lenny had stashed.

Parker called Ito to find out if he had developed the negative, but he got Ito's voice mail instead. He left a message for Ito to call him ASAP.

He needed to know what he was up against. The clock was ticking for him to close the case on Lenny Lowell. As comeback cases went, this one was shaping up to be a doozie. Ironic, Parker thought, that if he was right about the target of Lenny Lowell's blackmail scheme, chances were good this case would be his last. In a city fuelled by fame and power, this message would be something nobody wanted delivered: the truth.

THE MEDIA ENCAMPMENT outside the courthouse looked like a techno-geek refugee camp. Lights on poles, generators, wire cable snakes running in all directions, guys in baggy shorts carrying video cameras with network logos. Parker punched Andi Kelly's number as he approached the scene.

'Andi Kelly.'

'This is so 1994,' Parker complained. 'Hasn't anybody come up with anything new since O.J.?'

'Celeb criminals are hot again, Parker. Where are you?'

'By the Channel Four news van. Meet me by the espresso guy.'

'You're buying.'

'Have you ever picked up a tab in your life?'

'Nope.'

Parker paid for a double tall espresso for himself and a grande triple caramel macchiato with extra whipped cream for Kelly.

'You have the metabolism of a gnat,' Parker observed.

'Yeah, it's great. What are you doing down here?'

'Talking to you,' he said. 'Take a walk with me. You won't miss anything, will you?'

She waved a hand at the courthouse and rolled her eyes. 'Cole's inside, trying to look bereaved for the jury pool. Scintillating, I'm sure.'

They walked a short distance down the street.

'You look a little rough around the edges, Kev,' Kelly said. 'Have you had to face your friends from RHD?'

'I won't give them the satisfaction,' Parker said. 'I took everything I had on the case and walked. They've probably got an APB out on me.'

'So who knocked you around?' Kelly asked. 'My keen investigative skills tell me someone wasn't playing nice on the playground.' She leaned down and plucked at his trouser leg where he'd landed on his knee in Davis's garage. A grease stain and a small three-corner tear marked the spot. Both legs were beige with dust over the expensive brown-pinstripe fabric.

Parker's eyes widened as if he were seeing himself for the first time. 'Aww, son of a . . . This is Canali!'

'Well, why would you wear a designer suit to a dogfight?'

'I'm a detective. When am I ever in a fight?' Parker said.

'Today, apparently.'

'Besides, my clothes are my disguise. No one thinks I'm a cop. I dress too well to be a cop.'

'Can you write your suits off on your taxes, then?'

'My business manager says no.'

'Everything has a trade-off.' Kelly shrugged. 'So what happened?'

'Eddie Davis caught me poking around his place. I took the opportunity to arrest him. Then he took the opportunity to try to kill me. He's at large now. He's a low-end petty criminal with delusions of grandeur. Until recently, he had a low-end defence attorney by the name of Lenny Lowell.'

'Surprise, surprise.'

Parker turned and walked down the block another fifteen yards. Kelly scurried to catch up.

'My friend who overheard my name in that conversation between Giradello and Kyle was at a fundraiser for the DA,' Parker said. 'The prominent guest of the evening was Norman Crowne.'

Kelly's brow furrowed as she tried to tie the pieces together. 'A low-end lawyer like Lowell, a cheap thug like Davis. Those guys are less than ants in the world of someone like Norman Crowne.'

'I think Lowell and Davis were blackmailing someone,' Parker said. 'I'm guessing Eddie got tired of sharing. So how does a goon like Eddie Davis come up with someone to blackmail?'

'Sixty-two percent of relationships begin in the workplace,' she quipped. Then realisation dawned. 'Oh my God. You think someone hired Davis to kill Tricia Cole.'

'And that someone couldn't be Rob Cole,' Parker said. 'Even he wouldn't be stupid enough to be in the house when the cops came. He would have been out establishing an alibi.'

Kelly tried to digest the idea. Parker started to pace, his thoughts racing. Black cars were lined up at the kerb with drivers at the wheel. Three limos, a couple of Town Cars, a black Cadillac.

Parker took in the details almost absently, then stopped abruptly. Slowly he turned back to walk past the last of the cars again.

'What is it?' Kelly asked, joining him.

On the lower right corner of the back window was a small purple circular sticker with a gold insignia and a row of black numerals. A parking sticker for a corporate lot. The scene came up in his memory: he was walking towards the black Lincoln Town Car, taking in details, filing them away in his brain but keeping his mind focused on Eddie Davis. He remembered the electric blue of the sky, the black car, the licence plate, the small parking sticker on the the back window. It was no bigger than a quarter.

Parker's breathing was shallow and quick, and he felt a strange light-headedness as he lowered his gaze to the rear plate. CROWNE 5.

Parker's first thought was a selfish one: *My career is over.*

'Eddie Davis is driving a black Lincoln Town Car,' he said quietly.

'You're out of your mind, Kevin,' Kelly said. 'There's no way a hit man is riding around in a Crowne Enterprises vehicle.'

'Crowne Enterprises has reported two black Lincoln Town Cars stolen in the past eighteen months,' Parker said.

'So Davis stole one.'

Parker gave her a look. 'Eddie Davis decides he wants to steal a ride, and the car just happens to be a Town Car owned by Crowne Enterprises. What are the odds of that?'

Kelly frowned. 'Well, if you put it that way . . .'

'You've been on this story since day one,' Parker said. 'If you had to pick a suspect other than Rob Cole, who would it be?'

She thought about it for a moment. 'Well, there's darling Caroline, who discovered her mother's body. Her relationship with Rob was certainly not father-daughter.'

'And then there's Phillip, Tricia's brother. I suppose living in the shadow of Saint Tricia had to get old. He had dinner with Tricia at Patina the night she was killed. A roomful of people saw them. He says she talked about divorcing Cole. She hadn't spoken to anyone else about it, so we've only got Phillip's say-so.'

Kelly paused and looked away and made a face as if she was trying to decide whether or not to share something with him.

'You might as well tell me,' Parker said. 'I know there's something more in that brain of yours.'

She sighed and said, 'OK. I heard a whisper once, back at the start of this mess, that Tricia had accused Phillip of skimming off one of the charities. I dug on that story like a badger, but I never could substantiate it. Phillip has an alibi for the time of the murder, but if he hired it out . . .'

'He could have paid Davis with a Town Car,' Parker speculated. 'Then had to account for the missing car and claimed it was stolen.'

'But you're forgetting something here, Kev,' Kelly said.

'Which is what?'

'Rob Cole did it. He was there, in the house, passed-out drunk, when Tricia's body was discovered. He has no alibi. He's well known for having an ugly temper. If Tricia wanted to be rid of him, then he would certainly have motive to want to be rid of her.'

The first limo in line started its engine and rolled forwards.

'They must be coming out,' Kelly said.

She started back towards the courthouse at a fast walk, which quickly broke into a trot. Parker followed her, holding up his ID, telling people to step aside. He found her because her head suddenly popped up between a pair of broad-shouldered men.

She turned to Parker. 'Bend over. I want to get on your shoulders.'

'What if I don't want you there?'

'Stop being such a baby, Parker. Hurry up.'

He hoisted her up just before the doors opened and the first of the procession emerged: Norman Crowne and his entourage of attorneys and assistants and bodyguards. Crowne had come to the courthouse as a show of support for his beloved daughter.

Parker had seen him in television interviews—a dignified man whose grief was almost palpable. It was a wrenching experience to watch him as he spoke about Tricia. None of the emotion was forced or disingenuous. It simply wasn't possible to imagine him having any connection to someone like Eddie Davis or needing to pay blackmail to a sleaze like Lenny Lowell.

On his arm: the granddaughter, Caroline, in a prim suit with a jacket tailored to minimise the roundness of her figure. Parker knew enough about psychology to know the idea of Caroline falling for her stepfather was not as far-fetched as it may have seemed. Caroline's biological father, an abusive bastard, had bowed out of her life early on, leaving her with a void where a parent should have been and a screwed-up idea of what made a good relationship. And Rob Cole had come along and looked past the mousiness, the awkwardness, straight to the billions of dollars behind her.

A couple of steps behind Caroline and her grandfather walked Norman Crowne's son, Phillip. The runt of the litter. He was a vice president of Crowne Enterprises, in charge of counting paperclips, or something to that effect. Norman was still in command.

Tricia Crowne's brother had expressed more anger than pure grief at his sister's murder. He was the one who spoke of revenge more than justice. He loathed Cole.

It was difficult to imagine any of the Crownes even knowing of a person like Eddie Davis.

They weren't all in the limo before the crowd's attention swung back to the courthouse. Rob Cole and his entourage had emerged.

Cole's attorney, Martin Gorman, was a big guy with red hair. He towered over his client, keeping a hand on Cole's shoulder.

Cole was the kind of guy Parker took one look at and thought: *What an ass*. Diane wasn't the only person who saw it. Parker recognised it instantly.

He just didn't quite let on to Diane, because he found her animosity for the man both entertaining and intriguing. But Parker knew the animal. He had been Rob Cole once, only younger and much better looking.

The difference was, a cute thirtysomething jerk could still get a pass for arrogance. There was time for him to evolve into something better. A fiftysomething jerk had passed the expiration date for change.

Parker had a bad feeling that although Rob Cole might be an ass, the one thing he wasn't was guilty.

Parker's phone rang as Cole passed him. Andi was on his shoulders, trying to turn him with her knees like he was an Indian elephant. He shifted positions and pulled his phone out of his pocket.

'Parker.'

'Parker, it's me, Ruiz. Where are you? At a riot?'

'Something like that,' Parker shouted. 'What do you want?'

'Your bike messenger called.'

'How do you know it was him?'

'He said his name was J. C. Damon. He said to be at Pershing Square at five twenty-five.'

'Hang on.'

Parker reached up and swatted at Kelly. 'Ride's over!'

She slid down his back. Parker walked away from the crowd and spoke into the phone again. 'J. C. Damon called you and told you to tell me to be at Pershing Square at five twenty-five. You think I'm an idiot, Ruiz?'

'It's not a set-up,' she said. 'Maybe I felt guilty and thought I'd do something decent. The guy asked for you, said he got your name from Abby Lowell. If you don't want it, I'll call RHD.'

'And you didn't tell any of this to Bradley Kyle already?'

'You know what? Fine,' she said, disgusted. 'You're not going to believe anything I tell you. Do what you want.'

She hung up on him.

Parker slipped the phone back into his pocket and stood there, watching the last of the black cars drive away. He would be a fool to trust Ruiz. She was an IA rat. Nothing she said could be believed.

Andi broke away from the media pack and walked over to him. 'Well, that's all the fun I can have here,' she said. 'Let's go someplace romantic, and you can tell me how one of the most beloved philanthropists in LA is hooked up with a homicidal maniac.'

'I've got to take a rain check.'

'Again with the rejection!' she said, rolling her eyes. 'Where are you going? Are you seeing another reporter?'

'I'm going to Pershing Square.'

'What's at Pershing Square besides dope dealers?'

'A circus,' Parker said, starting towards his car. 'You should bring a photographer. I think there might even be clowns.'

PERSHING SQUARE is an oasis of green in the middle of downtown LA, a draughtboard area of the best and the baddest. Across Olive Street stood the grande dame of 1920s luxury: the Millennium Biltmore Hotel. A block in the other direction, unemployed men with hungry eyes loitered outside cheque-cashing places with heavy iron bars over the windows.

The park was drawn out in rectangles of grass divided by strips of concrete and broad steps that transitioned one level to the next. Brightly coloured square concrete structures hid the escalators down into the parking garage.

From his vantage point, Jace could see most of the park. It was just past five. The sun had set behind the tall buildings. Jace had stashed The Beast between two equipment trucks parked across Fifth Street. He'd been hanging around since three, keeping his eyes open for anyone who looked like a cop, watching for Predator to cruise past, waiting for Abby Lowell to show.

If she was involved in the blackmail plot, she would come alone. She wouldn't want the cops looking at her, and Predator had threatened to kill her, so she couldn't be in on it with him. Whether or not she brought the money was something else.

Tyler would be worrying by now. Thinking about his brother, Jace felt a terrible sadness. Even if this scheme worked, Jace didn't know that the cops wouldn't still have an interest in him, that they wouldn't then find out about Tyler. His instincts were telling him he and Tyler would have to run.

The idea of tearing his brother away from the Chens made him feel ill. Tyler was probably better off with them than he was with Jace, living like a hunted criminal, but Jace couldn't leave him. He had promised their mother he would look after his little brother.

But Jace wondered if his reasons for sticking to his promise to Alicia weren't more self-serving than serving Tyler. His brother was all he had. Because of Tyler, he had the Chens. Because of Tyler, he had goals and hope for a better future. Without Tyler he would be adrift.

There was no point in thinking about it, and no time. Abby Lowell had just emerged from the parking garage.

She was wearing camel-tan slacks and boots, a black turtleneck sweater, and a pale aqua quilted vest. The girl had style.

Parker watched through high-powered field glasses as she walked towards the Fifth Street end of the park, where a guy with lime-green hair sat on a bench. She was carrying a small nylon tote.

Parker stood in a beautifully appointed room at the Biltmore, overlooking Olive Street. Pershing Square was stretched out before him.

He didn't believe Ruiz with her cock-and-bull story of Damon calling in. Parker's take was that Abby Lowell had gone to Robbery-Homicide, and RHD had set up this tableau to seduce Parker so they could throw a net over him and get him out of the way. If Damon really was going to show, if Bradley Kyle knew that, there was no way they would have invited Kev Parker to the party.

Abby Lowell eyed the guy with the green hair, went to the other end of the bench and sat down, putting the tote on her lap.

Payoff, Parker thought. That's how they were setting it up: making it look like she was there to pay off Damon in exchange for the negatives. He scanned the perimeter of the park with the field glasses, looking for Kyle or Roddick. Nothing out of the ordinary.

5.10. On the low wall near the statues sat a guy in an army jacket, a black ball cap pulled low, his head down. Then he turned his head a little to the side. Towards Abby Lowell. Parker caught a glimpse of the face before it lowered again. Caucasian, young, beat-up.

Damon. Parker had never seen the kid, and yet he knew in every fibre of his being it was J. C. Damon. Parker drew a line with the glasses from Damon back to Abby Lowell, then past Abby Lowell to the area behind her, a wide half-circle, looking for cops. No sign of anyone Parker knew.

5.12. Parker dropped the glasses around his neck, turned, and hurried out of the room. He found the stairs and raced down them, jogged into the Olive Street lobby and out of the door.

5.14. As he came up from street level, he saw that Damon was moving towards Abby Lowell. The guy with the green hair got up off the bench and turned towards her as well.

Parker hurried. Green Hair was not part of the equation.

Damon kept coming. Abby Lowell stood up.

In his peripheral vision, Parker caught someone coming from the alcove hiding the escalators to the underground parking. Bulky trench coat, collar up. Bradley Kyle.

Parker hesitated. A motorcycle engine revved nearby. The scene froze for an instant in Parker's head.

Then someone screamed, and all hell broke loose.

12

Jace didn't care about the kid with the green hair. The guy was just trying to panhandle. Besides, he created a little diversion.

Jace's heart was thumping. Shove the envelope at her, grab the black bag, run. He reached a hand inside his shirt and started to peel back the tape that held the envelope to his belly.

A sound like a chain saw registered in the back of his mind. Then a scream. Then everything seemed to happen at once.

'Freeze! Police!' The guy with green hair had a gun.

'Down on the ground! Down on the ground!'

The motorcycle roared from the Olive Street side of the square, coming straight for them.

Jace didn't have time to even draw breath or to think that the green-haired cop would shoot him. He lunged for Abby, knocking her to the park bench, just as the cycle hit the cop with the green hair and blood exploded in every direction.

People were running, shouting, screaming. Guns were popping.

Jace scrambled to get his feet under him. His eyes were on the cycle. Red bike, black mask, helmet. The driver had already swung it around. It came back at Jace like a rocket. He went over the bench and ran for his life.

PARKER STARTED RUNNING the instant he saw the motorcycle. A red Kawasaki Ninja ZX12R. Eddie Davis. Parker sprinted, opened his mouth to shout. He never heard the sound. The bike hit Green Hair. A body bending the wrong way, blood everywhere. People were screaming, some of them running towards the bike, some running towards the street.

Parker pulled his gun.

To his right, Bradley Kyle had his weapon out and was firing.

Damon went over the back of the park bench.

Abby Lowell tried to follow.

Davis roared past.

Parker fired. *BAM! BAM! BAM!*

The cycle swung hard right and went after Damon.

JACE HEARD HIM coming. He hit Fifth Street. The equipment trucks seemed a mile away. He veered right in a wide arc so he could get a look back without slowing down. The headlights blinded him. Way too close.

Four more strides to the trucks.

Three more strides. Then two strides.

The cycle came up over the kerb, onto the sidewalk, and around the back side of the trucks. Jace grabbed The Beast and mounted from a run, fumbling to catch the pedals, to start pumping. If he could stay hidden by the trucks, if he could get to the other side of Olive Street before the motorcycle came around . . .

He stood on the pedals, ran on the pedals, down Fifth to Olive, through the intersection, horns blaring, lights coming at him, lucky he didn't end up on a windshield. He jumped the kerb onto the sidewalk. Glancing over his shoulder, Jace could see the red cycle racing up the opposite side of the street. He would make it to the intersection before Jace did.

The light at Olive and Fourth turned red. The motorcycle hit Fourth, screamed into a hard left turn. It ran the intersection, and horns blasted as it split the oncoming cars on the one-way street.

Jace made the corner, went left, stuck close to the meters so he couldn't get pinned against the buildings if the cycle made it to the sidewalk. Turning again, Jace cut through a small plaza with a fountain and came to a halt. Before him was the precipitous drop of the Bunker Hill Steps, a stone double staircase with a waterfall running between the two sides. It dropped like a cliff down to Fifth, where traffic was now gridlocked. Sirens were screaming.

Jace looked down to the bottom. It would be his death or his salvation. He swallowed, took a deep breath, and went over the edge.

SEVERAL PEOPLE rushed to the aid of the guy with green hair. Kyle ran past him, chasing the motorcycle, chasing Damon. Parker went to Abby Lowell. She lay over the back of the park bench.

'Ms Lowell? Are you all right?' he called.

Blood stained the back of her aqua vest where she'd caught a bullet. He rested a knee on the bench, bent over her.

The brown eyes that rolled to look at him were wild with fear. 'I can't move! I can't move!'

'We'll have an ambulance in two minutes,' Parker said. 'Did you feel something hit you from behind?'

'In my shoulder. Yes. In my back. Twice. Am I shot?'

'Yes.'

She was sobbing now, hysterical.

'Why did you come here?' Parker asked. 'Who set it up?'

'He did!' she said on a wail. 'Oh my God, I'm going to die!'

'You're not going to die,' Parker said calmly. 'The paramedics are here. They'll be with you in a minute.'

The EMTs had run to the fallen Green Hair and were trying to revive him. He lay on the ground like a broken doll.

'Hey!' Parker called. 'I've got a gunshot wound here! She's bleeding!'

One of the EMTs acknowledged him. Parker turned back to Abby. She couldn't have cared less about what Parker wanted to know.

It didn't matter anyway. He had simply been shocked to see Damon show, and he wondered if the kid really had tried to reach out to him. And what it meant if he had.

He hoped he would get a chance to find out.

THE BIKE banged down the steps, back end threatening to overtake the front. Jace shifted his weight, and the bike kicked out from under him and tumbled the last fifteen steps to the sidewalk. Jace rolled and bounced after it.

He landed at the bottom and looked back up towards the fountain. The motorcycle sat at the top. Even as he watched, the lunatic with the throttle in his hand made a decision, and the angle of the headlights tipped dramatically downwards.

Jace grabbed his bike, climbed on, pointed it down Fifth. He raced around the corner at Figueroa. He lost himself then, in the same spot he had started his day, under the tangle of bridges that connected downtown to the

Harbor Freeway. His pursuer wouldn't think to look here, Jace hoped.

He hid the bike and himself behind a huge concrete footing, out of sight from the street. He stripped off his backpack, then stripped off his coat, feeling so hot he thought he was going to vomit.

Who the hell was the guy on the motorcycle? Predator?

How had he known to be there? How had the cops known? It didn't make sense to Jace that Abby Lowell would have tipped them off. Why would she? She was in on it, whatever 'it' was.

Jace had tried to call the detective she had told him was in charge of the case—Parker. But he hadn't got him, and even if the woman he'd spoken to had acted immediately, there'd been no time for them to get people set up in the park. The green-haired guy had been there an hour *before* Jace had made the call. Abby Lowell had double-crossed him. She had thought she could get him arrested and walk away scot-free. But if she had set it up, she would have walked away without the negatives, and the negatives were what everybody wanted.

And even if she had called in the cops, that still didn't explain Predator, if that was even who had been chasing him.

What the hell could he do now?

He pushed himself up onto his knees, shrugged into his coat, reached for his backpack, and dug out his space blanket. The walkie-talkie fell out of it as he unfolded the blanket.

Jace picked it up, turned it on, and held it next to his face, but he didn't press the call button. What could he say to the kid anyway?

'Scout to Ranger. Come in, Ranger. Do you read me?'

The walkie-talkie crackled into the side of Jace's head. It was as if his mind had conjured his brother's voice.

'Ranger, do you copy? Come on, Jace. Be there.'

He could hear the worry in Tyler's voice. But he didn't answer. What could he say to Tyler after screwing up their lives this way?

He just whispered, 'I'm sorry. I'm so, so sorry.'

TYLER PUT THE RADIO in his backpack and tried hard not to start crying. He went back inside the Central Library, his base of operations for most of the day. It made him feel calmer to be in this big, solid building full of things he loved: books. But he was really tired now, and he still didn't have a plan. He kept thinking if only he could talk to Jace, but Jace hadn't answered a single radio call all day, and that made him worry.

Did the fact that he wasn't answering mean he was out of range or that his batteries were dead? Or did it mean he *couldn't* answer?

Tyler had thought that maybe if he went to the places he knew the bike messengers hung out, he would find Jace. So during the afternoon, he had gone back and forth between the hangout spots and the library, each time thinking he would see Jace, but he never did. He had tried to get him on the radio, but he never had. Now it was dark. Madame Chen would be worried about him, he knew. The idea made him feel really bad.

Tyler stuck his hands inside the pockets of his sweatshirt and fingered the business card Detective Parker had given him. He didn't seem like a bad guy. He was kind of funny in a cool sort of way. And when he'd told Tyler he didn't want to see anything bad happen to Jace, Tyler had wanted to believe him.

Always trust your instincts, Jace told him.

It was now six nineteen. His instincts were telling him he wanted to go home. Maybe if he went up the fire escape onto the roof, he could sneak back into the building and let Madame Chen know he was OK. He could sleep in his own bed, then sneak out really early and come back downtown to try again to find his brother. It wasn't a master plan, but it was a plan.

Tyler wriggled into the straps of his backpack and headed outside. There was some kind of commotion going on across Fifth Street, at the foot of the Bunker Hill Steps. Two police cars sat at angles to the kerb, lights flashing.

Tyler hurried up the sidewalk towards Olive Street, his backpack bouncing as he went. The closer he came to Olive Street and Pershing Square, the more cop cars and disorder there were.

The square was bright with floodlights and full of activity and yellow crime-scene tape and people shouting at one another. Tyler felt like he was walking onto a movie set.

He worked his way up to the yellow tape. Then twenty feet in front of him he saw two men having an argument, and he knew them both: Detective Parker and Detective Kyle. Good cop, bad cop.

Pin prickles raced up Tyler's back. The two detectives had one case in common that Tyler knew about: Jace.

Tyler tried to back up a step and banged into someone who had come up behind him. Parker was still yelling at Kyle. Kyle was yelling back at him.

Then Parker turned and looked right at Tyler.

PARKER HAD STAYED with Abby Lowell until the EMTs loaded her into the ambulance and drove away. She would go directly to surgery. It would be hours before anyone could talk with her.

'What the hell are you doing here, Parker?' Bradley Kyle said, red-faced, with steam coming out of his ears.

'I know I declined your invitation to this little soirée,' Parker said, 'but you can't seriously be all that surprised to see me.'

Kyle didn't bother to deny the accusation. Another black mark against Ruiz. He looked away and called out, 'Did anyone get a plate number on the cycle?'

'It belongs to Eddie Davis,' Parker said. 'Did you invite him too? Congratulations. You damn near managed to kill someone. Or did you mean to hit Damon? He's the perfect fall guy if he's dead.'

'I didn't shoot anyone.'

Parker looked around, feigning shock. 'Did I miss the guy on the grassy knoll *again*? I didn't fire until Davis turned and was clear. You were shooting before I was.'

Kyle wouldn't look at him.

'Are you going to try to tell me the dead guy did it?' Parker asked, incredulous. 'His death grip pulled the trigger and shot Abby Lowell in the back—twice?'

Jimmy Chew stepped between them then. 'Hey, fellas, let's cool it down. One dead cop at the scene is enough, right?'

'I wasn't firing at her!' Kyle shouted, like an imbecile. 'How many times do I have to tell you that? You're not on this case, and if I have anything to do with it, you're not on the force.'

Parker laughed. 'You don't have any power over me. Nothing you could say or do could make any more impact on my life than a mouse dropping.'

He held his hands up to Jimmy Chew to say he had no violent physical intent and took a step back and then around the officer.

'Too bad Ruiz didn't come,' Parker said. 'She could confiscate your weapon and start the IA investigation right now.'

'Yeah?' Kyle sneered. 'I hear she's got her hands full already.'

'She's got nothing. She's wasting everybody's time, including mine. I haven't shot anybody. I'm not slinking around like Tony Giradello's lapdog.'

'You don't know what you're talking about, Parker.'

'Don't I? I know Eddie Davis is driving around in a Lincoln Town Car just like the Crowne Enterprises Town Cars. I know Davis and Lenny Lowell were blackmailing somebody, and I've got a good idea why. How about you? What do you know about that?'

'I know you took the paperwork on a murder investigation and stole evidence out of Lowell's safe-deposit box, including twenty-five-thousand dollars cash,' Kyle said. 'That's a felony.'

'I had a court order,' Parker said. 'The money is sealed, signed for and safe. It hasn't made it to Property yet because I've been busy getting stabbed in the back by my partner and my captain and trying to keep from letting Robbery-Homicide screw me over again.'

Disgusted, he turned and started to walk away from Kyle, looking for Andi Kelly in the crowd and finding the kid from the alley staring at him with big eyes. Andi was standing right behind him.

Parker didn't want to react. He didn't want Bradley Kyle wondering what he was looking at.

His eyes went from the kid to Andi, back to the kid, back to Andi. Telepathy would have been a good thing, but he hadn't mastered it. Kelly probably thought he was having a seizure.

'Parker!' The voice came from behind him. Kyle. 'You can't just go. You're a police officer. You drew and fired your weapon.'

Parker unholstered and handed Chewalski his SIG. 'You'll take that to Ballistics for the purpose of elimination in an officer-involved shooting. Let Internal Affairs know where it is.'

'Will do, Boss,' Chew said, and walked away.

Parker tried to find his little friend again, but the kid had gone, and Kelly too. Parker ducked under the tape and walked away from the lights and the noise and the people. He was going back across the street to the Biltmore to sit in a civilised place and have a civilised drink.

He exited the square, stepped onto the sidewalk and glanced left. The city was doing some kind of work to a retaining wall. Someone had seen a need to throw up a lot of plywood and make a tunnel of the sidewalk for twenty yards or so. The kid was standing in the mouth of the tunnel.

Parker stopped and put his hands in his pockets. 'Funny meeting you here,' Parker said. 'You don't work for Internal Affairs, do you?'

'No, sir.' The boy nibbled on his bottom lip. 'If I tell you something, will you promise not to arrest me?'

'That depends. Did you kill somebody?'

'No, sir.'

'Then whatever you've done, I'll give you a pass.'

'I don't like that other guy,' the boy confessed. 'He's mean. I saw him at Chen's Fish Market this morning.'

Parker arched a brow. 'Really? And what was he doing there?'

'Well, he came to see Madame Chen's car, only some other cops had already taken it, which made him mad.'

'Mmm . . .' Parker leaned a little closer. 'I think he has self-esteem issues. So what is it you want to tell me?'

The boy looked all around and up and down.

'I'll tell you what,' Parker said. 'I was just on my way across the street to grab some dinner. You want to come? The cheeseburgers are on me.'

'I'm an ovo-lac-to vegetarian,' the kid said.

'Of course you are. All the tofu you can eat, then.'

The boy fell into step beside him, but just out of reach. As they waited at the corner for the light to change, Parker said, 'You know, we should be on a first-name basis by now.'

The sideways suspicious look.

'You can call me Kev,' Parker said.

The kid swallowed hard. 'Tyler,' he said. 'Tyler Damon.'

TYLER DAMON gave Parker the saga of the Damon brothers, picking like a bird at a plate of pasta in Smeraldi's. Parker's heart went out to him. The poor kid was terrified for his big brother, and terrified for himself. He had to feel like everything about his life was changing on a dime, and here he sat, telling it all to a cop.

'What's going to happen to us?' he asked miserably.

'You're going to be fine, Tyler,' Parker said. 'We need to find your brother so he'll be fine too. Can we make that happen?'

The skinny shoulders went up to his ears. He stared at his plate. 'He hasn't answered any of my radio calls. What if that guy with the motorcycle got him?'

'The guy with the motorcycle doesn't have the motorcycle any more,' Parker said. 'According to what I was hearing, your brother was hauling ass on that bike of his. The bad guy took a dive off the Bunker Hill Steps. He should have died.'

'But he got away?'

'Your brother was long gone by then.' Parker got up. 'Come on, kiddo, let's blow this shack. You're riding shotgun.'

Tyler Damon's eyes went huge. 'Really?'

'You've got to be my partner.'

'I have to call Madame Chen first.'

'We'll call her from the car.'

They went out through the main lobby, where Andi Kelly was loitering. Parker raised a hand and gave the universal sign for 'I'll call you', but didn't pause. He needed Tyler's trust, and he wasn't going to get it by giving his attention to other people.

They got in Parker's car, the boy trying not to make a big deal of being impressed with the convertible. Parker made a mental note to take the kid out in the Jag after this mess was over.

'So,' he said, 'does Jace have any friends he might stay with?'

'I don't think so,' Tyler said. 'He's too busy to hang out.'

The boy explained where he had been looking for his brother and why. Parker thought about it for a minute.

'Do you know if he was carrying much money with him?'

'We don't have very much money,' the boy said.

'Credit cards?'

Tyler shook his head.

Parker made a call to Madame Chen to allay her fears that Tyler had been abducted, or worse. She asked to speak to the boy, and they conversed in Mandarin. Then the boy handed the phone back to him.

'Take care of him,' Madame Chen said. 'Take care of them both.'

'I will,' Parker said, and ended the call.

Tyler was watching him, trying to read him the way he would figure out a maths problem. It had to be frustrating, Parker thought: having that big IQ but still being a kid with no real power over his life.

'You got a nickname?' Parker asked.

The boy hesitated for a minute. 'On the radio, my name is Scout,' he said, brightening. 'Jace is Ranger.'

'Scout. I like that. Buckle up, Scout. Let's ride.'

HE NEEDED to get rid of the negatives, just get them to someone who didn't want to kill him. He'd been stupid to try to get something for them, but he had wanted someone to pay for Eta.

The evening chill had grown damp. He could smell the ocean in it. When he wasn't sitting under a concrete bridge cocooned in a giant piece of aluminium foil, Jace loved evenings like this.

Stiff joints and tendons stretched reluctantly as he pushed to his feet. He needed to keep moving or he wouldn't be able to move at all.

'Scout to Ranger. Ranger, do you read me?'

The muffled voice came out of Jace's coat pocket.

'Pick up, Ranger!' Tyler's voice pleaded. 'Jace! I'm in trouble!'

PARKER GRABBED the boy by the shoulders and pretended to jostle him. Tyler put his own hands around his throat and made a sound like being strangled.

'Tyler!'

'Ja—' He clamped his hand over his mouth, cutting off the sound.

Parker snatched the walkie-talkie. 'I want the negatives or the kid dies.'

'Leave him alone!'

'I want the negatives!' Parker shouted.

'You get the negatives when I get my brother.'

Parker gave him instructions to meet them on the lowest level of the parking garage beneath the Bonaventure Hotel in half an hour.

'If you hurt him,' Damon warned, 'I'll kill you.'

'If you screw this up, like you screwed up in the park,' Parker said, 'I'll kill you both.'

He turned the radio off and looked at his young cohort.

'That was mean,' Tyler said.

Parker nodded. 'Yeah, it was, but if you had just radioed him and told him to meet you because you had a cop sitting here telling you to, do you think he would have come?'

'No.'

The boy was silent for a moment as Parker started the car and pulled away from the front entrance of the hotel.

'I wish this wasn't happening,' Tyler said.

'I know.'

They sat in silence for a moment, waiting for Jace.

'Kev?' the boy asked in a small, shy voice.

'Yes, Scout?'

'When I asked you before what's going to happen to Jace and me after it's over . . . will Jace and I get to stay together?'

'What do you mean?'

'Jace always said that if anybody found out about us, Children and Family Services would come, and everything would change.'

'You're my partner,' Parker said. 'I'd never rat you out.'

'But that other detective knows I live with the Chens, and he knows Jace is my brother. And he's pretty pissed off at you.'

'Don't worry about him, kid. Bradley Kyle is going to have a lot of other things to worry about. Trust me.'

Tyler sat up, suddenly at attention. 'There's Jace!'

'OK. Down in your seat,' Parker said, putting the car in gear.

They rolled into the garage, well behind Jace, following from a distance, letting him move down from level to level to level.

'Does your brother own a gun?' Parker asked.

'No, sir.'

'Is he schooled in the ways of killing men with his mind?'

'People can do that?' Tyler asked.

'I saw it in a ninja movie.'

The boy chuckled a little. 'That's not real.'

Only a few cars occupied spaces on the lowest level. Parker slowed his car to a stop and popped the automatic locks.

'OK, Scout, you're on.'

JACE SAT ON The Beast, barely moving, going just enough so that he wouldn't have to start from a dead standstill if he needed to move fast. Then suddenly Tyler was running to him.

'Tyler! Run!' Jace called. 'Go to Security!'

Tyler ran straight for him instead. Jace dumped the bike and grabbed his brother, shoving him towards the doors to the elevators.

'Tyler! Go!'

Tyler spun around. 'Stop yelling! You have to listen to me for a change!'

What a nightmare, Jace thought. He reached inside his coat, pulled out the envelope with the negatives in it, hurled it as far as he could away from the two of them and away from the guy getting out of the silver convertible Tyler had tumbled from.

Not Predator.

The guy at the car held his arms out. In one hand he held a badge. 'Jace, I'm Kev Parker. I'm here to help you out of this mess.'

13

Eddie Davis had been told numerous times that he would never amount to anything. Some people blamed him. Other people—his mother, specifically—had always blamed fate. Eddie chose to believe the second reason.

This mess he was in now was a perfect example. He had masterminded a brilliant plan. And the one person he should have been able to trust had turned on him. His own lawyer.

A person was supposed to be able to trust his lawyer. There was that confidential privilege thing, right? That had been the genius of the plan—he hooked his lawyer in when the game was already in motion. The murder had already happened. Whatever he told Lenny was confidential, so the lawyer couldn't rat him out. Eddie had needed someone to take the pictures of the client paying him off. He would split the money 70–30. Of course he deserved more, since it was his idea and he had done the killing. The deal was too sweet for Lenny to resist.

They had milked the client a couple of times, then agreed to one final big payday in exchange for the negatives. It was then that Eddie had heard detectives were nosing around. That meant one thing to Eddie: Lenny had dropped the dime on him and figured to end up with all the money and the one negative they had saved. A man's lawyer was supposed to take his secrets to the grave, right?

Lenny Lowell had taken Eddie's there early.

Eddie had set up the final drop, told Lenny the client would be there, told the client nothing. His plan had been to intercept the negatives and kill the messenger as a warning to Lenny. Then he'd have the lawyer in his pocket.

But everything had gone wrong, and it was all Lenny's fault anyway, so if he couldn't kill the messenger, he might as well kill Lenny. Get the lawyer to give up the last negative, then beat his head to a pulp.

'Ouch!' Eddie howled, twisting around to give the woman stitching him an ugly look. 'That hurts!'

One of the cops had nicked him good. The bullet had torn a gash in his side three inches long, and it felt like it had chipped a rib.

Now he sat in this backdoor 'clinic' in East LA, getting stitched up by some woman who probably spent her days cleaning toilets.

Hector Munoz, the guy who ran the place, sure wasn't a doctor, but he would keep his mouth shut for a couple of hundred bucks, and he always had a supply of oxycodone—Eddie's drug of choice.

Eddie's cellphone lying on the metal table beside him went off. He knew who it was. He'd been waiting for the call. His client was expecting the negatives. Now Eddie had to break the news that that wasn't going to happen.

He grabbed the phone. 'Yeah?'

'You can have the negatives.' He'd never heard the voice before, young, male. The bike messenger. 'I just don't want to die, that's all. It's not worth it. I thought Abby Lowell would pay for them. I never figured she'd call the cops. She told me she was in it with you—'

'How did you get this phone number?'

'From her.'

He sounded scared. He should be. This kid had caused Eddie nothing but grief. And now the kid thought he could shake him down.

'What do you want?' Eddie snapped.

'I want out,' the kid said. 'I don't even know who's in the damn pictures. I just knew if the negatives were worth killing for, they had to be worth money. Throw me a couple grand. Enough for me to get out of town—'

'Shut up,' Eddie snapped. 'Be at Elysian Park in twenty minutes.'

'Go out there so you can kill me? You can come to me.'

'Where are you?'

'Under the bridge at Fourth and Flower.'

'I don't like it,' Eddie said.

'Then don't come. You know what? Forget it.'

Eddie wanted to choke the little creep. 'I can get you five grand, but you have to give me a couple hours, and the meet has to be somewhere cops aren't driving by every minute. Olvera Street Plaza. Two hours. Double-cross me and I'll skin you. Got that?'

'Yeah. Whatever. Just bring the money.'

Eddie ended the call and got off the examination table. The door cracked open and Hector came in. Eddie shrugged into his shirt.

'Hector, I need to borrow your car.'

'Sure, man, whatever.' Hector flashed a nervous smile, pulled a set of keys out of his trouser pocket and tossed them to Eddie. 'It's the blue Toyota with the flames all down the sides. What you gonna do, man?'

Eddie looked at him with dead eyes and said, 'I'm gonna go kill somebody. I'll see you later.'

AT WEEKENDS the plaza on Olvera Street is ringed with tourists and Mexican families listening to mariachi bands. On a week night in the dead of winter, there are no tourists, only transients.

Jace paced a slow half-circle at the edge of the plaza, feeling like a goat that had been staked out as lion bait. He had brought Tyler here a million times. It was an easy walk from Chinatown and an inexpensive day out.

If anything happened to that kid, Jace was going to dismember Kev Parker with his bare hands. There had been no time to take Tyler home. They had to set up, get into their positions, and do it before Davis could arrive. Parker had given Tyler the job of lookout and had left him in the car with his walkie-talkie.

A big black guy was lying on a bench that Jace had walked past twice, snoring, reeking of bourbon. He looked like a sea lion flopped on the beach, the moonlight washing over him and the rags he had covered himself with. *An innocent bystander unwittingly waiting to die,* Jace thought.

Jace walked away. A dot of light flashed at him from across the plaza. Parker. Davis was coming.

THE EXCITEMENT built in Eddie's gut as his nerve endings started to buzz. He loved his work.

He'd come up with the perfect plan to cut away all the loose ends of this deal and ride off into the sunset. He could see the kid pacing around the plaza. Stupid kid. Except he probably wasn't so stupid that he hadn't brought a gun or something to protect himself. What he hadn't brought with him was cops. Eddie had done his recon.

Eddie himself was travelling light. The only thing he carried with him was his knife.

PARKER HAD GIVEN Jace a gun, a .22-calibre handgun he had taken out of a case in the trunk of his car. It seemed a pretty wild thing for a cop to do, but Jace had figured out quickly that Kev Parker was not a mainstream kind of guy. They had also stopped en route and picked up a crazy woman who was a newspaper reporter.

He could see Davis coming, the shape of a small vending machine in a long dark coat. His palms started to sweat and acid rose in his throat like the red stuff in a thermometer.

PARKER WATCHED Eddie Davis through night-vision binoculars as he crossed the plaza. Clipped to the binoculars was a small, wireless parabolic microphone that fed him sound through a discreet earphone. In his other ear was an earbud for the walkie-talkie that connected him to Tyler, in the car.

He had left the boy with Andi Kelly and didn't know which one was more liable to keep the other out of trouble. They had picked Kelly up on the way. If Parker's hunch paid off, she was going to get one hell of a story.

'WHERE'S THE MONEY?' Jace asked. Davis was still ten feet away.

'It's on the way.'

'What? You never said anything about anybody else,' Jace said.

'You never asked,' Davis said. 'I don't carry that kind of cash around. What did you think? That I'd rob an ATM? So where are the negatives?'

'They're safe,' Jace said. He rubbed his hand over the gun in his pocket. He didn't know anything about using a gun. Parker had said, *What's to know? Point and shoot.*

'There must be someone big in those pictures to be worth all this, for people to be killed over them,' Jace said now.

Davis smiled like a crocodile. 'The killing's the fun part.'

He started to take a step closer.

Jace pulled the .22 out of his pocket. 'Stay right there.'

'I HOPE MY BROTHER doesn't get killed.' Tyler tried to sound matter-of-fact about it.

'Kev won't let that happen.'

They sat hunched down in the front seat of Parker's car.

'Are you his girlfriend?' he asked.

'Naw, Kev's a loner. Until this week, I hadn't seen him in a long time,' she said. 'He's a good guy. He didn't used to be.'

'And then what?'

'And then he took a long look at himself and he didn't like what he saw. I'm pretty sure he's the first man in history to make the decision to grow and change and actually pull it off.'

Headlights flashed as a car turned towards them. Tyler fumbled for the walkie-talkie, pressed the call button.

'Scout to Leader, Scout to Leader! Bogie! Bogie!'

One thing Parker hated was a wild card, unless the wild card was himself. Davis had called in a ringer, and what the hell was that about?

He touched the button on his mike. 'Roger that.'

Countdown to showtime.

JACE'S ARMS were getting tired holding the gun out in front of him. Where the hell was the guy with the money?

Headlights bobbed nearby. He almost made the mistake of turning to look. The air around them seemed as thick as the ocean. Hard to breathe. The only sound he could hear was the black guy snoring on the park bench.

'Here comes the money, honey,' Davis said.

PARKER WAITED for the new member of the troupe to appear. His money was on Phillip Crowne. Andi had told him Phillip had been having dinner with his sister the night she was killed. Phillip claimed Tricia had talked about divorcing Cole, but the discussion could just as easily have been about Tricia wanting to blow the whistle on her brother's siphoning of funds from the charitable trust.

No one had ever been able to prove that Phillip had been helping himself, but then, everyone had been focused on stringing up Rob Cole. A celebrity scandal was so much more interesting than plain old vanilla embezzling.

Besides, Rob Cole had motive, means and opportunity. Parker was willing to bet Phillip Crowne hadn't got more than a perfunctory look from RHD, if that. And it hadn't hurt him to be the son of one of the most influential men in the city either.

If Eddie Davis and Lenny Lowell had been blackmailing Phillip, was it such a stretch to imagine Phillip Crowne going to his old buddy Giradello for a favour? It wasn't that difficult for Parker to imagine Giradello selling justice to Crowne. There wasn't a man on the planet hungrier or more ambitious than Anthony Giradello.

All of it fell into place like the heavy, glossy pieces of an expensive puzzle. Giradello couldn't let a couple of mutts like Davis and Lowell bring down his well-heeled pal or ruin the trial that would make his own name a household word. If he sent in Bradley Kyle and Moose Roddick, who also stood to benefit from convicting Rob Cole, he could manipulate the situation, make it go away.

Parker's blood went cold at the idea that maybe Kyle hadn't meant to miss anybody he'd been shooting at in Pershing Square. Davis was a big loose end. Jace Damon had the negatives. Abby Lowell was a wild card.

He had wished for a case to make a comeback. This one was an embarrassment of scandalous riches and human tragedy.

A figure was walking towards the plaza, towards Davis and Damon. The moment of truth was at hand.

Parker raised his glasses and focused in . . . and the world dropped from under him.

JACE DIDN'T RECOGNISE the person coming towards them, coming from behind Eddie. The light was too poor.

'This guy had better have the money,' he said.

The other person spoke. 'Where are the negatives?'

'Where's the money?' Jace asked, allowing himself a second to register that the third person turned out to be a woman.

She looked at Davis. 'Who's he? Can't you do anything right?'

'I did OK killing Tricia Cole for you.'

'I paid you for that. And that's all I've done since,' she said.

'Hey,' Davis said. 'You want to run with the dogs, that's how it goes, honey. You had someone whacked. There's consequences.'

'I can't do this anymore,' she said, choking back tears. 'It has to stop. I just wanted him to pay. But when do I stop paying?'

'Now,' Davis said. 'This is it. The kid has the negatives. You pay him his five grand, you pay me my finder's fee, and that's the end of it. Cole goes to trial next week. You did your part making sure he doesn't have an alibi. Giradello can't wait to hang him.'

The woman held a black nylon gym bag. She swung it out to the side and let go. The bag hit the ground four feet away.

Jace nodded to Davis. 'See what's in it.'

Davis went to the bag, squatted down, and unzipped it. 'Here it is, kid. See for yourself.'

Jace took a step to see inside without bending over.

It happened so fast, he barely had time to register as Davis came at him and rammed the knife into his belly.

PARKER SCREAMED into the mike, 'Go, go!' He bolted out of cover.

Even as he shouted, 'Police!' Diane Nicholson pulled a gun and shot Eddie Davis in the head.

Dan Metheny rolled off the park bench, weapon in hand, shouting, 'Freeze!'

But Diane was already running as Metheny fired five shots.

Parker screamed at him, 'Don't shoot! Don't shoot!'

He sprinted after Diane as hard as his legs would pump. She had twenty yards on him and was athletic and fast.

She skidded around her Lexus, yanked open the door and got in. The engine fired; then the car was coming at Parker.

He went up on the hood, grabbing on with both hands as Diane spun the wheel. The turn threw Parker off the side. But the Lexus didn't make it a hundred yards. Jimmy Chewalski's black-and-white came screaming from the other direction and skidded to a stop, blocking her escape.

Parker reached the back of the car, panting, as Diane flung herself out of it. She turned to face him. A gun was in her hand.

'Diane,' Parker said. 'My God, drop the gun.'

Chewalski and his partner both had their weapons out.

Diane looked at them, looked at Parker. Her expression was one of anguish and a kind of pain Parker had never imagined until now. Her face was mirroring the emotions tearing through him.

'Diane, please,' he begged. 'Drop the gun.' His heart was in his throat as he held his hand out. 'Diane. Honey. Put the gun down.'

Behind him, Jimmy Chew said, 'Kev, don't get close.'

Parker took a step.

The emotions on his face broke her heart. She looked at him and said, 'I'm so sorry. I'm so, so sorry . . .'

'It's OK,' Parker whispered. Stupid thing to say. What was OK about any of this?

The gun dropped from her hand, and she melted into his arms.

Parker held her as tightly as he could. He was shaking. Behind them, he could hear the radio chatter coming from the black-and-white. Chew's partner was calling for back-up. Parker hoped to God they didn't send Ruiz.

An ambulance siren was already wailing, coming from the other side of the plaza. Metheny would have called them in and requested back-up, detectives and a supervisor. Soon the plaza would be ablaze with lights, alive with people. He wished he could make it all go away. Diane wouldn't want anyone seeing her like this.

It was a strange thought, he supposed. She had shot a man. She had as much as confessed to having paid Eddie Davis to murder Tricia Crowne-Cole. But he didn't know the person who had done those things. He knew the woman he held.

'Kev,' Chew said quietly. 'They're coming.'

Parker nodded. He led Diane to the black-and-white and put her in the back of the car. He walked a few steps away, took a deep breath, and let it out. He had a job to do. That was the only thing that was going to keep him from falling apart.

He returned to the plaza, where Metheny knelt on the ground with Eddie Davis's head in his big hands.

'Is he alive?' Parker asked.

'So far.'

Metheny pressed a thumb against bullet holes on either side of Davis's forehead. Diane's shot had gone in one side and out the other. Parker couldn't tell if Davis was actually conscious or not.

'That chick was a wild card, man,' Metheny said. 'Did you see that coming?'

'No,' Parker said. 'I didn't.'

He stepped over Davis and went to Jace Damon. The kid was lying on his back, staring up.

'Knocked the wind out of you?' Parker asked.

The kid nodded.

Parker kneeled down and helped him onto his hands and knees. Jace sat back on his heels and wheezed.

Parker said, 'I told you not to get close. I gave you the gun so you'd stay back from him. Of course, it wasn't loaded . . .'

Damon glared at him, mouthing the word 'What?'

'I'd never give a loaded gun to a civilian. Get my ass fired,' Parker muttered. 'Not that that won't happen anyway. Metheny had your back.'

The kid finally got his breath. 'Who the hell is Metheny?'

Parker nodded in his former partner's direction. 'I didn't want you to know he was there. I didn't want you glancing over at him, tipping Davis.'

'Well, thanks for thinking about me,' Jace said finally. He opened his coat, revealing the Kevlar vest Parker had strapped him into. Davis's blow with the knife could well have broken a rib, but the blade hadn't penetrated the material of the vest.

'We'll get an EMT to check you out after they take care of your friend here,' Parker told him. He put a hand on Jace's shoulder. 'That was a really brave thing you did, Jace.'

'For Eta,' Jace said. 'Partly anyway.'

Parker nodded. 'I know. But it's not your fault she died.'

The kid nodded, but with his eyes pointed at the ground.

'Jace,' Parker said. 'I'm telling you, you did what you believed you had to do through all of this. Not what was easiest or best for you. And I don't know ten men who would be brave enough to do that.'

'Jace!'

The excited shriek arrived about a nanosecond before Tyler hurled himself at his brother.

Parker ruffled the boy's hair. 'Good work, Scout.'

Tyler beamed. 'Me and Andi let the air out of the tyres on that Lexus!'

Parker turned to Andi, who shrugged and made a face, waiting for him to yell at her. Instead, he took a few steps away from the boys and rested his hands on his hips.

'Well, this is a hell of a mess,' he said.

She studied his face. 'Who's down there, Kev? Phillip?'

'Diane Nicholson.'

'What? I don't understand.'

'Yeah, well, that makes two of us,' Parker said. 'It looks like she hired Davis to kill Tricia, and she set up Rob Cole to take the fall.'

'Oh, my God. Diane Nicholson? From the coroner's office?'

'Yes.' He watched the paramedics swarm around Eddie Davis. Numbness had begun to set in. Thank God.

Kelly touched his hand. 'Kev? Are you all right?'

'No,' he whispered. 'I'm not.' And he turned and walked away.

RUIZ CAUGHT THE CALL to the shooting. She showed up in a white suit and sandals. Parker, sitting back against the hood of a black-and-white, didn't have the energy to comment.

She walked over, shaking her head. 'What were you thinking?'

'Shut up. I don't need a bunch of crap from you, Ruiz.'

The sharpness of his tone set her back a step.

'You put a civilian in harm's way,' she said.

'He's not going to sue the city, if that's what you're worried about,' Parker said. 'The kid had a stake in this. He did it for Eta. There are a few people left in the world who know the meaning of honour and duty.'

'Don't bag on me, Parker,' she bitched. 'You could be blackmailing the preppie killer. You could be up to your ass in drug money, for all we know.'

'"All you know" doesn't amount to much, does it?' he said. 'Tell me, was Kyle standing there when you called and tipped me on Pershing Square?'

She didn't answer, and that spoke volumes.

'Who tipped Kyle?'

Ruiz took out a cigarette and lit it. 'I did,' she said on a stream of blue smoke. 'Damon really did call for you.'

'And you called Davis so RHD could set up the whole thing,' Parker said. 'In a public park at rush hour. I would say that trumps what I did.'

He reached out and yanked the cigarette from her lips.

'Don't smoke at a crime scene, Ruiz. Haven't I taught you anything?' He crushed the cigarette beneath the toe of his shoe, took it to a trash can and threw it away.

'Parker! I'm not done talking to you!' she said, doing the high-heel jog to catch up with him. 'I need to get your statement.'

'I've said everything I have to say to you.' Parker started to walk away again, then hesitated. 'That's not exactly true.'

Ruiz waited, stiffening for a tirade.

'I doctor scripts for Matt Connors.'

He might have told her he was a hermaphrodite. Her expression would have been the same. 'What?'

'My big secret,' Parker said. 'I doctor scripts and serve as a technical consultant to Matt Connors.'

'The movie guy?'

'Yeah. The movie guy.'

'Why didn't you just tell us?' she breathed.

Parker smiled a bitter smile and walked away. In this town, he probably would have received a promotion if he'd let on he was connected in the industry. He hadn't wanted the attention. All he had wanted from LAPD was a chance to make it back from purgatory and to do it through his own sweat and brainpower. The bitter irony was, in fighting for his own resurrection, he had ultimately revealed the fall of a woman he cared about.

'I want my money back,' he mumbled as he approached Bradley Kyle.

Kyle stood amid a tiny forest of evidence markers, trying to boss one of the SID people around. He turned and smirked at Parker. 'I hear you and Nicholson—'

Parker hit him so hard with a right cross, Kyle spun halfway around before he hit the dirt. Everyone stopped what they were doing, but no one made a move towards him.

Parker turned to Moose Roddick and said, 'All the paperwork on the Lowell homicide is in my trunk. Come and get it.'

The news vans had rolled in. The choppers were swarming, just in time for the eleven o'clock news. The feeding frenzy would begin.

Parker turned his cellphone on as he walked towards his car and hit the button for voice mail. He had one message. Ito had the photograph ready.

DIANE SAT on a chair in the interview room, her feet tucked up, her arms around her legs, her cheek pressed to her knees.

Parker closed the door behind him and sat on the table.

'Hi,' she said in a voice so small it seemed to have come from another room. Her gaze moved from point to point, not lighting on his face at all.

'Are you cold?' he asked, already slipping off his jacket.

It wouldn't have mattered if she had said no. He wanted the excuse to touch her. He wrapped the jacket around her shoulders and touched her cheek with his fingertips.

'Who's watching?' she asked, looking across the room at the two-way mirror set into the wall.

'No one. It's just us. Do you have an attorney?'

She shook her head.

'I'll take care of it.'

She sighed and looked away. 'Thank you.'

'So . . . you hired Eddie Davis to kill Tricia Crowne-Cole and set up Rob Cole to take the fall. That's a pretty harsh sentence for having a married guy hit on you.'

She looked away and closed her eyes. It was late. Parker had had her shipped to Central Division before RHD could make a move. The territorial dispute was being left until morning. Spending the night in one holding cell was pretty much the same as spending the night in another. And no one was going to question her without an attorney present.

'I play it through in my head,' she murmured. 'I can't believe it's me in those memories. I've listened to women friends cry about this guy or that guy, and the promises they made, and the excuses the women made when none of it happened. And I'd think, What's wrong with her? How stupid is she? And then I found out. It's some kind of insanity. The passion, the unbridled joy. It's like a drug.'

'What's *it*?' Parker asked.

'Love. The kind people write about, but no one really believes in. I always wanted to know what it was like to feel that, to have someone feel it for me.'

'Cole told you he did.'

'No one has ever made me feel the way you make me feel. I've never loved anyone the way I love you.' Her mouth twisted in a bitter smile. 'I know. I look back now, and I say the same thing. But I believed everything he told me. I should have seen him coming a mile away.'

'He's an actor,' Parker said. 'He's been playing that role for a long time.'

'The poor, misunderstood bad boy from the wrong side of the tracks,' she said. 'Trapped in a loveless marriage. If only we could be together. But I was married . . . and he was married . . . and Tricia was "fragile". And then suddenly I wasn't married . . . and things became difficult . . . and Tricia was practically suicidal, he said . . . and he had to sacrifice himself . . . and do what was right . . .'

She closed her eyes, and the fluorescent lights hummed. 'You can't know the rage I felt,' she whispered. 'My marriage was already falling apart when I met Rob. I was vulnerable, lonely. He knew just how to prey on those feelings. And then, when Joseph died . . . The guilt was terrible. Not that I'd caused his death, but that I hadn't been a very good partner, that I'd cheated on him. And Rob knew just what to do with those feelings too. I gave him everything I was. How dare he take that gift and break it?'

She was trembling. She squeezed her eyes shut, straining against an inner pain.

'Then one day, I got in an elevator at the Crowne building, something to do with Joseph's pension. There was Tricia,' she said. 'Just the two of us. She had this smug, evil look on her face.'

'She knew?'

'Oh, yes,' she said, laughing without humour. 'She knew things she couldn't possibly have known without having witnessed them happening. You see, I wasn't a game just to Rob Cole. I was a game to them both.'

'Oh God,' Parker breathed. Nausea washed over him.

Fat tears rolled like pearls down Diane's cheeks. 'And she said: "He always comes back to me." There was nothing fragile about her.'

Parker could picture the scene in his mind. Diane would have pretended not to react, because she was proud and controlled. While inside she would have shattered like glass.

'A couple of days later I got a package in the mail. A videotape of me and Rob in bed, him telling me all those things I wanted to hear. Then there they were, the two of them—Tricia and Rob—re-enacting that very same scene, line for line, and laughing.'

Parker's stomach turned at the cruelty.

'Something inside me just broke,' she said. 'I started drinking. I was in a bar one night crying to the bartender. There was a man listening. He told me he could help me, for a price.'

'Eddie Davis,' Parker said.

'I think about it now and I can't believe I hired a killer, and I came up with a plan, and I went through with that plan. I asked Rob to come to my house for dinner the night Tricia was killed. To talk about things, I told him, smooth things over. No hard feelings. He actually thought we could still be friends.' She laughed at that.

'It was so easy,' she continued. 'He drank too much, because he always drinks too much. I slipped some GHB into his last drink. Just enough to know that by the time he got home, he would be ready to pass out. Later that night I got called to a murder scene.'

'Tricia,' Parker said.

'Davis had killed her with Rob right there in the house. He staged it to look like Rob did it.'

'And Cole didn't have an alibi, because he was there, and he couldn't tell anyone he'd been with a lover scorned just prior to the murder. Even he had to know you'd be called as a corroborating witness, and you'd crucify him.'

Methodical, cool, smart.

'Why kill Tricia, though?' Parker asked. 'Why not Rob?'

'Because to die quickly wasn't punishment enough. But to send him to prison where he would have to face a life in hell, where being Rob Cole would never, ever be an advantage . . .'

'And the blackmail?'

'Started shortly afterwards. I had money. Joseph left me well taken care of. Davis thought he deserved a bonus, so I paid him. But then he wanted more. He sent me a photograph of me paying him off. The trial was coming up. Everyone said Giradello had a slam dunk. Davis said he could ruin it.'

'By incriminating himself?' Parker said.

'He didn't care. He said he'd disappear. But that wouldn't stop him from putting the photographs and the story out there. I gave him Joseph's Lincoln. That wasn't enough.'

She went to the darkened glass and stared at her reflection.

And then there was her lover, Parker thought, investigating the crime, working to tie two seemingly disparate crimes together. His big comeback case. He wanted to throw up.

'I just wanted him to pay,' she said softly, her voice strained. 'I wanted them both to pay for what they'd done to me.'

The last threads of her control shredded, and tears came in a torrent. The sounds were of something dying inside her.

Parker turned her to him and held her gently, as he would a child. He couldn't connect the woman he knew to the things she'd done. Yet the woman he knew would pay, and there was nothing he could do except be there for her as her demons raked her with their claws.

PARKER LEFT the building and just stood for a while in the night air. It was closer to morning than to midnight. The streets were shiny black, wet with sea mist. No one was around.

Andi Kelly was curled in the passenger seat of his car, huddled in a microfleece jacket he kept on the back seat. She jumped awake as he unlocked the doors and let himself in.

She turned sideways on the seat and stared at him for a moment. Parker started the engine and turned on the heater.

'How are you doing, Kev?'

'No comment. I can't talk about this, Andi. It's too raw.'

'Diane Nicholson is a friend?' she asked carefully.

Parker nodded.

'I'm really sorry, Kev.'

Andi pulled out a flask from her bag and offered it to him. 'Have a wee nip, as my grandfather used to say to us as children. He taught us how to play poker so he could cheat us out of our allowance money.'

Parker managed a chuckle, took the flask.

'Eddie Davis is conscious and talking,' Andi said. 'Unnamed hospital sources say he'll be released in a matter of days.'

'He's not worth the powder to blow him up, and he walks away from getting shot. Rob Cole screws up people's lives right and left, and he'll walk out of jail tomorrow, a free man,' Parker said.

'Well, it turns out he didn't kill anybody,' Andi said.

That wasn't exactly true, Parker thought.

'Any word on Abby Lowell?' Parker asked.

'She's stable. They won't know until the swelling goes down around the spinal cord whether she has any permanent damage. You're done in. Go home. Sleep. Call if you want company,' she said, and waggled her eyebrows.

Parker smiled. 'I'm glad we found each other again, Andi. I'll walk you to your car.'

'I'm right here,' she said, gesturing to the next car down. She leaned over and kissed his cheek, then gave him a hug around the shoulders. 'Take care of yourself, Kevin,' she said as she got out of his car.

He nodded. But as he drove the deserted streets home to his loft, he wished he didn't have to take care of himself. He had won the battle and lost the war. This was a night for a soft place to fall, but the person he wanted to share his victory with was gone. Lost to him. Lost to herself. For ever. There was nothing to do but mourn.

14

Another gorgeous southern California morning. Sunshine, traffic jams and sensationalism. Every early news show in the city was running footage of 'Peril in Pershing Square', followed by 'Shoot-out on Olvera Street'. Parker watched TV with the sound muted.

One of the things he loved most about LA was the sense that every day was new, brimming with the possibility of dreams coming true. Today, all he could feel was the opposite of hope. Today, he would in all likelihood lose the career he had fought so hard to resurrect. Today, a woman he cared about would be charged with murder, and a morally bankrupt, emotional rapist would be set free.

Parker sighed and prepared to face it all. The best thing to do with a bad day: get through it and hope tomorrow would be better.

PARKER MADE his first stop of the day the hospital. Abby Lowell was a ghostly figure under the white sheet, the machines monitoring her vital signs the only things that indicated life.

Her eyes darted towards him. She didn't say anything.

'I'm told your prognosis is good,' Parker said, pulling over a stool. 'You have feeling in all extremities.'

She just looked at him for a moment, trying to decide what to say. 'Thank you for staying with me in the park yesterday.'

'You're welcome.' He gave her a smile. 'See? I'm not all bad.'

'You're pretty bad,' she said. 'You treated me like a criminal.'

'I can apologise now,' Parker said. 'But it's my job to be suspicious of people. Nine times out of ten I'm proven right.'

'Did you get the bike messenger?'

He nodded. 'He had nothing to do with your father's death.'

'He tried to sell me the negatives. I thought he was in on it with Davis.'

'Why would you have wanted them? Did you have any part in the black-mail scheme?' He wasn't sure she didn't.

'I found out what Lenny was up to,' she said. 'I confronted him, begged him to put a stop to it. He told me he would, but he had got caught up in it and he was afraid of Eddie.'

'How did he get involved in the first place?'

'Davis was already a client. He came to Lenny and confessed to the murder, bragged about it. He didn't think Lenny could do anything because of privilege. Then he asked Lenny to help him with the blackmail. He needed someone who wouldn't rat him out to take the photographs.'

'And Lenny said yes,' Parker said.

A nurse came in and gave Parker the eye. He could see by the strain on Abby's face that she was running out of gas.

'Did Lenny give up Davis to the DA's office? He wanted the last big payoff to himself?'

Tears brimmed over her lashes. 'I did,' she confessed in a hoarse whisper. 'I thought if Giradello could go after Davis . . .'

Then Davis would have been arrested for Tricia Crowne-Cole's murder. The negatives showed only Davis and Diane. Maybe they wouldn't find anything against Lenny, except the word of a hit man. But Davis had had other plans.

'Did you speak to Giradello himself?'

'No. To his assistant.'

'Did you give your name?'

'I couldn't.'

And how seriously would Anthony Giradello take an anonymous tip on a case that was a lock to convict and a lock to launch his own political career? Not very. It was a wonder he'd even bothered to put Kyle and Roddick into the field to nose around.

Parker looked at Abby lying there looking young and crushed at the losses she had suffered. Her eyes closed. The nurse scowled at Parker. He murmured a goodbye and walked out of the door.

'I THINK the unemployment office is in a different building,' Andi Kelly said as Parker walked towards her through the mob outside the Criminal Courts Building, where Rob Cole and his dream team would be emerging shortly to tell the world he was a free man.

Parker's suit was rumpled from sitting in a conference room for two hours. 'Suspended,' he said. 'Thirty days without pay.'

'Never mind that you cleared about three cases in one fell swoop.'

Parker had brought up the subject of Robbery-Homicide's shadowy involvement in the Lowell homicide investigation. He had pointed out that a lot of people could have been killed at Pershing Square. No one wanted to hear it. He mentioned that Kyle had shot a woman in the back. Internal Affairs would investigate the shooting. Kyle would be on desk duty pending the outcome and would likely be suspended afterwards.

At least Parker had the satisfaction of knowing Bradley Kyle would not be advancing his career.

When Parker's sentence had been pronounced, the chief of detectives had asked him if he had anything he wanted to say. Parker stood up and asked Kyle directly, why, if Giradello had been given a reason to suspect Davis for the Crowne homicide, had he not had them pull Davis in for questioning.

They had all looked like they were trying to pass a hot potato with telekinesis. They hadn't taken the threat of Eddie Davis seriously on the weight of an anonymous tip. And Tony Giradello wouldn't have wanted it to get out that another suspect was being questioned on the eve of his opening statement to the jury, telling them Rob Cole was a murderer.

So Kyle and Roddick had dragged their feet, and a lot of people had paid a terrible price.

'I quit,' he told Andi. 'I took off my service weapon, took out my ID, left it all on the table, and walked.'

Kelly was wide-eyed. 'But you worked so hard to make it back, Kev. After they're done being pissed off, they're going to see—'

'I don't need them to see anything, Andi,' he said, shaking his head. 'They don't matter. I thought I had to prove something, and I did, to myself. Now I can move on with my life.'

'Wow,' she said. 'That's one of the most mentally healthy things I've ever heard anyone say.'

The commotion began at the courthouse doors and rolled through the crowd on a wave. The doors swung open, and Good Man Wrongly Accused emerged with his entourage.

Parker stood at the edge of the madness, watching women hurl themselves at Cole, screaming. It turned his stomach. He glanced to his right. There was a tall, striking woman with sandy hair standing a few feet away, staring at Cole with grey eyes as cold as ice. Andi made a comment, and he had to lean over and have her repeat it.

In that split second, the woman with the grey eyes pulled a gun from her handbag, pointed it at Rob Cole and started shooting.

The scene was chaos. People screaming, people running. The woman just stood there, gun in hand.

Parker knocked her to the ground. The gun flew out of her hand. She began sobbing, saying over and over, 'Look what he did to me!'

A SUBSEQUENT SEARCH of the home of Rob Cole and Tricia Crowne-Cole yielded a treasure trove of X-rated videotapes. Most were of Cole with other women—Diane among them—having sex, having dinner, telling each of them she was his soul mate, that no one had ever made him feel the way she made him feel.

And there were the tapes of Cole and Tricia, shot in their bedroom. Tricia mocking the other women, begging Cole to love her, begging him to stay. The two of them laughing like jackals.

And a fresh scandal was born.

The press demanded to know why the tapes hadn't turned up during the initial investigation of Tricia's murder, but there had been no reason to look for them. In the investigation of Tricia's death, there had been no reason to search for anything.

Parker hired Harlan Braun, attorney to the stars, to represent Diane. On Sundays, he would go visit her in jail.

Andi Kelly was writing a book.

The laws of nature dictate nothing go to waste when an animal is killed. Rob Cole was feeding the scavengers, all eager to pick their teeth with his bones. In the end, there would be nothing left of Cole but his infamy. He deserved nothing better.

JACE SAT ON THE roof of the Chens' building, watching Tyler and Grandfather Chen play with a pair of remote-control cars. Both the old man and the boy were laughing as the cars careened around.

It was a perfect Saturday morning. The sun was already warm and felt good on his body. After several days of rest, the aches had begun to subside, and some of the tension had left him.

Parker had taken him to the Robbery-Homicide offices the day before so Jace could give his statement of everything that transpired in those few days. He'd held his breath practically the whole time, waiting for someone to ask him about Tyler, but it hadn't happened.

Besides, Parker had said, if Jace really was nineteen or twenty-one, or any of the ages he chose to tell people, he was legally an adult and entitled to custody of his brother.

The focus of the interview had been narrow and on point. What had happened and when. Parker had stayed right there with him the whole time.

Afterwards, Parker had taken him to lunch and filled him in on the case. Davis was being charged with four counts of murder. A one-man crime spree, fuelled by greed and the sheer joy of taking lives. Three of those lives, including Eta's, could have been spared if Giradello had had Davis picked up immediately after Abby Lowell had tipped him off regarding Davis's involvement in the Crowne murder. An investigation was under way.

The most important thing to Jace was that he was out of it, and his odd little patchwork family was safe.

Where he would go from here, he wasn't sure. He wouldn't go back to being a messenger. The stress would be too much for Tyler.

Jace should have been anxious about the future, but for now he was content to watch his brother being a kid. He was content to think that they had a home and a family, and to know that family didn't have much to do with blood but had everything to do with heart.

PARKER TURNED the green vintage racing Jag down the alley and parked behind the Chens'.

'Kev!' Tyler's shout came over the side of the roof. Half a second later, the boy came bursting out of the door. 'Wow! Cool car!'

'You think?' Parker said. 'I came to take you and your brother for a ride.'

'Excellent!'

Ten minutes later they were on the road, the Jag growling beneath them, the wind in their hair. Parker found he liked playing uncle very much. Tyler was a terrific little person. And Jace was something too. Brave and good. Both of them were pretty amazing.

Parker suspected that Jace had been born an adult. At nineteen he had a larger sense of duty than ninety per cent of the people Parker knew. Jace had geared his life to raising and protecting his little brother. He was working two jobs, taking the train to Pasadena City College a couple of times a week to work towards getting a degree.

It seemed to Parker that no one deserved a break more than Jace Damon did. And he was about to give him one.

He turned the Jag in at the entrance to the Paramount lot and pulled up at the guard shack.

'Hey, Mr Parker. Good to see you.'

'You too, Bill. My friends and I are here to see Mr Connors.'

'Who's Mr Connors?' Tyler asked.

'A buddy of mine,' Parker said. 'Matt Connors. I do a little work for him on the side.'

Jace looked over at him, suspicious. 'Matt Connors the movie director? What kind of work do you do for him?'

'I . . . consult,' Parker hedged. 'I was talking with him last night. He's anxious to meet you.'

'Why?'

'Because you've got a hell of a story to tell, kid.'

He parked the Jag, and they all piled out. Having been alerted by Bill at the gate, Connors met them at the car.

Matt Connors was handsome enough to work in front of the camera but smart enough not to. On the list of successful people in Hollywood, Connors's name was not far down the list from people like Spielberg.

'Kev Parker, my long-lost friend and script saviour!' Connors rejoiced, throwing his arms around Parker. Then he stepped back and said, 'Where the hell are your notes on *Prior Bad Acts*?'

'I've been a little busy saving the city from violence and corruption,' Parker said.

Connors rolled his eyes. 'Oh, *that*. Are these your deputies?' he asked, looking at Jace and Tyler.

'More like secret undercover agents,' Parker said. 'This is Jace Damon and his brother, Tyler. I was telling you about them.'

'Right,' Connors said, sizing them up as if he was already casting their roles in his head.

The three of them shook hands. Tyler was wide-eyed.

'So, we get to look around?' Jace asked. He was, Parker noticed, trying very hard not to appear excited.

Connors spread his arms. 'Matt Connors, tour guide, at your service. Let's take a walk. I'll show you where the magic happens.'

They started down the lot, Parker and Connors flanked by the two boys, the California sun spilling over them like molten gold, the world of dreams spread out before them.

Parker put a hand on Connors's shoulder and said, 'My friend, have we got a story for you. And for a generous price that would put him through college and graduate school, I'm guessing Jace here would be happy to tell it to you.'

Connors nodded, turned to Jace, and said, 'How about it, kid? You want to be in the movie business?'

Jace stared at him, his brain stalling out. 'A movie? About me? About what just happened?'

'Right,' Connors said. 'I already have the perfect title. We'll call it *Kill the Messenger . . .*'

TAMI HOAG

Born: Cresco, Iowa, January 20, 1959
Home: Los Angeles
Former job: horse trainer

Tami Hoag began her writing career as a romance author, publishing her first book, *The Trouble With J.J.*, in 1988. She went on to write nineteen more romances but found herself increasingly drawn to crime writing. 'It was a gradual progression in my work. I started adding bits of suspense to the romance and as I grew as a writer and wanted to do bigger, more complex stories, that was the direction which was natural for me to go.' *Night Sins*, published in 1995, was her first real suspense story and was very successful. A year later, Hoag set a publishing record when three of her books hit the *New York Times* best-seller list within ten months.

The idea for *Kill the Messenger* came to her some years ago when she was watching a programme on television. 'It was about bike messengers in Los Angeles and the role they play in shuttling documents between lawyers and the courts. There seemed to be a lot of possibilities for stories there, but it wasn't until I moved to Los Angeles that all the pieces came together for me. I had to make some new contacts for the research, but I enjoy that. It's always interesting to sit down and talk with cops. Probably my biggest challenge was to limit myself, to keep the story in focus and not let the city take over the book.'

A love affair had taken her to LA and, even when the relationship ended, she was happy to remain in the city. 'There's an energy and enthusiasm here. Everybody comes with a big dream, and while a lot of them don't happen, there's always a chance that they will.'

Hoag, who was brought up in a small country town in Minnesota, loves the out-doors, especially horses and riding. Before moving to LA, she lived on a horse farm in Virginia, training show horses and competing in dressage events at national level. She has recently recovered from a serious riding accident in which she fractured several vertebrae, but even that hasn't put her off the sport. 'My horses are my passion away from my work; my joy, refuge, therapy, salvation and comfort.'

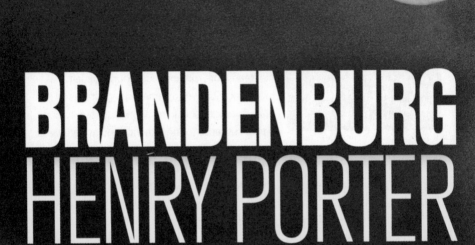

BRANDENBURG
HENRY PORTER

Dr Rudi Rosenharte, a former agent for East Germany's secret police, thinks he's put his spying days behind him – until his former masters cleverly blackmail him into one more mission.

Events are unfolding in Leipzig and Dresden, however, that will soon change the world. And with border security tightening, and political tensions mounting, Rosenharte finds himself less concerned with the familiar East–West spying games and far more preoccupied with the safety of his brother, Konrad, and his family

PART ONE

The man in the straw hat dogged his footsteps from the first, keeping his distance, yet never bothering to hide himself. Rosenharte saw him loitering outside the hotel when he checked in, then at the conference centre and later sitting at a café in Piazza dell'Unità, a mournful fellow with a washed-out face. Once or twice Rosenharte thought he was going to approach, but then he seemed to decide against it and darted away into a side street.

He wondered if the man was the visible part of the Stasi's surveillance operation in Trieste, put on his tail to remind him of their presence. Or perhaps the man was being fielded by a Western agency as some kind of ploy to draw out the Stasi surveillance.

He ignored the man and threw himself into the conference on the rise of artistic conscience in the late Renaissance, a theme that had drawn 150 academics from all over Europe. Between lectures, Dr Rudi Rosenharte explored the streets of the hot, carefree city, marvelling at the unbelievable fullness and plenty of Italian life and the contrast with life in East Germany.

Yet never for a moment did he forget that he had been brought to Trieste to rendezvous with an old lover—a lover who he knew had been dead for the best part of fifteen years but who the Stasi believed was alive.

On his third day in Trieste she made contact. Inside an envelope containing the daily conference bulletin was a handwritten note from Annalise Schering, which instructed him to walk unaccompanied to the end of 'Molo IV'—Pier Number Four—in the Old Port, where she would be waiting.

He reread the note several times. The handwriting was perfect, the romantic urgency of the sentiments just right. Using the phone in the hotel lobby he called Colonel Biermeier of the Stasi Main Directorate for Foreign Intelligence, the HVA, who was running the operation in Trieste.

Biermeier came to his hotel room just after three that afternoon.

'It's an obvious fake,' Rosenharte insisted to the back of Biermeier's head as he read the letter on the little balcony. 'It's a trap. We should go back and forget the whole thing.'

The colonel shook his head and turned to him, his unhealthy white face and brilliantined dark grey hair shining in the sunlight. Biermeier was unprepossessing and oafish, yet he was far from stupid.

'No, Comrade Doktor, this is no fake. The handwriting matches our samples. We will go ahead as Brigadier-General Schwarzmeer has ordered.'

'But if anything goes wrong, I'll be held responsible. You've got my brother in jail and he'll be punished. What justice is that?'

Biermeier smiled, came over to him and put an arm round his shoulder. 'Go, Rosenharte. See what the woman has to say.' He paused. 'Look, what's the problem? You give her dinner, win her affections and bring her back to us. Make her yours again.'

Rosenharte laughed, momentarily recalling the 'love tutorials' of the Stasi spy school. 'Make her yours again! You're still living in the fifties, Colonel.'

'You know what I mean. You used to do this for a living. You, above anyone, know what to do with this woman. I don't have to remind you that you have an obligation to the state equal to that of a serving officer.'

Rosenharte lit a Marlboro, then said, 'You'll allow my brother Konrad and his family to go free if I meet her?'

Biermeier closed his eyes and nodded.

'I don't want your people following me. Pier Four is deserted and very exposed. I went there earlier. She'll spot anyone on my tail.'

'That's doubtless why she chose it. No, we won't follow you. We're relying on you to bring her to us. It's all on your shoulders.'

There was a knock at the door. Biermeier opened it to a young officer. 'This is Schaub. He will show you how to operate the listening device.'

'You expect me to seduce this woman wired up to Normannenstrasse?'

'When it comes to that part of the evening you take it off in the bathroom. It's the conversation before that interests me, not your lovemaking.'

Rosenharte sat down on the bed. He removed his shirt and submitted with mild protests as Schaub taped the equipment to his chest and back.

'Some part of you must feel pride,' Biermeier told him. 'After all, you're going back into harness for the state.'

'Nothing could be further from the truth,' said Rosenharte. 'I was never any good at this kind of work.'

'Ah well, now you count yourself a member of the intelligentsia. You affect an air of superiority, but I know the man behind the façade. I've read your file. What was it one of your girlfriends said? "A clever, selfish bastard."'

Schaub smirked, then got up and left.

'You mean she didn't mention my lovable sense of humour?' said Rosenharte. 'My skills as a cook, my sobriety, my modesty . . .'

Biermeier shook his head disdainfully, and then checked the transmitter. 'Remember to press the button at the side once you see her,' he said.

Just before six Rosenharte dressed, checked himself in the mirror and then left the hotel. Did the Stasi know? Had they faked the letters from Annalise Schering to expose his great lie? No, no one in the GDR could possibly know that she had killed herself fifteen years before.

He saw Annalise now, as he walked. The little apartment in Brussels on a winter's evening, finding her in the bath surrounded by candles and roses, her head resting on one arm lying along the side of the tub. Dead. Bloodied water. Vodka bottle. Pills. Needle of the stereo clicking round the centre of Mahler's Fifth. His feelings then, as now, were guilt and a kind of horror at the operatic bathos of her death scene. Annalise always overdid things.

He passed through a series of parallel streets that led down to the sea, and made for the deserted quays. Konrad would shake with laughter at the idea of his brother's tryst with a dead woman. Rosenharte allowed himself a rueful smile, until he thought of his twin's plight as the Stasi's hostage. To ensure his cooperation and that he wouldn't defect, they were holding Konrad in prison. For good measure, they'd taken Konrad's wife Else in for questioning and placed Konnie's two boys in the care of the state.

Ahead of him was Molo IV, a broad stone structure that protruded into the harbour with quays on both sides and a huge single-storey warehouse along its spine. He passed through a gate near the old seaplane terminal, and turned left to walk up the pier. On the way, he noted a man rigging a fishing rod, and some teenagers kicking a ball in the abandoned marshalling yard. They all looked plausibly engrossed. He trudged on up the pier, picking his way through the rusting iron debris and tufts of dead weeds that grew in cracks between the stones.

'HERE HE IS,' said Macy Harp, nudging Robert Harland with his elbow. 'Bang on schedule like the bleeding Berlin Express.'

They both moved back from the doorway that led onto one of the iron walkways running along outside the disused warehouse by Molo IV. They were about 200 yards from Rosenharte, who was moving away from them. Harland trained his binoculars on him and reflected that both he and his quarry had much to lose if this went wrong. He had only been British Secret Intelligence Service station chief in Berlin for a year, and in many ways he was still on probation. The head of the European desk had given him a certain amount of support together with Macy Harp—the best odd-job man that the service had to offer—but Harland knew that many in Century House were actively hoping for the operation to fail.

He shook himself and concentrated on Rosenharte. At the time of the Schering operation in Brussels his fake passport had put him at thirty-two, which would put him in his late forties. He had looked after himself: he was tanned, still slim and there wasn't a trace of grey in the sandy hair. But he betrayed a certain edginess and Harland could see he was moving without enthusiasm to the rendezvous point. 'How many Stasi have we got?' he asked quietly.

Harp squinted into a notebook. 'About a dozen, maybe more.'

'And what do we make of the character with the straw hat?'

'At first we thought he was Stasi because we've seen him a couple of times. Jamie Jay followed him to a hotel in the New Port this morning.'

'But how does he manage to be here ten minutes before Rosenharte?'

Macy Harp lit a cigarette. 'Simple. He saw Rosenharte out here when he did his recce this morning, realised he had started off on the same route this evening and decided to get here ahead of him.'

'Right,' said Harland doubtfully. 'Where's Cuth Avocet?'

'Having a drink over there on the seafront.'

Harland nodded. 'Are we certain Rosenharte didn't make any calls from his hotel phone once he had found the note?'

'Can't be sure,' said Harp. 'The Stasi are likely to have set up a way of communicating with him without us knowing.'

'I bloody well hope they don't think we're here. The idea is that it's just Annalise. If they get any hint of us we're finished.'

Harp nodded. 'Tell me about chummy down there. How come he's going to meet a woman he knows is dead?'

'Because he didn't tell them she was dead. He couldn't—not back in 1974 and especially not now. We'd put him in—'

'An impossible position. I see that, but how . . . the girl's death? Was he compromised? Has he been working for you?'

Harland remained motionless behind his binoculars.

'There's something I'm not getting,' said Harp.

'That's right, Macy.' He wasn't about to tell him everything, and anyway it was far too complicated.

Harp nodded. He knew better than to press the point.

ROSENHARTE CAUGHT SIGHT of the man with the straw hat issuing from a building on his right and weaving drunkenly down the pier straight towards him. Rosenharte slowed, then stopped and pressed the little button on the device taped to his chest. As the man got closer Rosenharte was able to get a good measure of him. The round beer paunch and poorly cut suit jacket unambiguously announced a citizen of the German Democratic Republic.

The man seemed to stumble, clutched at his thorax and cursed before rushing the few feet to where Rosenharte was standing. At the last moment, Rosenharte tried to dodge out of his path, but the man snatched at his shirt and gripped it with such force that Rosenharte instinctively lashed out. The man looked aghast, and only then did Rosenharte understand that the face below him was contorted with pain and fear. He kept putting one hand to his throat and was searching wildly about him. A part of Rosenharte registered disgust at his breath and the foam that had gathered at the corners of his mouth, but he gripped the man by the shoulders and told him in German to be still and he would try and find him some help.

The man's body began to shake with a series of convulsions that forced them both towards the edge of the quay, where a few fishermen were sitting. They staggered in a drunken waltz for a few seconds, kicking up swirls of dust, until the man suddenly collapsed into his arms and pushed him against a large iron mooring bollard.

Some words came from him. 'Rye . . . Ryszard . . . Kusimiak.'

'Be still, for God's sake, or . . .' At that moment Rosenharte lost his footing and together they toppled over the bollard, rolling down the four or five feet of the quay wall into the water like a weighted sack.

More angry than shocked, Rosenharte surfaced and struck out to a chain that was hanging down from the top of the quay. He grabbed it and began to haul himself up. He heard a voice and looked up to see a man holding out his hand, yelling something in Italian. Rosenharte reached out for the hand, and a few moments later he was kneeling on the quay, hacking seawater from his throat. Around them stood a semicircle of teenage boys with fishing rods. Rosenharte wiped his eyes and nodded to show he was OK. The man put a hand on his shoulder and said, 'Just stay there for a bit.'

Then one of the boys caught sight of the body in the water and started shouting. All five stripped off and dived in. One yanked the man's head up by the hair while the others pushed the body towards the chain.

'Perhaps it's better that I speak German,' hissed the man after he'd instructed the boys in Italian to loop the chain under the body's arms.

It was the last thing Rosenharte wanted. He shook his head furiously, put his hand in his shirt and ripped the wire from his chest.

The man showed little surprise. 'Don't worry, it won't work after that soaking.'

'Who are you?' Rosenharte asked.

'A friend of Annalise.'

'You're English?' said Rosenharte.

He nodded. 'Is he one of your people?' he asked, pointing to the water.

'My people? No.'

'Look, we're about to be joined by the police.' The Englishman gestured with his chin. Rosenharte turned to see a navy blue Alfa Romeo threading its way through the scrap iron. 'Be at the Ristorante Grand Canale by nine thirty. Take a table on the canal pontoon. Just make it seem as though you happened on the restaurant by chance. You got that?' He punched Rosenharte lightly on the shoulder. 'Good fellow—everything will be OK.'

At that moment one of the boys shouted for them to take up the slack on the chain and help pull the man over the edge. The Englishman knelt down and began rhythmically pumping at the man's back. When the cough he was hoping for didn't come, he rolled the man over, took hold of his nose and chin and pushed the head back slightly. No sooner had he touched the man's lips with his own than he recoiled, wiping his mouth furiously and spitting on the ground. One of the policemen attempted to take over, but the Englishman pulled him back saying there was something wrong.

Rosenharte looked down at the body with a lack of emotion at first, but then bafflement and shock hit him. He wondered what the sudden extinction of this human being meant for him. Things like this didn't just happen.

FROM THE WAREHOUSE, Robert Harland watched the police car with Rosenharte inside disappear through the Old Port gates, followed by the ambulance carrying the body. He turned to Cuth Avocet, the gaunt figure known throughout British SIS as the Bird. 'We'd better get back to the van and start preparing the watch on the restaurant,' he said.

The Bird put out an arm. 'Perhaps you should wait for the area to clear first. There's another couple of bogies down there.' He pointed to two men who'd materialised from beneath them and were making for the dock gates.

Half an hour later, Harland sat in the back of a black Volkswagen van with Jamie Jay, sorting through the contents of the dead man's black leather wallet. Harland held up an identity card and read out the name Franciscek Grycko. 'What's a bloody Pole doing here? The Stasi and Polish spooks are barely on speaking terms. Normannenstrasse wouldn't involve them in something like this. It's a pity you didn't get his passport.'

Jay looked offended. 'You try kissing a dead man with vomit in his mouth and see how long you can stand feeling him up at the same time.'

'You think they knew each other?'

Jay shook his head. 'Rosenharte said the man had an attack of some sort—practically fell into his arms foaming at the mouth.'

'What about the taste you mentioned? You think it was poison?'

Jay wrinkled his nose. 'Dunno. I feel OK.'

'Good. So who's monitoring Rosenharte's phone at the hotel?'

'Cuth has gone to take over from Jessie.'

'Christ, I hope Jessie's changed by now.'

'Of course. She'll look just the part. Rosenharte's going to fall in love all over again.'

'We don't need him to. All that matters is that the Stasi believe she really is Annalise. And that will depend on Rosenharte's reaction. If for one moment he looks like he doesn't recognise her, he's lost and might as well defect tonight. He won't last a minute under Schwarzmeer's interrogation.'

'Schwarzmeer?'

'Yes, Brigadier-General Julius Schwarzmeer, director of the Hauptverwaltung Aufklärung.' Harland paused and looked at Jay's confused face. 'Sorry, I forget that you're rather rusty on all this. The HVA is the foreign arm of the Stasi.'

'And the purpose of all this? I mean, what's the bigger picture?'

'If it comes off, you'll see. It may even help in your patch.'

'With all respect, I very much doubt Oman is going to benefit from this.'

'You'd be surprised. There's a lot to connect the problems in your part of the world with the Stasi. That's what this operation is all about.' He stopped. 'Look, I'd better be getting along. I want to hear what the Italians have got to say about Rosenharte's state of mind after that business out on the pier.'

ROSENHARTE ARRIVED at the restaurant with his hair damp and his shirt still showing the signs of compression in the suitcase that he'd brought from Dresden. He was led to a table at the far end of the pontoon, where he sat down and ordered a bottle of wine.

All but two of the ten tables on the pontoon were occupied, mostly with young couples. He slipped down in his chair a little and watched the people drift along the canal banks, noting that the instincts that he had been taught to use at an almost subliminal speed in Stasi training school were coming back.

He was there ten minutes before he became aware of a woman standing on the gangway leading to the pontoon. Her gaze came to rest on him and she gave a shy little wave. For a moment he stared dumbly at her, then gave a halfhearted wave himself. She was heavier than Annalise but her hair was about right—dark and pulled back by a clip, and her outfit—the white linen skirt, loose jacket and sagging shoulder bag—was what the middle-aged Annalise would have worn. But she wasn't as beautiful as Annalise. She was now beside the table, wreathed in smiles and holding out both hands.

'For Christ's sake, stand up,' she hissed in English without losing the pleasure in her face. 'Stand up and give me a hug and kiss me.'

He did as instructed, feeling that anyone watching would immediately see beneath this phoney reunion.

'Rudi darling,' she exclaimed, 'it's so wonderful to see you.' She clasped him to her one more time then she let him go and stepped away, seemingly to absorb her first sight of him for fifteen years. 'Well, are you going to give me dinner, or what?'

Realising that she was waiting for him to pull out her chair, Rosenharte scurried round to help her.

'I think we both need a drink, don't you?' she said. 'I'll have some wine.'

He filled her glass.

'Did they give you another transmitter?'

He shook his head.

'Good. My people can hear us, but it's just one way.'

'You're not Annalise,' he said. He had to put on record that this was not her because a vague suspicion that he had been set up by his own side still lurked in his mind.

'Of course I'm not her,' she said with a puzzled look. 'Oh, I see. Christ, this is complicated, isn't it? You think you're being set up by your own side?'

At least the woman was quick. He nodded.

'Put your hand on mine,' she said, gazing into his eyes. 'We're being watched. There're about a dozen Stasi. That's good, because we want them to see us getting along and then you beginning to seduce me.' She gave him a mischievous smile.

He smiled. 'I hope I'm up to it,' he said playfully.

'Of course you are,' she returned. 'You like women, Rudi, and even if you don't fancy me, you're going to look as though you do. Now, light my cigarette.' She exhaled the first drag. 'The wind's getting up. It's a relief after the heat.'

'You Brits always have something to say about the weather.' He paused. 'I don't know your real name and I cannot call you Annalise, but—'

'Then use a pet name.'

'I called her Anna.'

'Then use that,' she said with a laugh.

'Your people—British intelligence—can hear me now?'

She nodded.

'They should know there are people's lives at risk.'

'If anything goes wrong, you can defect,' she replied. 'We've got enough people here to help you at the first sign of trouble.'

He looked at her without bothering to mask his feelings. 'My brother Konrad is in jail. They will hold him there until I return to the GDR.'

She absorbed this without changing her expression. 'All the more reason to make this work without raising their suspicions.'

'Already your operation is compromised. That man dying at the pier: the Stasi will know that something is wrong. Why did you ask me to go there?'

'We wanted to see how many people were following you.' She brushed the back of her hand against his cheek. 'Let's order, shall we?'

'The man who died—who was he?'

'We don't know yet. Look, leave all this to later; these questions are showing in your face. Just keep to the script and begin sweet-talking me, honey bun.' She winked at him. 'Relax, and tell me about your work.'

ALMOST DIRECTLY above the restaurant there was an ornate first-floor balcony running along four shuttered window bays. Behind these was a drawing room where Harland had set up his forward observation point. In the room with him were Macy Harp, Alan Griswald of the CIA, and his Italian counterpart, Ludorico Prelli, with two of his assistants. From here they monitored the movement of the Stasi team; the area was crawling with East German intelligence officers.

There was silence in the room while Harland listened to the couple talk. He watched the waiter take their order, then turned to Griswald. 'So what do you make of this thing about his brother being in jail?'

'It may be to your advantage, Bobby. It means your fellow's gotta go back East if his brother's in the slammer. And if he *does* go back, he's gotta work for you. There's no way out for him. Tell me about the brothers.'

'They're identical twins. Our friend has made a name for himself as an art historian. A lot of bearing. He looks like a damned prince down there. He's kept his nose clean, but the brother is a dissident. In and out of jail, including spells in Bautzen and Hohenschönhausen.'

'What was his crime?' asked Griswald.

'Consorting with demagogic and hostile elements—something of that nature. He's a film-maker. We don't know much more about him.'

They heard Rosenharte tell Jessie about the lecture he was giving the following day. The conversation was moving along quite well now. A radio crackled and Cuth Avocet, hidden in the van a little distance from the side of the canal said, 'One of those bogies is walking over to them.'

Harland moved his face up and down the slats. He saw a slim, middle-aged man in an open-necked shirt walking towards the table.

ROSENHARTE PLACED his hand on top of hers. 'We're about to be joined.' Then he cupped her chin in his hand and leaned over to kiss her.

'That's nice,' she said, smiling. 'You are rather good at that.'

'Thank you.' She was not the first to say it.

The man was within a few feet of them. He hesitated, then approached the table. 'Annalise!' he exclaimed. 'Annalise Schering, is this really you?' He spoke in English. 'It can't be!'

She stared at him. 'I'm sorry . . . do we know each other?'

'The Commission in Brussels! Don't you remember me? Hans Heise. We worked in the same unit, the Directorate General for Development.'

She looked at him hard, then glanced at Rosenharte, who smiled politely. 'I'm sorry, I simply can't place you. Which office did you say?'

'The Development Directorate, under the Dutchman—Jan van Ostade. Surely you remember?' He gave her an indulgent look.

'I certainly remember him, but, forgive me, I . . .' she shook her head. 'I'm sorry, it must seem rude, but I don't remember your face.'

He looked troubled. 'But you remember my name, surely. Heise—Hans Heise. We used to meet at parties held by the Russell-Smiths.'

'His name wasn't Jan van Ostade,' she said. 'It was—'

'Ugo van Ostade,' said Rosenharte, shooting a firm smile in Heise's direction. 'You introduced me once. He was drunk, I seem to recall.'

She turned from Heise to Rosenharte, a look of relief beneath her smile. 'Yes, exactly.' She turned back to Heise. 'I remember that office. So where did you sit? Not on the right, because the Italian and Spaniard were there. What were their names? Carlo and . . .?' She was playing him at his own game. Heise opened his arms as though to say that he couldn't be expected to remember everything. 'Then on the left,' she continued, 'were the secretaries and the research group. Perhaps you were part of the research group?'

Heise hesitated. 'No . . . I did not have my desk exactly there.'

'Perhaps she will remember you later,' said Rosenharte helpfully. 'I should explain that we are seeing each other for the first time in fifteen years. Maybe one ghost from the past is enough this evening, eh?'

The man straightened. 'You will excuse me for interrupting. *Bon appétit.*' He nodded to both of them before retreating to his own table, where he joined a younger man with a pallid face and glasses.

'Thanks,' Jessie said. 'I know what this means to you now.'

'Do you?' asked Rosenharte under his breath. 'Do you really know what has just taken place? I mean, really?'

'Yes. You supported my identity as Annalise, so you are now committed.'

'You understand it intellectually.' He put his hand up to her face again, hiding his own expression from the men at the other end of the pontoon. 'I will listen to what your side have to say, but they must give me an assurance that they will do nothing to endanger my brother or his family. That's the condition of my cooperation. He has two children. If anything goes wrong, the children will be taken from him and their mother for good.' He brought his hand down and studied her. 'There can be no mistakes. Until we get out of this restaurant you must do what I say. Remember, I know the way

Annalise would have behaved in this situation. You must be guided by me.'

She nodded. 'I hear what you're saying, but you really must stop showing it in your expression.'

They continued with their meal, drinking more than was good for them and occasionally managing uproarious laughter. Just after eleven the wind changed. Instead of a sea breeze, much cooler air came straight from the mountains. Rosenharte moved his chair closer to hers, brushed the hair from her ear, whispered urgently and looked into her eyes. Then he pushed the chair back and took up his glass of wine, still smiling.

She spoke into her lapel. 'Hope you heard all that. We're going to have a row and I'm leaving.'

Half a minute later she straightened in her chair and brought down her glass. 'You haven't changed, Rudi. You used me and left me all those years ago, without a thought for my feelings. And now you want me to do your dirty work for you again. I won't be used like this. I won't be!' She had begun quietly but now her voice was rising.

'Hey, hey. Do you want the whole restaurant to hear?' He gave an embarrassed smile. 'Look, I'm sorry. You knew the circumstances were difficult. It wasn't possible for me to act in any other way. Please, Anna, be reasonable.'

'Not until you admit that you ran away instead of behaving like a man.' By now she had the complete attention of the other diners. Fighting back tears of anger, she leaned forward and slapped him. Rosenharte's glass fell from his hand and drenched his lap. She stood up, turned on her heels and marched indignantly towards the gangway.

Rosenharte picked up his glass and filled it with the remains of the wine.

A few minutes later, Heise slid into the chair opposite him. 'You screwed that one up, Rosenharte. The General will not be happy.'

Rosenharte set down his glass. 'What could I do after you scared her with all that crap about the Commission? She knew you were checking her out and she accused me of being involved in an operation to trap her.'

'Where's your microphone? Why isn't it working?'

'It may have escaped your notice but I was thrown in the water. You should have realised it would be ruined and I would be out of contact.'

'Never mind that now. Colonel Biermeier says you must go after her.'

'How? I don't even know where she's staying.'

'You didn't think to ask her the name of her hotel?'

'She was hardly going to tell me after you'd announced your presence,

Heise. She accused me of bringing you here. She says I've betrayed her. You screwed up, Heise, not me.' A few drops of rain began to splatter around them. 'Look, I don't understand any of this. I don't understand why you're interested in this woman. She's a drunk. She's crazy. You saw.'

Heise got up. 'These are judgments you're not competent to make, Rosenharte. Go. You'll find Knef, the man dining with me, at the entrance of the restaurant. He'll lead you to her.'

'Wouldn't it be better to do this in the morning? She's upset now.'

'Go.'

'Do I have your assurance that you will keep your men back?'

Heise said nothing.

'You do it my way or it won't work. Call General Schwarzmeer and tell him this is what I said. Call Biermeier. He'll say that I'm right.'

The man seemed to accept this. 'You have until tomorrow afternoon.'

JESSIE WAS SITTING in the hotel bar near the entrance, a picture of alcoholic deflation. The barman looked up at Rosenharte as he wearily filled the glass in front of her.

'I'm sorry about the restaurant,' she said, when Rosenharte slid onto the stool next to her. 'It was stupid of me. I just wanted to . . .' Her head lolled forward while she made a hash of stubbing out a cigarette.

'We'll talk about it in the morning. Now what you need is sleep.' He paid off the barman and guided her to the lift, where she made a very credible display of needing his support.

In the lift, she moved away from him, straightened and smiled.

'What's your real name?' he asked.

She shook her head. 'Sorry, can't say. We're in suites four-one-five to four-one-seven. They're waiting for us there. You'll find three rooms and two bedrooms if you need to rest at some stage. I'll be on hand should we need to convince anyone else that we're lovers.' They got out of the lift and walked quickly to suite 415. 'The floor is secured,' she told him. 'There are no other guests here. Everything's been done with the maximum of discretion.'

'They'll already be watching the building,' he said.

'Let them. The place is totally secure. The Italians are cooperating.'

'They know about me?'

'How else do you imagine you weren't held for questioning over that man's death?' She touched him on the arm. 'Everything's going to be fine. Really.'

She unlocked the door. 'Dr Rosenharte,' she announced, and without waiting, walked through the suite and left by another door. There were just two men. A tall, well-built Englishman with a shy smile stepped forward and offered his hand. 'I'm Robert Harland. This gentleman is from the CIA.'

Declining Harland's hand, Rosenharte took time to appraise the American: a large, shrewd-looking individual with possible German ancestry. 'And your name?' asked Rosenharte.

'Maybe later,' said the American.

'Can I give you a drink?' asked Harland.

'Scotch,' Rosenharte replied, looking round the luxurious suite.

'You handled that very well out there,' ventured the CIA man.

Rosenharte took the drink and regarded him. 'Whereas you don't impress me. You start out on an operation with only a vague idea of how it will be executed. And with this craziness you risk my family's security.'

'Why don't you hear what we have to propose?' suggested Harland, gesturing to a chair.

Rosenharte shrugged. 'Who was the man who died?' he asked quietly.

Harland sat down. 'His name was Grycko. A Polish national. Does the name mean anything to you?'

'No.'

'Not ours, and not yours. Did he say anything to you?'

'A name. He mumbled a name, but I forget what it was. The man was dying. He made no sense.'

There was silence in the room. 'Look, we understand the risks, and if you're not willing to help us, well, you still have time to get out. It's a simple matter to arrange for Annalise to behave so unreliably that even the Stasi won't think of touching her. You can go back and tell them that the stuff in the letters hinting at NATO secrets was just a come-on to entice you to Trieste.'

'Letters? I saw only one. There was no hint of secrets in that.'

'There were three—one in July, the other two in August.'

August was when the Stasi picked up Konrad. 'You knew they would be intercepted by the Stasi before they reached me. You were relying on that.'

Harland looked up at him. 'I'm afraid that's exactly right. But—'

'Do you have any idea of the damage you've done? My brother is in prison. What seems an ingenious game to you spies in the West is life and death to us in the East,' said Rosenharte. 'Because of those letters a mother and father are being interrogated and their children have been put into care.'

The American loosened his tie. 'I think Mr Harland appreciates that. But we're in this situation now. We have to keep our heads, move on with caution.'

'Caution!' Rosenharte spat the word out. They had shown no caution whatsoever. He sank to a chair. 'I'm an art historian these days. I don't have access to the sorts of things that you want. Why pick me?'

'We have a particular and limited task in mind,' said Harland. 'And you are the only person who can do it for us.'

'What is it that you want?'

Harland said, 'We believe that you may be able to help us gain some information on the whereabouts and intentions of a man named Abu Jamal, a Syrian terrorist who is financed and given safe haven by the Stasi in East Germany. We know he's been receiving medical treatment for a kidney complaint, maybe even a transplant. He pays regular visits to the Leipzig area.'

'You brought me here for this! I have no knowledge of these things. I haven't had any contact with the Stasi for a decade and a half, apart from the usual requests to act as an informer on my colleagues.'

'Yes,' said Harland patiently. 'We know who you are, Dr Rosenharte.'

'There's another man we're interested in,' said the American. 'He moves between Dresden and Leipzig, like you, and he is a professor of international relations. His name is Michael Lomieko, known to his friends as "Misha". Misha and Abu Jamal are close associates and have developed a policy of revolutionary intervention, which, put simply, is to attack Western targets and cause chaos and terror. It's the apparent scale of the plans that's worrying us. Both men have the tacit support of the Party high command— Schwarzmeer and the head of the Stasi, Erich Mielke.' He paused. 'We're eager to catch Jamal and, if possible, Misha, but we would also like to prove the state sponsorship of terrorism. Have you heard of Professor Lomieko?'

'Yes,' said Rosenharte. 'I know him. But only because we sometimes travel on the same train between Dresden and Leipzig. I have exchanged perhaps two dozen words with him in my life.'

'That's a good thing,' said Harland, moving the bottle towards him. 'Have another drink. We've got a long night ahead of us.'

Rosenharte studied him. 'Tell me, Mr Harland, how old are you?'

'Forty this year.'

'Yes, I thought so. You see, my brother and I were born in 1939, just after the outbreak of war. We will both be fifty in December. At that age you lose the taste for intrigue and adventure.'

The American shook his head. 'This isn't a game, Dr Rosenharte. We're trying to prevent people being killed. Your government has a record of supporting Libyan and Palestinian terrorists. Abu Jamal is just the latest manifestation of this. Misha is the interface of that relationship, passing information, help, inspiration, money, from the Stasi to Abu Jamal. Even by the peculiar standards of East Germany this is criminal behaviour.'

'If I help you, I want an agreement that you will bring me, my brother and his family out to the West, find us homes, jobs and medical treatment for Konrad. These are my conditions.'

'To get your brother out of prison is a tall order,' said Harland. 'We're not going to promise something that we can't deliver. But if our plan works, you stand every chance of getting your brother released because we're going to give you something they really want. It's the best way out for you all.'

They were right, Rosenharte conceded, there was only one way to go. 'But do I have your agreement on the other things?'

'Yes, you do. We will meet all your demands.'

'Then I'll help you. But there is one further condition. When I go back I must take something to convince them that Annalise is an important source.'

Harland nodded. 'Of course, and we already have something in mind.'

'And whatever happens, you'll bring my brother's family out as soon as possible, regardless of whether my brother is still in Hohenschönhausen.'

'That shouldn't be a problem,' said Harland. 'The Hungarians took down their border with Austria in May. Thousands are leaving the GDR and going through Czechoslovakia to Hungary every day. We've already got people out that way. How old are the children?'

'Eight and six years old.'

'Then no problem at all.'

'So what am I taking back?'

'The only things they care about,' said the American, 'are computers, software, programs. Defence programs from NATO would push all their buttons at once. We have something very special. We'll give you a disk we have had prepared with the help of Langley and NATO.'

'Who's running this operation?' asked Rosenharte. 'The CIA or British Intelligence? Who am I doing a deal with?'

'Me,' said Harland. 'The CIA is helping and will benefit from the information that you provide.'

'How many people know about it?'

'As few as possible.'

He nodded. 'It's well known that the Stasi have penetrated your services. I insist that if I agree to this plan you never refer to me by name.'

'Naturally, we'll give you a code name—what about Prince?'

'Whatever you like. Now I want you to order up from room service. A bottle of champagne, two glasses and caviar.'

'You don't have to do this now. The hotel is secure. The management is well aware of the need for discretion.'

'But not every member of the staff is. The Stasi will come in a few weeks and ask questions. They'll find one person who remembers something.'

Having taken some money from Harland, Rosenharte moved to the bedroom next door and, with the woman, began creating a scene of abandoned love. They undressed—she to a slip and he to underpants—then lay on the bed until the doorbell rang. Anna chucked him the white bathrobe provided by the hotel. An elderly waiter brought in a tray and smiled benignly at the scene of middle-aged passion. Rosenharte gave him a tip as he left.

'You know,' she said, her eyes dancing, 'if I wasn't a happily married woman, I'd be very content to be in a hotel room with you, Rudi.'

He smiled. She may not have been the beauty that Annalise was, but she was attractive and intelligent, and she was beginning to grow on him.

He dressed and returned to the sitting room, where Harland continued his briefing. 'This is what we know about Misha,' he said. 'He has a room at Leipzig University and he meets Abu Jamal in a safe house in Leipzig. He has also visited him in hospital over the summer. We know that he spends about twelve days a month in Leipzig. The rest of the time he's on the campus at the Technical University at Dresden, researching explosives and so forth.'

'That's more information than I could ever have acquired,' said Rosenharte. 'Why do you need me?'

'We want you to make contact with someone who has proof of the involvement of Abu Jamal and Misha in at least one bombing. More important, this contact may have information about plans for future attacks.'

'How will I find this person?'

Silence. 'You are not going to find them,' Harland replied. 'All we have is a code name: Kafka. He or she will find you.'

'If that means you have to give this individual my name, I can't allow it. What will happen if this person is questioned by the Stasi?' He paused. 'I think it would be better if you told me everything, don't you?'

Harland inhaled deeply. 'We wouldn't dream of giving your name to anyone. Besides, how could we give your name to someone whose identity we don't know?' He stopped and leaned back in his chair. 'A month ago, a British woman was visiting Leipzig as part of a Christian Fellowship group. This person works for us, mostly as a courier. Before leaving Leipzig she carried out the usual checks on her luggage to ensure nothing had been planted on her. She found nothing until she reached a hotel in the West, when she found some very interesting documents and a letter to us in her bag.'

'And you believed this?' asked Rosenharte incredulously.

'At first we were inclined to think that this was one of the Stasi's little pranks, but then the names in the documents proved very useful. The US government was able to make an arrest of one man and to begin tracking another. Both are connected with Abu Jamal. It turned out to be very valuable intelligence indeed—but we had no idea who gave it to us.'

'So why didn't you send your courier back to Leipzig?'

'We did. She came back with a message delivered the same way. Kafka wanted a German, someone with good cover who could travel to Leipzig as often as they liked without raising suspicion. Then a member of our outfit remembered you from your time in Brussels. We did some research and found that everything fitted perfectly.'

Rosenharte did not hide his scepticism. 'You recalled that you had something on me and thought you could force me to do this?'

'No,' said Harland. 'We are not going to force you. But if you want to be involved we will do as you ask as regards your brother and his family.'

'I need to think about this,' Rosenharte said. 'I'll take some rest now.'

'Go ahead,' said Harland. 'We'll make ourselves scarce until about seven—does that suit you?'

ROSENHARTE SLEPT LITTLE. By dawn he understood that cooperation was the only way, because at least it offered some hope of freeing Konrad and slightly better odds of bringing Else and the two children to the West. He had to do it, even though the operation seemed vague.

At six thirty he gave Harland his decision. By seven he and Anna had played their role for the benefit of the young man who brought them breakfast, which they consumed like a married couple, saying little.

He returned to the room to find Harland and the American having coffee and pastries. Immediately he launched into the thing he had been turning in his mind. 'When the real Annalise died you decided to keep her alive. I imagine it was an extensive operation. Why? What purpose did it serve?'

Harland picked the crumbs from his chinos. 'She transferred to NATO in the early part of 1975, to the department of Defence Policy and Planning, where she was mostly involved as a translator.'

'And you fed intelligence to the Stasi through a new controller?'

'Yes, as a matter of fact a man named Kurt Segler, a gardener at NATO headquarters. It proved a very reliable arrangement.'

'But the Stasi are not fools. They'd have suspected something when the substitute Annalise gave them false information.'

'That was the whole point.' He stopped and gave Rosenharte an oddly apologetic look. 'It wasn't false information. We used her as a truth channel. She was the most accurate source they had ever had. You see, we needed a way of telling the Russians what our actual intentions were. We knew that if they trusted Annalise as a spy, we could feed them stuff that was unambiguous about the Western position, and they always believed it.'

Rosenharte got up and poured himself some coffee from the flask. 'The Stasi does not simply accept what it's given,' he said. 'They give their agents tasks to gain specific intelligence for them. They wanted me to test Annalise in that way during the autumn of 1974, just before she died.'

Harland nodded. 'Similar demands were made on Annalise's substitute and in the spring of '75 we orchestrated appropriate responses which seemed to satisfy the Stasi. It was a collaborative effort, involving several nations, and it only worked because they believed she was their spy.'

Rosenharte leaned forward and asked, 'How did you explain Annalise's disappearance? One moment she was working for the Commission, the next she was in NATO handing over secrets to a gardener.'

'After the suicide, we had to work very hard,' said Harland. 'When Annalise Schering went off the radar screen we put it about that she had suffered a breakdown. A few months went by and she resigned from the Commission to take the job at NATO. She was, as you know, a fairly solitary person and had few friends. Her mother was dead by then and she had no other family. The Belgian authorities were helpful because at that time Brussels was full of Stasi Romeos trying to bed every secretary in town. What worked for us was that the only East German agent who knew her was you. When she went to NATO, it was explained that her collapse had been brought about by an unsuitable affair. You were that unsuitable affair.

She told her new controller that she had lost her heart to you, but that you drank too much and were therefore a security risk. They were impressed by the self-sacrifice entailed in dropping you.' He looked at Rosenharte. 'It was all very neat . . . though I do appreciate it was painful for you.'

'Indeed,' said Rosenharte, not letting them see his anger. Just after he had left Annalise's apartment on that dreary evening, he was picked up by the Belgian police. Two days of interrogation followed, at the end of which they told him he was to be charged for the murder of Annalise Schering. They said he had faked her suicide by forcing her to take an overdose of sleeping pills and then cutting her wrists as she lay asleep. It would be difficult to contest in court, particularly as it would be shown that Rosenharte was a Stasi agent who'd been trying to make Annalise Schering work for East Germany. He faced twenty years in jail.

Then two British spies and a Belgian intelligence officer came to the police station cell and put a proposition to him. He would be released without charge, as long as he remained in Brussels and filed regular reports of his contact with Annalise. Thereafter they would provide the pretext for his return to East Germany. If for one moment they suspected that he had told the truth to the Stasi they would release tapes proving his cooperation with the West. He had no choice. For the first three months of 1975 he maintained the fiction of his affair with Annalise in his messages to the East.

He looked at Harland through the smoke of his cigarette. 'I have always wondered what your side said about me to the Stasi through the substitute Annalise. They would have nothing to do with me when I got back.'

Harland coughed awkwardly. 'I understand there may have been some allegations of a sexual nature. And, of course, there was your drinking.'

Rosenharte had always suspected this but again decided to keep his anger to himself. 'When did the arrangement with the replacement finish?'

'When the woman became pregnant by her real husband. We couldn't have her meeting her controller with a bump. Security measures were increased in NATO headquarters, with several people being investigated. When the gardener was arrested, Annalise sent word to the Stasi that she risked being exposed and could not continue. Later it was put about that she had left to marry a Canadian businessman. End of story.'

'When was this?'

'Late spring, 1985.'

'And in that time, do you think that they did not take photographs of her?

What if they took pictures last night? All they have to do is compare the two.'

'We hope they did.' Harland looked at Griswald and grinned. 'She worked for us in NATO. She was the second Annalise. She came out of retirement for this job. As far as they're concerned, it is Annalise. That's why I believe you'll be safe for as long as it's necessary. Then we'll get you out.'

Rosenharte got up, walked to the window and looked down into the street, which was now beginning to fill with people. It was Sunday, September 10, and church bells were tolling across the city.

'What do you want me to do? How do I communicate with you?'

'Are you a religious man, Dr Rosenharte?' asked Harland.

'No.'

'Well, we need you to be converted to the cause of Christian brotherhood and peace. It is in this context that Annalise has offered to help East Germany. As she explained in the letters she sent you in the summer, she wants to help rectify the technological imbalance between West and East. That much the Stasi know, though of course you don't because they intercepted the letters. It's the old argument about preserving peace by equalising military power. You must put some time into thinking about this before you go back. But first we need to discuss how you're going to meet Kafka.'

HARLAND AND GRISWALD said goodbye to Rosenharte at the hotel, having drilled him in the procedures to be followed for contacting the West and making himself known to Kafka in Leipzig. They waited for an hour before leaving by the service entrance and making their way to the conference centre where Rosenharte was due to talk. After the first lecture had started they slipped in and joined Prelli of Italian intelligence in the projection box at the back of the lecture hall. Prelli pointed out the two Stasi agents in the audience. Harland watched as Jessie entered and took a seat near the front. Rosenharte turned in his seat and nodded discreetly to her.

At three, Rosenharte rose and walked to the podium. An effusive Italian academic introduced him as the premier authority on early seventeenth-century drawings in East Germany. The lights dimmed and Rosenharte began speaking without notes and in English; he pressed a button on the slide projector and on the screen there appeared a drawing of a crippled boy.

'Ten years after this was made by the young Annibale Carracci, some words were written by William Shakespeare: "Cheated of feature by dissembling nature, deformed, unfinished, sent before my time into this breathing world, scarce half made up."' He paused. 'Beautiful words. And a beautiful drawing to describe deformity? But this sketch is also revolution- ary in its compassion. The artist has written beside the boy's head, "*No so se Dio m'aiuta*"—I don't know if God will help me. The artist provides a chal- lenge to God and to the religious authorities. Why are people born like this? These are the questions of a revolutionary conscience, and I maintain, a socialist conscience. Carracci calls God and the Church to account.'

Over the next forty minutes he developed the theme of artistic con- science. When he reached the end he said, 'No, God does not help this man. But we must. That was Carracci's message.' With a tip of the head he thanked them for their attention. The hall burst into spontaneous applause.

'It's the same lecture he gave in Leipzig in the early summer,' Harland said. 'It's why he was chosen by Kafka.'

'He was chosen by Kafka!' said Griswald.

Harland nodded. 'You see the lecture can be read two ways. If you are an unimaginative commie it appears to comply to the usual Marxist theories about the suppression of the masses and the rise of capitalism et cetera, et cetera. But it can also be seen as an argument against persecution by the state and the stifling of free expression.'

'A bird who can sing several tunes at once,' said Griswald. 'Hey, look, Jessie's on the move.'

She had left her chair and was on the edge of a group of admiring acade- mics gathered round Rosenharte. He went to greet her. They kissed and she gave him a congratulatory hug. Then she tapped her wristwatch to say that she had to leave. As she went she blew him a kiss. Harland spotted the small envelope that she had slipped into his hand.

'The ball's in play and our man's on his way,' said Harland, noting the two Stasi agents hurrying down the central aisle to be near Rosenharte.

As THE FIRST LIGHT was beginning to show in the east, the old Antonov 26 circled three times, then landed on a runway at a military base somewhere in the south of the GDR. Two Ladas and a military truck were waiting, but only Biermeier and three Stasi officers got off the plane with Rosenharte. Then the Antonov prepared to take off again, he assumed for Berlin, where Annalise's material would be examined.

Now back on German soil, the Stasi had become a degree more officious than they had been in Trieste. They drove off through what he knew must be a restricted zone. About forty-five minutes on, they reached a gateway and two men appeared from a hut behind some bushes. After checking their credentials, they opened the gates. A long drive led to a clearing in beech woods where there were four well-tended, single-storey summerhouses, all with verandahs. He was led to the furthest house and down some steps to a basement, where he was shown to a large room with a bed, table, chairs and a glass bowl in which there rested a solitary apple. 'You will remain here until they call for you,' said Biermeier.

For the next three days Rosenharte saw no one apart from the men who brought his meals and escorted him for a daily turn in the grounds. It took all his self-discipline to avoid worrying, telling himself that he was being held while Annalise's material was assessed. But he also understood they would be checking on every detail concerning Annalise's position at NATO, her life in Canada and her present circumstances in Brussels. A single error, the slightest hint of incongruity and he would be done for.

After breakfast on the third day—Thursday, September 14, he noted—a man came and silently indicated that Rosenharte should follow him.

It was no more than a hundred yards to the next house, and the moment after Rosenharte reached the top of his basement steps, he saw a figure on the verandah, lounging in wading boots that had been rolled down to his shins. General Schwarzmeer, the head of the HVA.

'How do you like our little retreat, Dr Rosenharte?' he called out.

'Why are you holding me, General?' he asked, on reaching the verandah.

'You know the drill, we have to make certain checks. I could not allow you to wander around Dresden with all that knowledge.'

'I don't have any knowledge. I took delivery of a package, that's all. I don't know what it contains.' He noticed two bodyguards lurking in the house. Biermeier was nowhere to be seen.

'But you know who gave it to you and what she does. That is knowledge of a very interesting kind to the spies that seek to destroy our country.' He pushed himself out of the wicker chair and gazed down a path cut through the beeches to a lake. 'Perfect conditions for angling,' he said. 'It's good for the soul to spend time out here, with nothing but the fish to try your patience.'

Schwarzmeer had changed little since the seventies, when Rosenharte had twice encountered the then Stasi lieutenant-colonel before leaving for Brussels. He had the same equable presence: the lips slightly parted ready to laugh; and the ingratiating manner which was all the more nauseating for his insistence that he was the sort of man who could only speak his mind.

'Come, Comrade Doktor. I have some people who wish to meet you.'

Rosenharte climbed the four wooden steps to the decking and entered a gloomy interior. Three men in suits and a starchy blonde woman in her early forties were seated at a table. Schwarzmeer gestured to another wicker chair in front of the table, taking one to the side himself. 'So, Rosenharte, you will tell my colleagues what you found in Trieste?'

'How do you mean?'

'What you saw. What you found. Don't be a fool now.'

'I found Annalise Schering and we dined together. She told me that she was willing to hand over certain information about some new computer systems used in NATO. Communication systems, I think.'

'You say you found her.' It was the woman. 'That's not true, is it? Unless you have failed to tell us something, you had no instructions to go to that restaurant by the canal. Only to go out on the pier?'

'Yes, you're right.'

'Then she found you?' said the man next to her, a clerkish individual with receding hair brushed forward. 'Are you suggesting that in all Trieste she happened upon the right restaurant?'

'No. I made a point of asking the hotel staff if they could recommend one. Annalise knew where I was staying and I realised that she would check with them to find out where I was that evening. I told them to tell anyone who asked for me.' It was a poor lie because the Stasi could easily check his story.

'Why didn't you simply stay in the hotel?'

'To tell you the truth I was rather shocked by that man dying. I decided to have a drink or two and get some air.'

'Yes, we wondered about that. We didn't find out who he was because the authorities in Trieste did not release any information about him. A man dies in the port and not one Italian policeman can say who he is. There is no record of his death. Nothing. Does that not strike you as strange? Perhaps he didn't really die. Perhaps he passed you information about the meeting place and was miraculously revived in the ambulance.'

Rosenharte shrugged. 'He was having some kind of convulsion when he approached me on the quay. I assumed he was one of your people.'

'But we have it that he mentioned a name to you.'

'That's true, but I can't remember exactly—Kusimack; Kusi-something.'

'And he said this word before he entered the water?'

'Yes.'

'Perhaps you would then explain why the microphone picked up nothing. This suggests, in fact, that you hadn't switched it on.'

'That's not true. In fact I switched it on as I went up the pier, even though Colonel Biermeier told me to do so only when I saw Annalise.'

'It's interesting, is it not, that you were required to meet Miss Schering on the pier but that at no time was she actually there? None of our officers saw her enter or leave the dockyard that day. How do you explain that?'

Rosenharte inwardly cursed himself for not thinking of an answer to this obvious question. 'She told me she was aware of the surveillance from the start; it nearly scared her off completely.'

'That isn't very convincing,' said a man who hadn't spoken before.

'Look, I can't comment on these things,' said Rosenharte. 'You compelled me to make the journey against my will, saying that it would be bad for my brother if I refused. I did what you told me. I saw this woman again. I had relations with her. Yet now you hold me here against my will and accuse me of treasonable activities. This was not my plan. It was yours.'

The expressions in front of him remained unmoved.

'Tell us about Schering,' said Schwarzmeer. 'It's some time since we were in contact with her.'

'She told me that she had worked for you at NATO until '85. You must know much more about her than I do. I only saw her for twelve hours. And she was pretty drunk for much of that time.'

Schwarzmeer did not respond. There was a silence in the room.

'She also told me about the gardener who was arrested and the security checks at NATO that made her work for you difficult.'

'This is something that puzzles us,' said the man who had made most of the running so far. 'If she was worried about being discovered, why return to NATO headquarters? And if she had left in a hurry, why did NATO not suspect that she was the source, and at the very least refuse to employ her in such a sensitive position? You must see it doesn't make any sense.'

'These things are not my area. I was suspicious about her letter—I said so at the time. Now you expect me to vouch for Annalise's good motives towards the state. That's not my responsibility, surely? And it isn't just that you make me answer for her; now my loyalty is called into question.'

'Don't get heated,' said Schwarzmeer. 'Did she say anything about the reason for contacting us, apart from seeing you again?'

'She is passionate about the cause for peace, and she wants to make contact with the peace groups in Leipzig and Berlin—confidentially, of course—in exchange for handing over the material.'

'That will be easily arranged,' said Schwarzmeer.

'She says that she wants to do it through me. She trusts me.' He wanted to provide himself with more cover for his trips to Leipzig but he regretted saying this as soon as it was out. Schwarzmeer's eyes darted round the table.

'And yet in 1974,' he said, 'she refused to deal with you any longer because you were a security risk. What has occurred to change her mind?'

'I don't know,' said Rosenharte.

'Another thing that doesn't make sense,' said the lead inquisitor. 'There are too many inconsistencies in this story of yours for us to believe you.'

'It's not my story!' he was almost shouting. 'That's the point. I refuse to be put in a position where I'm defending Annalise Schering's story to you. If you don't trust her motives, don't deal with her. It's as simple as that. Believe me, if you weren't holding my brother I'd have had nothing to do with this operation.' He got up and walked around. He could tell that they were surprised, but what did it matter if they saw he was agitated?

'Sit down and stop being so hysterical,' said Schwarzmeer quietly.

Rosenharte returned to the chair. 'I have never shown anything but loyalty to the state. All I want is to be treated with respect.'

Schwarzmeer got up and, after giving Rosenharte a weary look, he pulled the wader straps up to his belt, fastened them and left, followed by one of the men and the woman.

'I am Laurentz,' said the older of the two men that had remained. He was in his forties and had the air of a practical man—an engineer or an administrator. 'This is Richter.' Richter was pallid and had wispy blond hair.

'At last, some names,' said Rosenharte. 'Are they real?'

'We are archival specialists, and we have real names,' said Laurentz.

'We specialise in people's lives,' said Richter. 'We construct a biography of a life, any life, in order to identify certain psychological traits, certain patterns. That allows us to suggest ways of addressing a problem with, say, an interview subject or someone who is harbouring a secret.'

So their speciality was suggesting ways of breaking people. 'Are you threatening me?' asked Rosenharte.

'No, we simply want to confirm a few things about your background,' said Laurentz.

'Right, the old stuff about my parentage.' His eyes drifted to the window and then to a room next door. He noticed through the open door a man sitting in a chair with his legs crossed and his hands folded in his lap. Rosenharte turned with an enquiring look to Laurentz and Richter but they ignored him.

'You and your brother Konrad were born on December 15, 1939,' Richter intoned, 'to Manfred and Isobel von Huth, both members of the National Socialist Party. Your father joined the Second SS Panzerdivision, in 1939. He saw action in Russia in 1942 and 1943 when he was linked with the massacre of thousands of civilians in the Ukraine. He rose to become Brigadeführer und General of the Thirty-second SS Panzergrenadierdivision in 1944. Your mother, Isobel, was an aristocrat, a von Clausnitz. She died in the bombing of Dresden on February 13, 1945 at which point it seems Marie Theresa Rosenharte, a housekeeper in the family home, took charge of you and your brother. In March 1945 your father died in mysterious circumstances and it is assumed that he was either executed by orders of the high command, or murdered by his own troops. Some time that spring Frau Rosenharte and her husband adopted you. There were no other children.'

'Is this necessary?' asked Rosenharte. 'Am I still to be held responsible for the actions of my parents?'

'Naturally, this is a sensitive matter for you,' said Richter. 'Fascist tendencies of that order are still an embarrassment.'

'I don't think of my natural parents from one year to the next. I cannot even remember them.'

This was not quite true. He held one image of his mother—a neat, slender woman, sitting in the window bay of a great house. She was looking down at a book. When they entered the room with their nurse she turned and smiled with a look of remote interest. He and Konnie would have been four or five years old. From then on the only woman whom he had called mother—and loved as a mother—was Marie Theresa Rosenharte.

'Perhaps you have subconsciously eliminated these memories,' said Laurentz. 'It would be perfectly understandable.'

Rosenharte shook his head.

'You both did well at your studies,' continued Richter, 'and attended Humboldt University in Berlin. Your brother studied political theory. You went on to gain a doctorate in history and taught at Humboldt. You were aged twenty-eight when you were recruited by the Ministerium für Staatssicherheit.' He stopped and consulted a thin blue folder. 'Your record as an officer with the MfS was well below expectations; you were on several occasions reported to be in breach of disciplinary and security rules. Finally, you were deployed in the West, first in Bonn then in Brussels. It was here that you met the woman known as Annalise Schering, but within a few months it was reported to us that you had mishandled the situation. When approached by another officer, the woman said that she could not trust you with the delicacy of the task ahead. Then, rather than returning to the GDR, you waited to be recalled and showed signs of reluctance to leave the West.'

'It was at this time,' said Laurentz, 'that your brother Konrad got into trouble with the authorities and was first arrested.'

'To ensure that I returned,' said Rosenharte.

They ignored him and peered into the file.

'You were married in 1980,' continued Richter, 'to Helga Goelkel. There were no children and you were divorced in 1982, just sixteen months later. Since then there have been a number of unsuccessful relationships which have all foundered because of your philandering.'

'For a man of your gifts,' said Laurentz, 'it is not an impressive career.'

Rosenharte smiled at them ironically. 'You missed all the good bits: my work at the Gemäldegalerie Alte Meister in Dresden, the papers on Dutch realism and the drawings of the collection. The essays and papers published in the West. They're modest achievements, I agree, but I am proud of them.'

'Let's face it,' said Laurentz, 'there is nothing in your work that distinguishes it as the product of a socialist living in a socialist state.

Then they asked him about women, naming one after the other with a prudish exactitude; the wives of friends, two students, a librarian, the girl who picked him up on the train from Berlin. They wanted him to know there was nothing they could not find in their files. They told him plainly that they were even acquainted with his sexual preferences. Rosenharte smiled at this. 'By "preferences" you mean that I prefer women to men.'

'You know what we mean,' snapped Richter. 'What you like to do in bed.'

'And what did these women report my preferences to be? Did you talk to my ex-wife, Helga? You would hardly get the most flattering portrait of me from her.' She had been a bleakly beautiful woman: tall, fine-boned with white skin and an air of tranquillity. But after a year or so there was never any real conversation and the sex had faded. What a fool he had been.

'It is understood that she left you because of your unreasonable demands and habitual intoxication.'

In a way they were right. After a period trying to find out what was wrong he gave up and spent his evenings with friends or reading and drinking in any bar that stayed open late enough.

The survey of his life moved to Marie Theresa Rosenharte's death of untreatable cancer three years before. It was said, by Richter's nameless sources, that Rosenharte had shown the poor woman not the slightest help or support. The lie was preposterous. He and Konnie had not left her bedside for three weeks and they had been devastated when she died.

He let them see that he was troubled and hurt by these accusations, but all the time he watched them with a grim detachment, recognising that what he was seeing now was an overture to the methodical dismantling of his personality that would take place if he made a mistake.

The leaden deprecation of everything about him and all he held dear dragged on until evening, when the interview suddenly ended as though the pair were meeting a prearranged timetable. When they had left Rosenharte turned to see if the silent observer was still there, but he had gone too.

FIVE MINUTES ELAPSED before two of the resident guards came and led him back to the basement. There was food—bread, sausage meat, cheese and another solitary apple—waiting for him, together with a packet of cigarettes. He ate the apple, then lay down on his bed without undressing.

As he expected, they came for him again. In the dead of night, two men rushed him, still drowsy, to what seemed like a fortified storehouse; inside there was a lot of equipment—hoses, protective suits, helmets and implements. He was roughly placed on a stool in front of three dazzling lights.

A voice came from behind them. For some reason, Rosenharte was certain that it belonged to the man who had sat in the adjacent room throughout the first interrogation.

'You met the woman known as Schering in August 1974,' said the voice.

'About then,' said Rosenharte, straightening his clothes. 'I had picked her up in a bar. You know all this: it was in my reports at the time.'

'How would you characterise her feelings towards you?'

'I believe that she became very attached to me.'

'She fell in love with you.'

'If you put it that way, yes.'

'When did you discuss working for the GDR?'

'I left it for about four weeks, then introduced the subject one evening.'

'She wasn't shocked?'

'No, but she said there was very little of interest for us in the Commission. She was hoping to land a job at NATO.'

'This was not mentioned in your reports.'

'I didn't want to say anything until she'd definitely got the job.'

'But when she did receive news of the job, she dumped you?'

'I don't know. Some time that winter she seemed to lose her enthusiasm for our relationship. Then she refused to see me. I tried to get in touch but she wouldn't answer her phone or the messages I left her. Now I understand that she had offered to work for you through another channel.'

'But this great love of yours had disappeared overnight? Evaporated?'

'Yes, I suppose so.'

'Then how do you account for the passionate sentiments that she expressed in her letter to you this summer?'

'She told me she had written more than one letter. If I had been able to see the others I might have understood her motives better. But now, having talked to her, I realise that the time we spent together all those years ago meant a lot to her . . . and, in retrospect, to me also.'

'Have you considered that she knew that her letters from abroad would be opened? In other words, she was making the offer to us, not you?'

'That has occurred to me, yes.'

'And have you considered the possibility that the gift she proposes to make the GDR could damage state security?'

'That possibility is implicit,' said Rosenharte. 'I myself pointed this out when you first proposed it to me.'

'So now we must decide on the nature of the person making this offer. And we conclude that this person is remarkably inconsistent. In some circumstances, she demonstrates prudence and foresight, for instance when she got rid of you in favour of a more reliable means of communicating with us. Indeed, all through the years of dealing with her she showed detachment and good judgment. But there's another Schering, who is given to emotional outbursts and to excessive drinking. When she left you in the restaurant in Trieste, that was most unlike the woman we knew.' The voice stopped. 'Although it was entirely like the woman that you wrote about in your first reports. It's almost as if we are dealing with two different people.'

They were so close. Rosenharte felt his pulse race. 'But your people saw her in Trieste,' he said at length. 'It is the same woman.'

'We know that. But how do you explain the difference in her behaviour?'

Rosenharte leapt in the only direction he could. 'Maybe,' he said, 'it has something to do with the way we respond to each other.'

There was a murmur behind the lights. 'It is odd that she refused to meet any of our people in Trieste—she specified as much in her letter to you— and yet for ten years she had no problem meeting different officers from the MfS. Why this sudden phobia for the very people that she wishes to help?'

'She did tell me that she had been scared by the lax security in your people at NATO. And when Heise approached us in the restaurant she expressed the same fears.' Rosenharte felt his stomach constrict; he had been forced into a space where it was impossible to manoeuvre.

'Which foreign intelligence agency are you working for, Rosenharte?'

'I am working for no one except the Gemäldegalerie in Dresden.'

At this, a large man appeared from behind the lights and walked to Rosenharte, took his face roughly in his hands and peered into his eyes.

'You are working for the Americans,' he said. 'I can see it in your face.'

'Maybe I am,' Rosenharte said and pulled back, out of the man's shadow. This brought silence to the room. Rosenharte held the man's eyes. 'But if I am, I don't know it. Only you can tell if I am being used.'

The man let go. 'What makes you think that you're being used?'

'I have repeatedly said that this could be a trap. It's for you to decide. I have told you everything I know.'

The man looked down at him, giving no hint of his feelings. It occurred to Rosenharte that he was at that moment fighting for his life. 'Look,' he said, 'you know what Annalise gave you before. Judge her on what your people are analysing in Berlin. But don't judge her on me. It's not logical.'

The voice came from behind the lights again. 'What do you know about her past work for us?'

'Nothing. But she did tell me to ask you a question.' He stopped, as though he was making sure he was getting something right. 'Why no thanks for her news on the Ides of March in 1985?'

'March 15th?' asked the voice. 'What happened on March 15th?'

Someone cleared their throat. Schwarzmeer. 'It refers to the death of Konstantin Chernenko and the succession of General Secretary Gorbachev.'

'Yes,' said Rosenharte. 'On the 15th, everything changed in the Geneva arms limitation talks and she gave you the updated briefing documents, the telegrams between Washington and Brussels, and the agenda of a meeting between defence ministers. You never thanked her and she hasn't forgotten it. That's why she wants to run this operation on her own terms. She will decide what to give you and when . . .'

'It's not for you to dictate terms to us,' said the voice behind the lights.

'I'm not. She is. I have no interest in this matter, other than seeing that you complete your side of the deal.' He paused. 'Now you must free Konrad as you promised you would.'

'You have not told us about the arrangements for taking delivery of the material,' said the voice.

'I will tell you when you have allowed Konrad to return to his family.'

The big man's expression didn't change as he stepped back and delivered a powerful blow to the side of Rosenharte's head, sending him sprawling from the stool onto the floor of the shelter. There was a scuffle as another man came forward to help beat him. Even in that moment he understood that each blow confirmed that the Stasi was, in its brutal way, showing interest in the material that Annalise Schering had to offer them.

HE SUPPOSED that he had been carried from the shelter unconscious, but that didn't explain the taste in his mouth, the heaviness in his limbs or the sense that a long time had elapsed. When he cracked open his eyes he saw that he was in a very light place. It was pleasantly warm. Then he became aware of someone beside him urging him to raise his head. 'Drink, Comrade.'

And he drank, cup after cup, before lying back and allowing his eyes to focus on a plaster roundel of a hunting scene set into the ceiling. It seemed familiar to him but he could not for the life of him think why.

'In this very room your father said farewell to your mother for the last time.' It was Schwarzmeer's voice, low and casual from behind his head. 'They drank champagne, brought up from the cellar on January 1st, 1945. One last toast to the Third Reich.' He spoke as if setting a scene for a drama.

Rosenharte blinked the sleep from his eyes and turned his head to see Schwarzmeer sitting on a lone chair, dressed in a dapper light grey suit.

'Why have you brought me here?' asked Rosenharte.

'As you know, we like to do research: prepare ourselves by entering the minds of our subjects, learn to predict their reactions.'

'This place has nothing to do with my life.'

'Oh, but it does, Herr Doktor. It was also in this room that you last saw your mother. It's all in your file. And do you know who furnished us with this information? It was Marie Theresa Rosenharte, the woman you called mother. She was the one who brought you here that day—but your real mother paid little attention to you. She was a cold and ruthless woman, little feeling for anyone or anything apart from your father and the Nazi party.'

'All the more reason for me to see them as irrelevant to my life.' He didn't show he was shocked that they had talked to Marie Theresa. She had been a chatty woman of limitless good nature, who almost certainly thought she was helping her sons in their careers by talking to the Stasi. After Konrad was arrested the first time, however, she had freely likened the Stasi to the Nazis.

Rosenharte had got to his feet and was looking through the window and across the lake to the grotto. He remembered the word 'grotto' from his childhood and the fun of playing at the foot of a fountain. The fountain was gone.

'So, it begins to return to you,' said Schwarzmeer. 'The last summer of the fascists.'

Rosenharte shook his head. 'I remember nothing of this place.'

'That's a shame because it represents your debt to the state—the state that overlooked the monstrous crimes of your family and gave you the advantages of a socialist upbringing, the best education in the world.'

Rosenharte looked at him, unable to express anything but disbelief. 'You criticise the Nazis. What about Bautzen, where you held and tortured my brother without even telling his family what he had been found guilty of?'

'He distributed fascist propaganda that endangered the peace.'

'How can making a private film and showing it to a few colleagues endanger the peace? How is that fascist propaganda? And for this, you sent him to a prison used by the Nazis.'

'Those observations alone are enough to earn you a sentence in the political section of Bautzen.'

'No,' shouted Rosenharte. 'You will not threaten me any longer. I have done nothing but comply with your wishes. All Konrad has ever been guilty of is bad judgment. He's a sick man, incapable of presenting the slightest threat to you. Let him return to his wife and children. Let him find the treatment he needs for his heart and his teeth.'

'Nothing stopped him when he was free before.'

'His teeth became rotten in Bautzen because of the beatings and the diet. When he got out, no dentist or doctor would see him, your people saw to that. Let him go home. He's suffered enough.'

'Who will look after him? His wife is helping with enquiries.'

The drab, brutal efficiency of it appalled him. 'OK,' he said at length, 'you win. If you return Else and the children to their home I will cooperate. Then we will talk about Konrad.'

'You do not make deals with us,' snapped Schwarzmeer.

'You promised to release Konrad if I went to Trieste. I did what you wanted. Now . . .' Rosenharte stopped to control the sense of helplessness that rose in him. 'You cannot do this thing without me. The security of the state is in your hands, not mine.'

'I warn you, this—'

'No, I warn *you*, General,' he said, raising his voice. 'If you don't free Else and the children, Annalise will never help you.'

He moved his aching limbs towards the door. 'I'd like to be taken back to Dresden now. I've lost several days already. I have work to do.'

Schwarzmeer blocked his way. 'Trick me, Rosenharte, and I will see your Nazi brains crushed from your head in a vice.'

Rosenharte smiled at the grotesque image and knew that Schwarzmeer regretted saying something so crude. 'I just want to live in peace and see my brother restored to health. That's all I want. And if I can help you in the process, then I will feel I've done my duty. May I now return to my home?'

Schwarzmeer said nothing, but stepped out of the way. Rosenharte walked to the open French windows and walked down a flight of stone steps into the garden. Three men were waiting for him at the bottom.

'We will be in touch,' said Schwarzmeer.

All Rosenharte heard was the birdsong coming from the great deserted garden that had been his childhood playground.

HE WAS RETURNED to Dresden in an unmarked delivery van late that Friday. Over the weekend he bought some food, slept a great deal and made one visit to a bar nearby, but had no contact with anyone. As the working week began, he set about a routine, taking the same route each day to the Zwinger, the baroque palace that housed the Gemäldegalerie's collection of old masters. He ate his lunch on the same bench and then returned to his apartment at about 8.30 p.m., after a drink or two in the same bar.

His purpose was to lull the Stasi surveillance teams as well as to get an idea of their strength. Very soon, he became used to the men and women around him touching their noses, sweeping off dark glasses and flourishing handkerchiefs. Had they forgotten that he'd received precisely the same training as they?

He moved through his life as though in a trance and completed his rounds in the Gemäldegalerie with unusually leaden diligence, attending the daily meeting with the director, Professor Lictenberg, and writing a report about bringing high art to the people with a socialist message.

On Wednesday, September 20, he decided to take his first risk. He made a detour on his round through the galleries and arrived outside Lictenberg's office where he found the professor's assistant, Sonja Weiss, alone. Sonja and he had once had a short, uncomplicated affair lasting six or seven months, which had ended without rancour when she found someone she preferred. Two years later, they were still firm allies and, because the Stasi hadn't named her during his interrogation a week before, he assumed she was not one of their informers.

Sonja gave him a mischievous smile and popped a kiss on his cheek. She experimented uninhibitedly with different hair colours. At the moment it was jet black with blonde streaks. Vulgar, perhaps, but nothing she did detracted from the natural prettiness which lay underneath.

They talked for a little while, then he cleared his throat. 'Sonja, can I ask you a favour?'

'And here I was getting all nostalgic. You want to use his phone? Right? Go ahead. Oh, I forgot to mention some weird guy came looking for you when you were away. He didn't leave a name, but said he'd be back.'

'One of our friends?'

She shook her head. 'No. I think he was a foreigner, maybe Czech or Polish. A country boy. You could see by his clothes.'

'I suppose we'll find out when he shows up again.' He paused. 'Now, you make yourself scarce for the next few minutes, OK?'

He went into the office and closed the door, praying that the place wasn't bugged. He dialled the number in East Berlin that he'd memorised in front of Harland and the American in Trieste and was put through to an answering machine. 'It's Prince,' he said. 'I need a delivery of material within the next week. Good material.' He hung up and slipped out of the office.

Sonja gave him a conspiratorial. 'Be careful, my handsome Doktor.'

'Thanks,' he said. 'I will.'

Two days later, on Friday evening, he remained in his apartment, cooked a meal and read the final draft of the lecture he was to give in Leipzig. As he worked he began to notice tiny discrepancies between the way he'd left the apartment that morning and its present state. Three books habitually placed beside the typewriter, on top of each other and always opened at pages 102, 203 and 304, had been moved. The shade of the table lamp was angled differently and some papers had been moved on the windowsill. He realised that the rooms must have been bugged and marvelled at the wasted effort. He had no phone, because he was on a list of thousands waiting to be connected, and it had been months since anyone else had been there with him.

Next day, he went out early to buy a packet of cigarettes and noticed that there were far fewer Stasi on his tail. He guessed that this was because there was so much talk of demonstrations. Sonja had mentioned it as she skittered past him in the Dutch collection on Friday afternoon. And now, as he walked through the park, about a dozen punks entered from his left. At the same moment, another group materialised from beneath the shade of some trees—skinheads with laced boots and denims held up with braces. Very soon a bottle arched through the air towards the punks and broke on the path in front of them. One of the punks picked up the broken neck and flung it back at them, and then more bottles and some stones started flying.

Rosenharte stopped and watched, bemused, then he noted that the Stasi team were consulting each other. One broke cover to use a radio, while the other two moved hesitantly towards the edge of the fray.

'You'd better stop those louts before someone gets hurt,' shouted a man in a checked shirt and a cream-coloured cap. 'Today's youth!' he said despairingly to Rosenharte. 'You'd think they'd got better things to do.'

Rosenharte nodded and then with astonishment saw the man wink at him. It was Macy Harp, a British intelligence officer he'd met briefly at the hotel in Trieste with Harland. With the cap and clothes, he looked fifteen years older. The accent was good too; exactly right for the region.

'Time to get going, Dr Rosenharte,' he murmured. 'Find your way to the Neustadt Bahnhof by five this afternoon. There's an old building opposite the station that was a restaurant before the war. You'll see the sign. To the right of the sign there's a door, which you can push open. I'll see you in there after five.' With this, he strolled away to talk to three or four onlookers who were shaking their heads.

Rosenharte moved quickly to the side of the park and, spotting a bus going to the centre of town, ran to catch it. As the doors closed he saw one of the Stasi men frantically looking around. He rode the bus for two stops, then boarded another bound for the suburb of Weisser Hirsch on the east of the city. At the last stop he got off and set out across the Dresdener Heide, the great heath to the north of Weisser Hirsch. He lay in the sun and ate the meagre lunch that he had kept in his pocket since leaving the apartment.

At four, he picked his way through the sleepy streets until he found the dilapidated restaurant near the station. He sidled up to the door, placed his back against it and lit a cigarette. Satisfied that no one was watching, he pushed the door with his backside and slipped through to find he was in a large space that was open to the sky.

'Thanks for being so prompt.'

Harp was now in blue overalls and was accompanied by a much taller man with a thin face, red complexion and a prominent broken nose.

'This is my associate, Cuth Avocet, known by all as the Bird.' Both men were grinning inanely.

'Where's Harland?' Rosenharte asked.

'In Berlin,' said Harp. 'It's not possible for him to get away at the moment, but we came as soon as we could after we got your message.'

They moved back to the dark area where there were three fishing stools, a bottle of wine and a candle. 'Rather festive, don't you think?' said Avocet. 'Would you like a drop of this lovely stuff before Macy polishes it off?'

Rosenharte accepted, thinking he had entered some bizarre British film. 'You understood my message?'

'Absolutely,' said Harp. 'We've fixed a rendezvous in West Berlin for a few days' time and Annalise will give you some material. Have you begun to make contact with Kafka yet?'

'How could I? I'm followed everywhere.'

'You think this new stuff will get them off your back? Current estimates put Stasi strength at about eighty thousand, which means they have the capacity to watch pretty much anyone that interests them. Maybe we have to face the possibility that you're never going to shake them off.'

'It will work,' said Rosenharte. 'They've got a lot to occupy them at the moment. People are very restive. They can see that nothing's working and the economy is in trouble. They're tired of queuing for everything.'

'I don't know how you've all stood it for nearly forty years,' said Avocet.

'Überwintern,' said Rosenharte. 'We are hibernating.' That was exactly it. Everyone was waiting for spring but had no idea whether they would live to enjoy it.

Harp smiled. 'But maybe the thaw will come one day soon.'

Rosenharte shook his head. 'Maybe,' he said. 'I've told the Stasi that I will continue to work with Annalise on condition that they release Else and the children. Once they're freed, I want to get them out.'

'And leave your brother at their mercy?'

'Konrad would want this. I know it. He won't be able to stand the idea that the boys have been taken away from Else and put in care.'

'It's not going to be easy to get him out,' said Harp. 'I don't want you to go away with any false hopes.'

'I understand. We'll concentrate on getting Else out first.'

Harp's tone changed. 'I'm afraid we won't be able to move them until there has been some progress on contact with Kafka.'

'You don't trust me?'

'No, it's just that if Else and the kids disappear to the West, they're hardly going to let you alone, are they?'

'How's Annalise going to contact me?'

'By mail. The letter was posted yesterday and the Stasi should intercept it tomorrow. Of course, you don't know anything about the trip to Berlin.'

Rosenharte couldn't subdue his impatience. 'They suspect that method of communication. They think it's been used to attract their attention.'

'Don't worry. What we're giving them is good enough for them to ignore any doubts they've got. Once we've got Else out, things may become more difficult for you and we have to come up with something to deal with that.'

The questioning by Schwarzmeer's people had exposed so many flaws and false assumptions in the British planning that Rosenharte had no confidence whatsoever. 'Do you have any ideas?'

'We'll have to wait and see how things turn out,' said Avocet.

'I'm afraid I agree. There's no point in planning anything now,' said Harp. 'So we'll see you in Berlin. All the instructions will be in the letters. You can make your way out the back.' He gestured behind him.

Rosenharte said goodbye and headed for the Augustus Bridge, wondering how long it would be before the Stasi picked up his trail.

THE AFTERNOON WAS still warm when he reached the Augustus Bridge, which crossed the sluggish waters of the Elbe. It was only when he had passed the figure standing midway across that he recognised Sonja. She was looking downstream.

He hesitated, then called out. She didn't turn so he crossed over to her side of the bridge. 'Sonja? Is there something the matter?'

She turned to him. 'They arrested my boyfriend. This morning.'

'Maybe they've only taken him for a short spell. They arrest people when they think there's going to be a demonstration. He'll be back next week.'

'How can I be sure?'

'Because it happened to me last week. I wasn't in Italy all that time: I was being questioned. Come on, tell me all about it over a drink. We'll buy some beers and go and see an old friend of mine. We can talk there.'

Half an hour later, having got hold of some beer, they walked along the riverbank until they came to an area of small allotments where those Dresdeners fortunate enough to acquire one, were allowed to grow their own produce and set up sheds. In the summer, many decamped to the gardens, sleeping in the huts and cooking their meals in the open.

Rosenharte noticed Idris's old bicycle roped to the fence and called out over a clump of bamboo. A rustle was followed by a black face appearing between the canes. 'Rudi, my friend, what pleasure is this! It has been many months since we have seen each other. Too long for good friends.'

The head disappeared, then popped out a few feet away above a little white gate. Before opening it he reached out, clasped Rosenharte's neck and kissed him three times. Rosenharte introduced Sonja.

He had first met Idris Muzaffar Muhammad when he intervened to stop a gang of racist youths wrenching his bicycle from under him. Idris had then invited him to his plot by the river. He told Rosenharte that he was the son of a wealthy Sudanese landowner who had come to the GDR in some kind of exchange programme and was then stranded after his family fell from grace in Khartoum. Idris was now in his early forties and lectured on irrigation and water conservation at the Technical University.

He led them into the little garden, which was spilling over with flowers and vegetables.

'We've brought beer for you,' said Rosenharte.

Idris flashed his white and gold teeth, showed them to a table made from salvaged planks and found stools for them. They opened the beer and looked at the river, and Idris told them that sometimes he fooled himself that he was sitting by the Nile, surrounded by the noises and smells of his childhood.

'Her boyfriend has been arrested,' said Rosenharte when there was a lull in the conversation. 'Can we have a few moments alone?'

'I shall cook a meal for us,' said Idris. He went off to the shed and soon a stream of smoke rose from a pipe that protruded from the roof.

'So, what happened?' asked Rosenharte.

'They took Sebastian this morning. I was there. They told him that he was under suspicion of "rowdyism and incitement hostile to the state".'

'What did he do?'

'He made some posters calling for freedom of expression and stuck them up at night. Someone ratted on him to the Stasi.'

An idea occurred to him. 'Did they have you in and ask you to work for them in exchange for letting Sebastian go?'

'Yes, they implied it would be better for him if I helped them.'

'Me too. You see, my brother's in prison. That's the way they do things.'

'Really, your brother?'

'Did you tell them about that phone call I made the other day?'

'No.'

'And what about . . .?'

She saw what he was thinking. 'No, I didn't tell them about us. Look, I wasn't going to admit to sleeping with an old guy like you.'

'Thanks,' he said, ambushed by Sonja's bluntness. 'Listen, if they take you in again, I don't want you to tell them about me at all. Do you understand? Say I'm a bore—whatever you need to.'

'Some other people came before that. I had to tell them about the guy who was looking for you. They wanted to know if I'd seen you with another man, plump guy in his fifties.'

'Who wore a straw hat?' said Rosenharte, thinking of the dead Pole.

'Yes, that's right. So who are these men?'

'I don't know. When did they ask you about the man?'

'Last week. When they searched your office.' She looked down. 'I'm sorry, I should have told you. They may have put a microphone in there too.'

'It's all right,' he said. 'But you're sure the professor's phone isn't tapped?'

'I can't be sure. But they ask me who he calls, so maybe not.'

'Or maybe they're testing you. Look, it's very important that you don't tell them about that call, Sonja. My freedom depends on it.'

She put up her hand as though taking an oath. 'I won't tell them.'

'Thank you.'

Idris emerged from the shed and hung four brass lanterns on the trees around them. 'Now we have a feast,' he said, and he started ferrying small dishes of food from the shed, giving their Arabic names and describing their ingredients: *adas*, a lentil stew with garlic which he had reheated; *fule*, dried broad beans, cooked and served cold; *tamia*, deep-fried chickpeas; and *tabika alyoum*, a mutton dish. After the meal, Sonja moved to a dilapidated chair in the shed and curled up. Idris threw a large piece of white cloth over her and returned to finish the beer with Rosenharte.

'Where do you get all this food from?' asked Rosenharte. 'I've never seen any of these things on sale in Konsum. How do you do it, Idris?'

'People brings it for me. A friend of mine he return from Yemen a few days ago. He bring me the meats. I am happy to share it with you, Rudi.'

Idris smiled. Not for the first time, Rosenharte wondered what went on behind his obliging eyes. Then something occurred to him. 'This man who brought you the food from Yemen, is he the man at the university? Misha?'

'Yes, of course,' answered Idris, as though it was the only answer that Rosenharte could have expected. 'He goes to many, many Arab countries. He visit Sudan and he come back and tell me it is safe for me there now.'

'I've travelled on the train to Leipzig with Misha. He seems a good man.' Rosenharte decided to take a risk. 'He knows an Arab gentleman called Abu Jamal. Have you heard of him? I think he stays in Leipzig sometimes.'

Idris turned to Rosenharte. 'Why do you ask these questions? You could die even for knowing his name in this country.'

'But how do you know him, Idris? You're a lecturer in irrigation. Why would you know these things? Has Misha asked for your help?'

'I can ask the same question to you, Rudi. How do you know this man? This is not your business.' He lowered his voice. 'This is business of terrorist and killers. Do not say his name again.'

Rosenharte poured the last of the beer. 'I need to find out where he is.'

'That is why you come here?'

Rosenharte shook his head. 'It was only when you mentioned Yemen that I thought of asking your advice. It was a shot in the dark.'

Idris said, 'The woman, Sonja, is she part of this enquiry that you make?'

'No, she just let me use a phone the other day.'

'She will tell them.'

'Did you overhear what she was saying?'

Idris gave him a furtive look. 'You must not tell her more. This woman loves another man and she will do anything to save him. Beware, Rudi.'

'You're probably right.' He wished that the light allowed him to see

Idris's face properly. 'Can you help me on this man Abu Jamal?' he asked.

'When you help me, Rudi, you expect nothing in return. So now I will help you. But you must tell me why you need to find this man.'

Rosenharte explained about his brother and his family and said he had a chance of freeing them if he acquired some information about Abu Jamal. When he finished, Idris asked, 'Are you a Marxist, Rudi?'

'I am a socialist, yes, but not like Lenin or Stalin or Honecker.'

'Herr Gorbachev—you think he is a good man?'

'He seems a decent man, yes. I think he is doing the right sort of things in the Soviet Union. Reform is needed everywhere in the East.'

'I am a Marxist and a Muslim,' said Idris. 'Does a man do the will of God or of the state? This is very, very difficult question.'

'It is,' said Rosenharte. 'Tell me, why are we having this conversation?'

'Because there are other people like you and me who want reform in communist countries, but remain socialist. They do not believe in terrorism either. It hurts us in the East and it hurts Arab countries.'

'Can you help me with hard information?'

'I will send someone. His name is Vladimir, a Russian. He's a good man and very clever man,' said Idris, tapping his forehead. 'He will help you.'

Rosenharte got up and thanked him. He thought how much he liked the man—a true affection that bridged every cultural and ethnic difference. He grinned and Idris acknowledged the sentiment with a wink.

'The Russian will find you and he will help you soon, Rudi. Soon.'

THEY WALKED to Sonja's apartment block on the south side of town, where he left her with a kiss of genuine tenderness. He hurried off to a dive he knew in the crypt of a bombed-out church and sat alone at a table, methodically draining one beer after another.

By one o'clock he reckoned that he looked drunk enough to persuade his Stasi surveillance that he had been on a bender all day. As he made his way to the door of Die Krypta, two men slipped from a table in the shadows, took hold of his arms and moved him expertly up the steps and onto the street. Rosenharte allowed himself to be led to a car, where there was a third man waiting at the wheel. 'Good evening, Comrade. My name is Vladimir. Can you come with us to a safe place?'

'You're the man my friend spoke of?'

'Yes,' said Vladimir. 'We found you soon after you left your girl at her apartment. We had to make sure you weren't being followed.' The car moved without haste, as if making for the Stasi headquarters in Bautzner Strasse, but then veered off to a building in Angelikastrasse, the KGB residence in Dresden, which stood just 100 metres from the Stasi. Vladimir and his men took him to a basement, and offered him a drink. Rosenharte asked for coffee.

'You were quick to find me,' said Rosenharte, thinking that Idris must have sped to a phone on his bicycle soon after he'd left.

The Russian smiled. 'It was a coincidence: we already knew about you. When the Stasi mounts this kind of operation we take an interest.'

'Idris said you could help me. Is that true?'

'It depends how,' said Vladimir. He had an interesting face, pale and unmistakably Slav, with a good deal of authority in his expression.

'I want news of my brother. He and his family have been arrested.'

'And your brother is?'

'A man who makes films. His name is Konrad Rosenharte. My twin. They're using my family's detention to gain a hold over me.'

'Why would they do that?'

'I'll tell you everything I know if you help me.'

'Do you have a lot to tell us, Doktor?'

'Yes.'

Vladimir circled him, with his hands thrust forward in the pockets of his leather bomber jacket. Rosenharte took him to be completely ruthless yet also someone with whom he might be able to negotiate. The KGB could be very useful to him. It had a vast station in Berlin and satellites in every major city. During Rosenharte's time in the Stasi, Normannenstrasse had deferred to the KGB in everything from training to the broad strategy of intelligence gathering in the West. But the KGB had moved on from its obsessions with fascists and class enemies to make a reluctant accommodation with the new Russia of glasnost and perestroika.

At length Vladimir spoke. 'Idris is a friend of ours and I trust his judgment. I'll see what can be done for you.' He looked at Rosenharte thoughtfully. 'He said you were interested in Abu Jamal. Why is that?'

'I wanted to know his relationship with Michael Lomieko—Misha.'

'Ah, Misha!' said Vladimir. 'Everything always comes back to Misha. I repeat the question: why do you want to know about him?'

'I travel on the train with him to Leipzig, that's all.'

Vladimir grinned and shook his head. 'Don't take me for a fool. I know that you went to Italy a week or two ago because we have done our research on you. I cannot guess at the relationship you have with the Western intelligence services, but that is why you want to know about Abu Jamal and Misha, is it not? Come on, let's be straight with one another.'

Rosenharte felt out of his depth, but he did have a glimmer of an insight. Idris must be watching Misha for the KGB, who were interested in him for exactly the same reasons as the British. Maybe the KGB disapproved of East Germany's support of terrorism, too.

Vladimir nodded encouragingly. 'Tell me your problem, Rosenharte.'

'This is difficult,' he started. 'I have been given hope that if I gain information about Abu Jamal I may be able to get my brother released.'

The calculation was visible behind the Russian's eyes. 'Abu Jamal is coming to a villa in Leipzig soon for consultations. Is that any help?'

'Why are you telling me this?'

'Because I expect an exchange of information. I want you to tell me everything that you pass to your friends in the West.'

'What is the villa's name?'

Vladimir spoke to one of his men. The man left the room.

'Are you a reformer?' Rosenharte asked after a few moments' silence.

'Everyone is a reformer today. Except the Party in East Germany hasn't understood this and won't implement the necessary modernisation programme. The writing's on the wall. Isn't that the way the Bible puts it?'

'Not on the Berlin Wall. Honecker says it will last another hundred years.'

The other man came back with a folder. Vladimir spent a few moments leafing through it before flourishing a map and spreading it on a table in the corner. 'These are the Stasi safe houses in Leipzig. There are seventy-eight in all,' he said, pointing at a mass of black stickers.

'Seventy-eight!'

'They increase every year. But we no longer have access to the latest information. We have three likely addresses.' He pointed to dots around the city centre. Then he turned and gripped Rosenharte's shoulder with one hand. 'No matter what complications you experience, our help must be kept secret. And I will not tolerate you keeping anything back from us.'

'I understood the first time you said it,' said Rosenharte amenably. 'I'm here to help you any way that I can. I will keep to my side of the bargain.'

'Good. The girl you were with earlier this evening, keep your distance from her. She's working for the Stasi.'

Rosenharte nodded.

'I'm glad we've got things straight. I'll find out about your brother, if I can.'

Rosenharte stood for a moment. 'Sometimes I feel this is like a novel by Kafka.' He watched Vladimir's face for a reaction.

'I don't read Kafka,' he said indifferently.

Rosenharte tried another tack. 'Have you had me followed? Did you send someone to meet me in Trieste?'

'Herr Doktor! I didn't hear your name before last week. How could I send someone to Trieste to watch you?'

'And you didn't send anyone to the gallery where I work?'

'Of course not. Why would I do such a thing? We don't operate like that.'

The interview was coming to an end. 'How will I contact you?'

'You won't. We will make contact with you in a week or so.' He paused. 'Now go off and read some good Russian authors. Forget the Czechs; they're too dark for these times of light.'

'Times of light?'

'Oh, yes, times of light, Herr Doktor.' He appraised Rosenharte openly, then put out his hand. 'I will see what I can do for you. Goodbye.'

One of the men gave him a piece of paper and he memorised the three addresses in Leipzig. Then they took him to within a mile of his apartment. and left him in a wasteland. It was past four o'clock when he turned the corner into Lotzenstrasse and saw a car waiting for him. He ignored it and shuffled with the unsteady purpose of a drunk to his front door.

HE SLEPT MUCH of Sunday and read through his lecture in the evening, making one or two cuts. Very early on Monday he packed a case and made his way to the Hauptbahnhof to catch the first service to Leipzig, surprised to see groups of Volkspolizei, the East German police, standing around with riot shields. As far as he could tell, there was no one following him.

The train reached Leipzig just after nine. At the station there were scores of Vopos in summer uniform, but no one seemed interested in him and he was able to walk unobserved towards Karl-Marx-Platz, where he bought a copy of *Das Magazin* at a newspaper stand. He walked a couple of hundred yards to the Nikolaikirche and stood for a few moments in the back row of pews, before moving to a small office at the back of the church where some religious books and postcards were for sale. As instructed by Harland, he bought three cards, all views of the church, signed a visitors' book with the name Gehlert and wrote: 'Mine eyes have seen the coming of the glory.'

The first postcard was posted in the door of number 34 Burgstrasse, bearing the same quotation, the second was left blank between two pilasters under the clock of the old town hall and the third, inscribed with the words 'To Martha with love', was deposited with a manageress at a café nearby.

This done, he walked to the Thomaskirche, the imposing church where J. S. Bach once led the choir, and repeated his words in a second visitors' book, signing as Harry Schmidt. Outside, in the thin autumn sunshine, he lit a cigarette and read *Das Magazin*.

Harland had told him not to expect Kafka to make contact immediately; he would make his move only when he was sure it was safe. After about an hour, Rosenharte made his way to the university canteen and ate an early lunch of stew and dumplings.

By two thirty he was standing at the front of a full lecture hall, slightly regretting the meal. He was always nervous before speaking. Then the lights dimmed and an image of a bull from the prehistoric cave of Lascaux in southwest France appeared on the screen. Rosenharte let his audience gaze at the bull for a few moments, then began to speak.

'This image was probably painted by a young man some eighteen thousand years ago. In the same cave there are other animals, which we know from radiocarbon dating were painted by other people much later. To us they seem all of a piece, the same period, but in fact two thousand years separate the artists.' He looked up. 'Those two men were as far apart as Karl Marx and Jesus Christ.' At this, some of the students smirked. 'Not in their nature, I hasten to add, but in time.'

He couldn't think what had got into him to make this aside, which would only weaken the message of his text. He asked for the next slide, which was of galloping bison from the Altamira caves in northern Spain. 'If the bull was a great work of art,' he continued, 'this one, painted about seventeen thousand years ago, is a masterpiece. Through the subtle application of tones and shading, and the skilful use of colour, the image reaches a perfection unequalled by any modern artist. This beast lives, my friends, and it is as great a work of art as any of you will ever see.'

Rosenharte moved to his theory. If the height of art had been 7,000 years before man planted seeds, millennia before he invented the wheel, how was it possible to think of art in terms of evolution? Evolution implied a gradual improvement over time. 'But in no area,' he said, 'has this painting been equalled in all the history of art—not in the simplicity of technique, the harmony of design or the expressive animation of form.'

He continued on this theme for twenty minutes, but before he could move to the final section of the lecture, a large man jumped to his feet. 'But what purpose did these paintings serve society, Dr Rosenharte?'

'None, because there was no society,' Rosenharte shot back.

'That's my point exactly,' said the man. 'We must all agree that the principal function of art is to serve society by expressing that society's aspirations and reflecting its achievements. If these primitive daubs bear no relation to any society, then they must be disqualified from the realm of art.'

Rosenharte shifted to his right so he could see the man. 'Why must we all agree? Do you really believe that all art, no matter from what period, is dependent on our views about what is and what is not a society? I have to tell you that it is a very old-fashioned view.'

A murmur of approval came from the students, who were clearly excited by this rare exchange of convictions. The man was having none of it. 'Is it old-fashioned to favour works of art produced by an advanced state like the German Democratic Republic against the graffiti of primitive tribesmen?'

Rosenharte's blood began to rise. 'The problem in the GDR is that we don't know what art this society has produced. Why? Because most of the artists who have anything to say are banned. They paint for themselves because our society cannot hear its own voice, will not listen to its own heart.'

The man started pushing along the row towards the exit. 'I will not listen to any more nonsense, and if people know what's good for them they will follow me from this hall.' One or two made to move, but the majority cried for them to stay and began a slow handclap. This was not at all what Rosenharte wanted. He put his hands in the air and appealed for silence, and when the room was quiet he resumed his lecture. At the end there was silence then a deafening round of applause. Reluctantly accepting the congratulations of the students, Rosenharte stepped down from the platform and joined the crowd filing through the door.

'Well, Doktor, I guess that's the last time we'll hear one of your stimulating talks here.' He glanced to his left. A woman in her mid thirties was looking ahead of them, smiling. 'I'm glad I came. It was the best so far.'

'Thank you. But I screwed up with that crack about Marx and Jesus Christ. I think that's what annoyed my critic. Do you know who he was?'

'Professor Böhme, a senior figure in the local Party.'

'Böhme! Yes, I've heard of him. What was he doing here?'

'Checking up on you. Your last lecture—the one about Carracci—it was thought by one or two people to be criticising the Party in a sly way.'

They reached the corridor. 'I always feel a sense of anticlimax after these things,' Rosenharte said. 'Would you like to go for a drink somewhere?' He noticed a very confident face, full lips and an acute expression in her eyes.

'Why?'

'What do you mean, why?' he said.

'I mean what is your motive?'

'I haven't formed a motive. Do you want a drink, or not?'

She gave him a long-suffering look. 'OK, I will take you to a place I know. We can talk there. My name is Ulrike. Ulrike Klaar.'

They walked to a place near the station, where they sat across from each other at a small round table. The arch of her eyebrows made him think he should watch what he said but there was also a humorous glint in her eyes.

'We can't be long,' she said. 'I have an appointment at five.'

'Anything important?'

'Yes, as a matter of fact, it's very important, Herr Doktor.'

'Rudi. My name's Rudi. And I have to go soon, too. I want to take a walk before I leave, maybe to the Clara Zetkin Park.' It was the first address on the list that Vladimir had given Rosenharte.

'Why do you have to go?'

'I don't have to. I just want to stretch my legs.'

'But you said you had to go.'

This was not going well. He took a mouthful of beer and watched three police trucks that were disgorging Vopos.

'What's up?' he asked. 'There were riot police at Dresden station at five thirty this morning. Do they think something's about to happen?'

'Monday evening prayers at the Nikolaikirche. That's where I'm heading after this. We meet every Monday to pray for peace. The authorities don't like it because other groups come—the environmentalists, people who want free speech and reform, people protesting about prisoners of conscience. Someday the Stasi are going to break into the church and take everybody. They've already arrested many of my friends.' She looked out of the window and suddenly straightened. 'Were you followed here?'

'I don't think so. Why?'

'There was a man looking at us from the other side of the street. You can't see him now because of the trucks. I think he was at the lecture.'

'Perhaps he's an admirer of yours. What did he look like?'

She gave him a withering look. 'He was tall, thin, and has russet-coloured hair almost like yours. Does it mean anything to you?' she asked.

He shook his head. 'No. Tell me more about these prayer meetings.'

'They started last year. Last January we tried to advertise them by leaving leaflets in people's letterboxes. But the Stasi got to hear of it and had the police remove the leaflets with long tweezers. They actually had a supply of specially long tweezers for this purpose!'

'So no one came?'

'No, about five hundred people showed up in the end. That was really the start of it.' She smiled and stirred her tea in silence, a good silence, he thought, because neither felt the need to say anything.

'A friend of mine,' she started, 'thought you might be the brother of Konrad Rosenharte, the film-maker. Are you?'

'He's my twin.' He paused and looked away. 'He's in prison.'

'What for?'

'The usual . . .' He stopped, suddenly overwhelmed by the thought of Konnie. 'You see, he can't take any more. They broke him last time.'

Her hand fidgeted indecisively on the surface of the table. 'I'm sorry. It's nearly as bad for the friends and relatives on the outside,' she said.

'What a country,' he said under his breath. 'They've got Konrad's wife, too. The children have been taken away.'

She shook her head in disbelief. 'Then why did you take such a risk today? It won't be ignored. Believe me. Not with your brother in jail.'

'I didn't intend to say anything,' he said. 'But then I made that stupid remark about Christ and Marx and when that fool started spouting, I—'

'I had the impression that you were cooler than that.'

'I should have been, but the attitudes of that man are the ones that imprisoned Konrad. His only crime was to make a private film that displeased the authorities—and for this they jailed him.'

'When will you return to Dresden?'

'This evening, probably, I'm not sure. I'm hoping to meet someone.'

'Oh. And in Dresden, what will you do when you go back?'

'My life is taken up with Konrad at the moment. It's a pretty complicated business.' He paused. 'Then I suppose I'll eventually get down to writing a book from these talks—a book that will never be published, of course.'

'But a book that will be read,' she said brightly. 'It will be a great book, an axe to the frozen sea inside us.'

'That's a wonderful phrase,' he said. 'I'd like to use it.'

'Then you must give credit to the author.' She looked up from her tea.

'I'm sorry, I don't recognise it. Who said it?'

'Kafka,' she said very quietly. 'Franz Kafka.'

OUTSIDE THE CAFÉ, Ulrike brushed stray wisps of her dark brown hair away from her face with a gesture of irritation. 'We don't have much time. Listen very closely to everything I say. But first, I must know how you heard about the villa in Clara Zetkin Park?'

Rosenharte had prepared his answer for when he met Kafka. 'I did my own investigations in Dresden. I found out from Misha's colleague at the university. It was by chance that I heard that Abu Jamal stays there.'

She frowned doubtfully. 'Nothing like that comes by chance.'

'Trust me, it's not important how I know.'

'It is important,' she said, 'but I'm going to ignore it. Now, listen. We'll walk to the park. I'll show you the villa, but don't be obvious. Remember, in this city one in four is working for the Stasi in some way or other.'

They set off, walking quickly, to the southeast of the city. 'I am a fluent Arabic speaker. I spent most of my childhood in Arab countries. I studied European languages at university and I was employed by the government as a translator. My position now is much less sensitive than it was—I am at the Central Institute for Youth Research—but I still have access to the Department of International Relations and I have a friend there.'

'And this friend has shown you proof that the GDR is supporting Middle Eastern terrorism? That doesn't seem very likely.'

'Please, everything will be clear, if you listen. They're going to do something big at Christmas in the Federal Republic and there'll be attacks on Western interests next year in the Middle East. The Arab has a list—the American embassies in Jordan and Egypt. Jordan will be in January, Egypt sometime in March. There's something planned for Vienna and maybe Paris, but we don't have details.'

'Exactly why would an academic doing youth research know about these things? The other side will need to know how you got this information.'

'The Arab drinks heavily. That's why he has problems with his kidneys and liver. My friend is the woman they have assigned to look after him while he's here in Leipzig. She has already got clearance to work with the professor. She was the natural choice.' She avoided Misha's name.

'You mean the GDR supplies a woman for him?'

'Yes, of course! A woman who speaks Arabic. He's become fond of her and she was with him in the hospital when he had a kidney transplant. He was on drugs and it was then that she began to learn the details. We acquired two names of his associates in the Middle East and these were passed to the West in the summer.'

'Yes, those names are what convinced them that your information was good. Are you sure that the authorities are involved?'

She nodded. 'But they keep their distance from the planning. Everything goes through the professor. That's the weak point. We know when the professor comes to Leipzig, when he goes to the villa, when he travels abroad. We know about his money, which all comes from the Party.'

'Is the Arab here now?'

'He comes next week, or the week after. We're not sure.'

They had skirted the centre of town and now reached the park where one or two couples sat on the grass. She turned to face him. 'Take me in an embrace and look over my shoulder.' Rosenharte held her lightly by the waist and shoulder. 'There is a large, dark green building on the far side of the park,' she said to his right ear. 'Next to that is the villa, but you can only see a little of it because of the high fence.'

'I see,' he said and let her go. 'There's something I don't understand. Why didn't you give all this information to the British woman who was here in the summer?'

'It was too dangerous for her to take this out. And, anyway, it wasn't until the Arab's medical operation in August that we had hard evidence about dates for these attacks.'

'What made you think of me?'

'We knew you came here quite often to teach your classes and lecture. You have a pretext for being here. You seemed perfect.'

Rosenharte didn't buy any of this, but decided not to press it. 'There's one other thing I don't understand,' he said. 'Why don't you leave? If you took this information out yourself they'd give you a place to live and a job.'

'Leave!' She hissed the word. 'I will not leave. I want to rid the GDR of these stinking old men who steal everything from us and give us platitudes about sacrifice in return.'

'If you go on like that, you will be arrested.'

'The time has come when everyone has to take risks. You know that.'

'But if we're going to work together on this thing, I have to know you're not going to put yourself in an exposed position. We're dependent on each other in a way that's dangerous for us both.'

'We're already exposed. We've reached the stage when it's no longer enough for an intellectual like you to make clever points that you hope one group of people will understand while the others don't. We have to occupy the streets and take possession of our city.'

'Well, that's for sure,' he said. 'But, Ulrike'—it was the first time he had used her name—'you saw the number of police we passed on the way here. They will never let you simply take the state from them. Look what happened in China. You must have read reports of Politburo members making threats about repeating Tiananmen Square in Germany?'

'We have to take risks. We will fight violence with non-violence. They can't massacre us in the middle of Europe.'

He shook his head. 'How will I get in touch with you?' he asked.

'By the same means as before, but don't go to the Nikolaikirche. Sign the book at the Thomaskirche, leave a postcard at the café, or wedged between those two pilasters. Then wait outside the Thomaskirche. I will find you.'

He gave his the address in Dresden, but left out the apartment number. 'If you want to contact me, send a postcard to Lotha Frankel. He used to live in my apartment. Sign it Ruth if you're in trouble, Sarah if you need me to come to Leipzig. I will see it without it being delivered to my apartment.'

'I'll see you, then,' she said, turning away. She set off down the street that would take her to the centre of town. Rosenharte watched her go. About fifty yards down the road she suddenly turned and smiled at him.

HE MADE HIS WAY to the station, unable to decide about Kafka. She certainly wasn't what he'd been expecting, but the more important thing was that her story didn't hang straight at all. No more than a handful of senior officers would be allowed to know that the GDR sponsored terrorism. It was simply unbelievable that a university worker had acquired this knowledge from a friend. But what did it matter to him? He'd made contact with Kafka, and she had coughed some very startling information. And in a couple of weeks' time he could give the British the precise location for Abu Jamal. They'd have to start moving on Konrad and Else then.

He crossed Dresdenerstrasse and moved on towards Karl-Marx-Platz. The Volkspolizei were mustered in the square in their thousands. A good number of Stasi were hanging around in civilian clothes. As he walked towards the station, he heard a voice shout his name.

It was Colonel Biermeier, who was pursuing him with four plain-clothes Stasi officers. 'Stop, Rosenharte. Stop now!'

He turned round.

'Where are you going?' demanded Biermeier. 'Where have you been?'

'I'm late for the train,' he said.

'You didn't answer my question. Where have you been?'

'For a walk in the park. I needed to calm down after my lecture.'

'I heard about that. You offended the locals.' Biermeier wiped his brow. 'Why did you evade your protective surveillance in Dresden?'

'Protective surveillance! Is that what you call it? I simply left my apartment early this morning. I can't help it if your men were asleep,' he said. 'Now you've found me, can I go back to Dresden?' he asked.

Biermeier shook his head. 'No, you're going to Berlin.'

'Why?'

'It's enough to know that we have need of you there.' He looked at his watch. 'We'll take the train; it will be quicker.'

Forty-five minutes later they were on the Berlin train. Biermeier sat across the aisle from Rosenharte, trying to ignore him.

'You should take some time off, Colonel,' said Rosenharte good-naturedly. 'You look stressed. Find yourself a mistress. Have a few drinks.'

'I don't drink.'

'Biermeier—a brewer who doesn't drink. It's odd how inappropriate some names are.'

Biermeier examined him for a moment. 'You're an arrogant bastard, Rosenharte. So damned sure of yourself, aren't you? Well, they won't be hearing from you in Leipzig again. You've blown that one.'

Rosenharte shook his head. 'Whatever you have heard was taken out of context. The man wanted to be offended. Besides, I need to make contacts with the church community there as agreed with our friend in Trieste. So I must return whether they want to hear my lectures or not.'

They said little more until they arrived at the Ostbahnhof in Berlin, where they were met by three cars, one of which contained a trim man in his early forties who introduced himself as Colonel Zank from HA II, the

212 | HENRY PORTER

department for counterintelligence. Zank took them to the Interhotel where they ate tasteless white fish in an empty dining room. As the colonel watched them with a bloodless smile, Rosenharte began to recognise something of this man's stillness and reserve, and he understood that the shadow who had observed him as he was interviewed by the archivists had moved into the world of substance.

They drove to Karl-Marx-Allee, then headed east to Lichtenberg. It was nearly fifteen years since Rosenharte had been to Normannenstrasse, but apart from the increased number of security cameras and one or two new apartment blocks, little had changed. At the barrier a camera swivelled in their direction. Rosenharte had to clasp his knees to stop his hands shaking. He would get through this for Konnie's sake. That was his mission—his life's mission—and if he held on to that thought, he'd handle everything well.

The guards checked each man's credentials, then waved the cars through to the main entrance. The car carrying Rosenharte pulled up just beyond the covered area. He got out and looked up at the seven-storey building that contained the minister's suite of offices. Most of the lights were on.

The escort peeled off and just one other man, apart from Biermeier and Zank, entered the building with Rosenharte. Zank nodded to the desk on the right and gestured to a lift, indicating that Biermeier should go first, followed by Rosenharte. They stepped off at the fourth floor and were shown to a characterless antechamber without windows. And there they waited.

Zank went off and came back several times, but said nothing. Biermeier seemed to enter a deep official torpor. Eventually Zank summoned Biermeier and Rosenharte into a dark passage, which led through an office with three secretaries and came to a door, which Zank eased open. On entering, Rosenharte saw a long, panelled room with a conference table on the right and a seating area on the left. From the way Zank and Biermeier had been touching their tie knots and smoothing their hair in the corridor, Rosenharte had known they were about to enter Erich Mielke's presence.

They came to a halt halfway along the conference table, but it was only after a few seconds that he saw a diminutive figure in uniform standing by the window, looking out into the night. No one spoke. Rosenharte stared at the man who had run the Stasi for thirty years, causing untold misery to untold numbers.

Zank spoke. 'This is Rosenharte, Minister.'

'I know it's Rosenharte. What do you take me for?' He moved away from the window and went behind his desk with short, quick steps. He looked at them. 'Where's Schwarzmeer? He was told to be here.'

'I believe he is on his way,' said Zank diplomatically.

'That's not good enough. I don't have time for delays.'

Rosenharte took in the man in detail: a permanently down-turned mouth, bristling grey hair and eyes that seethed with offence and hatred. Every kind of medal ribbon was stitched to the breast of his summer uniform.

'In Leipzig, what are they doing, Biermeier?'

'Everything appears to be under control, Minister. It seems they have put the lid on these demonstrations for good. But we must remain vigilant.'

Mielke shook his head and shot him a derisive look. 'They are traitors. They should be locked up. Shot, if necessary. They bring disgrace to the GDR. What do you say about these people, Rosenharte? Are you a member of the hostile forces ranged against the socialist state?'

'No, Minister.'

'But it's people like you, isn't it? People who don't know what hard work is. People who want to read books all day while the state provides for them.'

Rosenharte wasn't going to rise to the bait. 'I think the important thing to realise, Minister, is that the demonstrators are not from one group, but a number of minority interests that have coalesced to cause this trouble.'

'How do you know so much about it?'

'I don't know much. I simply observe that there is very little homogeneity among the demonstrators. They all seem to want different things.'

The little goblin clapped his hands. 'Exactly right. See! I have to go to an outsider to tell me these things. Every type of antisocial element is using this excuse to cause trouble on the eve of the fortieth anniversary of the GDR.' He banged his desk with a small clenched fist. 'That is our opportunity, Comrades: to drive a wedge between these groups, compel them to tear each other part. Zank, I want your proposals on a strategy. This paper has top priority.' He looked at a calendar on his desk. 'Today is Monday, September 25th. I want it on my desk by Wednesday morning.'

'Certainly, Minister,' said Zank. 'It is an exceptional insight of yours.'

Biermeier risked an incredulous glance in Zank's direction.

They heard a door open softly behind them, and Schwarzmeer greeted the minister and moved to the other side of the desk in order to whisper in his ear. Rosenharte caught the words, 'briefing for the general secretary . . . from hospital'. Honecker was ill: that was news.

When Schwarzmeer finished what he was saying, Mielke gestured to the conference table behind them, and told them all to sit down. He took the chair at the end, Schwarzmeer sat to his right, Zank to his left. Rosenharte sat opposite Biermeier.

Mielke looked at him. 'So, Dr Rosenharte, we must decide tonight whether we believe you, or whether to throw you in jail with your brother.'

Rosenharte knew that he had to take the initiative. 'Minister, I have said nothing that can be believed or disbelieved. As General Schwarzmeer will tell you, I never wanted anything to do with this operation because I didn't want to be held responsible for things outside my control. However, the general has persuaded me that this is my duty and I am therefore happy to serve as an implement of your policy. But, Minister, I cannot answer for the truth of what has been passed to us by Annalise Schering. I don't know whether she is genuine in her desire to help the state, or is working against us.'

'That's a clever answer,' said Mielke. 'But it's not a convincing one.'

'I can't give any other. I cannot vouch for her motives.'

'You are to be sent to the West to make contact with her again and receive more material. Before you leave, I want to know more about you.'

'But I have received no word from her.'

He dismissed this with a wave of the hand. 'She has made contact, but I suspect you knew that would happen. You probably even knew the date.'

Rosenharte shook his head. 'No, Minister. I knew nothing.'

'My view, Rosenharte, is that you're a gifted wastrel. You are the son of an SS general who has inherited a degenerate character. Isn't that true?'

'It doesn't matter if you disapprove of the way I've led my life—believe me, I have my own regrets. Neither my character nor my actions are at issue here. It's whether you believe that what you're getting from Annalise Schering is true. Speaking for myself, I wouldn't trust something that comes so easily. But that's just my suspicious nature.'

The minister nodded. 'We'll go ahead with the plan tomorrow. See to it that I'm kept informed throughout. If you're playing a game with us, Rosenharte, you will pay for it with your life. Understand that.'

The room seemed to have got darker, the atmosphere closer. The others began to move, but Rosenharte remained seated. Now. He had to say it now.

'You want something?' said the minister.

'If you want me to go to the West, I have conditions.' He turned his head to face the terrifying old man squarely. 'I want Else and the two boys returned to their home immediately. And I want to see my brother.'

The minister got up. 'You deal with it, Schwarzmeer. This is an operational detail.' He walked to a door in the corner of the room and disappeared.

They took Rosenharte to another, less well-furnished room. The three officers sat opposite him, with Schwarzmeer in the middle.

Rosenharte wasn't going to wait for them to speak. 'If you want this material, you must release Konrad and allow him to regain his health.'

Schwarzmeer's face resembled a clay mask in the half-light of the room. 'You do not come here and make deals, Rosenharte. You *will* go and you *will* return with the intelligence. And that is all there is to it.'

'No,' said Rosenharte quietly. 'I am prepared to suffer anything. Unless I have what I want, I will not go. And Annalise will not help you without me.'

Schwarzmeer looked at Zank.

'These difficulties you face now with demonstrations,' Rosenharte continued, 'are nothing compared with the perils represented by the West's technical superiority. Annalise's material is immensely important to you.'

'So what exactly do you want?' asked Zank.

'Before I leave, I want half an hour with Konrad in private. I will tell him that he is to be released, because that's what you are going to do. When I'm in West Berlin, I'll make a call to the neighbour of my brother at six in the evening—Else does not have a phone. I will bring the material back with me only if she answers and tells me that she and the two boys are home.'

Schwarzmeer moved to protest.

Rosenharte put up a hand. 'Then I shall request a second collection from Annalise in two weeks,' he continued. 'By that time, Konrad must be with Else and receiving medical and dental care to correct the harm done to him owing to his mistreatment by the state. During the period before and after my second visit to the West, my brother's family will be left in peace, unmolested by surveillance or harassment. They are to be treated with respect.'

'And if there are problems with the material,' said Schwarzmeer, 'then we revert to the status quo as of tonight.'

'There won't be.' It had been almost as though someone else was speaking for the last twenty minutes. But now he heard his voice falter and he coughed to cover it. Zank's anaemic features twitched with understanding.

Nothing more was said. Rosenharte was taken to another part of the building and placed in a holding cell. He sat down on the bed and, to the embarrassment of his rational self, prayed to Ulrike's God.

PART TWO

On the morning of Tuesday, September 26, Rosenharte rose from the narrow iron bed. He would neither eat, sit nor lie any longer because it indicated an acceptance that locking him up was reasonable. He knew the deliberation that would decide his and Konnie's fate was still going on and he had now given up all idea of predicting which way the decision would fall.

Then three men came, unlocked the door, pulled him from the cell and frog-marched him along the empty corridor to a loading bay where a white van waited. Three steps led up to an open door in the side. Rosenharte saw the tiny compartments and a row of key hooks by the door. He demanded to be told where he was being taken, but they said nothing, forced him up the steps and into the nearest cubicle and slammed the door.

The journey lasted just twenty minutes. After a series of abrupt turns the truck slowed and the engine was shut off. The door to his cubicle was opened and he was beckoned into the gloom of a large garage.

A little way from the bottom of the steps, Colonel Zank stood with his hands clasped behind his back. 'Never say that we do not keep our word,' he said. 'Welcome to Hohenschönhausen.'

A metal door rolled back with a low rumble. Zank gestured Rosenharte out into a large courtyard. Three sides were occupied by uniform blocks rising five storeys high. Nowhere in the GDR was there a building more expressive of the state's ponderous brutality.

'This is our main facility,' said Zank. 'We can take pride in the work that's done here. Without Hohenschönhausen the hostile negative forces would have overrun the state years ago.'

They turned right to walk away from the interrogation blocks. Zank threw out an arm to a long, low, red-brick building to his left. 'This was constructed by the Nazis as a kitchen. The Soviets used it to detain objectors to the de-Nazification programme after the war. There were cells in the basement, named the U-boats by prisoners. Perhaps you've heard of them?'

Rosenharte nodded. He had heard of the unspeakable tortures practised by people who proclaimed liberation from Nazi barbarity yet employed the

Gestapo's methods. Hundreds, maybe thousands, of martyrs had been destroyed in the U-boats, their spirits broken in the underground hell.

They took a left turn and came to the main entrance where there were two electronically operated gates for vehicles, a small gatehouse and a side entrance for pedestrians.

'And over here, beyond the reception centre, we have the prison hospital building, where we are heading now. Oh, yes, we have a hospital here, too.'

Zank pressed a bell and a tall, cadaverous attendant in a white coat appeared behind the glass, drew several bolts and turned a key.

The man turned out to be a Dr Streffer, a Stasi officer with the rank of lieutenant-colonel. He led them along a corridor to a glazed door.

Streffer turned and, avoiding Rosenharte's eyes, said, 'Prisoner 122 is a very sick man and he will tire easily. You would be well advised not to place any further strain on his heart.'

He turned the handle and pushed the door open. Konrad was seated at a table in filthy pyjamas, and his head was drooping. When he looked up, his expression remained blank, as though he was struggling with delusion.

'Konnie. It's me—Rudi.'

A smile began to shine in his eyes as he took in Rosenharte's features. 'Is it really you?' he asked. 'Good Lord, it is you, Rudi. Am I going to die? Is that why they let you in?'

'No, Konnie, you're not going to die. I have done a deal to see you. I'm doing all I can to bring you home.'

Nothing could have prepared Rosenharte for the sight of his twin. He had lost twenty pounds since the summer, his eyes had retreated into his skull; the veins stood out on his hands, his forearms were like an old man's.

'What deal have you done, Rudi?' He smiled—that old sceptical smile that he used to tease Rosenharte when he was being dogmatic or pompous. 'What deal can you do with these people?' His eyes moved to Zank. 'All they want is to finish me off. That is their only objective.'

'Enough,' said Zank. 'You may not utter defamations against the state.'

Konrad bowed his head. 'I'm sick, Rudi. Maybe I don't have long.'

Rosenharte shook his head. 'I'll get you out of here and find you proper treatment, Konnie. Else and the boys will be free by this time tomorrow.'

Konrad's eyes rose to meet his, hope gleaming through the pain. 'How . . .?'

'Don't tire yourself, brother.' Before Zank or Streffer could intervene, he moved forward, grasped Konrad's shoulder and looked into his face.

'Unhand the prisoner. Step away now,' Streffer commanded.

Rosenharte did as he was told. 'I am rendering services that are important to the state.' He glanced at Zank. 'Look, they know Else is a loyal citizen; they understand the boys deserve to be with their mother. This will happen.'

'That's good, Rudi; you've done well.' Konrad smiled again. Rosenharte noted that even now he enjoyed the warmth of his brother's approval. It had always been like that. However much he had achieved, Konnie's praise was the only thing that mattered. Now, as his brother suffered for his beliefs, it made Rosenharte feel shallow and inadequate. In his *Überwintern*—his hibernation—he had shirked his moral responsibilities, and instead retreated to an inner sphere, taking his pleasures when he could, with women and drink and the exquisite proximity to the work of great artists, whereas Konnie had remained true to himself.

They looked at each other for a moment and Konrad understood what his brother was thinking. He saw the fear and guilt in his eyes and assuaged it with a humorous wink. Just a few minutes into the meeting and they were in each other's minds—back on the old wooden jetty near the Rosenharte farm, looking at their identical reflections in the water of the lake and watching sticklebacks glide between the weeds.

'We'll have a picnic on the jetty yet,' said Rosenharte. 'Next summer we'll take the boys and Else there and show them how to catch trout.'

'Good,' said Konnie. 'That's good.'

'The interview is terminated,' Streffer said. 'The prisoner is tired.'

Before Rosenharte could say anything, he had been guided out of the door by Zank. In the passage he shouted, 'Hold on, Konnie. Just hold on!'

Outside, Zank escorted him to the main gate, where Biermeier was waiting with a car. Rosenharte suddenly turned and gripped Zank's shoulder. For a moment he thought he would kill him. 'You'd better make sure that my brother receives the proper treatment, because I am holding you personally responsible for his well-being.' Zank shook himself free. 'Remember, Zank,' he hissed, 'you can never be sure of the cards you're dealt in life.'

He didn't know what he had meant, other than that the system from which Zank drew his power was no longer an eternal certainty. Zank's features hardened and for a brief moment a chilly, sadistic mediocrity was revealed. Then, spinning on his heels, he walked off in the direction of the administration block.

Biermeier let Rosenharte watch him go and in that moment, Rosenharte knew of his own deep conversion. If ever there was a 'hostile negative element', it was him. From now on he would oppose these people, their prisons and their muffled brutality with everything in his power.

'Come on,' said Biermeier. 'Let's get in the car. We've got work to do.' Then, as he opened the door, he added, 'This place gives me the creeps.'

Ten minutes passed before Rosenharte absorbed that remark and turned to look at Biermeier with interest.

ROSENHARTE CROSSED the Berlin Wall for the first time in his life two hours later. It took about half an hour, while the border police on the eastern side looked over his credentials and exit visa. Then he followed the trickle of old people who were allowed to visit relatives in the West. He carried a case and a copy of *Neues Deutschland* tucked under his right arm, as instructed by Annalise in the intercepted letter. In his wallet were 600 German Marks, which he had signed for at Normannenstrasse.

He walked over the white line painted across Friedrichstrasse, noting a sign that declared 'You are entering the American sector'. A few yards on, he came to a modest hut in the middle of the road, and showed his passport and waited while an American major examined it. 'Welcome to Checkpoint Charlie, Dr Rosenharte. I've been told to tell you that your friend will be waiting at the Café Adler as you expected.' The officer handed back the passport. 'Have a good day, sir.'

Rosenharte entered the Adler by the side entrance. The café was full, but Annalise's stand-in had a table to herself by the window. She lowered a newspaper and waved. Rosenharte glanced around the tables as he walked over, furiously kick-starting the pleasure in his face. She rose from the chair and hooked her arm round his neck and kissed him most tenderly. 'It's just marvellous to see you,' she whispered. 'We have a lot of company in here. It's all going to be OK.'

He smiled at her. 'It's good to see you,' he said.

She placed the back of her hand against his cheek. 'Are you OK, Rudi?'

'I'm fine.' He nuzzled her. 'They've just let me see my brother. It's not good news; he's very sick.'

She nodded, her eyes registering concern, and they sat down.

She glanced left and right. 'I want to talk to your side directly. I have to make new arrangements.'

He nodded, crossed his hands on the table and looked at the overnight case on the chair next to him. Biermeier had taken it from him at Leipzig station, and one of his men had handed it back just before he crossed the Wall, saying his clothes had been laundered. Rosenharte had immediately guessed that it had been fitted with a microphone and a transmitter. He waggled his thumb in its direction. She gave him an imperceptible nod.

'I'm sure they would like to talk to you,' he said quietly, 'but we should go somewhere more discreet. I will have to make a call.'

She leaned forward and rested her hand on his. 'You know I've never been to the Tiergarten. We could have a picnic. The weather's not too bad.'

Rosenharte glanced out of the window at the grey sky and said yes, that would be a splendid idea.

A few minutes later they left the Adler and stood outside, waiting for a cab to come. A beige Mercedes cab pulled up. The driver got out and, without asking, took Rosenharte's case and put it in the boot.

The moment the car moved off, Annalise snuggled up to Rosenharte and began to feel his chest. 'Are you wired?' she mouthed.

'No, but I think the suitcase is.'

'I thought that was what you meant. It won't pick up anything in the boot.'

Rosenharte darted a look at the driver.

'It's OK,' she said, 'he's one of us.' She leaned forward. 'Is the radio on, Tudor?' The man nodded. 'Bobby, can you hear me?' she asked.

'Yes, go ahead,' came Robert Harland's voice over the cab radio. 'I'm in a car in front of you.'

'We're going to get some food and then make for the Tiergarten for a picnic. Got any suggestions where?'

There was a pause, then Harland's voice came back on the radio.

'Tudor, drop them to the north of the Neuer See in the Tiergarten. You two can cross to the south by one of the bridges. There's plenty of cover there. We'll have Griswald's people all around. How will you make sure they know to approach you there?'

'They already know. The suitcase has a microphone,' said Rosenharte.

'Fine,' said Harland. 'But it's important you keep on demonstrating that you are relative innocents in this business.'

'I have a number,' said Rosenharte. 'A number to call in an emergency.'

'Right,' said Harland, 'so, while Annalise goes to buy the food, you find a phone and call them to say she wants to talk. Now, what have you got for us, Dr Rosenharte?'

'I've made contact with Kafka and I have important information. But now you must keep your side of the bargain. My brother's family will be released by this afternoon. I want to hear your proposals for freeing my brother from Hohenschönhausen. He's very sick. If he doesn't receive proper medical treatment soon, I think he will die.'

'We'll start working on that right away. But you have to realise that this is a very tall order, Dr Rosenharte. We can get his family out, but your brother is a different matter entirely. We'll work on this, but we need to concentrate on the few hours ahead of us. Is that OK?'

Rosenharte said yes, reluctantly.

'Right. Basically, Jessie is going to make a proposal to them and she will hand over certain items today. You will take the more important material back with you tonight or tomorrow. She's got to do a lot of bullshitting. Just stay on your toes and we will get through this. Have you got anything more for us on the Arab gentleman, Rosenharte?'

'This is for later,' he said firmly, noting that Harland had let slip Annalise's real name. 'But I can tell you that the material you have given to my side caused the Minister for State Security to interview me last night. So I think they believe in this.'

'Good, we'll talk later.'

They stopped at a grocery store. Rosenharte found a payphone and dialled the number in West Berlin he had been given by the Stasi. A woman answered, and after a few seconds he was put through to Biermeier, who said there wouldn't be a problem finding them in the Tiergarten.

Less than ten minutes later, Tudor dropped them in the park, near a secluded path that led to a large lake. Rosenharte was carrying his case, so they kept the conversation to a minimum until they found a spot beneath some beech trees overlooking the lake.

Rosenharte perched on a rough wooden bench, opened the bottle of wine and filled two paper cups. As Jessie set about slitting bread rolls and filling them with ham and cheese, Rosenharte caught sight of a yellow bird flitting in some saplings about thirty feet away. 'It's a young bird,' he said. '*Ein Grasmücke*. I think you call it a werbler. Something like that.'

'A warbler!'

They smiled.

He handed her a cup of wine. As she thanked him, her eyes moved to the path behind them. Rosenharte turned to see three men approaching. He got up when they were twenty yards away and called out, 'Can we help you?'

'We were sent by Biermeier,' said the one in a fawn mackintosh. 'Miss Schering, it is a pleasure to meet you.'

Jessie did not take the hand that he had offered. 'I have asked to see you because I'm not satisfied with the way you're treating me,' she said in perfect German.

'Fleischhauer. My name is Fleischhauer,' said the man in the mackintosh, returning his hand to his pocket. 'May I?' He sat down beside her. 'I'm sure we can settle any problems you have.'

'I have given you so much over the years,' said Jessie exasperatedly, 'and yet I learn you are making enquiries about me. Two weeks ago, a friend of mine from Canada called to say there had been a man snooping about in my past. Only the Stasi, it would seem, treats one of its most loyal informers like this. I can't walk down the street in Brussels without being followed. Your men are swarming all over the place. This whole operation will be blown if you can't control them.' She stopped. 'I take it that you have examined the material I gave Dr Rosenharte in Italy. You understand its importance?'

Fleischhauer nodded. 'It's useful, as far as we can tell.'

'Useful! Is that all you have to say? Do you people have any notion of the technological revolution in the West? You're being left behind.'

'We have a good idea of certain advances.'

She shook her head. 'I doubt it. In March, two scientists working at the Research Centre of the European Organisation for Nuclear Research in Geneva produced a paper. They propose a way of managing information in a network of computers, a way of keeping track of the vast flows of data that are generated at CERN. They call it a web. I've got you a copy of a NATO paper on this. You should read it because we're on the threshold of a revolution. It'll transform the military planning of the West. The Warsaw Pact countries will be left in the dust.'

'Don't be so sure about that,' said Fleischhauer.

She got up. 'Well, if you're not interested, there's really no point in continuing this conversation. We can all go home.'

'I didn't say we weren't interested. It's just—'

'It's just that you don't want to admit how far behind you are. Look, I understand that. That's why I'm here. I am a pacifist. The only way to ensure peace between East and West is to make certain that your side keeps pace with ours.'

'We understand that, Miss Schering. And my government would like to arrange a full briefing by you in the GDR. If you will come with us now, we can have you back in West Berlin by tomorrow without anyone knowing.'

She glared at him. 'I'm a pacifist but I'm not a fool. I want Rudi's brother released and until that happens I will limit my cooperation.'

'These arrangements are already in hand.'

This was Rosenharte's cue. 'I saw the minister himself last night with General Schwarzmeer,' he said. 'Nothing certain was agreed about Konrad.'

'And Konrad's family?' asked Annalise.

'They have already been released and are on their way home at this very moment.' He swung round to Rosenharte. 'Tell her, Rosenharte. Tell her about your arrangement to call Else this evening.'

Rosenharte nodded. 'It's true.'

'Still, there's no need for me to go to the East,' said Jessie. 'I am telling you everything I know. The technological aspects are beyond me.' She delved into her bag, then flourished a sheaf of paper. 'I have this for you. It's the paper I mentioned, plus a diagram of the network. This has all the information you need about NATO's proposed non-linear text system. It originates from a man named Berners-Lee at CERN and is known as hypertext.'

Fleischhauer slipped the document inside his raincoat. 'This is not a good place for passing such information. We should go to a safe house.'

'Look, to be quite honest,' she said, 'I want to spend as much time as I can with Rudi. That's why I came to Berlin. There's a package in my bag. It contains six disks with a third of the source code for the proposed NATO network. When Rudi returns to the East he will bring six more disks.'

Fleischhauer hesitated. He was plainly under orders to convey Annalise back to the GDR, but she had been smart enough to bring only a portion of the secrets with her. Fleischhauer now had to calculate whether to remove her forcibly to the East and risk losing the final delivery of disks, or leave her in the West and so earn the displeasure of his masters.

'This arrangement is surely agreeable to you?' said Rosenharte.

'This arrangement is nothing to do with you,' said Fleischhauer. 'What you know about, Dr Rosenharte, are pictures and little birds in the woods. So please leave us to discuss this matter . . .'

Jessie looked at Fleischhauer. 'You mention Rudi's interest in ornithology: *little birds*. How would you know that if you weren't listening to our conversation before you arrived? Rudi, are you wired with a microphone?'

Rosenharte patted himself all over and emptied out his pockets.

'Then it must be in your case,' she said with fierce indignation. She picked it up and tossed it twenty feet away, then turned to Fleischhauer. 'Have you any sense of the risks I've taken for the GDR? And this is how you repay me.' She was trembling with indignation.

Fleischhauer was unmoved. 'As you say, what you are doing for us now could be of the utmost importance to the state. That is why we must take all precautions: maybe it explains our haste and lack of gratitude. But deep down, you know that the state, the ministry and the first secretary himself appreciate your devotion. That is why they want to see you in person.'

'Let's drink to that,' said Rosenharte, seizing the tube of paper cups and prising three from the top. He lined them up precariously along the edge of the seat and began to pour the wine.

Rosenharte stepped back and prepared to make his toast. 'Hey, come on, boys, hand the drinks around.' He could see that the two men felt a little silly, but the one nearest to him leaned forward to give his boss a drink. At this, Rosenharte dropped his own cup and plunged his hand into the man's left-hand jacket pocket where he had seen the weight lying and pulled out a handgun. He flourished the gun, before pointing it at the other man, who was reaching to the back of his waistband.

'No,' he said, wagging his finger at him. 'Put your hand in your trouser pocket.' He paused, and examined the gun. 'Now, what are you doing with this? The PSM—the Pistolet Samozaryadnya Malogabaritniy—the handgun of choice for the quiet assassin, I seem to remember from the Stasi firearms course.' He turned to Fleischhauer. 'This woman has risked her life for a decade and a half and you have the gall to come here and threaten her?'

'It's obvious to any sane mind that we were not threatening her,' said Fleischhauer, shaking his head in disbelief. 'We were issuing an invitation.'

Rosenharte demanded the second man's gun and threw it into the lake, then told him to pick up the suitcase and hand it to Fleischhauer. Turning to Jessie, he said, 'Now, why don't you put the disks in the case, my darling, and these gentlemen can go home.'

Fleischhauer unzipped the top and Jessie gave him the package. 'I hope you possess the hardware to run these,' she said.

'Be sure that we have it,' said Fleischhauer.

'Now, be off with you,' said Rosenharte. They watched them go.

'That's a high-risk strategy you're following there, Rudi.'

'Yes, but if they had forced us into a car and driven us over the border, we'd both be lost.'

'But it wouldn't have come to that. They would have been intercepted by our side.'

'And then where would I have been?'

'I take your point. Now, we should go and find Harland.'

LATER THAT AFTERNOON, flanked by Harland and the Bird, Rosenharte walked to a pay phone and dialled the number for Biermeier.

'Did you get the message that I will be coming tomorrow with the complete set of new tyres?' he asked.

'Yes, but we were wondering why you didn't use the opportunity to complete the delivery today. Our representatives weren't pleased.'

'Your representatives frightened her. But, look, you have the material now and the delivery will be completed tomorrow as long as Else is home.'

'I hope you're not playing any games with us, Rosenharte. The boss is keeping abreast of developments hour by hour.'

'Tell him I am fully aware of that. All I want is to get my family mobile. I hope the delivery tomorrow will further establish my good faith.'

'When will you come over tomorrow?' demanded Biermeier.

'Sometime near one. It depends on her travel arrangements.'

He hung up. Harland unplugged the sucker mike from the handset and they got into the car with Jessie and slipped into the afternoon traffic. Before long the car plunged into the entrance of an underground car park and an electronically operated gate opened. The Bird dropped them at a lift, which took them to a large, modern apartment on the top floor.

The American was there along with two men Rosenharte didn't recognise, and he came to meet him as the lift doors opened. 'My name's Alan Griswald. I don't think I told you before. By the way, you did absolutely the right thing in the park,' he said, pouring Rosenharte a whisky. 'They were about to take Jessie on a scenic tour of the Eastern sector. We'd have had to intervene, and then where would we be?' He gave Rosenharte an open smile as he handed him the drink. 'So, Bobby, how do you want to handle things?'

'This is Mr Phillips and this is Mr Costelloe,' said Harland. 'They run the German desk in London. They've come to hear about Kafka.'

Rosenharte was angry that these two Englishmen had been sprung on him. 'You should have told me about this arrangement. Too many people know this secret. If there is just one mistake my entire family is in danger.'

Costelloe got up and approached Rosenharte. He was stout and wearing glasses, a grey pinstripe suit and burgundy knitted tie. He looked straight into Rosenharte's eyes and said, 'Mike Costelloe. I have been with our service for twenty-eight years—I joined as a young man in 1961, six months before the Berlin Wall was put up on August 13th. That forged my hatred of communism and it has been my life's mission to resist and to do harm to the system that you've had the misfortune to live under.' He paused. 'Please understand that I am here as your ally, and that the undertakings that we have given you are the pledges made by Her Majesty's government. We will indeed try to release your brother and we will certainly bring his wife and children out of the GDR as soon as you require.' He stopped and gave him a smile. 'Now, why don't we all sit down and talk about Abu Jamal, because at bottom we're all here to try to stop that regime destroying more innocent lives.'

Rosenharte sat down by Jessie and Harland started speaking.

'We need to know how solid Kafka is,' he said. 'You're the only person to have met him. We want to know your judgment about this source.'

Rosenharte thought for a few moments, then lit a cigarette. 'Kafka is a woman. She's engaged in the peace movement in Leipzig. As far as I can tell, she is a genuine source.' Their surprise was palpable.

'Name,' said Harland. 'Her name?'

Rosenharte shook his head. 'You can have it when Else is out of the country.'

'What did she tell you about Abu Jamal?' Costelloe asked.

'In August he had a kidney transplant in Leipzig, or at least recuperated there. The woman who has been assigned to look after his needs has spoken to Kafka. Abu Jamal is expected in Leipzig during next week or the week after. I know where he will be. He'll meet Misha Lomieko there and discuss plans for future actions.' Rosenharte had memorised this part of Ulrike Klaar's information. 'Attacks on the American embassies in Jordan and Egypt, planned for January and March next year. There are two more attacks to be staged in Vienna and Paris but she has no details or dates about these. There is one planned for West Germany at Christmas.'

'Jesus . . .' whispered Griswald. 'Are you talking bomb attacks?'

'That is what I assumed. There were many questions I wished to ask Kafka myself, but time did not permit it. She had to leave to attend a prayer meeting in Leipzig. Does this tie in with your information?'

'Yes,' said Costelloe. 'We have sources that confirm parts of the plan. Clearly we need to know much more—identities, money supply, et cetera.' He paused. 'How old is Kafka?'

'Between thirty-five and forty. It's not easy to say.'

'And her background?'

'A translator and interpreter. She's an Arabic specialist, but speaks all the major European languages. Her father was in the diplomatic service and she spent a lot of her childhood in Arab countries. She worked in the Department of International Relations, the faculty to which Misha Lomieko is attached, though her security clearance has been in some way impaired.'

'And she has this friend . . . this close female colleague?' Costelloe asked. Rosenharte nodded. 'And she is feeding her information about Abu Jamal's intentions?' Costelloe continued. Rosenharte nodded again. 'I suppose it has occurred to you that this other woman may not exist; that Kafka may be the companion assigned to Abu Jamal for his stays in Leipzig?'

'Yes, that is a possibility.'

Phillips, a slight, dark man who had not stirred until then, said, 'But if Kafka's security clearance is no longer valid for her to work in the faculty, they would hardly allow her contact with this source.'

'I couldn't explore these inconsistencies. I had very little time with her.'

'Where's the safe house?' asked Harland. He had moved to a table in the centre of the room and was making notes on a pad.

'A villa on the edge of Clara Zetkin Park. I can show you on a map.'

'We'll do that later,' he said. 'What plans can Kafka tell us about?'

Griswald stirred. 'This is not making any sense,' he said. 'Why would anyone hoping to pass information of this sensitivity to the West try so hard to be noticed by the Stasi at those weekly prayer meetings, for chrissake?'

'Let me tell you something,' said Rosenharte. Wearily, he prepared to issue the same disclaimer as he had repeatedly given to the Stasi. 'I cannot guarantee this information. I act merely as the messenger.'

'We should discuss the other end of the operation,' said Harland. 'Are they buying the story?'

'For the moment, yes,' replied Rosenharte. 'The minister took a look at me last night in the company of Schwarzmeer, Biermeier and Zank.'

'Zank!' said Costelloe. 'If he is in on this, he's watching Schwarzmeer. Zank will find something wrong, because that's what he is programmed to do. It's the Stasi testing itself. If Zank is involved, it will be only a matter of time before his doubts are allowed to prevail. So I would suggest it's wise to decide on a deadline, by which time Rosenharte and his family are brought out and people are placed around Kafka—say four weeks.'

Costelloe turned to Rosenharte. 'I want you to think about your decision not to tell us Kafka's true identity. That information could save scores of lives.' He rose from the sofa. 'Right, you've a lot to get through. We're going back to London. Keep in touch, Bobby.'

He shook hands with Griswald and then turned back to Rosenharte. 'In your opinion, will these demonstrations about democracy and peace in the East amount to anything?'

'I'm sure the Stasi will act forcefully to suppress at least one demonstration to send out a message to dissident groups all over the country.'

Costelloe nodded. 'But there is a groundswell of opinion?'

'People are coming together, but one determined use of force will end it.'

'I'm afraid you're probably right.' Costelloe took Rosenharte's hand. 'You're doing a very remarkable job, sir. It's been a pleasure.'

Rosenharte watched as he ushered Phillips into the lift. Costelloe's eyes came to rest on him before the doors closed and Rosenharte had the impression that he saw right into him. For a moment he experienced a vertiginous fright. He was now playing off four intelligence services against each other across the Iron Curtain. With individuals like Zank, Vladimir and Costelloe involved it was not a situation that could continue for very long.

BY SIX THIRTY they had been joined by Macy Harp, the Bird and Tudor Williams. Griswald showed Rosenharte to a phone in the bedroom and told him that Harland would listen in on the set in the sitting room.

Looking out on the enticing lights of West Berlin Rosenharte dialled the number of Frau Haberl, a Party member who lived near Else but who was well disposed to her and took messages for her. On the third attempt he got through and it was Else who answered. She sounded cowed and he realised that she had been told that he would ring, but had no idea of the circumstances of the call.

'How are the boys?' he asked straight away.

'They're better now. Florian says he hasn't been sleeping. Christoph doesn't seem to have taken in what happened. They were both shocked by the experience of being . . .' She stopped. 'Of being away.'

'Give them a hug from me,' he said. 'I don't want to raise your hopes, but we should see Konrad soon. They let me see him, Else. Do you understand?'

The whole tone of her voice changed. 'Thank God! How was he? Is his health standing up? Tell me.'

'He'll need rest when he comes home—your cooking and seeing the boys will do the trick. Else, I'm working very hard to achieve this.'

'Thank you, Rudi . . . we can't thank you enough.'

'Send the boys my love and tell them we'll go on a hike at the lake. I hope to be with you very soon.' He waited to see if she understood. Konrad and he used the word 'lake' as a code to indicate that they couldn't talk and that an explanation would follow later. It was no more than an alert.

'Yes, the lake. That will be fun. Maybe I'll come too.'

'Everything is going to be OK,' he said. 'I'll ring again and leave a message with Frau Haberl.'

'Thank you, Rudi—we send our love to you.'

Rosenharte replaced the handset with a sense of his enormous responsibility. Else was not robust. If this went wrong, what the hell would she do?

He took himself next door to the sitting room, where Harland had begun unfolding a large map of Leipzig. 'Well, that's some cause for a small celebration, isn't it?' Harland said. 'Did everything sound all right to you?'

Rosenharte poured himself another drink. 'It means nothing that the Stasi have kept to their agreement by releasing Else,' he said. 'They know they can pick her up any time they want. That's why I want her and the kids out as soon as possible.'

'We'll talk about that in a minute. First, your brother. Al, have you got those photos?'

Griswald picked up an envelope and withdrew several satellite images.

Rosenharte peered at them, then pointed out the main entrances to Hohenschönhausen, the interrogation centre and the hospital building.

Macy Harp and the Bird got down close to the four photographs. 'One thing is obvious,' Harp said. 'We only stand a chance of pulling this off while he's still in the hospital. Once he's been transferred back to the main detention centre, there will be little hope of locating him quickly enough.'

'How sick is he?' Harland asked. 'Was he in bed when you saw him?'

'No, he was sitting at a table. I think it was a room they use to continue interrogations while prisoners are receiving treatment.'

'So, we can assume he walked. That's good to know,' Harp said.

'What's the earliest you'd be ready to go?' Harland asked him.

Harp frowned. 'Seven to ten days. Maybe more. It depends how long we take to exfiltrate Konrad's family. Cuth is going to handle that.'

Harland glanced at Rosenharte, then spoke. 'One thing occurs to me straight away. Once we get Konrad and the family out, there's absolutely nothing to keep you in the GDR. We'd lose our contact with Kafka.'

'That's correct.' It was pointless to deny he would leave for the West.

Griswald rubbed his hands together. 'Rudi—may I call you that?—you gotta have some faith in us. We're going to a lot of trouble to help you and it doesn't look good to our governments if you continue to hold out on us. We have to equip ourselves with all the information.'

All eyes rested on Rosenharte expectantly. 'I have one good card in this game,' he said pleasantly. 'You all understand that once I give it to you, I may be condemning my brother to rot in that place.'

Griswald started shaking his head. 'You got it all wrong. None of us enters an agreement that we can't keep. If we say we're going to get your brother out we'll all do our damnedest to get him out.'

'I understand what you're saying but I don't have Kafka's permission to reveal her name. And I have a responsibility to protect her.'

'No, *we* have a responsibility to her and to the people who wind up at the end of one of these terrorist attacks, Rudi. That's what this is about. She understands that by giving you the information she has put herself on the line.'

Rosenharte put his hands up. 'All right. I'll think about it. But if I do give you her name, I'm going to need certain guarantees about her safety.'

'That goes without saying,' said Harland. 'There's just one more area I want to explore. When the Bird and Macy came back from Dresden they told me about the surveillance deployed against you. They said it was truly impressive. What I don't understand, therefore, is how you were able to slip away to travel to Leipzig and to contact Kafka without being observed.'

'I caught the earliest service to Leipzig. There was a car in my street, which I assumed was Stasi, but they didn't stir when I left the building.'

'When were you picked up again?'

'In the main square going back to the Bahnhof. About twenty or thirty minutes after I left Kafka.'

'And up until that time you had not sensed you were being followed?'

Rosenharte shook his head then remembered the tall man. 'That's not entirely true. There was one man who appeared while I was speaking to Kafka. It seems the same man went to the Gemäldegalerie.'

'Was this man Stasi?'

'No, he was far too obvious, too big to be a surveillance officer.'

'Have you any idea who he was?'

'No. He spoke to one of the assistants at the Gemäldegalerie. She took him to be Polish or Czech.'

'And that didn't ring any bells?' asked Griswald.

'Of course it did, but even in this affair I cannot believe the man who died in Trieste and this individual were associated.'

'I'd put money on it,' said Harland, 'though I don't know what it means. But let's just get back to the square in Leipzig, shall we? Who spotted you?'

'It was Colonel Biermeier. He needed to find me urgently because they wanted me in Berlin. The Stasi knew I was giving this lecture. That's how they tracked me down to Leipzig.'

'Certainly,' said Harland. 'But if they were so desperate to apprehend you, why not go directly to the lecture theatre?'

Rosenharte had to admit that it didn't make sense but he needed food and rest. He was not going to make this his worry.

Harland persisted when he gave no response. 'There's something here that none of us are seeing, Rudi. Both Alan and I feel there's a hidden hand at work. We need to understand who it is and why. Someone is helping us.'

ROSENHARTE SLEPT until after nine the next morning. When Harland returned it was agreed that there might be the need for one more meeting with Annalise, though they would wait to see how things went with Konrad before this was arranged. Rosenharte would tell the Stasi the next rendez-vous was set for the middle of October in the West. After that he would make it plain that she was willing to undertake the trip to East Germany.

At eleven, Jessie returned with some new clothes for Rosenharte: a jacket, a pair of shoes and two shirts. Rosenharte needed to be able to take money back with him, so the Bird set about making neat incisions along the line of the front seam and the collar of the short blue overcoat and inserted the $2,000-worth of high denomination Deutschmarks. He dissected the insoles of the new shoes and padded each with five $100 bills. The remaining $2,000 was stitched into the backing of a broad leather belt. While this went on Harland schooled him in the new procedure to make contact with them, which involved a code that changed each week.

At the end of the morning, Rosenharte was introduced to two men and a woman, all agents on loan from the BND, the West German intelligence service, who would slip into East Germany and find their way to Leipzig over the coming weeks. They were already familiar with the procedure for contacting Kafka. Rosenharte knew it was only a matter of time before they identified her, but he had no choice other than to go along with the arrangement.

Just past one o'clock, Tudor Williams drove Jessie and Rosenharte to Friedrichstrasse, where they got out and entered the Café Adler. Jessie was subdued. She avoided Rosenharte's gaze and looked out at the traffic passing through the checkpoint. Gradually her hands moved across the table to touch his. Their eyes met. 'What I'm going to say now is me,' she whispered.

'The real you?'

'Yes, the person inside Annalise.' She looked down. 'I wish you all the luck in the world with this, Rudi; I want it to work for you. And I hope your brother recovers when he gets out.' She stopped and stirred her hot chocolate. 'With this information, you never know, they may let him go.'

'They only let people go when they are *gleichgeschaltet*—pulled into line—that will never happen.'

She raised her head, then bent down even lower. 'Give my regards to the other woman. I feel a connection with her.'

It was an odd request but he nodded. 'I will. Look, I should go.'

'Yes. Got the package?'

'Yes.' He leaned forward and gave her a peck on the cheek.

'Good luck,' she said. 'I won't come out with you.'

He left the Adler, showed his passport at the checkpoint, then began the walk through the Death Zone to the Eastern border control.

THE STASI were full of surprises. On the other side of the checkpoint they were waiting for him—six men in two cars—yet not with the usual sullen superiority. Now they were all grins and congratulations. Even Biermeier's face had cracked to express a rough pleasure. Rosenharte gave his hand to Biermeier. 'I've got it in my inside pocket. Do you want it now?'

'Wait until you get in the car. They're very pleased with the material.' He opened the car door. 'Now get in, we've got a lot to do.'

Twenty-five minutes later the two cars pulled into Normannenstrasse and drove to the HVA block, which Rosenharte took as another good sign. They were shown to a meeting room where coffee and cakes were laid out. Five minutes later Schwarzmeer appeared with half a dozen men and a woman.

'Ah, Rosenharte. Welcome back. Good work, good work. These people are from the Department of Cryptology and the Department of Political Espionage Two. They are interested in what you have brought with you— very interested.' He was in an ebullient mood.

Biermeier handed over the second package of disks with some ceremony.

'Sit down, sit down, we haven't got all day,' Schwarzmeer said. 'These people have questions to ask you. But before that tell us when we can expect the final delivery.'

'We can expect the remaining six disks in a few weeks—by mid-October at the latest. As I understand it, you will then have the source code for the whole system. Then our informant wishes to come to the East to clear up any matters outstanding. That will be in November.'

There were many questions, chiefly from the armed services. Plainly all that Annalise had said to Fleischhauer in the park had sunk in, and they understood the grave implications for the Warsaw Pact military.

Then they went away and Rosenharte was left with Biermeier, Schwarzmeer and one of his aides. It was then that he felt his energy quit and he began to feel ill, nausea coming in waves. He clenched his fists and summoned the strength to ask Schwarzmeer about Konrad's release. The general cut him off, saying they couldn't let him go now, while he was still ill.

Rosenharte slammed his hand heavily but without strength onto the table. 'The deal is that Konrad is sent home now.'

'There is no deal, Rosenharte,' snapped Schwarzmeer. 'He goes when we say he can. For goodness' sake, man, understand that he is ill and that he is receiving the best medical attention available in the GDR.'

'Nothing could be better for him than to return to his family.'

'That is not the opinion of his doctors, Rosenharte.'

The skin of Rosenharte's scalp prickled with sweat. He searched fruitlessly for a handkerchief to mop his brow, then mumbled something about establishing a date for Konrad's release, but Schwarzmeer would hear no more. 'Colonel Biermeier, get this man out of here. He's ill.'

Biermeier took him to the Interhotel near the Ostbahnhof and arranged a room for Rosenharte. Before leaving, he had some tea brought up and said he'd get the hotel staff to look in on Rosenharte that evening.

Rosenharte raised his head from the pillow. 'Before you go, tell me about the park. Why were Fleischhauer's team preparing to snatch her?'

'It was the general . . . He's a hothead. He couldn't wait, but then reason prevailed and this morning he had forgotten he even gave the order.'

After Biermeier had left, Rosenharte forced himself from the bed, undressed and laid his new overcoat under the mattress. The shoes Jessie had bought were placed beneath the centre of the headboard, together with a plastic bag containing a new shirt. He didn't want anyone helping themselves to his possessions while he slept. He washed his face, drank several glasses of water and retreated shivering to the bed.

For the next twenty-four hours he knew little. He was unaware of any member of the hotel staff coming in, though at six in the evening he did notice several aspirins left by the bed. He took three pills with several glasses of water, and returned to bed for another delirious night.

ON THE FRIDAY—September 29—he woke and knew that the worst of the fever had passed. At eleven, Biermeier appeared with a waitress in tow. She placed a tray on the table with some soup, bread, raw carrots and a triangle of hard cheese. He also brought Rosenharte's suitcase.

'You need to shave and clean yourself up,' he said. 'You look half dead.'

Rosenharte eyed the case suspiciously. 'Is that still wired?'

Biermeier shook his head. 'You can check it if you want. We haven't the resources to waste a good transmitter on you now you're back in the GDR.'

'I have to put in an appearance at the museum. I've been away for so long.'

'Don't worry. They understand that you have been working on important matters. It's all been settled.'

'I don't get you. First you hold me prisoner and give me the third degree, now you're sorting out my problems at work.'

'We're pleased with you. That's why. Now you need to look after yourself.'

'I need to get Konrad out. He was arrested to make sure that I worked for you. Now I have done what Schwarzmeer asked, why doesn't he let him go?'

Biermeier threw him an awkward look. 'I'm sure he will when he can.'

Rosenharte washed, shaved and dressed, then left the hotel and walked to the station, where he boarded a train home to Dresden.

The moment he stepped off the train he encountered a vast crowd milling about the station. Whole families were on the move, their valuables stuffed into suitcases, looking to make a new life for themselves in the West. And they didn't seem concerned to hide their intentions either. But how long would the Vopos and Stasi stand by? The state couldn't haemorrhage these kinds of numbers for long without the already stricken economy feeling it.

Rosenharte went out into the rain and found a taxi. He told the driver to drop him a few blocks away from a foreigners' hostel where Idris lived. He found Idris sitting in the communal TV room with some Vietnamese students. Rosenharte beckoned him out into the corridor and began to speak, but Idris put his hand to his lips and led him to the back of the building.

'You want to take that flight to Khartoum, Idris?'

He nodded.

'Here's the money for it—three hundred dollars. That'll buy you a seat.'

Idris took the money that Rosenharte had extracted from his coat on the train, and shook his head in disbelief.

'I want you to do something for me this weekend. Will you travel to my sister-in-law and take a letter from me that no one else must see? Can you do that? Her safety and her children's depend on your discretion, Idris.'

He nodded. 'And your brother. Where is he? Is he free?'

Rosenharte shook his head.

Idris nodded sadly. 'My sorrow for you,' he said.

'Thank you. I will call Else tonight and leave word that you will be coming.' He stopped and smiled at his friend. 'Tell her that I'm doing all I can for Konrad. Will you tell her that, Idris?'

'No problem, my friend. Where is letter?'

'I have to write that now. Can we go to your room?'

When he handed the letter to him ten minutes later, he said, 'This is private—not for Vladimir's eyes. OK? But I do want to talk to him. Can you arrange that for this evening? I will be at the same bar in one hour.'

Idris agreed. Then Rosenharte hugged him and wished him Godspeed.

He jogged the few blocks to his street in heavy rain. When he got there he took his time to creep along a wall to see if the Stasi were outside his building. They weren't.

On the table, just inside the front door, lay a postcard addressed to Lotha Frankel: *I hope this finds you well. I saw Ruth yesterday, but everything is all right with her now. I thought you would be pleased to know. With kind regards, Sarah.* From this he understood that Ulrike had experienced some kind of trouble, but was now free of it and needed to see him.

In his apartment he burnt the card, and flushed the ash down the lavatory before leaving for the bar.

Die Krypta was packed with groups of middle-aged men. As Rosenharte sat alone at the bar, he overheard snatches of their conversation about the rush to the border. He drank three beers and began to despair of the Russian coming. He also decided that the man in the group of five, right next to him, who was wearing a blue corduroy cap, was taking too much interest in him. He sank the last beer, nodded to the group, and left.

The rain had been replaced by a thin drizzle that shrouded the city in mist. He pulled up his collar and set off gloomily in the direction of his home, but it wasn't long before he became aware of the sound of footsteps some way behind him. Maybe it was the character from the bar who had shown so much interest in him. He doubled back and sprinted alongside the Zwinger complex. There he retreated to the shadows and waited.

He heard the footsteps slow to a walk and Rosenharte saw a man in silhouette, wearing a cap and raincoat. He leapt forward with his arm raised, but the man turned, crouched, then grabbed the arm descending on him, ducked to Rosenharte's right and pulled the arm into his chest. He had moved with such speed that only when Rosenharte's face was an inch or two from the ground, and his arm was being forced back excruciatingly, did he understand that he had attacked Vladimir.

The Russian let him go and Rosenharte fell towards the stone.

'You are fortunate, Doktor. I omitted the disabling part of that move— the knee to the groin. Come. Let's get out of this rain.'

Rosenharte got up and apologised. 'But why didn't you come to the bar?'

'The Stasi drink there. I would have thought you knew that. Let's get to the car. It's over by the Catholic church. My two colleagues are waiting.'

As before, they drove to Angelikastrasse and went down to the basement. They all sat down round a table; a bottle of vodka was produced.

'OK,' said Vladimir. 'I want you to be utterly frank with me, Rudi. Time passes. I have demands on me.'

Rosenharte lit a cigarette. 'You know the only thing that matters to me is my brother,' he said. 'When I've got him out, you can have everything.'

'We would like to hear it now.'

'But you haven't helped me yet. What I need to hear from you is how you're going to persuade them to let Konrad go.'

Vladimir withdrew an envelope from his inside pocket and placed it on the table. 'This letter was written by your brother the day after you saw him. We arranged that. I tried to deliver it before now, but we could not find you.'

Rosenharte reached out, but Vladimir's hand remained on the envelope. 'I'm sorry. I can't let you have this until you tell us what has been going on.

Why don't you begin by telling us about the British and Americans?'

'Let me read the letter and I will talk to you alone,' he said.

Vladimir nodded and slid the letter across the table. 'I'll be back in a few minutes,' he said. All three Russians left the cellar.

Rosenharte opened the letter and saw that Konrad precise hand.

My dear Rudi,

I will be amazed if this finds you, yet since I have nothing to lose by putting down my thoughts and sending my good wishes to you, my dearly beloved brother, I sit here and write. The sight of you heartened me, though during the last few days I have become convinced that I am nearing the end of my life and that I should put my affairs in order and make my peace with the world.

It sounds melodramatic. I can hear you chiding me, yet the truth is that I do not look forward now, except to think of my sons' future and Else's happiness. In the event of my no longer being here to look after them, I know that you will nourish them with your love and your care. This knowledge gives me strength. I know that you are doing everything in your power to free me but I beg you not to risk your own freedom in this enterprise; nor to jeopardise Else and the boys.

I close now by sending my love and gratitude for the comradeship of the last fifty years; the memories of our times together have preserved me during the dark nights passed in places such as this. Send my love to my beautiful Else, kiss her for me and hug the boys as if they were yours. You are now the channel for my love, Rudi.

Your ever-loving brother, Konrad

Rosenharte folded the letter and replaced it in the unaddressed envelope, then brushed an angry tear from the corner of his eye. Staring at the envelope he repeated the words he had shouted in the hospital corridor as he was ushered out. 'Hold on, Konnie. Just hold on.'

VLADIMIR ENTERED with a knock, an oddly courteous gesture, given they were in the KGB's cellars. He slipped off his watch, which he placed on the table. 'So, we have much to discuss,' he said.

Rosenharte nodded. 'But before we speak of the other matters, I need to outline the problem with Konrad for you. Then I'll ask what you may be able to do to help me. After that I will tell you all I know about this affair.'

He began the story of how Konrad had been arrested when the second letter arrived from Annalise Schering and how the Stasi's promises to release Konrad had been broken. He described the deal he'd done with the British and Americans, but said that he now believed that they would not succeed on their own in getting Konrad out. The KGB, on the other hand, might be able to acquire the necessary release forms. Rosenharte would give them to the British who would never be any the wiser.

'You have a very devious mind, Dr Rosenharte. You're perfect spy material: a loss to the profession.' Vladimir grinned. 'Maybe there is a way we could help, but you have to make it worth my while.'

Rosenharte gave him a detailed outline of the Anglo-American operation to trace Abu Jamal and Misha. He gave no clues as to the identity of their British source in Leipzig, but he did tell him the nature of the information he had passed to the Stasi. He knew that Vladimir would be able to piece together the history of Annalise Schering, so he told him about the way the West had used her as a truth channel in the seventies and eighties. At this the Russian cocked an eyebrow—the only sign of surprise he permitted himself as he wrote notes in Cyrillic script.

At length, when the bottle of vodka was half empty, Vladimir flipped through his notebook. 'The operation against the Stasi is clever,' he said, 'because it preys on their sense of technological inferiority. Did the idea of tempting the Stasi with this bait while retrieving information about the MfS relationship with Jamal, come from the SIS chief in Berlin, Robert Harland?'

Rosenharte nodded.

'Someone we must watch,' said Vladimir. 'On the other hand, the man *you* have to watch is Colonel Zank. He's the one who stands between Harland and success, and the one who stands in the way of your brother's freedom. Perhaps he senses that it is the only way the Stasi can retain some hold on you.' He pondered the notes for several minutes. 'You're running against three clocks attached to detonators.' He picked up his watch. 'The first clock is your brother's failing health. The second is the security of the informant in Leipzig; a source handing secrets like this over to the West won't last long in the GDR. The third is the one ticking away in Stasi headquarters. It's only a matter of time before you're under arrest and being questioned by Zank about the computer program.'

'The only clock that matters is my brother's failing health. Once he's free, we can all leave the country and to hell with espionage.'

'Yes, I understand your focus, but you will appreciate my surprise that you are attempting to get three of the world's major intelligence agencies involved in the release of a prisoner held by a fourth agency. One mistake and . . . well, you know the risks. And those risks are to some extent mine too.'

Rosenharte nodded and said that it was all a question of timing.

'But what about the Leipzig connection?' the Russian asked. 'You say you want to leave immediately, but surely it would be regrettable if the information this person apparently possesses does not reach the West?'

Rosenharte looked at him intently. 'What do you mean?'

'What I say. It must be against everyone's interests if Abu Jamal is allowed to carry out the attacks you've told me about. You're the informant's only link to the West. It is your duty to stay with the case.'

Rosenharte studied him. 'Does your government want this to happen?'

'In the new era of the Soviet Union, there are reformers who regard this arrangement with a terrorist as very unhelpful.'

'I see.'

It was now six thirty in the morning. Rosenharte got up and stretched. 'There's one other thing I want to ask of you,' he added. 'Well, a couple of things, actually. May I use the telephone to call my brother's wife to tell her to expect Idris to visit her with a note?'

Vladimir smiled. 'Soon we'll all be working for you, Dr Rosenharte. Yes, you may make that call.'

'And I need to make contact with the West.'

'From a phone here?' He paused. 'You're out of your mind.'

'It will be untraceable but I must be alone. It won't compromise you.'

Vladimir shook his head and thought for a moment. 'Very well. You make your call to your brother's wife and I will find us some coffee.'

Rosenharte called Frau Haberl's house and after a wait of ten minutes spoke to a drowsy Else. In the most coded way he told her to expect Idris later that day and to follow all the instructions that he would bring.

'I'm sorry,' she stammered. 'Your friend has already been here and I turned him away. I didn't know that you had sent him.'

'The foreigner has already been to see you? It can't be so.'

'I didn't know his name but yes, he came yesterday.'

'That wasn't Idris. I only asked him last night. Who was this other man?'

'I don't know. He said he wanted to talk to you and Konrad on a personal matter. A tall man, reddish hair, a foreigner. I told him to go away.'

Rosenharte recognised the description. 'We'll talk about it when I see you. But please give my friend a proper welcome. He's a good man.'

'Of course, Rudi,' she said, then hung up.

Vladimir returned with two mugs of coffee. He sat down and leaned on his desk with his fingertips pressed together. 'You're taking them out this week? You'd better be quick about it. We're expecting them to close the borders.'

'May I make one other call? Alone?'

'We will record the call so you might as well tell me how it's done. Otherwise, I will not allow you to use the phone again.'

Rosenharte shrugged. 'OK,' he said.

As he dialled the number, Vladimir leaned forward and scribbled it on a pad. There were a number of clicks and the sound of another phone dialling. When this stopped, Rosenharte entered an eight-digit number.

'Is that the access code?' Vladimir asked, copying the number.

Rosenharte nodded. He saw no reason to tell him that it changed within twenty-four hours and then again in seven days' time.

He heard the answering machine and repeated the sentence Harland had drilled into him. 'This is Mr Prince. I am calling on behalf of my aunt who wants to rearrange her appointment.' He waited.

The voice of a woman, unmistakably English, came on the line. 'Hold on while I connect you.' More clicks, and then he heard Harland say hello.

'My aunt wishes to change her appointment to October the 4th, early in the day. That's the only day she can make it.'

'I think we can manage that. And what about your uncle?'

'At the end of the week. Everything must happen by the end of the week.'

'But we'll need a name in order to make a proper appointment.'

'You'll have the name. I'll give it to your representative.'

'It's good to get that straight, Mr Prince. Goodbye.'

Rosenharte hung up.

'So you're planning to finish everything by the end of this week?' said Vladimir. 'That's going to be very hard.' He got up and pointed to the calendar. 'The end of the week is October 7th—the fortieth anniversary of the GDR. It's a bad idea. I and most of my colleagues will be in Berlin. Believe me, Rudi, there will be more Stasi on the streets that day than at any time in the last four decades. Use your head.' He tapped his temple.

'What about the next week then—the 9th, 10th or 11th? I was hoping you could arrange release papers that say Konrad has been summoned to the KGB headquarters on the instructions of the MfS for interviewing on Friday night.'

'That would be better. But it's still going to be difficult. It's well-known that the KGB and the MfS are not as close as they once were. And the guards may have their suspicions when you get inside Hohenschönhausen.'

'Look, it's just to get the vehicle inside the compound, that's all.'

'What do we get in exchange?' Vladimir asked.

'The name of my contact in Leipzig and full details of what the British and Americans plan to do about Abu Jamal.'

'Call this number on Monday morning—in nine days' time,' Vladimir said. 'I will tell you then whether I have permission to go ahead. The delivery of the release forms will follow. They won't be good forgeries, just enough to get you into Hohenschönhausen. I can't guarantee they will get you out.'

'I'm sure they'll work. The people in this operation will also need Stasi ID photo cards with the appropriate coding and department stated.' Rosenharte got up and went to the door. 'One last thing. I'd like to know the name of the man I have entrusted my life to. You have enough knowledge to have me executed.'

A smile twitched at the corners of his mouth. 'I do not like to be exposed. However, since you ask, it is Major Vladimir Ilyich Ussayamov.'

'Vladimir Ilyich—the name of a loyal communist.'

He opened the door. 'I will have one of our people drop you near to your home. You look as though you need a long rest, Rudi.'

A few minutes later the car left Angelikastrasse with Rosenharte lying low in the back, wondering why the Russian had lied about his name.

While he had been talking to Harland on the phone, Rosenharte's eyes had strayed to Vladimir's bookshelves, where he saw a silver medal displayed in a blue satin upholstered box. He knew enough of the Cyrillic alphabet to see that it was a first prize awarded in a judo tournament to a man with the initials V.V.P. Vladimir Ilyich Ussayamov was his cover name.

HE WANTED TO LEAVE for Leipzig that day, but he succumbed to the fever again and took to his bed. The next morning, Sunday, October 1, he got up, flung the windows open onto a moist autumn day, then packed the clothes he'd need over the next few days in a rucksack and walked to the station.

When he arrived in Leipzig, Rosenharte followed the procedure to contact Ulrike and waited outside Bach's church, the Thomaskirche. He had been there for nearly an hour and a half when a young couple approached him. The boy told Rosenharte to follow them at a distance of thirty yards and to pass them if they were stopped by the Stasi.

They walked for fifteen minutes until they reached a once-prosperous area in the southeast of the city, where there were a number of Alpine-style chalets, each with two or three large trees in their garden, and a flight of steps running up to a first-floor entrance at the front. The girl turned to him and signalled to her right with an almost imperceptible tip of the head. Then she took her boyfriend's arm and they vanished into the dusk, laughing.

He came to a gateway bridged by an ancient wisteria vine. He ducked and walked down a path that led him to a door at the side of the house. There were no lights on. He knocked tentatively, but no one came. He knocked again, louder. Just as he decided that he must have got the wrong entrance, a bulb above him came on and the door squeaked open. Ulrike's face appeared, looking pale. She beckoned him in, then bolted the door.

'I would have come sooner, but I've had flu and was laid up in Berlin.'

'You must have given it to me. I was in bed for two days.'

'I'm sorry. Is it difficult now? I can always go and find somewhere to eat and come back.' He grinned, hoping to defuse the tension.

'At this time on a Sunday you won't find anywhere open.' She looked him up and down. 'You've lost weight. Come and have something to eat.'

Rosenharte followed her into a neat sitting room that looked like a set for a 1930s film—cream sofas, framed photographs on the wall, two porcelain figurines, a pair of tall brass lamps and a worn-looking walnut-veneer desk. Rosenharte liked the place and felt it displayed an elegance he would not have associated with Ulrike's rather worthy activities at the church.

They went into a small, draughty kitchen that was papered with a montage of postcards, recipes and pictures from magazines. Rosenharte opened the bottle of wine she handed him. He watched her with pleasure as she prepared dinner. He liked her new, shorter hairstyle, with the hair pushed back into a fine, electrified brush. It made her face younger and more dramatic.

He told her about seeing Konrad in prison as she fried up some potato and onions.

'I know people who've been in there. They're never the same. It destroys a basic faith in humanity. It's irreversible.'

They ate in the sitting room, opposite each other with three candles between them. Rosenharte talked about his contacts with the Stasi. Then he came to the point. 'The result of all this is that I must give your name to the British and Russians.'

Her eyes flared. 'No, Rudi. Give them some other name. Not mine.'

'The British and the CIA will only help me to free Konrad if they have your name.'

She shook her head.

'But without knowing the source, they cannot assess the intelligence.'

'You mean they say they don't know whether to believe it?'

'Yes.'

'There were things I told them in July and August that they can check on, things that no one could make up. So they don't need to know my name, because they already know what I'm saying is true. Though I see that you're in a very difficult position with your brother.'

'Which you put me in. The moment I started receiving those letters from the British, they arrested Konrad and locked up his family. I'm sorry to lay this at your feet, but there's no other conclusion. You have to help me out.'

She thought about this for a while. 'If I let you give them my name I will have to leave Leipzig. I need to stay here. This is where the struggle between good and evil is taking place.'

'But there is another contest between good and evil and that is the modern one between terrorism and the free society that you yearn to build here. You acknowledge this yourself because you were responsible for telling the West about Abu Jamal.' She shook her head. 'And what happens if they start shooting? Mielke will do anything to keep his power.'

'They can't do that in the middle of Europe.'

'We might as well be in Albania for all the contact we have with the West. Where are the foreign camera crews? Mielke can do what he likes.'

She stared at her wine for a while. Minutes passed.

Rosenharte studied her. 'The British have a theory that you're the person assigned to look after the Arab. Is that true?'

'Partly, yes.' She paused. 'But I have a collaborator. If I allow you to use my name, I will endanger that person too.'

'But you're the person who has most contact with Abu Jamal?'

'Yes.'

'Who gave you the assignment?'

'No one. He picked me. We had some contact two or three years ago. I told you, I speak Arabic and I can talk to him. He likes me.'

'And finds you attractive.'

'Naturally, that was part of it. But he's a very sick man now. His kidney problems may have been cured, but nothing can be done for his liver—he has cirrhosis. These attacks he's planning are his last throw of the dice.'

'When is he due here?'

'After the anniversary. They don't want him anywhere near the GDR when the other leaders are here. He will be here from Tuesday, October 10th.'

'In the villa?'

'Maybe. I will know by the end of the week.'

Suddenly he could hardly keep his eyes open. 'I'd better find somewhere to stay,' he said, looking at his watch then his rucksack.

'Don't be an idiot. You're staying here.'

She showed him to a bed that lay behind a thick green curtain in the passageway between the sitting room and her bedroom. Within a minute or two of her leaving he had washed, undressed and was falling asleep to the sound of branches scratching at a window somewhere.

He woke at four to find Ulrike had curled into the contours of his body, apparently asleep. Her hair touched his cheek and he smelt her soft scent. For an hour or so he remained awake, feeling her breath on his neck. Then, without warning, she hopped from the bed. As her feet touched the ground, tiny snakes of static swarmed inside her nylon shift so that her entire body was revealed in silhouette beneath the material. She giggled, then bent down and kissed him on the forehead before leaving for her own bed.

BY FIVE the following evening, the Nikolaikirche was filling up. Rosenharte went to the upper of two galleries that surrounded the nave and chose a place in the front row so he would have a clear view of the congregation. He leaned over the edge and picked out the middle-aged men scattered around the pews, all studiously ignoring each other, all obviously Stasi. A nervous hubbub rose from the body of the church, and Rosenharte noted the youth of the rest of the congregation and the hope on people's faces.

As he waited for the service to begin he went over in his mind the conversation he'd had with Harland that morning on a phone in the institute where Ulrike worked. Harland told him that he planned to move Konrad's family to the Czech border the following evening. 'Can you give us the name of your contact?' Harland asked once again.

'Of course,' replied Rosenharte without a qualm. 'Everything is in order.

I have a new means of taking delivery of the Berlin package next week.'

Harland seemed to understand what this meant and had hung up without saying any more.

A few moments later he saw Ulrike pick her way through the people sitting crosslegged in the main aisle to a place at the front.

Then the pastor walked to the altar table and a hush fell on the congregation. He introduced himself and explained that the service took the form of prayers, followed by an open discussion on matters that were relevant to the themes of peace and freedom.

Someone began to read from St Matthew: '"Blessed are the poor in spirit: for theirs is the kingdom of heaven . . . Blessed are the meek . . ."'

The Beatitudes had not run their course before Rosenharte's eyes came to rest on a familiar profile on the other side of the aisle from him. It was Biermeier. What the hell was he doing there?

He had hardly had time to speculate when he realised that tucked in behind a column on his side of the church was Colonel Zank. This really shook him. He listened to the remaining prayers and the beginning of the discussion. Only when he followed Zank's gaze did he see that Ulrike had risen to her feet and was upbraiding a man who wished to leave the GDR. 'This is not simply about *your* freedom,' she said. 'We're fighting for a new relationship between the state and the people that guarantees *everyone*'s basic civil liberties. The people who run away are selfish.'

As Ulrike took her seat again, a man stood up and said haltingly, 'No man searching for the personal fulfilment that has been denied him all his life and will be denied to his children, can be accused of being selfish. How can a person with no influence, like me, hope to have any effect on the Party?'

Ulrike was on her feet again. 'By staying and adding to the numbers who stand in peaceful defiance of the state and demand change here in the GDR.'

The discussion came to an end, and after a final prayer the congregation began to move towards the doors. Rosenharte jumped up from his seat, but by the time he reached the bottom of the stairway he found that most of the congregation had left the main space and had disappeared into a wheeling mass of people on the Nikolaikirchhof, the square beside the church.

Over the next few minutes he saw Ulrike several times, before losing her completely and becoming stalled in a group trying to light candles. The Vopos stood two or three deep along the perimeter of the square to prevent the demonstration from sprawling into the city. At the centre, the crowd was in a state of heady disbelief. Chants of 'We're staying here!' and 'We are the people!' rippled through the mass. Cheers, catcalls and applause filled the air.

Rosenharte reckoned that Ulrike must have moved towards Ritterstrasse, which was acting as a safety valve for the Nikolaikirchhof, feeding people towards the open plain of Karl-Marx-Platz. He made for the part of the street where the current seemed to be moving quickest.

It was then that he saw Biermeier and a sidekick moving with a steady purpose up Ritterstrasse. He crouched down, waited for them to pass ahead, and slipped in behind them. They had to be following Ulrike too.

He lost them when they reached Karl-Marx-Platz, where a vast number were milling about. In the distance, police cars and trucks were parked at random with their lights still on. Some kind of operation to muster the forces of the state was under way, yet everyone seemed oblivious. A free territory had been established in the heart of the crowd where it was possible to make an impromptu speech, brandish a slogan that would have been unthinkable a few weeks before. It was clear that the crowd was trying to get the measure of its own power, probing the defences of the authorities.

A few minutes later he saw the first spout from a water cannon arch through the air and then train on the people about seventy yards from where he stood. He went forward and saw about half a dozen dog handlers and a line of police with batons and shields had moved into position. In front of them people were being skittled over by the jets from three water cannon. The ones who didn't get up fast enough were dragged away and beaten.

Rosenharte jogged over to a row of benches just in front of the university building and mounted one. He had to find Ulrike. His eye was drawn to two men moving from beneath one of the huge streetlights towards a group of women. In the middle was Ulrike, who was gesticulating enthusiastically. Right up until the moment when one of them snatched a sheaf of leaflets from her hand, and the other took her by the arm, she seemed unaware of their presence. Within a short time they had dragged her from the group and were hurrying her towards a truck parked in the shadows beside the Opera House. Rosenharte jumped from the bench and walked smartly towards them, not knowing what he intended to do, but taking some heart that neither Biermeier nor Zank was anywhere to be seen. He shouted after them with a booming military command which made them stop and look round.

'Leave that woman,' he shouted. 'Let her go immediately!'

'Who says so?' shouted one with lank, black hair.

'I do!' Rosenharte was within yards of them now.

'And who are you?'

'Colonel Zank from HA II, acting on the orders of the Minister for State Security. So is the major here,' he said, gesturing to Ulrike.

Ulrike shook herself from their grip. 'Colonel, I was told that everyone had been briefed. Weren't the orders passed on?'

'Evidently not to these louts.' He looked at them. 'Your names?'

Neither one said anything.

'Show me your MfS IDs,' he bellowed. 'Now!'

As they reached into their pockets, Rosenharte said, 'Major, get back to your work immediately. I will deal with this pair.' Ulrike moved away.

'Why didn't the major say who she was?' asked one plaintively.

'Operational security,' said Rosenharte. 'Look, there's a lot going on tonight and I'm prepared to accept that the orders and photographs of my officers were not passed on to you. I'm willing to overlook this matter.'

Both nodded and shuffled away. Rosenharte turned and walked back to the edge of the crowd. Just as he reached it he heard one of the Stasi shout after him: the penny had evidently dropped, but it was too late. Ulrike and he melted from sight among the crowds around the Nikolaikirche.

THREE HOURS LATER they reached Ulrike's home with some people she'd met at the demonstration. They were in a triumphant mood and Ulrike— flushed, with eyes burning—insisted on telling the story of her rescue several times. Rosenharte spoke little until the others drifted off in the early hours, leaving him facing Ulrike over some empty beer bottles.

'I don't understand you,' he said quietly. 'After all the warnings you gave me about security, you mark yourself out at the church and get yourself arrested. If you behave like this, what the hell is the problem with me giving your name to the British?'

'I would have been all right. They let people go after a bit.'

'But Ulrike! I need you to keep a very low profile until I get Konrad out. That's the priority. OK?'

She got up and paced around the sitting room, lit up with passion. 'You saw how many people were out on the streets tonight: twenty or thirty thousand. That's incredible. Nothing like it has been seen for years in the GDR. You can't ask me to leave Leipzig now. We won tonight and next week—'

'Next week they will crush you,' he said. 'The only reason you weren't clubbed down tonight is because Gorbachev is arriving at the end of the week for the anniversary celebrations. Next week they won't be so restrained.'

She tilted her head to one side, smiling. 'You're really angry, aren't you?'

'No, just very disappointed. Our lives, my brother's and his family's, depend on us keeping our heads over the next few weeks. If it had been Biermeier or Zank, you would have been under interrogation now.'

'You mentioned them before. Zank is . . .?'

'Counterintelligence. If Zank and Biermeier are here, they are here for a reason and I think they're onto us.'

She shook her head. 'If they had the slightest suspicion about me, I'd have been arrested by now.'

Rosenharte opened his hands in a gesture of frustration. 'I'll leave early in the morning. I will return to Leipzig in a couple of days when I'll hand over my role to professional agents. Is that clear?'

'That means you will give my name to them?'

'Not necessarily. You can meet them without them knowing your name.' He got up. 'I need some sleep if I'm to catch the early train.'

'You can take my car. I don't use it much. It's an old Wartburg that belonged to my father. He gave it to me before he died. It's running OK.'

This was a peace offering of sorts and he accepted it gracefully. A car would make life a lot easier over the next few days.

They went to bed after that, bidding each other good night with abrupt formality. He lay awake thinking about Biermeier and Zank, although it was the former's presence in Leipzig that disturbed him most. Biermeier had no business in the city unless it was directly related to him.

He was still awake when she came to his bed and stood looking down at him in the dark. 'What is it?' he asked.

'You have to have faith in me. It will work.'

'It's not that I don't trust you. It's that I don't understand you. Every time I see you, you seem to be a different person. I find you hard to assess.'

'I have more information for you. I forgot to tell you. The Arab will be here for two to three weeks from next Monday. He will stay at the villa and I will see him there. It's all settled. I heard late this afternoon from a coded text to Professor Lomieko.' She knelt down and cupped his head in her hands. 'Trust me and this *will* work out.' She kissed his eyes and his lips, then felt his face with her fingertips. 'It's going to be all right. Believe me.' Then she slipped away.

Satisfied that he was not being followed, Rosenharte headed out of the city and flogged the Wartburg towards the hamlet where Konrad had sought refuge to bring up his family. In the late afternoon, and after several hours driving, he began the climb through the pine plantations to Holznau. The first house was Frau Haberl's place on the right, and after passing two smaller houses on the left he let the Wartburg freewheel down a narrow track that glanced off into the pine trees. Within a few seconds he came to a wide, open meadow, at the far end of which was a traditional farmhouse.

As Rosenharte bumped down the track, he caught sight of Florian and Christoph with a football, and then, to his surprise, Idris wading carefully in the uncut hay crop, carrying something in the skirts of his robe. The boys stopped playing and looked anxiously at the unfamiliar mustard-coloured car, until Rosenharte shouted and waved from the wheel.

He pulled up behind a large brick and timber barn, so the car would not be visible across the fields, then ran round the side to scoop the boys up in his arms. Their excited squeals brought Else to the door. Rosenharte saw her expression light up, her hands reach to her mouth, then her shoulders sag. She had thought he was Konrad. He set the boys down and took her in his arms.

'I'm sorry,' she said. 'You just looked so like him. For a moment I was sure he had come back to us.'

'He will come back. I'm doing all I can to bring him home,' he said.

Else was fighting back the tears.

Idris moved to her side and craned his neck to look into her face. 'Konrad will come. I know this, Frau Rosenharte. Idris know this.'

She smiled at him and said to Rosenharte, 'Where did you find this wonderful man? He's been so very kind to us.'

Idris looked down at the boys. 'One day Rudi finds me floating down the river and he picks me up and cleans me and gives me the name Idris and I am his friend for ever.' The boys goggled at him and consulted each other on the likelihood of this being true.

'Come on in,' said Else, 'supper is nearly ready.'

Rosenharte lingered for a moment and watched the mist creep over the trees that bordered the meadow, and he prayed that the two British spies would find their way to the rendezvous by four the next morning.

After beer and a risotto, and when the boys had gone off to bed, Else indicated that they should go to the barn so they could speak freely. She wasn't sure whether the farmhouse had been bugged while she had been detained. In the barn she lit a hurricane lamp and they sat and listened as Rosenharte began to explain the plan to take them across the border.

But Idris shook his head incredulously, interrupting, 'You have not heard, Rudi? They close border today.'

'It's true,' said Else. 'Didn't you know?'

'How could I? I've been in the car all day. It has no radio.' He walked to the door. 'I'd better find a phone.'

'The only telephone round here is Frau Haberl's.'

'There's no way I can let her hear this,' he said.

Else thought, then clapped her hands together, smiling. 'It's Tuesday night. The Haberls go to a Party meeting twenty kilometres away every week on a Tuesday. I suppose you could break in and make your call.'

Ten minutes later Rosenharte parked near the house and walked round it, checking that there was no sign of life inside. Then he prised the window open and climbed inside. The house was dark, but he groped his way to the front door where Else had said the phone rested on a table. He dialled the number and waited. Eventually he heard the clicks that prompted the code, and soon he was talking to the woman with the English accent. She put him through to Griswald, who was helping out in Harland's absence.

'This is Mr Prince. I can't make the delivery as planned,' he said.

'We know there have been problems but it goes ahead anyway. I have a map reference for you. You're to deliver the goods there by seven o'clock. Our mutual friend will meet you and provide transport. I have instructions.' He gave Rosenharte the name of a village close to the border with Czechoslovakia and told him they should cross the bridge and climb up the hill. On the other side of the border he would find a small road. The contacts would be waiting there in a red Volvo estate car with Austrian plates.

Rosenharte hung up and stole out of the house.

In the barn he told Else of the new arrangements. 'Are you sure you still want to do this?' he asked her.

'I love my home,' she said simply. 'But my first duty is to the boys now. I have to get them out. You know, they took them in the middle of the night and told them they might never set eyes on us again. Can you believe that?'

'Where did they hold you?'

'In Dresden for most of the time. They took me to Bautzen for eight days. I was locked up with criminals, Rudi. Monsters, perverts, murderers.'

'You've done well to keep your sanity,' said Rosenharte quietly. 'Konnie would be proud of you. Now, we'd better talk about tomorrow,' he continued briskly. 'We may have to do some walking, so you should keep the luggage to a minimum.'

She replied that she had got everything ready. The boys had a knapsack each and she was going to take a backpack and a grip with food and drink already packed. 'Has Idris told you that he's coming too?' she said.

Idris dipped his head apologetically. 'I go to Sudan with the money you gave me, Rudi. I go see family.'

Rosenharte considered this.

'Let him come, Rudi,' said Else. 'The boys will think it's an adventure with Idris there. Besides, we need someone to carry Konnie's films.' She got up and walked to an ancient barrel, pulled away some sacking and hefted out a sports bag. 'This represents Konnie's life's work—all the films that have never been shown publicly.'

'I assumed the Stasi had confiscated all this,' Rosenharte said.

'No, everything is here, and the equipment too.' She took the hurricane lamp to a container once used for animal feed, and told them how Konrad had fitted it with a false bottom and a hidden drawer. She crouched down and, grasping both ends of the container, pulled hard. Eventually the drawer came away, revealing a projector and Konrad's old Wollensak Eight camera.

'We see film now,' said Idris. 'Yes? We see film now.'

'Why not?' said Rosenharte. 'We've got plenty of time.'

Else shrugged. 'Most of the canisters contain negatives. But there's one I could show you.' She went to work setting up the projector and unfurling a white cloth, which she hung on the wall of the barn. She chose a canister marked *Sublime No. 2* and threaded the film through the projector. 'There's no soundtrack,' she explained to Idris while she switched on the projector.

Sublime No. 2 began with the camera moving over a pedestrian concourse, lingering on patches of lichen that grew on the concrete and stone. People seen only from the waist down crossed the camera's field at random, women with shopping bags half full, men with walking sticks, children with bruised knees. The camera moved across the ground as though sweeping it like a metal detector. For a few seconds it was diverted to track a dandelion seed bouncing over the concrete, and in the distance some buildings were glimpsed. Rudi knew the film had been shot in Dresden's Altmarkt.

Dusk came and pools of light appeared on the ground. The film cut to a pair of old-fashioned women's shoes and suddenly the washed-out palette of the daylight footage was replaced by luxuriant colour. The camera inched up the woman's legs to a floral patterned dress, also prewar, and then to a bodice and a head that was turned away. The whole image was lit from above by a streetlight. Then the woman turned to the camera and gazed into the lens. Her lips were very red and slightly parted; her hair was dark and worn curled in the style of the thirties. It took a few seconds for Rosenharte to see that it was a younger, slimmer Else wearing a wig.

She opened her arms and from each side of the frame a boy appeared and clutched at her legs and skirt. The dark Else smiled. The camera focused on her face. Then the image faded, bleached out by an intense white light.

'This was made before the boys were born,' Else said. 'It's as though he had a vision of our life.'

'I don't think that's what it's about,' said Rosenharte gently. 'I think you were playing the part of our natural mother and the boys are Konnie and me. The Altmarkt, or somewhere like it, is where he thinks she was killed in the firestorm of 1945. Why is it called *Sublime No. 2*?'

'I don't know. He never explained.'

The film fascinated Rosenharte because Konnie knew as well as he did that their mother had not been a warm, beautiful figure.

Elsie started packing away the equipment and then stopped suddenly. 'Oh, I almost forgot,' she said. 'The man who came here the other day—the one I told you about. He left this.' She took a piece of paper from her pocket. 'It is addressed to Konnie, but it concerns both of you.'

Dear Herr Rosenharte,

For several weeks I and members of my family have been trying to contact you regarding a private matter. My uncle, Franciscek Grycko was hoping to contact your brother, but died suddenly of a heart attack. I now must return to Poland. I leave you my address and telephone number at the base of this page with the hope that you will get in touch. It is important to both of us.

Leszek Grycko

Rosenharte read the letter again, then asked Else what it meant.

'He would not tell me,' she replied. 'I thought he was the Stasi playing one of their games so I told him to leave. I'm sorry.'

'It doesn't matter. I've got his number now. I'll call him over the next few days.' He folded the note and slipped it inside his jacket pocket.

By the time dawn rose on Wednesday, October 4, the little Wartburg had already passed through four or five villages. The village of Herrensbach lay about twenty-five miles to the southeast of Holznau, but it took them the best part of an hour to reach it by the exceptionally tortuous road system in the Erzebirge Mountains. Rosenharte was thoroughly familiar with the area and knew that the border lay just over the hill beyond a bridge, though the top of the hill was hidden by mist. He drove through the village then took a lumber track on his left. He parked behind a stack of timber, hopped out and put on his walking boots and anorak. Taking his camping knife, he unscrewed the Wartburg's registration plates and hid them some way off in the undergrowth. If the car was found, he didn't want it to be traced back to Ulrike. Finally, he covered the rear of the car with boughs cut from the trees nearby so it wouldn't be seen from the road.

Before shouldering his own rucksack, he checked Else's and the boys' shoes. They couldn't take their eyes off Idris, who was dressed in a long, tailored prelate's coat and a turban. On his back he carried a large grip, with the long handles acting as straps.

Keeping hidden from the road, they made for the bridge, crossed it and entered a patch of open and very marshy ground at the base of the slope. Then Rosenharte led them into the dark, silent forest, along a steep path. The hill was higher than it had seemed from the bridge, and since Else had already broken out in a sweat they sat down on a tree trunk and had a drink. Idris wandered a little way up the path to see how far there was to go, while Rosenharte, encouraged by Else, talked to the boys about the long journey ahead of them and their new life in the West.

Suddenly they spotted Idris sliding and tripping down the path, waving his arms. Rosenharte grabbed the boys by their hands and led them to a spot where the boughs of the pines touched the ground and made them lie down. Else and Idris followed and they all three flattened themselves to the bed of pine needles and waited, panting.

It began to rain. Within a few minutes it had turned into a downpour and the mist rolled down the hill, filling the forest. They remained dry under the trees, but visibility was reduced to about forty feet.

'Did they see you?' Rosenharte whispered.

Idris shook his head.

'How many were there?'

Idris held up four fingers, then made a sign to indicate that the men were carrying weapons. Rosenharte cursed and indicated to the boys that they must stay quiet. They waited for an hour under the trees, until the mist had lifted and the rain had stopped. Rosenharte rose to his knees very slowly and crawled out of the shelter to see if there was any movement above them. It was only then that he saw one of the boy's knapsacks propped up against the tree where they had stopped. Anyone coming down the path would see it immediately. He cursed and moved forward, but just as he was about to reach out, he heard voices coming down the path and scrambled for cover.

It was in fact a party of six guards. Evidently they had been sheltering somewhere on the top of the hill, because their uniforms were barely wet. When they reached the knapsack, one of them spotted it and picked it up. They crowded round and looked inside, but it didn't seem to occur to them that it had been left there recently or that the owner might be close by. One man then flung it high into the trees, where it dangled from a branch by a strap. This seemed to amuse them and they continued on their way, laughing.

Rosenharte waited a quarter of an hour more before moving again and summoning the others back onto the path. They climbed the next 200 yards quickly, carrying the boys up the steeper parts. Eventually they reached a large rock, from where they were able to look down into the cauldron of mist that was Czechoslovakia. Else bent over to clutch her knees and asked if they had arrived. Rosenharte told her that there was just one more obstacle which he was going to look at. He urged them to stay hidden while he was gone.

He jogged the fifty or so yards and came to a rusty mesh fence topped by three lines of barbed wire. Compared with the defences along the East–West border, this was pretty rudimentary. He felt the spring of the mesh and realised it wouldn't take much to dislodge it from the fittings on the posts.

A little way up he had noticed a fairly sizable log, which he now dragged down to the fence. Aiming one end at the point where the mesh was fixed to the fence, he jabbed at the mesh and burst the fitting with little difficulty. Very soon he had pushed the mesh over with the log so that it lay at an angle of forty-five degrees from the ground. He called to the others and they were able to scramble under the barbed wire and drop down on the other side.

Griswald had said that the road clipped the border about 500 yards down the slope. If they followed an easterly route they would find it. Rosenharte took his compass from the side pocket of his rucksack and they walked until they came to the road, where they miraculously found a red Volvo estate. Inside, the Bird and Harland were sharing a flask of coffee.

Rosenharte knew there would be a difficulty about Idris and there was. Harland got out, shook his hand and explained that Macy Harp was ill with flu. Then he let his eyes run over the figure in the long flowing robes.

'Who's this? King Melchior? The bloody Lion of Judah?'

Rosenharte made the introductions and explained that unless they dropped Idris near Prague they wouldn't hear Kafka's information.

'I don't mean to be rude, Rosenharte,' said Harland, 'but I'm not fucking around here. I want the information now, or I'll leave your brother's wife and kids on this road. Tell me what you've got and then we'll talk about your friend.' He led Rosenharte thirty feet beyond the car. 'Well?' he said.

Rosenharte had no option. 'Her name is Ulrike Klaar. She works in the Central Institute for Youth Research in Leipzig. She's heavily involved in the liberation and peace movement based around the Nikolaikirche. I believe it's only a matter of time before she's arrested for these activities.'

'Right. What do you make of the information? Do you think it's likely she has access to Abu Jamal?'

'She says Abu Jamal will be in Leipzig from Monday, 9th October. He will be staying at the villa in Clara Zetkin Park.'

'How's she getting this information?'

Rosenharte shrugged. 'I think she has been his mistress at some point, but I'm not certain. There's a part of this thing that I don't understand. Do you think there's some kind of trap?'

'That's about the sum of it, yes. Do you have a good feeling about her?'

'It's hard to say. I like her, but I don't trust her. There's too much that's unexplained. However, I believe she's sincere about the peace movement.'

Harland absorbed this. 'What about the Annalise side of the operation? Are they buying it?'

'So far, but I saw Biermeier in Leipzig. It doesn't make sense that a member of the foreign intelligence service was there. Maybe he's onto her.'

'And he saw you?'

'No, no.'

'Good. I wonder what's going on.' He looked back down the road, where Idris was playing with the boys, while the Bird and Else watched. 'OK, Cuth, you can go ahead!'

'Righty-ho, but I'm afraid I can't do a new passport for King Melchior.'

'That's fine,' Harland called out. 'He says he wants a lift to somewhere near Prague and that's what he's going to get.'

The Bird lifted the tailgate of the Volvo and started taking pictures of Else, Florian and Christoph against a dark blue cloth that he hung from the car. Harland's eyes returned to Rosenharte.

'I've now given you everything you asked for,' said Rosenharte. 'It's time for us to discuss when you're going to bring Konrad out.'

'I will do all I can, but something like this is very out of the ordinary for us. The Berlin Station is a minute operation compared to the Stasi.'

'I've found some help from a friend,' said Rosenharte. 'I can get you two good-quality passes—a vehicle pass and a docket authorising the collection of Konrad by the KGB—from the beginning of next week. All you need is a truck like the ones they use, a couple of men with good German and a way out of the East. And with the Stasi totally distracted by the demonstrations, it shouldn't be too difficult.'

Harland shook his head. 'But one check and our men are lost and your brother never gets out.'

Rosenharte looked back down the road at Else and Idris. 'That's true,' he said, 'but that's the deal we struck. Listen, I've seen the Stasi at very close quarters over the last week or so and they are flawed. They are preoccupied by these demonstrations. So let us decide on a date.'

Harland looked doubtful. 'Saturday the 14th is probably the best for us. We'd aim to get him through the border by midmorning.'

'OK, but no later. How will I get the passes to you?'

'We'll fix a rendezvous in Berlin for the Friday afternoon. You'll call that day using the same system.' He paused and looked at Rosenharte. 'There's one more thing. I'd like you to go back to Leipzig and effect contact between Kafka and our people next weekend in order to allay any fears Kafka may have. Will you do that?'

Rosenharte nodded. He had to return Ulrike's car in any case.

'Right, we'll fix the meeting for Sunday. You'll find an agent from the West German intelligence service at the main entrance to the park where the Leipzig trade fair is held—the Altes Messegelände. He will be there at five. He'll fix a meeting with Kafka later. Now that I'm able to give these guys her name, the BND can find out exactly who she is and, well, if she's for real.'

Rosenharte turned to the car. 'You still have doubts?'

'Not really, but I am baffled by her.' He kicked the gravel on the road. 'There's one further thing, Rudi. We've got to keep the Stasi off your back, so we're going to arrange that Annalise makes the final delivery in early

November. She will write to you in the usual way and they will intercept the letter. By that time we will have sorted Konrad and the Arab, and we'll just give them some crap that will foul up their computers for a few months.'

Rosenharte turned and walked back to the others. The Bird was handing over the new joint British passport for Else and the boys. 'You are now indubitably a legal British citizen, madam,' he said.

Harland offered his ungloved hand to Rosenharte. 'Good luck, Rudi.'

'Yes, Godspeed, old son,' said the Bird, seizing his hand in an iron grip. 'We'll look after this lot for you.'

Rosenharte went to the boys and crouched down. 'Look, take good care of your mother for me and your father, eh?' They nodded solemnly. 'And I will see you very soon in the West.'

Else kissed him and made him promise to bring Konrad to her. Before he had let her go, Idris had fallen on him and was also kissing him. 'We will see each other again,' said Rosenharte. He shook Idris's hand and palmed the two $100 bills he had ready. With a final kiss to Else, he managed to plant $500 in her coat pocket, which he indicated with a wink.

It was time to go. He turned and was moving quickly up the slope before they had even thought of settling into the Volvo. By the time he heard its engine start and turned to look, the road had vanished in the mist. Life was a hell of a lot simpler now. His only objective was to get Konrad out.

PART THREE

Sonja sat down on the bench beside him. 'You should look after yourself, Rudi. One sandwich and a piece of old sausage. No fruit, no protein to speak of. What's the matter with you?'

Rosenharte gazed across to the Opera House. It was a beautiful day and he could do without an ambush from Sonja.

'When did you get back?' she asked.

'Wednesday.' He turned to look at her.

'So you got back the evening of the big riot at the Hauptbahnhof?'

'Yes, I saw it.' He had seen the trains carrying the East Germans from Prague to the West. God knows how many Dresdeners had tried to board at the station and on the approaches to the city. The police used their batons without mercy, but those with serious head injuries declined to receive hospital treatment because they didn't want to be turned in to the authorities.

'You saw it all? Why were you at the Hauptbahnhof?'

'I just happened to be there.'

After the journey from the border he had parked the Wartburg in an old goods yard. He wanted to keep the car out of sight so the Stasi wouldn't make any connections with Ulrike, and he also thought the Hauptbahnhof was still the best place to lose surveillance when he wanted to leave the city.

'You "just happened to be there",' she said. 'You're a mystery man, Rudi.'

He ate the remains of his sandwich. 'Talking of mystery men,' he said, 'do you remember the man who came to see me? The country boy?'

A flicker of worry crossed her eyes. 'Sure. I remember him.'

'I believe he left something for me: a letter?'

'I don't remember. Maybe he left it with one of the other girls.' Her cheeks betrayed a slight flush and she looked away.

'It's OK,' he said. 'I know the pressures. Did you give it to the Stasi?'

She nodded. 'They told me that if the man showed his face again I should call a special number.'

'Do you know what was in the note?'

'Yes, something about your family.'

'What was the name of the officer you gave it to?'

'Someone from Berlin—a cold bastard called Zank. A real Nazi.'

Rosenharte put his hand on hers. 'Thank you. It's good you told me. But don't tell them that you have spoken to me about this. Act ignorant.'

He returned to the gallery, where he found a note asking him to attend a meeting of the committee at five o'clock.

At the appointed time he presented himself in the committee room to find Professor Lictenberg at a table, stroking his little grey goatee beard and peering over his glasses. Three other members of the gallery's committee, two men and a woman, were also there. Rosenharte sat down on the chair in front of them, wondering why he'd been summoned.

'Certain things have come to our notice, Dr Rosenharte,' said Lictenberg.

'Oh? What things?'

'Your lectures, Doktor, in particular the talk you gave at the University of Leipzig several days ago. Professor Böhme has written to us to complain about your attitude.'

'It was an aside that caused the offence, one which he wilfully misunderstood. It was nothing to do with the main body of the lecture.'

'Are we to believe the professor invented the whole incident?'

'Believe what you like, but it was a serious lecture that embodied my views and I have a right to express them whether they offend a pompous fool like Böhme or not. I invited him to debate the matter, but he was incapable of uttering anything but Party slogans.'

'We have our reputation to think of,' said Lictenberg, leaning forward. 'When you give these lectures you represent this institution and all the people who work here. You must understand that, Doktor.'

'I represent no one but myself.'

'An individualist through and through!' said the woman triumphantly.

'Not an individualist, but an individual. You wouldn't know the difference.'

Lictenberg had raised a hand. 'There's little point in continuing this discussion. The Gemäldegalerie no longer requires your service, Dr Rosenharte. Is that clear enough for you? You will leave at the end of this hearing and remove your personal possessions from your desk.'

Stunned into silence, Rosenharte moved to the door, then stopped and turned to them. 'Look around you. Barely a day goes by without a demonstration. People have had enough. The world is changing.'

Lictenberg put on a hurt expression. 'Why this sudden defiance? These are the views of a rebellious teenager!'

'Why? My brother is in Hohenschönhausen, the place where the Party crushes its opponents. He is being held without trial there and he may be dying. In his life he has never expressed anything remotely as controversial as I have just uttered in this room. That explains my change of attitude.' Without pausing he left the room and went to collect the books from his office.

HE ENTERED HIS OFFICE to find Colonel Zank standing at the window with two other men. 'What are you doing in my office?' he demanded.

'Your office?' said Zank. 'Surely it's no longer yours?'

'Until I leave it is.'

'We want to ask you some questions about your trip to Trieste,' said Zank. 'There're things that do not satisfy us. For instance, how Annalise Schering knew that you were at the restaurant by the canal.'

This threw him. 'Why are you asking this now? Surely you've got better things to do.'

'I do, that's for sure. But please answer the question.'

'I don't remember. No, wait, someone at the front desk recommended the place and I told them I would be there if anyone called for me.'

'That's odd,' said Zank. 'Because we had two people try the same thing—an experiment, you understand. They reported that the hotel recommended an entirely different place.'

'All I can say is that the man in the red and black jacket told me that it was a fine place. Maybe he got a kickback for sending people there.'

Zank's lips parted, but there was no smile. 'I don't believe you,' he said.

'Well, it's the truth.' Rosenharte turned to the bookcase and started taking books from the shelves. 'You're trying to frame me to discredit General Schwarzmeer's operation,' he continued. 'I will not be used in the internal battles of the ministry. Last time I saw the general—you were not there, of course—he expressed his pleasure with the intelligence from the West. His scientists are looking forward to the next delivery. But there won't be one unless my brother is released. You'd better be sure of what you're doing, Zank.'

'The man who died on the quay in Trieste was called Franciscek Grycko. Does that mean anything to you?'

'I had no knowledge of him. I've said that before.'

'He was once an operative of the Polish state security service,' said Zank. 'I believe the same man visited this office. How did Mr Grycko know that you were going to be in Trieste? What did he want? And how does he fit into the business of Annalise Schering? At HA II we are trying to make sense of it all, Rosenharte, and we want your help.'

'But I can't help you. You're trying to make something out of nothing when you know that all I have ever wanted is the release of my brother. I know you're the one who stands in the way of his freedom.'

Zank gave him a chilling look. 'I am merely doing the best I can to protect the state, Rosenharte, and I assure you I will find out what it is that you're hiding. Who can say how many people are involved in this plot?'

'There is no plot! I am working for General Schwarzmeer, but I will cease to cooperate if my brother is not released.'

There was a knock at the door. Another young Stasi thug said something quickly in Zank's ear. Zank nodded and moved to the door. 'I must return to Berlin,' he said. 'The rowdies are on the streets again causing trouble for tomorrow's celebrations. What a world we live in, eh?' One of the men opened the door for him. Zank faced Rosenharte. 'Oh, yes, your pleasant friend Sonja told me you made a call from the director's office two weeks ago—something you were anxious to keep secret. I have learned that it was to a Berlin number but we have experienced difficulties in tracing it. Odd that.'

Rosenharte thought quickly and looked him in the eye. 'I have been told to say nothing about this.'

'Are you saying that the number belongs to the ministry?'

'I cannot say.'

Zank considered him for a moment. 'We will continue this conversation at the earliest opportunity.'

After they had gone, Rosenharte stood staring out of the window. When Zank found out that there was no such number at Normannenstrasse, his suspicions would be confirmed. But he already had enough information to hold and interrogate him. So why didn't he? Maybe he was simply letting Rosenharte know what he knew. Maybe he was also trying to panic him into taking precipitate action.

Two things were clear: Zank hadn't managed to discredit Schwarzmeer's operation, and the Minister for State Security wasn't yet willing to abandon the hope of gaining more information about the NATO system.

He walked straight to Angelikastrasse without bothering to check if he was being followed, and rang the brass bell at the door. Within a few seconds the door had been opened by a thickset man in his early thirties with a small scar on his chin, who showed him into a little interview room on the ground floor. A couple of minutes later, Vladimir appeared.

'I thought you were away in Berlin,' said Rosenharte.

'We're leaving any second. How can I help?'

'They're moving next week. All their people will be in place in Leipzig by Monday evening. I've been told to contact a member of the BND Sunday evening at the trade fair ground.'

'And you are to take them to Kafka. You were going to tell me her name.'

'Before I do, I want to know I have your agreement about the passes. The date has been set for a week tomorrow, Saturday, October 14th.'

'What is it you want, exactly?'

'A vehicle pass, a release form for Konrad, specifying the KGB's need to question him, and two passes for the men whose names I'll supply this week.'

'I think we can do this. Saturday the 14th should be possible.'

Rosenharte thanked him, then gave him Ulrike's name and explained who she was. It troubled him greatly but he had to get Konrad out of prison.

'That's all good,' Vladimir said at length, 'and they're going to take some kind of action next week? I'll want to hear details of that the moment you learn of them. The Stasi have no hint of what's to happen?'

'They're close, but Colonel Zank hasn't made all the connections. I think they're preoccupied with what's going on. The riots at the station . . .'

'To say nothing about the demonstrations in Berlin. You should be careful in Leipzig, Dr Rosenharte. We think they will use force on Monday. Mielke means business this time. If you survive Monday, call me here, at any time.'

Rosenharte was aware that the interview had come to an end, but he had one last favour to ask of Vladimir.

He listened impatiently, but eventually agreed to help. 'Now, please go, Dr Rosenharte,' he said, 'and keep in touch.'

ALL OVER DRESDEN that night, groups of youths were gathering to jeer at the Volkspolizei, who responded by running them down and beating them. It was plain that feelings had not dampened after the mass arrests on Wednesday and Thursday. The people seemed to have lost their fear: it was as if they wanted to be attacked, to hold up the mirror to the police and show them the reality of the state now celebrating its anniversary.

Rosenharte got home late and turned on the BBC World Service news. There was a short item about the celebrations in Berlin, including a suggestion that the young people had turned it into a pro-Gorbachev demonstration shouting, 'Perestroika! Gorby help us!' A West German radio station ran an interview with Gorbachev that had been given at noon. Rosenharte heard a reporter ask, 'Do you feel threatened by the situation in Berlin?'

'No,' replied Gorbachev. 'It's nothing compared to the situation in Moscow. We are prepared for anything, and we've learned a lot too. For instance, how to initiate and carry out reform programmes and how to defend our policies. Danger threatens only those who do not react to life's challenges.'

If that wasn't an instruction to Honecker to initiate reform, he didn't know what was. The world was changing, but would it change fast enough for Konrad?

NEXT DAY he packed both his suitcases and the rucksack with everything of importance in his life, for he knew he would not return to the flat. He took his luggage down to the hallway at three in the afternoon. With up to 30,000 expected on the streets in Dresden that day he was assuming the Stasi would have no men to spare to watch him. Nevertheless he knocked on the door of the ground-floor apartment and an eager young face appeared— Willy, the son of the bakery manager. Rosenharte asked if he wanted to earn some money. The boy nodded. At three forty-five Willy left with the bags and rucksack, then Rosenharte sauntered out in the same direction, apparently unaware of the two pairs of eyes following him. Only when he rounded a bend about 100 yards from his building did he begin to run.

At the last bend he saw the black car with diplomatic plates waiting with its boot open. Beside it stood Willy, looking doubtful. Rosenharte thrust some notes into his hand, slung his luggage into the boot, then slid into the back. The car moved off into the sparse Saturday-afternoon traffic, leaving Willy to join a bus queue not far away.

'It's OK, they don't follow,' said the driver. It was the same man who had opened the door to him at Angelikastrasse. Rosenharte nevertheless stayed on the floor until they arrived at the goods yard and pulled up next to the Wartburg. A few minutes later he was travelling on the road to Leipzig.

Zank would now consider him to be on the run, and infer guilt from his disappearance. If Zank argued his case well, the minister might even abandon the whole Annalise operation. And this would not help Konrad. On the other hand, he could not help Konrad if he was followed to Leipzig; he had to remain free and unobserved for the next seven days.

As he went, he listened to his transistor radio, picking up a West German station broadcasting news bulletins every hour. Reports through the afternoon stated that spontaneous demonstrations had flared in Leipzig, Magdeburg, Karl-Marx-Stadt, Halle, Plauen and Potsdam. In Berlin thousands of arrests had been made, and nothing had been missed because so many Western journalists were present to cover Gorbachev's visit.

By the time Rosenharte slipped into the suburbs of Leipzig, he was almost convinced that the revolution had begun. The impression soon left him when he saw half a dozen blue and white buses containing hundreds of Volkspolizei parked up in a street not far from Ulrike's place. He circled her block once or twice to make sure nothing untoward awaited him there, then parked across from the wisteria gateway. Sitting in the shadows he watched the house for about an hour before knocking on Ulrike's door. No response. It hadn't occurred to him that she would be out. Cursing himself for not taking a phone number where he could have left a message, he walked back up the little brick path. At the gate he nearly ran into a tall young man who loomed from nowhere.

'Ulrike's not in,' Rosenharte said. 'Have you got any idea where she is?' The man turned. 'No.'

'Do you know if she's coming back this evening?' The man looked shifty. Rosenharte realised what he was thinking and introduced himself. 'I was hoping to catch her. It's quite important.'

He took a few paces towards Rosenharte. He was extraordinary-looking. Standing at six feet four, his hair was dyed black and cropped at the sides. On top was a streaked mohican, which ran front to back like an ancient Greek headdress, and both ears were clipped with rings and studs.

'You're her friend?' he asked softly. 'A real friend?'

'I'm not a member of the Stasi, if that is what you're asking.'

'OK, I can see you're not Stasi.' He grinned. 'I'm Kurt—Kurt Blast.'

'That's a good name.'

'That's why I chose it. It's my name. You won't find it in the Stasi files.' He looked to his left and right edgily. 'Ulrike's in Berlin at the demonstrations.'

'I see,' said Rosenharte.

'You have any cigarettes?' he asked.

Rosenharte gave him one. 'I don't think we should be talking out here,' he said and moved into the gateway.

'Where are you going to stay now?' Kurt Blast asked.

'Probably in the car. It's difficult for me to go to a hotel.'

'Maybe you can stay with me. It's dry and warm and you can pay me a few marks for the night. I'll throw in some food for a little more money.'

Rosenharte considered this. 'Are you under any kind of surveillance?'

'No, they had their fun with me long ago. They don't bother me now.'

They drove to a strange, mutilated house on the very edge of Leipzig, which had been boarded up and abandoned by the authorities. Inside, Kurt Blast had made it remarkably snug. There were two guitars hanging from hooks in the wall, a portable amplifier and neat stacks of records and books.

He turned out to be a rather thoughtful man and a diligent cook. He made Rosenharte a meal of soup and risotto, which they washed down with Marzen, the amber-red beer sold during *Oktoberfest* in the West. Later, Rosenharte bedded down quite comfortably on the couch.

Next morning he made arrangements to leave his things with Kurt and went in search of Ulrike. Overnight he had been gripped by the morbid certainty that she was being interrogated. He needed to find out where she was.

He went to her home twice more. Both times he knocked and got no answer but the process took an hour or so each time because he made sure the place wasn't being watched. Before he knew it the day had disappeared and he had to start making his way to the trade fair ground.

He arrived at the gates a little early, so he stood by the entrance and lit a cigarette. He was there just five minutes before a large truck pulled up and began to reverse into the opening so that it could turn. The door was opened by one of the Germans Rosenharte had seen in Griswald's apartment in Berlin, who offered him a hand and pulled him in. The doors banged shut and as the truck drove off one of the men guided Rosenharte to a crate and gave him some black coffee. Eventually the truck pulled off the road, then came to a stop. Both doors were opened, and standing in front of a car's headlights were Robert Harland and the short figure of Macy Harp.

'What the hell are you doing here?' Rosenharte said, jumping down. 'Isn't this too dangerous for you?'

'Things have changed quite a bit,' said Harland, putting out his hand. 'But I think we're OK. Look, I have something for you.' He took a picture from his wallet and handed it over. 'That's Else and your two nephews in their new home. They arrived on Thursday morning. They seem to like it a lot.'

Rosenharte slipped it into his wallet and looked around. There were eight of them, including Harland and Harp. 'What are you . . .?' he started.

'We think tomorrow is the ideal time for us.'

'Abu Jamal isn't here.'

'He's been here all along; at least since last week when our German friends moved in to do the recce.' He pulled a large black and white photograph from out of his pocket and gave it to Rosenharte. He saw a middle-aged man with a comb-over sitting in a wicker chair. Ulrike was standing a little apart from him, gazing somewhat vacantly towards the camera's lens.

'That was taken last week. We've now got a mini-camera in the garden which we can operate remotely,' said Harland.

'So, how does this concern me? You have all you need.'

'We want you to get her out of the villa before we make our move.'

'She's there now? I was told she was in Berlin.' He shook his head. 'She was quite specific about Abu Jamal not being allowed into the country until the fortieth anniversary was over.'

'Maybe she wanted to keep us at arm's length to allow her to stay in Leipzig; after all, we know that's her priority.'

'It means she'll have to leave, then. Does she know that?'

'We haven't been able to get to her to warn her. That's why we need you. You see we have to move tomorrow night.'

'Going tomorrow will put her under suspicion immediately.'

Harland shook his head regretfully. 'We have to move against Abu Jamal now. There's talk of him blowing up the Paris Métro. This man is a serious threat to Western security and I'm afraid that sweeps all other considerations aside. Besides, the GDR won't make a fuss, believe me. If they kick up about the snatch, it's as good as admitting their involvement.'

'Why can't you wait until Wednesday or Thursday?' asked Rosenharte.

'Because we've decided to deploy the same team to extract your brother. And the overriding reason to move now is that the Arab's health is fading: we need to keep him alive so that we can find out what he has planned— where, when and with whom. You understand that.'

'So what do you want me to do?'

'Warn Kafka so that she can leave the city.'

Rosenharte laughed bitterly. 'You've heard the slogan "We're staying here!" She all but invented it.' He paused. 'Anyway, do you imagine the Stasi guards will allow me just to walk in and speak to her?'

'There are a couple at the front,' said Harland. 'They watch the house but rarely go inside. You'll go through the garden. There's minimal risk.'

'That I don't believe.' He looked at Macy Harp. 'And are these people to help with my brother?'

Harland nodded. 'We think a team of three: a driver and two men to make the pick-up. What's our cover story?'

'A request for Konrad to be interviewed by the KGB at the Karlshorst HQ.'

'And these passes—where are you getting them from?'

'That's my secret. But they're the real thing.'

Harland handed him a small bottle of brandy. 'You realise that this whole thing is about to come off? We're about to beat the bastards.'

Rosenharte handed the bottle back, feeling the warmth in his stomach. 'Getting Konrad out is my only definition of victory.'

'What are you going to do after tomorrow? You know you will have to lie low whatever Ulrike decides to do. You could do worse than come here.' Harland swept the beam of a torch over a squat single-storey farm building.

'The beauty of it is that it is totally surrounded by trees, it's got about three ways in and out. And you can see for miles around. We'll leave the food for you and some other supplies.'

'I don't know where we are.'

'I'll show you on a map. That reminds me to tell you where we want to pick you up on Saturday morning as well.'

They went to one of the cars and Macy Harp showed him their position. Then he got out a large-scale map of East Berlin. 'You see this church just off Kopenickerstrasse? You have to be there from six thirty onwards at the back of the church. You got that? Saturday at six thirty,' he said emphatically. 'And no passengers. OK?'

'How will we leave the GDR?'

'We'd prefer to keep that to ourselves,' said Harland quickly. 'What about the passes? How are you going to get them to us?'

Rosenharte thought. 'There's a train—the Dresden to Berlin service. It stops at six o'clock at Berlin-Schönfeld. That Friday evening I will board the first carriage, carrying the passes in a plain white plastic bag. At ten past six I'll go to the toilet. I will leave the bag in the towel disposal bin.'

Harland nodded. 'We need a back-up plan. Trains get cancelled.'

'The newsstand at the Ostbahnhof. I will be there at at seven thirty. I will have a copy of *Neues Deutschland*. The passes will be in that. We will have to contrive to make a swap.'

Harland nodded again. 'So, let's talk about tomorrow and how you're going to get Kafka out of the villa.'

ROSENHARTE SCALED the wall with help from two BND officers and slipped into the shadows of an overgrown garden that was bordered on three sides by shrubs. He could make out the sliding door at the rear of the villa which led onto a small patio area. If surveillance reports from the previous days were anything to go by, Ulrike would rise early, shower, make a light breakfast and read for about an hour before the Arab stirred from his room and began the painfully slow business of his own toilet. At some stage before he appeared she usually went out onto the patio. That would be Rosenharte's only chance to speak to her because at eight thirty a nurse arrived.

He remained for an hour crouching in the bushes, anxiety nipping at his insides. A glimmer of dawn showed in the east and began to fill the garden with a greyish light. He noticed a movement behind a curtain on the first floor, then Ulrike's face appeared at the window. A few minutes later, wearing jeans and a mauve sweater, she opened the sliding door and came out. When she was about twenty feet from him, he called out to her softly. She seemed not to hear him, but stepped onto the grass and walked towards him.

'What are you doing here?' she hissed without looking down.

'They're going to take him today. You have to leave.'

'Go!' she said. 'I'm not leaving until I'm ready.'

'There's nothing you can do to stop them. Please, Ulrike, come now.'

She moved a few steps closer, glanced back at the house and then sank down beside him. 'The Arab isn't even here. He went for treatment at the hospital last night. He won't be back until late morning or early afternoon.'

Rosenharte wondered what else the surveillance team had missed.

'I don't understand why you have to wait for him to return,' he said. 'It's Monday. It would be natural for you to go to work.'

'I'm waiting for information. A contact will visit this afternoon and we'll know if they plan to use violence tonight. That's more important than this.'

'Forget your contact, Ulrike. We already know they're going to use force. Everyone knows it. There are army trucks everywhere.'

'Don't lecture me about what's going on in this city,' she said fiercely. 'This is my city. Your British friends are jeopardising everything. Did you give them my name?'

'Of course. I had to. You know what matters to me is getting my brother out of Hohenschönhausen and sending Else to the West. That was the deal.'

She turned to him, her expression furious. Rosenharte wondered why he'd found her attractive. 'You go back and tell them that they move only when I say so. Today is the day. Everything will be won or lost today. Nothing else matters. They must not interfere.'

'I must be able to explain to them why this contact is so important.'

She glanced towards the house. Nothing was moving. 'At the institute where I work there's a professor. He has a close relationship with one of the highest members of the Party—Egon Krenz, the man who they say will succeed Honecker. They're close. The professor is driving to Berlin to argue that military force will be counterproductive. Krenz will pay attention.'

'So what's to stop you learning this information by phone?'

'Here? On this phone? Don't be stupid. I repeat, I instigated this operation and I will decide when they move on the Arab.'

He shrugged. 'How will you let us know?'

'I'll leave a white towel on the back of his chair. They can move then and only then. Is that understood?'

He nodded.

'And then, Rudi, I will meet you at the church door. Now go.'

She looked at him for a few seconds then walked back inside.

Rosenharte waited a little while, then crawled back into the shrubs and, using the trunk of a lilac tree, climbed the fence and jumped down.

AFTER DEBRIEFING Rosenharte, Robert Harland returned to the back of the truck. Macy Harp and another West German sat in the front wearing overalls, listening to the watchers call in from their positions around the park.

By three in the afternoon there was still no sign of Abu Jamal and they began to fear that he would remain in hospital overnight.

At four the watchers reported that the villa received a visitor, a young woman in a headscarf and a dark raincoat, who showed her identity card to the two Stasi men at the front. Harland knew it must be Kafka's contact.

The woman hurried away shortly afterwards. Through the window, Kafka was observed picking up the phone, speaking for a few seconds and replacing the receiver. A minute later she was hurrying towards the centre of Leipzig.

'Fuck,' said Macy Harp. 'No white towel; no Arab. We might as well go and join their effin' peace demo.'

THE MIDDLE PART of Rosenharte's day was spent talking to Kurt Blast. In the afternoon, they left the house and walked briskly to a bus-stop. On the way, Rosenharte spotted a phone box and dialled Vladimir's number in Dresden. A Russian answered but it wasn't Vladimir. Without waiting to be put through he said, 'This is Rudi. It's all happening in Leipzig this evening. You understand?' and hung up.

They took the bus and arrived outside the hospital on the southeast of the city at 3.30 and headed for the Georgi Ring, the road that encircled the heart of Leipzig. Kurt had done his best to tone down his appearance by cutting an inch from his mohican and removing some of the rings from his ears.

At 4.15 they began to walk slowly towards the Nikolaikirche. It wasn't just the absence of rush-hour noise—the buses and trams having been taken out of service—or the massive presence of the security forces; there was something profoundly different about Leipzig which Rosenharte likened to the peculiar heaviness that silences birds before an electrical storm. The people now making sombrely for the churches had evidently taken all their courage in their hands, because it was clear that something would be settled that night, one way or the other.

They reached the Nikolaikirche and found Ulrike standing just inside the door, gesturing to a group of men. Her eyes lit up when she saw Rosenharte. She continued talking for a few minutes, then broke away, wishing them all good luck and peace.

'It's over,' she said as they hurried up the stairway, her fingers digging into his arm. 'Don't you see? It's coming to an end.'

He said nothing because he was convinced still that it would crumble in the first volley of gunfire. But he smiled a truce.

They climbed to the first gallery and when they had settled in the beautiful old painted pews she popped her head over the parapet. 'Look, the entire Party membership is down there. That's why we can't sit there.'

'What's going to happen?' whispered Rosenharte.

She bent towards him, her eyes darting around the congregation.

'My informant says Krenz was persuaded by the argument. But there's a rumour that the orders were given out by the Minister for State Security anyway. These may have been countermanded, but we don't know for certain. We do know that the Stasi are all carrying weapons.'

He moved closer so he could speak into her ear. 'What about the Arab?'

'He hadn't returned by the time I left, so I guess your friends are just going to have to wait. But that's not our problem now, is it? We've done what we can. That part of my life is finished.'

'I'm glad,' he said. She had deceived him about the presence of Abu Jamal in Leipzig and her attendance on him. What else was she concealing?

Rosenharte scanned the congregation for Biermeier and Zank, but didn't see them. Maybe they were directly below him.

All eyes had turned to the front and a sudden calm settled over the congregation as one of two pastors got up, greeted the packed church and began to read. 'Jesus said, "Love your enemies," not "Down with your opponents." Jesus said, "Many who are now first will be last," and not, "Everything stays the same."'

It seemed a little simple to Rosenharte but it was the essence of the protest. Prayers followed, then a preacher named Wendell spoke. 'The reforms will come if we allow the spirit of peace, calm and tolerance to enter us. The spirit of peace must go beyond these walls. Take great care you are not rude to the police officers. Be careful that you don't sing songs or chant slogans that could provoke the authorities.'

It might just work, thought Rosenharte.

AT 5.10 P.M., one of the watchers on the far side of the villa reported that a car had drawn up and a man in an overcoat had been helped from the front seat. He wore a cap and carried newspapers and a folder under his arm. A nurse accompanied him inside and stayed for about half an hour, during which time she made him a sandwich and a glass of milk.

An identification was made in the interval between the man lowering himself heavily to the chair and the nurse walking to the sliding window and drawing the curtains before leaving. He was still wearing his cap and a straggly beard covered his chin, but it was undoubtedly Abu Jamal.

At 5.55, Harp and Harland transferred to a dirty cream-coloured Lada saloon while a BND agent named Johann Horst climbed into the driving seat of the truck. Both vehicles rolled to the end of the street without turning on their engines or lights. Harland listened to the watchers reporting in for the last time. Four of the BND team were in the garden at the rear of the villa.

Harland nodded to Harp, who flashed his headlight at the truck, which moved off ahead of them. 'Right, let's get on with it, shall we?'

A FEW SECONDS before the end of the prayers, they slid from their seats and went down the stairway so that when the final blessing was over they were at the main entrance before the rest of the congregation. As the doors opened a sea of faces greeted them, many lit in the dusk by candles shielded in people's hands. Ulrike had told him about this—if the people were holding candles there could be no mistaking their peaceful intentions. A cheer went up and as the congregation spilled out into the square the rush of benevolence made even the grim Party loyalists smile.

Ulrike took all this in with an ecstatic, slightly manic grin, then linked arms with Rosenharte and Kurt and they surged through the crowd towards what appeared to be the head of the march. The demonstration moved off northwards from the Karl-Marx-Platz towards Leipzig's main station. The aim was to march round the four sides of the Georgi Ring without being stopped—and so achieve the symbolic encirclement of the city.

'What are you going to do afterwards?' asked Rosenharte.

272 | HENRY PORTER

'Celebrate,' she said, as though he was being stupid.

He bent down to her. 'But if they've removed our friend, life is going to become very difficult for you. You have to hide.'

'We'll see.' Her expression was so exultant that he wondered whether she was absorbing anything he said.

She took his hand and looked at it, then let her gaze travel up to his face. 'When you arrived at the Nikolaikirche I told you that everything was over. If the foreigners managed to take our friend, which I imagine they did, then it is over. My life of deceit is over. And with this demonstration,' she gestured at the crowd with her free hand, 'everything changes. Where are the Stasi now? Nowhere. Things have changed for good tonight.'

'Don't talk too soon. Violence is still a possibility, and it doesn't mean you're safe. When they find the Arab missing, they'll know you had something to do with it. That's why Zank has been in Leipzig. We must hide.'

She looked up into his eyes, gently shook her head. 'I'm staying here.'

'Then I will go without you.'

'If you want. But you must stay tonight and drink to our victory and remember every minute for when you return to Dresden. Your city will have its own moment too, but we have set the pattern.'

'I won't be returning to Dresden. They've fired me from the gallery.'

'You told me you had some kind of protection.'

'What protection was that?' he asked.

'You said someone squared the director of the gallery so you could be absent for long periods.'

He shook his head. 'Ulrike,' he said firmly, 'I didn't tell you that.'

'I'm sure you did. But if you didn't, I must have imagined it,' she said nonchalantly.

The rest of the march passed in a pleasant blur for Rosenharte. He relished the sudden affection that sprang up between strangers all around them. Sometime after midnight they said good night to Kurt. Rosenharte told him he would collect his things and the car in the morning and they set off for Ulrike's place. She put her hand through his arm and looked up at him occasionally and smiled, but they did not speak of the Arab nor of Konrad, nor of the extraordinary events of that night. Eventually, they reached the wisteria gateway and walked to her door. As she placed the key in the lock, she said to him, 'I have never seen you smile, not properly. You are always holding something in reserve.'

'You could say that about everyone.'

She wrinkled her nose and pushed the door, pausing to listen.

'I'm beginning to think you had the same training as me.'

'You're right. I did. But like you, I didn't fit.'

'You're telling me you were in the Stasi?'

She turned to him with a look of amusement. 'Who do you think gave me all this training in languages? My father was in the diplomatic service, for goodness' sake. I thought you had put all that together. It wasn't so difficult.'

Rosenharte shrugged and said he hadn't.

She laughed. 'Maybe you're not the sharpest knife in the drawer after all.'

They went inside. She switched on a table lamp and went to her little kitchen to find a drink and some glasses and returned clanking a bottle of red wine. She opened the wine and came to rest her head on his chest, handing him a glass at the same time. He took a mouthful and put his arm round her. 'When did you stop working for the Stasi?' he asked.

'I lasted just three years before I was thrown out. That was a long time ago.'

'Why?' He felt her stiffen.

'I had a baby . . . a baby who died. But I wasn't married and, well, I wasn't in love with the father and he wanted nothing to do with it. They told me to get rid of it but I refused and they got rid of me.' Her head remained on his chest and she spoke without looking up at him.

'Did you sleep with the Arab?'

She inhaled deeply. 'No, by the time he started coming to Leipzig and I became his regular companion, he was so debilitated from the years of drinking and cocaine that he wasn't up to it. He liked my company.'

'If he's been taken tonight, they'll come after you. You're an obvious suspect. How else would the West know where and when to find him?'

'If they've done it intelligently, no one will know where he's gone. He's a free agent. He comes and goes as he pleases.'

He put down his glass and slipped his hands under her shirt, trying to engage her eyes while feeling the suppleness of her back. 'Ulrike, you're in danger. They know who you are and where you live.'

She put her finger to his lips. 'Nothing's going to happen tonight. They won't check on him until morning.' She began to kiss his neck. 'Take me to bed,' she whispered.

He cupped her face in his hands and looked into her eyes. 'Seeing you this morning at the villa and then later at the church was like meeting two completely different people. You change so often that I wonder if you have multiple personalities.'

'You're confusing personality with behaviour,' she said sharply. 'Anyway, let me assure you that you're with the real me now. This is me.'

'How can I tell? I feel there's so much that you're keeping from me,' he said. 'Why Kafka? Why did you choose the name Kafka?'

'Because he predicted the world we live in today: the secrecy, the men who ruin a person's life with rumours and lies, the mysterious persecutions, the senselessness of it all. He got it exactly right.' She paused. 'Drink with me, Rudi, to the end of the lying old crows and the beginning of us.'

He picked up his glass. 'To the most puzzling person that I've ever met.'

She shook her head vigorously. 'I just know what I think about things. And this—you and me—is right.' She took a mouthful then put down her glass and came to him. She led them to her bedroom, then turned and pulled her shirt off in one motion, which made her hair shimmer with static. Without seeming to notice she undid her bra and removed it. 'Hey, look, you're smiling!' she exclaimed. 'Is my body really that funny?'

He held her lightly above her waist. 'No, it's beautiful. I'm smiling at your static. I've never seen anyone with their own electricity supply before.'

'Yes, but you smiled, Rudi, and you look a different person when you smile. I love that.' She clasped her hands together. 'Wasn't tonight wonderful? Can you believe what we witnessed? It was a miracle, wasn't it?'

He nodded, then undressed and sat down on the bed. He watched her draw the curtains and switch on a lamp. She slipped off her jeans and pants and stood before him to let his eyes run over her body. He began to kiss her, his hands not exploring, but rather gauging the warmth and shape of her body. It moved him like no other experience with a woman, made him love humanity and its vulnerability. He said something of this and she mocked him, told him that he didn't have to articulate every absurd thought that came into his head; nevertheless it seemed to please her.

'This is different, isn't it?' she whispered and he nodded in reply.

ROSENHARTE WOKE with a start, aware that someone was in the room. A man was calling Ulrike's name and fumbling his way to her bed in the dark. He lifted his head from the pillow, cursing that he hadn't made Ulrike leave the night before. Then she stirred and sat bolt upright.

'Who . . .? What do you want?' she hissed back.

'You must leave at once,' said the voice.

She climbed over Rosenharte, taking a sheet with her, and approached the outline of the man.

'Who's with you?' the voice demanded. 'For Christ's sake, have you got someone there?' Rosenharte was struggling to process what he was hearing because he was now sure that Biermeier was in the room. But instead of arresting them, he was warning them of an impending danger. The light came on. Biermeier was standing in the middle of the room. 'If he's found here, we'll all be shot,' he said when he saw Rosenharte. 'Come on.'

'Tell me what's happened,' said Ulrike, calmly picking up her jeans.

'The Arab's gone. Zank has been found unconscious in the safe house by the park. He was drugged and tied up. When he comes round all hell will break loose. You must go into hiding.'

'What was he doing at the villa?' she asked.

'I don't know. He must have got wind of something. But the fact that he was there and someone tied up and drugged him means that he's made discoveries that we never thought he would.' He picked up her shirt and threw it at her. 'You've got to get out of here. You too, Rosenharte. I'm giving you this chance because you're with Ulrike.'

Rosenharte began to protest about Konrad.

'Forget your brother. Leave by the window at the back where I came in. If you don't, in five minutes I will come back and kill you both.'

He vanished into the dark passageway and a couple of seconds later they heard the window in the sitting room open. Ulrike started to stuff a rucksack with her possessions, while Rosenharte got dressed.

'The car's at Kurt's place,' he said.

'That's good. There can be no danger of them following us from here. Go to the kitchen, put as much food as you can find in the shopping bag. Pasta, eggs, oil, candles—anything. We'll need it if we're going to stay hidden.'

He tipped the box where she kept her provisions into a big canvas bag and added a pan, torch, cups, knives, and all the alcohol he could find.

Ulrike eliminated all trace of his being there before turning the lights off in the sitting room. Then, heaving her rucksack through the window, she jumped down into the garden. Rosenharte followed with the bag and pressed the window shut.

Not far from the house she told Rosenharte to wait while she fetched the car. She left him with the bags in the cover of some laurel bushes. He began to consider the implications of Biermeier's appearance in the apartment. Clearly he was involved with Ulrike in passing the intelligence about Abu Jamal to the West. Rosenharte thought back to the hotel in Trieste and realised that while checking the microphone and transmitter Biermeier had sabotaged it because he thought Rosenharte would give everything away in the first encounter with Annalise's substitute. That's why no one had heard the Pole blurt out the name in the last moments of his life. How much more of the last few weeks could be explained by his involvement? Was he working with the British? How did the two Poles fit in? Was Schwarzmeer involved as well?

In the centre of this mystery was Ulrike. Now he understood how Ulrike knew that the gallery in Dresden had been squared about his absences. Perhaps some kind of struggle was going on in the Stasi between the forces of crude decency as represented by Biermeier, and Zank's unwavering zealotry. When confronted with the evil of Abu Jamal's plans, Biermeier had decided to do something about it. Rosenharte couldn't help but admire his courage and his planning. Yet the fact was that Biermeier and Ulrike had used him and Konrad ruthlessly. If Zank really began to see all the connections, it would put Konrad in terrible danger.

He was beginning to wonder whether Ulrike would ever return, when the little beige Wartburg trundled into the road. She flung open the passenger door and yelled, 'I had to get your stuff from Kurt's apartment. It took for ever to wake him.' He slung their bags in the back and climbed in.

'Where're we going?' she asked, pulling an old dogeared fold-out map from beneath the driving seat and handing it to him.

'Go southwest. Take minor roads.'

As soon as they were out of Leipzig, Ulrike's eyes left the road for a second. 'I guess you want an explanation?' she said.

'Don't bother,' he said sharply, 'unless you're going to tell me the truth.'

'I couldn't tell you about Biermeier's involvement before. You would've reacted differently to him and Zank would have spotted it in your eyes.'

'How long has this been going on, this private operation to expose the Stasi's use of Abu Jamal? Was it Biermeier's idea?'

She nodded. 'Nearly two years—for as long as he's had medical treatment in Leipzig. Biermeier set me up as Abu Jamal's mistress. Though what I told you before was true. He's incapable of physical love. He had put someone close to Misha Lomieko and he needed someone next to Abu Jamal.

'The Party had no idea what Abu Jamal was doing—the extent of what he and Misha planned, although it was the Party's machinery and money that enabled him. Biermeier wrote one memorandum to Schwarzmeer and was told it wasn't his business, so he decided to get evidence. This he fed into the information chain anonymously, but still nothing happened. That was in the spring. So he—no, *we*—decided that there was only one way of stopping the Arab. In May we began to plan how we could do that.'

'When did you think of using me?'

'Later. Early June. We wanted someone who could visit Leipzig legitimately. Biermeier did some research after I suggested you and discovered you had a very interesting past.'

'You mean he went into my Stasi files?'

'He didn't manage to pull all of them. Just the one that said you had been in the HVA. The rest are in some ultra-secret section. We wondered why?'

'So you must have known about Konrad; you knew I had a brother they'd imprisoned once before?'

She shook her head. 'Only when he was arrested. Rudi, I want you to know that I'm truly sorry. I wish I could change what's happened.'

Rosenharte wasn't listening. He saw his brother's drained, lifeless features in the hospital wing at Hohenschönhausen. There were just four days before they would enter the prison with Vladimir's fake documentation, and for the thousandth time he prayed Konnie would hang on till then.

Ulrike knew what he was thinking. 'I'll do anything I can to help you.'

In the cold light of day he knew that he could not trust her with the plan. Now that they were on the run, with Zank not far behind, the less she knew the better. He changed the subject. 'The two Poles—where do they fit in?'

'We didn't know who they were. The man in Trieste very nearly spoilt all our plans. We couldn't work it out.'

There was only one other solution Rosenharte could think of: the poles were somehow connected to Vladimir. Though Vladimir insisted he knew nothing of the operation in Trieste, Rosenharte was now inclined to disbelieve him.

About thirty miles from Leipzig they filled up with petrol and bought two cups of black coffee. Then Rosenharte took the wheel. After trying several tracks, he found a turning which he thought looked promising because recent tyre ruts had been left by a large truck. They glimpsed part of a wooden roof, at which point he pulled up and turned the car round so that it faced the direction they had just come. They got out and approached the top of a hillock through some trees. The roads leading to the farmhouse came from four directions, each one hidden from the others. If they kept watch, they would stand a good chance of escape were they to be cornered there.

The house was in worse repair than Rosenharte remembered from his night visit. They unpacked their food and a few other items from the car, then concealed it in some bushes. Rosenharte suggested they make a meal in the open rather than use the kitchen stove. That way he could keep an eye on the amount of smoke they were producing. He made a fire using dry kindling and they sat sharing a bottle of beer and devouring the contents of several cans heated in pans. Rosenharte dispersed the smoke by fanning it with a piece of board.

He knew very well that Ulrike was still hiding a lot from him, but unless this had a direct relevance to Konrad, he wasn't interested. The only thing that mattered now was collecting the documents from Vladimir, getting to Berlin and handing them over to the British.

'I find myself in an odd position,' he told her. 'I've fallen for someone who's lied to me about the most important thing in my life.' He looked into her eyes. 'If there's anything you know that is relevant to Konrad, I want to hear it now, or I will not answer for my actions.'

She shook her head and said there was nothing more. After a moment's silence, he said, 'Come with me to the West when I take Konrad out. You'll be welcomed as a hero now that they've got the Arab.'

'One day, maybe. But for now I am staying here. I want to see it through. Last night was just the beginning. We have to keep up the pressure.'

He knew she would never be persuaded and when it began to spot with rain they went inside the farmhouse and drank beer at the table, keeping an eye on the tracks and the road across the fields to the north. Very little traffic passed on this road, and in the fields there was no sign of activity.

When night fell, Rosenharte got the old cast-iron stove burning and made a meal of pasta. They drank one of the two bottles of wine they had and toasted recent events. She sat down on their makeshift bed and began to undress in the light from the open mouth of the stove. Rosenharte watched her, then did likewise and held her, seeing a look of wonder mixed with uncertainty in her eyes. They slept until midnight when they both awoke to the sound of a phone ringing. Rosenharte went to investigate and found a telephone inside a cupboard under the stairs. He picked up the handset.

'Is that Prince?'

'Yes.' Rosenharte recognised Harland's voice.

'The news is very good. The package proved more than we expected. We're very pleased. Everything's set for Friday. But during the removal we were disturbed by certain parties and we now believe the situation's extremely volatile. You understand what I'm saying? We want you to make sure Kafka comes with you.'

'We know about the problem. That's why we're here.'

'Glad you've taken action. Our feeling is that the parties who disturbed us will now understand all the implications. They'll put things together.'

'Understood.'

'So we'll see you at the place you specified on the day you specified. If you don't show, we'll take it that it's off.'

'Agreed,' said Rosenharte.

'Pass on our congratulations and thanks to Kafka.'

Before he hung up, Rosenharte asked whether they could use the phone, and if so what codes they should use to dial a number in the GDR. After giving him the codes Harland said, 'Keep your calls short, and don't use the phone continuously at the same location unless you're about to move. We'd like the set back, so bring it with you to our meeting.'

Rosenharte replaced the handset and wrote the codes on his hand.

THEY ROSE EARLY the next day, stiff and cold. Rosenharte made a drink of beef stock for Ulrike, who perched on the table, blowing steam from her cup.

'You make the call, then we should go,' she said.

She started picking up things from the floor and packing them into the two bags they had brought from the car. Rosenharte returned to the phone and dialled Vladimir's number as instructed. Vladimir picked up. 'Yes?'

'It's me—Rudi. Did you get my message that everything was happening on Monday night? It all went as planned.'

'Yes,' he said. 'What kind of telephone are you using? It sounds different.'

Rosenharte read off the name Inmarsat.

'We shouldn't speak long on this phone.'

'Have you got the papers I asked for?'

Vladimir hesitated. 'There may be a problem. Call me later on an ordinary telephone. I can't speak now.' There was a click as he hung up.

Rosenharte replaced the receiver feeling troubled, but he decided to put

Vladimir's manner down to routine cautiousness. He unplugged the phone from the electricity supply and placed the phone on top of the bags ready to take out to the car. Ulrike was staring out of the window.

'What's the matter?' he asked.

'I don't remember more than a couple of cars passing on that stretch of road yesterday, but I've just seen a van and three cars pass in the last minute.' She motioned him over. 'And is that a vehicle parked by those trees in the distance, or am I seeing things in the mist?'

Rosenharte cursed. 'We've got to get out of here. They must have picked up the phone call last night.'

A minute or two later they were crab-walking to the car with the bags. Rosenharte opened the driver's door and beckoned Ulrike to climb across into the passenger seat, then he gently pulled the door to. Releasing the handbrake, he nosed the car onto the track with almost no sound. At the bottom of the hillock he turned the ignition key and hit the accelerator.

In a few seconds they reached the golden cover of the great beech forest and were heading for somewhere that Rosenharte knew would be the very last place the Stasi would search for them.

HARLAND TOOK no part in the interrogation of Abu Jamal. A team from London was flown in to the military base sixty miles from the BND headquarters at Munich-Pullach. As well as the SIS and BND officers, the CIA had conjured a dozen antiterrorism and Middle East specialists to comb through the documents taken from the villa.

Two men had been picked up, one in Vienna and the other in Italy, and now that the identities of Abu Jamal's main contacts were known, the embassies of six nations had been alerted across the Middle East to pay special attention to the comings and goings at East German missions, and to the movement of known Stasi operatives. Harland's stock was high in London and he had received a congratulatory note from the Chief of SIS. He went to seek out Alan Griswald, whom he hadn't seen since he got back from Leipzig, and found him in a corridor of one of the low wooden buildings, reading a magazine.

'Hey Bobby, that was a wonderful operation. Just beautiful.'

Harland nodded his appreciation.

'Is he talking yet?'

'Not much, but we got his address book, a fake passport or two and, most important, papers relating to the bank accounts. It's all there.'

'You know, Bobby, we've had formal contact with the Russians on this. They were aware of the situation and had a very good estimate of Abu Jamal's plans. And get this—they knew when and where you were going to snatch him, and didn't inform the Stasi. We took that as a sign of their good faith and had a little talk yesterday.'

'And . . .?' Harland knew Griswald enough to know that there was more.

'Well, we think that your man Rosenharte told them everything.'

'That makes sense,' said Harland. 'He's managed to get some passes into Hohenschönhausen for Saturday morning which only the Russians could supply. He did a deal. That was very smart of him.'

'Yes, there's a KGB man in Dresden who he's been talking to, and you're right—they're helping him.'

'So what's going on?'

'There's been some pretty high-level contact with the Soviets on terrorism for a couple of months now. You see, for the past fifteen years we've been pushing the idea that every bad thing that came out of the Mid East was the Soviets' fault. They're kind of pissed about that. Gorbachev has decided to show they're whiter than white. They're really helping now.'

Griswald looked left and right along the corridor. 'Let's take a walk, Bobby,' he said. 'I need to see the daylight.'

They left through a door where a couple of armed US military policemen stood guard. Griswald said, 'Because I like you, Bobby, I'm going to tell you something interesting. The other side have got someone in here. A senior BND officer is reporting straight to Schwarzmeer.'

'Jesus, which one?'

'The woman sitting in on the interrogation, Dr Lisl Voss.'

'Their chief analyst! Do they know?'

'We just told them. That's really why I'm here.'

'Does she know that Kafka and Prince are still in the East?'

'Well, that's why I'm telling you *entre nous*. I'd hate to see you end up in Hohenschönhausen, Bobby. The BND don't know what you're planning in Berlin, so you can use Voss to your advantage, perhaps.'

'How?'

Griswald grinned. 'It's simple: we let her know that the two people responsible for the operation against Abu Jamal are being brought to the West at the moment. That way the Stasi will stop looking for them.' His expression became serious. 'And make no mistake, when Zank found you at the villa it was a racing certainty that he would put the whole thing together.'

'You're saying that he knows all that bullshit in Trieste with Annalise and the extraction of Abu Jamal are one and the same thing? How could he?'

'Believe me, he does. The Stasi know the disks are baloney and that they've been had.' He put his hand on Harland's shoulder. 'Still, you're riding high and you've got permission to get Konrad Rosenharte. But don't get caught. We don't want to have to swap you for Abu Jamal.'

Harland looked across to a stand of pine trees. 'So, let me get this straight. Lisl Voss is passing them everything we're learning here.'

'Fortunately she has been involved in just one part of the interrogation. She doesn't know about the documents you found and she's ignorant of the methods used in this exfiltration. So you see there's a real good opportunity to mislead the GDR while the West Germans build their case against her with phone taps and the usual surveillance. It's a gift.'

'So who's going to do this?'

'You are. When they break for lunch, you join them and let it be known that Prince and Kafka are due to arrive in the West. She'll be wetting herself to make the call to her controller to tell the Stasi that the Arab isn't talking. At the same time she will let them know that Rosenharte and Kafka are out.'

'You don't think this will jeopardise the brother's situation?'

'Look, I can't tell you how they're gonna react, but I do know that you can help your operation immeasurably by doing this. The Stasi are in chaos and they'll be thankful that the Arab isn't talking and that they've got time to get their act together to distance themselves from any fallout.'

'How long are the West Germans going to let Dr Voss run?'

'They gotta get the evidence to make charges stick. So my guess is that they'll wait for a week or two.' He punched Harland on the arm. 'Off you go, sport. I'm going to catch my ride to Berlin. You stay safe now, Bobby.'

ROSENHARTE WATCHED the blackbird wipe its beak on the side of a branch, then straighten and sing for a few moments before dropping into the air.

They were in the car waiting for the dark. Ulrike watched him watching the bird. 'When did you become interested in birds?' she asked.

'When Konnie and I were boys, I suppose, but it wasn't until I was in my forties that I really came to love them—their defiance of gravity, the mystery of migration and their sudden reappearance in the spring. Fascinating.'

'You said "when we were boys", as though you did all your thinking with your brother.'

'I suppose that's right. My interests were Konrad's, and vice versa.'

'Like having another self.'

'Yes.'

'But you must have had arguments, like all children?'

'We did, but intellectually Konrad always beat me and when I won, well, he would usually make me feel so guilty that I would concede in the end.' He smiled. 'Should we be going? It's nearly dark.'

They had already passed through the village once and had noticed that the public phone by the church was not overlooked by any houses. They parked on the far side of the church and Rosenharte approached the phone booth via an alley without street lighting. He dialled the number and Vladimir came on the line.

'I'm using a public phone,' said Rosenharte.

'Good, that's good. Thank you.' His voice was different. Hesitant.

'So is everything arranged as we agreed?'

'There is a problem,' said Vladimir. 'I'm sorry to be the one to break this to you, but your brother has died. He died of natural causes—a heart attack—the day after you saw him.'

Rosenharte couldn't react.

'Rudi, are you there?'

He was doing all he could to remain on his feet.

'Yes, I'm here,' he said slowly.

'They kept it from you because they wanted you to work for them,' continued Vladimir in his factual monotone. 'They needed the third delivery. It seems that he died after composing that letter to you. They're very angry at being fooled by these disks. They are prepared to do anything to harm you, Rudi. You have to cross the border tonight. Do you understand?'

'Yes.' He fought to keep his voice normal. 'What happened to his body? Where did they bury him?'

Vladimir coughed. 'Rudi, I'm afraid they cremated your brother a few days later. It's said that they tried to contact his wife, but that she'd already fled to the West. I have no reason to disbelieve this.'

Rosenharte's rational part was functioning, like a wounded animal still running on adrenaline. 'So, there's no proof that he was killed by them?'

'Ultimately, no. But I believe my source on this. He's always reliable.' He stopped. 'I'm sorry for you. Truly, you have my deepest condolences.'

Losing his composure, Rosenharte muttered something and Vladimir said goodbye. The line went dead. Rosenharte sank to a squatting position still holding the receiver, then he let go of himself completely.

HE GOT DRUNK on the bottle of Goldi brandy Ulrike had put in the back of the car, and spoke without stopping because it meant he didn't have to think. The talk was automatic, a free association of tales from his boyhood about school, their hide-out on the lake, the first girls who came their way. He even laughed in the hour or so it took to travel to the place where he knew they would never be found, a place he now also had an urgent need to see. Ulrike followed his directions, occasionally glancing at him with concern.

At length they found the gateway he was looking for and Ulrike crept along the lane until they saw some abandoned farm buildings in the headlights. They took a right and proceeded up an overgrown driveway until they came to a mesh fence. Stapled to one of the posts was a notice that read '*Verboten—Ministerium für Staatssicherheit*'.

'Where the hell are we?' she asked Rosenharte as he almost fell out of the car. He did not answer, but ran to the fence and started working with a blind fury at the post immediately in front of them until he felt the wood give beneath the soil. The wire came away easily and he rolled it back.

'Where are we?' she repeated, as she looked up at the façade of a great ruined house.

'Schloss Clausnitz. The ancestral home of my family that was stolen by the Stasi. It's now Schwarzmeer's country retreat. But he stays way over on the other side of the estate. It's the last place they'll look.'

'We can't stay here!' she said, placing a hand on his arm.

'We can,' he said, wresting his arm free. He rushed to the steps and quickly broke through the French windows with his knife. Ulrike followed him into the dusty blackness.

The beam from his torch skidded along the floor as he stumbled from room to room, clutching the bottle of brandy. He paused in the dining room, and then in a reception room, before coming upon a double staircase leading up from the grand entry hall.

'We used to play here,' he said, his torch sweeping wildly across the stairway. Around the walls the old mirrors had been vandalised and bits of glass hung from plaster frames and flashed in his beam.

They turned to the entrance, where someone had attempted to prise the marble from the floor. 'And here was the front door where we lined up to watch our parents arrive.'

'Who was your father?' she asked.

'I thought Biermeier had seen my file and told you everything?'

'Not everything. I knew they were Nazis and that they both died at the end of the war.'

'My father, General Manfred von Huth, was in the SS,' he said savagely. 'History does not relate how he died, although the Stasi have a theory that he was killed by his own troops. My mother was a von Clausnitz. This place belonged to her family. She died in the Dresden firestorm.'

'And that's when the Rosenhartes took you in?'

He took a swig of brandy but didn't answer her, then he staggered down the corridor to find a kitchen, pantry, larder, storage and laundry rooms. All of them bore the signs of abuse and sudden evacuation. Ulrike did all she could to keep up as he roamed through the house, cursing the ghosts of the von Clausnitz family.

In the end she said it would be best if she left him alone while she found somewhere for them to sleep. She touched him before leaving and said, 'Be careful with yourself, Rudi.' He brushed her away and went up a back stairway. He had no idea what he was searching for, but as he went he was conscious that he was mapping the extent of his loss.

He had arrived in a room, at last, at the front of the house which had four windows, inlaid mirrors on two sides and the remains of a chandelier that dangled from the ceiling. He lowered himself onto a wooden window seat.

The clouds had lifted and the night had become lighter. He took out Konrad's letter, unfolded it carefully and read it in the moonlight. The first tears of his grief soon hit the paper, and he hurriedly wiped them away so there would be no stain. Then he sat with his head in his hands as Konrad's loss, rather than his own, assumed its rightful place in his mind. His brother had lost everything, from the sight of his children and the comfort of his wife to the hopes of his own creative impulse. Against this, Rosenharte had merely lost his twin—the person he had relied on all his life. But he hadn't suffered like Konrad and he hadn't lost his life.

He stayed there for several hours. His rage began to pass, although he was no less stricken. He moved from the window to escape a draught and slid to the floor so his back rested against the seat. At some point he noticed that part of the front of the seat and the top lifted up. He turned his torch into the space and saw a lot of documents. It took only a moment to discover that they were the personal papers of Isobel von Huth—bills from her dressmaker, old invitations, old diaries, correspondence from lawyers.

He was thumbing through the 1938 diary absently when he realised that several small snaps had dropped between his legs. There were five in all, three of an elderly man with a walrus moustache, and two of a woman with a horse. He assumed that this must be his mother, and even though it was the first image he had ever seen of her he felt nothing stir in his heart. He flipped over one of the pictures. An ink inscription read: *Myself and Schnurgerade, September 1939.*

He slipped the pictures into the little flap pocket at the back of the diary and put it into his coat. Then he got up, rubbed his buttocks and legs into life and, feeling the weight of his grief, made his way along the vast corridors to the main staircase, in search of Ulrike.

AT DAWN ROSENHARTE slipped from Ulrike's cold embrace and went to urinate from a window. He looked out over the courtyard, feeling the effects of the brandy at the base of his skull, and cursed himself, not quite remembering why he had sunk the majority of the bottle of Goldi. Two or three minutes elapsed before Konrad's death hit him and he revolved from the window and slumped against the wall.

What stopped him from complete collapse was the sound of a voice echoing round the walls of the courtyard outside. A man was musing about the presence of the car. He nudged Ulrike with his foot. 'Get up, we've got company,' he said roughly, as though it was her fault.

She leapt to her feet and followed him into a passage that led from the kitchen to the dining room. They heard a dog scampering along the corridor. Then came a voice ordering it to heel. There was nowhere for them to hide, and a second or two later a man appeared at the dining-room door.

'Hey, this is state property. You're in a restricted area: authorised personnel only. We don't allow vagrants here.'

'Good morning,' said Rosenharte. 'Sir, let me assure you we aren't vagrants. This house belonged to my mother's family—von Clausnitz. So you could say I've every right to be here.'

The man entered the dining room and examined them. He looked to be in his seventies, and was wearing an old traditional leather jacket with horn buttons, corduroy britches and brown leather boots.

'This is all owned by the state now. The von Clausnitz name counts for nothing here.' He looked at him. 'Besides, you can't be a von Clausnitz.'

'I'm not,' he said. 'I was originally given my father's name—von Huth. I am the son of Manfred von Huth.'

'Then worse luck for you. The man was a Nazi, a butcher.'

'Indeed, sir, but we cannot choose our parents.'

'That's true,' said the man, melting a little.

'I'm trying to do a little research,' said Rosenharte. 'You know how it is when you get to middle age: you want to try to understand your past.' He pulled out the picture of Isobel von Huth. 'This is my mother. Did you by any chance know her?'

The man peered at the photograph, but it was plain that he couldn't see properly. 'Yes, yes, I remember her. I used to work on the estate before joining up in 1938. Her heart was as cold as a winter's night.' He looked up at Rosenharte. 'And you're her boy? You don't look like her.'

'Perhaps that's a good thing. So you're the caretaker now?'

'I keep an eye on things for them.'

'There are some houses at the other end of the estate. Are they occupied?'

'How do you know about them? This place is supposed to be secret.'

'I was the guest of General Schwarzmeer a month back. I wanted to return and take a look in my own time.'

The man looked doubtful. 'Are you a friend of his?'

'No, I couldn't honestly claim to be that,' said Rosenharte, hoping that he had judged the man right. 'To be frank, I am no friend of the Stasi. They were responsible for my brother's death two weeks ago and I cannot forgive them.'

Ulrike stepped forward with a smile. 'Can we level with you, Herr . . .'

'Flammensbeck—Joachim Flammensbeck. Go ahead.'

'Herr Flammensbeck, my friend has just received the terrible news of his brother and he needs peace and quiet. We'll pay any money you need. We appeal to your good nature to allow us to remain here out of sight for a while.'

'What've you done?'

'Demonstrated for peace, liberty and democracy. That's all. We were part of that march in Leipzig and things got difficult. We need to lie low for a bit.'

He looked at Rosenharte. 'So all that stuff you just told me about being Manfred von Huth's son was a lie?'

'No, it was the complete and utter truth,' said Rosenharte. 'Do you have sympathy for the marchers? Do you think they have a case?'

Flammensbeck blew out his cheeks and exhaled. He seemed to be weighing something. Eventually he addressed them both. 'In the spring of 1945 I was in a prisoner-of-war camp in the east. At the end of April it was announced that the Führer had committed suicide. We were stunned, but after a bit we fell to asking each other what it had all been about. So much death and destruction. Each one of us with innocent blood on our hands. What was it all about? Nothing! We'd been had. The same question came to me the other day. What is this socialism all about? This supposed equality? There's no equality in the GDR. The Party bosses come here and they screw like goats and drink themselves into oblivion. I'll tell you what—we've been had again! Another gang of criminals has been taking us for a ride.'

Rosenharte nodded grimly. It was all so simple, so easily reduced.

'So we can stay here?' asked Ulrike.

'Yes, but you must hide the car and if they catch you, I have never seen you. Do I have your agreement on that?'

They both nodded.

'Are there guards at the Stasi compound?' asked Rosenharte.

'An idiot named Dürrlich who thinks he's my boss. But he's away in Berlin at the moment filling in as Schwarzmeer's driver.' He called the dog to come to him. 'Move the car and I'll go and mend the fence you broke.'

LATER THAT DAY they made their way across the von Clausnitz estate to Schwarzmeer's hide-out in the forest.

'Why did you want to come here?' she said.

'It's the one place we can make a phone call without being eavesdropped.' He was aware of her flinching at his harsh tone. A lot had fallen into place overnight, though he hadn't had time to articulate it to himself other than knowing that she was as much responsible for Konrad's death as the Stasi. He found that he felt little more than a distant contempt for her.

There was no problem gaining entry. Rosenharte found an ancient hoe to lever the doors apart and burst the lock. He went straight to the phone and, remembering the code for that week, dialled Harland. The SIS man came on the line. 'Konrad is dead,' said Rosenharte. 'The operation is off.'

There was a pause. 'You're certain?'

'Yes, it happened when I was in Berlin that day. They kept it from me because they wanted me to continue working for them.'

'I'm so sorry. How did you learn?'

'The Russians told me. They have sources.'

'Please,' said Harland sharply. 'Be careful not to use any names or specific details from now on. This call may be intercepted.'

'I'm not using the satellite phone. This phone is safe. You need to tell Else what's happened,' he said urgently. 'You have to tell Else and the boys.'

'Of course,' Harland replied. 'But there's no reason for you to stay now. Cross the border and bring your friend.'

'No,' he said quietly. 'I am staying here. I am staying here until this thing is over. It's what Konrad would have wanted.'

'Surely what he'd have wanted is for you to look after his family in their new home,' Harland retorted. 'You've done everything you can there.'

Rosenharte looked at Ulrike. 'No, we're staying here,' he said heavily. Ulrike saw he was about to collapse and rushed to catch him. He pushed her away then rolled onto a chair.

She picked up the receiver, which had fallen to the floor. He heard her say: 'It's not possible for your friend to travel, you understand. He's taken it very badly . . . Yes . . . We'll call again . . . Yes . . . Goodbye.'

She put the phone down, crouched in front of him and held his hand.

'Get away from me,' he mumbled.

FOR THE NEXT thirteen days Rosenharte moved in his private limbo of guilt and anger, knowing little of what was going on around him. He drank Flammensbeck's sweet and deadly home brew and he roamed Schloss Clausnitz, by turns raving and silent. He was vaguely aware of Ulrike always there a few paces behind him, watching that he did no harm to himself.

It was odd how much he heard Konrad's voice during this time. It was as clear as if his brother was in the room with him, but for some reason, the Konrad he saw in his head was the boy of thirteen or fourteen.

Flammensbeck seemed to be there a lot with his dog, which had formed an obsession with Rosenharte and would sit for hours looking at him with his head cocked to one side. Occasionally, Rosenharte would sit watching Ulrike, searching her face for signs of the personality that he had so badly misjudged. Yet he could not entirely expel the feelings he had for her, and he recognised that he would not have survived these past weeks without her.

One day he stood in front of her and said, 'Why did you choose me, Ulrike? What's behind it all? Are you still working for them?'

'Rudi,' she implored. 'You're still not yourself. Of course I'm not.'

'Oh, but I am myself, which is why I'm asking these questions. I need the truth, Ulrike,' he said, grabbing her. 'No more lies. You put Konrad in prison—you and Biermeier.'

She pulled away from his grip and looked up at him. 'Before I tell you everything, you should know that I love you more than I have ever loved anyone. I hope you still feel something because I cannot stop loving you now.'

'All love is conditional. Mine is dependent on the truth.'

'OK, I'll tell you. I matriculated top from the language course at Humboldt University and was immediately taken up by the Stasi, just as you were. After training I was sent to Brussels undercover. That's when I first set eyes on you. I was just twenty-four years old. A translator.'

'Like Annalise Schering!'

'Yes.' She paused. 'I knew her.'

'How did you know her?'

'By that I mean I knew the second Annalise, the one who took the place of the first. I still do, Rudi. I know Jessie. Do you understand what I'm saying?'

He remembered the remark Jessie had made at the Adler just before he crossed over to the East. She seemed to be telling him to pass on her regards to Ulrike. If he hadn't immediately had to face the Stasi on the other side of the Wall he would probably have thought more about it.

'I was her contact at NATO. I passed the stuff back to Biermeier, who was the case officer. In fact, a lot of it was Biermeier's idea.'

'Biermeier! How the hell did he get Jessie's cooperation?'

'He didn't need to. The letters came from British Intelligence, not her.'

'But somewhere along the way she must have been involved.'

'He got word to her. She's a member of the British Campaign for Nuclear Disarmament. The Stasi keep an eye on such people, so Biermeier had no problem discovering her address and telephone number.'

'But why would she trust an oaf like Biermeier?'

'Because she trusted me. You see, I knew that she wasn't the real Annalise Schering. Do you understand what I'm telling you? I knew, and I told no one on our side. You know why? Because we were both convinced members of the peace movement. That was our first loyalty. Jessie was worried by the rumours of the deployment of cruise missiles in Western Europe. We had our own secret pact.'

'What was she telling the East? Why was she so valued?'

'Annalise was the truth channel, but at that stage only I had guessed she was being used to tell the Soviet bloc the real intentions of the West.'

'You're not telling me she just blurted this out to you.'

'No. I discovered it for myself.'

He shook his head. The thing still seemed highly improbable, another pack of lies. 'She isn't the sort of person to make mistakes.'

'But she did. At the end of 1980 she gave me an advance copy of NATO's annual communiqué and I realised that she could not have acquired the sensitive sections about the arms race without official help. I told her I knew and she implored me to allow the truth channel to continue. And why not? It served the interests of peace. That was our shared priority.'

'And Biermeier? When did he get into the picture?'

'Much later. By '86 I'd told him everything. At that time I was back in Leipzig and out of the Stasi. The baby—all that had happened by then. Biermeier was working on the Middle East section, and that's how he got to hear about Lomieko and Abu Jamal's plans.'

'Who did he think was sanctioning this stuff?'

'Schwarzmeer and his predecessor, maybe Erich Mielke too. Biermeier never knew who was running things. That's why he arranged for me to get the job of looking after Abu Jamal; he had to find out what they were planning. I had clearance, though I was still in disgrace for my immoral behaviour. But Biermeier argued that only a woman of loose morals would be prepared to befriend the Arab and so I got the job.' She stopped. 'Look, the only way we could get this information out was through an intermediary like you. We had to improvise as we went along. You were perfect. The fact that you'd never told them about the death of the first Annalise would mean that you'd have to go along with it.'

'And look what your "improvisation" did. Konrad lost his life. Else and the boys lost a husband and a father.'

She looked down. 'I know. I understand how bitter you must feel, but you must believe me when I say that if I'd known what would happen to your family, we would have found another way of getting the information out.'

They were silent for a few minutes.

'You're in touch with Biermeier?' he said.

'Yes, I've spoken to him several times since we've been here.'

'He can help me find Zank.'

'Zank's under investigation,' she said. 'Two weeks ago he disappeared on sick leave. By some miracle all this seems to have reflected badly on him. You don't have to bother with Zank any more. He's finished.'

Rosenharte shook his head. Zank wasn't finished.

THAT AFTERNOON they took the car the long route round the lake to Schwarzmeer's compound. They knew Dürrlich was still in Berlin because that morning he had sent orders to Flammensbeck telling him to carry out some repairs to a broken cistern. When Rosenharte pulled up outside the building where he'd been questioned in the middle of the night, he saw that it had been disguised to look like an aircraft hangar.

'The old man said there's enough stuff in here to equip a small army,' he said to Ulrike. He placed the crowbar Flammensbeck had given him to the padlock, jerked upwards and the lock fitting burst from the door. For the caretaker's sake it needed to look like a break-in.

Rosenharte threw a light switch and they both exclaimed at the same moment. When he had been interrogated, he had seen some of the equipment and luxury goods there. Now he saw biohazard suits, hoses and ropes all jumbled up with boxes containing tape decks, cameras and video recorders, alongside a gun case containing hunting rifles and pistols.

Ulrike hunted round for a paint sprayer and the tins of paint Flammensbeck had said were there, while Rosenharte approached a wine rack. 'It'd be good to drink some of the bastard's wine,' he said.

'Come on, Rudi, keep your mind on the job. We shouldn't stay here long.'

'Nonsense,' he said, gathering up several bottles of French wine and some vintage champagne. 'Besides, it's rightfully mine.'

He placed the drink in the car, returned to the gun case and smashed the glass, selecting a couple of SIG-Sauer pistols and boxes of 9mm shells. He stuffed these in his pockets and went back to the car.

'You don't need a gun,' Ulrike said.

'I'll tell you when I want advice at every turn.'

She looked as if he had slapped her. 'Really, you don't have to be so unpleasant. Look, Rudi, we don't have to be lovers but can't we be friends?'

'Friends! Men and women want too much from each other to be friends. They fall in love or they make alliances, but they're never friends.'

'No wonder you didn't stay married long,' she said.

'Ah, well, there you have the advantage over me; I haven't yet had the pleasure of reading your Stasi file.'

He could see that that had hurt her but she said nothing and picked up the spray gun and started to paint the car. He unscrewed the number plates and replaced them with a pair from a pile inside the door. They worked in silence before standing back and looking at the matt-black Wartburg.

'You can be a real bastard when you want,' she said without looking at him.

'Maybe it's the Nazi in me.'

She shook her head, dropped the spray gun and walked into the woods. He didn't see her for several hours.

THAT EVENING, after Flammensbeck left, Ulrike pulled a chair in front of Rosenharte. He was mildly drunk and the fury had left him.

She held out her hands to touch his. 'I need to go back to Leipzig,' she said, 'back to my old life.'

'You'll be arrested.'

She shook her head. 'No, Rudi. I won't be. Things have changed.'

'But there is still a risk.'

Slowly she shook her head. He looked intently into her eyes. 'That stuff you said about relationships when we were painting the car makes me, well, doubt who you are. You made yourself out to be a misogynist.'

'Perhaps I am. Perhaps it's because I have been disappointed. What you did to me, the way you lied to me about your involvement . . . I mean how can I trust you after that?'

'You don't have to trust me. You can go your own way, although I hope you don't. I think we had something that . . . could last. And . . .' She stopped and looked up at him. 'Before I go, I feel I must say this, Rudi. You need to become a whole person without your brother. I know you worshipped him, and plainly he was a remarkable human being, but you make him out to be a saint. You're clever and funny and kind, but you have to go on without comparing yourself with your brother.' She paused again. 'And you should stop thinking about yourself. Call his wife, comfort her and her sons instead of wallowing in your own grief. Do it now.'

'Enough of the lecture. I'll do it tomorrow.'

'Why not now?'

'Because I need to think what to say: to offer her some hope.'

'Hope? There's no hope. Just say that you're going to be there with her. Forget this obsession with Zank. Men like Zank aren't worth your time.'

'I can't. Konrad died primarily because of him. Zank must pay for that.'

'You're going to shoot him? Konrad would say you've lost your mind.'

'Maybe I have.'

'No, Rudi, you're just very, very sad. That won't be cured by killing Zank.'

He shook his head, got up and opened another bottle. He gave a glass to Ulrike. They sat in silence drinking and listening to the pine kindling snap in the fire. Eventually he set down his glass, leaned forward and kissed her tentatively. She pulled away to read his intent, and after a few seconds seemed to settle something and offered her cheek. He brushed his lips across the patch of down in front of her ear and she murmured her pleasure.

NEXT MORNING he saw her standing in a huge old bath, bending down with a pail to scoop up the warm water they'd heated on the range. Things were easy between them now. As she emptied the pail over her the light from the mottled glass of the bathroom windows fell across her slim white body. She caught him smiling and flung some water in his direction. 'What is it?'

'It's just that I saw a painting in my mind—the picture Rembrandt did of his wife Saskia in that exact pose. You know the one?'

'No.' She stepped out of the bath and wrapped herself in the length of sheet they used as a towel. 'I know the exact moment when I completely fell for you. It was when you looked at that bird and talked about your brother. When was it for you?' she asked rather earnestly.

'I felt something in the café that first day but resisted it.' He took her hands and held them. 'I can only say this: that I've never loved a woman like I love you.' He searched for the right words. 'Your conviction and tenacity, your brilliant, eccentric courage, and your beautiful body that leaves me helpless with desire. You simply overwhelm me, Ulrike.'

LATER HE WALKED to Schwarzmeer's house and broke in again. He dialled Harland and was put through to Else very quickly. They spoke for fifteen minutes, which included some long, painful silences. He read her Konrad's letter and apologised for not giving it to her before. When he came to the end, she said that Konrad never wrote anything that better caught his nobility and generosity. She told him Harland had been to see them and had set up a bank account for her. She was arranging for Idris to get a visitor's visa. He was so good with Christoph and Florian that she wanted him to stay for a few weeks and help them settle down. He said goodbye and told her he would be with her as soon as he could.

That evening Flammensbeck came over to tell them Dürrlich was returning the following day. It was time to move on. It took no more than fifteen minutes to load the Wartburg. Before getting into the car, Ulrike hugged the old man and kissed him on both cheeks. Flammensbeck's eyes watered up. He had enjoyed having them there more than he could say. It had been the best time he'd had in years, he said.

They spent the next few days touring the sites of Rosenharte's boyhood—the house that once belonged to the Rosenharte family, the school and sports ground where the Rosenharte boys starred, and finally Konrad's last home. Rosenharte knew that he was saying goodbye to it all because he'd decided to go to Else in the West.

THEY WERE SITTING at the top of a valley on the Sunday afternoon when Rosenharte turned and touched Ulrike's cheek with the back of his hand. 'Come with me,' he said suddenly. 'We can get over the border no problem.'

'I can't. I must attend the demonstration tomorrow. This is my destiny, to stay in Leipzig and see it through.'

'If you choose to go to Leipzig, I'll come too and march for one last time. Then I want you to think about leaving with me. Because this—us, you and me—is your destiny now.'

They left early the next day and found a phone. Ulrike called several friends and when she returned to the car she could barely contain herself. The leadership was in a state of paralysis and across East Germany the people were in a state of open defiance of the authorities: peaceful demonstrations were occurring in every major city.

'The beast isn't slaughtered yet,' said Rosenharte. 'We must be careful tonight.'

'How are they going to find me in a hundred thousand people?'

'Still, they may be looking, so I think we should stay apart.'

In Leipzig, Rosenharte parked a few streets north of Ulrike's place and they went straight to the Nikolaikirche. When they joined the huge crowd outside the church she lifted his hand and placed it to her lips before disappearing inside.

Rosenharte hung around in the crowd uneasily. At the end of the service the congregation surged out joyfully. He fell in behind the group of people surrounding Ulrike and followed them to the rally in Karl-Marx-Platz. There were three or four times the numbers of October 9. Yet the atmosphere was far less charged by the fear of official violence, and Rosenharte began to feel the battle had been won. At about ten the crowd began to thin. The people had made their point, pushing their numbers towards the critical mass necessary for permanent change. Rosenharte told Ulrike it was time for them to be going. 'We should leave the city too,' he said.

'No,' she replied firmly. 'I need my own bed. It will be fine.'

They walked briskly from the city centre, heads bent against the sharp breeze. As they entered her street she slipped her hand in his hip pocket for warmth then withdrew it and looked down. 'What's this? Ah, the picture of your mother.' She handed it to him. 'I wanted to ask you about that. It says September 1939 on the back. That can't be right.'

'Why?'

'Well, look at her, Rudi! You were born three months after that picture was taken. She should have been five or six months pregnant with boy twins that September but she's as thin as a rake.'

'It's dated wrongly. I found it in a diary for 1938.'

'You're probably right, but what mother makes a mistake like that?' She smiled. 'Wait a few minutes then follow me. If the outside light is on you'll know the coast is clear.'

He watched her disappear into the wisteria gateway then he began to move slowly up the road. He was less than fifty yards from the entrance when a car came to a stop outside Ulrike's house. Rosenharte backed into the shadows, his heart pounding. He reached for the gun and fumbled with the safety catch. A man got out and held the back door open. Then two men emerged from the gateway with Ulrike between them. They bundled her into the back seat and the three men climbed in, but during that time Rosenharte registered that the man who had opened the door was Colonel Zank. He raised the gun and aimed, but knew he couldn't fire. He might hit Ulrike and the sound of the shots would certainly bring a response from Zank's men. He would be killed or taken prisoner. Neither would help her, and that was why she didn't cry out for his help.

VLADIMIR DROPPED the phone onto its cradle and looked him straight in the eye. 'She's been taken to Hohenschönhausen. Biermeier also. They're both being held in isolation.' His steady gaze betrayed no feeling.

'Is there anything you can do?' Rosenharte asked.

The Russian grimaced. 'You must understand that I can't interfere in the affairs of a sovereign state. You're mistaken if you think you're going to walk into Hohenschönhausen and rescue your girlfriend.' He stopped and softened his tone. 'You achieved what you set out to do: Abu Jamal has been dealt with. You should leave now. The borders are open again.'

Rosenharte shook his head. 'I'm not going to lose anyone else to that place,' he said quietly. 'One way or another I'm going in to get her, and it's in your interest that I do this with the minimum of risk. It's very important to you that I don't get caught, isn't it?'

'In our game we always need a return on risk, Rudi. I can't help you unless I'm able to show my superiors there's a substantial advantage.'

'I've told you everything. I have nothing more to give.'

'The man Harland—could you get him here?'

'Why here?'

'It doesn't matter. Bring him here and I'll help you. Tell him there's something in it for both of us. And for the Americans too.'

Rosenharte was now beginning to understand the strength of his position. Vladimir hadn't agreed to speak to him because of Ulrike, but because he wanted him to act as an intermediary.

'What about our exit—can you help with that?'

'I can provide the release documentation in Ulrike's name. You'll have to ask the British to help you get her out.'

Rosenharte nodded. 'There's one other thing,' he said. 'Members of the Polish secret service have been trying to contact me for the last two months. I haven't had time to discover why. Can you find out what they want? The Stasi were interested in them. They may have something on them.'

Vladimir smiled. 'When we discovered Zank was interested we did some digging ourselves. The Pole who followed you to Trieste, Franciscek Grycko, was a fifty-eight-year-old veteran of the Polish secret police. A tough character who entered the camps as a ten-year-old, survived and became one of the service's best operatives. He used his contacts to see some of the files on you. We know that.'

'How could you know that?'

Vladimir looked at him with his poker face and shrugged.

'Whatever he wanted to say must have been important, for him to travel when he was so ill to try to speak to me,' Rosenharte said.

'You're convinced he died of natural causes, that he wasn't murdered?'

'Yes, for the simple reason that no one had a motive to poison him. No one knew who he was.' Rosenharte paused. 'What's interesting is that the second man, Leszek Grycko, who is much younger, also seemed to want to contact either Konrad or me. You've got contacts, influence.' He withdrew the note Else had given him and handed it to Vladimir. 'I'd like you to make some enquiries on my behalf.' Vladimir took the note and copied the number.

'I'm not promising anything,' he said.

'I understand,' said Rosenharte, 'but, thank you. I'll call later about the meeting with Harland and about my own operation at Hohenschönhausen. I need time to carry out a recce, so I won't make my move until next week.'

'That's sensible. Those disks you got from the West were a Trojan horse; they screwed up the mainframe in Normannenstrasse and now they are having to rebuild it. If the Stasi arrest you they'll torture you and shoot you.'

Rosenharte felt his neck and back go cold. He looked away. 'I need to know where Ulrike's being held,' he said. 'What room, what floor? Anything that might be of use to me.'

'Phone Harland now and I will see what I can do.'

ALAN GRISWALD nursed a cup of coffee and examined Harland over his reading glasses. 'I can't go. Langley won't allow it. And nor should you consider it, particularly if you haven't got any kind of diplomatic cover.'

Harland stroked his chin. 'I've got cover as a TV journalist next week. London wants to know what's going on in East Germany so I said I would cover the demo in Berlin tomorrow. What's the problem if I have a word with the Sovs' man in Dresden? I mean, they did help us on Abu Jamal.'

'Go and hear what the man says but don't get near that damned jail. Send one of your people. You're not a knight in armour, Bobby.'

'But what if the Sovs really have something to offer us?'

'That's a different matter. The Soviets look after themselves. Never forget that. This guy in Dresden, he's small time. What can he offer?'

'Access,' replied Harland testily. 'Access to the Stasi files. Things are unravelling there. I just have this feeling something's going to happen.'

ROSENHARTE DROVE through the night to Dresden, where he dug in for the weekend in Idris's snug cabin by the River Elbe.

On Monday morning he ventured out to buy some more provisions and have his photograph taken. While he waited for the picture to be developed he read *Neues Deutschland*, and noted a small item that referred to the resignation of the Minister for State Security, Erich Mielke. Rosenharte could not but hope that the absence of Mielke and the general turmoil would mean that summary executions would be less likely.

That evening, he left Dresden for East Berlin with a form requiring the presence of Ulrike Klaar at KGB headquarters in Berlin-Karlshorst on Wednesday, November 8 at 5 p.m., and a docket authorising the transfer of the prisoner, which was countersigned by the Stasi official responsible for liaison with the KGB. Also in his possession were two Stasi photograph ID cards in the names of Bernhard Müller and Werner Globke.

Vladimir had got his meeting with Harland and was happy to provide the documentation. Harland was providing help in the form of Cuth Avocet, who was due to meet Rosenharte in Berlin. This would give Rosenharte time to recce the area in advance of the operation.

Rosenharte was well rested after the weekend and content to go through Monday night without sleep. By six in the morning on Tuesday, he slipped into the outskirts of the city and parked the car some distance from the huge Stasi complex north of the Frankfurter Allee.

Throughout the day he walked in and out of the area near Hohenschönhausen prison. By the end of the afternoon he had learned that whatever routes the Stasi trucks took in the early stages of their journey to the prison they usually approached it by crossing Konrad-Wolf-Strasse. This last stretch of road offered several possibilities for interception, but he would wait until he had consulted the Bird before settling on a plan.

At midday on Wednesday, Rosenharte went to the Ostbahnhof—the main station in East Berlin—to meet the Bird. When he spotted the British agent striding through the crowds he hastened towards him and they greeted each other like old friends.

'Where's the truck?' the Bird asked in English when they had climbed into the Wartburg.

'We have to hijack it first. I know the routes.'

'Jesus, when are you hoping to do this?'

'In the next couple of hours.'

'Got any kind of weapon?'

Rosenharte turned round and lifted the back seat to show the guns and boxes of ammunition.

'Right, well, that's something, I suppose.' The Bird looked to the front and sniffed. 'What happens after you've got her out?'

'Harland gave me these when we were in Dresden.' He showed him two British passports, complete with East German entry visas dated the week before and laminated strips that peeled back so that the picture could be fixed underneath. 'I don't have a photo of Ulrike yet.'

The Bird nodded. 'All right, I'm in but it's against all my better instincts. We'll leave this car near the prison. At the first sign of trouble we'll have to ram or shoot our way out.'

Rosenharte nodded.

'Afterwards we'll all go our separate ways. You've got your passports. You make your own way out of the country. Right, we'd better get a move on.'

'Do you speak any German?' asked Rosenharte, as he pulled out into the traffic on Muhlenstrasse.

'No, I'm like most Englishmen: I can order from a menu and ask for a lavatory quite convincingly, but beyond that I'm rather at sea.'

They parked about a mile from the prison in Friedrichsfelde and, after ripping one of Rosenharte's shirts into several lengths of cloth, they took a gun each and walked the rest of the way to Hohenschönhausen.

They reached the spot that Rosenharte had chosen, a narrow right-angle bend, where the trucks slowed to a walking pace. It wasn't overlooked by any of the houses in the area.

'How many Stasi do we expect on board?'

'Two, maybe three if they've got a guard in the back.'

Rosenharte explained his plan and they split up to wait at different positions around the right-angle bend. Rosenharte stood beside a wooden fence and watched the incline the truck would climb before reaching the bend.

It was just past nine when the lights swung into the road from Frankfurter Allee and the truck began to grind up the gentle slope. The vehicle was almost upon them when the Englishman loped at great speed from the shadows and jumped up to the driver's door at the point where the truck was moving at its slowest. Rosenharte drew his gun and ran to the passenger side, reached up and wrenched it open to find no one there. All he saw was the astonished face of the driver as the Bird hauled him out on the other side. The vehicle juddered to a halt as the engine stalled.

Rosenharte scrambled quickly through the cab, turning off the lights on the way. 'Where are the keys for the back?' he demanded. 'Tell us and we won't kill you.'

'There's no one in the back!' the driver protested. 'I'm just leaving the vehicle at the prison for tomorrow morning. They need it first thing.'

'Why?'

He looked down at the gun. 'I don't know! I'm just a driver.'

'Where're the keys to the back?'

The man pointed to a hook above the driver's door. Rosenharte reached up and then got out of the cab. They frog-marched the driver round to the right side of the truck, unlocked the door and placed him in one of the open cells. The Bird gagged him with one of the strips of cloth, and tied his hands behind his back, running the cloth through the bar on the side of the cubicle.

'Now, you listen to me,' said Rosenharte. 'Any sound and you'll die. Keep quiet for the next two hours and you'll remain unharmed. Understood?'

The man nodded and they slammed the door on him.

'I'll drive into the prison,' Rosenharte said. 'I know the way and I may need to speak to the guards. Then you drive us out. Is that OK with you?'

'Righty-ho,' said the Bird. 'Let's go and get your friend.'

As the cumbersome truck neared the prison entrance, the gate inched back and let it move forward into the garage space. They stopped in front of a second door that led into the compound, and a man came running down a short flight of metal steps. 'Hey, what's going on? We're not expecting any more deliveries,' he called. 'Let's see your ID.'

'This isn't a delivery,' said Rosenharte. 'This is a collection.' He waved the papers at him. The Bird got out and nodded to him.

'You'd better come to the office. We don't know about any collection.'

'This is a special collection. The prisoner was meant to be at Karlshorst at five.' He followed him into an office where there was a table, a bank of four black and white TV monitors, two telephones and a single desk light.

The man ran his finger down a list, then looked at the forged papers. 'I have no record of this.'

'You mean to say that the prisoner isn't ready for immediate transport? We're already four hours late. Have her brought down here immediately,' said Rosenharte testily.

The man's hand went to the telephone. The Bird darted a warning look to Rosenharte, but it was too late; the man had begun speaking. When he put the phone down, he said, 'She's still in interrogation. You'll have to wait.'

Rosenharte leaned forward confidentially. 'Colonel Zank is being as diligent as ever, eh? You'd better take us to the interrogation room. It is a matter of national security.' He drew the man aside. 'My companion is from the

KGB. He is their chief interrogator and he has come to take delivery of the prisoner. Let's not waste any more time.'

The man nodded, picked up the phone again and barked an order. Very shortly a younger man appeared in an ill-fitting dark suit. 'Take these men to the interrogation wing. Forty-two A.'

He beckoned them down a flight of five steps and out into the U-shaped courtyard formed by the sinister interrogation cell blocks. They walked across the yard to a door on the eastern wing, which the man unlocked. They entered a gloomy stairwell and climbed to the second floor. They were taken through an iron gate and past twenty or so identical doorways. The guard stopped at a heavy, padded door, and pulled it open to reveal a second door. He knocked. 'Do not interrupt us!' came a command from within.

The Bird drew a gun and put it to the man's head.

Rosenharte whispered, 'Open the door or he will shoot you now.'

The man unlocked the door and pushed it open. The Bird flung the man into the room and stepped inside, moving the gun between the three inter-rogators. 'Move and I'll fucking kill the lot of you,' he said in English.

Rosenharte looked down. Ulrike was crouching, bare feet on the floor, torso wobbling, grimacing like a child trying to hold a pose, her face streaked with tears that shone in the single desk light trained on her.

He rushed to her and lifted her in his arms. 'It's OK,' he said. 'We're taking you away from here. It's OK—I'm here, my love.' She looked at him with incomprehension. There were bruises round her eyes and her neck was ringed with a chain of strangle marks.

The Bird glanced round. 'Here, give her one of these.' He passed a blister pack to Rosenharte. 'It's a painkiller and light opiate. There's some water on the desk. Then give her one of these. It will keep her awake.'

As Ulrike took the pills, Rosenharte went over to the lead interrogator at the head of the table, pulled his head back by his hair and put the gun to his ear. 'You people killed my brother. I told Zank I'd hold you responsible; now I'm here to keep that promise.'

Ulrike said, 'Don't, Rudi. This isn't you! Konrad wouldn't want this. He's not worth the trouble it will cause your conscience.'

He looked down at the man. The other interrogators had imperceptibly moved away, believing that he was about to pull the trigger. Instead he raised the gun and let it come down very hard just above the man's ear. He fell forward with blood seeping from a deep, curved gash, still conscious.

'Where's Biermeier?' Rosenharte demanded.

'He's dead,' Ulrike said. 'They shot him. Zank showed me his body.'

Rosenharte turned to the man he had hit. 'Is that what you did with Konrad—put a bullet into the back of his head? Is that what you did, you filthy piece of scum?' But by now he was watching himself at a distance, perhaps with Konrad's eyes. He knew Ulrike was right: this wasn't him.

While Ulrike hobbled to the door, where her shoes were, the Bird took the keys from the guard. Backing towards the door he held a hand over his nose and mouth and sprayed the room with an aerosol canister. Rosenharte slipped into the corridor and saw the three remaining men slump to the floor before both doors were shut and locked.

'We won't be hearing much from them for a while,' the Bird said. 'Right, let's get out of here.'

Outside in the yard nothing stirred as they made their way to the van bay.

'I'll go ahead and get the truck started and the gate opened up,' said the Bird. 'I'll sort the guard out. Leave it two minutes, then come.'

A minute passed before they moved out of the shadows. As they reached the open, Rosenharte heard some movement off to the left. He turned to see a group of three men running from the shadows of the kitchen block. He raised his gun and took aim, protecting Ulrike with his body.

Two men with pistols emerged into the light, with Colonel Zank following. He was smiling. 'Put down your weapons. You cannot escape.'

'We may be outnumbered,' Ulrike said, 'but we'll make sure you die with us.'

'You're a pacifist,' said Zank teasingly. 'You only take punishment; you don't hand it out.' He looked at Rosenharte. 'You should have seen what I did to her; I began to wonder if she got off on it . . .'

'There's no question you will die,' said Rosenharte, moving closer so that his gun pointed at the middle of Zank's forehead. 'Your world is over—your power to destroy good men like my brother, your delight in tormenting a beautiful and brave woman. You're a sick bastard, Zank, but more important you're the past, a leftover from the time when this disgusting place was built.' He gestured with his left hand at the Nazi kitchen block to divert attention away from the Bird, who had slipped without a sound from the office above the van bay and had rolled a clutch of round objects behind the men. 'And that's why you're going to let us walk out of here.'

Zank was saying that they'd never get past the gates, when three small explosions occurred behind him, causing his two companions to reel backwards and start shooting wildly in the direction of the watchtower. Rosenharte spun round and saw that Ulrike had fallen to the ground. As he moved to haul her up, he was aware of the Bird rushing at Zank's men, hitting them with terrifying force, one in the throat and the other in the small of his back, then rising behind Zank to hook an arm round his neck and place a gun beneath his chin. He waved to Rosenharte and shouted for him and Ulrike to make for the truck. With his left hand he chucked two more objects into the compound, then delivered a single blow to the crown of Zank's head. Zank crumpled at the base of the steps.

A few seconds later they were crowded into the front of the truck as it reversed furiously out of the bay. The vehicle spun round and they caught a glimpse of dense white smoke leaking over the prison walls.

'Well, what now?' said the Bird with a lunatic grin. 'Know anywhere you two can put up for the evening?'

'WHERE ARE THEY?' demanded Harland.

'Somewhere in Prenzlauer Berg, being sheltered by friends of Kafka,' the Bird said.

'Why didn't you get the address?'

'Because we had to split up. Half the bloody Stasi were pursuing us at one point. We did pretty well to get away in that little car.'

They were standing in a car park near the building that housed the endless deliberations of the Central Committee. Theoretically, Harland was there to cover the meetings as a member of the press corps, so when the Bird's call came through it had been the best rendezvous he could think of.

'I could do without this today. I'm meeting the Russian and I still haven't heard from Griswald. Why the hell didn't you take them over last night?'

'Keep your shirt on, Bobby.' The Bird shook his head in annoyance. 'We couldn't go last night because Kafka needed a picture for her passport.'

Harland made an apologetic nod. Cuth was right; and he had done magnificently to spring them from Hohenschönhausen.

'You seem out of sorts, Bobby. Is there anything I can do?'

'No, I've got a lot on, that's all. We're on the threshold of the greatest intelligence coup in the history of the Cold War, and those bloody idiots in London are still scratching their heads wondering about flaming cost benefits. This could save millions.'

'It's that good, is it?'

'Better.'

The Bird smiled. 'So we just wait for the call from Rosenharte?'

'Yep, then you arrange the reception committee the other side. Put them in a hotel. And we'll follow up from there in a few days.'

ULRIKE'S FRIENDS, Katya and Fritzi Rundstedt, were two mathematicians who lived on the top floor of a building in Prenzlauer Berg. From the fifth-floor windows you could follow the line of the Berlin Wall as it continued its jagged path through the city. Rosenharte spent some time with Fritzi early on the morning of Thursday, November 9, picking out the crossing points and a corner of the Brandenburg Gate.

Ulrike was still asleep on the floor in the adjacent room. Her feet were very painful and Katya had borrowed some crutches from a neighbour to help her move around.

'Your friend is a woman of rare spirit and very special qualities, Dr Rosenharte, but I'm sure you already know that.'

Rosenharte had nodded and found himself suddenly overwhelmed by the thought of how close he'd come to losing her.

At midday a photographer came to take a passport picture of Ulrike, who was made up by Katya with foundation to cover her bruises. The photographer returned at two with the photo and Rosenharte was able to fix it into the passport of Birgit Miller.

At four he went to a phone box and dialled in the code. He was told that they would be expected to cross by Checkpoint Charlie any time after six. An ambulance would be waiting for Ulrike.

'It's good you have come through all this in one piece, sir,' said the English voice. 'Many congratulations.'

Rosenharte acknowledged this, thinking that in truth half of him was still missing. He returned to the Rundstedts' building, where he was let in by a neighbour with an impressive moustache. 'There's trouble,' he said. 'The Stasi have traced the car to a street nearby. Two of them are here now.'

'Where is my friend?'

'She's fine. We have decided to entertain the Stasi while you make your way from here.'

'What do you mean?'

'Well, we are putting them right about certain things that we in this building feel strongly about. Your friend Fritzi is plying them with a cheap brandy and giving them a piece of his mind in the basement apartment.'

Rosenharte realised that Zank must have worked out they were using number plates stolen from Schwarzmeer's retreat in the country, and put out a general alert for the missing pair. 'OK, we'd better leave.'

'Leave separately,' said the neighbour. 'Then meet up somewhere.'

Rosenharte thanked the man and tore up the staircase, the noise of his pounding feet reverberating through the tired old building.

HARLAND FILED into the press conference at 5.45 p.m. with members of both the Western and communist media. Already twenty or so TV crews had set up, and the air of expectation was palpable. This would be the first time that a member of the Politburo had taken part in a news conference broadcast live to the people of the GDR.

For Harland the only thing that mattered was picking up the documents from Vladimir, but he was interested in Schabowski, the man whom Krenz had appointed to handle the media. MI6 had reports that suggested that the East Berlin Party chief was one of the key figures in the putsch that had ousted Erich Honecker.

Schabowski entered in a grey checked suit and threaded a route through the journalists. Just as he arrived, Harland spotted Vladimir standing on the far side of the room, merged into the media throng. Their eyes met for a second or two and looked through each other. Harland turned to the dais.

Schabowski communicated unease as he began to speak about the 'intensive discussion' at the Central Committee. The new proposal on travel regulations was being dealt with and it was understood that Krenz would confront his colleagues with the bleak facts of the East German economy.

At 6.30 p.m. Harland noticed that Vladimir had left his position. Next thing he knew, the Russian was sidling up to him with a folder of holiday brochures in his hand. He tipped his head to the rear of the room.

'We hear they got away last night,' he said when they reached the back wall. 'All except the man they executed last week. A good result for you.'

'Yes, it was, and thank you for your help.'

'It's nothing. This is the first delivery. There are details of cases you know about so your side will realise that what we're offering is very, very important information. The crown jewels, as you say.'

'What cases?' asked Harland, his gaze returning to Schabowski.

'You've got everything you need on Abu Jamal and Misha. In other words, the documentary proof of the GDR's official involvement. Oh, yes, and there's one other file in there. Rosenharte's personal file. You should give it to him at the earliest opportunity, then telephone me.'

'What do you mean?'

'We can't talk about that here.' He slipped the file into Harland's hand and then turned his attention to a question from an Italian journalist.

Schabowski seemed rattled by the Italian's point, which had referred to mistakes in the release of the draft travel law a few days before. 'No, I don't think so,' he was saying. 'We know about this tendency in the population, this need of the population to travel or leave the GDR, and we have decided to adopt a regulation that enables every citizen of the GDR to leave the country by means of GDR border crossings.'

Harland began to say something but Vladimir put up his hand. 'Listen.'

'When does that take effect?' someone called out.

Schabowski had put on his spectacles and was reading from notes. 'Trips abroad may be applied for without meeting preconditions. Permission will be given forthwith. Permanent emigration may take place at all border crossings from the East to West Germany.'

'When does it take effect?' came the call again.

'As far as I know, immediately,' Schabowski replied.

Vladimir turned to Harland. 'The man's an idiot. There was a press embargo on this until tomorrow morning.'

Harland had been so focused on how he was going to get the documents to West Berlin that he had not seen the significance of the statement.

'He hasn't mentioned passports or visas,' said Vladimir. 'The Central Committee has revised the travel laws so that people can apply for visas without preconditions. But it still means they have to have a passport to leave. Most East Germans don't have a passport. He's screwed up.'

A rather studious-looking journalist in the middle of the room got to his feet. 'Herr Schabowski, what will happen to the Berlin Wall now?'

The room was suddenly electrified. It was the question on everyone's mind. Schabowski could not escape the logic of the young man's question. If people could travel whenever they wanted without preconditions from that moment on, what indeed was the point of the Wall?

'What will happen to the Berlin Wall?' he mused. 'Some information has already been provided regarding travel activities . . . the question of the permeability of the Wall from our side does not yet or exclusively answer the question of the purpose of this . . . let me say . . . the fortified national border of the GDR.'

With this baffling statement the press conference ended and the reporters surged forward to the dais. Vladimir shrugged his astonishment and then glanced at Harland. 'We'll speak. I'd better let my people know that Gunther Schabowski has single-handedly torn down the Berlin Wall.'

'They already know,' said Harland. 'It's on live TV.'

THEY WERE DRIVEN separately from Prenzlauer Berg to a neglected court-yard off the Hackescher Markt, near Alexanderplatz. Then they were shown to an apartment belonging to a violinist named Hubert. Moments after Rosenharte arrived in the musician's tiny flat he received word that Colonel Zank was now questioning everyone in the Rundstedts' block. This worried Rosenharte and Ulrike. Both knew that the Stasi would consult records held in Normannenstrasse and draw up lists of known contacts of the Rundstedt family, and sooner or later Hubert would show up on that list. More trou-bling was the certainty that every border post would now be on alert and in possession of photos of them.

At 7.20 p.m. Rosenharte used Hubert's phone to call Harland. A woman answered and said that everyone dealing with the operation was out.

'How are we expected to come across?' asked Rosenharte.

'Haven't you heard?' she asked. 'All travel restrictions have been lifted. There was an announcement by Gunther Schabowski just before seven—twenty minutes ago.'

'But we still have to go through checkpoints. They'll be looking for us.'

'The situation's very fluid. Call again in an hour's time.'

Rosenharte turned to the others. 'Something's happened. No one knows what's going on. There's been an announcement about the travel laws.'

Hubert turned on his television and tuned it to an East German state channel. At seven thirty the blue logo of the *Aktuelle Kamera* show appeared, and after a prologue about the Central Committee meeting, they heard the words: 'Immediately effective, private trips abroad may be applied for without specifying a particular reason.'

Ulrike rose. 'Can anyone travel at any time? It can't be true.'

Hubert rang round his friends, who were all confused as to what the government had actually said. Some had heard rumours that people were beginning to gather at the main checkpoints with nothing more than their identity cards and demanding to be allowed through.

It was now 8.45. Rosenharte called the British again, but got no further information. Hubert's phone rang several times. Brisk, incredulous exchanges took place. At Bornholmerstrasse crossing, they learned, thousands had already gathered. Then at 9.15 another caller told them that the Stasi officer in charge of passport control at Bornholmerstrasse was easing the pressure by allowing a trickle of East Berliners to pass into the West with nothing more than a stamp on their identity cards. Hubert arranged to go to Bornholmerstrasse with friends. 'You must come too,' he said.

Rosenharte shook his head. 'No, we'll head for Checkpoint Charlie. It's the closest.'

Hubert snatched up a coat, but just as he was about to leave they heard shouts from below. A man was calling up to Hubert that four Stasi cars had pulled up in Rosenthalerstrasse and were preparing to enter the yard.

They crashed down the rickety stairway and at the bottom Hubert led them to a dark opening at the far end of the yard. A minute or two later Zank appeared in the courtyard and started to organise half a dozen men to search the buildings. Zank vanished into Hubert's stairway then reappeared, brandishing the crutches that Ulrike had left in Hubert's apartment.

'We missed them,' he shouted. 'They've only just left—the coffeepot's still warm. They'll be making for the Wall. We'll search the area west of here.'

Ulrike and Rosenharte waited a few minutes then left the yard, and hurried as fast as Ulrike could manage towards the cold, friendless heart of the old city. Rosenharte's plan was to keep to the smaller streets until they hit Friedrichstrasse. At this intersection was Checkpoint Charlie, a twenty-minute walk away. Ulrike slipped her hand into Rosenharte's. 'It's so near and yet so far,' she said.

Plenty of people were milling around, among them some West Germans who had crossed over and were intent on a party. A young man came up to them and asked where he could get a beer at this hour. He told them his name was Benedict and that he'd just walked straight through Checkpoint Charlie without anyone asking for his papers. 'There are more people on the western side than on the eastern. We're waiting for you.'

'You're drunk,' said Ulrike with a broad grin.

'And why not, on a night like this?' asked Benedict good-naturedly. 'The Wall is wide open. Come and help me get your comrades out of their beds.'

Rosenharte smiled. 'If you don't mind, Benedict, we have been waiting all our lives for this moment, so we'd like to go and see it all for ourselves. But we may need your help because there are people pursuing us.'

'The Stasi?' said Benedict excitedly. That was the difference with Westerners. They had no fear because they didn't understand the reality of the Stasi. 'I'll bring my friends over here. We'll all go together to the Brandenburg Gate.'

He whistled to a group across the street. Soon six eager students had joined them and they headed for the intersection with Friedrichstrasse, where they paused in a darkened part on the north side of the street. It was with a grim lack of surprise that Rosenharte spotted Zank on the other side, scanning the crowds that were making their way to Checkpoint Charlie.

He consulted Benedict. Three of the young students agreed to set up a diversion while the remainder of the party would crowd round and convey them across the intersection, then to the Brandenburg Gate. The three young men approached Zank and begin to caper around him insisting he pose for a picture with them. His attention was drawn long enough for them to have moved out of sight. The diversion worked well.

Cut off from the West by the most massive and impassable stretch of the entire Berlin Wall, the Brandenburg now stood stark against the white haze of TV lights hurriedly set up on the other side. The dark hero of the Cold War was illuminated like an opera set. The few guards visible from the East moved between the six Doric columns like stagehands.

They covered the open ground between the end of the boulevard and the Gate feeling desperately exposed. Rosenharte put his arm round Ulrike and glanced back several times, but Zank was nowhere to be seen. They came to a low metal fence—the Grenzpolizei barrier which had denied Easterners contact with their own landmark since August 1961. It was easily climbed and then they pushed on across another stretch of tarmac towards the death zone immediately in front of the Gate. Ulrike stopped and gasped at the sight of a thousand people straddling the wall, silhouetted against the lights.

Rosenharte pulled her closer and spoke into her ear. 'It's amazing, but let's get over the other side.'

'Let's go and join the party,' shouted Benedict enthusiastically.

Until now they had attracted little interest from the Grepos, but when they got to within fifty yards of the Gate, two dozen troops appeared from the guardhouses either side of them and shouted for them to go back.

'Shit, they don't seem too pleased to see us,' said Benedict. He called out,

'Lads, come and join the party. We'll find you some good West Berliner girls.'

Rosenharte turned to Ulrike. 'What we have to do now is seem as drunk as Benedict and his friends. Remember, we've come through Checkpoint Charlie and now we're on our way back to the West. OK?' Ulrike nodded.

Benedict turned to them. 'Well, are we going?'

Rosenharte nodded. They passed through the unblinking line of guards without one of them raising his gun.

Halfway under the Gate, an officer ran to them holding up his hands. What were they doing there? Where had they come from? Benedict became their spokesman again. 'We're exercising our right ashhh citizens of free Berlin to walk under shish monument of peace.' He gave a rather drunken bow at the end of this speech.

The officer lost patience. 'You better get back to the other side or there'll be trouble for you damned Western agitators.' With this he hurried back to the line of troops, ordering them to prevent further encroachments from the East.

They emerged on the other side of the Brandenburg and found themselves not in the death zone, but a playground. People wandered around, chatting up the guards, swigging from beer and champagne bottles.

Rosenharte turned from the jubilant faces and looked up at the Gate, where the shadows of the people on the top of the Wall were projected like a huge Chinese lantern show. He would never know what made him turn to look down through the columns, but in the Eastern lee of the gate he saw Zank gesticulating to the officer who had stopped them a few moments before. He took Ulrike by the arm and spoke to Benedict. 'We've got to get out of here. Come on.'

Benedict shook his head. 'You go,' he shouted. 'I'm shtaying here.'

They hurried into the shadow of the Wall, which now seemed every bit as forbidding as a cliff face. Rosenharte crouched with his back against the Wall and cupped his hands in front of his knees.

Ulrike placed one painful foot in his hands and he hoisted her bird-weight without difficulty to a height of about nine feet. The hands of the people on top came down to meet hers and she was pulled the last few feet. From the corner of his eye, he saw Zank and an officer coming towards him.

'You must arrest this man,' he was shouting to the officer. 'This man is an enemy of the state—a spy. Arrest him now. Or I will.'

'You have no authority here,' the officer told Zank, before turning to Rosenharte. 'Who are you?'

He proffered the passport. 'I'm a British citizen. It's my first time in East Germany.'

'Nonsense. This man is a spy. He must be arrested.'

This all seemed very much beside the point to the Grepo officer and he threw out his hands in despair. 'I leave it to you.'

Then someone on top of the wall aimed the beam of a powerful flashlight at Zank. At the same time Ulrike started up a chant of 'Sta-si! Sta-si!' Soon hundreds on this section of the Wall had joined in. Zank reached for something in his breast pocket, but then he seemed to think better of it and backed away, his gaze never leaving Rosenharte. 'You think you've won,' he shouted. 'But you haven't.'

Rosenharte moved a few paces towards him, at which point the baying of the crowd became deafening.

He gestured upwards at the crowd. 'These people have won, but I haven't. I lost my brother—remember? If I had obeyed my instincts last night, I'd have killed you there and then in Hohenschönhausen. That's where you deserved to die. But at least I know you'll live to see everything you believe in crumble. That's good enough revenge for me.'

He didn't wait to hear Zank's retort, but returned to the Wall and, using one foot to power himself upwards, he stretched and found the hands reaching down to grab hold of his arms. Then he was on top, dusting himself off and looking down at the sea of happy faces on the other side.

Ulrike's eyes were filling with tears. 'Is this true?' she asked. 'There's never been a moment in history like this. Are we dreaming?'

He shook his head very slowly and bent to kiss her.

AN HOUR LATER Rosenharte followed Ulrike through the door under the letter C of Café Adler. Robert Harland and the Bird were sitting at the corner table by the window on Zimmerstrasse.

They ordered champagne and brandy chasers on the British government and made toasts to Berlin, freedom and a united Germany. They marvelled at the story of Schabowski's gaffe.

'Was it planned?' asked Ulrike. 'Surely, he knew what he was doing—an experienced Party official like that?'

'Who knows,' said Harland, 'but here we are in a new world. What's happened tonight is irrevocable. Without the Wall, there's no East Germany, at least not one that will function as a viable state. The game is up.'

For a further half-hour they sat huddled round the table, but then Harland insisted that Ulrike should go and get the medical attention that had been arranged. He rose to his feet, but not to usher her from Café Adler. 'I would like to offer you both a toast—to your indomitability, your courage and endurance. What you did is very important, even in this new era of ours.'

Rosenharte looked at his companion. 'I know I speak for both of us when I thank you each for your role in getting us out. Without your help, Mr Avocet, my friend here would still be in Hohenschönhausen. We thank you from the bottom of our hearts.' The Bird began to redden from the neck up. 'And I want us to toast Ulrike, one of the true founders of the revolution.' He raised his glass to her. The others followed suit.

'You'd better be off before we're all in tears,' said Harland briskly. 'I'd like to have a word with Rudi in private, if that's all right with him.'

Rosenharte nodded.

When they were alone, they ordered more brandy and Harland delved into a plastic bag. 'This is your Stasi file,' he said quietly, handing Rosenharte a folder. 'I acquired it this evening from the Russian, who made it plain that his motive in handing it over was his concern and liking for you.' He pushed the file across the table. 'Before you read it, I must warn you that there are a number of shocks in here—things that will change your life. I haven't read all of it yet, but I think it's perhaps best to start at the back. The last sheet will set everything in context.'

Rosenharte glanced at him then turned to the back of the file. It was a letter from the Stasi headquarters in Dresden to Normannenstrasse HQ. It was dated May 1953.

We have made extensive enquiries into the two young men known as Rudolf and Konrad Rosenharte and have found that there are good reasons for taking no further action on the request from the Polish authorities for investigation and repatriation were these enquiries to be fruitful. Both young men have attained an exceptionally high academic standard, which is matched by their physical prowess. There is no telling what they may achieve for the state in future years. Since the war they have been brought up in a good socialist home. Their adoptive parents Marie Theresa and Hermann Rosenharte are robust working-class stock, ideologically staunch and active in the Party's cause. On the question of their time in the household of the fascist general and his

wife—Isobel and Manfred von Huth—we believe it is safe to conclude
that there has been no negative influence of any sort in the formation
of the personalities of the twins or of their political consciences.

We recommend informing the Polish authorities that we have been
unable to trace the children on the information supplied.

Rosenharte hardly knew how to react. Then he blurted, 'I knew it. Both of us felt that we couldn't have been born to that woman.' He took out the picture from his hip pocket and flattened it on the table. 'This is Isobel von Huth. Ulrike noticed that the photograph was taken in September 1939, when, of course, she should have been six months pregnant. But she's not. I thought it must have been a mistake in the dating. The man Grycko—this is what he was going to tell me in Trieste, wasn't it? He must have been some kind of relation, or closely associated with our family there.'

'Yes, I think that's plain,' said Harland. 'Maybe later you should talk to the Russian. He knows more about this than I do.'

Rosenharte returned to the papers and began to read the letter that had been sent by a Monsieur Michel Modroux from Red Cross headquarters in Geneva on December 3, 1956 to the Foreign Ministry in Berlin.

We again communicate with you on the matter of two twin boys taken
from the Kusimiak family home near Bochia, Poland. Ryszard and
Konstantyn Kusimiak were kidnapped in November 1939 by German
officers working for the Germanisation programme, known as
Lebensborn. They were the only children of Dr Michael Kusimiak and
his wife Urszula, both academics at the University of Kraków. After the
execution of their father and the imprisonment of their mother, it has
been ascertained that the boys were taken to Lodz concentration camp.
Having been assessed as racially valuable, soon after they were moved
to a Lebensborn home and given new names. Documents in the
Ministry of Interior in Warsaw suggest that the Kusimiak boys were
found a home with a senior-ranking Nazi. The Red Cross hope that the
time will now be found to research this case as it is believed there is
every chance the Kusimiak boys survived the war and were settled in
the GDR. We would urge you to expedite this matter.

'They knew the whole time! Those bastards in the Stasi knew the whole time that we had been taken from Poland. And if the Polish were making enquiries, it means that a part of the family survived the war. We have relatives. They denied us contact with our own flesh and blood.'

'Do you think your adoptive mother . . . did Frau Rosenharte know?'

Rosenharte shook his head. 'She only went to work at Schloss Clausnitz very late in the war so she wouldn't necessarily have known. She was a good woman and a very good mother. It wasn't in her nature to deceive.'

'They kept you for your talents,' said Harland, 'and it explains why you were allowed to join the Stasi in the first place. No one with an SS general as a father would have been allowed to join the HVA.'

'It's a tragedy that Konrad did not live to see all this tonight. He would have been amazed.'

Harland nodded. Rosenharte studied the British spy's face and wondered at the tension around his eyes. He asked him why he seemed distracted.

'I may lose the deal I set up with the Russian. Five hours ago it looked sweet, but then this happened and, well, it seems that the Americans are going to step in with their money and gather up everything I was working for.'

'Does it matter? After all, you achieved the arrest of Abu Jamal. You got Konrad's family out. And without your friend, Cuth Avocet, I would never have managed to release Ulrike.'

Harland pursed his lips. 'You're right. But my pride is offended. I wanted to pull it off. Still, when history takes over we all have to stand aside.'

He signalled for another round. When it came he said, 'My instructions from London specifically require me not to tell you the thing that I believe you ought to know.' He stopped, swirled the brandy in front of his nose and glanced out of the window. 'However, watching you go through that file, I realised that tonight I also have a duty to the truth.'

There was another pause. Then he said, 'Annalise Schering never died. There was no suicide.'

Rosenharte felt himself stiffen. 'No! She was dead. I saw her.'

'But you didn't touch her.' He paused. 'You left immediately. We had people in the apartment. You saw our little tableau with Annalise in the ice-cold bath and panicked, just as we hoped you would.'

'Why? It doesn't make sense.'

'She wasn't up to dealing with you. She wasn't sharp enough and she wanted out. We didn't know how you'd react. When you didn't immediately tell your people that she was dead and that you had in effect failed, we knew we could use you. We got the police involved and put a deal to you. Then we made sure they got rid of you by using the second Annalise to feed some bad stuff back to the Stasi about your drinking and your lack of discretion.'

Rosenharte was still dumbfounded. 'But the risk! I might have told the Stasi at any time.'

'There was no risk. The only person who was exposed was you. The longer the operation went on, the more important Annalise became to us, the Stasi and, of course, the Russians. You've got to remember it was the only method of telling your side what we actually intended without them putting it through the filter of suspicion. Because she was a traitor they trusted her.'

He opened his hands to invite reaction. Rosenharte said nothing.

'You have every right to be angry about this,' said Harland. 'I know how much that little stunt affected your life, but then . . . but then you have to appreciate that to us you were just another communist spy, a Romeo sent to the West to steal our secrets.' He paused. 'Look on the bright side, Rudi; at least you have no death on your conscience. The real Annalise Schering is living happily in the English shires with three teenage children.'

Rosenharte shook his head. He could have sprung his own shock on Harland by telling him how Ulrike and the second Annalise had worked together in the cause of peace for so long. But it wouldn't serve any purpose to reveal that a young Stasi translator had seen through MI6's great subterfuge. He rose from the table and threw back his brandy. 'That was another time—an age ago. Right now, Mr Harland, I need some sleep.'

'You're not angry?'

'In some ways. But remember I was able to leave the Stasi and devote my life to the study of art. Where would I be now without your spy games?'

ON SATURDAY, NOVEMBER 11, some thirty-six hours after the Wall fell, Rosenharte got up early in the hotel and put on the dark grey suit that he'd bought with Ulrike the day before. Then he sat at the desk and read the notes he'd made while on the phone to Leszek Grycko the previous evening. After about an hour Ulrike came in from the adjoining bedroom.

'How're you feeling?' he asked.

'Not great. It's unnatural to sleep for twelve hours.'

'You've woken from a long hibernation,' he said and touched the faint crease made on her cheek by the pillow. 'We all have.'

'Have you talked to Else?' she said, nuzzling him.

'Yes, they'll all be here by early evening.'

'Explain this to me,' she said, pointing at the crude family tree he had made while she slept.

He placed his finger by the name of Dr Michal Kusimiak. 'This is my father. He graduated from the Cieszyn Business School and in '36 went to teach politics at the University of Kraków. There he met my mother, Urszula Solanka, who was a nineteen-year-old student of literature. They were married almost immediately and on July 5, 1938 she gave birth to me and Konrad. We were named Ryszard and Konstantyn after our grandfathers.

'Come the war, my parents went into hiding at the Kusimiak family estate near the city of Bochia. They were hunted down. My father was summarily executed on November 7, at the age of thirty-one; Urszula was sent to Ravensbrück then Auschwitz. Konrad and I were taken to Lodz, then very soon afterwards to the von Huths at Schloss Clausnitz.'

He moved his finger to the name Luiza Solanka. 'This is my mother's older sister. She married a man named Grycko at the age of eighteen and had one son, Franciscek, who was born in 1930. She and her husband both perished in the camps, but their boy somehow survived. This was the man who died in my arms in Trieste.'

'Your first cousin!'

He shuddered. 'That's one of the things that I can't really absorb. The fact that he came so close to telling me all this. Franciscek joined the Polish Foreign Intelligence Service and began to make representations through his government and the Red Cross about the lost Kusimiak children. But it was useless. You see, about two hundred thousand Polish children were kidnapped in the Germanisation programme. Only thirty thousand were ever found and returned to their natural parents. But it seems that Franciscek couldn't let go of this thing, and when he retired he devoted all his energies to tracking us. It was he who made the breakthrough by finding a contact in Schwarzmeer's office. When he died, his son Leszek seemed to have inherited the cause. He was the man who followed me to Leipzig that day when we first met, and then he went all the way out to Konrad's home.'

She kissed the top of his head. 'How odd this must feel to you—seeing a life that was yours but that you haven't lived.'

'You could argue that if we hadn't been taken by the Nazis there would be no life at all. We might have died with the others in the camps.' He lit a cigarette and blew the smoke away from her. 'Shouldn't you be getting ready? Harland will be here soon.'

'ARE YOU NERVOUS?' Ulrike asked him as they waited for Harland at the entrance to the hotel.

'Yes and no. I don't know what I feel. I don't know what I should feel.'

It was a glorious autumn morning. As they drove southeast to Wannsee, Harland told them that the first sections of the Wall had been winched out of place at Potsdamerplatz to make a new crossing and that the Russian cellist Mstislav Rostropovich had played for the crowds streaming through another opening.

Rosenharte murmured interest in these bits of news, but said little.

They drove along Konigstrasse, the long, straight drive that cuts across Wannsee, and parked a hundred yards from the Glienicke Bridge.

'This is the only crossing point controlled by the Russians,' said Harland, as they all got out. 'Maybe Vladimir is making some kind of point.'

'Vladimir is the KGB spy from Dresden?' Ulrike asked Rosenharte.

'Yes,' he said. 'Major Vladimir Ilyich Ussayamov.'

'His name isn't Ussayamov,' said Harland. 'It's Putin. Lieutenant-Colonel Vladimir Vladimiric Putin.'

Rosenharte turned to him and shrugged.

'Do you want me to come?' Ulrike asked him.

He shook his head, turned and began to walk towards the old iron bridge over the Havel Lake that marked the border between the city of Berlin and the state of Brandenburg, between the territories of West and East. He reached the bridge and moved to a stone parapet on the right where there were fewer people.

No one, least of all Rosenharte in his rather uncertain state of mind, could fail to be moved by the scene. Westerners stood clapping as each little Trabant car passed over the line at the centre of the bridge. Red roses were flung at the cars and pedestrians and once or twice the women from the East stooped to pick them from the road and pressed them to their hearts.

Harland had followed and now passed him on the other side of the bridge. They nodded to each other. Rosenharte watched as he came to a halt by a figure who was leaning over the railings, looking down on the sparkling waters of the Havel. The figure straightened, and they shook hands. It was Vladimir. Harland gestured in Rosenharte's direction. Vladimir put his hand to his forehead and then held it high above him in a kind of salute. Rosenharte returned the wave but didn't move from his spot.

Turning, he spotted Leszek Grycko on the other side of the road. The tall young Pole saw him and waved back with a broad grin. Beside Leszek stood an elderly woman who was looking at him with intense curiosity. She brushed away a strand of dark grey hair that had come loose from her bun, nodded, then seemed to smile at him. For his entire life he had seen precisely the same expression of clever, restrained interest in Konrad's face. Here it was again in Urszula Kusimiak—his natural mother.

She waited for him to cross. Then, as he approached, she held out both her hands. He took them and she absorbed the face of the child she had lost almost fifty years before.

'I'm sorry,' he said. 'I'm sorry I couldn't bring my brother Konnie with me.' She nodded and shook her head and the corners of her mouth trembled with emotion. But her eyes remained composed, watching him with growing love. 'I wish he could have met you.' He suddenly thought of *Sublime No. 2*, the film Else had shown him. 'But I'm sure he knew instinctively of your existence. I believe he was aware of you in some deep part of himself.'

She put her head to one side. In deliberate German she said, 'We've both lost so much these past years. But now I have found you and I've gained two grandchildren. That is more than I could have ever hoped for.'

'You speak German. I was thinking it would be the final irony if we weren't able to communicate.'

'I learned in the camps in order to survive. I knew also that I would need it to find you after the war.' She stopped. 'And now I have.'

Out of the corner of his eye, he saw Ulrike approach. He turned. 'This is my friend Ulrike—the woman I hope to make my wife.'

Ulrike was shaking her head and pointing towards the bridge. They all turned. Standing in the middle of the bridge, oblivious to the traffic, was Colonel Zank. Rosenharte's hand moved to the pocket where he kept the gun.

Ulrike put her hand up. 'He's not coming; he's watching, Rudi. Leave him.'

Urszula Kusimiak seemed to know exactly what was going on. 'I suspect he is one of the few people who cannot cross the Glienicke Bridge today.'

'You're right,' said Rosenharte, noticing that Harland had left Vladimir and approached Zank from behind. Now he was saying something and patting his own pocket to indicate that Zank shouldn't try anything. Zank looked away.

Then Urszula Kusimiak took her lost son's arm and they turned to walk the gentle incline away from the bridge, leaving Colonel Zank trapped behind the force field that was once the Iron Curtain.

AFTERWORD

We have forgotten the tragic power of the Berlin Wall and also, perhaps, what it meant when, on Thursday, November 9, 1989, East Germans massed at the border crossings and West Germans climbed onto the Wall in front of the Brandenburg Gate to demand its destruction. Few who were there will ever again experience the surge of joy and optimism of those hours. Or the incredulity. For even after one million East Germans demonstrated against their government in Alexanderplatz, no one would have dared to predict that within a week those same people would be shopping in West Berlin.

People were bent on change, and came together around the thriving evangelical churches of the East, particularly the Nikolai Church in Leipzig. As the Monday evening demonstrations there swelled with crowds chanting the simple self-assertion, *Wir sind das Volk*—we are the people—Honecker seemed incapable of acting. It's interesting to speculate what might have been if a younger generation of hardliners had succeeded at the beginning of the decade. Honecker was seventy-four and had undergone an operation that summer; Erich Mielke, the Head of the Stasi, was eighty-one. The other members of the Politburo were mostly over sixty-five. In the face of such orderly and disciplined defiance of the state, they simply froze.

We have also forgotten the curious nature of the East German state. The GDR possessed the most formidable intelligence services the world has ever seen. A population of just over 17,000,000 was served—if that's the right word—by 81,000 intelligence officers belonging to the Ministerium für Staatssicherheit—or Stasi for short. Some estimates put the number of informers at 1,500,000 million, which meant that every sixth or seventh adult was working for the Stasi, making regular reports on colleagues, friends and relations.

Run from a vast complex in Normannenstrasse, Berlin, the Stasi was a state within a state. It had its own football team, prisons, special shops selling foreign luxuries, holiday resorts, hospitals and sports centres. Large and well-equipped regional offices were in every city. In Leipzig, where part of my story is set, thousands of pieces of mail were opened every day, over 1,000 telephones were tapped, and 2,000 officers were charged with penetrating and monitoring every possible group and organisation. Their efforts were augmented by as many as 5,000 IMS—*Inoffizielle Mitarbeiters*, or unofficial collaborators—who were debriefed by Stasi controllers in some seventy safe houses around the city.

The dismal paranoia of Erich Mielke's organisation is hard to imagine today. Even schoolchildren's essays were examined for signs of political dissent at home, and in museums in Leipzig and Berlin you can still view the sealed preserving jars containing cloth impregnated with the personal smells of targeted dissidents. There is no better symbol of the Stasi's powers of intrusion and their absurd levels of obsession. The special equipment they made for themselves has a comic ingenuity about it: the cameras hidden in briefcases, petrol cans or the headlight of a Trabant car; a bugged watering can, which lay unregarded in one of the garden allotments outside Leipzig to catch anyone being disloyal as they tended their vegetables. East Germany was a truly dreadful place to live if you objected to the regime, or showed anything but craven loyalty to the state.

I have tried, as far as possible, to thread my story through the actual timeline of events that occurred between the beginning of September and the weekend of November 11–12, 1989. Although this is clearly a work of fiction, some real people are portrayed. Erich Mielke, the head of the Stasi, makes a cameo appearance. I hope that I have done him justice. Lt Colonel Vladimir Putin was at the time a KGB officer stationed in Dresden. Of course, his role in this plot is entirely made up. My character Colonel Otto Biermeier is very loosely based on Colonel Rainer Wiegand, a courageous member of the Stasi's counterespionage directorate who revealed details of East Germany's collaboration with Middle Eastern terrorists in the West.

The characters of Mike Costelloe and Lisl Voss are based on real people. When news of the Wall coming down hit London on November 9, 1989, both were attending an informal dinner at Langan's Brasserie in London for the West German intelligence service.

Schloss Clausnitz, the grand country house where Rudi and Konrad Rosenharte were taken as babies at the beginning of the war, is based, brick for brick, on Schloss Basedow, a huge pile in the Mecklenburg-Vorpommern region. I have moved it to the beech forests of southern Saxony.

Henry Porter, London, 2004

HENRY PORTER

Home: London
Likes: P. G. Wodehouse & Graham Greene
Hates: reality TV; 'British yobs abroad'

RD: How did your writing career start?

HP: I began as a journalist. I wrote a play or two and some short stories, and a lot of long and, I hope, amusing poems to celebrate various occasions. Then I had an idea for my first novel, *Remembrance Day* [published in 1999].'

RD: All your books are about espionage. What is it that fascinates you about the subject?

HP: I have always been a great admirer of John le Carré's early work. But more important is the fact that spies generally have something to hide, whether it's history or a motive, and I find that interesting. I like their world. I know quite few and am always fascinated by the difficulties, drudgery and lack of reward or recognition that constitute the average spy's life.

RD: Where were you the night the Berlin Wall came down?

HP: I was actually in Berlin. Something was obviously going to happen, though at the time we expected only demonstrations. My feelings were total shock and joy. I remember letting myself down into the East, having climbed the Wall, fully convinced that I was dreaming. But of course my feelings were as nothing compared to the delirious reaction of the East Germans. It was difficult not to have a lump in your throat that whole weekend.

RD: Apart from conveying the events of that emotional night, what else did you set out to do in *Brandenburg*?

HP: I wanted to weave a plot through what were effectively the last eight weeks of the Communist era in the German Democratic Republic, and to explain the sudden collapse of a fierce Communist dictatorship. I was also taken by the idea of the hero's enlightenment about his own life in some way keeping pace with the extraordinary events of those weeks.

RD: Did you spend much time in Germany researching the book?

HP: A great deal of time. I was born in England, but I spent the early years of my life in Germany. I love the country and am interested by its haunted corners—

ruined houses that still stand after the bombing of Dresden in 1945, abandoned railway sidings, disued facilities, and so on.

RD: How did you set about researching the book?

HP: I interviewed former members of the East German Government and spent a lot of time soaking up the atmosphere of the place, much of which is unchanged. I found visiting detention centres and former government buildings almost as valuable as the interviews. You really get the texture and feel of the GDR from them.

RD: Is Rudi based on anyone in particular?

HP: There is quite a bit of me in Rudi. I am an art historian by training and I know about the things he knows about. I spend a great deal of time in galleries looking at pictures. So, his sensibility and tastes are mine. He is a spy who has reservations about the business (as I do) and he can be rather thoughtless, perhaps like me . . . I hope not! But he has the ability to listen and to think his way out of a problem. His looks are based on a rather distinguished man I once saw in Dresden.

RD: What led you to incorporate the Lebensorn programme into the plot?

HP: I had read about it in an excellent study of the Red Cross by Caroline Moorhead, *Dunant's Dream*, and realised that almost nothing had been written about the 250,000 children who were stolen from Poland, Hungary and Czechoslovakia for 'Germanisation' by the Nazis. Only ten to twenty per cent were returned, and when the Iron Curtain fell across Europe there was little incentive for either side to repatriate citizens. I find their story almost unbearable to think about. Now, of course, those who did return are all in their sixties.

RD: What do you find the hardest part of writing a book?

HP: The first two chapters. They take months. Then I usually get lost in the middle and think the whole book is useless. I worry about publication and dread the reviews. Then I start it all over again, wondering if I should do something sensible like drive a cab for a living.

RD: If someone offered you a job in British intelligence would you take it?

HP: Errr . . . I'm not sure. It can be very dull and, if you're in an embassy pretending to do one job while your main job is spying, it can be rather a lot of work.

RD: You must have written about many different subjects during your journalistic career. What gets you most heated?

HP: The current attacks on civil liberties, the bone-headed attitude to the environment, and unnecessary intrusion of Government into personal choice.

RD: Other than writing, what gives you most enjoyment in life?

HP: Family, looking at pictures, travelling, walking in the Pyrenees, painting (when I have the time), gardening, and my dachsund.

DIGGER

MAX ANDERSON

Gold. For centuries, men have fought and died for it, used it to build their palaces and temples and to create symbols of enduring love. To this day, it remains an absolute measure of wealth and power with an irresistible lure.

One of those smitten by gold fever is Englishman Max Anderson, whose obsession with finding his own share of the earth's treasure took him to the far side of the world on a real-life adventure.

PROLOGUE

Listen carefully and I'll tell you where the gold is.

Deep inside Western Australia, in the semiarid lands of the North-eastern Goldfields, there's a tap. It's an ordinary metal tap, with small cauliflowers of mineral growing on its spout, and it sits in the shade of two iron water tanks raised on wooden towers. When the winter breezes slither over the red soils, a tin windmill creaks and clanks and draws water from deep underground to replenish the tanks. Sometimes the tap is hard to see, so it's best to look for the frenzied, shrimp-pink figure dancing naked before it.

I splash myself with the frigid bore waters, clenching my teeth, hot-footing around thorns and a swelling mud pool the colour of tomato soup. Then I shudder, gulp in some air and stick my head under the tap: the icy water shrinks my scalp and makes me hoot and pant and curse.

Suddenly there are voices from the east. I stand up and peer out over the clearing, but see no one, only the railway line at the far edge and beyond that the corrugated iron roof of the one-hundred-year-old Grand Hotel pub. It's pub noise I can hear, the faint sounds of an approaching Friday night, the *whump-whump* of car doors, bawdy 'G-days!' and the nasal click-clack of Wongutha native language. It's Friday night in the town of Kookynie, a night when the population soars. To around twenty-five.

Kookynie's thirteen permanent residents live in eight buildings, the only structures left standing in a town that once served 7,000. Everything else is foundations, rubble and mining waste. Tour maps mark Kookynie as a ghost town, but it can't be, because the ghost hasn't been given up.

I return to my tap wash, satisfied that no one is paying a surprise visit.

I'm afforded some privacy by a fuzzy green curtain of peppertree that circles the water towers. The peppertree is home to birds, lizards, insects and me. One side gives shade and wind protection to my tent, another forms a dangling green awning under which I park my Toyota four-wheel drive.

The winter sun is a clipped coin on the western vista. Some evenings I climb the water tower until I'm above the peppery fuzz and watch as the sun melts into a sea of mulga trees. A single mulga is a hunched, mean-leaved tree that can turn its ugly back on drought, but en masse it glints silver, ripples away to far horizons and makes you think hopeful thoughts. The people of Kookynie occasionally refer to it as the mulga and more often as the bush. They treat it with respect. 'You wanna be careful in there,' they say.

I'd like to go into the mulga. Not yet and not lightly, because it's huge, about 2,500 square kilometres of waterless lands, punctuated throughout with abandoned mine shafts. But I want in, as deeply as any has dared. I want to find a patch, too, and score an X with my heel in the rough red earth, and I want to dig up gold. I can picture it: a place where, beneath the black, snakelike pebbles and the iron-rich ochres, there lies a rock shot through with yellow signatures. And I'm a broad, solid figure, standing over my X, with my long-handled shovel raised high over my head, thrilling that I'm going somewhere that no one—no one—has ever been.

I straddle the mud pool once again and bend low before the tap to rinse soap from my hair. I start to wail and blow, then I stop. It's time to square my shoulders. There's only one way I'm going to find where the gold is, and that's by washing out the dirty labours of my day and taking my place at the bar among the prospectors drinking at the Grand Hotel, Kookynie.

AT THE AGE of seven, I spent weeks digging a hole at the end of our very long, thin and often ramshackle garden. If television wasn't serving or if the children next door had been packed off to church, I'd find my grandfather's old spade and drag it noisily over the paving-slab path. The path ended at a wall of raspberry plants that cordoned off an area of turfed ground, far from the busy workings of the brick house. Here I worked at digging my hole.

Dad made the long trek one afternoon to see the shaft I had sunk. He was only thirty-one, and he spoke with gentle enthusiasm to his unusually small, rather excitable young son: 'Hiya, Max,' he would have said, or 'Ey-up, Son,' which was the Derbyshire way. 'Ey-up, you're a good way down!'

I looked up at him from the mouth of my hole, swallowed nearly to my shoulders, and his surprise at the progress of my project caused me to puff inside with stuff I'd later recognise as pride.

'Found anything?'

'Not really,' I said. 'I found this. Is this something?' I let my spade fall, turned to the north rim, where I'd placed various treasures, and took a blob of material the size and colour of a sucked Toffo.

He crouched down, took the blob in his hands and split it with his large, hard thumbnails. It crumbled somewhat disappointingly and I wished he'd asked before he split it. 'No . . . It's an oxide, I think. Like rust. Might have been attached to a piece of metal.' Dad knew about metal; he worked with it in the factory, trimming curls and burrs from the edges of finely cast parts, before skilled engineers assembled the pieces into Rolls-Royce aero-engines. At the factory, men like my dad were called semiskilled.

'Is it old?' Old would be OK. Viking old or Roman old would be good. Dinosaur old would be really good.

'I don't think so, Son.'

'Dad,' I said, 'what would happen if I struck oil?'

'Oil?' Dad took the question seriously, as he took all my questions. 'Well, we'd call the oil company, and they'd measure to see how much oil was down there. If it was a large amount, they'd come and build an oil pump over it and run a pipe to a refinery. But raw oil . . . It'd be a lot of trouble.'

I looked up at him. I'd really wanted to ask how *rich* I would become.

'It'd be better if you struck water,' he continued. 'To use in the garden.'

But I didn't want to strike water; I wanted to strike oil, or gold, or things that the Derby museum would gladly pay for, something that would be displayed in a glass case, with a small plaque with my name on it.

'If you go much deeper, you'll need shuttering,' he added.

'What's that?' I asked. But I already knew it for what it was, a dull thing among shiny plans.

'Shuttering,' he continued. 'Planks of wood to hold back the walls. If it rains, the soil might be washed back into the hole.' He pointed to my clayish spoil heap. 'The walls might come down on top of you.'

He explained how shuttering worked, how it could be built, but I'd stopped listening. I stopped listening often, usually when he was explaining how to fix his car. He believed I was absorbing everything because I opened my eyes wide and inserted noises into all the right pauses. It's a skill I haven't lost, though I pay a fortune in mechanic's fees.

We left the hole for lunch. But the shuttering caused this particular project to lose its sparkle and I abandoned it, allowing it to weather at the sides and slowly fill itself in.

So I dug another hole.

One summer evening, in half-light that swarmed with gnats, I sank a narrow shaft. I dug it quickly, punching through the tight turf and scooping down and down. Eventually, my top half was entirely swallowed while my legs lay flat against the lawn: anyone looking on would have seen half a boy. From my perspective, however, I was upside-down in a dark, cold-smelling cavity with my checked shirt falling loosely round my shoulders. The sensations convinced me I was a miner down deep. And it was electrifying.

This time I was burying treasure—a crinkly white plastic bag containing a trove of large coins of little value.

Steven Betteridge, who lived next door but one, was kneeling beside me, acting as custodian of the bag. He was five, a little kid, but his witnessing of the treasure burial was essential. At regular intervals I would extract my upper half from the shaft, clutching handfuls of excavated soil. Soon it was time to lower the bag of coins into the hole. Grunting in the small clammy space, I called up a narration to Steven so he could monitor our progress, before finally surfacing so we could infill and plug the swatch of turf back into the lawn. Then there was a loud whistle of summons from a far silhouette in a lit doorway, and we returned to our homes.

Mum was furious that I was filthy and ordered me into the bath, then to bed, but I didn't sleep. Outside lay the bag of coins deep in the cold, black ground. There was treasure buried in my back garden. My excitement wouldn't be overcome and I dug up the bag first thing in the morning.

My subterranean proclivities were variously expressed in the construction of trench networks, underground dwellings, even a swimming pool, when a shallow pit was fed with a hosepipe. While certain rules were enforced, I was never totally discouraged from making forays into the ground. But eventually, my zest for digging holes, my urgency to find *something*, fell into a doughty wooden chest, to be hasped, locked and left to sink out of sight beneath time's strata. And certainly the layers piled on—a friable teen-hood, the moist loam of university, some shifting sands of travel, a few ashes and a flinty pursuit of career. But like all good buried treasure, it would sit, perfectly undisturbed and at a slight angle.

Waiting.

1

After London, I thought the provinciality of Adelaide in South Australia would benefit my head like nutcrackers benefit a walnut. I was wrong. The city was unhurried and well mannered, ringed by generous parklands where kids practised soccer at nights and grown-ups played cricket at the weekends; a thirty-minute drive and you were at the beach or among vineyards or in oak-shaded hilltop villages that might have been in Wiltshire were it not for the koala road signs. Adelaide had space; its people had time. Here was a city with the keys to urban contentment.

I arrived in January 2002 and stayed until April, enjoying a late but splendid antipodean summer. In four months, my face was pumiced clean of its grubby London dermis and revitalised with fresh air, sea salt and good food. And in those four months three new things came into my life. The first was a Toyota 4.2-litre Land Cruiser Troop Carrier with twin tanks, spotlights and a sleeping space where rear seats had been removed. The second was a small orange dog. And the third was a woman with a heart as big as a milk pail.

A pity, then, that only two of these would be accompanying me to the goldfields of Western Australia.

'You'll be my Turon Widow,' I said, hoping the thin historical association might bind her to the project, and distract her as I hammered some final kit into the Troop Carrier before driving away from our months of happiness.

'What's a Turon Widow?' said the Turon Widow, her question unmarked by any wanting to know.

'It's what they called the women left behind by men who went digging for gold in the Turon fields in the . . . ahh . . . 1850s. The Turon River is in New South Wales. I've been there. Beautiful area . . .' The Widow was looking at the ground. 'Come on,' I said softly. 'Just keep thinking about that thirty-ounce nugget. Twenty thousand dollars. A deposit on a house. Only yesterday I was reading about a bloke who found a fifty-ouncer near Kalgoorlie.'

'Yeah, and I bet he was using a metal detector.'

'Tourists and part-timers use metal detectors,' I said. 'You think the prospectors in Kookynie use metal detectors?'

'Yes.'

'No. Deep veins of gold aren't found with a metal detector.'

She folded her arms. 'So how are they found?'

I heaved my heavy suitcase of books into the back of the vehicle, knowing I didn't have a precise answer to her question. 'Look, a hundred years ago the old-timers had a pick and shovel and they found tonnes of gold. There's no reason why I can't do the same. And anyway, there's plenty of idiots who'll rush out and buy a detector and never find a single speck. And that's five thousand dollars down the toilet.'

The books in the suitcase were written by men who had prospected during the 1890s, the 'roaring days' of the West Australian fields. I'd spent weeks buried in their exploits. I believed that the books would serve as my treasure maps, help me count the paces to where X marked the spot.

'Here,' she said. 'I bought you this.' The one-cup Bodum coffee plunger was cute and thoughtful, a practical memento of the big plunger pot I'd taken into the bedroom on Saturday mornings along with newspapers and ideas on how to spend the day. I kissed her and tucked the little pot safely into a plastic bin of utensils, stowed in a long steel drawer that slid out from under the bed in the back of the Troop Carrier. Aussie blokes called the vehicle a Troopie. You could hear some mute approval in the way they said it: 'Got y'self a Troopie, eh? Jeez, she's well kitted out.'

'Dog, stop that.' The small orange dog looked up. She wasn't so small. Like a Labrador not quite grown. But she acted small in the way she sat, keen to please and smart as carrots, her neat white bib showing like a dress shirt in an orange tuxedo. Sensing something was amiss, she'd begun to fret. The Widow bent to give the dog's limp ears a fondle, said her name softly to reassure her. I liked the way the Widow said the dog's name, quickly, with two little beats. But I made a habit of rolling my eyes when I told people what the dog was called, indicating I wasn't to blame for the name.

The Widow stood and said, 'You'd better get going soon.'

She'd frequently asked, 'How long will you be gone?' to which I'd replied, 'I don't know,' or, 'However long it takes to find us some gold.' Closer to my leaving, I'd agreed to, 'Maybe six months. Maybe less, maybe more.' I'd glanced into her eyes, and remembered to look deeply so the guilt wouldn't show. Hers were soft grey eyes, enormous things, though sometimes they'd light with flashes of green if she was tired or livid. It was a shock when those eyes spilt enormous teardrops. We'd been standing under the shower, two hours before I was going to take the Troopie north to steal a few hours of night driving away from the city. I marvelled at the tears, so large that they maintained their shape and course, even under the shower stream. She looked away and swore, promising she wouldn't cry again. Not when night fell and it was time to throw the dog into the truck. And not when I slammed the dual rear doors shut, one of them hung with a magnificent spare wheel.

The once cavernous vehicle now sounded dead with stuff: 'provisioning', I called it, but in reality it was boxes of guesses, racks of contingencies, cases of just-in-cases, all acquired by the unknowing in anticipation of the unknown. The small orange dog didn't like her allotted space in the back and leapt into the passenger seat. She pressed her moist nose to the window and watched as the Widow and I kissed and hugged goodbye, our figures lit by pale light coming through the door of the rented terrace cottage.

'See you soon,' I said and climbed into the cab, smelling its vacuumed interior. 'Dog, get in the back.' There was a loud cough of ignition.

'Bring me back some gold!' she called over the engine noise. She waved and smiled as her man and her dog ground their way up the street in the growling Troop Carrier. Then she folded her arms, turned back into the lit doorway and quickly shut down the rectangle of light, as my heavy, bloated wagon slogged into the night streets.

After an hour driving north, the lights of Adelaide had long dribbled away and the highway was black as oil; only the Troopie's high beams forged between the fenceless fields of grain stubble. Two hours more, and I turned off the highway into a lonely dirt road to park beside a gum tree. I slid out of the cab, opened the rear doors to fix my bed, cracked my shin bone on the tow hitch, bashed my head against a stereo speaker screwed into the ceiling and emptied a glass of water over my rucksack of clothes.

It wasn't until I wormed into the Widow's eiderdown sleeping-bag beneath a row of cool windows that I relaxed. I stared at a slim swatch of constellations and an idle thought lit up, about the Victorian explorer-hero of the 1800s. I pictured him leaving his wife and family, declaring bitter regrets at being forced to abandon love and comfort for pain and peril, all at the behest of queen, God and nation. Me, I just wanted to dig up some gold. But I'd stolen an insight, and I'd lay money that, however hard the adventurer pounded his breast, his heart was filled with a dull and filthy awareness that the sacrifice was really being made by the person he'd left crying on the doorstep.

I winced at the idea of the Widow sitting alone in the quiet little terrace, and vowed I'd make it up to her. I'd find her a huge gold nugget. I really would.

AFTER REPORTS of 'Gold!' in 1851, hundreds of thousands of men left their homes in the cities, towns and villages of Britain to dig the fields of the Australian colonies. Tens of thousands more came from Europe, Asia and North America. And in Australia itself, previously sedentary people began streaming across the face of the continent. Gold caused changes to the embryo nation that were radical and perverse.

For sixty-five years, from 1787 when the first convict ship sailed for the colony, Britain conducted a sociopathic programme to cleanse itself of riffraff by piping it offshore like sewage. Transportees—killers and horse stealers, but also the political undesirables of Ireland and maids caught pilfering hand-kerchiefs—faced a punishing three-month sea voyage followed by hard labour under a harsh regime in an isolated, alien and often hostile environment.

But when the eucalypt forests were rolled back, along with their pesky insects and 'troublesome' black people, there came to light a fruity loam capable of raising fine pasture, plus a handsome amount of coal. As time was served, the convicts were let out. Some were given the freedom to take a little land or seek paid work under the pioneering free settlers, who had estab-lished a lucrative wool industry. The ex-convicts bore free children, and by 1850 Australian towns were rapidly succumbing to the civilising influences of growth, prosperity and moderate government.

The first acknowledged Australian gold strike was made in February 1851 in Bathurst, New South Wales, by Edward Hammond Hargraves, who chased up rumours of the metal's whereabouts and, with two locals, succeeded in panning a few paltry specks from Lewis Ponds Creek. Hargraves spread the word and incited a rush to the place he named Ophir, eventually netting himself £10,000. Some 2,000 people left Bathurst and Sydney to camp along the creek of the Ophir valley, helping themselves each day to an ounce or two of Queen Victoria's gold using simple tin dishes as pans. The governor, unwilling and unable to enforce Crown entitlement, resorted to selling miner's licences. Thus the great chapter of Australian gold was begun.

A rash of fields was quickly discovered, fantastic tales of treasure reached London, and gold fever swept through the nation's farms, mills, mines and workshops. Lord Grey, secretary for the colonies, was quite content for work-ing people to sail south and invest their labour in the profitable taming of Australia; the champions of an uncompromising penal system were less so. They were already concerned that their living hell offered ex-convicts good land, good food and a modest living. Now it was providing gold.

The last convict ship bound for the penal colonies of NSW and Van Diemen's Land (Tasmania) sailed in 1852. In the same year, Australian gold worth £2 million sailed into British ports and more than 5,000 British emigrants *paid* to sail across the globe every week. Between 1851 and 1861, half a million people sailed from Britain alone. By 1856, ninety-three tonnes of gold had been unearthed, more than during the earlier Californian rush and more than the Yukon rush would yield at the end of the century.

At first the gold seekers headed to New South Wales, but when bubbles of alluvial gold were found in the dun gullies of Ballarat and Mount Alexander there was a great rush southwards, into the fledgling colony soon to be named Victoria.

As foretold, the labour market imploded when men ditched their stock whips, meat cleavers and forges—and even stethoscopes, legal gowns and police batons—to take up a shovel. The infant government of Victoria was besieged by soaring labour prices, a chronic revenue deficit and a rash of lawless areas requiring expensive policing. In a bid to stop the rot, it enforced a punitive mining tax of thirty shillings (half an ounce of gold) a month. When police moved into the canvas shanty towns to collect, some diggers bolted in the opposite direction. But in 1854 the tax met more serious resistance in the form of Australia's only armed rebellion.

The muddled uprising at Ballarat's Eureka field is sometimes regarded as the moment when ordinary men from disparate nations resisted British rule. When a detachment of soldiers was ordered to quell the uprising, they found 120 diggers camped inside a crude stockade armed with pikes and a motley assortment of guns. The rout left twenty diggers and four soldiers dead, all martyred at the birth of Australian nationhood. But while some of the leaders held loftier ideals, Eureka was mostly a rebellion of Irish diggers agitating for the removal of a tax that was especially hard on men looking for deep veins of gold, men who had to invest months sinking shafts before locating a shred of metal. The tax was scrapped within half a year.

Diggers across the colonies were meanwhile causing a subtler and more lasting change. Out of the shallow alluvial burrows and deep clanking shafts emerged a new breed of people, a white, resilient, self-assured people who would come to proclaim themselves 'Australian'. Gold betrayed no class bias when delivering itself into the pan or shovel, even favouring the calloused land labourers and navvies who worked their claims faster and deeper. Rewards were accorded on the basis of sweat and ingenuity, a

336 | MAX ANDERSON

'shammy' pouch of nuggets engendering independence and respect in a world away from the stifling class system of Britain.

A letter to *The Times* described a disgraceful episode in which a gentleman farmer had offered a shilling if a digger would help him lift a heavy sack. The digger proffered his boot, the lace of which was untied: 'Do you see that? I'll give *you* three shillings to tie it.'

AFTER a ten-hour trip and another night in a South Australian parking bay, I'd crossed into Western Australia. Ahead of me was a long drive through the country's biggest state: 700 kilometres west across the Nullarbor to Norseman, 200 kilometres north to Kalgoorlie, and 200 kilometres more to Kookynie, deep in the goldfields.

The nothing of the Nullarbor was crushing, and I swear it bent my faculties out of shape. How else to account for my lunatic programme of fuel efficiency, for my scrutinising needles and clocks while sticking doggedly to eighty kilometres per hour on one of the straightest roads in the world. Only months earlier I might have drawn a rich travel story from the drive. I'd have stopped to look at the ocean from dramatic cliffs, cut metaphorical slices in the blank limestone to reveal cataclysmic geological dramas, sat in grim roadhouses listening to local talk while drinking slow beers under neon mozzie zappers. I'd have peeled back the emptiness and let the reader gorge. Right now, I couldn't be arsed. It was interminable. And any brighter horizons were dimmed by a grim slab of cloud extending further than the road. Besides, I'd ditched my travel writer's pen to take up a shovel and dig for gold.

In December 2001, I'd resigned as the deputy travel editor of one of Britain's Sunday national newspapers. Six of us were charged with compiling a travel section that met exacting standards of insight and erudition. We achieved this by throwing things at each other and swearing a lot. It was the perfect job. When I wasn't laughing I was editing, and when I wasn't editing I was travelling. I hiked in Tanzania, sailed in the Caribbean and cruised to Antarctica. I skied, snorkelled, went salmon fishing in helicopters and punctured the earth's atmosphere over South Africa in a Lightning jet.

On assignment, I'd keep my eyes on the ground; I found pottery in Iran, some rusted militaria in Haiti, relics of the penal colony in French Guiana. But just when I'd fashioned a digging stick for myself, it was always time to go and do something else.

It was obvious what I really wanted. I daydreamed a short list—Russia,

Brazil, Zaire, South Africa, Canada, Australia—all the countries in my atlas speckled with mineral icons and all appealingly remote, suggesting a man and his spade might be left undisturbed should they spend a few months turning a sod or two. Slowly the daydream became a serious consideration. I revisited my short list, discounted Russia and Brazil on account of language barriers, struck off the African countries for safety's sake and thought a North American working visa might be problematic.

Which left Australia. One afternoon, with my feet on my desk, I was flicking through the newspaper's glossy supplement. I found a feature on small-time prospectors pulling gold out of the West Australian deserts, a feature that mentioned an outback ghost town called Kookynie, a pub and a windmill. By coincidence, I'd been assigned down under on a two-week press junket to drive cattle in South Australia. I stayed on my horse but fell heavily for the PR manager herding the journalists. She lived in Adelaide.

So Australia it was. I resigned from the newspaper, delighted to be digging a hole for myself.

Rain fell hard on the Nullarbor, stiff pellets of wild rain that rapped on the white shell of the Troopie. I stopped for lunch at a roadhouse, one of the older Eyre Highway rest stops where chronic isolation is reflected in the stale decor, languorous service and sky-high prices. The dining room was empty except for a woman at a window table smoking sad cigarettes. She wearily asked where I was headed.

'A place called Kookynie. North of Kalgoorlie.'

She exhaled smoke at the window, looked out at the grey sky rolling over the plains of pale yellow grasses. 'Y'hoping to find gold, are ya?'

'Yep,' I said.

'Got a detector, have ya?'

'Actually, no; I want to do it the old-fashioned way. Dig for gold.' Then I quickly added, 'I'm thinking I might get myself a lease so I can work on it properly.' I had no idea what I was talking about.

She took a drag on her cigarette. 'Mining companies got all the land stitched up. And there ain't no gold left anyway. All the easy gold's bin found.'

I forked something greasy into my mouth.

'You got friends out there, have ya?'

'No,' I said. 'Never been. I'm just going to turn up.' My voice had unconsciously adopted her own flat tones. 'Maybe stay a few months.'

The woman gave a little twist of her head, kinking her exhaled smoke.

I wrapped a piece of toast in a serviette for the dog and said I had to get going. 'See you later.' The expression was sometimes used between strangers on parting in this sprawling, empty continent. I never worked out whether it was underpinned with polite hope or laconic irony.

'Good luck,' she said.

As usual, the dog was behind the steering wheel, looking like it was her turn to drive. She gently took the toast. I went to the back of the vehicle, hauled myself onto the spare wheel and then up onto the roof rack. I checked that the tent, tarpaulins and jerry cans were roped tight and began climbing down. But I slipped off the wheel and, still gripping the roof rack with one hand, swung out and slammed against the side of the vehicle. A muscle in my armpit stretched painfully and a splinter of unease lodged in my stomach.

Was I ready for the wilds of WA? Just how equipped was I to do this? In my years of travel writing, I'd regularly sleep under the stars, but only five of them, awarded to the hotel or resort for unstinting excellence. I'd never camped longer than two days, couldn't cook and didn't know how to fix a two-tonne Land Cruiser Troop Carrier if it broke down in the bush. I couldn't gut a fish, I blenched at blood and the nearest things I had to a working man's calluses were inflamed tendons from typing on laptop computers.

These doubts were nothing as to the misgivings I had about the locals. What did I know about prospectors, miners, drillers, jackaroos, shearers, roo shooters and other people of the bush? In the early 1990s, I'd muddled along quite successfully as a Brit among Australians, working and playing among Sydney's creative types. But rural West Australians would call these Eastsiders 'tall poppies', 'big-noters' and 'poofters'. And what—don't say it too loudly—about Aboriginal people? I'd seen a few. I'd met one. But other than that my knowledge was a map of white space, a *terra nullius* where neither myself nor my Sydney friends ever seemed to go.

None of my concerns were alleviated when, soliciting advice about the goldfields trip, I'd been counselled to get a gun. Not once, but many times.

'What do I need a gun for?'

Wry grimaces, crinkled eyes and tugs at extended chins all suggested situations that might be resolved with a gun in my truck, my tent or my hand. Then someone elected to be succinct: 'Look, you're going for six months into the bush and there'll be some mad bastards out there. I'd get a gun.'

But a gun was absolutely out of the question. If security was a problem, I'd deal with it another way. I'd get a dog.

The Widow's brother, who lived in Darwin, had undergone a family breakup. An offshore fisherman, he'd been left with the family pet and the problem of what to do with her. 'She's a good dog, mate,' he'd told me on the phone. 'She'll do you right . . .' I collected her at Adelaide airport in February. She was a funny-looking thing. You could see she had Alsatian in her, but where there should have been stiff Colditz-patrol ears, there hung lame, floppy flaps. It looked like she'd failed alertness class. The rest of her was either Labrador or ridgeback. And her small nature soon peeped out. A blind terrier bumbled up to her in the park one day and made off with her tennis ball. She never barked, and she would shrink if I picked up a rake or, more depressingly, my gold digger's shovel.

The road before me was dark, smothered by a great black weather front so huge that it seemed another continent was hovering a few centimetres overhead. I inspected my fuel needle and the minutely rotating kilometre wheel and listened to the patient noise of the big diesel engine.

And the woman's nicotined words curled into view: 'There ain't no gold left anyway. All the easy gold's bin found.'

AUSTRALIA'S diggers were a ragtag bunch of nationalities bound together by experience, knowledge and a readiness to move wherever the gold was richest. Successive strikes had drawn them in an anticlockwise direction round the continent. After the rushes of NSW and Victoria, they moved north into Queensland and then, in 1886, Hall's Creek in the tropical ceiling of Western Australia. From here the pioneer parties would circle south again, opening most of WA's gold regions within five years.

They travelled by horse, by dray, by bicycle and on foot, some pushing an iron-wheeled barrow containing pan, pick, shovel and roll of bedding or 'swag'. Blinded by the dazzle of gold, some of the diggers underestimated distances, misunderstood climate and miscalculated their ability to survive. Tramping from the north of Western Australia to the south was like slogging from Stockholm to Sicily or from Vladivostok to Hong Kong. It's not recorded how many died, but they became known as the Legion of the Lost.

In 1892, Arthur Bayley and William Ford found 554 ounces of gold on Fly Flat. Worth £2,000, ten times a working man's annual salary, it triggered a frantic gold rush, and a diggers' camp swelled at a place called Coolgardie. Again, gold seekers poured in from overseas, but reports of 'nuggets lying on the floor like spuds' also provoked adventuresome Australians to arrive in their tens of thousands. It would be described as the greatest single movement of people in the nation's history.

Joining the savvy old diggers were legions of 'new chums', novices in clean clothes with shiny shovels and fresh swags, keen as mustard. They sailed from Adelaide, Melbourne and Sydney to land in Perth and Esperance, then sped by train to Southern Cross. There they were at the mercy of the horse-drawn coach companies. Some 600 unsprung vehicles shuttled back and forth to Coolgardie, a miserable four-day journey for which the roguish teamsters charged exorbitant fares and villainous cartage fees. Not a few diggers slung their swag on their backs and made the journey by foot.

But in and around Coolgardie, men staked their claims and got to work. At first they sifted the dusts with pans and dry-blowers, looking for nuggets, the nodules of alluvial gold washed free and worn smooth by ancient rivers. Then they dug deeper, sinking shafts to chase the lodes or reefs, the veins of gold trapped in quartz and dark ironstone. Some diggers hit the sort of pay dirt that aroused the interest of London speculators, who sent representatives to assay, risk-assess and ultimately buy. Soon, gold was doing for Western Australia what it had done for the eastern colonies in the 1850s: in 1891 the population of WA was 49,700; in ten years it had soared to 184,100.

Boom towns were well named. Coolgardie's population exploded from a handful of prospectors to a canvas settlement of 4,000 in a matter of weeks. The racket of miners ripping gold from the earth was accompanied by the noisy industries of builders, smiths, saddlers, millers, woodcutters, teamsters, scalpers, hawkers and roadside quacks. Adding to the din were fights spilling from the twenty-six pubs, and great lines of gargling camels being provisioned for trips to hunt out new fields.

In 1896 the first steam locomotive coughed and hissed into Coolgardie, greeted by rousing choruses of 'Hoorah!' and 'Three cheers!', not least because the town was no longer at the mercy of the piratical coach companies. Gold drew the rail networks deep into the dry interior.

I ARRIVED in Coolgardie, the old prospecting capital, and found it sweet and deathly. It still has an imposing Victorian courthouse, it still attracts enough tourists to warrant a caravan park and the main street is still broad enough to turn a team of camels, but the railway no longer runs through the town, the population of 500 is served by two pubs, not twenty-six, and Bayley Street's grand parade of buildings has been left gap-toothed by fire and demolition. Coolgardie's roaring days exist only on laminated information boards posted along a tourist walking trail.

The cemetery, however, is a huge and lively affair, divided into great paddocks of Protestants and Catholics, with two smaller resting places for Muslims and Jews. Latter-day prospectors are also buried here, including a man who died in 1980, commemorated by a memorial constructed from his pick, shovel and a steel pan framing a photo of him working a dry-blower.

While poking among the headstones, I was listening to my short-wave radio, tuned to Goldfields Radio, a Kalgoorlie station. A newsreader supplied the gold price: 'Three hundred and four, US.' Nearly $550 Australian, or £200 sterling. I sat on the low cement wall of a grave, looking down between my boots, and considered that a one-ounce nugget is a little smaller than the round flat toffee you find in a box of Quality Street and the weight of half a Mars Bar.

I scraped aside some ochre dusts with the edge of my boot and inspected the ground. My gold books were filled with tales of good fortune, accounts of men stumbling over a rock, disturbing a tree root, taking a second glance.

'Bugger it,' I said, standing quickly. I had as good a chance as any of finding gold, and I wanted to start looking *now* . . . But my destination, Kookynie, was still 300 kilometres ahead of me.

2

I unplugged my hat from my head and placed it on the bar, then quietly perched myself on a stool. The barroom was tiny, more bar than room: line six gold-diggers along the bar, place another row of six behind them and the place would be full. But as the clock struck noon, mine were the only boots planted on the old wooden floorboards.

The barmaid placed a beer on a freshly laundered bar towel. 'There y'go.'

My hand wrapped round the glass. 'Thank you,' I said and sucked down the sharp, fizzy beer. A gentle country and western track played on the satellite TV mounted high in a corner above the bar. 'It's hot out today,' I said, choking a little on the coldness of the beer.

'Yeah,' she said. 'But thirty-two degrees isn't hot for round Kookynie.'

342 | MAX ANDERSON

Her voice had a low, earthy register, like the dust had got to it. 'It gets way hotter in summer. You come up from Kalgoorlie?'

'No, Coolgardie.' It was strangely intimate, just the two of us and the crooning cowboy music. 'Tell me,' I said, trying to sound matter-of-fact, 'do people ever come into the pub with . . . er . . . with gold?'

'Yeah, they do,' said the barmaid. She swivelled towards the till and made the tray spring open. 'Here, look.'

I did. She was in her mid-twenties, dark brown eyes, bottle-blonde hair tied into a tail, high cheekbones with a few freckly motes. Her black T-shirt was tight over her chest and cropped above her hipster jeans to reveal a four-inch belt of pale tummy. I hadn't seen anything like her since leaving Adelaide seven days ago.

She dropped something beside my glass onto the hundred-year-old bar top. It made a *clunk*, though the size of it, less than a thumbnail, suggested it should have made a *clink*.

I'd seen and handled maybe half a dozen nuggets, all in the past year. All had been encouraged to a supreme lustre by overnighting in little baths of hydrofluoric acid. But the gold I picked off the bar top wasn't like that. It was raw gold. The metal had some vitality, but it wasn't quite full-flushed, like a baby yet to have air shocked into it by the slap of a midwife's hand. Its tiny creases and folds were webbed with earths of brown and black and some of its cheeks and dimples were a mucky red, the colour of old blood. This thing had been delivered 'Yesterday, somewhere near the pub', but it was born ancient, already 2.6 billion years old, and conceived not in the rocks of Australia, the great south land, but in Gondwana, an extinct mega-land moored elsewhere on the earth's oily mantles. The dirty little nugget in my palm was a souvenir from somewhere we can no longer visit.

'People *pay* with gold?' I asked.

'Yeah, sort of. They come in and sell it. Kevin'—she thumbed over her shoulder—'the manager, buys it by the gram and then takes it to sell in Kalgoorlie. Sometimes he wins, sometimes he loses. The Wongis sell their gold here cos it's too expensive for them to drive the two hundred Ks to Kal. So they sell it here and use the money to buy food and grog.'

I knew grog was an Australian relic word for alcohol, but 'Wong-eyes' was a new one. 'What are Wongis?' I asked.

'It's what the Aboriginal people are called round here. They're Wongutha tribe. They don't like to be called Aborigines; you call them Wongis.'

'They look for gold?'

'Some do. Some have got metal detectors.'

I'd never pictured Aboriginal people using metal detectors.

She collected the nugget, popped it back in the till and returned to lean her hip against the bar, arms folded. 'You a prospector?' she asked.

I looked at my beer, worrying I might have blushed at the question. 'Sort of. Well, I'm actually wanting to dig . . . for gold. Actually, I'd like to stay around here for a while.'

'Oh, good one. Well, there's rooms for fifty dollars a night,' she said. 'Or you can pitch a tent round the side of the pub for seven dollars. It's a great town.' Then she laughed at herself. 'OK, so it's a bit quiet at times.'

'How many people live in town?'

She counted through names on her fingers. 'Thirteen. And the Wongis up at the Morapoi community and the prospectors camped out in the bush— they all drink here. Friday and Saturday nights are great. But I've only worked here two weeks. Me and another girl, we both come up from Perth.'

'I'm Max, by the way,' I said.

'Hi, I'm Nic. Nicole. Would you like another beer?'

The wall behind Nic was lined with shelves supporting glasses, bottles, sweets, cigarettes and tinned foods, and there was a hatch through which customers in the adjacent larger bar could be served. Lying before the beer taps was a metre-long stone lizard, painted green and black and wearing a necklace of wooden beads. Suspended by fishing line from the ceiling was an Aboriginal spear with a rifle scope taped to its middle. The wall on my left was hung with rusted mining implements and leather horse tack. On the right were two old shotguns and a 1940s painting of a woman with a serene expression and bare breasts. And looking down over the bar was the moth-eaten head of a kangaroo wearing an eye patch and with a broken cigarette dangling from its mouth. This was not orchestrated decor, it was larrikin aesthetic.

'How are ya, bloke?' A man with a swarthy face had appeared at a half-door connecting the service area with the main corridor. He was lighting a chocolate-coloured cigarillo.

'I'm very well, thanks. How are you?'

'Oh, three steps forward, two steps back.' His words came from way down, through pipes behind the solar plexus, catching on tar. He paused after inhaling, performing a mock calculation while the smoke loosened his lungs. 'Which puts me about one step ahead!' And he cracked a beaming smile.

Kevin, I thought, Kevin Pusey, the owner and landlord of the Grand Hotel. He was of moderate height, with a substantial beer belly pushing at the fabric of his grey polo shirt. But the gut was supported by an equally substantial frame packing a considerable amount of working-man's muscle. The hands were big and hairy-backed; each of his forearms was three of mine taped into a bundle. His bearish appearance was not lessened by his face: stolid and hugged by a well-groomed, tightly cut beard. Greyness in the beard suggested he was in his late forties, but his hair was black and combed back with oil, giving the impression that he'd just stepped out of a shower to rid himself of a hangover. Blacker still were his eyes, which were constantly surveying and assessing from behind silver-framed glasses.

'Go for lunch if you like, Nic,' he said, entering the bar.

Nic left, and after some small talk with Kevin I raised the subject of leases. Had the big companies sewn up all the land?

'No,' he said, 'not altogether.' He mentioned numerous lease types issued by a government office in Leonora, a mining town seventy kilometres north; he talked of permits and papers and a computer data base that pin-pointed lease availability and land access. Then, levelling me with his dark eyes, he asked, 'So you've got a metal detector?'

I tilted my beer so I could look into it. 'Ah, no. I haven't got much of any-thing except some pans and a shovel. But I want to find some gold.'

He smiled briefly. 'There's a few round here that want to do that.' And he levelled me again, this time with a look that said, 'And?'

'Well, um, I was wondering if . . . Do you know of any blokes around here who might need someone to help out on their leases . . .?'

He began lighting another cigarillo, still observing my performance.

'Because, to be quite honest, I haven't got a bloody clue what I'm doing. I probably want the learning as much as I want the gold.'

He put away his lighter. 'You're looking to do a bit of brain-bleeding. Come in here one of these nights and say what you just said to me. There's one or two'll point you in the right direction. Y'looking to stick around for long?'

'Maybe a few months.'

He looked over his glasses. 'Got a tent?'

'Yes.'

He withdrew the cigarillo from his mouth and pointed through the win-dow. 'There's a borehole past the railway line. If you like, you can camp over there by the windmill. You'd have water, and trees for a bit of shelter.'

'That'd be great,' I said. 'Course, I'm happy to pay for the site . . .'

'Well, you'd be doing us a favour. People drive over there to drink and leave shit all over the place. If someone was camped there for a while it'd be good for us. Just keep it tidy, maybe give it a clean, pick up the cans lying around. And don't piss in me water supply.'

Walking out into the bright slab of light, I stopped to count my luck.

Two four-wheel drives were parked to face the hotel like horses hitched to a rail, the sun jouncing off their hot paintwork. Three men were talking, deciding how long they should stop at the Grand. One of them was roughing the neck fur of my dog, who was sag-eared and half-lidded under his caress.

'Hello,' I said.

'How are ya?' called the man in a loud, assertive voice. Nic appeared under the verandah with a mug of coffee. The man noted how good she looked and became extra gruff. 'Whassa dog's name?'

'Her name . . .' Oh God. 'It's, ahh . . .' I scrambled for a lie, an Aussie working-dog's name, one of those whipcrack names—Jess, Red, Jack, Sam, Zack. 'It's, ahh . . .' Hurry, anything—Killer, Fan, Ripper, Mauler. 'I didn't actually name her . . .' I rolled my eyes extravagantly but no one saw.

Small silence.

'It's Lala.'

Lala hiked up her ears a fraction. The man straightened from patting. The dog wagged slowly over to me.

'*Lah-lah?*' repeated the man.

I started to explain that the original Lala was a Teletubby, one of the big-eyed anthropomorphs that had TVs in their bellies. 'It's a Tele—'

'Who the fuck gave it that name?' said the man. And disappeared into the front bar with his mates.

I twiddled one of the dog's floppy ears. 'A three-year-old,' I replied.

Nic was laughing, a low, well-exercised laugh. She turned to follow her customers, but she stopped to extend her hand and lower her face, forming a space into which the dog quickly inserted her soft, orange head.

'Hello, Lala,' she said gently. 'Hello.'

THAT AFTERNOON I set up camp. Tent, folding canvas bed, sleeping-bag, diary, low-amp fluoro lights leading to twelve-volt battery, doormat for dog (under bed) and, most importantly, my suitcase of books written by old-time prospectors. Over the tent was a large tarpaulin supported on six poles and guyed

tight into the earth. This in turn was partly shaded by a luxurious green peppertree and two iron water tanks raised on wooden towers. These formed a
cool green enclosure, and within this was a tap. I hung my flannel on a low
bough and found a bark concave in which to sit my soap and toothbrush.

To one side of the towers was a windmill. Not the sort you get in
Holland, but one of the implacable sentinels that look out over American
prairies. And all around was a hummocky clearing the size of a football
pitch. I deduced that I was camped at the old margin of the town: a hundred
metres across the clearing to the east was the railway line and the pub, and
behind that the brick ruins of Kookynie; a few metres from the windmill to
the west was where the great ocean of mulga trees began.

There were shafts in there, there had to be, for these were the Northeastern
Goldfields, home to Kookynie, Menzies, Leonora, Laverton, Sandstone,
Wiluna, Burtville—glorious names all, placed on the map by the old-timers
as they pushed through 160,000 square kilometres of dry lands and thorny
trees, sinking their shafts and extracting their gold.

For now, however, I would concentrate on pulling something else from
the ground. Over the course of the afternoon I filled a dozen large garbage
sacks with beer cans. Some were whole, others buckled into small cakes or
pancaked flat. There were also beer bottles, whisky bottles and wine boxes.
I dragged my clinking sacks out into the clearing, bending to discover more
caches of tins beneath clumps of saltbush, water bush and prickly wattle.

Then I picked up a different sort of vessel—it was squat and brittle with
rust, and had a lid reading NEAVE'S FOODS FOR INFANTS AND INVALIDS. It was
undoubtedly early 1900s, and I was pleased with this bit of history, so I put
it to one side. Where it promptly grew into a rust-brown pile of tobacco
tins, cocoa tins, horseshoes, shovel heads, axe heads, broken brace drills, a
saw, a panning dish, hasps, handles, brackets, hinges, chains, a padlock, a
home-made birdcage, glass marbles, glass stoppers, teacup handles, teapot
spouts, kettles, broken plates, broken bowls, broken clocks, broken glass . . .

Strange, I thought—what was the difference between these oddments
and the contents of my bulging garbage bags? What made one pile trash
and the other treasure? Some history, a little endeavour—it'll gild anything.

But all of Kookynie felt gilded to me. My eyes had never felt so full of
sky and light. I turned to watch the wide open west where the sun was slipping through crimson oils, then spun on my heel to watch the equally
candid eastern rim, an inky wash of royal blue from which had bubbled a

profound silver moon, rising boldly over the iron roof of the pub.

Lala was running through the saltbush, tail up, ears flapping, almost a rocking horse of doggish delight as she whooped up the space. And her delight was my own, so I ran alongside, urging her into a greater, faster frenzy—'Go on, Lala, go on, *go on* . . .' We ran far enough to look back at my camp: at the tent beside the branches of the giant tree, at the rear doors of the Troopie poking from a car port of leaves, and at the crown over it all, the signal silhouette of the windmill, clanking faithfully in the breeze..

It looked like a home.

I DON'T think I ever saw Lazy Les's face square-on. It was only ever in three-quarter profile, and usually angled up towards the TV in the corner of the front bar. No matter what was screening—half-dressed pop kittens, slippery octopus antics on the National Geographic channel, dreadful Perth-based news—he talked to me through the TV. On top of this, indeed on top of Lazy Les, was a wide-brimmed Akubra hat that he never removed.

The rest of Lazy Les, however, was plain to see. He was a big bloke. He drank steadily through a supply chain of small-glass beers, swallowing the liquid into a stomach swollen like a prize pumpkin. It filled T-shirts bearing motifs and messages better suited to a young person on a busy high street, not a prospector over fifty-five living in a bush camp fifteen kilometres outside Kookynie. He also wore shorts, and, at the end of his thin, white legs, a pair of gaiters, small elastic skirts worn about the ankles to keep loose dirt from falling into his boots.

His face was usually pale with white stubble covering much of the lower half. Perched on a nose whose complexion betrayed a pious and steadfast consumption of alcohol were great plastic-framed glasses with lenses like windscreens, often spattered with teeny specks. Sometimes you could steal a glance behind them at his eyes—I think they were blue but they were often screwed tight from grinning, or else squinting up at the TV screen.

If the mood took him, Les could be loud, calling through his wide, peggy grin, super-stretching the diphthongs like he was extra-authenticating his Australian-ness. Lazy's opinions on any race or nationality outside Australia were indictable offences. He did, however, love heavy metal, and if he'd had enough to drink and AC/DC was playing, he'd turn his pumpkin belly away from the bar to rest his air guitar upon it and pick along with Angus Young.

'Why do they call you Lazy?' I asked, finishing my fifth beer.

'Cos I'm bone idle,' he told the TV. The word 'bone' was a great moan. 'Bohhhhhhhn idle. I'm so lazy I can't even get out of bed. And when I do, I want to get back in.' Les delicately swallowed some more beer, looked back up to the TV and said, 'So why y'here, young fella?'

'I'd like to dig a hole. Find some gold.'

'You wanna sink a shaft?' The 'a' sound in shaft sounded like an *aaaagh*, like he'd already fallen headlong into my pit.

'I do.'

'Y'got a miner's licence?' asked Lazy, staring up at three young girls called Destiny's Child on the Virgin video channel.

'Yes, I have.' My fifteen-dollar Miner's Right, posted by the WA Department of Minerals and Petroleum Resources, was folded in my wallet. 'But I've got to get myself a lease. Are they hard to come by?'

'Aww, y'can still get a lease. Just gotta know how to get one.'

'Another beer, Laze?' This was Rebecca, the other barmaid. A tiny, birdlike woman in her early thirties, she had long blonde hair and fierce energies.

'Yes, thank you, moi dear.'

I conversed with Les through an hour of Madonna's greatest hits. He'd been looking for treasure for forty years: opals in the east, precious stones in the north, gold in the west. He'd been in the goldfields for some of the latter-day rush that happened in the early 1980s, when gold soared to US$850 an ounce. For the mining companies, the metal price outstripped extraction costs to such an extent that even the meanest rock could be made to pay. And small operators—the prospectors—were cashing in, too.

'Y'got a detector?'

I winced. 'No.'

'Gotta gitch y'self a detector.'

'I've got a shovel. And I've got pans.'

'*Pans?*'

'Pans. But I'm happy to start out small. Anything would do, even a speck.'

He muttered a perplexed '*Paaaans?*' and exhaled smoke. 'You wanna know where you should go?'

I swallowed a mouthful of beer and nodded.

'Only, don't say I toldya, cos it's probably owned by a company, and if they catch ya, y'could git foined . . . And y'moight not git much, at least not big stuff, but you'll certainly git colour . . .'

It was that easy.

'BEAUTIFUL GOLD,' I said, shouldering a backpack with water bottle and sandwiches.

'Lovable gold,' I said, taking my long-handled shovel.

'Spendable gold,' I said, collecting the steel pan I'd blackened over burning gum leaves in my breakfast fire, exactly as I'd read in a book.

I glanced at the clouds over Kookynie and smiled. 'A man has his creed'— I tum-te-tummed some honky-tonk piano—'and mine is all greed . . .'

Tunes from the movie *Paint Your Wagon* would accompany Lala and me for much of our two-kilometre walk to work. It had rained overnight and the great skies of yesterday were blotted out by brooding clouds. But no matter. I strode into the morning, clanking and singing as I went, as happy as if the horizon was alight, a shining dawn, an *aurum*. The word that gave gold its chubby chemical symbol.

So what is it about gold? What makes it so beautiful, lovable, spendable, so terribly *fabulous*?

Gold comes from the old English word *gelo*, meaning yellow. But gold isn't yellow, it's gold. When ancient populations held gold they thought they had the sun in their hands, and the sun meant life, which meant God. So uniquely and powerfully suggestive was its lustre that peoples in both the Old World and the New separately concluded that gold conferred power, potency and passage to the ever after. The ancients were so sold on gold that even people with a very practical sense of what a cow, a wheat bushel or a man's labour was worth came to take this undrinkable, indigestible and noncombustible metal happily in trade. By 500 BC, along with silver, it had become the key to humanity's greatest ever conjuring trick, the concept of money.

But why, I thought, why do *I* think it's fabulous?

It's not an elemental thing. I'm not captivated by the ring given to the Turon Widow by her mother, nor am I in thrall to the smooth crown clamped onto a stump once occupied by my right molar.

No, I'm taken with the stuff that fills stories and books and movies, the twinkling nests of gold coins on which smoking dragons doze, the treasures strewn blithely about Nemo's Underwater City, the gold dust sluicing into a stone tomb in Tarzan's lost city to suffocate the raider who'd dared enter.

But walking along the dirt road out of Kookynie, my shovel beginning to cut into my shoulder, I began to consider an uncomfortable truth—that fabulous gold was just that: fabulous, fantastic, un-credible. Even in the goldfields, gold for me did not *demonstrably* exist; it was as fanciful as the smoking dragon on its shimmering heap. I turned off the road through a gap in a run of wire fencing. If my shovel and pan could uncover gold for me to see and touch, then I'd see and touch fantasy.

The black headframe of the mine looked magnificently appalling against the grey sky. It was a wooden superstructure, crowned by huge spoked wheels and once responsible for raising the little trucks that carried men and ore out of the earth. A wedge-tail eagle sat at the top of the frame, watching me and my dog as we moved through the litter of mined earth.

In 1912, when the Altona mine gave up the last of its gold, the scavengers took away the mine office, the pumping station and buildings housing engines, tools, lubricants and explosives. But they left the headframe. The shaft at the base of the tower was a wide mouth punched into the ground. Its extracted guts had been piled alongside in huge humps of earth. I climbed one to locate the marker that Lazy Les said would lead me to gold.

And there it was, zigzagging in the dull morning light, a thin red scar describing two edges of the mine site. It was a dry creek bed, shin-deep and mostly wide enough to jump across, clogged with river sands and cemented muds washed downstream by the furious but infrequent rainstorms.

'Y'gotta dig down to the cap rock,' Lazy had said. 'Gitchya spade down to where it gits roolly haaaaard. Gold's *heavy*. It *sinks*. Then you'll git colour.'

I quick-marched to a bend in the creek. Then, for one of the very few times in my life, I applied my degree. I studied geography at Lancaster, and the course was partly dedicated to how rivers shape the landscape. A body of flowing water can carry material in suspension as long as it has the momentum to do so; put an obstacle in its path—slow it down—and it will begin to shed that load. Of course the heaviest particles go first, and gold is right up there with the densest of metals. A tonne of gold will form a thirty-seven-centimetre cube, the size of a portable TV set.

I found a rock bar stretching across a wide piece of creek. An obstacle, I thought, enough to persuade rushing water to give up its freight of gold.

It wasn't long before my spade had chuffed into coarse river sand piled upstream of the bar. Beneath this was darker, more compact earth. My spade bit into this, too, freeing chunks of soap-sized cakes. And beneath was a surprisingly flat and solid bed. This was Lazy's cap rock, and if it was the limit to where gold could sink, then the cakes of earth should have my gold. Into my flat-bottomed panning dish they went, where I ground them up, first with my boot heel, then with my hands.

Now here was a problem.

'Y'won't do it without water,' Lazy had said, squinting up to Madonna as she affected an austere mistress figure and flexed a riding crop.

I'd protested at this. I knew from my reading that some of the old boys had dry-panned for gold, using wind to do the job of water. Why couldn't I? It was a simple enough process: take a dish of fine, dry dirt, then stand and pour it gently into another pan on the ground. Listening for nuggets clanging into the lower tin, allow the breezes to winnow out the lightest dirts. Repeat— swapping the pans—until the heavy grains of fine gold have accumulated.

'Y'can *troi* it,' Lazy had said. 'But y'won't do it without *water*.'

There were no puddles at the mine site, since most of last night's rain had been blotted by the parched soil the minute it fell, but a short distance from the creek I found little canals of water trapped in the corrugations of a sheet of discarded roofing iron. Carefully lifting the sheet, I decanted some water into my pan. Then walked back to the creek and began panning for gold.

You forget how pleasant it is to be intimate with the earth. I plunged my hands into the water and mashed the slippery soil cakes between my fingers, mixing them into a rich soup. It was a primal delight. But I'd read enough about panning to know that dishing dirt was a serious business. Sloppy panners lost gold over the pan's edge—hurry the slurry and it'll slip from the lip. So I concentrated and worked slowly, swirling the fluid round the tilted dish so that the least dense matter spilt over the edge, splattering the toes of my boots. Meanwhile, gold was given all the time it needed to sink into the seam of the pan, where the rim wall joined the flat bottom.

After half an hour I had a smaller, finer and more concentrated amount of 'heavies' in the pan. I drained off a fresh litre of water from the corrugated iron, diluting the concentrates to allow the swirl-and-separate process to begin again. The more refined the residue, the more exciting it became. After an hour and a half I'd washed—for that's what it was—a panful of thick red mud until it was a small crescent of what looked like iron filings.

These were black sands, the heavy residue of water-eroded ironstone. Ironstone, Lazy had told me, was the rock I should learn to love, especially when it was cheek to cheek with quartz. The magic formula, he said: two rocks notorious for hosting gold.

But no matter how much I swirled and peered and tipped and shook out the finger-width curl of black sands, the only colour I saw was black.

I projected some more theoretical hydrodynamics onto the creek bed, picked my spot and gathered another panful of dirt. The dud pan was forgotten, for this new pan was brimming with promise . . . Yes, *this* was the pan.

It was a dud, too. But each new digging, each new panful brought the same expectancy. Which is why I worked constantly for over six hours, washing just five pans. I'd forget to stand to relieve the muscles in my back until they locked and I'd have to ratchet myself painfully out of a crouch. I didn't eat lunch because every time I stopped to reach for my sandwiches I'd think, I'll just do one more pan . . . And all the while the cloud layer had thinned until the sun came out, first in hot patches, then in a solid and very surprising scorch—spiriting away the corrugated puddles in a flash.

I returned to my sheet of iron to find the dog helping herself to my shrinking water supply. 'Gahhh! No! Out!' I shooed her away. She looked at me, making big brown eyes that said 'thirsty'. But the water was gone. I needed to locate another source.

'Of course!' I said, and triumphantly snatched the bottle of drinking water from my backpack.

As the water glugged into the pan, I was delighted at my resourcefulness and quickly resumed swirling. But as I worked I got thirsty. And as I got thirsty, I got despondent. The skin of my hands had dried into taut, liney parchment. And I became aware that the flies were bad. Then one buzzed up my nose, making me snort and swipe angrily at my face. I jumped up and dropped my pan. Red slurry dribbled onto the ground.

'Ahh, shit!' I snatched up the bottle of water irritably and began sucking its contents in great slugs. 'Here, Lala.' I turned. 'Dog?'

She was under a bush, tongue out, panting in the humidity. She came over, her tail wagging lamely, and I felt shabby. I let her lap from the mouth of the bottle as I poured water into my palm. 'There y'go,' I said, and tutted, which was the best I could do for an apology. 'Tomorrow we'll bring our own water, OK?' I tugged her soft ears and made her tail wag. Then I sighed loudly and began gathering my few things.

The mathematician Archimedes needed water. He reputedly settled into a tub full of it to consider the problem of how to determine pure gold from gold debased by other metals. On displacing his body weight in water, he hit on the notion of density and reputedly yelled Eureka!, the word much used in the journals of the Victorian diggers.

I didn't yell Eureka! when I approached my abandoned pan, I was too astonished by the certainty of recognition. Five steps away from the tilted dish drained of slurry, I saw two pinheads beaming brilliantly. And I knew absolutely what those two pinheads were.

I didn't yell Eureka! I just jumped and hoooo-ed and laughed and shook the dog's head and held the pan so close to my nose that it filled with the smell of wet dirt. Then, very carefully, I dabbed the two motes with the paper-dry tip of my finger.

NIC WAS laughing at me, Rebecca was going Wow! Lazy Les squinted at the motes of gold lying in my plastic film canister and said, 'That's the stuff. Good on yer, young fella.' Kevin took a look too, and smiled, saying, 'Well, at least it's a start . . .' Kevin was in high spirits because it was a Friday and the two bars of the Grand were filled—thirty people making a happy clamour, each group shouting at or outshouting another.

A group of young Wongi men wearing sports shirts and long surfing shorts came into the pub. They were from the Morapoi community. They said, 'How are ya?' to Kevin and Kevin said, 'I'm good, thanks,' and asked how they were doing. They trooped through into a side room with a pool table. An older Aboriginal man, perhaps in his late forties, came into the pub to play darts. His face was hawklike and beguiling; he had shoulder-length hair hanging in curling strands from a battered drover's hat. His name was Clarry and someone said he was an Aboriginal lawman, that under his moleskin trousers were wounds in his legs where he'd been speared as part of the initiation into the office. He challenged me to darts and bet a beer on the outcome. He beat me hollow. Never play darts with a man who's voluntarily had spears driven into his legs.

'HEY, GUESS what!' I yelled into the receiver. I was pretty merry on beer but had gathered myself enough to disguise the fact with a happy weariness so she'd never tell. The glass phone booth was outside the pub; I could smell the night air mixed with the cigarette butts ground into its concrete base. 'Guess what! I've found us some *gold*!'

'Woo-hoo!!' cried the Widow, 'How much, how much?'

'Two pieces! Each one about . . . 0.001 of a gram.'

She laughed. 'Yeah, that'd be right. And it's worth what . . .?'

'Ohhh, maybe half a cent?'

She laughed again. 'So how long d'you reckon before you get back the fifty bucks you've obviously blown on beer tonight?'

TOWARDS THE END of the night I took a stool at the bar next to a bloke called Ron. He was taller than me, but short for an Australian. He was in his early forties, with cropped hair, fierce blue eyes and a biker's goatee suffused with grey. He had beefy arms poking from a military shirt, the sleeves of which had been torn off. A tattoo of a naked woman covered one of his biceps.

'How's things?' I slurred.

He stopped drinking to look at me sideways. 'Yeah, good.'

'Didn't I see you on a four-wheeled bike, coming along the track?'

'Maybe,' he grunted. 'Lookin' for gold are ya?'

'Just started.'

'So y'gotta detector.'

I shifted on my stool. 'No.' I laughed at myself. 'Pans!'

He shook his head. 'Whoi'—some of his vowels had the same crow calls as Lazy's—'whoi would ya wanna use pans when the only way to make a quid is by usin' a detector?'

I babbled out some confused ideas about finding gold the old-fashioned way but he wasn't listening.

'Tourists,' muttered Ron.

'Eh?'

'Tourists.' He nodded towards a couple of clean-shaven men in casual shirts ordering drinks at the bar. 'They're detecting over near Birmingham Hill. *Hate* fackn tourists. They come here in their fancy four-wheel droives and caravaans, asking, pleading, *begging* for ya to tell 'em where the gold is, and cos y'wanna do the right thing, y'tell 'em a few spots . . . Then they turn up later in the bar showing off a seven-ounce fackn nugget. An' these *bastards* are on fackn holiday; they're not doing it for a livin'. And that's one more seven-ouncer I'm not gettin' . . .'

I quietly drank the remains of my beer. 'So are you originally from WA?'

Ron was from Melbourne. He used to work as a long-distance truck driver, but he gave it up to become a full-time gold prospector.

'And now you live round here?'

'Yeah. Next block behind the pub. I'm buildin' me own house.'

I told him I was interested in doing some digging, maybe sinking a shaft.

He swallowed the last of his beer and stroked his goatee. He said he was doing some digging himself, but couldn't say much—except that it was gonna be big, he was gonna 'kill the pig'. The gold was gonna pay for his new house. 'Gonna kill the fackn pig, mate.'

3

A banshee shriek, prolonged and fierce, ripped across the clearing. It was the screech of steel against steel, a sound I could feel in my teeth. I woke to darkness. The screeching ceased and in its place was a contented hiss of air and the sound of large, idling engines.

I raised myself onto one elbow to squint blearily through the tent's mesh window. Stretched across the horizon was the 5.30 a.m. nickel train: two diesel locomotives, powerful American workhorses, sitting at the head of thirty wagons loaded with sulphur, ammonia and acid. A small figure clambered down to the concrete platform, dropped a bundle of newspapers and made a phone call from a galvanised broom cupboard. The platform and the cupboard were Kookynie Station.

I sniffed the night scents of cold soil and still plants and remembered I was wearing something weird, something I'd never worn before. A beard. It was, however, an impoverished one; I was old enough to grow better.

'Just how old *are* ya?' Ron had asked.

'I'm thirty-six.'

'Fack me, y'look twenty-six. Y'can't even grow a fackn beard.' It was easy to spot me among the prospectors of Kookynie: while their luxurious growths flourished like summer vines, thick enough to prune and train, mine was an overgrazed paddock. With crop circles.

I stopped pinching at the coarse hairs and looked at the black anvil of the east, where the day's first fiery glints were being struck. 'My God, it's cold,' I whispered, thudding back onto the pillow and pulling up the Widow's sleeping-bag, unzipped to make an eiderdown. I dozed for a few minutes. Then the locomotive engines were revved into a howl until there was power enough to forward-snatch the freight, setting off a Mexican wave of booms and crashes as thirty heavy wagons were dragged into the dawn.

It was going to be another warm day; I could tell by the glow creeping across the tent's canvas. It had been this way for the past three weeks: no cloud, no rain, just cold night skies soupy with stars, and days that were 26°C by midmorning. I thought it all sublime, but the weather was making Marg uneasy: 'We need rain,' she'd mutter, 'proper rain. The ground's too dry.'

Six a.m.: time to get up. I dressed in shorts, khaki shirt and warm fleece. I unzipped the mesh door, banged my boots together to shake out scorpions or pencil-long centipedes and happily found neither. Then I began unfolding the camp, like a snake-oil quack sets up his roadside stall, splitting open the back doors of the Troopie, switching on the fridge, angling my twin solar panels eastward to catch the first rays, and finally sliding out the long steel drawer containing food, gas bottle and Primus stove, all with a little drum and cymbal noise—ba-dum-dumm, crash.

My first month of living under canvas could have been a long, dull squat full of hapless predicaments, regrets and embarrassed requests for help and advice, but it had been none of these. I was completely self-sufficient.

I could store perishable food for weeks in the car fridge-freezer. The clearing was strewn with slow-burning mulga wood and building materials: I arranged three railway sleepers atop three upended oil drums and made a kitchen area between the tent and the peppertree. And I had water. Not only to drink and wash with, but water to sustain a small garden sown with silver beet, lettuce and radishes, and to fill jerrycans carted to the mine site.

So it was never simply a tent. Within a month I'd established a comfortable bush camp that served me well after long days of looking for gold. I wasn't exactly devoid of creature comforts, having a hundred-year-old pub at the end of a hundred-metre walk, but I was surprised at how few things I missed.

As I searched out the Widow's one-cup Bodum coffee plunger, a thin voice floated across the clearing: 'Hello, Lala!' The dog was already bounding merrily through the saltbush to meet Marg's approach.

'How are you, Marg?'

'Ohhh, I'm OK, thank you. Here, I brought you these.' She handed me a paper bag. 'They're ginger snaps; I baked them yesterday. Actually'—she giggled—'you ought to dunk them if you don't want to break your teeth.'

Marg Pusey, joint owner of the pub, was just five feet tall. I once saw her husband Kevin place his fingertip on the top of her head, at which she obligingly turned like a music-box figurine. She had a short woman's intense energies, enough to see her through six fourteen-hour days and an eight-hour Sunday, a brutal schedule for anyone, especially a woman of sixty.

'And how's your panning coming on? Are you still over at Altona?'

'Yeah,' I said, igniting propane gas and setting a pan of water to boil.

'Well, be careful. There's shafts everywhere round there and some of those holes go all the way to China. You're not going too close, are you?'

God, yes. The abandoned mine shafts were everywhere, on hillsides, in gullies, on plains, between creek beds, beside salt lakes, everywhere.

'No, Marg. I'm always careful.'

'And if you're going to be later than six o'clock, call us on the pub radio, Channel 20. Remember, you're either at Altona or *in* Altona. After dark we come looking. And if you've fallen into a shaft, well, we'll chuck down a six-pack and go get the Mine Rescue.'

Marg's face was framed with fine grey hair, but her Melbourne complexion was smooth and her eyes could sparkle with wickedness, especially at a little innuendo. Her vocabulary was incredibly chaste. I rarely heard her use a word spicier than 'damn' or 'hell'.

Once divested of her roster of toil, Marg was entertaining, insightful and enlightening. She was avidly interested in the town's short history and sometimes I'd see her wandering over the clearing, stooping occasionally to rescue an object from the dirt. If she liked the thing, she'd take it back to 'the shops', the row of six original Kookynie stores converted into the house she shared with Kevin. The house was a sanctuary for abandoned memories. Toys, jewellery, porcelain, glassware, all were washed clean and ranged on shelves. She also took in rusted and broken things, finding new duties for them: bicycle wheels were arranged as a fence round a cactus garden; bent silver cutlery was strung with fishing line into a tinkling wind chime. Surrounded by her treasures, Marg typed letters in the predawn hours, corresponding with a hundred veterans of the town, people who'd resided here as infants. She was compiling their reminiscences in a book she was paying to have published.

But right now Marg was bending low, inspecting Kookynie artefacts I'd collected into a heap outside my tent. 'Now,' she said straightening up. 'Would you like to do some work for us on Friday?'

I WAS STANDING in the pub garden talking to a man dressed as a dog. 'Gimme another scone, mate,' said the dog.

Other men were laughing and joking, filling polystyrene cups with tea and coffee, helping themselves to paper plates loaded with precisely one ginger snap, one muffin and one scone.

'I'm sorry, I can't,' I said. The dog wore a black plastic nose held on by elastic, his whisker holes were eyeliner dots and he had long basset-hound ears of limp brown cloth. 'I mean, I could, but what's that Mohican or that caveman going to say when they find out we've run out of scones?'

The dog moved off dejectedly, his tail dragging on the grass.

The square of lawn at the side of the Grand was well watered, fenced by tall corrugated sheeting and shaded by gum trees. It was possibly the only lawn for fifty kilometres. Two hundred 'Outback Trek' drivers had arrived from Laverton at 9 a.m. in a smoking fleet of seventy pre-1971 cars, most of which were dressed as garishly as the drivers. There was a Batmobile, a car with a dinosaur fixed to its roof and a dog van completely covered in brown shagpile carpet except for its windscreen eyes, a large nose at the end of the bonnet and a pink tongue hanging from the radiator grill. A leg above the rear bumper could be automatically lifted and a jet of water fired from a nozzle. The garden quickly filled with hyperenergetic people suffering from sleeplessness and hangovers. Those who weren't in fancy dress wore team shirts or shirts bearing company logos. 'They're raising money for the Royal Flying Doctor Service,' murmured Kevin as he topped up a tea urn with more water. 'Though for some of 'em I wonder how much of it's for charity and how much is just an excuse to stay pissed for two weeks.'

'Any sugar, mate?' asked a man in a poor Batman outfit. 'For me tea? And I'll take another one of those scones . . .'

I didn't want to be here; I wanted to be at the creek bed, panning.

'Marvellous event!' boomed a man dressed as a politician, raising his polystyrene cup of tea. 'But, you know, Kevin and Marg always do a great job at this place. I love coming to Kookynie!' He was dressed as a politician because he was a politician. The Federal Member for Kalgoorlie. 'So . . . you're working at the Grand, then?'

I took a slow breath. 'Yes, I do some work now and again . . .'

Sweeping up leaves, towing stinking garbage to the dump, removing cobwebs from tall ceilings on the end of an Aboriginal spear, paint-scraping mutton fat from the bottom of an aluminium spit-roast, doling out sausage and steak from the garden's smoking barbecue plates . . .

A plump man swaddled from head to foot in a shapeless brown cocoon pushed up to the kiosk, huffing and puffing through a broad smile. I couldn't figure his costume. 'Give us another scone, mate,' he said.

I pushed my tongue into the corner of my mouth and poked at bristles of hair. Two hundred kilometres from Kalgoorlie and the richest gold-bearing mile in the world, and I was wasting precious time being a scone cop.

'Can ya, mate? Just one?'

But I'd earn $120 for my morning's work—enough to buy food for two weeks. For every day that Marg and Kevin hired me to do odd jobs at the Grand, I could spend two weeks digging. So perhaps I should shut up and be grateful. After all, I was a gold prospector. I needed the money.

'Yeah, mate,' I said. 'Help yourself.'

BY 3 P.M. the last of the Charity Trekkers had headed south for Kalgoorlie. After Kevin handed me a small curl of notes, I left the pub for my camp, stepped out from under the verandah and walked into Luke.

Luke was in his early twenties and lived with his parents, working casual jobs on three sheep stations in the area. He came to the Grand fairly often, usually at night. He was a nice bloke, casting himself in the role of bashful bushman. He liked to take mechanical things apart, but it was well known that he was quite hopeless at putting them back together.

'Hello, Luke!' I said. 'How's life?'

'Awww, nobbad,' he said quietly. 'Hey, do you wanna . . . buy some gold?'

'What have you got?'

He tugged at a pocket in his filthy jeans and pulled out a few single-gram nuggets. One was the size and thickness of my little fingernail. He smiled sheepishly. 'I'm broke . . . Looking to make m'self some beer money.'

'How much for that one?'

'Aww . . . I dunno. Fifteen bucks?' The gold price worked out about eighteen dollars to the gram.

'That sounds fair. Go on then, I'll have that bit.'

The deal was done.

I crossed the railway and began the walk over the clearing. The afternoon was still warm, the light soft. There was still time to make a quick run out to Altona, do an hour's panning.

As the little nugget grew warm in my hand, I thought out a letter to the Widow. *How bloody stupid is this stuff? Not having found any gold, I take a job to make money . . . then use the money from the job to buy gold.*

I'd fix the nugget onto her letter with a square of sticky fabric cut from an Elastoplast. I wouldn't tell her I'd grown a beard.

WHILE LOOKING for gold, I was amazed at how often the same question would pop into my head, demanding a specific answer from the experts, the prospectors: 'OK, I've tried there, there and there and I've not found it, so I give up. Where is it?'

An impatient new chum fronting up at the Grand with 'Hi! Where's the gold?' gets short shrift, or at least some barely disguised irritation and a variation on 'If I knew, don'tcha think I'd be there instead of here talking to you?' But a canny new chum sits tight, keeps quiet and listens.

'Gold's where y'foind it, young fella,' said Lazy Les to the TV.

'Gold is where ya find it,' said Ron, draining his beer.

'Gold's where you find it,' said Mike, a station hand working at the Yerilla homestead.

'Where she be, there she be,' said the prospectors of the 1890s.

This isn't a glib epigram to hand off interlopers, it's a basic truth dearly held by the goldfield diggers. And buried within is a key orthodoxy. You, the seeker, searching among the exposed mulga roots, kicking aside rocks, are helpless here. You may be amply equipped with electronic technology, aerial magnetic surveys, decades of experience and a PhD in geology, but at the end of the day the gold decides whether you'll be any wealthier because gold chooses where, when and even by whom it will be found.

Mike was a man with his feet on the ground. He earned a very certain income undertaking very certain duties on the Yerilla station, east of Kookynie: keep the water pumping, keep the sheep fat, keep the fleeces rich. But Mike detected in his spare time, and even this quiet, practical man was flummoxed by gold's spooky caprice. 'The biggest nugget I ever found was a seven-and-a-half-ouncer,' he said one afternoon in the bar. 'I found it in the middle of a paddock. And it was a bloody beauty. But that was it. Not another gram in the whole paddock. I went back over it twenty, thirty times in all directions. *Nothing.* Now, you tell me how that nugget got there.'

And he was not averse to appeasing its caprice. 'I wouldn't do that,' he told me. I was flipping a disc-shaped nugget like it was a small coin. 'You've got to respect your gold or you won't get any more.'

Gold, I learned, had to be flattered and sated in small ways. Nic gave me a small nugget, one of a pair she'd found while detecting with a visiting prospector: 'It'll bring you luck,' she said, putting it on the bar. 'And anyway, gold probably attracts gold.'

I was very touched by the gift, but before I could thank her, Ron said, 'You're a smart girl. Y'dead right. Always carry gold if y'wanna find gold. Y'won't get much without it.' I thought the growling ex-truckie was buttering her up. But he wasn't. Many prospectors religiously carry nuggets, on chains round their necks or wrapped in handkerchiefs. These serve as trophies and mementoes, but are primarily talismanic, acting as magic magnets.

The prospectors' faith in the metaphysical properties of gold is unshake-able; I heard evidence of it all the time: 'It won't let me find it . . .' 'Shh, shh, don't say that; it'll hear you and we'll be jinxed . . .' 'I *knew* I was going to find it. I knew it the moment I got close to it . . .' 'I don't know why I went back to look there, but something inside me said, "Go look . . ."'

And at the end of the bar, under the wide brim of an Akubra hat: 'Never want it too badly, young fella,' said Lazy Les, peering through a cloud of smoke at Britney Spears. 'Cos y'won't git it. Y'can be out there for weeks, but if y'want it too badly'—he exhaled an untidy cloud—'yer buggered.'

EVERY YEAR, American copper miners extract around 1.5 million tonnes of copper. To date, the total amount of gold unearthed throughout human history is estimated to be just 132,500 tonnes. Cast this into a cube and each edge would measure just over nineteen metres.

Ironically, the planet is literally covered with the stuff. The oceans alone are believed to contain 20 million tonnes of dissolved gold. But we're not very good at profitably rescuing it when it's present in tiny amounts. Of the world's gold reserves, we've secured only 0.00002 per cent.

The bulk of Kookynie's gold (among the world's purest) was located and extracted between 1900 and 1912 and probably added ten TV-sized blocks to the nineteen-by-nineteen-by-nineteen-metre cube. It came from seven shafts driven into a rich haunch of land at the northeast corner of town, registered as the Cosmopolitan Lease. Miners drilled into the auriferous quartz and granite, hoisted the ore to the surface, crushed it to a powder, chemically rinsed it of gold using cyanide and dumped the tailings in hills up to five metres tall. So many hills that the area eventually became a veritable necropolis of barren heaps.

One warm afternoon I decided to visit what I'd come to regard as Kookynie's dead lands.

The entrance was guarded by a DANGER KEEP OUT sign and two car wrecks gazing eyeless and open-mouthed at the sun. Beyond these were shaft entrances of varying size and the broken bones of a large above-ground operation—massive tanks held together with fat-headed rivets, concrete pylons that had once supported sluices and rusted boilers of thick steel plate.

The glory years of the West Australian goldfields lasted barely two decades. By 1900, the easy gold had been located and the fast money made.

Kookynie's mines on the 'Cos' were closed by 1912. The Great War did nothing to help the struggling towns scattered through the goldfields. Mine companies lost their chemicals, steel, horses and explosives to the war effort, all redirected to the fronts of Europe. They also lost their work forces.

The fit, lean fellows who'd dug through the strata of Western Australia were eagerly signed up by the 11th and 16th Battalions of the Australian Light Infantry Force. The 84th Infantry (Goldfields Regiment) was among the first to storm the beaches of Gallipoli. But ironically for the diggers, the Turks dug deeper and rained carnage down upon the Australians trying desperately to sink their shafts to safety. Today, many Australians continue to associate the term 'digger' solely with the slouch-hatted servicemen of the First World War, not the earlier pioneers of the goldfields.

The shafts of the Kookynie dead lands still look like trenches of battle: broken parapets are topped with curling barbed wire and lopsided DANGER signs, all preserved by the ossifying climate in some incidental homage. By the 1920s, Kookynie's population, once as high as 7,000 according to some reports, was reduced to a skeleton staff working the sheep stations.

But the gold hadn't been entirely purged from the Cosmopolitan Lease. Over the decades, companies made periodic forays into the dusty shafts, and in the 1970s people figured there might still be gold in the dead hills, gold that the old mining processes had missed.

All you needed was a bulldozer and some basic ingredients to execute a reasonably simple process: gouge out a shallow pit, line the pit with plastic sheeting and lay a network of perforated piping. Bulldoze dirt straight from the old heaps into the pit to create a flat-topped hill. Soak the plateau (now called a slime dump) with a weak sodium cyanide solution until it leaches down to the pipes. As the solution soaks through, it finds any remaining ore and dissolves out the latent gold. Collect the run-off from the pipe mouths and treat with zinc to harvest the precious metal.

I climbed an inert white mound. It was so high and so large that the town and its brick piles, even the mighty mulga oceans, disappeared from view. This elevated landscape was bare and Saharan, but the sands weren't soft and yielding; they were set hard. And trapped in the white crust, stirring and crick-crackling in the breeze, were torn hems of black plastic sheeting; pipes with cartilaginous ribbing poked into the air like ripped throats.

The glare of the powders was fierce. I screwed up my eyes, felt the skin of my face dry. 'Jesus. I hope it was worth it.'

'G'NIGHT, REBECCA,' I called.

'Night!' she replied, already gathering the bar towels for washing.

I left the front bar, pausing in the hallway to look briefly over the pin boards. They were covered in business cards, community messages, Larson cartoons and photos of people.

There were also photos of gold. A nugget for sale (1.3 ounces, $1,200). A nugget covering the back of a hand like a tarantula. A nugget in the fingers of a bearded man wearing an expression somewhere between insouciance and guilt. And the picture that always caught my eye: a young woman looking coyly up to the camera, proffering a solid bar of grubby yellow metal.

I pulled a torch from my pocket and went out into the cold night. Kevin was slouched on the squat, square petrol bowser. He was smoking a cigarillo, absently watching the stars, waiting until it was time to shut down the pub's big electric generator.

'How are ya, Kevin?'

'Yeahhh,' he said, flicking ash into the darkness. 'Still 'ere.'

Kevin had an excellent mind, and if the time was right he'd share it, holding forth on a huge variety of subjects: on complex things, from auto-electrics and satellite communications to Aboriginal law and customs.

'Tomorrow's the day,' he growled softly. He pointed with his cigarillo up into the blackness and the crystal dusts. 'Mars, Venus, the moon and Saturn, all perfectly aligned. And it's taking place in the Taurus constellation.' He affected some comic mysticism to suggest great fortunes coming his way: 'And Taurus is my sign.'

Before he and Marg bought the pub in 1998, Kevin liked to study the stars through a powerful telescope he kept at the shops. Before Kookynie, from what I could gather, he'd had a colourful working life. He'd been a diver, working deep beneath oil rigs in the North Sea and the Pacific. He'd also managed an explosives team that blasted a pipeline trench across a sea floor.

I folded my arms against the cold—it was down to five degrees again—and noticed he was wearing a short-sleeved shirt and had no socks under his sandals. 'Kevin, d'you know who treated the sands over the other side of town?'

'You mean the tailings on the Cos?'

'Yes.'

He smiled briefly. 'Me.'

'You treated all of it? All those hills?'

'Pretty much. Me and a partner. It was a good living. Did it for about thirteen years. For every tonne of tailings we averaged 1.1 grams of gold.'

'*Grams?*' Each time his bulldozer shovelled up a load of rock dust he was hoping to extract a wheat grain. 'How'd you make money from that?'

'You'd be surprised. Wait here a minute.' He walked back into the pub, returning with a small plastic calculator. 'One point one grams multiplied by . . .' And he tapped in the hundreds of thousands of tonnes he'd treated over thirteen years. 'Now divide all that by 31.1 grams . . . and that's how many ounces we got.'

He held out the calculator to show a long row of LCD figures, the total ounces of gold squeezed from the dead hills of Kookynie. It made my jaw drop. If you multiplied it by the current and rather modest gold price and split it with a partner, you'd still get change after you carried out expensive restorations on hundred-year-old shops and bought the local pub.

I frowned. 'There's a picture on the pin board in the corridor, the one of a young woman holding the bar of gold . . .'

'That's Marg. I had to take the photo pretty quick. She was struggling to hold it.'

'Christ, I didn't recognise her at all. Did you keep the gold bar?'

He flicked the butt of his cigarillo into the road. 'No.'

'Didn't you want to keep it?' I would have wanted to keep it.

'Nope.' He swept his hand across the top of the bowser. 'Sell it. Get rid of it.' There was a moment's quiet while he took a packet of Captain Blacks from his top pocket and withdrew another cigarillo.

'It's strange stuff, gold,' he said. 'Y'get prospectors coming in here when they're on the bones of their arses—in worn-out clothes, driving worn-out old cars, haven't even got the money to buy a few drinks. So they come in to sell some of their gold.' I could see his eyes roving over the constellations. 'And they put it on the counter with the most miserable look on their faces, hating having to give it up. Not that they're broke. Some of 'em have got gold stashed all over the place. They just can't bear to part with it.'

He shifted his weight against the petrol bowser. The cigarillo dangled from his lips. 'Y'know the only decent use for gold?'

I knew that 90 per cent was in jewellery boxes and bank vaults. Most of the rest ended up in the world's teeth.

'No, what?'

'Weights for beach fishing.' He made a cast with an invisible fishing rod over his head. 'Straight out to sea. Go for *miles*.'

4

Every day, I dug the goldfields, usually at 6.30 a.m., when I would collect my long-handled shovel and walk about thirty metres from the tent into the red shallows of the mulga ocean. I'd spear the sands with the nose of my shovel, looking for soft tillage, but more often than not the spade clanged against hard cap rock beneath. My toilet digging would sometimes be delayed by minutes of walking and spearing, spearing and walking, but once the hole was dug I'd lay the shaft of the shovel across it and perch my backside on that. The operation was not without hazards, namely rogue thorn stems, the dog misconstruing my crouch as a signal for a playful tussle and, worst of all, redback spiders in the saltbush. Small and black with red-dot signatures, redbacks are known for their untidy webs, bad temper and painful bite.

The only recompense to crapping in the bush was that I might find gold. Nuggets have been uncovered by prospectors taking a leak and plenty more have been spotted by diggers squatting down and staring blankly at the ground between their feet.

But this morning, gold was not uppermost in my mind. I'd slept badly, and on waking to the 5.30 a.m. nickel train, my skin felt sticky.

In some reverse alchemy, thick cloud turned the silver mulga and golden dawn to lead. I took a bowl of cereal and sat on a canvas stool. The cereal tasted dead, the milk sour. My guts were cramping. I glanced at a small pile of dishes and recalled last night's meal of pork chops. Pork chops saved from four nights previous.

'Oh bloody hell,' I groaned, 'not now, not here . . .'

I walked to the front of the truck, grabbed the long-handled shovel and dashed for the mulga to find soft ground, hotly pursued by the excited dog. The spade's edge rang out against the hard cap rock, all stubborn clangs and dangs, while a traffic of velvet bubbles slipped through my intestines, sending messages to hurry, hurry, hurry. Panicked now, I settled for a shallow depression and ripped at my belt buckle, tugged at my zip . . . then endured a livid evacuation accompanied by the sort of heraldic blasts that start Robin Hood films.

HOME, LOVED ones and family; tin baths of steaming water and cold compresses; starched sheets, professional diagnoses and safe medication. These were the things a sick digger missed. Sorely.

Instead he had only the comforts of his swag, the roll of hard, unwashed bedding, and maybe a canvas tent freezing in winter and stifling in summer, all doubly punishing if he was feverish, shivering against the cold or spaghetti-limp from a burn-up and greased with sweat. In high summer the temperature reached between 37 and 45°C, a still, brutal heat that robbed energies as quickly as it sapped fluids.

The sick digger's mates would care for him as best they could, keeping the latrine trenches powdered with ash, attending small fires to boil tea and smoke out blowflies, giving up extra water rations, and maybe improvising medication from health salts and cure-all powders fashionable at the time.

The diggers were tough men, so chances of recovery were probably good. They regularly weathered ague, fever, venom and broken bones. They endured 'sandy blight', the temporary blindness caused by having their eyes scoured with wind-blown sand, and they lived with long bouts of scurvy provoked by lack of fresh fruit and vegetables.

Underground they fell victim to explosions and cave-ins. Above ground, their steam-powered rock-crushing contraptions—driven by huge leather belts, spinning fly wheels and gears with fearsome teeth—harvested fingers, hands, arms and scalps. They also suffered poisoning through cavalier use of cyanide and mercury in the separation of gold and crushed ore.

And there was drought. Lack of rain quickly drove men from fields ill-supplied by ground soaks or wells. But the diggers were at greatest risk when moving between fields, on long rushes, or when prospecting for new ground. It didn't take much: a moment of poor navigation, an oversight with water provisioning, a dependable water hole gone bad. A man can live three weeks without food, but without fluids he's good for only five days.

It was the death they feared more than any other, not only because of the agonies but because it was especially inglorious. In his final moments, a man dying of thirst would turn crazy as a dog, and strip. I'd read several accounts of searchers arriving upon a starkly twisted figure surrounded by a halo of clothes. The corpse would be naked except for a gauzy body stocking of ants, gently fussing into pale flesh.

Those lucky enough to survive were laid up for days, not only from the effects of chronic dehydration but also from gastric complications resulting from swallowing terrible substitutes for water. A digger stumbling into camp with a black and clotted beard would have drunk the blood of his slaughtered horse, the animal having succumbed more quickly to thirst. But there were also reports of men drinking the slime from water holes rancid with rotting animals, hair tonic and, in the case of a lost cyclist, machine oil.

Some sick diggers had access to rudimentary treatment. Larger fields attracted the attention of charitable Christian societies, which set up tented mission stations and nursing outposts. Fields that spawned mining towns inevitably evolved their own hospitals to care for mine-workers. They were funded at first by subscriptions and monies raised by the diggers, and later by the West Australian government. But nurses were still occasionally obliged to clean patients with whisky or brandy when water became scarce.

It was 9 a.m., an ugly, very wrong time to be in bed in the goldfields. The day was mild but I was cold. I still wore my shirt and trousers and the bag was zippered tight.

An angry buzz began at the pub, then got louder, swelling with thrumm and thump before it passed by my tent. It was Ron on his quad-bike, diving back into the mulga. Where was he going? What was he finding? How did he do it? What did a patch *look* like? How did he recognise it in the first place?

A week ago I'd fronted him in the bar. It was late afternoon, I'd been doing some work for Kevin and I felt a bit sure of myself, of my place in the pub's routine. 'So how's it going, Ron?' I asked. The brazen familiarity was out of all proportion to our association.

He fixed me with his fierce blue eyes and gave me the usual silent assessment, drew the usual conclusions. 'I'm good, mate. How *you* goan?'

'Long day, actually,' I said airily.

He nodded. 'Hm-mm.'

Silence.

I sniffed. 'Heard you found another patch.'

The eyes again. Some outrage. A quick stroke of the greying goatee. 'Y'heard that didya?'

'Yeah.'

Silence.

'So . . .' I continued, 'are you getting anything out of it, or what?'

Ron put his glass down and looked hard at me. 'Actually, I am.' And without ceasing his glare, he tugged a handful of nuggets from a pocket in his black denim jeans. Among a few grubby peanuts of gold was a spike, three centimetres long, with an elegant twist in it.

'Shit!' I said. 'That's a nice-looking piece of gold.'

'Maybe eight grams.'

'Can I . . .?'

He nodded. I cupped it in my palm, then turned it in my fingers, struck silent. I returned the nugget to him and mumbled, 'Thanks.' Then left the bar.

I pulled the sleeping-bag shut over my head to trap some extra warmth. The buzz of Ron's bike soon drowned in the ocean of mulga. 'Bastard.'

THE SYMPTOMS of my gastric bug were loss of appetite, exhaustion, chronic diarrhoea and an all-over feeling of stupidity.

Struggling from a tent, hopping rabbit-like between holes in a mulga plain and firing off fifteen calls of nature a day was a pathetic state for a man to find himself in. It was even more risible given that he could have been with his girlfriend, dining in a cliff-top restaurant or watching dopey videos with two pairs of slippered feet resting on a blanket box strewn with coffee mugs. My adventuring suddenly smelt like my tent: rotten.

I irritably grabbed another book from the suitcase open beside my bed. I'd declined Marg's offer of medication from the pub's huge Royal Flying Doctor Service pharmacopoeia, instead confining myself to bed.

Between bouts of sleeping and reading I lay with a book butterflied on my chest, watching the antics of my new housemate, a praying mantis. The big green insect moved stealthily through the canvas loft. She was a female; I knew this from her size, about eight centimetres long, the larger of the sexes and given to devouring her much smaller mate after copulating. I liked her a lot. She was strong and ruthless, devoting weeks to eating small insects that gathered about the fluorescent light hung in the apex. But she was an extra-welcome housemate because she disposed of the animal I most feared and loathed, one that could bury my gold-digging days for good.

The goldfields are not short of venom sacs. Lazy Les and another local prospector, Russell the Kiwi, had both been bitten by redback spiders, and Marg had been stung by a scorpion. None sought treatment, and all said the bites felt like having a lit cigarette pressed against your skin, later mitigated to hours of throbbing pain. But the most dangerous sacs of venom were installed in snakes. 'It's the little fellas y'wanna watch for,' said one prospector, 'yer dugites and yer gwardars. It's a *little* bite, feels like you've been scratched by a thorn. Y'might not even know it until you start to get sick . . .'

I wasn't bothered by snakes, not least because they were hibernating; I was preoccupied with a far more insidious creature: the mosquito. Every time I angrily slapped one into a squit of blood and black fibres, every time it raised a pale, rubbery welt bloated with irritant, I was jabbed by the same tiny, needling fear. Have I just been injected with the Ross River virus?

There's still no cure for Ross River fever and it's uncertain how many people have contracted it. But I met three sufferers in Kookynie, and that struck me as a lot. 'I think I got Ross River one night sleeping out,' said Rick, a retired sheep shearer. 'Me and a mate, we got drunk and slept out on the roadside. Only there was a water hole nearby and I got eaten alive by mozzies. I reckon I caught it right after that. It's a terrible thing. The pain travels up from my ankles, then it gets into my hands and wrists and then it knocks me flat on my back. Can't do anything for weeks. Then it just goes again, and I'll get nothing for months.'

I asked how many years he expected it to last. He shrugged. 'No one really knows. You've just got it.'

The water towers high in the peppertree nursed a thriving community of mosquitoes. Like malarial mosquitoes in Africa and Asia, only a few insects might be hosting the parasite, but it was a lottery game I didn't want to play: I burned citronella candles and green spirals of scented card, rubbed myself with insect repellent, kept the tent door zippered and wore long trousers and long sleeves at sunset. But a few lone raiders invariably snuck into the tent. Which is when the mantis would turn her beautiful alien face and begin stilt-walking over to the light.

'That's it,' I'd say, looking up from a book. 'Eat 'em all.'

FOUR DAYS later, when I walked back into the camp from a trip into the mulga, I noticed something strange sitting on the canvas roof of the tent. It looked like a novelty oversized pencil, about twenty centimetres long, resting on a delicate frame of wire. But at the end of the pencil was a head the size of a large button, and it was looking directly at me. I've never had an insect look at me before. The face was triangular with monstrous almond eyes, like the Roswell Alien.

'Shit a brick,' I breathed. '*You're* the female.'

She left after two days. My smaller housemate disappeared too. Though probably not into the sunset.

AFTER RECOVERING from the bout of 'gastro', I had high hopes and set about things with renewed vigour. I scrubbed the tent throughout, built a west-facing 'verandah' using a guyed tarpaulin, and stretched another tarp to roof over my kitchen. I also made a doghouse by draping a heat-reflective sheet over my foldaway kitchen table and laying a fat square of foam on the floor. 'Dog, you're out of the tent.'

But I focused most intently on my pursuit of gold. I pestered Lazy for new leads, followed up whispers and developed ideas. I climbed down into the Champion Mine open-cut pit, where, among dried animal carcasses, I ground up rock using a steel pestle and a steel mortar—or dolly pot—and pan-washed the fine grey powders of crushed quartz. I spent a week digging into stinking boglands under the railway line near Turkey Nest, a place scattered with iron pins from the railway gangers and therefore off-limits to metal detectors. I got little. Or nothing.

Hunting through my gold books for clues on how the old-timers sighted gold-bearing country, I discovered that they looked for 'breakaways', rocky outcrops whose lode-bearing geologies poked above the mulga. Every morning I'd jump in the Troopie, switch on the GPS and turn off the dirt road, always moving towards the ridges of higher ground from which quartz and ironstone had washed down in broad swaths. Deep in the mulga I would come upon great nests of old shafts with their little volcanoes of excavated soils, forgotten landscapes, lost worlds, and I felt rewarded, that I was on the same trail as the original diggers. But inevitably, while scouting for a dry creek, I would find tyre tracks left by detector operators.

And still I got nothing.

The effect of not finding gold was complex. After a long fruitless day, my wanting gold would deepen into a powerful need, like a hunger. So I'd race back to Kookynie, screech over to Altona and beat up the old creek, rob a few more particles from its exhausted body. The specks slipping from my fingertip to the bottom of the canister settled my immediate hash. But there was no satisfaction, just like there was no unnatural density to the canister's slender contents. Only resentment was beginning to weigh.

ONE AFTERNOON, on my way to Altona, I stopped at the pub to get some diesel. Rebecca asked if she could come along. 'OK,' I said. 'Jump in.' Her powers of observation at the mine site were surprisingly acute: she offered ideas on rock formations, on plant species and mining processes among the ruins. I dropped her back at the pub, and an hour later she came over to my camp as I was starting the evening fire.

'Y'got a beer?' Rebecca laughed, helping herself to a seat.

She was singsong cheery, chain-smoking with a hint of tremble in her hands. As the flames gobbled up my stash of firewood and Rebecca gobbled up my stash of beers, so she began slowly raising the lid on a tray filled with bleak personal histories. Each was lifted out for my inspection: there was a detailed portrait of a 'whore' relative; there was a screaming four-letter phone fight (energetically re-enacted, with her clearly relishing the drama and her own importance in it); and there was a string of ugly abuses, made more ugly by the flippancy with which they were relayed.

I poked the fire, squeezing out sounds of interest, regret and concern, but my face was soon sagging in despair. It was Jerry Springer by firelight.

'Your truck's got scabies, eh,' she said.

I looked up from the fire. 'What?'

'Your truck. It's got scabies, eh. I felt them biting me when I was sitting in your truck.'

'Wh— what are you talking about?'

'Scabies. I've got scabies and I know all about them.'

I let the poker droop to the ground, I was open mouthed, flabbergasted.

'There's a lot of scabies about. A pharmacist told me. But I itch a lot, eh. I'm very sensitive to stuff like that. So I know there's scabies in your truck.'

'You're talking crap!' I spluttered.

'No,' she said. 'My pharmacist told me, eh. That's why I itch all the time.'

'If you've got skin problems, why the hell are you going to a pharmacist?' The register of my voice was climbing: 'See a bloody dermatologist!'

'But they're doctors. And you can't trust doctors, eh.'

'Then get used to having skin problems,' I snapped, rising smartly.

I led her across the clearing back to the pub, where she retreated to the staff caravan at the rear.

Then I stepped into the phone box to make a call to the Widow. As I heard the phone ringing in Adelaide, I looked over the glass panes of the kiosk, richly etched with nicknames, initials and dates.

'Hi,' I said.

'Hey,' she said. It was a bad start. It meant, 'I'm not happy.'

Nearly three months had passed and the Widow was feeling the strain. I'd insisted on calling her every day, but it had become more principle than necessity. We were reduced to trading pedestrian details, or feigning care about people and places with which neither of us could identify. Privately, I thought I did a good job of sounding interested in her various work contretemps; for her part, she thought I 'crapped on for ever' about Kookynie.

She said, 'So, how y'doing?'

I gave a long groan and started recounting the fireside encounter with Rebecca, clearly relishing the drama and my own importance in it. Here, I thought, was a topic that might raise some interest, arc a connection from Kookynie to Adelaide. 'But, y'know,' I said, 'Nic always said Rebecca was a nutcase. In fact, Nic reckons—'

'You keep mentioning Nic.'

'Eh?'

'You're always mentioning Nic.'

I paused. 'Nic?'

'Yes, *Nic.*'

I'd picnicked with Nic, I'd grown vegetables with Nic, I'd caught tiny lobster 'yabbies' in Niagara dam with Nic. And Nic had cooked me a meal on my campfire—a night with wine, when she'd shown me the spectacles she'd never dare wear in the pub. It was the night I thought, God, you *are* attractive. One of the few nights I remembered I had a libido, or a portion of libido that hadn't been suffocated by my rampaging gold lust.

It was probably the night when most of Kookynie had made up their minds that the 'young fella' under the windmill was shagging the blonde barmaid. When I first had this suggested to my face I was astounded. And then disconcerted. Having sex in other people's minds made me feel like I had something to hide from the Widow.

'She's just a friend,' I said. 'Come on, you know me . . . I mean, look, it's quite interesting that you're worrying, because it's exactly what happened for years when men left their wives to go to the goldf—'

'*And I don't like being part of your stupid project!*'

She was a decibel shy of phone-slam. I shut my mouth.

'While you're out there having a wonderful time, I'm going to work every day. *I'm* the one coming home to an empty house, I'm the one waiting for the phone calls because I can't call you at your stupid pub and I'm the one waiting for this bullshit to finish—and all the while I'm hearing about *Nic.*'

The call ended.

I went into the pub, scratching aggressively at my hairline.

'Arghghghggh, Maahhhh!'

(Oh God.) 'Hello Luke. You've had a few, then?'

Nic was against the bar with her arms folded. She dropped her jaw and half-masted an eyelid, either communicating Luke's drunkenness or her own despair at having to listen to him.

'Yrrr, I arghh a foooo!'

I winced. There were three of us in the pub. In a town of thirteen. Surrounded by 2,500 square kilometres of little else except a few other towns of thirteen. I felt a constriction in my guts, only this time it wasn't the work of a gastric coliform. It was a hug of claustrophobia.

AFTER MONTHS of working on remote fields, stir-crazy diggers moved into town, to stock up on supplies and kick up their heels. Depending on the fullness of their shammies, they would gorge on food, company, alcohol and women. And by the late 1890s there was one town laying on more unwholesome distractions than any other: the gold-diggers' capital of Kalgoorlie.

I said goodbye to the dog, and to Marg, who said, 'You be *care*ful, and even though you're only going for three days, I'd better give you a hug.'

And I said goodbye to Nic: 'Thanks for looking after Lala.'

'No worries,' she said, bending to fluff the head of the orange dog, who was tidy, seated and alarmed. 'Just make sure you have fun.'

I didn't know it, but I really was saying goodbye to Nic. Rebecca had moved to Perth, after announcing that Kevin's bar had scabies, and Nic had taken on Rebecca's shifts. This would double her workload and cause her to disappear from view. Any time off she got, she spent sleeping.

Then I drove south to Kalgoorlie. With tarmac beneath its tyres, my truck was fleet. It didn't bounce, it didn't rattle, it didn't blaze red dust. I swigged coffee from a truckie-sized thermo-mug and listened to Vaughan Williams and then Robbie Williams, by which time I was wired and singing and on the northern margins of Western Australia's second-largest city.

A sign said, WELCOME TO KALGOORLIE-BOULDER. POPULATION: 30,500 PEOPLE. And I thought thirty *thousand*. Oh wow oh wow oh wow.

I WONDERED if the citizens of Kalgoorlie could spot exiles returned from the bush. Did they notice our smile for every stranger who passed, our professorial curiosity in swept pavements, watered lawns, the stencilled names on office windows, the skies that occasionally rumbled with the ascent of jet aircraft?

The official name of the conurbation, Kalgoorlie-Boulder, is unerringly filleted to Kalgoorlie or Kal. Boulder is the powerhouse, the labour pool and the remains of the original Great Boulder gold mines, now quarried into a single huge pit. Boulder's gold paid for the building of Kalgoorlie. Today the desert city was adazzle with new-car showrooms, DIY super-stores, a hospital, a museum, hotels, churches, a university, schools, parks and a modern art gallery. It had a grid of roads so broad you had to con-stantly scan the verges for stop signs or risk an intersection smash.

The architecture was ebullient. Hannan Street was a carnival parade of turrets and domes, cupolas and façades, painted in pale candy colours. It was frontier-town folly, but as I sat with my nose in the dust of a cappuc-cino in Basil's Cafe, I found it all very grand.

In 1895 this was trophy architecture, the best money could buy. Small outposts of the British empire could afford one or two pieces to house their offices of law, administration or rail transport, buildings that became monu-ments to the civilising effect of Britain. Kalgoorlie had the stuff erected all over. And some of the showiest pieces housed not bureaucrats and clerks but beer-guzzling diggers. Deserts were dug so Kalgoorlie could look like this; the diggers and miners bankrolled it, bought rights to it. Perhaps I'd had too much coffee, but after three months in a tent I felt entitled to enjoy it too.

I strolled into a giant air-conditioned supermarket, took a shopping trol-ley by the handle and swung it like a dancing partner through the aisles. Between the hedges of splendid comestibles I hummed madly to piped pop, my conductor's arms plucking out exotic soups, choice teas, olives, dips, pâtés, crackly packets of seaweed wafers and the entire suite of Arnott's Timtam biscuits. From frilly slopes of plastic lawn I harvested shiny fruits and green-jacketed vegetables, from the deep refrigerators I pulled plump slabs of raspberry-coloured meat, chilled foursomes of Cadbury's mousse and a fine champagne that broke an icy sweat before I reached the check-out.

Then I went to the Palace.

THE PALACE HOTEL is one of Kalgoorlie's old warhorse hotels. That after-noon I checked into a $120 room. On the wide double bed I laid out a sunny orange flower, a silvery new gold pan and an old-fashioned hurricane lamp. As I showered, carefully combed my hair and groomed my beard to cover the bald spots, I could feel the excitement rising. I dressed in khaki shirt, jeans and boots, and at last I felt ready to pick up a girl.

She was easy to find, leaning against a wall, idly scanning the traffic with that look of one waiting for her finder. She wore a short-cut corduroy jacket over a pale blue T-shirt with the number 83 on her chest, and tight jeans. Her short blondeish hair was cut at the front into a sprightly cowlick. I liked this, I approved, and felt all my casual words of introduction pushing forward to come out. (God, don't jumble them up.) Another step, and she still hadn't seen my approach. She bent her head and I noticed that her mouth— with a very demure top lip—had been sexed up with red lipstick.

Perhaps she saw my boots first. 'Hello,' I said.

She looked up, relieved to be found.

'Hel*lo* . . .' she said. Her beautiful smile gave way to a look of confusion and in a split second her eyes—enormous grey eyes with their own lights inside—began to rove my face, to find out what it was that was so wrong. 'Oh my God!' she said, and a hand went up to her mouth. 'Oh my *God*!'

And we stepped into each other, arms wrapping, faces touching, and while I apologised for the beard in case it made me unkissable, she stepped back to review it all over again, laughing and exclaiming, 'No, it looks wonderful! You never *said*!'

5

There was a film called *Paint Your Wagon*.' I spat out a small bolus of white bread and pressed it onto a hook, shaping it into a doughy teardrop, then dangled the bait to inspect my work. The Widow peered over her sunglasses. I trusted she was impressed by my resourcefulness.

'It was about these blokes who—'

'Yeah, I know it.' Her words echoed up the rock walls, chasing mine.

'Eh?'

'*Paint Your Wagon*. With Lee Marvin and Clint Eastwood. "Wandrin' Star" and all that. I used to love it. My Grandpa and I used to watch it together.'

'Good God. Most people think it's crap.'

'So what about it?'

'Eh?'

My careful prep had gone to pieces. I'd forgotten that the Widow was capable of surprises. I thought I held all the keys to new worlds, new experiences. I was the one who knew which open-cut gold mine was stocked with fish, *I* knew the secret to fishing in the semiarid goldfields.

But surprise me she did. Instead of smiling in polite forbearance on seeing my camp of dirt and make-do, she'd quietly cooed approval at its alfresco accommodation—the little plastic basket of utensils hanging from a branch, the kitchen table that doubled as a dog kennel, the water-tower platform high among the pepper seeds where you could watch the sunset. At night, when a hurricane lamp was lit above an enamel basin of hot water, I heard her sigh with deep and private pleasure. When we woke and she saw my tins of food shelved along the railway sleeper outside the tent mesh window, she went, 'Awww,' and hugged me and hid her face in my neck.

I was doubly surprised at how quickly she got gold fever. She got it the moment her wrists were sleeved in mud. She forgot to eat the sandwiches I made beside the Troopie; she let her tea go cold and wanted to wash just one more pan when I said we'd call it a day. And she let out great shrieks of joy when she found it, never again needing to ask, Is this gold? Is this gold?

I handed her the fishing rod. She triggered the line with her forefinger and cast a few metres into the pale blue-green waters of the lake.

'What about *Paint Your Wagon*?'

'Um . . . you remember how they find gold in the end?'

'Don't they tunnel under the town and up under the saloon or something?'

'That's it. And they catch the gamblers' gold dust that has spilt out of sacks through the floorboards. Well, I was in the Grand the other day with Lazy Les and we were talking about it. And I said, "There's a cellar under these floorboards, isn't there?" He said there was, so I asked him if he thought a bit of gold could've fallen through the boards, what with a hundred years of diggers coming through and all that.

'And Lazy says, "I know for a *fact* there's gold under here." One night his partner was roaring pissed and he spilt a bag of nuggets on the floor. He started with six ounces but by the time they'd gathered it all up he was two ounces short. Which isn't surprising cos there's holes all over those boards. But he also said the old-timers used to pay in gold sovereigns and there might be a few of those down there too.'

'So, can we get under there?'

I grinned. Amazing. Just amazing. She was already sold. No need for the soft soap, ('Look, I know you're here to relax and I'll completely

understand if you'd rather do something else . . .') and no need for the
faintly tiresome two-week itinerary of hill walks, long drives and picnics.

'I asked Kevin about his cellar and he said it was filled with mud from
winter flooding they'd had a couple of years back. I can't see him being
happy about us hauling out stinking flood mud while he's trying to serve
customers. And Marg would be none too impressed.'

'So you didn't actually ask him.'

'Mmmm, no. But'—I lofted my eyebrows to telegraph inspired cunning—
'I had a better idea. Kookynie's big mining area was on the Cosmopolitan
Lease, over where I showed you those big piles of yellow sands. Next to
that are the ruins of a pub called the Cosmopolitan. It's a shell. The walls
are still there but the roof's gone and so has the floor. But when you stand at
the doorway of the old bar, guess what you look down into.'

'A cellar.'

'Yup. And it's chock-full of rubbish. Hundred years of rubbish and dirt
and rubble, almost up to where the floorboards used to be. We could dig it
all out. Get down to the original cellar floor and pan the lowest few inches
of dirt for gold. What d'you reckon? You up for it?'

'God, yeah.'

We plotted on until the small red float was tugged slowly beneath the surface. The water was clear enough to see a fish idly swimming away with the
bait. The Widow gave a gentle pull, then reeled in about twenty centimetres
of perch, madly squirming and flexing a comb of sharp spines on its back.

I stood and said, 'Here,' a handsome, generous sound, then removed my
hat and stripped off my T-shirt to use as a glove.

'No,' said the Widow, circling the fish's head with thumb and forefinger
before firmly smoothing down the spines. 'Haven't you caught perch before?'

ON THE FIRST day we cleared garbage.

I rolled out the rusted remains of a rainwater tank, an operation of tremendous violence and noise. The Widow dragged roofing timbers and buckled
sheets of corrugated iron, which sent crashes and clatters across clearings
ordinarily disturbed only by birdsong. Then we stuffed dozens of garbage
bags with bottles, cans and other detritus left by people in recent decades.
The rubbish was extracted through a car-sized hole in the pub wall and
loaded into Kevin's trailer hitched to the Troopie. I couriered the trailer
twice to Kookynie's dump, a place to make you depressed for the planet.

After several hours of bagging rubbish we straightened our stiff backs to survey the walls. We were standing in a small yellowish landscape a full metre lower than the ghosts of drinkers past. 'I reckon the bar ran along here,' I said, pointing up to shadowy recesses in the walls. 'You can see where the counter ended. They'd have served behind there, where you're standing.'

'So all those nuggets and sovereigns would have dropped . . . here.' She pointed along the broken wall to what had once been the corner door, where a young peppertree now grew.

'Y'know, Marg said they used to bury sovereigns under the hearthstone for good luck.'

We grinned at each other and continued clearing until it was dark and we were filthy and tired. 'You ever showered under a cold tap?' I asked.

ON THE SECOND day, the dog found shade from the gentle 24°C sun and watched while we cut back the peppertree and tossed hundreds of red bricks through the door well. As we dug down, our brick hills piled up, until they got so high that tossed bricks started rolling back on top of us.

At 2.30 we clapped the dust from our leather gloves and, looking grey from top to toe, took lunch in the Grand. Kevin smiled to himself, a press-lipped smile, and he kept smiling as he served us beers and meat pies.

'Is that you over at the Cosmopolitan?' asked one of two out-of-towners sitting at the bar. He was in his fifties.

'Yeah,' we said through mouthfuls of pie.

'If you're waiting for it to open, you'll wait a long time,' said the other.

We laughed a few pastry flakes onto the floor.

'I remember playing in that ruin as a kid,' said the first man. 'I don't know if it's still there, but round the side there's a collapsed gutter. One day we were playing next to the wall and the guttering fell down and out came all these old pennies.' He made a big circle with his fingers to illustrate the size of the coins. 'It was probably where the old miners used to play their games of two-up. They'd toss the coins in the air and lose a few in the guttering. Loads of 'em, there were!' He was smiling now. 'All spilling out!'

ON DAY THREE we really got to grips with the body in the cellar—a hummocky yellow-grey fill, sometimes spongy and aerated with bones of timber or metal, other times compacted with dense matter, stewed into pale cement by loitering rainwaters.

The Widow raked at the sides of hills, collapsing them, sifting out rusted remains for inspection. I shovelled the waste into two bins cut from thirty-litre plastic barrels scrounged from the dump, and hauled them to the trailer. Our excavation was beginning to concentrate in one half of the cellar; the other half was developing into a well-trodden ramp leading out of the cavity and through the gaping entrance in the wall.

Suddenly the treasures started coming, and not the broken detritus found around my camp, but complete, recognisable things. Whole bottles pressed with logos and words from the 1920s. A motorbike contraption that was really a push-bike with an absurdly small motor. Tools, a cache of them, perhaps from a rotted trunk. Small medicine bottles with their papery labels partially intact. And then we were like two kids unwrapping presents under the Christmas tree.

'I've got a spoon. There's a hallmark. It's silver . . .'

'A pill bottle . . . *Dr Morse's Indian Root Pills* . . . Hey! It's still got pills in it! It's full!'

'Another button.'

'Drill bit. And the brace.'

'Look at this . . .' A heavy brass plaque, *J Barre Johnston & Co., Engineers and Importers, Fremantle.*

A bottle: '*Effervescing saline . . . for biliousness, indigestion, headaches, giddiness, lassitude and general feelings of . . .* er, something.'

'The front half of a toy car, made of tin.'

'Wow.' A hand-forged wheel from a wheelbarrow, the Irish locomotive, a true goldfields icon.

'Look at the size of this spanner!' It was nearly a metre long, open-ended, rotten with rust. A mine-sized tool.

We arranged these along a shelf where the top of the stone cellar wall met the plastered brick footing of the bar. Soon, there were dozens of pieces, over a hundred. Their recovery cost me five exhausting runs to the dump, and what I had to shovel in I had to shovel out.

That night, while the Widow doused herself under the freezing tap, I wrapped four perch in aluminium foil and baked them among hot coals, uncorked a bottle of white wine and warmed a towel for her over the fire. After dinner we lay on a tarp under a blanket and, using a winter sky constellation map she'd torn from the Adelaide *Advertiser*, found Virgo. Cosy in her dark green plaid pyjamas, she was asleep before 9 p.m.

ON DAY FOUR my shovel reached the original cellar floor, a level of sandstone rock three metres beneath the defunct Cosmopolitan Hotel.

The Widow got down on her knees to sieve the last ten centimetres of dirt after I scraped it up off the stone floor with the shovel. The dust was fine and smoked terribly. When the wind blew, it sent grit roaring round the cellar walls, forcing us to shield our eyes and noses.

Nic popped over to introduce her mother and her friend, both visiting from Perth. They opened the back of their hire car and broke out tea and cakes.

The Widow was filthy with dirt, but too exhausted to be embarrassed. After six hours, her sieving had yielded little except glass marbles and metal buttons. No sovereigns and no nuggets. We found an 1820s shilling, and a small moustached face made of clay, not much bigger than the coin.

Marg brought a bag of banana and date muffins and inspected the little face. 'Oh goodness,' she said. 'That might have been attached to a cloth doll.' She then inspected the collection, pointing out things and explaining their use, like a fairy godmother bringing dead bric-a-brac to life with her history wand.

Then she looked sadly up into the space where the roof had once been.

'Kevin and I wanted to restore this place. It was a beautiful building in its day, with huge verandahs all around . . . But it's too far gone now. The structure's shot. Have you seen out the back? There used to be rooms all along there; I remember waking up one morning and finding that a storm had knocked them all down. All gone. Such a shame. Such a shame.'

ON DAY FIVE we panned the sieved dusts for gold. On canvas stools we sat beside the ruined pub where the penny-laden guttering must have fallen, and mixed pans of grey dirt with water. But it yielded nothing, not a speck of gold. We panned and panned, and soon I was brimming with irritation, looking with distaste on the entire process. It was all my worst panning sessions in a single morning: filthy, dull and fruitless.

'Sod it,' I said, clanging my pan onto the ground. 'I think it's time to draw the great Cosmo caper to a halt.'

'Ohh, come on,' said the Widow. 'Let's just dig into another pile.' She pointed to another bank of cellar filth. 'Come on. Just one. You never know.'

That afternoon I was descending the slope into the pit with my empty buckets, sore and weary, when I stopped. The Widow was ankle deep in raked matter. 'Is that . . .?' I said. 'Is that a gun by your feet?'

She looked to where I was pointing, at what appeared to be a barrel poking from the mire. And she retrieved the rusted skeleton of a short-barrelled rifle. I took it from her.

I examined the lever action and the hexagon cross-section of the short barrel. 'Fuck me,' I said quietly. 'It's a Winchester.' The Widow clambered up to the starry look of astonishment on my face. And kissed it.

ON THE LAST day we stood looking down on the cellar from the hole in the wall. We'd cleaned out over forty per cent of the sandstone earth floor. And in the morning light, we saw the truth of our labours, that we'd unearthed something of considerable beauty: the Cosmopolitan cellar. The walls were blocks of cut rock, all mortared together superbly and precisely dovetailed at the corners, the work of goldfields craftsmen.

'It really *is* amazing,' said the Widow.

I mentioned again the lucky sovereign set under the hearth. I'd already lifted a stone, but found nothing and put it back. 'Shall we keep looking for it?' I asked. We pursed our lips, looked again at the freshly exposed walls of the cellar, the yellow sandstone floor and the line of treasures ranged like knick-knacks on a long shelf.

'Nah. Let's leave it be.'

IT WAS FRIDAY night, my favourite night at the Grand, fat with atmosphere, crackling with good cheer, with a log fire and everyone upending drinks or tucking into plates of Marg's fish and chips. The TV was showing a World Cup semifinal, there were people playing darts and the young Wongi blokes in their surfing and basketball gear were shooting pool. Lazy was invigorated after three weeks of detecting in the bush; there was Luke, happy and mostly coherent. The Widow moved between the bars, laughing, drinking beer, stopping to talk, shooting pool with the Morapoi lads, joking with Lazy.

Ron was standing at the bar, his huge arms resting on the counter, his head sunk a little into his shoulders. He was with another bearded man wearing a hat of soft khaki cloth. I suspected this might be Ron's brother.

'How are ya?' asked Ron.

'I'm . . . I'm good.' Actually I was more surprised by Ron's greeting than I was good. 'How about you?'

'Yeah, good,' said Ron. 'Heard y'found a Winchester. Is that roight?'

'Yeah, I did,' I said. And I told him what I knew about it.

'Wouldn't moind seeing that,' he said.

'No problem. Y'know where I am.'

'Y'met my brother, Pete?'

'No,' I replied, 'Nice to meet you, Pete. How are ya?'

'Yeah, good thanks.' Pete was slighter than Ron and older, mid to late forties and softly spoken. He was a prospector of some repute but intensely private. He'd load up his Land Cruiser and stay in the bush for months. No one knew where he went, or what he got. 'You're the bloke who's been doing the panning over at Altona, arntcha?' he said before swigging from his bottle. 'How's that goin' for ya?'

'Oh, pretty badly,' I said. 'I'd be lucky to have half a gram.'

'Pans ain't gonna get ya gold,' he said. 'Get a detector. It's not as easy as people think. But if you've got the patience to pan, you've got the patience to swing a coil.'

I was taken aback at this. It was almost an endorsement. 'Er, thanks,' I said, 'I'll think about that.'

He raised his bottle again and winked. 'But come on one of my patches and you'll find a hole.'

'Really?' I asked. 'Why, is the gold deep there?'

'No!' He began by sounding mildly irritated, but then he was smiling. 'I mean if you come looking on one of my patches I'll fuckin' *bury ya*!'

I RETURNED the Widow to Kalgoorlie airport.

'How much longer?' she said quietly.

I parted my lips to show that my teeth were clenched, that she'd asked a hard question. 'Just . . . a few more months,' I said.

She looked into my eyes. Waited.

'Um, until, maybe . . .' I rolled my eyes upwards. 'Until . . .'

'OK, look, I'll do you a deal,' she said. 'You keep looking until you think it's time. *Don't* make it too long or God help you. But after that we meet up somewhere neutral—not the goldfields, not Adelaide, somewhere in between. We'll spend a week together. Maybe on a beach. How's that sound?'

'Sounds like a good deal to me.'

She'd flown into a bright sky and I went back to Kookynie and stood at the ruined wall of the Cosmopolitan.

I looked into the hole in the cellar, at the incredible cavity and the walls that so perfectly described it, and my heart sank to meet the uneven floor.

I'd returned to a *de*-spirited camp. The Widow had taken away her big grey eyes and big smile and her dark green plaid pyjamas and her star map, and this made me miserable.

But here was the hole we'd dug, the project she'd thrown herself into, the ridiculous project of excavating the ruin of a cellar to find buried treasure. And suddenly I was smiling. I'd found a woman who would follow me into a hole. Keep digging to the end. Perhaps into the last hole.

*T*he mug of tea has grown cold. I lay my book flat on the Formica-topped table and pull a blanket tighter round my shoulders. The dog is snoozing at my feet on the linoleum floor. She too has a blanket insulating her from the cold. Somehow she knows I'm looking at her, and in that uncanny dog way wakes to meet my staring eyes.

'More tea,' I sigh.

Wrapped like a wintering Cherokee in my blanket, I collect the mug and set about making a fresh cup. The kitchen is the most furnished room in the empty homestead and certainly the warmest at 4°C. There's a table, four chairs and sideboards. I've ranged my possessions on the floor near the sink, including my car fridge, my food containers and my suitcase of books.

'Now, Dog,' I say. 'D'you want to go outside?' I shuffle to the fly-screen door and pull it open, a sound of stretching springs. She must choose: stay in or run out to sniff over the back yard. A back yard of 100,000 acres of empty red bushland. This homestead is Mount Remarkable Station and I'm its caretaker for three weeks.

Some days, I've interpreted 'caretaking' to include careering over the property in my Troopie, bursting through overgrown tracks, getting bogged in sand, exploring the infinities of the massive salt lake. But caretaking has also left me bored and lonely. So bored that I bury myself in books and make windy entries in my diary. So lonely that I've thrice driven the 110-kilometre round trip to the nearest pub to consume beer and company.

The pub, of course, is the Grand, where, on each occasion, Marg has come from the kitchen, thrown open her arms and said, 'Ohhh,' before giving me a huge hug and a brick of freshly baked fruit cake. Then, looking over her spectacles, has added, 'Are you being careful? Are you eating properly? Are you OK out there on your own?' And I feel like I've returned home.

But there's change afoot in Kookynie. Goldfields change. People move on, move out, heading for elsewhere.

Nic was the first to go. On her last night the temperature sank like a stone, but the pub was warm with well-wishers drinking to her health and pressing bourbon on her. Plenty of people leave Kookynie, but the barmaid got clean away. Kookynie was a refuge for Nic as much as it was for the tremulous, birdlike Rebecca. But she stashed her overtime cheques, invested in a little raw gold to resell and left to start anew—in Norway, working on a horse farm with pastures overlooking fiords.

The other one to leave was Lazy Les. 'Hate the cold,' he told the girls of Atomic Kitten. 'Bladdy hate it. I'm goan back to the opal fields. Warmer.'

'Why do you do what you do, Les?' I asked.

'Just chasing a quid. Y'only gotta foind two thousand ounces and that's a million dollars. And y'can foind it; it's out there. It's easier still when it comes to sapphires and opals . . .'

Later, he shook my hand and said, 'Well, was noice to meetcha, young fella. G'luck.' But I followed him outside and interrupted his squeezing himself into his flat-bed Holden.

'Hey, Les,' I said. 'I . . . um want to say thanks. Thanks for helping me out. I didn't know what I was doing when I got here, but you gave me a hand.'

The prospector looked up from under the wide brim of his felt hat. His heavy red face was whiskered snow-white, his square glasses were enormous, and his eyes were blue. 'No, I didn't,' he said. 'I didn't do nothin'.'

And he drove away.

Even though the old homestead reeks of loneliness, it doesn't spook me; it has an appealing melancholy. The owner, 'Old Tommy Lowe', died a year ago at ninety-eight. He ran the station all his life, inheriting it in 1920 when his father and older brother died within weeks of each other. Tommy was seventeen. His stained and battered hat keeps vigil from above the kitchen door.

My reward for being here is $100 a week. I'm being paid to sit tight while Iain—the owner of both Remarkable and the sheep station at Yerilla—looks around for a full-time caretaker. My duties are to crank-start the black oily Lister generator every morning and let the bush telegraph take care of the rest, spreading the whisper there's someone on the property.

I cut a piece of Marg's fruit cake and push it into my mouth. 'So, Lala,' I say through a black mouthful, 'are you going to look after the ranch while I go to the pub tonight?'

She wags.

'Correct answer. You may have a piece of cake.' She gently takes a chunk from my fingers. 'Good girl.' I shrug off the blanket, and resolve to check the oil and water in the truck before my absurdly long drive to the pub.

The last time I visited the Grand, a stranger asked if I was the bloke whose dog had a funny name. Yes, I said. Someone else asked if I was the bloke looking after Remarkable. And another asked was I the bloke under the windmill who'd been doing some panning.

I realise it's all part of the change, the goldfields change that's brought new people into Kookynie, people cautiously putting new faces into spaces left vacant by the old. And then I realise something else: these people have known about me before I've known about them. They know me because I've been here a while, I've been around and I might have a bit of information about the country. I might know where the gold is.

'So, are you the bloke . . .?'

Yes, I'm the bloke. The bloke with the awful beard and shabby shirts with sleeves rolled to the elbow and a dent in his Troop Carrier from taking a fence post too tight on Mount Remarkable.

I tug one of my dog's ears and she closes her eyes, lets her tongue hang out. 'Guess what, Lala,' I say softly, bending to put my head close to hers. 'We're no longer the new chums.'

6

The winter rains wouldn't come, despite Marg's frowning sunset vigils. She would stand beside her pub to encourage the pinking horizon to swell with sour black thunderheads. She wanted clouds, armies of them, to sally over the silver seas of mulga until they bunched and bulged and towered overhead, and let fall their great leaden chains of water, lashing the dusts of Kookynie to the bedrock.

Once I looked up from the pool table to see her outside the window, going eye to orange eye with the sun. Its levelling rays blackened the lenses of her glasses. She looked an even match for a stubborn season.

But it was a cold, dry July, and at the end of it three things had become starkly apparent: (1) diesel expenditure on far-flung panning trips plus the beer levy raised by the 2002 World Cup had sent my monthly tab at the Grand into orbit, over $800; (2) the gold powders and niblets in the bottom of my film canister would probably raise about $7 for its repayment; and (3) my panning days were finished.

One quiet afternoon I was plumbing Kevin's depths for guidance and received a thing rarely given in the Australian bush. A compliment.

'I take my hat off to you,' he said, leaning on the bar top, looking down at his big hairy hands knitted together. 'There's not many would go with the pans. But you've stuck it out and you've probably learned some basic knowledge that a lot of people never get.'

I twisted my mouth, unsure what to say to this.

'And that's good. But now you're wanting to go to the next stage, right?'

'Right.'

'Well, big money isn't won from panning. It never was, not around here.'

'But they used pans. I've found old pans lying in the bush.'

'Yeah, they did. But they used them as a tool, to find the source of the payable gold. Before Altona was ever found they would have been doing exactly what you're doing: working up a creek bed or a slope. They'd take a sample of dirt and pan it, then count the number of gold specks they found. The more specks, the closer they were to the source. It's called loaming and it's pretty much what you're doing. Only you're doing it backwards, cos the bloody gold mine's already been found!'

He said I needed a detector. I gave a small groan of assent.

'But don't forget, a detector in the right hands is just a sophisticated pan. Most tourists out there are wandering aimlessly around with their detectors picking up stray nuggets. And most of the time they're finding nothing more than places you don't go back to. But with a bit of knowledge and a good eye you can use the detector to loam up to where the gold's coming from—and that's where the money is. That's when you sink your shaft. *That's* when you call in the mining companies and start talking the big dollars. The nuggets you find along the way are just a bonus.'

'So the blokes round here are doing that?'

'Not many. A couple. Get yourself a detector. Spend time learning how to use it, tune your ear to it. Give yourself twelve to eighteen months and with your appetites you could be working a field with a million dollars beneath it.'

Twelve months? I could do that.

As WELL as interrupting Ron's midmorning efforts to install a toilet system, I'd brought an uncomfortable truth to light: that his consistently nice, grounded, *sane* wife Jane didn't actually like detecting for gold.

Ron paced in the sunlit orange dirt, looking conspired against and pissed off. Jane and I stood with arms folded, watching his mobile fulminations.

'Look,' he said, chopping the air with his hand. 'I bought it as a present for her, an' it's a bloody good machine, an' I don't want her t'sell it.' He milked his long goatee. Then he raised an open palm to Jane and twisted his face away. 'But Jane, it's yours. If y'wanna sell it, well, *foine* . . .'

'Ronnie, I don't *use* it any more,' she said. 'When Max told me he was looking for a detector I thought we could get rid of it. We could do with the money to get the toilet finished. I mean, it's been taking you *for ever* . . .'

His pale blue eyes threatened to white out altogether.

'Look,' I said quickly, 'I don't want to get in the middle here and if you're not sure, then let's leave it. Really, it's OK . . .'

We stood for fifteen minutes, each leaving it up to the other, until Jane started to lose her patience and to my surprise caused Ron to acquiesce—to dampen his mania and begin glumly pointing out the metal detector's virtues.

It had been a special test machine, ramped up in the manufacturer's test labs. 'It's quoi-it,' he said, his beefy arms folded across his chest. 'Loike, *really* quoi-it.' A quiet machine reduced ground interference, leaving only the noises emanating from ferrous and nonferrous metals. Crucial, he said.

Which was just as well, because the Minelab SD 2100 Super Detector looked like crap. The extendable aluminium arm had peeling tape round it; the Super Goldsearch plate had peeling tape round it; and a fluffy padded sleeve lining the elbow support was held on by peeling tape. The backpack containing the battery bore a camouflage pattern, but this was coated with red dust thick enough to conceal a few nuggets of its own.

I looked at Jane, whose eye-rolling during the earlier pacing display had confirmed her as a reliable ally. 'Honestly, Max,' she said gently, 'it's an excellent machine. I've found gold with it, and if *I* can find gold, anyone can.'

'Well, mate,' said Ron, 'take it or leave it. But I think it's a fair proice at two thousand dollars.'

'Hm,' I mused, aware that it was probably worth $500 less.

'Tell y'what: if y'loike, we'll take it out into the bush tomorrow morning and you can troi it, see how it feels. We'll see what we can foind with it.'

'Done,' I said. For the chance to see Ron at work I'd have paid $500 more.

HE ARRIVED at my camp at 9.45 with wraparound sunglasses and well-meant apologies for being late. 'Have y'got y'self a lunch?'

After recovering from the shock of his apologies, I answered in the negative. But then I'd assumed that the trial wouldn't go much beyond an hour.

'Well, make y'self some sandwiches, and don't rush; there's no hurry. We'll take my truck, OK? Y'wanna take y'dog?'

'No, no. I'll tie her on the line.'

Ron's Land Cruiser was protected by fat steel pipes; two of these ran like wedding ribbons from the top of the windscreen to the bull bar. Behind the two-seater cab was a box cage covered in reinforced khaki canvas. The canvas unzipped and two sides of the cage lifted on gas suspension arms to reveal solar panels, boxes of tools, two detectors and a fridge in which he stowed my lunch.

'Don't moind the mess,' he said as we climbed into the cab.

Everything had a dusting of ochre: seats, dashboard, satphone, notebook, high frequency radio and mounted GPS unit. Strapped to the ceiling were scrolled maps, ten or so of them, which fell on my head with regularity.

Ron drove east out of my camp, along the track he used on his quad-bike. It was deeply cut by creek beds, and the prospector had to work the gearbox hard to negotiate gullies and fractures. I was going deep into the mulga ocean, deeper than I'd gone before, places where the mulga trees stood taller and sturdier than those at my camp's shoreline. A few kilometres on, we passed through a gate in wire fencing, then found a track that led to a clearing of black ironstone pebbles. The collars of old shafts erupted everywhere, the little volcanoes with timber-lined mouths, their flanks of waste soil compacted by weathering. I couldn't help expressing my liking for them.

'Yeah,' said Ron. 'Fack, the old fellas were good.' He must have seen these mounds a thousand times, but he was shaking his head in admiration.

We drove on and I asked questions about the shafts, about how the old-timers knew where to start digging. Ron was happy satisfying these questions, even stopping the truck to jump out and scratch a diagram in the dirt.

The object, he explained, was to locate a buried reef, an ore body of ironstone or quartz, micro-peppered with gold or shot through with yellow veins. In the early days, gold-bearing outcrops poked above the ground, waiting for a lucky prospector to walk past and spy them glinting in the sun. But the underground stuff had to be located by deduction, by loaming with the pan, counting specks. They dug wherever they found the surface soils richest in eroded gold, hoping to strike the source underneath. The shallow shafts I'd seen dotted around, some just a few metres deep, were often no-shows or else suggested only poor prospects. To improve the odds of cutting across a vein of gold they dug long, open trenches, or 'costeans'. Once they'd located a buried reef, the chase was on: wherever the ore body went the diggers followed, tunnelling like crazy rabbits in all directions.

When Ron steered off the track into thick bush, he stopped driving the vehicle and began operating it. He was constantly moving, twisting in his seat, monitoring ground to the front and to the sides, peering up over the end of the bonnet, scouting routes of least resistance. Vegetation thrashed over the bonnet and its steel piping.

We crossed a narrow clearing that ran in both directions, rapidly greening with mallee, acacias and mulga. 'This probably runs for forty Ks. But it's pretty old. Y'can see the bush growing back.' Then Ron crashed and mowed his way for another thirty minutes, stopping abruptly in an area where the bush was thinner. He cut the engine. The ground was red and black and warming under the midmorning sun. And he said, 'Inneresting.'

He reached for a grubby notebook and riffled through pages of numbers, hundreds and hundreds of them, in black Biro, blue Biro and pencil. They were latitudes and longitudes, occasionally marked with an asterisk and written with 'granites' or 'strike line', or two asterisks and 'must check'.

'Very inneresting.'

I quietly looked around, trying to discern what was so inneresting. This place looked little different from anything we'd seen for the past half-hour. But Ron was craning his neck this way and that.

'No one been out here for a while,' he said, more to himself than to me.

He got out and went to the front of the vehicle. I joined him at the bonnet. 'See those tracks?' Faint depressions coated with smooth ironstone pebbles curved away into the mulga. 'They're old wagon tracks. From horse and cart. But I don't reckon anyone's stopped here.'

Then he was nodding. 'Here. Let's give this place a go.'

I was flaring with excitement but I was confused. 'Can you . . . um . . . tell me what it *is* that's interesting about here?'

He sucked his bottom lip. 'There's ironstone alongside the laterites.' He waved his hand over the black-bubble rivers of ironstone abutting great swaths of orange dirt. 'I'm no geologist, but that suggests, loike, some contact between the rock—an' that's good for gold. But it also means movements, over toime, where the rock's been eroded away and washed over the land-scape. Maybe gold has been washed down from an outcrop; maybe there's a trail round here. We don't know. Did y'see that white quartz back there?'

'Those rocks in a pile?'

'Yeah. Well, the old fellas found that for sure. You can see they've napped it, broke it up lookin' for gold. But I reckon they gave up on it, thought there was nothin' here.' Then he paused. 'And I just—I dunno—I just feel it's here . . .' He was grinding his fist into a socket made from his other hand. He, too, was excited. 'Let's get the detectors out.'

Ron strapped me into the detector's backpack and placed vinyl head-phones over my ears before jacking a number of leads into sockets. It all felt comfortable. 'Here, you'll need this.' He handed me a small mattock and quickly stepped me through what I had to do.

Then he buckled himself into his machine, a GP Extreme worth $5,000, supported by a harness he'd engineered himself. The detector looked like a cyber-prosthesis. As Ron walked off into the bush, he creaked like C3PO.

'How's your sense of direction?' he called back.

'Awful.'

'Aw fack. Well . . . well just follow yer shadow, stay in a straight line. And let's do an hour at a time, OK? Back at the truck in an hour.'

'OK.'

'Good luck.'

I watched him move and saw that the detector *was* an extension of him-self. He didn't carry it or swing it; he executed a series of manoeuvres, probing at the ground, asking rapid questions with the white plate. These plates, loaded with sensitive magnetics, were always referred to as coils.

I set off after my shadow, swinging the detector, feeling its weight. My ears were filled with a tiny dull whine, blocking out all the pleasing sounds of the bush. The ground was quiet and the machine was quiet, the whine always dull, always tiny. Sometimes I'd pass the coil over the metal eyelets in my boots, setting off a looping scream closely followed by an angry squawk, just to wake myself and be assured the electronics were still working.

It was an hour before the first thrilling swallow dive of sound looped and crashed through my headphones. I removed the mattock from my belt and knelt clumsily, pulled this way and that by the cords and extensions of the detector. I scratched a neat square round the source of the sound and chopped five centimetres down, heaping the red soil beside the hole. Reaching for the detector, I awkwardly waved the plate over the hole—nothing—and over the heap, which returned the noisy signal. I divided the pile in half and reapplied the coil, discarding the half without the signal. I divided a few times more until I was left with a small inverted bowlful of dirt. From this I took a handful at a time, waving my fist over the coil until a signal told me I was holding the metal. I opened my hand and pushed the red dusts around with a fingertip.

I picked out two millimetres of rusted wire. Half an eyelash, a minuscule thing in miles of red dirt. It was quite a result.

Then there were tiny words in my warm headphones. 'Over here! Here!'

I found Ron crouched near a bush of thorn. 'Got a piece,' he said. He held aloft a gleaming shred of gold, all the while speaking in fragments: 'Knew it . . . Yep. S'round here . . . F'sure . . .' He stood up from his crouch, started sweeping with his coil. A few paces. And stopped. 'Here.'

He squatted and dug, then separated the dirt into piles, poured dust between his hands, waved his fists over the coil, opened his hand and picked out a reddish clot. He put the clot into his mouth, swished it around—and spat out another gleaming piece of gold.

'I fackn *knew* it!' And he was standing again, only this time he was abruptly switching the detector from side to side, almost with the stiff urgency of a blind man using a cane on an unreliable surface. 'I know I'm doing this too quickly,' he sputtered, narrating now, 'but I'm excoited . . .'

I started to say something but he was already digging out his third piece.

'Troi over there!' he urged, like the gold might be gone if I didn't hurry.

I took up my detector and began checking among the thorn bushes. Within ten minutes I had a signal. It was pure squeal. I called Ron as I began whittling down the dirt, hand-shuffling and discarding. And then I felt something in my palm. And uncurled my fingers.

Ron was grinning his delight, congratulating me, shaking my hand, swearing the whole time. He pushed his sunglasses up on his head and I saw his pale eyes were glowing. 'You know what we got?'

My eyes, too, were wide, my head swirling. I shook—no, no, I don't know.

'We've got a new . . . *fackn* . . . *patch*.'

MY NUGGET was 3.4 grams, smaller than a five-cent piece, maybe $80. I offered it to Ron. His navigation, his fuel, his detectors, his patch.

'Nah, mate. Fack that, my four pieces add up to the same. And you should keep it; it's y'first. Just don't tell anyone about that patch, OK?' He packed his digital weighing scales back into a box. 'I mean, it's great to get these little bits of gold, but they could just be the beginning. We'll follow 'em up and, who knows, the trail might take us somewhere. We'll work it. Could take toime, cos y'gotta do it carefully, slowly, foind the edges of the patch and close into the *source* . . .'

He'd said 'we'. I heard him. 'Ron, it's your patch; you found it, I didn't. If you want to work it on your own, then I understand; it's not a problem.'

'No, no. We found it together so we'll work it together. That's how it is.'

Jane brought out some cold beers. We clinked bottles and sat and talked. The night developed into a 2 a.m. drinking session over by my campfire, one that swelled steadily as more people drove up to spill out of their vehicles bearing cartons of beer and Tupperware containers of steaks, chops, sausages, salad, coleslaw.

As well as Jane and Ron, there was Russell, Cath and Joe.

Joe was all of eighteen. He was gangly, thin as a whip, especially in his white moleskin trousers and cotton shirt. His narrow, angular face hadn't yet recovered from the trauma of hormonal surges, but it promised to be a handsome one, split by a wide, expressive mouth.

Actually, Joe was all of seventeen; he'd lied about being eighteen. He had a yellow Daihatsu Rocky four-wheel drive, and in the back he carried a swag, some recovery gear and a stock whip. He was a man of the bush.

But really Joe was all of sixteen; he'd lied about being seventeen as well. He'd been schooled in Perth and the busy town of Esperance. But he really did love being in the bush. It allowed him to be who he wanted to be: at sixteen he could be eighteen; he could sit in a bar, push back his hat, light up a Marlboro and shoot the shit with other blokes, telling how he was a larrikin, a roustabout, a hard-drinkin', hard-smokin', hard-drivin' man of experience: 'I remember once, when I was doing a bit of rally driving . . .'

I always smiled at his onces remembered, his recollections, his delving into long histories. Joe's lying was shameless and constant, but it was done with conviction and some flair. And when he was finally rumbled for flagrant invention—which came to be often—he adopted a look of hurt and affront. And then he'd grin, and shrug, and ask, 'Who wants a beer?'

Joe's dad Russell (Russell the Roadman, not Russell the Kiwi) was a courteous, kind man with large unblinking eyes. He'd been contracted by Menzies Shire Council to grade hundreds of kilometres of local dirt roads until they were flat again. He'd driven his Mack truck 600 kilometres from

Esperance, trailer-hauling fifty tonnes of road grader, living quarters, Land Cruiser, two border collies, his wife Cath and their thin son.

Now Russell threw open the doors of the Land Cruiser and started playing tapes on the car stereo, and my dog chased around with the two collies, raising happy hell in the firelight shadows and the red dust.

THE GUNSHOT echoed across the clearing.

CRACK.

The dog shrank under the truck. Gangers working on the railway line looked up from their labour. The barking of the Puseys' dogs carried across to my tent. I circled the whip again, once, twice, three times, until all seven feet of leather filament was occupied with the graceful business of tracing a wide overhead arc. With a breakneck flick I snapped it down to the ground, shocking the frayed tip of nylon twine into breaking the sound barrier.

CRACK.

Again: up with the whip, only harder, faster, so the arc sounded a low whistle, and down. But I mistimed the wrist flick and the energy was concentrated instead in cracking the skin on my bare forearm. The graze was stinging. Three pink welts marched in lines towards my elbow.

The Widow had sent me the hand-plaited stock whip for my thirty-seventh birthday and young Joe showed me how to use it. I practised in the evening, because after just fifteen minutes the aerobic workout left me hot and breathless and made it easier to endure the freezing wash under the tap. But this morning I was using it because I wanted to work off some frustration.

Ron had disappeared into his toilet and was not coming out. Three weeks had passed, and though he occasionally held up his hand at the bar and said, 'Now, don't worry, I haven't forgotten,' I felt there'd been a distinct cooling off in commitment. This morning I'd heard his quad-bike buzzing up the track. I'd summoned all my realism and reasonableness, but when I poked my head out of my tent, listening to the fading drone, I groaned, 'You're going to the patch.' And I cursed him black and blue.

Detecting, meanwhile, was proving to be an exercise in misery.

Dropping the 3.4-gram nugget into my film canister—splash, clunk among my panned particles—had been the most profound pleasure. For days afterwards, I'd pop the top and look down on the piece, observing the red and black dirts dissolving out of its wrinkles. Sometimes I'd carefully change the water like it was a little fish tank.

And now I wanted more. I'd found a place about three kilometres from Kookynie, a hill pimpled all over with shafts. The hill was called McTavish. The track was rough and twisting but the mine site was deserted. The first day I pulled the detector from the back of the Troopie and slotted myself into the exoskeleton, I felt heady and wondered why I hadn't taken it up earlier. Then it all went wrong. It didn't work.

But there was nothing amiss with the machine. It was the ground that was all wrong.

At first glance, here was a peaceful mine site with silent shafts and the calming natter of birds. Through the detector, however, it was the soundtrack to Picasso's *Guernica*: a ranting, bellowing, snorting topography of metal.

From hobnails to half-buried sheets of corrugated iron, it was everywhere. There were rusted tins, horseshoes, pots, pans, lead bullets, brass cartridges, the heels of shotgun cases and great pools of millimetre-long filaments shed by rotting steel ropes used for winching ore trucks and buckets. Ore trucks and buckets gave off a signal, too.

The patch Ron and I had found was virgin, untrodden and noiseless except for gold nuggets. But it was an exception, so rare that it practically didn't exist. Most prospecting ground was like McTavish.

I tried burying my nugget among a circle of other metals, to learn to discern so I didn't spend all day unearthing old buttons from decayed denim trousers. But the complexity was bamboozling. The signal was affected not only by an object's metal type, but by the size of the object, depth of the object, shape of the object and how that object was sitting in the ground. Even at its simplest, it was frustrating: a blob of nonferrous gold sent out a solid, sweet note, but so did a nonferrous lead bullet. A rusted tobacco tin lid made the same vandal's howl as a glittering ten-ounce gob of Au.

Lazy Les, who was bohhhhhhn idle, used to put in an eight-hour day of detecting. At the end of four hours I was a scowling, sweating curmudgeon and driving for home at top speed.

I coiled the whip and hung it on a tent pole. As Lala emerged from underneath the truck, ears down, tail cowed, I made a cup of tea and retired to the verandah of my tent. I thought about spending a few hours at McTavish. But three weeks of raking the goldfields clean of rusted crap was beginning to take its toll. 'Bollocks to it,' I said. 'I'll take a day off.'

I settled into my collapsible canvas chair, the one that looked out over the clearing, and began reading one of the books from my suitcase.

'GOOD GOD,' I said, looking up from the book. 'Do you exist outside the pub?'

'Yeahhhh,' drawled Kevin, stepping through the clearing, a cigarillo in one hand. 'Y'not at McTavish today?' he asked.

'No,' I sulked. 'I'm taking the day off.'

'Been some good gold come out of McTavish. Back in the eighties it was being worked over by a group of blokes. It was small stuff but they'd come back to the pub with a fair old bit. Where you working?'

My descriptive locators weren't the best. 'Sort of west of the hill, near the big mine shaft that's full of dead goats—where the track cuts through . . .'

He grunted. 'So you've not quite made your millions.'

'No,' I said. 'Hey, Kevin'—I'd remembered something—'have you ever had biltong? Y'know, jerky. Dried meat.'

'Ohhhh yes,' he rumbled approvingly.

'So, do y'know if you can make jerky out of kangaroo meat?'

He pursed his lips. 'Beee*yoodiful*,' he said. 'Kangaroo makes bloody *lovely* jerky. Rub in some spices, bitta pepper, string it up for a few days . . . Old fellas used to make it.'

'Well, how about this? Kookynie Kangaroo Jerky. We'll dry it in the pepper tree and sell it in small packets. Three dollars a packet. We'll sell it through the pub! Make a fortune!'

Kevin smiled at the suggestion. Then he began to chuckle, his eyes crinkling behind his glasses. 'Not bad,' he said, shooting me with the two fingers that held his cigarillo. 'Processing and selling meat for human consumption without a licence would of course land me in jail, destroy my livelihood and ruin my life. But not bad . . .'

I CLOSED my book. It was getting cold. Evening was creeping over the clearing, colouring the dirt russet, making the shadows black. A breeze was pushing at the windmill, nudging at the blades to start their singsong of creaks and clanks.

There was buzzing from the mulga ocean. It was Ron on his bike, emerging at speed. I turned in my seat and waved as he passed forty metres away. But he didn't look and he didn't wave. I twisted my mouth and sighed through my nose. The orange dog with the small nature was lying faithfully by my side, so I leaned down and scratched her soft floppy ear flaps.

'Tell you what, Lala, how about I get myself a beer and we go for a walk?'

She jumped up, shook herself all over and wagged alongside as I went to the fridge in the back of the Troopie to search out a tin. Pushing through bags of vegetables and packets of Timtams, I heard another noise, an unfamiliar one, a long, low rasping noise coming from the pub, then a string of fat coughs interspersed with extruded farts.

I looked up to see a face that cheered me immediately: the square muzzle of an old British Land Rover, only the vehicle had no top; it was just a body and a windscreen and a chunky spare wheel strapped to the bonnet.

Kevin drew up beside the tent, his long fag drooping down his beard. 'C'mon,' he growled. 'Geddin.'

This was the sum total of conversation as we drove into the mulga with enough noise to raise the dead in Kookynie cemetery. Every surface of the open vehicle was covered in junk—dice, dart flights, key rings, fag ends, rocks, washers and inches of brown dust. It was obviously much loved, like a man's shed, only on wheels.

We passed the McTavish mine site and went a little further into the bush. Then Kevin stopped and pointed to a coarse stretch of land, maybe an acre. 'There. That's where those blokes worked it. They pushed it—got a grader and cleared away the bush.'

I looked and listened as he explained what I should do, before venturing, 'Some fellas in the pub reckon McTavish has been flogged to death.'

'Nah, bullshit. Blokes say this place has been flogged, that place has been flogged. They usually say it cos they're too lazy to work it properly. If you work it carefully, slowly, little steps at a time, you'll get gold.'

He then drove his farting, belching monster-car, the only thing in the goldfields that smoked more than he did, north along other tracks, pointing out areas for gold, pointing out possibles, maybes, worth-a-gos.

And then he cut the engine again, carefully stepped through the little metal door and gently extracted a glossy high-powered rifle from a long flat case. He pulled down a lever to expose the chamber and inserted a long cartridge tipped with a copper-jacketed, hollow-nosed bullet. Replacing the lever with an oily click, he laid down his cigarillo, leaned on the bonnet and put his eye up to the telescopic sight.

Fifty metres across a clearing, a small grey face was poking up from behind a bush. The face was still. Watching.

CRACK.

The gunshot smashed across the clearing. It sounded nothing at all like my whip.

7

I laid the steel baking tray in the dirt and took from it a long, sticky strap, plum-red and gritted with spices. I tied it to a low branch with string, where it hung, safe in the shady interior of the peppertree. I reached for another strap and thought again of the high-velocity killing of the kangaroo.

A sudden bang, a yellow-white lightning flash, a squirt of cordite gas. Fifty metres from the Land Rover there were only speech marks of fur, floating in the space where the small grey face had been.

Kevin had worked quickly and quietly on the warm carcass using a hunting knife. He needed strength and technique to cut back the animal's stubborn architecture of hide, sinew, tendon and bone.

This morning the publican was master of happier ceremonies, snatching up his great pepper grinder and crunching the corns with rapid twists of the wooden head, dusting the meat straps from tins of salt, cayenne and ground chilli. Then he rolled and pressed the cold fillets between his palms, encouraging the savoury granules to penetrate the flesh. It was a joy to watch.

Fourteen pieces of kangaroo were hung in the tree. I stepped back to admire them. Just three days of air-drying and . . . Beee*yoodiful.*

Despite her preoccupation with chasing them pell-mell through the bush, the dog was not at all interested in kangaroo meat, only in what I was doing. She watched me wipe my hands on my shorts then followed me to the rear of the open-backed Troopie, where the long drawer was open. I groped among lost cashew nuts, dried leaves and coils of wire and found a small glass bottle containing Heinz baby food. I ate the puréed contents, stripped the bottle of its label, washed it and half-filled it with water. Then extracted my nugget from the film canister and dropped it into its new home.

Big nuggets have names: the Bobby Dazzler, the Latrobe, the Welcome Stranger. My nugget was the One That Ron Helped Me Find. It looked like a bunch of grapes in miniature and made a forlorn *clack-clack-clack* against the glass of the Heinz jar.

I returned the jar to the long steel drawer and slid it shut, before checking the battery charge on my metal detector. 'OK, Dog, get in the truck. Let's see if we can make this bloody thing pay for itself.'

OF THE WORLD'S ten largest alluvial nuggets, eight were found in Australia, all in Victoria, all before 1871. The biggest was the Welcome Stranger, found by Cornish partners John Deason and Richard Oates in the Moliagul area. On 5 February 1869, Deason struck a hard object with his pick and bent down to find a huge piece of gold clinging to a substantial chunk of quartz. The nugget survived intact for only ten days but sketches suggest it was a complex butterfly-shaped mass some sixty centimetres across. It was heavier than two sacks of cement and yielded 2,283 ounces, 6 pennyweights and 9 grains of gold. At the August 2002 gold price of US$320 an ounce it would be worth US$725,000—around AUS$1.3 million or £470,000.

The Holtermann nugget was the world's biggest single *mass* of gold, a slab of quartz rock shot through with metal. It was dug out of the Star of Hope Mine in Hill End, NSW. A montage photograph depicts Bernard Otto Holtermann standing beside the golden rock, his hand on it like it was the shoulder of an old friend; the obelisk stands 1.5 metres tall, only a head shy of Holtermann. Twelve miners struggled to bring the quarter-tonne rock to the surface, where it would eventually yield over 3,000 ounces.

Western Australia's biggest nugget was found in 1931 by the seventeen-year-old son of digger Jim Larcombe. The lad was working on his father's small lease in Larkinville, south of Kalgoorlie. He hit the nugget with his pick and called out, 'Dad! I've got a nugget!' His father called back, 'Well, pull it *out* . . .', but the youth was unable to lift it from the hole: the Golden Eagle, a great flat plate of gold, weighed 1,135 ounces, over thirty-five kilos.

All these champion gold specimens were sold to the government, melted down and shipped back to Britain as bullion. If found today, they would exceed their gold value many times over, purely for their collectability. Prospecting and souvenir shops sell small nuggets for 30 to 60 per cent above their metal value. Nuggets over an ounce are increasingly rare. 'They're not like mushrooms,' say the prospectors of Kookynie; 'they don't grow back.' Collector-investors pay handsome premiums.

The 1.3-ounce nugget pictured on the notice board in the Grand Hotel was for sale, price $1,200. At the end of August 2002, the gold price was still pushing upward, to US$320 an ounce, around $575, making the 1.3 ouncer's metal value (its 'scrap' value as the refineries have it) $750. An American visitor thought the gold price still had a long way to go and came through the pub looking to invest in nuggets. He haggled with the nugget's finder, who finally agreed to let it go for $1,000.

Parking the Troopie, I strode away to mentally cordon off half an acre of Kevin's scraped ground, then began detecting in long strips, as a ploughman might work a field. I was soon excavating the usual metal rubbish, albeit in smaller amounts, and my hands became pinched and parched, my shorts stained with brown hand-wipes. Lately, the days had begun to warm again—today was 27°C—and my shirt was languid with moisture and quite wet beneath the backpack.

After the first hour, I found myself lost in rich landscapes of thought. Other detector operators had spoken of these, the places they escaped to when the going was tedious. The clarity of these mental vistas was amazing, sometimes real enough to provoke physical reactions: a face-crease of embarrassment, a fist-clench of resolve, a belly-shake of laughter.

The dog spent her hours happily scampering through the bush, exploring, sniffing out trails, but never letting me out of her sight. After two hours it was 11 a.m. and we met back at the truck under the shade of a mulga tree for 'smoko'. Smoko was traditionally a break from work to enjoy a cigarette and billy tea; today it still means a break and is used in Australia's city offices as readily as in the outback.

Lala took some water and part of my peanut butter sandwich; I sipped from my truckie's thermo-bucket filled with tea. I felt good—fresh, interested, convinced there was gold to be found. This last was critical; I knew so from panning. The second you think it's only soil, you're crushed by the ridiculousness of it all and it's time to pack up, because it's over, at least for today.

'Righto, Dog. Let's do some more.'

I shrugged myself back into the apparatus, donned the clammy headphones and switched on the machine. The detector instantly began screeching and shrieking, beside itself with something metal and massive.

It was two tonnes of Toyota.

'Shit.' I stepped away from the vehicle and moved off towards my delineated square. But just ten metres from the vehicle's bull bar I collected a calm, clear signal, so calm that I wasn't able to relocate it at first, thought it might be another insect leg of fly wire. I waved the coil repeatedly over the spot, then bent—pushing away the dog's snuffling head—and dug a shallow hole until the metal object was in a small heap of excavated soil.

And soon it was in my open palm.

'Lala,' I said plainly. 'I've found one.'

It was a raised shape in the dirt, a fat button, but the weight was telling.

And from its tight red jacket of earth poked the smallest nub of gold. Rubbing the button on my shorts, I encouraged a little more metal to appear. Then I remembered how Ron had done it, and popped the nugget into my mouth.

I vigorously swished it around, rinsing it in spit, letting the dirty red accretions dissolve in the saliva. The smallest grits would crunch between my molars for some minutes after, but for now the flat mineral taste was honest, wholesome, even a bit familiar. But it was the delicious heaviness knocking against the inner enamel surfaces of my teeth that I relished most.

Then I spat it out so it lay in my palm, shrouded in a bubbly, blood-coloured froth until the bubbles slipped aside to reveal a gleaming brilliance. In two billion years, my eyes were the first to acknowledge its form: a small fat disc of bright, ponderous metal. Looking closer at one surface I decided I could see a scorpion in relief, with curved tail and curved claws encircling the button of gold. The Scorpion. I drew a breath that was part rapture, part gratitude. And mostly relief.

I returned to the Troopie, retrieved the Heinz jar from the steel drawer and dropped the Scorpion into the water. I lifted it to the light like a crystal glass and swirled it, watching as the palest red began to infuse the waters around my two nuggets.

THE EXTRAORDINARY thing about finding gold is the twin urges that immediately follow the discovery. The first is to disguise all evidence of finding anything, the second is to find someone and boast about it.

The old-timers understood how important it was to keep news of a strike absolutely quiet. Perhaps there were some who kept mum about a patch of gold-bearing reef, some who extracted their riches before tiptoeing away, carefully closing the door on their secret behind them. But not many. Diggers invariably succumbed to excitement, vanity and alcohol – and then blurted. Reliving their most recent glories, usually at a bar, usually before a host of rambunctious new friends all eager to buy the lucky prospector another drink or two, cost them dearly. Soon afterwards they might fall victim to thieves, but more often they simply had their patch overrun by frantic diggers, before the hangover had abated.

For me, it wasn't unlike running up the long path from the bottom of the garden yelling, 'Mum, Dad, look what I've dug up in me hole . . .'

I broke open a beer, climbed into the Troopie and rocked happily down the broken track from McTavish to the pub. Fighting back a smile, I entered the bar and carefully placed the nugget on the counter in front of Kevin.

'Ahhhhh,' said Kevin, '*there* you are . . .' He was talking to the nugget.

I wanted to stay and unload all the precious details leading up to the find, but I'd promised Joe and his parents that I'd join them for dinner (and I was already impatient to show the Scorpion to someone else) so I paid for two six-packs and walked the few metres through town to Russell's camp.

Russell's set-up reminded me of a wagon circle in a cowboy flick. On one side were long aluminium sheds mounted on a semitrailer. On the other were two yellow road graders, the big Mack truck, a Land Cruiser and Joe's tin four-wheel drive.

And to my surprise here also was Ron's Land Cruiser, driving slowly out of the camp towards me. Ron halted his car, a thick arm resting on the open window. 'How y'goan!' His face was open and cheerful.

'I'm pretty good! Yourself?'

'I'm fackn good, mate! So why you so good?' He had a glint in his eye. He was close to smiling. And I realised at once: we'd both got gold.

'Here.' I released the Scorpion into his proffered palm.

'Aw, wow! That's a *noice* piece of gold. Maybe six grams? Good on yer!'

'It's a start,' I said.

'Yeah, well good on yer. And . . . Now listen, mate, I'm really sorry about not being able to get out lately. I've been working on me fackn toilet, and it's taking for ever. You been back to that patch?'

'Eh?'

'You been back to it? Where we found those bits of—'

'No, no. I thought *you* had.'

'Christ, no. I'm doing a bit of work over somewhere else with Gary. We're troin' out some new coils he's desoigned. Y'know Gary?'

'Yeah, met him in the bar once or twice.' Gary was from near Bunbury. He spent half his year designing extrasensitive plates for detectors and the other half testing them out in the bush. 'But look, don't worry about the patch,' I said disingenuously. 'Whenever you're ready, OK?'

'No worries . . .' Ron handed back the nugget, and now he *was* smiling.

I looked him in the eye. 'You've got gold.'

He laughed, and nervously milked his goatee. 'What makes y'say that?'

'You've got it written all over your face! Come on, show me.'

'Hey,' he said quickly, craning through the window to the rear of the vehicle. 'Here's young Joe.'

'G'day, Max,' said Joe. 'How's it going?' Joe, too, was beaming.

'Good, but Ron's onto something, and I want to know what it is . . .' Joe widened his eyes and glanced at Ron. 'Aw, *c'mon guys*, you know I won't say anything.'

There was a pause. Ron glanced briefly down to the passenger seat of his cab. 'Watcha reckon, Joe? Shall I show him?'

'Yeah, go on.'

Ron lifted out a gold pan. 'Here. Careful with it.'

The matey banter of the exchange, the glee at finding my own nugget, the gratification at hearing I'd been wrong about Ron and the patch—all of it wiped away in a second.

The dish was dead-weight heavy, but what lay in the bottom was baffling. At first I thought it was a layer of solid gold, so thickly did it cover the pan's base. But it moved like a sluggish gel or heavy magnetic paint, and seemed to repel the water sitting uneasily on top. I nudged the yellow sludge with my finger and it shifted reluctantly to reveal larger splats and blots, like molten solder dropped onto a cold surface, only they were splats and blots of pure gold. I'd never seen so much. 'What . . .?'

Ron apologised repeatedly but said he couldn't, just couldn't say any-thing—not where, not what, not even when.

I looked at Joe and he shrugged. 'I dunno where he got it.'

But my speechlessness must have been gratifying. When I carefully handed the pan back to Ron, out it came. The blurt. 'Reckon there's a few ounces in there,' he said. 'And another hundred and fifty ounces where that came from.'

I looked again at Joe. Joe looked away. Joe knew.

KEVIN TOOK the slip of paper. It was a small flyer that I'd designed in black pen. It read:

KOOKYNIE KANGAROO JERKY
Dried among the peppertrees of the historic Grand Hotel,
Kookynie, heart of the Northeastern Goldfields

Underneath was a cartoon of a heavy-faced man with a beard, genially winking from behind his spectacles. A quote alongside read: '*Three days hanging around the Grand Hotel will cure anything* . . .' It wasn't a good likeness; Kevin never winked genially, and leaving out his cigarillo was like leaving out his nose.

But Kevin's eyes were creased at the corners; he was smiling at the flyer, his press-lipped smile that recognised illicit or nonsanctioned fun. He retreated to a small office, scanned it into his computer, printed off a copy and hung it on the notice board.

'MAX? MAX, are y'there?'

The electronically piped voice came from the Troopie. I always left the radio switched on, tuned to Channel 20 in case the pub ever needed me.

I dropped the bough of mulga I was breaking into kindling and took up the handset. 'Yeah, Joe.'

'Mate, whatcha up to?'

'Getting my fire ready for tonight.'

'Mate, I've got something for you. I'll come over. And I'll bring beer.'

'Right.'

I spent a few more minutes snapping mulga, then a thundering roar came over the railway line, accompanied by the sounds of gouging and scraping and a great steely clanging. I looked up and let go a burst off laughter, then watched as the fourteen-tonne yellow grader, slung underneath with a three-metre knife blade, made its way slowly towards my camp. In its wake was a trail of pale orange dirt, as clean and flat as a ribbon of rolled pastry.

Joe cut the engine and blinked like an owl from behind a thick mask of dust. 'There y'go, mate! I've given ya a nice new road!'

'You're a lunatic, Joe.' I smiled, shaking my head as he jumped from the cab. 'Come on, let's open that beer.'

We talked over our respective days—my getting more gold from McTavish, him helping his father to grade the Yerilla road.

'So,' I said, 'tell me, where the hell did Ron get that gold?'

Joe hesitated and looked a bit nervous.

'C'mon, out with it.'

'Well—and y'can't say anything cos Ron will kill me—but y'know the Orient Well mine up the road?'

It was an astonishing story. Ron had heard that the mothballed Orient Well processing plant was being disassembled. He'd raced the fifteen kilometres north and talked with someone at the dead plant, specifically about a huge stack of 1,500 solid rubber sticks. Each stick was a metre or so long, forty centimetres wide, and so heavy you could only lift one at a time. They were going to be scrapped, buried in a giant pit. Ron had said, 'I'll take 'em.'

To extract gold from ore, the rock must first be crushed to fine powder. In the old days, the diggers used a pestle and a steel dolly pot. Modern plants load the ore into a house-sized rotating drum containing hundreds of steel balls, and their constant tumbling pulverises the rock. To insulate the drum from the balls, it's lined with thick rubber sticks that interlock like tiles.

Powdered gold gets into every conceivable pore of these rubber liners.

Joe and Russell had helped Ron load the sticks and cart them home. Ron's pan of gold was the result of scrubbing the surface of three especially rich rubber sticks, using a wire brush and a paint scraper. A man from Kalgoorlie who specialised in rescuing gold from dead mining equipment would pay a lot of money to relieve Ron of his giant pile of rubber liners.

'You've got to admire him, Joe.' I raised my beer to my mouth, but stopped to say, 'Hey, how'd you like some kangaroo jerky with that beer?'

'Is this your Kookynie Kangaroo Jerky?'

'It certainly is.' I beamed. 'A million-dollar enterprise in the making. You can be our test market.'

I led him into the peppertree—and found that fourteen straps of spicy, dried-black meat had been reduced to just four. Ten pieces of green string hung lamely from a branch.

'Nooooo!' I wailed. 'Bastards!'

The million-dollar Kookynie Kangaroo Jerky industry had been brought to its knees. By crows.

THROUGHOUT AUGUST I detected five days a week, and, if the mood took me, half a day on Saturday. I got gold. Usually one or two small pieces in the space of five or six hours. The nuggets were usually only five centimetres or so into the ground. But unearthing each was a special moment, for they came bearing information, clues to where other nuggets might lie. All of them went into my mouth for a rinse, shooting me through with a rich thrill.

None of the nuggets was as big as the Scorpion, and sometimes hours and even days would drag by when I found not a thing. But I schooled myself to relax about time spent strapped to the machine. When nuggets wouldn't come, I scanned the ground for indications of where gold might have shed from higher ground; I squeezed myself into awkward spaces.

Walking through thick spider webs stopped bothering me; I stopped wincing when I grabbed handfuls of dirt filled with evil curara needles; and I took time out at regular intervals to make tea, eat sandwiches and be nice to my dog, whose happiness I could sometimes call upon to boost my own.

The jar grew heavier and brighter with nuggets—a threesome, then a family, then a gang, eventually a crowd—nuggets that sounded a small knobbly gurgle when I swirled the glass, or a hiss when I accelerated them into a smooth centrifuge. Each new nugget was a prize that lodged fat clots of pleasure in my heart. Each was distinctive. Each had its own story . . .

The Laughing Boy, a two-gram sunflower seed of gold a centimetre long. I prised him out of the dirt, then with the very next step, walked into ground that swarmed with fly wire. He was the needle I found sitting next to a haystack of sound.

Orion's Belters, three one-millimetre pips, each just 0.2 of a gram. I found them within metres of each other, all tiny and insignificant, which somehow made me all the more grateful for finding them.

The Skull, round, smooth and over four grams. He'd travelled so far over the millennia that he'd become abraded and graced with a dome. One of his eye sockets held a jet-black eyeball. Prospectors call it an inclusion; in the case of the Skull, it revealed that the gold had once been held captive in an ironstone reef.

The Map of Ireland, only a couple of grams, but he almost cost me a broken nose. The flies were bad that day and one tickled so insistently that I swiped at it with my hand. Only I'd forgotten my hand was holding a small mattock. My eyes watered from the pain.

The Sunbaker, my first specked nugget. I spotted him sitting brazenly in the red dirt, gleaming like a small coin in the oft-tramped, century-old mine site. Gold. Gold lying on the floor.

And the Afghanis from Afghan Hill. They were the result of four days' work on a long, exposed flank of gully, hard-skinned with beads of iron-stone, the backside of a place so 'flogged' and worked over that prospectors rolled their eyes at its name. But here was where I found my patch. I looked at the broken, crumbling uplands and imagined gales and torrents and the giant hands of time that could uplift and excise landforms like modelling clay, leaving riverbeds where there were once mountains and mountains where there were once rivers. I pictured the swirling processes and thought, *If this was a huge pan, where would the gold gather?* The Afghanis came out in a string, eight of them over a line of twenty metres. They totalled nearly twenty grams. Nearly two thirds of an ounce . . .

I was completely lost to gold, often oblivious to the date or even the day.

One date—11 September 2002—only became apparent in the weary evening when, straining to write by firelight, I glanced at the top of my diary page. Though satellites were showering the planet with reports and analyses and live memorial broadcasts, I was deaf to them. My ears were filled with signals from below, not from above.

THE PRISON was a small, one-felon cell made of thick wooden slabs. The only light came through a hole set with iron bars in the heavy door. Despite its cartoonish appearance, it was a bona fide piece of goldfields history, though none of the Gwalia Day crowds seemed particularly interested. I was sitting in its shady lee, drinking beer with Russell the Kiwi and his wife Jude. It was Sunday, traditionally the diggers' day of rest.

Jude was selling jars of homemade preserves and pickles from a stall under a sign that read *Jude's Jars*. 'Not doing so bad today, Russ,' she said, tucking notes into a pouch at her waist. 'But I think we had a better position last year. More people walking past.'

'Yeah,' said Russell. 'But we get a better view of the billy cart races here.'

It was the tenth heat; two carts were whizzing down the steep curving hill from the Gwalia Museum to the finish line. The cart in front was silver, sleek as a dart and low to the ground. The mining company had engineered it to run on racing-bike wheels, and it was swishing gracefully to victory.

Metres behind trundled a cart that gave enormous pleasure to Russell. 'Ha! Look at this! Aww . . . *Go on mate! Go!*' Descending with the speed and elegance of a cow on skates was a wide-load vehicle: the driving seat was a sofa occupied by a lad of generous weight. The dart cart was long home but Russell wasn't giving up on his champion: 'Go on, mate, y'can *still do it*!'

I rarely saw Russell the Kiwi in Kookynie, but when I did he was laughing. He was built to laugh: tall, six feet two inches, and thin, all long bendy limbs and amiable gestures. He had a large smile full of unnaturally perfect teeth, surrounded by a red beard that exploded outwards as though blown that way by his laughter. Russell and Jude lived in one of Kookynie's eight standing structures, but Russell worked a lease 120 kilometres northeast of town. He worked it with an expensive metal detector and, since he'd often be gone for months at a time, I could only assume he was getting good gold.

But today we were in Gwalia, four kilometres south of Leonora, amid Gwalia Day celebrations, a day when another dead goldfields town was brought back to life.

The late-nineteenth-century shanty town of timber and hessian had been restored by Leonorans—restored in the sense that they'd used the same dirt-poor materials and half-arsed techniques as those living here a hundred years ago. The effect was one of superb authenticity. The one-room hovels leaned and buckled, had little or no glass, and their walls were whitewashed or papered with 1900 editions of the *Kalgoorlie Miner*. Even the more solid cottages leaked, smelt of rot and collected thick layers of dust—mining dusts, blown in from the neighbouring Sons of Gwalia mine.

The open-cut pit was nearly a kilometre wide, and beneath were a hundred kilometres of shafts and drives tunnelling away in twelve subterranean storeys. The mine operated 365 days a year. Even on Gwalia Day.

While the miners laboured deep beneath our feet, the township was all bunting-flutter and festivity under a regal blue sky. There was a funfair with jewellery-box twinkles and music that waltzed through the air. Between the shanty restorations were trestles loaded with homemade produce, bric-a-brac and fried food; people moved among them buying, chatting and guessing the weight of a gold bar that was actually brass.

I bought us a round of beers from the Sly Grog Shop and returned to watch heat eleven of the billy cart races.

'Russell,' I said, handing him his drink, 'you know where I got that string of nuggets on Afghan Hill?'

'Ye-ah.'

'Well, parts of that area are leased by companies, right?'

'Some. Not all.'

'So . . . by taking out a handful of nuggets, was I taking a huge risk? Or what? It all seems a bit grey to me.'

'It's pretty unlikely a company would find you, but if they did, you'd most likely get a warning and be told to clear off. But some companies are tougher than others. And if they catch you they can take you to court. And then you'd be looking at a hundred-thousand-dollar fine.'

I winced.

'You're more likely to have a run-in with someone who works a small lease. A bloke from New South Wales was detecting over at Afghan Hill recently, on a local fella's lease. The lease owner caught him and gave fair warning to clear off. Next day, the owner caught him again, so he called in the Gold Police.'

'The *Gold* Police? Really?'

'They're based in Kal. They usually deal with gold theft, but they also handle lease infringement, stuff like that. Anyway, they came up and confiscated this bloke's detector and impounded his four-wheel drive. They told him to hand over all the gold he'd found on the lease and said he'd better be honest about it if he wanted to see his vehicle again.'

'What happened to him?'

'He got his vehicle back, but he was prosecuted for carrying an unlicensed rifle. And I tell you what, the bush telegraph really works after something like that. It makes people stop and think before they go off detecting just anywhere. Which is good for me—I've found people on my lease and told 'em to clear off. They come sniffing around while I'm dry-blowing, trying to see if there's—'

'Dry-blowing? You've got a dry-blower?'

'Yeah. Had one for years.'

'I thought you detected on your lease.'

'Well sometimes I do, if it's raining or if the wind's no good. But it's a dry-blowing operation.' He shrugged. 'Dry-blowing's what I do.'

8

I watched the dust column; it was fifty metres high, like an immense orange bloom or a serpent rearing up into the spring sky. Once, there would have been hundreds of them, twisting, waving their engorged heads over the dun fields. And at the base of each would be a man, maybe two, busy as ants, rocking a small timber-framed cabinet to sieve dirt and blowing away the dusts with simple canvas bellows.

Today, among the expanse of plains, ridges and barren slopes, there rose only one column of orange dust. It was, however, an exceptionally large one, created by furious and ungodly contraptions.

'WAH-HEY!!' shouted Russell the Kiwi, standing in the seat of what looked like a moon buggy fitted with an earth mover's shovel. His cry was almost drowned by engine combustions, the thunder of wide leather conveyors and a dull gravelly chunter.

I climbed from the Troopie and immediately tasted dust. Russell loped over to meet me, pulling down a face mask and lifting a pair of goggles; with his khaki shirt and peaked cap he looked like a tank commander in the Afrika Korps, but his beard and the dust rendered most of his face bright orange.

'Ha-ha!' he yelled, pumping my hand. 'Good to see ya, Max!'

'Russell, how are you!' I yelled back. Russell's nature and the clatter of his machines had put a smile on my face. He'd invited me to stay for two weeks.

'And who's this?'

'Lala!' I yelled.

'And Lala! Ohhh, Lala, yerra beautiful girl, arn'tcha?' He bent low to ruffle the dog all over.

'Great set-up!' I called.

'Come on! I'll show you how it works!'

The dry-blower was big enough to fill a room. It shook and turned and spilt dirt from everywhere into smooth-sloped piles. It was endearingly, eccentrically, gorgeously homemade. Pinned all over its panels and frames were essential maintenance tools to keep it alive: a hammer for bashing, a long stick for poking, a roll of stiff wire for repairing.

Russell's lease was about an acre, scoured flat, an umber scab among rolling valleys of parched grey grass dotted with thorny trees. It was set against a magnificent hogback range of ironstone hills. He'd bought the lease seven years ago from the man who first pegged the land and built the machines. The gold had shed and variously dispersed into the soils from an underground reef source that no one had managed to pinpoint.

We inspected separate mounds of soil—dirt gouged fresh from the ground, dirt spread over the ground to dry, dirt being crushed by a heavy concrete roller ready for blowing—then looked over the moon buggy. It was a chassis with four balloon tyres: at the rear was a V6 engine, at the front a hydraulic bulldozer shovel, and in the middle a driver's seat enclosed in a cage and crowned with an extravagant pair of bull's horns.

Russell beamed. 'This is Chev!' he said, then noticed that the dry-blower's labouring was growing quiet. 'Aw, she's running out of dirt . . .'

'You get back to work,' I said. 'I'll watch.'

Russell used the buggy to hoist half a tonne of dirt into the dry-blower's overhead hopper, sending dust roiling into the air. The dirt dropped onto a conveyor, then fed into a horizontal forty-four-gallon drum rotated by engine-driven rollers. The middle section of the drum had been cut away and replaced with windows of mesh. As the soil rumbled through the drum, the dirt was sieved out and dropped onto the eaves of what looked like a dog kennel. Bellows inside the kennel puffed air through cloth filters in the roof. The lightest dirts were blown away or sent spilling down the sloping eaves, while dense, heavy particles were trapped by lateral partitions of wood.

'This is the exciting bit,' said Russell after dismantling the roof. It was quiet now; the engines shut down, the smudgy dust column slowly clearing away on the breeze. 'I just can't help having a little preview.' He poked a finger into a wooden partition and nudged some dust aside. 'There . . . See?'

A thin line of golden grains and granules trailed along the wooden seam.

'Wow, there's more there than I panned in three months. It's quite . . . Hello,' I said, looking up quickly. 'Who's this?' An air-conditioned luxury coach swung off the dirt road and pulled onto the lease.

'It's the tourists,' said Russell. 'The bus driver brings 'em here to let 'em have a look. They lap it up.'

A group of fifty pensioners from Perth clambered out of the coach, offering cheery hellos! and g'days! before bunching around the dry-blowing machine. Russell greeted them all before happily explaining again how his incredible, noisome contraption worked.

RUSSELL'S CAMP was half a kilometre from the lease; Lala and I were driven there sitting in the shovel of Chev.

The camp was in a peaceful copse of mallee trees at the base of the splendid hogback ridge of ironstone. An old caravan served as the prospector's sleeping quarters; in front of this was an area of beaten earth, wetted down and well swept, furnished with a fireplace, table and chairs. Blackened cooking utensils hung tidily on a tree beside the table. Under another tree was a shower, screened with sheets of tin and primed with hot water boiled in a fire-heated drum; the shower head let fall its piping-hot water at the flick of an old Bakelite switch wired to a small pump. Electricity came from a Honda two-stroke generator, located some distance from the camp.

'You've got everything but the kitchen sink.'

'Got that, too.' He indicated an aluminium sink without taps. It was set against a bush and plumbed so waste waters drained away onto a veggie patch, a small cactus garden and a bed of sweet peas trained round sticks.

'So does Jude always stay in Kookynie?'

'No, she comes up when she can, but she's in Kal at the moment.' He collected an ice-cream tub of fine dirt from Chev. 'Wait till you see this next bit; it's bloody magic.' He hunched over like a happy hermit and loped across to a leafy corner where a small gizmo was installed on an upturned drum.

'It's me gold separator,' he breathed, his eyes alight, his grin spreading to reveal his perfect teeth. He pressed a switch and the machine—similar in appearance to an old gramophone player with a speaker horn, but fed all over by pipes and chutes—began nimbly performing like a clockwork Victorian curio. There were whirrs and clicks; there were miniature movements and trickles of fluid. It had the same serenities as a well-appointed train set or an indoor water ornament.

The speaker horn was a cone of thin metal lying on its side and rotating on rollers. The dry-blower fines were automatically fed, small amounts at a time, into the cone, where they were sluiced with water. The simple physics of the cone's rotation and a delicate tilt of the axis meant the water-washed fines separated: less dense matter spilled in an orangey wash from the mouth while the super-heavies were dragged upwards into the nose.

After fifteen minutes, we were mesmerised by the rolling cone. The fruits of Russell's labours, the filthy processes of excavating and preparing the earth, the infernal noise and smoking dusts of the dry-blower, all were brought to a delicate point.

'Bloody hell,' I said. 'It's . . . beautiful.'

Marching like a file of single-minded beetles were wet beads of ironstone and gold, all winking and twinkling as they crawled and rolled inexorably into the nose. The *coup de théâtre* was their falling through a hole at the tip, into a waiting jam jar of water: *plop-plop-plop.*

After half an hour the machine was switched off and the jar emptied into a gold pan. The small scree of black pebbles and sands was studded with nuggets and peppered with gold dust. Russell picked out the biggest nodules and we ducked into his caravan to weigh them on a set of analogue scales.

'Twelve grams. Not . . . *great.* But that's how it goes. On a really good day I'll clean up thirty-odd grams, nearly an ounce. But I've gotta get at least two grams a day to cover costs—fuel for Chev and for me blower and the genny. I reckon on average I earn about fifty dollars an hour.'

Outside again, he collected up the pan of ironstone sands. They were speckled with gold dust. 'This all goes into me poverty pot.' The poverty pot was a round glass jar, leaden with black powder like a bowling ball. 'All prospectors used to have a poverty pot for their black sands. It may not seem much at the time but it really adds up.'

Russell fed one of his poverty pots for two years. Then he chemically extracted the gold and converted it into two twenty-four-ounce gold bars. 'I got twenty-five thousand dollars, cash. I remember, I had the dollar bills in a bag and I took it to a Kalgoorlie car dealer and emptied the bag on the table. Ha! Always wanted to do that!'

IN TWO WEEKS I'd detected more than ten grams in the valleys around Russell's dry-blowing lease. These pushed the Heinz collection to over thirty-two grams—my first ounce. But today we were heading out on a joint search, so the pool-and-divide rule applied: we'd split whatever we found, regardless of who found the million-dollar nugget and who found nothing.

The forecast had predicted rain, so Russell covered his soil mounds with heavy tarpaulins and unsheathed his detector, a $5,000 model like Ron's. We drove cross-country to a broad valley, its dry floor running with a dark green river of acacia trees. 'I've been all over here but never got anything,' he said. 'But I'm sure there's gold here somewhere. Has to be.'

He had a hunch, a feeling; he especially liked the quartz 'blows' dotted across the slopes. Blows were surface eruptions of the crystalline rock. Under the onslaught of sun, rain, chemicals and extreme temperatures, they would fracture and erode, extending great skeins of dirty ice over the red and black ground. They were beacons of contact, betraying sites where quartz rubbed shoulders with granite or ironstone.

Within ten minutes of leaving the truck, I ducked into a patch of thorn bushes and detected a very small, very bright piece of gold. 'Russell! Here!'

'I don't believe it!' he said, examining the piece. 'We got a start! Well done! Oh Jesus, I'm gonna start shaking. I start shaking whenever I find bloody gold.' But he tried to contain his enthusiasm, not wanting to subvert our luck with undue optimism. He began working upslope through patches of quartz and basalt, and a few metres away found another small nugget.

And sure enough, he started shaking.

At lunch we returned to camp and weighed in nine pieces of gold totalling fourteen grams, over $250 worth. 'Sorry Russell,' I said. 'You found the better part of these. You sure you want to split it?'

'Mate,' he intoned with mock seriousness, opening his eyes wide, 'we'll split it. We'll split it because you might find the big one this afternoon.'

After lunch we returned to the valley and spent four infuriating hours finding nothing. The slope yielded not a single piece more. 'That's how gold is,' said Russell. 'You get everything. Then fuck all.'

But when the sun was low to the horizon and casting coppery outlines on the undersides of rain clouds, I wandered into the creeklands. This looks good, I thought, eyeing a small, slightly elevated patch of flood plain. I began slowly waving the coil.

I got a signal; it was big, too loud in fact. I kicked away the grey grass and chopped with my mattock until I had a mound beside a shallow hole. The signal was in the mound. I grasped a handful of dirt and waved it over the coil—nothing. I grasped a second handful and waved it over the coil—still nothing. I grasped a third—and pulled up a dense brown rock the size of a golf ball. One that was showing yellow metal.

'Oh God,' I said, and bellowed once more for the lanky prospector.

He came running. 'HA-HA!' he cried, taking the brown ball from me.

'Half an ounce?' I gibbered. 'Y'think? Maybe half an ounce?'

'Ohhh,' he said, chuckling. 'Methinks more than that.'

We dollied the specimen at the camp, the steel pot ringing like a bell as I crushed up the rock ball with the steel pestle. It crunched like brittle toffee, releasing chewy gobs of gold, and I stopped frequently to pick out scabs of squashed metal and drop them onto the scales.

Slightly under two ounces. Around $1,150—plus the $250 from the other pieces. The gold was shared out. Caps were prised from bottles of beer.

'HERE, LEE. Got something for you. Thought it might cheer you up.' I placed a single-gram nugget, one of my early finds, on the bar counter.

'Awww, thanks Max,' said Lee, and she blushed. 'Thank you so much.' The barmaid took the piece of gold in her fingers and looked carefully at its small faces. 'My first gold nugget.'

Like Nic and Rebecca before her, Lee had her problems and her share of debts, and two months at the Grand had afforded her plenty of time to dwell on both. She was a pretty, friendly girl with bright blue eyes and high cheekbones, though she wrestled with her weight. Lee usually kept her troubles hidden, preferring to present a robust, jolly nature to the world. But one night at the pub, I'd found her staring glumly through the window.

'What are you worrying about?' I asked.

'My dad,' she said, looking down at the bar. 'He's coming to Kookynie.' Lee's father had spent four years in jail for dealing drugs; she made no secret of it. 'Don't get me wrong, I love him, and all. But he can be . . . Whenever he's around, things can get . . . difficult.'

414 | MAX ANDERSON

'You're worrying over nothing,' I said. 'He'll be fine.'

'I hope so.'

Kevin was away, towing a trailer to Perth to collect 1,500 copies of Marg's new book, *Niagara, Kookynie, How it was*. Marg, Lee and Sarah—the most recent barmaid, a quiet, self-assured university student—were minding the pub for two days. But Kevin had also asked me to 'stick around. Just in case.'

Marg gave me a string of tasks for the morning: I made a sixty-kilometre trip to collect bread and milk from a delivery truck pulled up on the highway; I uprooted weeds; and I burned a mountain of cardboard boxes. She then asked me to take 'the Ford' and tow a trailer-load of garbage to the dump.

The Ford Falcon Tradesman was a new, low-slung, racing-line pick-up truck, or 'ute' as they're called in Australia. It was painted in a rich blue metallic paint and was sometimes referred to as 'Kevin's You-Beaut Ute'. I hitched the trailer onto the vehicle's tow ball and made an easy run to the dump. But on returning, the trailer refused to unhitch; the ball and tow hitch were stuck fast, no matter how much tugging and hammer-bashing I administered. I informed Marg of this, who said, 'Why don't you free it using a counterweight on the other end of the trailer?'

'A counterweight? Like what?'

'Well, how about Lee?'

Marg meant this practically rather than unkindly, and when I put it to Lee she laughed. 'God, the things I get asked to do round here . . .'

Lee climbed uneasily onto the back end of the trailer while I tugged at the release handle of the tow hitch.

'Try jumping up and down,' I called. 'When I say! Y'ready? OK! Jump!'

Lee jumped, the trailer unhitched and seesawed in her favour. She shrieked and toppled back into the dirt, relieving the trailer of its counterweight and sending it crashing back into Kevin's shiny You-Beaut Ute, causing the steel tow-hitch to behave like a well aimed pick.

While Lee lay giggling uncontrollably with her legs in the air, I stooped to inspect the fifteen-centimetre gash down the metallic blue tailgate. And, making a face like the tragic theatre mask, softly breathed the word *shiiiiiiiit*.

I WOKE to the banshee shriek of the 5.30 a.m. ore train and was suddenly aware of being ready to leave Kookynie and the Northeastern Goldfields. This sudden readiness came as a surprise. I knitted my hands behind my head and tried to understand it as dawn light crept over the tent.

Was it, I thought, something to do with the temperature? Winter had passed and every day was over thirty degrees. I was sweaty before 10.30 a.m. Water from the tap had lost its chill and made washing less insane, but my wet legs were now constantly assaulted by ants.

Was I listless in the wake of a recent two-day visit by friends from Sydney, Peter and Charmaine and their eight-year-old son Elliott? They found me sitting outside my tent beside the windmill and the peppertree, with my books and my beard. They watched politely as Russell the Kiwi drove up to give me a pile of plaid shirts that had once belonged to an old prospector who had died of cancer in 2000, and saw how grateful I was to have them. When Pete asked, 'How do you cope with all the dirt?' I was confused by the question, then realised I coped because I no longer saw it.

Or was my unease something to do with the two-ounce specimen?

Except for affording me the exquisite pleasure of popping a fresh nugget into my mouth, the McTavish kernels were no longer shooting me up with any kind of rich thrill. The panicky lusts and hungers for gold hadn't abated, but their scale had shifted: only big nuggets would do. But finding another big specimen was unlikely because the gold had spoken and my allocation had been awarded.

Then I started doing my sums, and I really knew it was over.

Tens of thousands of diggers before me had done their sums, balancing expenses and incomes and finding that, not counting gained wisdom or lost years, they'd pretty much broken even. They'd arrived with nothing, found a little gold, spent it trying to find more gold, and ended with nothing.

In six months I'd found 2.5 ounces of gold worth approximately $1,500 at nugget prices. In the expenses column was a metal detector ($2,000), a dent in the Troopie ($300), four staked tyres ($400), a solar panel smashed in high wind ($600) and a bar tab at the Grand Hotel for diesel, cooked dinners and beer ($5,000 minus $600 wages).

To cover costs like these I needed to have located a payable gold source and sunk a shaft. I'd done neither. Kevin said I had the appetites to strike it rich in twelve to eighteen months—a million dollars, he said. But those appetites had gone. And at the bottom of my reckoning sheet, there was one more cost. Only it was more like a dangerously diminishing return.

In the three months since she'd flown back to Adelaide, my phone calls with the Turon Widow had been steady and placable, certainly more relaxed thanks to our shared knowledge of Kookynie. But after a total of six months apart, some unspoken ennui had begun to take hold. Times shared, passions indulged, adventures embarked upon; all these were being imperceptibly supplanted, in my case by lengthy quests for gold, in her case by the dull routine of loyal widowhood. Midway through the sixth month, we were increasingly devoting our calls to imagining a reunion on a remote South Australian beach where we'd camp and fish and eat oysters. And I realised—perhaps she did, too—that our prolonged isolation had become a state of emergency: we'd broken the glass and were sharing out survival rations, hoping they'd sustain us until we were found again.

Later that morning I looked at dates in my diary and phoned the Turon Widow: 'You know that beach we've been talking about? Well, what are you doing on October the third?'

THE MOMENT I was ready to leave Kookynie, the gleam went from my eye. I started playing truant. I'd shrug off the metal detector before lunch, abandon the field on any pretext—too hot, too noisy, too many flies. I'd spend afternoons mooching around the pub, putting beers on my tab and shooting pool.

At night I drank with Ron. He visited the pub more frequently now because Jane was staying with her family in another part of the state. He'd sit and reveal fresh plans to find gold, *big* gold, and talk of pending leases and operations involving heavy earth movers and shafts. 'Enough of this fly shit, mate,' he'd say. 'It's time to kill the pig.' And I felt envious and a little cheated because these plans lay in the future, but it was his future, not mine.

One morning Ron took me back to the long-dormant patch we had found nearly three months earlier. It didn't look so remote and incredible as it had then, but we noted our original tracks and the shallow scars where we'd dug our first nuggets, checked that no other bastards had been there since. And we detected for five hours, looking for the golden trail to take us to the source.

We found nothing.

Sensing my frustration, Ron took me to a remote series of gullies he'd been working, a tight network of spurs and slopes and ridge lines, black as night with ironstone, all braced by mulga and saltbush and a few looming salmon gums with copper-coloured trunks.

After finding a small nugget, he broke open a couple of beers and led me onto a ridge, to look over an empty landscape already acid-yellow before the setting sun. 'Look addit,' he cried. '*Look addit!* There's gold here, I tell ya! And it's never been detected!' Like a wild-eyed wall artist, he began painting the possibilities, sweeping his beefy arms this way and that. 'Now cummen look over 'ere . . .' He turned to stride back through pressing clumps of saltbush and claws of mulga, noisily expounding his theories on mineralisation, gold runs and ridge lines.

I followed some way behind, with my Carlton Cold beer in one hand and a roll-up cigarette in the other. Some rare wanting inside me had idly put its hand up for a smoke. And as Ron continued his happy rant, I noticed that my black T-shirt was filthy, a palette of squalid tones. And my khaki shorts were waxy with barbecue grease and car oil. My legs were brown from soil and sun, my expensive R.M. Williams leather boots scarred and scuffed. I looked at my hands, at my forefingers, fissured and caulked black; the lines of my palms were clogged with sweaty grime, my future occluded by muck.

And I was suddenly overcome by the fact that I was somewhere in the bushlands of Western Australia, walking, smoking, looking over scant clues left by inhuman time on a shifty geology, being led by a wild-eyed ex-truck driver who trusted me enough to reveal his hidden valley of gold. Perhaps energised by the nicotine, I started to laugh. Here I was: a man unrecognisable to me six months ago. So I raised my beer bottle and quietly toasted people far away, feeling it important that I wish them all long life and hoping we'd meet again soon.

'Y'havin' a bit of a yarn to y'self?' called Ron, turning briefly in a narrow corridor of mulga.

'Oh . . . yeah,' I said. 'Y'know.'

'Yeah,' he said, marching on, 'I know.'

'MAX, THIS is my dad, Roy,' said Lee.

'Nice to meet you, Max.'

'Hello Roy, how are ya?' I was on my ninth bottle. Roy settled at the bar and ordered a bourbon and Coke from his daughter while I glanced anxiously around the room, watching for Kevin. The publican had returned from Perth, driving 800 kilometres in eight hours. At this moment he was in the kitchen with Marg, getting an update on everything that had happened in his absence. God only knew how pissed off he'd be about the gash down the back of his metallic blue You-Beaut-Ute.

The stranger turned on his stool. 'Now,' he said, 'I hear you used to be a bit of a writer . . .'

Roy was a man of wild appearances. Wild red hair, wild red beard, small blue eyes set close together and a boxer's nose, smashed flat at the bridge. He wore a T-shirt, shorts and flip-flops, and at first I thought he was wearing long, lurid undershorts that reached to his knees, only they were great swirling tattoos in pale reds, blues and greens.

'Yeah, I used to do some travel writing.'

'Well, I've been doing a bit of writing myself,' he said, knitting his hands round his glass. 'So tell me, whadd'ya reckon makes a good writer? How would someone go about making himself a *better* writer?'

I swigged at my beer. Put the bottle on the bar. 'A good writer's probably a good reader. You've gotta read, read and then read some more.' I could hear myself, hear weariness with the day but also with the question, because I knew from experience that my answer was unlikely to be well received.

Sure enough, Roy was irritated and brushed off my opinion, said I was limiting a writer's creative flair, stifling his expression with old stuff.

'You've completely missed my point,' I said. 'In *my opinion*, a good writer is someone who reads because . . . they learn to be a better judge of writing. If you can judge the work of other people then you can create your own standards. If you don't develop an idea of what you think is good, and *why* you think it's good, then you're probably stuffed.'

He thought about this. 'OK,' he relented. 'I suppose that makes sense.'

While in jail, the man with the broken nose had earned a sociology and anthropology degree. Before this, he had known mining—and drug dealing. 'And in the end I just got tired of counting money . . . I mean, *physically* counting it.' But now he was travelling around Western Australia, filling his days with politics, Aboriginal affairs and youth work, and developing literary projects on an old blue-screen 486 laptop.

'So what books do you think I should read?' he asked.

In fact I soon found Roy engaging and stimulating company. And he reminded me how wonderful it was to be with someone who delighted in digging up novel ideas and insights. We drank late into the night, and on other nights. A pity, then, that in a matter of weeks one of us would run the other out of town.

I WAS SLUMPED against a doorway, talking with Joe and Ron, when a large pair of hands grabbed the back of my neck. They were soft, fleshy and warm. I stuttered apologies and offers of payment to cover the damage to the metallic blue Ford.

The hands squeezed and squeezed—and then dropped to my shoulders. 'Nahhhh,' said Kevin. 'It was an accident, wasn't it? At least I assume it was an accident.'

'Yes!' I said quickly.

'And you've learned a lesson from it?'

'Yes!'

'Cos if you haven't'—he took a heavy drag from his cigarillo—'I know how to teach you a lesson.'

LALA JUMPED into the passenger seat of the Troopie. I started to say, 'Dog, geddin the back,' but instead I put my elbow on the open window, rested my head on my fist and let out a long sigh.

I was badly in need of quiet, and perhaps the gentle ear of someone to whom I could lament the passing of my time among the diggers. So I headed for the hogback hill of ironstone, to Russell the Kiwi's bush camp.

But Russell wasn't home. His caravan in the little copse of acacia was locked up; the camp was bereft of his grin, his exuberant arms and his explosive laugh. There was only one thing to do. Start a campfire. Then I opened all the doors of the Troopie and found an ABC station on the car radio, broadcasting a very civilised retrospective on the fairly uncivilised musician Frank Zappa. And with Frank and the firelight and Lala, with the smell of chops sizzling in a pan and the sight of silver dusts constellated in the blackness into Virgo, Scorpio and the Southern Cross, I had all the company I needed.

At 8 p.m. I undressed, climbed into the back of the Troopie and lay with the rear doors open to the night. Happy that the benign spirit of the Australian goldfields was watching over me, I passed deep into sleep.

'LOOK OUT! He's here again!' said Russell, as he and Jude arrived the following afternoon. I began accounting for my being in their camp; Russell needed none of it. 'Whatcha been up to?' He beamed. 'Found the big one yet?'

'Nahh,' I replied. 'I did a few hours detecting over in the valley but it didn't come to anything. I dunno. It just didn't feel right.'

'Yeah, sometimes it's like that.'

Jude was ill with flu and retired to bed in the caravan while Russell and I sat to catch up, helping the sun into the horizon with a couple of beers. When there was an hour of light left, I suddenly realised it wasn't just any hour of light, it was the last hour of my days as a prospector. Tomorrow would be spent dismantling my Kookynie camp.

'Y'know, Russell, I think I'll grab the detector and get out there one more time. It's my last chance.'

'Good on ya! I'll drop you over there, if y'like.'

Russell ferried Lala and me to a patch of grassy ground within sight of his dry-blower, then returned to the camp.

As I began swinging the coil, I looked around, savouring the moments, smiling at a mob of kangaroos that upped and loped away to a low valley ridge. 'Go on, Lala,' I said. 'This is your last chance, too.'

After a few paces, a loud signal flashed through my headphones and I unearthed a bullet. I thought briefly about keeping it as a memento, before flipping it back into the shallow hole and covering it over.

Ten minutes later I received another signal: a clean, though rather vague sound. I bent among the grasses and marked a small square with my pick. I dug a few centimetres into the square and detected again; the signal was just as clean and just as vague. I dug deeper, five centimetres, then ten, and the signal remained unchanged. When I'd widened the hole to the size of a dinner plate, it was the most lavish I'd dug while wielding the detector.

The dog came sniffing. 'Don't get too excited, it's probably a bottle top.'

Twenty centimetres down, I was getting hot and the signal was getting loud, its fluty note fattening with growls and honks. The digging was awkward again, so I widened the hole once more until I was looking at a small hill of soft red soil beside a generous bucket-shaped excavation. I lowered the detector's plate to the floor of the bucket. The signal was shockingly loud: *WEEE-WA-WWWW*.

'It's a bullet,' I breathed. 'It's a bullet.'

At half a metre down, I was on my knees, reaching deep into the hole to claw out the earth with my hands.

'It's old-timer's crap, it has to be, it has to be . . .' I could feel the pumping of my heart. I began to whisper, 'Come on, come on, *come on* . . .'

I stopped and raised my face from the hole and wiped a hand over my forehead, scoring myself with earthy warpaint. I knew this hole, I'd been in it before—as a small boy, burying my bag of old pennies beneath a curl of willow plate. How brilliant my visceral belief in treasure had been, even treasure I'd buried myself. Did I still believe in treasure? Or had I given it too much shape and form, reducing it to hourly rates and heartache?

'It can't be gold, Lala,' I said, twisting my mouth and tugging one of her ears. It couldn't be. Not in the last hour. Not after six months. So I promised—promised myself, promised the goldfields, promised the gold—that I'd take whatever was down there with good grace.

I tightened my grip on the pick and drove it hard into the bottom of the hole. I heard a small clunk. I reached down into the bottom. And withdrew a nugget the size of a pocket watch.

Big. Bigger than any nugget I'd seen brought into the pub—the most beautiful thing I'd ever seen. My stomach was hollow, my mouth chattering out words of shock and delight. I laughed because there was no way this nugget was going to fit in my mouth, and then, 'Russell . . . gotta show Russell.'

With the detector carried low like a rifle and the headphones hung round my neck, I quick-marched back to camp.

'How'd you go?'

I dropped the nugget into his open hand.

'Ohh, my God,' he marvelled, his eyes and grin and beard all alight in the sunset. 'Ohh, my *God*, Max! She's a bloody *beauty*!' And then he laughed, so loud that Jude struggled out of bed to see what was happening.

'Hah! My God! Good on ya!' she cried.

Russell went to the water tank, took up a toothbrush and scrubbed away the red dirt. 'Just look at it! Oh! Can you bloody *believe* it?' His hands were shaking, the skin on his forearm was rigid with goose pimples.

I was too stunned to do much more than burble about being stunned.

9

People were filing into the back bar, saying 'How are ya!' and shaking hands, sharing news. Music was playing, everyone had drinks.

'It's a wonderful piece,' said Marg. The 1.5-ounce nugget looked even bigger in her small hands. 'You know what I see in it?' She indicated a line of bumps trailing across one side of the gold, shrinking into a vanishing point. 'I see the animals going into the ark.'

'Y'know what I see?' said Kevin, looking over the top of his glasses through a lazy twirl of cigarillo smoke. 'About fifteen hundred bucks . . .'

'Y'can see where he caught it with his bloody pick,' said Russell.

'Jesus, Anderson, you're an arsy bastard,' said Joe.

'Ohhh,' said Lee, putting an arm round my shoulders, 'I saw your tent's gone. It looks so empty over there now.'

'Yeah. It took me longer than I thought.' It had taken a day to dismantle the camp, wash everything clean of dust and pack it into the Troopie. Just before the clean-up, and with timing as curious as the nugget's unearthing, I heard a furious whipping sound. Streaming across the clearing was a small whirlwind, a 'willy willy', five metres tall, a fat orange vortex spinning with grit, vegetation and rubbish. It was heading for the mulga, but at the last minute took an absurdly personal left turn and slammed into my tent.

Its whirring Vishnu arms threw everything into chaos: guy ropes broke, aluminium poles clattered to the floor, canvas awnings flapped and snapped like angry sails and the contents of my kitchen tumbled across the clearing.

'Yeah, all done, Lee,' I said. 'OK, who wants a drink?'

Here were most of the friends I'd made in six months: Lee, Joe, Ron, Jane, Russell, Mike from Yerilla, Lee's dad Roy, Sarah, Kevin and Marg, the latter according me the greatest of Kookynie honours by hanging up her kitchen apron to take a stool at the bar.

But before the drinking could begin in earnest, Kevin stopped the music and made a generous speech about my coming to the town, about looking for gold and about friendship. Then Ron came forward and said, 'Here y'are, mate. We got y'this t'sorta . . . t'say . . . good luck. An' all that.'

I unfolded a paper carrier bag and withdrew a long stockman's coat. It was brown, thickly oiled and essentially Australian. There was also a stockman's hat to match.

'To keep off all the bloody rain we're not getting,' said Mike.

'Aw, thanks, guys, they're great. They'll go great with my stock whip.'

'Well, we reckon you're a proper bloke of the bush, now,' said Marg.

I felt happy and complete. And my completeness was embodied in the handsome gold nugget still being passed around the bar. It was my ticket of leave. 'Have you given it a name?' asked Russell. 'Ya gotta give it a name!'

'Yeah,' I said, and admitted it was named for the Widow. 'It's hers.'

'Ohh,' said Marg, beaming, 'she'll love it.'

'She probably deserves it.'

At some stage of the night, I slipped the nugget into the top pocket of my cotton shirt.

I WOKE fully clothed at 6.30 a.m. on a bunk in Lee's caravan. Joe was asleep on the floor, Lee was in her bed and her father was outside, under a lean-to.

My feeling of alarm was immediate: 'Oh Christ,' I mumbled, sitting up quickly, 'I think I said the f-word in front of Marg . . .' I struggled to think back, remembered wearing my new stockman's coat and joining with Kevin in performing the actions to a song, 'The Man From Snowy River'. Then I'd danced Scottish reels with Marg and Joe, before executing a slew of appalling karaoke songs with Ron. After midnight, I left with Ron and Jane and Joe and Lee to continue drinking outside Lee's caravan, under the lean-to. Roy, who was asleep in the lean-to, had been woken when Ron and I entered into a heavily intoxicated wrestling match.

My hand flew up to my shirt pocket.

Nothing.

I searched the bunk, rifled under cushions.

Nothing.

I dropped heavily onto Joe's chest, grabbed his shirt lapels and shook him awake. 'Come on, where is it?'

'Whurgh-urgh . . . Where's what?'

'You know what . . .'

He didn't know what. 'It . . . it's got to be around,' he said. 'Probably outside the caravan, where you and Ron were wrestling . . .'

It wasn't.

'Ron! Get up! Have you got my nugget?'

'Fack! FACK-FACK-FACK!' Joe and I stood outside his trailer listening to muffled thumps, as Ron tried to hop into jeans with twisted legs. The aluminium door swung open and he blinked into the hard morning light. 'It's fackn seven o'clock, fack yez!' He was boggle-eyed and stiff-haired. But on hearing the nugget was missing, he roused Jane, grabbed a mug of coffee and set about assisting with what he reckoned would be its simple recovery. 'Don't worry,' he said. 'It's gotta be somewhere outside the caravan.'

By 10 a.m. every possible path between the pub and the caravan had been minutely picked over. Kevin and Marg had joined the search party, combing the floor of the back bar, even sifting the ashes of the fireplace.

We asked Roy what he could recall after being woken by our invasion of his lean-to. 'Well, a few of you were pretty drunk. You two got into a wrestling match, and I got out of bed to move a few things out of the way. I thought someone was going to crack their head open.'

But Lee and Roy had to turn their attention to other things, a drive up to Leonora. Before departing, Roy presented me with a poem. It was a nice tribute and I was touched he'd taken the trouble to write it. I thanked him and we wished each other good luck. Then Lee gave me a long hug goodbye.

But I felt removed from the scene. My towering energy of the early morning, fuelled by alcohol sugars and the certainty that my nugget would be found, had become a low and bitter sickness.

By 1 p.m. I should have been on the road. I wanted to make Norseman by evening: the drive to South Australia was timed so I would arrive at Ceduna airport within forty-eight hours, where I would meet the Turon Widow's flight. So time was up. Six hours of searching had left us tired, irritated and confused that a shining 1.5-ounce piece of metal could escape all eyes.

Joe put his hands deep in his pockets. 'Have you . . .?' he began. 'Did you ever think, maybe . . .?' He looked awkward. 'I mean, you know that Roy was awake this morning before all of us. And he could easily have seen the nugget lying on the floor and picked—'

'No,' I said.

Ron folded his arms across his barrel chest. 'I'm sorry, mate, but I bin thinking the same thing.'

'No.'

'And, like, he has been in jail . . .'

I spun on my heel, waved away flies that weren't there.

'No, no, no.'

'DOG! GEDDIN THE BACK, DAMMIT!'

The Troopie felt swollen with rolled tent and tarps, heavy with solar panels, food bins, books and select treasures like the rusted Winchester rifle. And somewhere in the back was the Heinz jar. The Heinz jar that last night had housed four ounces of gold but now held a mean two and a half.

My anger burst out in evil-breathed spurts during the five-hour drive. It had me thumping the steering wheel, whacking my forehead with the heel of my hand, spitting out venomous oaths of contempt. It was all aimed at myself, a stinking wreck who hadn't even showered or eaten, so consumed had he been with trying to recover his nugget. But I was also crushed by hangover and sleep loss and gnawed by the sadness of a goodbye marred by a grotesque six-hour comedy. So much for relaxing with everyone over breakfast, joking, recalling drunken jinks and committing to visits and reunions.

It was a small, sombre group that saw me off. The missing nugget had cast a pall. Jane looked upset before hugging me for the last time; Marg was sorry about everything, and sorry when she patted Lala's happy face poking from the truck window. She choked when she said, 'Take care and drive carefully.'

'Come back soon,' said Russell.

'Come back and ya'll foind an even *bigger* nugget,' said Ron.

Kevin wore his gruff demeanour and shook my hand. 'See ya later, bloke,' he said.

And I'd driven out of Kookynie.

It was dusk when I reached Norseman. There was something I needed to do. It had taken me 400 kilometres to work it out, but now I had it clear in my head. There was a way I could fix everything.

Yes, Roy could have pocketed the nugget after chancing upon it where Ron had tipped me upside-down. It was entirely plausible, a credible solution to a conundrum, and the people who'd first suggested it were no less decent for doing so. I'd even come round to believing it myself. 'Roy. Roy took my gold,' I muttered, seeing the theft as clearly as the road before me. 'Or Joe! Yes, Joe. He knows how to lie, perhaps he took it and used Roy to cover his trail. And what about gold-hungry Ron? He could've found it on the way home to his trailer. And Lee, she had debts to pay . . .'

And there I was, hunched over the wheel, a vile character with black eyes, licking my sneering lips and sensing villainy everywhere. The *bastards*.

But no. None of them took the nugget. This was the truth. People who write poems with one hand don't steal gold with the other. There was only one corrupt element at work here, and that was gold. And I realised it hadn't yet finished with Roy, nor the people of Kookynie.

The circumstances surrounding the missing nugget still pointed to Roy being culpable. Even as I drove, I knew it was being debated and steadily built into a barroom case until Roy's guilt would be judged likely, and in some minds, conclusive. Inevitably, then, he would be obliged to leave Kookynie, perhaps run out of town by small-town suspicion. And soon after, unable to bear the idea that her father was considered a thief, Lee too would leave.

But I knew I could draw the whole thing to a happier conclusion. With one phone call, I could relieve Kookynie of its angst, release Roy from suspicion and spare Lee certain unhappiness. One call. That's all it would take.

I dialled the pub's number from the park call box and prepared to report with tremendous relief that I'd found the nugget in the glove box of my truck . . . Yeah, must've stashed it there last night for safe keeping! That's right, even though I was drunk as a rat! Amazing!

'Hello, Marg!'

'Ohhh, hello, Max. We've been thinking about you all day.'

'That's nice, Marg, and I—'

'But look, I'm sorry, we haven't found it. I went all round the pub this afternoon, Kevin had another look, and there's nothing.'

'I—'

'But don't worry, we haven't given up! We'll keep looking.'

'Yeah, but I—'

I pictured the search. Heard the cry 'Fouuuuund-itttt!' greeted with groans and sounds of relief. Saw the beautiful nugget sealed in a padded envelope and posted to the terraced cottage in Adelaide, where it would drop through the letter box onto thick carpet. Saw myself extracting it and excitedly showing it to the Widow, who would laugh and take it in her hand, happy because I was happy.

'Well, thanks, Marg. I'd really appreciate that. You've got my home number if anyone finds it. Y'just never know . . .'

I slunk back to the Troopie, exhausted to the point of shaking, and lay in the rear. I turned over on the mattress, pressed my face into the pillow and thought about gold.

About gold changing a man's soul so he's not the same kind of a man as he was before finding it.

THE PLAINS of the Nullarbor looked richer. And the kilometres were less of a drudge because I was flying towards the Turon Widow, who even now was swapping her widow's weeds for a bikini top and beach shorts.

Less than two days out of Kookynie, the thought of my red lands and my silver mulga oceans filled me with a sweet feeling of loss. But as quickly as these feelings came, so too did feelings of rancour. My joyous six months in the goldfields had been poisoned by a single night.

I struggled to find antidotes. I pretended I'd never found the nugget. I concocted a generous saga of a needy wanderer spying it outside the pub. I considered logging onto the Internet, contacting a nugget broker and simply buying myself a replacement.

But none of these worked. So I turned to the old diggers. What, I thought, would an old-timer have done in the same circumstances?

Well, he'd curse, and curse richly. And he'd tell his mates about it, who'd commiserate and slap him on the back and say, 'Half y'luck, mate!' And later on, perhaps round the campfire, the digger would relay the tale again, this time rolling his eyes, shaking his head and producing a theatrical groan.

Of course, I thought. He'd turn it into a *story*, a bit of a yarn about a bloke who spent six months looking for gold, who found it in the very last hour of searching, then got drunk as a skunk and let it slip out of his pocket. And the story would be taken by others and told round other campfires, and grow in the retelling, gaining layer and depth as it spread across the camps.

And soon it would become part of the landscape of the goldfields. Losing my treasured nugget had cemented me, if only for a couple of weeks, into the landscape of story that surrounded a small town called Kookynie. I'd become a landmark by which a few modern diggers might navigate safely through an evening at the bar. I'd reassure them that there really was gold out there, if only they'd keep looking and believing.

I laughed, happy with this. I called the dog into the front of the truck and ruffled her soft orange head and said, 'Good Lala.' And I accelerated east towards a woman with enormous grey eyes.

At which, my nugget winked its farewell and sank slowly back into the earth.

MAX ANDERSON

Career highlight: flying in a Buccaneer jet at 40 metres above a Cape Town beach
Ambition: to live past 100

RD: Where did you grow up?

MA: In the suburb of Allestree, just outside Derby. Actually, I grew up in the back garden, which was so long and so far away from the house that it was perfect for gangs of small kids to construct their various worlds without adults spoiling it. Digging into the ground was all part of the magic. And, unlike our other imaginary indulgences—headquarter dens, impossibly convoluted traps—this one actually promised a tangible result. Every spadeful could have yielded something to make me rich.

RD: Do you think the fact that your father worked as an engineer at the Rolls-Royce engine factory influenced your passion for precious metal?

MA: Yes, but not in the way you might think. My old man was a semiskilled labourer and not very well paid, so we were always broke (the big house and garden belonged to my grandfather with whom we lived). All the kids at school seemed to have pots of cash, whereas we were always 'on skinnies'. I think a little bit of want puts an extra gleam in the prospector's eye.

RD: What sort of kid were you?

MA: Talkative, risk-taking, desperate to be liked—looking back on it, probably exasperating and a bit irrepressible. I was intrigued by the way adults seemed to communicate so richly, and was always getting into trouble for chiming in with some sage bit of advice or choice gossip. Not good from an eight-year-old.

RD: Why do you think you got hooked on treasure hunting so early in life?

MA: I loved TV. And comics. In fact, I'm amazed I ever got into writing, given the amount of crap culture I consumed. I just got hungry for gold and treasure-heaps of it. I wanted to plunge my hands into a chest of coins, to run around a vault or cave piled high with priceless stuff.

RD: How did you get into travel writing?

MA: In my early twenties I naively thought I'd write about the thing I liked most—travelling. Naive, because it's a supremely difficult business to succeed in. Actually,

I started out writing professionally for computer magazines and did a bit of travel-writing on the side. My first travel pieces were published between the girly spreads in *Mayfair* magazine.

RD: What do you like about Australia, now that you live there?

MA: Space. Sunshine. Roads less travelled. Spare time. It's getting to be a well-worn phrase but this is very much a country for living. I've found my perfect life in the Adelaide Hills, fifty minutes drive from a surfing beach, and every evening I grab a beer and walk the dog along a bushland creek, looking for koalas and black cockatoos in the gum canopies overhead.

RD: Does gold still fascinate you, or have you 'been there, done that'?

MA: No, the gold fever is still rampant. I was signing books at the 2005 Perth Writer's Festival and a bloke dropped a two-ounce nugget on the desk. Beautiful piece. I think there're drool marks next to the signature I put in his book.

RD: Have you any other colourful ambitions?

MA: I've just bought a 1969 Aston Martin DB6 MkII. I want to make it Kensington Silver, which means I need to find a twelve-ounce nugget to afford the $12,000 bare-metal respray.

RD: What advice would you give other gold hunters?

MA: Get yourself to the nearest pub. Introduce yourself to the locals. Tell them you know bugger all. Buy them a beer. Buy them another one . . .

DID YOU KNOW?

• A quarter of the world's gold lies eighty feet beneath the streets of Manhattan in the gold vault of the Federal Reserve Bank of New York, which is half as long as a football field. Staff who transport the bars wear shoes made of magnesium, which is very light and strong, to protect their feet.

• It is estimated that mankind has secured only 0.00002% of the world's gold. Since it was first mined in 4000 BC, only 132,000 tonnes of gold have been extracted from the ground; American copper producers mine that much metal in a month.

See the World Gold Council's website at www.gold.org for more fascinating facts about gold.

ROBERT GODDARD
SIGHT UNSEEN

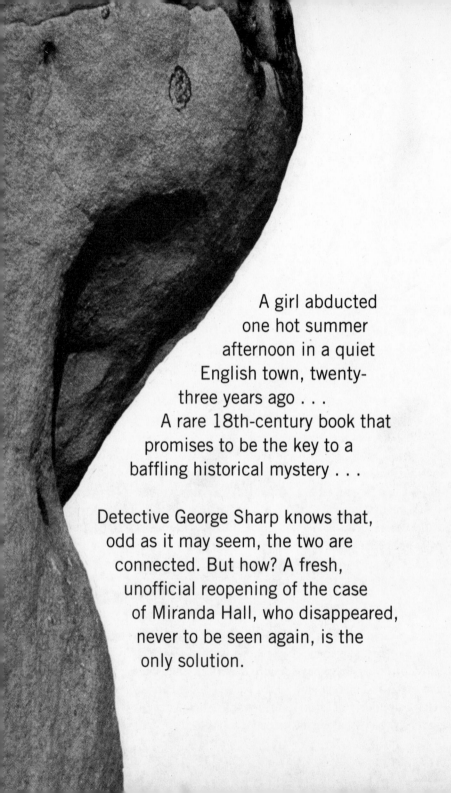

A girl abducted
one hot summer
afternoon in a quiet
English town, twenty-
three years ago . . .
A rare 18th-century book that
promises to be the key to a
baffling historical mystery . . .

Detective George Sharp knows that,
odd as it may seem, the two are
connected. But how? A fresh,
unofficial reopening of the case
of Miranda Hall, who disappeared,
never to be seen again, is the
only solution.

PROLOGUE

It begins at Avebury, in the late July of a cool, wet summer turned suddenly warm and dry. The Marlborough Downs shimmer in a haze of unfamiliar heat. Skylarks sing in the breezeless air above the sheep-cropped turf. The sun burns high and brazen. And the stones stand, lichened and eroded, sentinels over nearly five thousand years of history.

It begins, then, in a place whose origins and purposes are obscured by antiquity. Why Neolithic henge-builders should have devoted so much time and effort to constructing a great ramparted stone circle at Avebury, as well as a huge artificial hill less than a mile away, at Silbury, is as unknown as it is unknowable. It begins, therefore, in a landscape where the unexplained and the inexplicable lie still and close, where man-made markers of a remote past mock the set and ordered world that is merely the fast-fleeing present.

Saxon settlers gave Avebury its modern name. They founded a village within its protective ditch and bank. Over the centuries, as the village grew, many of the stones were moved or buried. Later, they were used as building material, the ditch as a rubbish dump. The henge withered.

Then, in the 1930s, Alexander Keiller, the marmalade millionaire and amateur archaeologist, bought up and demolished half the village, raised the stones, cleared the ditch, restored the circle. The clock was turned back. The National Trust moved in. The henge flourished anew.

Nearly forty years have passed since then. A kestrel, soaring high above on a thermal, has a perfect view of the banked circumference of the henge, quartered by builders of later generations. The high street of the surviving village runs west–east along the diameter, crossing the north–south route of the Swindon to Devizes road close to the centre of the circle. East of this junction, the buildings peter out. Green Street, as the lane is aptly called, dwindles as it leaves the circle and winds on towards the downs.

As it passes through the village, the main road performs a zigzag, with one angle being occupied by the thatched and limewashed Red Lion Inn. On the other side of the road are the fenced-off remains of an inner circle known as the Cove—two stones, one tall and slender, the other squat and round, referred to locally as Adam and Eve. There is a gate in the fence, opposite the pub car park, and another gate in Green Street, on the other side of Silbury House, formerly a minister's residence.

It is a little after noon on this last Monday of July 1981, and visitors to the henge are few. At one of the tables in front of the Red Lion, a solitary drinker sits cradling a beer glass. He is a slim, dark-haired man in his mid-twenties, dressed in jeans and a pale open-necked shirt rolled up at the elbows. Beside him, on the table, lie a notebook and a pen. He is gazing vacantly ahead of him, across the road, towards the stones. As a glance at his wristwatch reveals, he is waiting for something, or someone. He takes a slurp of beer and sets the glass down. Sunlight glistens on the swirling residue.

A child's voice catches his ear, drifting across from the Cove. The man turns. He sees a woman and three children approaching the Cove from the perimeter bank. Two of the children are running ahead to the stones: a boy and a girl. The boy is nine or ten, dressed in baseball boots, jeans and a red T-shirt. The girl is a couple of years younger. She is wearing sandals, white socks and a blue and white polka-dot dress. Both have fair hair, cut short on the boy but worn long, in a ponytail, by the girl. The woman is lagging well behind, her pace set by the youngest child, toddling at her side. This child, a girl, is wearing grey dungarees over a striped T-shirt. There can hardly be any doubt, given the colour of her hair, tied in bunches with pink ribbon, that she is the sister of the other two children.

The woman escorting them appears too young to be their mother. Slim, fine-featured and dark-haired, she is surely not beyond her early twenties. She is dressed in cream linen trousers and a pink blouse. Her attention is fixed largely on the little girl beside her.

As the other two children approach the stones, a figure steps out from the gap between Adam and Eve, hidden till then from view. He is a short, tubby man in hiking boots, brown shorts, check shirt and multipocketed fisherman's waistcoat. He is round-faced, balding and bespectacled, aged anything between thirty-five and fifty. The two children stop and stare at him. He says something. The boy replies and moves forward. The man takes something out of one of his pockets. The boy steps closer.

The woman is hurrying to join them now, not alarmed, but cautious, her attention diverted from the infant, who follows at her own dawdling pace before abruptly sitting down on the grass to inspect a patch of buttercups.

The man outside the Red Lion watches all of this for lack of anything more interesting to watch. He sees nothing sinister or threatening. Even when another figure enters his field of vision from behind Silbury House, he does not react. The figure is male, short-haired and stockily built. He is wearing army-surplus clothes and is moving fast, at a loping run, across the stretch of grass. The woman, who cannot see him moving behind her, is talking to the man in the fisherman's waistcoat.

And then it happens. The running man stops and bends over, grasps the seated child beneath her arms, lifts her up as if she weighs little more than the buttercup in her left hand, and races back with her the way he came.

The man in the fisherman's waistcoat is first to respond. He says something to the woman, pointing. She turns and looks. She puts her hand to her mouth. She begins running after the man who has grabbed the child. Screened by Silbury House, he can no longer be seen by the man outside the Red Lion. The roaring passage of a southbound lorry further confuses the senses. Everything is happening very quickly and very slowly. The beer-drinker does no more than rise and gape as the next minute's events unfold.

A white Transit van bursts into view round the corner from Green Street, its rear door slamming shut. The child and her abductor are inside. That is understood by all, or intuited, for only the woman has seen them scramble aboard. A second man is driving the van. That is also understood, though no one catches so much as a glimpse of him amid what follows.

The boy is standing stock-still between Adam and Eve, paralysed by an inability to decide what to do. No such indecision grips his sister, though. She is running towards the gate onto the main road. She knows her sister is being stolen from her, and seems determined to try to prevent the theft. She flicks up the latch on the gate and darts through.

The van turns right onto the main road. A northbound car, slowing for the bend, brakes sharply to avoid a collision and blares its horn. The driver of the van pays this no heed as he accelerates through a skid, narrowly avoiding the boundary wall of the pub car park.

The girl does not pause at the edge of the road. She runs forward, into the path of the van. She turns towards it and raises her hands, as if commanding it to stop. The van surges on. The girl holds her ground. In a breathless fraction of a second, the gap between them closes.

There is a loud thump as hard steel hits soft flesh. There is a blurred parabola through the air of the girl's frail, flying body. There is the speeding white flank of the van and the slower-moving dark green roof line of the following car. Neither vehicle stops. The car driver does not have to swerve to avoid the crumpled shape at the side of the road. The van and the car vanish round the next bend in the road. All movement ceases.

It is only for a second. Soon everyone will be running. The boy will be crying. The woman will be screaming. The man who was drinking outside the Red Lion will be hopping over the wall of the car park, his eyes fixed on the place where the girl lies, the tarmac beneath her darkening as a pool of blood spreads across the road. And her eyes will seem to meet his. And to hold them in her sightless gaze.

But that is the future, a future forged in the stillness and the silence of this frozen moment.

It begins at Avebury. But it does not end there.

ONE

It had been a fickle winter in Prague. Yet another mild spell had been cut short by a plunge back into snow and ice. When David Umber agreed to stand in for the day as a Jolly Brolly tour guide, he had not reckoned on wind chill of well below zero, slippery pavements and slush-filled gutters. But those were the conditions. And Jolly Brolly never cancelled.

A lean, melancholy man in his late forties, his dark hair shot with grey, Umber turned up the collar of his coat, exited his apartment and headed for the tram stop. God, it was cold. Not for the first time when such weather prevailed, he silently asked himself, 'What am I doing here?'

The answer, he knew, was best not dwelt upon. He had stayed on after the end of his teaching contract last summer because of Milena. But Milena had gone. He had a small circle of friends and acquaintances in Prague, including Ivana, the Jolly Brolly coordinator. But he also had plenty of evidence to strengthen his sense of purposelessness.

He stood at the stop, shifting from foot to foot to keep warm, or at least to avoid getting any colder. The heating in his apartment block was in dire need of an overhaul, like pretty much everything in the block. He had moved there as a stopgap measure when his flat near Grand Priory Square had vanished under the waters of the Vltava during the cataclysmic flood of August 2002. He had been in England at the time, but virtually all his possessions had been in the flat. The flood had claimed those tangible reminders of his past, leaving a void that the sixteen months since had failed to fill.

The red and white nose of a tram appeared through the murk. Those waiting at the stop shuffled forward. The tram, a number 24, pulled up and the passengers piled aboard, Umber hopping onto the second car, where there were more vacant seats. He slumped down in one and closed his eyes for a few moments as the tram started away. As a result, he did not notice the short, barrel-chested man muffled up in parka, gloves, scarf and woolly hat who jumped on just as the doors were closing. He had no cause to be on his guard, after all. A Prague tram at the back end of winter was hardly where he would have expected the past to creep up on him.

When the tram reached Wenceslas Square, Umber got off and headed for the Wenceslas Monument in front of the National Museum, the appointed meeting place for those hapless tourists who had decided to spend a thousand koruna on a six-hour walking tour of the city's principal attractions. About a dozen tourists, the usual mix of ages and nationalities, were waiting by the statue of Bohemia's patron saint, clutching their guidebooks.

Ivana, who was in the process of unburdening them of their cash, acknowledged Umber's arrival with a smile. 'You're late,' she whispered as she handed him his staff of office—a rainbow-patterned umbrella.

'*Je mi líto*,' he replied, apologising being one of the few aspects of Czech he had mastered. 'I overslept.'

Ivana's smile stiffened only slightly as she set about introducing him to his charges. A doctor of history, she called him, to forestall any complaints about his clearly not having been born and bred in Prague.

There was one latecomer who settled up with Ivana after she had said her preliminary piece. Having failed to register the man's presence on the tram, Umber naturally made nothing of his last-minute arrival. Ivana wished them a good day and bustled off to the Jolly Brolly office. A phone call to the proprietor of U Modré Merunky, where they were scheduled to stop for 'a typical delicious Czech lunch', and her duties would be concluded.

Lucky her, thought Umber, as he took a deep breath of cold air and launched into a commentary on the Prague Spring of 1968 and the Velvet Revolution of 1989. He *was* a historian, after all, albeit not as well qualified as Ivana had implied, for he had never finished his doctorate.

The tour proceeded. They reached Old Town Square in good time to see the Astronomical Clock's march-past of apostles when it struck the hour, crossed Charles Bridge, popped into and out of the Church of St Nicholas, then took the funicular railway up to Petrín Park. The snow was ankle-deep in the park, which slowed their progress, those inadequately clad and shod only now realising what they had signed up for. But Umber made some deft abridgments to their visits to the Strahov Monastery and the Loreto and had them at U Modré Merunky more or less when they were expected.

The deal between Ivana and the Czech innkeeper was certainly not predicated on the quality of the food. The roast pork was gristly, the red cabbage vinegary and the dumplings unyielding. But no one complained.

The latecomer to the tour, a short, broad man of sixty or seventy, sat at a different table and said little to his companions. Removal of his woolly hat revealed a bald head with a dusting of shaven white hair, piercing blue eyes and hollow cheeks. His gaze appeared to be fixed, throughout the meal, on the back of David Umber's head.

LUNCH OVER, the group slithered down to the Castle in time for the two o'clock Changing of the Guard. Then, after a circuit of St Vitus's Cathedral and the Royal Palace, they crossed back over the river to the Jewish Quarter. Three synagogues and a cemetery later, they returned to Old Town Square, where the tour ended at the birthplace of Franz Kafka. Umber cracked his customary joke about hoping nobody had found the day too much of a trial. There were more smiles than laughs, a few expressions of thanks and one very modest tip. Then the group dispersed.

It was late afternoon now and growing colder. Umber hurried to U Zlatého Tygra—the Golden Tiger, the Old Town's most famous drinking establishment—which was its normal smoky self. At this hour he could be sure of a seat, which, after foot-slogging round the city all day, he needed. He settled himself at a table next to the window. Half a litre of cellar-cooled Pilsner was swiftly delivered to him, and he took a deep gulp.

A bulky figure loomed above him. Umber looked up and, to his surprise, recognised the newcomer, or at any rate recognised the outfit of maroon parka and matching woolly hat. He was one of the tour party.

'Hello,' said Umber. 'What brings you here?'

'You do.' The man pulled off his hat and unwound his scarf, fixing Umber with a steely blue gaze.

It was the quality of the gaze that clinched it—and the faintly menacing tone of voice. True recognition dawned now on Umber. 'I don't believe it,' he murmured. 'Chief Inspector Sharp.' Even as he spoke the words, Umber realised that the man he knew as Detective Chief Inspector George Sharp of the Wiltshire Constabulary could by no stretch of the imagination still be a serving police officer. He must have retired long since. 'Here on holiday?'

'Let's get one thing straight.' Sharp discarded his parka and sat down. 'This isn't a chance meeting. I followed you from your flat this morning. I just didn't know I was going to have to wait this long for a word in private. And you can drop the "Chief Inspector". I was put out to grass years ago.'

'I suppose you must have been.'

At that moment Sharp's beer arrived. He eyed it suspiciously. 'Don't they ask what you want here?'

'It's taken for granted. Beer or nothing.'

Sharp took a gulp and grimaced. 'Not a patch on Bass.'

'What do you want . . . Mr Sharp?'

'What do you think I want?'

'After more than twenty years? Search me.'

'It's not that hard to work out.'

They looked at each other for several seconds in uncongenial silence, then Umber said, 'I thought your people reckoned they had the truth when they put Brian Radd away.'

'My people? I'll give you that. But not me. I never swallowed Radd's story. Not for a second. Did you?'

Umber shook his head. 'Of course not.'

'There you are, then.'

'You still haven't told me why you're here. You could just have phoned me without leaving England.'

'I like to know what I'm dealing with.'

'And what are you dealing with?'

'Unfinished business.'

Umber was beginning to feel angry now that the shock of Sharp's appearance had faded. 'You're not serious, are you?'

'Why do you think I'm here?'

'Bored by retirement. Writing your memoirs. God knows.'

Sharp smiled. 'Memoirs. That's a good idea. I handled quite a few big cases over the years. Mostly with the Met, before I transferred to Wiltshire. I put a lot of evil people behind bars. There were a good few more I couldn't pin anything on, but *I* knew what they were guilty of. As far as murder goes, there wasn't one I didn't crack. Not one. Except . . .'

'Avebury.'

'You said it.'

'Well, you'll just have to live with that, won't you? Like the rest of us.' Umber sat back as his empty glass was collected, letting slip the chance to decline a refill and take his leave.

'I should have got to the bottom of it. It may not be as hard to bear as the what-ifs of those who were there, of course, but—well, you must have said to yourself often enough over the years, "If I'd reacted faster, if I'd moved more quickly . . . I might have saved the girl."' Sharp broke off as Umber's second beer arrived, then went on. 'She'd be thirty this year. If she'd lived.'

Umber closed his eyes for a second. 'Oh, Christ.'

'What's the matter? Is that the sort of thing Sally used to say?'

There was another wordless interval. Umber swallowed some beer. 'I don't have to listen to this.'

'I only realised you'd married her when I heard about her suicide. The change of surname. It was a surprise, I don't mind admitting. How did that happen—you and her getting together?'

'None of your business.'

'Orphans of the storm, I suppose. But maybe the storm never quite blew itself out.'

'You don't know what you're talking about. It wasn't—'

'Suicide? Not according to the coroner, no. But that's what it sounded like to me. And to you, I'll bet.'

This was too close to the bone—and to the truth. Umber stood up and grabbed his tab. 'I've had enough,' he declared.

'Mr Umber, all I'm asking you to do is to sit down and answer a few questions. Help me with my enquiries. As the saying goes.'

Umber hesitated. Why was Sharp determined to put him through this? It was so pointless, so pitifully late in the day. What was he trying to achieve?

'Sit down.'

With a sigh, Umber obeyed. 'I could do without going over it all again,' he said, almost to himself. 'I really could.'

'So could I.'

'Then spare us both.'

'Not in a position to, I'm afraid.'

'Why not?'

'All in good time. Besides, I'm not convinced you don't know why.'

'You're making no sense, Mr Sharp.'

'All right. Let's just run through a few of the facts. Avebury, Monday, July 27th, 1981. Sally Wilkinson, nanny to the Hall family, takes the Halls' three children—Jeremy, aged ten, Miranda, seven, and Tamsin, two, to Avebury for fresh air and exercise. They walk around. They look at the stones. Everything's very normal, very peaceful. But a man gets out of a white van parked in Green Street, grabs little Tamsin while Sally's back is turned and drives off with her. Or is driven. We'll come back to that later.'

'You're not telling me anything I don't already know,' Umber pointed out wearily.

'Tamsin's sister runs into the road, presumably to try and stop the van,' Sharp pressed on. 'She is struck. And killed. Outright.' He paused. 'Witnesses. Other than Sally and Jeremy, we have Percy Nevinson, a local man with a comprehensive knowledge of the circle, who spoke to Sally and the boy just before the incident. Not exactly levelheaded though. Tells me he's working on a theory that Martians built Avebury. That puts him in the nutter category, in my book. Then there's Donald Collingwood, who drives through the village as all this is happening, but doesn't stop and only comes forward three weeks later. Explains he was afraid of losing his licence on account of his dodgy eyesight. As a result of said eyesight, he isn't too sure what he saw or where the van went. Finally, there's—'

'Me.'

'That's right. David Umber. Sitting outside the Red Lion. With a ringside view of the whole thing.'

'I told you every single thing I could remember at the time.'

'Which didn't amount to much. And the same goes for the other two witnesses. No registration number for the van. No decent description of the abductor. No nothing. Result: one traumatised boy; one guilt-ridden nanny;

a devastated family; an unsolved murder. What happened to Tamsin—we have no idea.'

'*You* have no idea. Officially, it's down to Radd, isn't it?'

'It's a grey area. He was never formally charged. But he did confess. The whole thing had a desk-clearing feel about it to me.'

'What do you mean?'

'Nine years after the event, and only a few months after I've taken early retirement, Brian Radd, child murderer, suddenly adds Tamsin Hall to his admitted list of victims just before he goes into court. Says he strangled her and buried the body in Savernake Forest. Can't remember which part of the forest, so a search is out of the question. My successor puts out a statement saying they're not looking for anyone else in connection with the murder. I smell a rat. Radd's confession gets the murder *and* the abduction off the books. Nobody cares whether it would stand up in court—whether it's true.'

'Sally cared.'

'Were you married by then?'

'No. Together. But not married. That came later.' Later as in too late, Umber thought. The marriage had been an attempt to deny that their relationship was falling apart. The disintegration would have been easier to accept if the reason for it had been something banal like infidelity or incompatibility. But no. The reason was Avebury, July 27, 1981. 'The police signing up to Radd's version of events really got to her, you know. She saw the bloke who grabbed Tamsin bundle her into the back of the van and climb in after her. Then the van took off. But Radd claimed to have been alone. No accomplice. Therefore Sally must have been mistaken. She had been blamed for not taking better care of Tamsin. Now she was being told her account of what happened wasn't credible. She never got over that.'

Sharp scowled into his beer. 'It would have been different if I'd still been on the force. But my old chief super asked me not to rock the boat.' He stared at Umber. 'Remind me why you were at Avebury that day.'

Umber sighed. 'All right. Here we go again. I was one year into a PhD at Oxford, studying the letters of Junius. I was spending the summer with my parents in Yeovil when I got a call from a man called Griffin, who said he was up in Oxford, had heard about my research and had something to show me that he thought would be helpful. We agreed to meet in the pub at Avebury. It's as simple as that. Though, as I recall, you never accepted my explanation at face value.'

'I kept my notebooks from the investigation. You're right. There were a lot of question marks in the sections relating to you.'

'Because Griffin never showed up? Well, you had roadblocks up within half an hour. He must have got caught up in the traffic jam and decided to turn round and go back to Oxford.'

'Plausible enough. But then why didn't he contact you again?'

Umber shrugged. 'I haven't a clue.'

'You had no phone number for him? No address?'

'I assumed I'd get the details when we met. I was more interested in what he was offering to show me.'

'Which was?'

'You already know. All this stuff is in your notebook, isn't it?'

'Junius was the pen name of the author of a series of anonymous letters to the press in the mid-eighteenth century blowing the lid on the politics of the day. Correct?'

'Yes. More or less.'

'What made him such a big deal?'

'For three years, from 1769 to 1772, he savaged the conduct of govern-ment ministers in the letters page of the *Public Advertiser* and succeeded in hounding the Duke of Grafton into resigning the premiership. The public lapped it up. Especially since he was clearly either a government insider or someone with access to extremely accurate inside information. He was never unmasked, and the mystery added to his appeal.'

'What exactly were you researching about him?'

'His identity. The classic unanswered question. Recent historical opinion favours Philip Francis, a senior clerk in the War Office.'

'Was it you or Mr Griffin who suggested meeting at Avebury?'

'Griffin. Avebury being about halfway between Yeovil and Oxford—'

'It's a good bit closer to Oxford.'

'Is it? Well, he was the one doing me the favour. I wasn't going to quibble.'

'And the favour was?'

'After Junius gave up his letter-writing campaign, Henry Woodfall, the proprietor of the *Public Advertiser*, published a two-volume collected edi-tion of the letters. He and Junius were in secret communication and Junius asked for a special vellum-bound, gilt-edged copy to be sent to him, which Woodfall duly arranged. It's never been seen since. If found, its provenance would obviously be a pointer to Junius's identity. Well, that's what Griffin claimed he had: the specially bound 1773 copy, with, he said, an illuminating inscription inside. It sounded too good to be true, but I wasn't about to pass up the chance, was I?'

'If Griffin had this . . . unique copy, why didn't he put it up for auction or something? Why involve you?'

'I don't know. He promised all would become clear when we met.'

'Did you try to track Griffin down when you went back to Oxford?'

'I asked around, but nobody had heard of him. After what had happened at Avebury, though, it seemed so . . . trivial. I mean, Junius, who really gives a damn? I suppose that was one of the reasons why I gave up on the PhD.'

'And the other reasons?'

'They were mostly to do with Sally.'

'I was told she went abroad after the inquest.'

'So she did.'

'You went with her?'

'Yes.'

'I'm sorry about her death. Was it suicide?'

'How would I know? We'd separated by then.'

'But what do you think?'

Umber took a deep swallow of beer and stared at Sharp. 'Same as you.'

Sharp cleared his throat. 'According to my notes, I considered the possibility that you'd made the Griffin story up to explain your presence at Avebury. But I never figured it out why you'd have wanted to be there.'

'That's because there was nothing to figure out.'

'It seems not. But I can't decide whether that's good news or bad.'

'What the hell does that mean?'

'I had a letter a few weeks ago, telling me I cocked up the Avebury inquiry and should do something about it. Anonymous, naturally.'

'Did you think I sent it? Is that why you came all this way to see me?'

'Yes. You were the obvious suspect. Because of the source of the letter.'

'You just said you didn't know who it was from.'

'I said it was anonymous. Maybe I should have said . . . pseudonymous. You see, the letter was from Junius.'

Sharp extracted a piece of paper from his pocket and handed it over.

Umber looked at it. Someone had cut various words and phrases out of a photocopy of an edition of the Junius letters, and had stuck them onto a sheet of paper to form this strangest of messages:

21. *January*

SIR,

IT is the misfortune of your life. that you should never have been acquainted with the truth. WITH respect to the Marlborough murderers

It is not, however, too late to correct the error. I am unable to correct it. It is time for those.

who have no view to private advantage, it is time for such men to interpose.

You have already much to answer for. The subject comes home to us all.

JUNIUS.

Umber read the letter several times and was still unable to offer an intelligent response.

'For God's sake, man, tell me what you make of it,' Sharp prompted.

'I don't know,' Umber said at last. 'I really don't know.'

'Are those Junius's words on the page or aren't they?'

'Oh yes. I recognise some of the phrases. I couldn't say exactly which letters they come from, but it's all Junius. And the date's authentic too. Junius's first letter was dated the twenty-first of January, 1769. These must be extracts from one of the early collected editions.'

'Like the one Griffin was offering to show you?'

'Like it, yes. But—'

'It's tied up with that, isn't it? And you are the Junius expert. That makes you one of the few people who could have put this letter together.'

'I thought you accepted that I didn't put it together.'

'I do.' Sharp sounded as if he almost resented his own exclusion of Umber as a suspect.

'How was it addressed to you?'

'See for yourself.' Sharp slid the envelope across the table.

It was white A5, bearing a first-class stamp with a smudged postmark and what looked like a computer-generated address label: George Sharp, 12 Bilston Court, Nunswood Road, Buxton, Derbyshire SK17 6AQ.

'London postmark,' said Sharp. 'Date barely legible. I received it on January the 22nd.'

'Derbyshire, Mr Sharp. What took you there?'

'A return to my roots. And you can call me George, since we're in this together.'

Umber tried to ignore the hint of an alliance between them. 'My guess would be that whoever sent this was trying to throw suspicion onto me.'

'If you're right, that means they know everything there is to know about the Avebury case. Your reason for being there didn't exactly make the newspaper front pages. The other implication is that I can find out what the truth is. "It is not too late to correct the error." And notice he says "the Marlborough murderers".'

'Junius would have mentioned the Duke of Marlborough. The town's only a few miles from Avebury, so—'

'That's not what I mean. *Murderers* plural. It rams the point home, doesn't it? It rules out Radd's confession.' Sharp frowned as he sipped his beer. The letter was a reproach as well as a challenge. And he was vulnerable to both.

'What do you mean to do about this?'

Sharp set down his glass with a clunk. 'Exactly what it dares me to do. "Correct the error". Dig out the truth. If it's there to be dug.'

'What can you hope to learn now that you failed to learn twenty-three years ago?'

'I'm not a policeman any more. I don't have to go by the book. And I have the advantage that nobody, other than this correspondent, will be expecting me to go down this road again.'

Umber grabbed the letter. A door had opened in his mind. The writer could reasonably have hoped that Sharp would bring this letter to him. It could therefore be a message to both of them. Indeed, the sentiments were in many ways more applicable to him than to Sharp. *The misfortune of your life.* What had happened at Avebury on 27 July 1981 was that all right.

'Bloody hell. Griffin must have sent this.'

'Aren't you the one who's jumping to conclusions now?'

'Maybe. But he didn't turn up that day, did he? He never intended to. He wanted *me* there. As a witness.'

'That makes no sense, Umber. No one could have known that Sally would take the Hall children to Avebury that particular morning.'

'God, no.' Umber dropped the letter. 'They couldn't, could they?' He fell back in his seat. 'I swore I was finished with this when Sally died. The wondering. The theorising. She never stopped doing that. But I did. In the end, I was just so weary of it that I felt . . . weary of her.'

'You're not going to go maudlin on me, are you?'

Umber's answer was a long time coming. 'I'll do my best not to.'

'I need your help to crack this. I can't go on drawing my pension and happily tending my allotment. Not now I've been reminded of what I did wrong all those years ago.'

'And what was that?'

'I gave up. I stopped looking. I wrote the little girl off. This is your big chance—and mine—to set things right.'

'I can't get involved, George. Not now. Not after putting it all behind me. Besides, you're the detective. What do you need me for?'

'Younger pair of legs. Keener pair of eyes. And the last word on Junius. I'll give you twenty-four hours to think it over.'

'It won't make any difference.'

'No. It won't.' Sharp slid the letter back into its envelope. 'Because you already know what you're going to do.' He smiled at Umber. 'You just can't bring yourself to admit it.'

HALF AN HOUR later, Umber was on the number 24 tram, trundling through the darkened streets of Prague—streets Sally had never trodden. Their wanderings had taken them to most of the capital cities of Europe, but never this one. That, he knew, was one of the reasons he had come to Prague—and stayed. He opened his wallet and took out the snapshot he always carried.

Sally's dark, shoulder-length hair cast part of her face in shadow, accentuating her high cheekbones and making her look gaunt and troubled, whereas in his mind's eye she appeared neither. He remembered her smile so very clearly. But she had seldom smiled for the camera.

He put the picture away again and looked at his own, ghostly reflection in the window. 'What do you want me to do, Sal?' he asked under his breath.

There was no answer. There could never be. It was too late for that.

HE WAS WOKEN by the telephone. Opening his eyes, he saw that it was light outside. According to his bedside clock, it was nearly ten. He had lain awake for what felt like hours before falling asleep.

He grabbed the telephone, wondering if it would be Sharp badgering for an answer, then realised that it could not be because he had not given him this number. '*Haló?*'

'*Dobré ráno.*' It was Marek, Ivana's assistant.

'What can I do for you, Marek?'

'Not for me, brother. For Ivana. She needs you to cover Tuesday.'

'Ah . . . Tuesday?'

'*Jo.* I can put you down for it?'

'I'm not, er . . . too sure I . . .'

'I need a decision, like, right now.'

'Then it's no.' Sharp was right, of course, damn him. There never had been any doubt about what Umber was going to do. 'Not Tuesday. Not any other day. For the foreseeable future.'

TWO

When Ivana heard that Umber was quitting Jolly Brolly, she rang to congratulate him on landing a full-time job, the only possible explanation for his conduct that had occurred to her.

When he assured her that he was going away for a while and would be back before long, she persuaded herself that the parting from Milena was what was driving him away. 'You think because things have gone bad for you here they will go good for you in England?' she asked.

'I don't think that.'

'Just remember. "*Dostat se z bláta do louze.*" It's an old Czech saying. Out of the mud into the puddle.'

'I'll remember,' said Umber.

And so he would.

SEVERAL LOUD BLASTS on a horn announced Sharp's arrival at dead on eleven o'clock the following morning. Umber looked out of the window of his flat expecting to see a taxi waiting below, but the vehicle that had pulled up was a blue and white camper van.

Sharp was waiting outside when Umber emerged, bags in hand, and caught at once his wary glance towards the van. 'A 1977 Volkswagen T2 in tiptop running order. I bought her secondhand when I retired and did her up proud. I've booked us on the midnight ferry from Dunkirk to Dover.'

'I thought we'd be flying.'

'Wait till we hit the autobahn.' Sharp winked. 'It'll feel as if we are.'

'TELL ME, George,' said Umber, as they made their way out of the city, 'what exactly are we going to do once we get to England?'

'You mean do I have a plan?' growled Sharp. 'I do, but that can wait. First I'd like a little background on you and the last twenty-three years.'

'I'm not going to talk about me and Sally, if that's what you're getting at.'

'Well, I'll hazard a guess and you can tell me whether I'm wide of the mark. The relationship began straight after the inquest?'

Umber was glad that Sharp had to concentrate on driving. Otherwise he would have noticed Umber's wince of dismay. The inquest *was* where it had begun for them. The coroner's summing-up had loaded an unfair amount of blame on Sally's shoulders. She had looked so young and alone, so helpless in the face of criticism. The Hall family had made no move towards her. The press had been lying in wait outside. On impulse, Umber had said to her, 'Come out the back way with me. We'll drive somewhere.' She had looked at him, her eyes full of gratitude, and simply nodded her acceptance.

'You whisked her away,' said Sharp. 'Where did you go?'

'The Kennet and Avon Canal. We walked along the towpath.'

'Nice choice. And what about the decision to go abroad?'

'You're not going to give up, are you?'

'Not for the next few hundred miles or so.'

'All right. I'll tell you.' Umber decided that an edited account of his life with Sally of his own shaping was better than whatever Sharp's guessing game might produce. 'Sally needed to get away. So did I. She rapidly became more important to me than a PhD. She'd abandoned a teaching degree before working as a nanny, so teaching English abroad seemed the obvious answer for both of us. We took a course in Barcelona in the spring of '82. We worked in Lisbon after that, then Athens, then . . . all over. The further from home the better. We had a few happy years.'

'Only a few?'

'We were in Turkey—Izmir—when we heard about Radd. Sally was pregnant at the time. Miscarried shortly afterwards. She got it into her head that she wasn't allowed to have a child of her own because she'd lost Tamsin.

It was crazy, and it went on that way. I tried to keep her on an even keel. Maybe I didn't try hard enough. Or maybe I tried too hard. We got married, but that made it worse. In the end, we felt trapped. We were in Italy at the time. I accepted a job back in Turkey, knowing she wouldn't go with me because of what had happened there. She went back to England, autumn of '98.'

'You were together a long time.'

'Nearly seventeen years. She lasted less than a year on her own.'

Blame had hung heavy in the air at Sally's funeral. Umber could remember the almost physical weight of it pressing down on his shoulders. He had been tempted to plead pressure of work and stay away, but that would have been one desertion too many. So he had gone. And seen the accusations hovering in the eyes of the other mourners. And known that he could not rebut them. He should have saved her.

Umber had returned to Turkey the following morning. In simple terms, he had fled. He had been home since, of course. But only now, on this long drive across half of Europe, did he feel that his flight might at last be over.

IT WAS AFTER DARK, in a service area near Aachen, over coffee and baguettes, that Sharp unveiled his plan.

'Checking facts and asking questions is what it amounts to. I want to know two things. One, who sent me the letter? Two, what *really* happened at Avebury on July the 27th, 1981? The great thing is to look on the passage of time as a blessing, not a curse. It means we can forget all that forensic crap. I never really trusted the white-coated brigade anyway. But time reveals a pattern. What the people touched by the abduction of Tamsin Hall and the murder of Miranda Hall have done in the years since is the evidence we're going to sift. How much do you know about the Hall family?'

'We heard the Halls had split up.'

Sharp nodded. 'It's not uncommon in cases like this. The death of a child. The loss of another. The parents' lives are shattered. In the end, it becomes easier to rebuild them separately. The Halls divorced while I was still in Wiltshire. Jane Hall married a local wine merchant. Name of Questred. He used to keep a shop in Marlborough. With any luck, he still does. They had a child of their own, you know. A daughter.'

'Yes. I did know. Sally had an aunt in Hungerford who seemed to think she needed to be kept informed about that sort of thing. What about Oliver Hall? He didn't register on Aunt's radar. Banker, wasn't he?'

'Not sure. Financial consultant. Something like that. A money man. Retired to Jersey, I gather. That must make him a mega-money man. Also remarried. But no more children.'

'And the son?'

'Went to live with his father after his mother remarried. Then . . .' Sharp shrugged. 'I never had any cause to find out. Until now.'

'None of these people are going to want to talk to us, George.'

'I can be very persuasive.'

'Who else do you intend to contact?'

'The other witnesses, if they're still in the land of the living. Collingwood was seventy-odd, so I'm not optimistic. But Nevinson still lives with his mother and sister on the council estate at Avebury Trusloe. Sending me a letter made up of Junius quotes could be right up his street. Could he be Griffin?'

Nevinson had been there, at Avebury, with Umber, standing helplessly by the body of Miranda Hall, while they waited for the emergency services. Everyone had been shocked, talking in soft, distracted undertones. He and Nevinson must have spoken to each other, but Umber could remember nothing of what they had said. He *could* remember the telephone conversation he'd had with Griffin, though, two days earlier.

'He can't be Griffin,' Umber concluded, 'I'd have recognised his voice.'

UMBER LEFT SHARP dozing in the passenger lounge during the ferry crossing and went on deck to watch the moonlight skittering across the Channel. Griffin's voice, he recalled, had sounded silken, faintly effete, the phrasing more eighteenth-century than twentieth. 'It won't be a wasted journey,' he had said. 'I think I can promise you that.'

Dover in the small hours of a chill March morning did not make for a gala homecoming. Sharp's doze had left him taciturn and liverish. Umber was tired and dispirited. Leaving Prague suddenly felt like a huge mistake. Little was said as they followed the signs for the motorway.

Sharp stopped at a service area near Maidstone and announced he would be stretching out in the back of the van for the rest of the night. Umber retreated to the cafeteria.

Come dawn, Sharp was as a bright as a lark, tucking into a full English breakfast after a wash and a shave in the toilets. Umber, bleary eyed and mentally drained, did not even ask where they were going next. Somewhere between Maidstone and the M25, he fell asleep.

'WE'RE THERE,' Sharp announced, some time later, turning off the engine and opening his window to admit a gust of cold air.

Umber woke with a start. 'What?' He blinked around him. 'Where?'

'Avebury.'

'Christ. You never said . . .' Umber struggled to compose his thoughts. They were in the high street car park, he realised. 'You never said we were coming straight here.'

'Where better to start? Let's take a walk.'

It was a cold, grey morning. A wind had got up, driving rain into their faces. They seemed to have the village to themselves.

Sharp led the way towards the Red Lion, but crossed the road before he reached it. Umber joined him beneath the trees on the opposite corner.

'Nothing much has changed, has it?' Sharp asked rhetorically.

Umber took a deep breath and looked across at the Adam and Eve stones in the field behind Silbury House, at the gate in the fence that Miranda Hall had run through that day. Then he looked along Green Street, towards the other gate, through which Tamsin Hall had been carried to the white van.

'If you'd been standing here rather than sitting outside the pub,' said Sharp, 'you'd have seen for certain whether there were two men in the van.'

'There were two.'

'Yes. Two.' Sharp nodded thoughtfully. 'Paedophiles don't generally work in pairs. And Tamsin was a lot younger than Radd's other victims.'

'He was lying, George. You know it. I know it.'

'But why?'

'I thought you reckoned he did a deal with your successor.'

'Who'd not have been above such a thing. But what was the deal? Radd was going away for life whatever he admitted to. So, what was in it for him?'

They started back along the high street in silence. But Sharp did not stop at the car park. He had something other than a swift departure in mind.

'I thought we'd pay the Nevinsons a call.'

'Now?'

'No time like the present.'

They crossed the churchyard and followed a narrow footpath between some cottages to the western edge of the old village. The footpath headed onto a bridge, then continued to a field gate. There the tarmac ended, leaving Sharp and Umber to dodge muddy patches the rest of the way to Avebury Trusloe, a huddle of utilitarian brown-brick houses and bungalows.

Sharp flung open the Nevinsons' gate and strode up the concrete path to the door. He had given the bell two jabs before Umber caught up.

A woman answered. Short and plump, clad in a voluminous sweater worn over track-suit bottoms and ancient plimsolls, she had iron-grey curly hair framing a round, placid face. Sixty or so, Umber would have guessed. She might well have attended the inquest, but he had no memory of her.

She, on the other hand, appeared to have a memory of him, of both of them. A smile dimpled her cheeks. 'Good morning,' she said, a local accent wrestling gamely with Home Counties elocution. 'I believe I know you gentlemen. But it's been a long time. Chief Inspector Sharp, isn't it?'

'Retired now, Miss Nevinson. Plain *Mr* Sharp.'

She looked intently at Umber. 'And you'd be . . .'

'David Umber.'

'Of course. Mr Umber. The other witness. We were never introduced, were we? I'm Abigail Nevinson, Percy's sister. What can I do for you?'

'We're looking for Percy,' said Sharp.

'I suppose you would be.' A thought suddenly struck her. 'You've not found her, have you? The girl.'

'No,' said Umber quickly. 'It's nothing like that.'

'Oh. What a shame. But it'll be about her you've called, I dare say.'

'In a sense,' said Sharp. 'Is Percy at home?'

'I'm afraid not. He's off on his morning walk. Could be back any minute, or gone till lunchtime. Would you like to step in for a cup of tea and see if he arrives meanwhile?'

'That's kind of you,' Sharp replied. 'We'd be glad to.'

The house was warm and comfortably furnished, albeit in a style several decades out of date. There was a brief discussion of milk and sugar requirements, then Abigail waved them into the sitting room and headed for the kitchen. Umber sat in an armchair by the fire, while Sharp prowled around.

'Nothing's changed here at all,' he said, softly. 'Except Old Mother Nevinson's not weighing down that chair you've parked yourself in.'

'Are you going to tell her—or him—about the letter?'

'Not until I rule him out as the sender.'

'How are you going to explain our visit, then?'

'Simple. I'll say it was your idea.'

A few minutes later, Abigail arrived with tea and biscuits. She distributed cups and plates, then sat down opposite them, looked solemnly at

Umber and said, 'I was very sorry to hear about your wife's death, Mr Umber. We both were. It's terrible how that one day ruined so many lives.'

'Actually, it's on Sally's account that we're here.' Umber launched himself at once into his hastily prepared cover story. 'Since her death, I've wanted to take another look at what happened and see if I can't resolve some of the doubts she always had about the official version of events.'

'I offered to help,' said Sharp. 'Least I could do.'

'I thought the police had decided that dreadful man Radd was responsible,' said Abigail.

'I don't go along with my former colleagues on that.'

'No? How interesting. Neither does Percy.'

'Oh? What's his theory?'

'You'd have to ask him, Chief Inspector. Percy has so many theories. About so many things. Will you be speaking to everyone involved in the tragedy?'

'If *they'll* speak to *us*,' Sharp replied.

'The Halls got divorced, you know. Mrs Hall—Mrs Questred as is—still lives locally.'

'Do you happen to know where?'

'Over near Ramsbury. It's a picture-postcard house at the bottom of Hilldrop Lane. Swanpool Cottage. Her husband keeps a wine shop in Marlborough, so I suppose it's handy, though how she can bear to stick so close to Avebury I don't rightly know.'

'Do you ever see her?'

'In Marlborough, from time to time. Shopping and such. She doesn't know me, of course.'

'But she'd know Percy?'

'I suppose so. But I'm not sure she'd show it.'

'Maybe she's trying to put it all behind her,' suggested Umber.

'Maybe she is,' said Abigail. 'And no one could blame her for that.'

'No,' said Umber. 'No one could.'

PERCY NEVINSON had still not returned when Umber and Sharp took their leave, half an hour later. Abigail noted down Umber's mobile number and assured them she would ask her brother to ring them as soon as possible.

Neither Sharp nor Umber noticed the figure in the telephone box at the corner of the lane that led them down to the footpath back to Avebury: a short, tubby man dressed in hiking boots, pale green corduroy trousers and a faded brown anorak. The brim of a dark green Tilley hat, worn low, obscured his features, and he had his back turned as they passed.

Once they had reached the footpath he put the phone down, exited the box and headed into the estate, moving at an anxious clip.

'WHERE ARE WE going now, George?' Umber asked as they drove out of Avebury.

'Worried I'll go straight to Swanpool Cottage and antagonise Jane Questred, are you?' Sharp responded.

'Well . . .'

'Credit me with *some* sensitivity, Umber. We'll drop in on Edmund Questred's wine shop and ask him—politely—if his wife will talk to us.'

'And if the answer's no?'

'It won't be.' There was the briefest of pauses before he added, 'Unless she's hiding something.'

Marlborough was much as Umber remembered it. A gently curving high street, wide enough to turn a coach and four in, was flanked by handsome buildings of several eras, housing a genteel assortment of shops and cafés. They drove in past Marlborough College, and found a parking space in the centre of the high street. Almost exactly opposite them, Umber noticed, was the Kennet Valley Wine Company.

'You a wine buff, Umber?' Sharp asked.

'Not really.'

'Nor me. More's the pity.' Sharp clicked his tongue. 'We'll just have to play it straight down the line.'

A bell rang as they entered the shop. From an office at the rear, behind the counter, a tall, thin man with wiry grey hair and a neatly trimmed beard emerged, stooping to clear the lintel. He wore a soulful expression, his face set in lugubrious, bloodhound folds.

'Mr Questred?' Sharp enquired.

'Yes,' Questred replied, cautiously.

'This is going to come as a bit of a surprise. My name's George Sharp. And my friend here is David Umber.'

A surprise it certainly should have been. But Umber felt, as Sharp's explanation of their visit proceeded, that it was a surprise Questred had somehow anticipated, as if they were fulfilling some gloomy presentiment that he only now recalled. Questred went to the door and flicked the sign round to read CLOSED. And then he turned to face them and sighed.

'You want to speak to Jane, to go over the same old ground again with her.'

'Just a few questions. That's all.'

'All? I doubt you have any conception of what "all" really covers for her. She hasn't got over it, you know. She never will. But she's learned how to survive it. We have a daughter of our own now. We're happy. We have a good life. Jane doesn't need any reminders of the life she used to lead.'

'Except she still lives in the area,' put in Umber.

'My business is here.'

'You could have relocated.'

Questred looked narrowly at Umber. 'She didn't want me to. She doesn't run away from things.'

'In that case, she surely won't mind speaking to us.'

'But you'll be encouraging her to run away, Mr Umber. From the truth. Which is that Tamsin's dead. That she isn't coming back.'

'Does she believe Brian Radd killed her daughters?'

'What difference does it make who killed them?'

'It made a difference to my wife.'

'Yes.' Questred's glance fell. 'I'm sorry.'

'We could have gone straight to your home, Mr Questred,' said Sharp softly. 'But Umber here insisted we consult you first.'

'I should be grateful, then.' But in Questred's voice there was far more resignation than gratitude. 'I'll tell Jane you want to see her. I won't try to stop her. It'll be her decision. You'd better give me a number where she can contact you.' He paused. '*If* she wants to.'

SHARP HAD EVIDENTLY noticed the Ivy House Hotel, a handsome red-brick Georgian building on the southern side of the high street, on their way into Marlborough. He led the way across to it, and booked them in for two nights. Then they headed back to the camper van, drove it round to the car park behind the hotel and unloaded their bags.

'I'm going for a walk,' Sharp announced. 'Want to come?'

'No, thanks. I need a break.'

A beer and a sandwich on room service, followed by a bath and a sleep, was the break Umber had had in mind. But a lot sooner than he would have wished, he was woken by the warbling of his mobile.

'Hello?'

'David Umber?'

'Yes.'

'Percy Nevinson here.' The voice was oddly pitched and breathily nervous, with the receiver held too close to the mouth, so that the P of Percy exploded in Umber's ear. 'I gather you want to see me.'

'If you don't mind.'

'Not at all. Pleased to help. Where are you based, Mr Umber?'

'Marlborough. Ivy House Hotel.'

'Righto. Well, I can come into Marlborough this afternoon. Why don't we meet in the Polly Tea Rooms? Four o'clock, say?'

'All right.'

'One thing, though.'

'Yes?'

'Just you, Mr Umber. I'll meet you. Not the policeman.'

SHARP, BACK from his walk, was none too pleased to hear Umber's news. 'Bloody nerve of the man! Who does he think he is?'

'Someone whose cooperation we need, I suppose.'

'Inflated idea of his own importance.' Sharp ground his jaw in frustration. 'All right. Let him have it his way. This time.'

'He might be more likely to let his guard down with me.'

'Maybe.' Sharp eyed Umber with no great confidence. 'I'll just have to hope you can take advantage if he does.'

The Polly Tea Rooms were close to the centre of Marlborough, and at four o'clock that Tuesday afternoon its doilied delights had drawn in a contented clientele, amid which Percy Nevinson looked by no means out of place. Kitted out in a tweed jacket and dogtooth-check-patterned sweater, he was already making inroads into a large slice of fruit-cake when Umber arrived.

'Mr Umber.' Nevinson degreased his fingers as best he could and stood up. They shook hands. 'It's been a long time.'

'The years look to have been kind to you, Mr Nevinson.' It was true. He was balder, though not much. That was the only detectable change. They sat down. 'It was good of you to come.'

'Oh, any excuse to tuck into one of the Polly's fruit-cakes.'

'Carry on.'

'Thank you. And, please, call me Percy.'

'OK. I'm David.'

'Yes. Of course. It's odd, isn't it, to wait twenty-three years before getting onto first-name terms?'

'It was a brief acquaintance.'

'But a memorable one.'

'True.' Umber broke off as a waitress approached. He ordered coffee. 'Your sister told you why Mr Sharp and I are here?' Nevinson nodded affirmatively. He had by now embarked on a last mouthful of cake. 'He retired from the Force years ago, you know. You have nothing to fear from him.'

'A representative of the authorities never truly retires, David,' Nevinson responded after a final swallow. 'You should tread carefully.'

'He's simply trying to establish whether there were any clues he missed—any leads he should have followed.'

'I gather neither of you believes Brian Radd was responsible.'

'Do you?'

'Certainly not. But who does, apart from the police? The authorities, you see. They're not to be trusted.' Nevinson leaned forward. 'We were there. We know what we saw. The question we must both consider—have both had to live with ever since—is what did it *mean*? Why was the child taken?'

'Because some sicko got it into his head to do such a thing.'

'You believe that? And your wife? Did she believe that? Please accept my condolences on your loss, by the way.'

'Thank you. As for what she believed, well, she could never quite bring herself to accept that Tamsin was dead.'

'Perhaps she was right not to.'

'Do you have some good reason, Percy, to say that?'

'I think I do, yes.'

'Care to share it with me?'

'It's in your own best interests that I should.' Nevinson pulled out a roll of thickish paper from the inside pocket of his jacket and spread out in front of Umber a large black and white photograph, which he proceeded to anchor down using the sugar bowl and the teapot. It appeared to be an aerial photograph of some desert landscape, buttes and mesas varied by what looked like craters and a couple of strange conical formations.

'What do you suppose you're looking at, David?' Nevinson asked.

'The desert somewhere. Egypt, maybe.'

'Interesting you should say that. In fact, this is a photograph of the surface of Mars taken by the *Voyager One* orbiter in July 1976.'

'Really? So, these shapes . . . are just freaks of nature?'

'What about this?' Nevinson pointed to a large, circular depression near the right-hand edge of the photograph.

'A crater.'

'And this?' Nevinson's finger moved to one of the conical mounds.

'An extinct volcano?'

'NASA would be proud of you.'

'Percy, what has this to do with—?'

'Avebury? Simple. It *is* Avebury. What you call a crater and an extinct volcano are perfectly scaled representations of the stone circle at Avebury and the artificial hill at Silbury. Or vice versa. They are precisely proportionate and have the same geometric relationship. Trace a line due north from the centres of the volcano and Silbury Hill and you'll find that the centres of the crater and the Avebury circle are offset by exactly the same angle. Nineteen point four seven degrees. Does that ring any bells? 1947?'

'The Roswell incident.' Umber's heart sank. Alien abduction. That was it, then. He sighed. 'So Tamsin was kidnapped by Martians?'

'Certainly not.' Nevinson frowned pityingly at him. 'Have you taken leave of your senses? Wessex is an encoded landscape, David. That's what you have to understand. Avebury. Silbury. Stonehenge. They're repositories of information—of ancient secrets. But not everybody wants those secrets to be uncovered.' Nevinson's voice dropped to a whisper. 'By the summer of 1981, I'd gone a long way towards cracking the code. I thought it my duty to notify the authorities of my preliminary conclusions. That was a mistake. Sadly, I fear Tamsin and Miranda Hall paid the penalty for it.'

'How do you figure that out?'

'I believe the incident was staged to demonstrate to me that innocent people would suffer if I continued with my researches. Of course, no one was intended to die. The driver of the van simply panicked. But Miranda's death complicated matters. I believe it's why Tamsin was never returned.'

'Did you tell Sharp any of this at the time?'

'I hinted at it. But I was left in no doubt that he'd been warned off by the powers that be. I suspect you've been manoeuvred into accepting his assistance. His role is to ensure you don't find what you're looking for.'

'I see.'

'And before you ask, I can't disclose what I've learned from my study of the henges. To share my findings with others would only be to endanger them.'

'Of course.'

'I strongly advise you to abandon your investigation. If you must persist, do so alone. But be aware of the considerable risks you'll be running.'

The man was mad. That was clear. Yet his madness at least ruled him out as Sharp's correspondent. His obsession left no room for Junian diversions.

'Your wife's sad example is a salutary one.' Nevinson continued. 'Neither of us believes she died accidentally, do we? Or by her own hand. She must have strayed too close to the truth—'

Umber stood up suddenly, banging his chair against the table behind him. Nevinson goggled up at him in surprise. 'What's wrong?'

'Nothing's wrong. I'm leaving. That's all.' Umber plucked a fiver out of his wallet and tossed it onto the table. 'I'll have to leave you to settle up.'

'But we haven't finished.'

'Oh yes, we have.' Umber smiled stiffly. 'I've heard enough.'

UMBER NEEDED a walk to calm himself before reporting back to Sharp. He suspected that he'd be criticised for failing to confine Nevinson to practical issues. But there it was. The man was impossible. He was also, Umber felt sure, irrelevant.

As it turned out, Umber had more time to prepare his excuses than he thought. At the Ivy House, he was handed a note from Sharp. *Have gone to Devizes. Back later.* As messages went, it was less than illuminating.

After awaiting Sharp's return for a while, Umber quit the hotel in search of dinner. On his way back from the restaurant he wandered into the Green Dragon, a quiet, smoky pub, where he sat by the fire with a pint and did his level best not to dwell on Nevinson's absurd notion that Sally had been murdered. Down that road, Umber feared, lay his own brand of madness.

At some point he remembered, to his irritation, a question he had meant to put to Nevinson. What had he wanted to show Jeremy Hall at the Adam and Eve stones that day in July 1981? Marks on one of the stones that he believed were Martian runes, in all likelihood, but—

'There you are, Umber.' George Sharp loomed suddenly into view. 'This is the third pub I've tried. Want a half in there?'

Taken aback as much by Sharp's unwonted jollity as his unheralded arrival, Umber mumbled his thanks.

Sharp was back within minutes. 'I've missed the Wadworth's up in Derbyshire,' he announced, taking a deep swallow of 6X as he sat down.

'Was it the beer that took you to Devizes, George? The brewery's there.'

'Very funny. I actually went to meet an old pal of mine. Johnny Rawlings. Just about the last serving police officer I still know. He's the only one there I can be sure will do his best to help rather than hinder, and keep quiet into the bargain. But what did you glean from Percy Nevinson?'

'He's convinced Tamsin was taken by government agents to frighten him into silence about his theory explaining the Martian origins of Avebury.'

'Still stuck in that groove, is he? Like I said, a nutter.'

'Fully paid up.'

'Then we'll put him on the back burner for the time being. Not off the stove altogether, mind. Now, as for Johnny Rawlings—he's had a squint through the files. I contacted him before I went to Prague, asked if he'd be able to swing a favour for me. Radd, according to the record, confessed out of the blue. No one here or at Thames Valley can understand why he should have done—unless he was telling the truth. I asked Johnny if he could fix it for me to meet the man, and he's come through with a visiting order.'

'When will you go to see him?'

'When it suits. Radd's in Whitemoor, up in Cambridgeshire. It'll have to wait until we've spoken to Jane Questred.'

'She hasn't called.'

'She will.' Sharp grinned at Umber. 'I'm banking on it.'

JANE QUESTRED never made the call Sharp had so confidently anticipated. But she was in touch, via her husband, who phoned Umber during a late breakfast the following morning. Hearing Edmund Questred's voice, Umber at once expected to be told that she had refused to see them. Not so.

Two hours later, Sharp was nosing the van through the open gate next to Swanpool Cottage. The cottage was timber-framed and thatched, every bit as chocolate-box as Abigail Nevinson had claimed. A swag of wisteria obscured the gable end.

The front door opened as they approached and Jane Questred stepped out to greet them. A slim, elegant woman in her mid-fifties with grey-blonde hair and delicate features, she was dressed plainly in a dark top and black trousers. She looked self-controlled and better equipped to cope with an intrusion from her traumatic past than her husband's protectiveness had suggested.

'Mr Sharp. Mr Umber.' They shook hands. 'You found your way, then.'

'Thank you for agreeing to see us, Mrs Questred,' said Sharp.

She led them into a surprisingly large sitting room that looked as photogenic as the exterior, pastel-toned sofas and downland watercolours blending tastefully with exposed beams and a big, rough-hewn fireplace. There was an aroma of freshly ground coffee, explained by a cafetière standing with some cups and saucers on a table in front of the fire.

'Would you like some coffee,' Jane Questred asked.

They accepted. Coffee was poured. Seats were taken. Umber's armchair put him at eye level with a silver-framed photograph of a blonde-haired teenage girl in riding kit. He half heard Sharp uttering some 'Nice place you've got here' platitude. But it at once became obvious that Jane Questred had no intention of trading in platitudes.

'Edmund advised me not to meet you. I generally take his advice. The only reason I didn't in this case . . . was you, Mr Umber.'

'Me?'

'You're here for Sally's sake, I gather. Well, Oliver and I . . . eased some of our grief by blaming her for what happened. I should have taken the trouble later to make it clear to her that I never truly held her responsible. When I heard she'd died . . . well, I'm so sorry I neglected her feelings.'

'It was only natural for you to blame Sally to some extent, Mrs Questred,' said Umber. 'She understood that—most of the time. What she couldn't understand was your willingness to accept Brian Radd's confession. She never wavered in her certainty that there were two men in the van.'

'It's easy to be confused in such a situation. I'm sure Sally *believed* there were two men. But eyewitnesses often contradict each other. Isn't that so, Mr Sharp?'

'It is, yes. But there's no contradiction here. There never were any eyewitnesses who swore there was only one man.'

Jane Questred spread her hands on her lap. She had schooled herself to remain calm, Umber sensed, to answer their questions coolly and rationally. 'Why should Radd confess to something he hadn't done?' she asked.

'I mean to ask him that myself,' Sharp said. 'I should have made it my business to question Radd a long time ago.'

'Do you really believe he did it, Mrs Questred?' Umber asked.

'Yes.' Her certainty was implacable. 'I do.'

'Your daughter, Mrs Questred?' Sharp nodded towards the picture Umber had noticed earlier.

'Yes.'

'Nice-looking girl. How old is she?'

'Katy's fifteen.'

'So, she must have been a babe in arms when Radd confessed.'

'Yes. I suppose she was.'

'You'd just made a new start in life.'

'What are you getting at, Mr Sharp?'

'You might have been ready to . . . draw a line.'

'Your colleagues were happy to assure me of Radd's guilt.'

'They hadn't worked the case, Mrs Questred. I had.'

'What did your husband think about Radd?' Umber asked. 'Ex-husband, I mean. Mr Hall.'

'He believed Radd's confession. Everyone did.'

'Your son too?'

'Yes.'

'What does Jeremy do these days?' asked Sharp.

'He runs a surfing and sailing school in Jersey. He's done very well. I'm proud of him.'

'It must be nice for his father, having him on the island.'

'Are you going to speak to them as well?'

'Probably, yes.'

'Jeremy didn't find it easy to cope with the loss of his sisters. His adolescence was . . . difficult. Oliver and I getting divorced didn't help. But Jeremy's put those troubles behind him now. I don't want him being forced to relive them all over again. Speak to Oliver if you must. But please leave Jeremy alone. People going over there to stir up the past to no purpose won't help one little bit.'

'I wouldn't say to no purpose,' Sharp commented.

'Wouldn't you? Then perhaps you'd like to tell me what you hope to achieve by going into all this again. I expected you to bring some compelling reason for reopening old wounds, but you've brought nothing. There's—' She broke off, her self-control faltering. 'Why are you doing this?'

A better explanation was clearly called for. Sharp cleared his throat and cast a darting glance at Umber—a warning glance, it seemed.

'I had an anonymous letter, Mrs Questred. It said the truth about the Avebury case had never come out, but could still be uncovered if I was willing to make the effort.'

'May I see the letter?'

'I'm afraid not. I . . . destroyed it.'

'*What?*'

'I threw it on the fire. It was . . . my instant reaction. Later, I . . . decided I ought to . . . do something about it.'

'I don't believe you, Mr Sharp. Destroying evidence would go against the grain even for a *retired* police officer. Either there was no letter and you've simply dreamt it up as an excuse or there *was* a letter, which you aren't prepared to show me.' She looked Sharp in the eye. 'Why, I wonder? Because you think I might have written it?'

'No, I don't think that. Mrs Questred, I—'

'I've heard enough. I must ask you both to leave.' Jane Questred rose to her feet and glared down at Sharp. 'I don't suppose there's anything I can do to stop you going on with this. But I'll try, believe me.'

Sharp stood up slowly and returned her gaze. He seemed minded to utter some retort, but he must have thought better of it. With a twitch of his head to Umber, he turned towards the door.

'I'm sorry, Mrs Questred,' Umber murmured as he moved past her.

'Mr Umber,' she said softly. 'Edmund said you seemed surprised that I hadn't moved out of the area. I have two daughters buried here, remember. Miranda, in Marlborough Cemetery. And Tamsin, somewhere in Savernake Forest. I often go there to be close to her. And to the cemetery, of course, to be close to Miranda. I failed them in life. I mustn't fail them in death.' She touched Umber's arm. 'Let them rest in peace. Please.'

'NOT AN ENTIRELY successful visit,' said Umber a few minutes later, as they started back along the Marlborough road.

'I cocked it up,' Sharp growled. 'You don't need to rub it in.'

'You shouldn't have lied to her, George.'

'I had no choice. We can't show her the letter. We wouldn't be able to trust her. She didn't send it. That's clear. But she might have good reason to protect whoever did.'

'Perhaps we should do as she asked. Lay off.'

'Not before I tackle Radd.'

'When will you go?'

'Right away. It's just possible Mrs Questred might be able to get me barred from the prison. There's no time to be lost. I don't know if I can make it up there before visiting hours end for the day. But I'm going to have to try.'

AFTER SHARP had dropped him off in Marlborough High Street, Umber walked up to the cemetery, set high on the hills north of the town. It did not take him long to find the grave he was looking for.

MIRANDA JANE HALL
1974–1981

From where he was standing there was a clear view across the valley of the grey-green swath of Savernake Forest. Whenever Jane Questred visited Miranda's grave she could also see the place where she believed Tamsin had been laid in the earth. And she had been to the cemetery recently. There were fresh daffodils in the vase beneath the headstone.

He walked slowly back down the hill into the town, turning over in his mind the question of what he should do for the best.

He did not hear from Sharp until early evening.

'The traffic was hell. I was way too late for visiting. I'm going to kip in the van and try my luck tomorrow. Anything to report?'

'Nothing.'

'I don't know when I'll get back to Marlborough. It could be late. Until then, just sit tight.'

'Will do.'

But Umber had no intention of sitting tight.

THREE

Shortly after daybreak on Thursday morning, Umber was standing outside Ladbroke's betting shop on Marlborough High Street, waiting for the number 48 bus. Just over an hour later he was pacing the platform at Trowbridge railway station, debating with himself whether there was any good excuse for the covert nature of his journey.

His parents would not think so, but explaining to them why he had come back to England was something he was willing to go to considerable lengths to avoid. However, he needed to establish who the mysterious Mr Griffin was—now more than ever, given that Sharp's approaches to the problem were generating more heat than light. Griffin brought him back to

Junius—and the necessity to revisit all he had once known about that enigmatic, unidentified figure from two and a half centuries ago.

The train reached Yeovil at ten o'clock. It was a fifteen-minute walk from the station to the red-brick semi in which Umber had spent his youth. His parents were creatures of habit. Mondays and Thursdays were shopping mornings. There was close to no chance of their being at home.

The street was quiet and empty when Umber hurried along it to number 36. He let himself in and stood in the hall for a few moments, testing the silence. It was total. He was alone.

He ran up the stairs to the landing, opened the door of the cupboard straight ahead of him and lifted out a metal rod with a hook on one end. Then he positioned himself beneath the loft hatch, fitted the other end of the rod to the hatch fastening and turned it. The hatch fell open. He used the hook to pull down the loft ladder and climbed up into the roof.

He pressed a switch to his left, and a fluorescent light above him flickered into life. The loft was much as he remembered, an elephants' graveyard of possessions his parents no longer had any use for: plastic bags full of old clothes, tea chests crammed with books, a gramophone, an ancient television. And there, in the shadow of the water tank, was the thing he was looking for: a white cardboard box, fastened with string. Written on the side in felt-tip capitals was the single word *JUNIUS*. And the writing was his.

He dragged the box to the hatch and, cradling it awkwardly in his arms, climbed down. Then he scrambled back up to switch the light off before pushing the ladder back into place and closing the hatch. He replaced the rod in the cupboard, then carried the box down to the hall.

It was going to be an arduous walk back to the station. The box was heavier than he remembered. But that could not be helped. He should be there in ample time for the 11.45 train.

He opened the front door, carried the box out and put it down on the doormat while he locked up. Then he turned and picked up the box again.

That was when Umber saw the man smiling at him from the front gate. He was tall, broadly built and middle-aged, wearing a dark suit and a sober tie, his grey-brown hair cut short, his tanned face split by a sparkle-toothed grin beneath darting, humorous eyes. His hand was curled round the handle of a black briefcase. 'Mr Umber?' he asked, his voice neutral and low-pitched.

'Er . . . No.'

'But this is the Umber house, isn't it? Number 36?'

'Yes. But . . .' Umber reached the end of the path, and rested the box on the gate between them. 'They're not in.'

The man looked quizzically at Umber. 'Any idea when they'll be back?'

'Not really, I . . .' An explanation was clearly called for. Preferably one close to the truth. 'I'm their son. David Umber. But I don't actually live here.'

'I see. Of course. My name's Walsh. John Walsh. Lynx Aluminium Windows. I have an appointment with your parents at eleven thirty, but my previous appointment has just been cancelled, so I called round in the hope of bringing this one forward.'

'I'm sure they'll be back soon if they're expecting you.'

'I'm sure they will. Can I give you a hand getting that box to your car?'

'I don't have a car.'

'No? Well, can I give you a lift somewhere? I may as well, with this gap in my schedule.'

'OK. Thanks. I need to get to the station.'

'No problem.'

Umber was happy to accept the lift for a reason unconnected with the weight of the box. He needed to give Walsh a good and compelling reason not to mention their encounter to his parents, and one began to shape itself in his mind as Walsh helped him load the box into the boot of his BMW.

'There's another favour I need to ask you, Mr Walsh,' he said as they set off. 'It's my father's eightieth birthday in a few weeks and we're planning a surprise party for him. I've been to the house making some preparations. I'd be awfully grateful if you didn't . . .'

'Spill the beans? You can rely on me, Mr Umber. Would it be better to say nothing about running into you?'

'It would.'

'It never happened. My lips are sealed.'

'Thanks.'

A few minutes later, they turned down the approach road to Pen Mill station. Walsh swung the car round in the forecourt.

'Need a hand with the box?' he asked.

'I can manage, thanks,' Umber replied.

'OK. Well, have a good journey. And don't worry. Your secret's safe.'

'Thanks a lot.' Umber climbed out, closed the door and walked round to the boot. His thumb was about an inch from the boot release when the car suddenly surged forward and accelerated away.

Umber started running after it but it was a futile effort. By the time he could see the top of the approach road, the BMW had vanished.

He could not believe it. Walsh had stolen his box of papers. But of course the man was not really Walsh. He did not work for Lynx Aluminium Windows. He had no appointment with Umber's parents. He had come to Yeovil for the same reason as Umber. And he was leaving with what he had come for. The word *JUNIUS* had been plainly visible on the box, so the man knew what was inside. Which meant that what was inside mattered.

Umber spread his fingers over his eyes, pressing them shut. 'What do I do now, Sal?' he murmured under his breath.

SEVERAL HOURS later, Umber was standing outside the Kennet Valley Wine Company shop in Marlborough High Street, a walk across the downs having cleared his mind. He had been stupid. But he did not have to go on being stupid. What Walsh had done he had been put up to do. And the list of people who might have put him up to do it was a short one.

The man Umber had seen entering the shop a few moments previously emerged and headed off along the street. Even before the door had swung shut behind him, Umber was through it.

He closed the door, slipped the bolt and flicked the sign round. Then he turned to face Edmund Questred, who was rounding the serving counter.

'What do you think you're doing?' Questred demanded.

With a shove in the chest, Umber pushed him back against the edge of the counter. 'You had me followed to Yeovil, didn't you?'

'What? I don't know what you're talking about.'

'Just tell me why. Why Junius. What in God's name is it all about?'

'You're making no sense. If you don't leave—now—I'll—'

'Call the police? It's me who should be calling them. I was followed and robbed. No one knows I'm in Marlborough except you, your wife and the Nevinsons. And I don't see Percy or Abigail hiring someone like Walsh—or whatever his real name is.'

'I can assure you I hired no one. I don't know anything about it.'

'I don't believe you.'

'That's up to you. But it happens to be true.' Questred did not look or sound as if he was lying. Umber's confidence faltered. Maybe he was on the wrong track after all. 'If someone's stolen something from you, you should tell the police. It's got nothing to do with me. Or Jane.'

The telephone in the office behind the counter began to ring. The two men looked at each other. Then Questred pushed past Umber, strode into the office and picked up the telephone.

'Jane? What's the matter? . . . I don't believe it . . . Yes, of course. I'll come straight away . . . Don't worry. I'll see you shortly, darling . . . Bye.'

Questred slowly put the telephone down and stared into space. There was an expression of shocked confusion on his face. 'It doesn't make any sense,' he murmured. 'Why now? After all this time.'

'What's happened?' Umber asked.

'Jane's had a reporter on to her. Asking for her reaction to the news. It was on the radio at lunchtime, apparently, but she hadn't heard. She's quite upset. I have to go home.' He frowned at Umber. 'Did you know about this?'

'Know what?'

'Brian Radd's dead. They say he was . . . murdered.'

WHEN UMBER switched his mobile back on, he found a message from Sharp waiting for him. He already knew, of course, what Sharp had to tell him.

'Radd's dead. Murdered by another prisoner, apparently. No point me staying here now. I'll head back. I don't know what to make of this, Umber, I really don't. We'll talk later. Bye.'

Umber went back to the Ivy House and learned a little more from the Ceefax service on the television in his room. Radd had been found bleeding from a stomach wound, in a toilet cubicle at about nine o'clock that morning. A police murder inquiry was under way.

Umber stared at the words on the screen, shock giving way slowly to something closer to fear. The media would regard this as rough justice for a child murderer and rapist, dispensed by a fellow prisoner. But they were unaware of the pattern. Both events that day seemed to imply that someone was on to Umber and Sharp. Someone had decided to stop their investigation in its tracks. And they were willing to kill to do it.

Umber switched the phone off and lay back on the bed. He was not thinking about Radd any more, or the theft of his Junius papers. It was Sally's death five years ago that filled his mind.

He had been in Turkey when it happened. Sally had been living in a flat in Hampstead, lent to her by her friend Alice Myers. Late June had not brought tropical conditions to London. And Sally had always felt the cold more than most. The flat's bathroom was unheated. It was possible to believe—just—that she had trailed a fan heater into the bathroom to warm it. There was a chair close to the bath, on which, the coroner theorised, she might have stood the heater, then somehow tipped it into the bath as she reached for a towel. Alternatively, she might have deliberately pulled the heater into the bath with her, knowing what the consequences would be. That was what most of her friends believed. The absence of a note and Alice's testimony that Sally had been in better spirits than for some time sufficed for the coroner to give her the benefit of the doubt. No one had suggested murder, of course. The idea would have been dismissed as absurd, not least by Umber. He had felt certain that Sally had taken her own life.

Now, five years later, he was certain of nothing. *She must have strayed too close to the truth*, Nevinson had said. Could he be right after all?

He headed out for dinner, the thoughts still running round in his brain.

BACK AT the Ivy House, the receptionist told him that Sharp had returned in his absence. He went straight up to Sharp's room.

Sharp looked weary. 'I didn't see this coming, Umber,' he said. 'It never crossed my mind.'

'Child murderers aren't top of anyone's popularity list, George.'

'That's not why he was killed and you know it.'

'I do, yes. You could say I've had independent confirmation of that.'

As Umber described his experiences in Yeovil, Sharp merely grunted and rolled his eyes.

'Shall I tell you where we are, Umber? Out of our bloody depth.'

'You ought to know I'm starting to think Sally may have been murdered.'

'I suppose you were bound to.' Sharp rasped his hand round his unshaven chin. 'Only bear in mind Radd may have been taken out to warn us off.'

'I can't let that stop me, George. Not if they killed Sally. You're not going to allow yourself to be warned off?'

'Good God, no. What do you take me for? My professional pride's been dented. I need to hammer it back into shape. Starting with the question of who tipped off these people.'

'Your friend Rawlings knew you were going to see Radd.'

'He promised to keep it under his hat. He wouldn't break a promise.'

'Are you sure about that, George?'

'A lot surer than I am about Jane Questred. She knew. She said she'd do whatever she could to stop us. So, let's find out who she contacted.'

'If anyone.'

'Like you say. If anyone. But everything we try is bound to be a long shot. Take Donald Collingwood. I checked his old address in Swindon.'

'Dead and gone?'

Sharp nodded. 'More than ten years.' He mulled over that for a moment, then said, 'What was in your Junius box that made it worth stealing?'

'I don't know. My PhD research notes aren't exactly state secrets.'

'Well, somebody wanted them, Umber. Badly. What were they about?'

'Well . . .' Umber rubbed his face. 'I'd started going through all the people who'd ever been accused of being Junius. There were fifty or sixty of them. My idea was to disprove each one conclusively. That involved checking their whereabouts at times when we could be sure where Junius was; comparing their known political opinions with Junius's expressed views; examining examples of their handwriting and prose style for similarities to—'

'Hold on. What about that War Office clerk you mentioned as odds-on favourite? Did his handwriting match Junius's?'

'No. But then it's generally assumed Junius wrote in a disguised hand. There's also the possibility he employed an amanuensis.'

'A what?'

'Someone to copy the letters for him before they were sent. There's a separate list of candidates for that role.'

'Can you remember all the names on these lists?'

'No. But I could reassemble them if I had to.'

'And your notes too, I suppose.'

'That would take months. You're not serious, are you?'

'No. But I was just thinking. Maybe the thief stole them to stop you looking at them rather than to look at them himself.'

'Does it make any difference?'

'Not sure. But we're on to something, Umber, definitely.' Sharp grinned ruefully. 'It's just a pity we don't have the first bloody idea what.'

IT WAS AGREED they would set off for Swanpool Cottage at nine o'clock the following morning. It was also agreed they would both benefit from an early night. Umber watched the ten o'clock news report on Radd's murder. It told him nothing he did not already know. Then he switched his mobile on and checked for messages. There was one.

'This is Edmund Questred, Mr Umber. We need to speak. Don't phone me. Come to the back door of the shop at eight thirty tomorrow morning. Please don't contact Jane in the meantime.'

Umber thought about phoning Sharp, then thought better of it. He might already be asleep. If so, it was a kindness to let him sleep on.

There was to be little sleep for Umber himself. He tossed and turned, counting Junius suspects like sheep, but to no avail. And then he thought about Sally again. It was difficult to remember how weary he had been of her inability to put the past behind her, and how relieved he had felt in the months following their separation. The guilt that had swept over him the minute he heard she was dead was clear in his mind, however. He pictured her, lying lifeless in the bath. He had loved her. He had abandoned her. There had been no excuse. But maybe now there could be the next best thing to reconciliation—reparation.

THERE WAS no sign of Sharp in the breakfast room when Umber left the hotel next morning. He followed a lane round to the rear of the high street shops. There was a small delivery yard at the back of the Kennet Valley Wine Company and the double doors leading to the storeroom behind the shop were ajar. He stepped through.

Questred was waiting for him inside, sitting on a wine box, staring listlessly at a newspaper folded open at an inside page. CHILD MURDERER SLAIN IN PRISON KNIFING ran the headline. He looked up.

'You got my message, then. Jane reckons you and Sharp will have taken it into your heads that something she did led to this.' He held up the paper.

'Well, it's quite some coincidence, isn't it?'

'The only person she told about your visit was her ex-husband. She phoned him straight after you left the cottage. But he wasn't at home. She left a message, asking him to phone back as soon as possible. She didn't say why. And Oliver didn't call until last night, so . . .'

'It really was a coincidence.'

'You obviously don't think so.'

'Do you?'

'No.' Questred smiled grimly. 'Does that surprise you?'

'Yes.' Umber sat down on the nearest box. 'It does.'

'There's something I have to tell you. In confidence. I don't want it to reach Jane's ears. I'd deny saying it if it did, anyway, and she'd believe me over you every day. It's, er, about . . . your wife.'

'Sally?'

'Yes. Well, the day she died . . .' Questred rubbed his forehead. 'That is, I realised later it was the day she died . . . She phoned here. She, er, wanted to speak to Jane, but she didn't have the number for the cottage and, er, well, I wasn't about to give it to her. Anyway, she asked me to get Jane to phone her. She didn't give a reason. I didn't ask for one. To be honest, I thought she sounded overwrought. I told her I'd pass the message on . . .'

'But you didn't.'

'No. I didn't want her upsetting Jane. In fact, this is the first time I've mentioned it to anyone.' Questred looked cautiously at Umber. 'I didn't expect you to take this so calmly.'

'What you've just said only reinforces my suspicion she was murdered.'

'Oh God. But that would mean . . . Christ knows what it would mean.'

'I intend to find out.'

Questred rose and moved to the door, where he stared out at the wedge of sunlight advancing slowly across the yard. 'Do you have to see Jane?'

'That's up to Sharp.'

'How would it be if I arranged for Oliver to speak to you? He's got state-of-the-art security at his place in Jersey. You won't get past the gate if he doesn't want you to.'

'In return for leaving Jane alone?'

'Yes.'

'That'd be up to Sharp as well.'

'But you could put it to him.'

'Yes.' Umber stood up. 'I could.'

AND HE DID, over the breakfast he found Sharp polishing off back at the Ivy House.

'We only have his word for it that Jane didn't speak to anyone else,' Sharp objected.

'He didn't have to tell me about Sally's call, George.'

'True.'

'And Hall could refuse to see us if he was so minded.'

'Also true.'

'So what do you think?'

'I think we'd better accept his generous offer.' Sharp eyed Umber over a jagged triangle of toast. 'Don't you?'

IT WAS UNCLEAR exactly how long it would take Questred to set up a meeting for them with Oliver Hall. Sharp gave him a twenty-four hour deadline to concentrate his mind, then booked Umber and himself out of the hotel and headed for London.

'We can stay with an old pal of mine from the Met, Bill Larter, while we wait to hear from Hall,' he announced as they drove towards the M4. 'I gave him a call from the hotel. He'll be glad of the company. Not that he'll let you know that. Besides, he won't see much of us—we'll be busy. And this time you'll be calling the shots. Who can we talk to about Sally's activities in the days and weeks before her death?'

'Alice Myers was her best friend. She owned the flat Sally died in. Still does, presumably. If anyone knows what was going on in Sally's head at the time, it's Alice.'

'We'll start with her, then.'

'But there's a problem. Alice is anti-Establishment to her fingertips. Spent a whole winter in the eighties camped out at Greenham Common. Obstructs the police on principle. I'll get more out of her on my own, George.'

'Huh.' Sharp said nothing more for a mile or so, then resumed, the affront to his status evidently shrugged off. 'All right. Leave me out of it. There's something else I need to do anyway.'

'What's that?'

'Alan Wisby. Does the name ring any bells?'

'I don't think so.'

'He was a private detective Oliver Hall hired when my investigation ran into the sand. You and Sally would have been in Spain by then, but if Wisby was doing a thorough job, which I—'

'Hold on. Yes. A private detective did come to see us. I can't remember his name. Insignificant sort of bloke.' Umber recalled a short, thin, whisper-voiced chain smoker. Sally had taken an instant dislike to the man. He had asked his questions and he had gone, with little to show for his trouble.

'That would be Wisby. According to Yellow Pages, he's still in business, so I was thinking of dropping by his office.'

'Do you think you'll get anything out of him?'

'Shake a tree, Umber, and it's surprising what falls out. He's worth a visit. You see, it's occurred to me that Junius may have sent the same letter I got to anyone else who was involved in investigating the case. And Wisby falls squarely into that category.'

SHARP DROPPED Umber in Hampstead High Street and headed on his way. They had agreed to meet later at Bill Larter's home in Ilford.

Alice Myers lived in a tall, elegant Victorian house halfway between the high street and Hampstead Heath. Umber had last set foot there, lingering for all of ten excruciating minutes, on the afternoon of Sally's funeral. Alice occupied the ground and first floors, while renting out the basement and the top floor. It was the top-floor flat she had given Sally the use of, following her return from Italy. And it was there that Sally had died.

Alice's multiple occupations of fabric designer, curtain-maker, cello teacher and political activist all had 22 Willow Hill as their hub. Umber was therefore confident he would find Alice in.

There was no immediate response to the bell. Then he heard a faintly vexed cry of 'Coming'. A second later, the door was yanked open.

Umber never ceased to be surprised by Alice's size. Her name and her feathery voice created in the mind's eye a slighter person than she actually was. Her outfit, a baggy, paint-spattered boiler suit, merely exaggerated her bulk. There were flecks of paint in her hair as well, flamingo-pink amid the pigeon-grey, and on her round gold spectacles, through which large brown eyes regarded Umber with dismay.

'Oh my God,' she said. 'David.'

'Long time no see.' Umber smiled uncertainly. 'Can I come in?'

'Sure. I'm . . . in the middle of decorating.' She led the way down the hall. They passed one room, bare of furniture, where a tide of pink had advanced halfway across the ceiling and a roller stood propped in a paint tray against a stepladder, and ended up in the kitchen. 'Do you want some tea?'

'All right. Thanks.'

Alice filled the kettle and switched it on, then gave him a long gaze of scrutiny. 'I heard you were in Prague.'

'I was.'

'Home for good?'

'I doubt it.'

The kettle boiled, and Alice dunked a couple of tea bags.

Umber sat down at the kitchen table. 'I owe you an apology, Alice.'

'You do?' She glanced over her shoulder at him.

'Leaving like that. Without even saying goodbye.'

'It was a tough day for everybody. Tougher for you than for most, I guess.'

'I bet that's not what you thought at the time.'

'It was five years ago. I'd just lost my best friend. I thought lots of things.' She delivered the mugs to the table and sat down opposite Umber.

'Do you know why I left so abruptly after Sally's funeral?'

'Afraid people would give you a hard time, I guess.'

'I reckoned I deserved one. I felt ashamed for running out on her. Guilty for what had happened. But I should have asked more questions. I should have forced myself to understand. We all should have.'

'Things just got too much for her. There's nothing else to say.'

'I think there is.' He folded his hands together. 'Has it ever occurred to you, Alice, that Sally might have been murdered?'

'What?'

'It's occurred to me, you see. As a very real possibility.'

'I don't believe this.' She shook her head. 'You turn up out of the blue after five years of silence and you tell me you think my best friend might have been murdered. In my house . . . Sally was alone when it happened. Have you forgotten that? Where did this murderer suddenly spring from? There was no sign of a break-in, down here or up there.'

'Perhaps he tricked his way in.'

'And she decided to take a bath while he was still there? You know as well as I do how ludicrous that would be. Her problem wasn't people coming to see her. It was people *not* coming to see her.'

'You said at the inquest she'd been in good spirits.'

'*Irrationally* good spirits, I thought, when I looked back on it. She'd broken her last appointment with Claire.'

'Who?'

'Claire Wheatley. Her psychotherapist. And a good friend of mine. She was at the funeral. I think you spoke to her. Don't you remember?'

'No, I can't say I do.'

'Sally had been doing well, according to Claire. They had regular Monday sessions, and Sally set off at the usual time. She got as far as the waiting room at Claire's practice, then walked out a few minutes before she was due to go in. Claire couldn't get an explanation out of her over the phone, so she asked me to find out why. But I got nowhere. Sally airily dismissed the whole thing. She was in a hurry to leave, said she was going to Wimbledon. But, hey, when was she ever interested in tennis?'

'Maybe she wasn't going to the tennis.'

'Oh, but she was. She told me so. I asked if she had a ticket and she said

"I don't need a ticket." It was all so unlike her. Claire thought she must have been yo-yoing by then—alternating between extremes of elation and despair. It was Wednesday morning when I spoke to her—the last time I *ever* spoke to her. By Thursday evening, she must have hit bottom.'

'Hard enough to kill herself—by electrocution?'

'You know she had a horror of pills. Maybe it was the only way she could think of.' Alice looked away. When she spoke again, her voice had thickened. 'I don't want to be reminded of this, David, I really don't. Why now?'

'Strange things have been happening. The policeman who investigated the Avebury case got an anonymous letter recently. Now Radd's dead. And I've learned Sally tried to contact the Hall girls' mother the day she died.'

'What did she want?'

'I don't know. But I think she may have been getting close to the truth. About what happened at Avebury.'

'You weren't here, David. I was. Sally wasn't chasing after answers. If anything, she was running away from them. You've got this all wrong. And she wasn't murdered. That idea's plain crazy.'

'Could you fix it for me to meet this psychotherapist?'

'What purpose could that possibly serve?'

'Well, you seem to think I'm crazy. Maybe I need some counselling.'

'Maybe you do. But you can arrange that yourself.'

'Look, Alice, you're right, I wasn't anywhere close when Sally most needed me. But let's be honest, you and Psychotherapist of the Month didn't exactly bring her through smiling and dancing either, did you?'

Alice compressed her lips. There was a brief, fragile silence. Then she said softly, 'All right. I'll ask Claire if she's willing to meet you.'

'Thank you.'

'Nothing you do can bring Sally back, so why stir it all up?'

'Remember what you said when I asked you what the point was of you and your peace sisterhood setting up camp at Greenham Common? "Sometimes the right thing to do is the only thing to do." I didn't understand what you meant, but I do now.'

UMBER TOOK the tube to Euston, then walked to the British Library. He did not know how easy reregistering would be. In the event, he was browsing the catalogue in the Humanities Reading Room within an hour of his arrival. Within another hour, he had placed his order for half a dozen

Junius-related books. It was too late to expect them to be available that afternoon, so he settled for first thing the following morning.

He switched his mobile on as soon as he was outside and checked for messages. There was one, from Oliver Hall.

'Mr Umber, this is Oliver Hall.' The voice was low-pitched and subdued, the enunciation surgically precise. 'Edmund's told me of your concerns. As it happens, I have to be in London on business next week. I'm flying over on Sunday. We can meet at my flat that evening. It's 58 Kingsley House, South Street, Mayfair. Would six o'clock be convenient? Perhaps you could leave a message for me there on the answerphone. 020 7499 5992. Thank you.'

Umber bought a coffee from the kiosk in the library courtyard and sat on a bench, drinking it, while listening to the message again. Oliver Hall sounded polite, even obliging. But his response was unmistakably calculating. Meeting in London rather than Jersey denied Umber and Sharp the opportunity to engineer an encounter with his son, Jeremy. And giving them only the London number to reply to meant they could not argue about it even if they wanted to. Umber rang and confirmed the appointment.

He was still sitting on the bench, finishing his coffee, when his phone rang.

'David, this is Claire Wheatley.'

'Thanks for calling, Claire. Alice must have spoken to you.'

'Yes. She has.'

'Can we meet?'

'If you like. I'm going away for the weekend and I'm fully booked for Monday. But we could meet during my lunch break. How would that be?'

'OK. Monday it is.'

UMBER REACHED Ilford with a trainload of weary commuters, exiting the station into a damp and windy twilight. Bengal Road was close by, a street of terraced, bay-windowed, red-brick houses. No lights showed at the windows of number 45, but a folded sheet of paper was wedged in the letterbox.

It was a note from Sharp. *Gone to the pub. Turn right into Riverdene Road and follow it to the Sheepwalk.*

The Sheepwalk, it transpired, was the name of the pub. It was full to bursting at the close of the working week, and Umber blundered around through a ruck of drinkers until he spotted Sharp in an alcove. Sharp's table companion was a big, broadly built man of about the same age, with greased, centre-parted grey hair, and a raw-boned, lantern-jawed face.

'You made it, then,' was Sharp's growled greeting. He looked glum. 'Bill Larter. David Umber.'

Larter gave Umber a crushing handshake as he sat down, and a peremptory nod. 'Want a drink, boy? Best bitter?'

'Er, yeah. Fine.'

Larter drained his beer glass. 'You ready for another, George?'

'Why not?'

Larter grabbed both glasses and steered a passage towards the bar. Umber looked at Sharp, whose expression suggested that his day hadn't gone well.

'To save you the trouble of asking, Wisby was a dead end. His ex-wife runs the business now, would you believe.'

'He's retired, then?'

'Yes. But not to any traceable address. Plies the canals on his narrowboat, apparently. How did you get on?'

'Do you want me to go into it all in front of Bill?'

'You can trust him with the secrets of your soul. He already knows a good few of mine.'

Larter returned with the drinks part way through Umber's report of what, by comparison with Sharp's search for Wisby, constituted solid progress. It was obvious that Sharp shared his suspicions of Oliver Hall.

'Business in London, my arse,' was his succinct assessment. 'He's trying to make sure we have no excuse to go to Jersey.'

'And what will we do until Sunday?'

'Well, you'll be busy poring over the archives. There's not a lot I can do. Looks like you get your wish, Bill.'

Umber watched the two old men exchange a smirk and waited for an explanation. Larter eventually supplied one after a lengthy swallow of beer.

'West Ham are playing at home tomorrow. George and me are going to take a stroll down memory lane.'

ANOTHER PINT later and Sharp and Larter had decided not to wait until Saturday to wander the byways of the past. Umber was left to sup in silence as they reminisced about crimes and colleagues of long ago. His attention drifted. He thought of Sally and their life together. He was tired and a little drunk by now, and could not seem to assemble all the implications of her death—and the manner of it—in his mind. He could not—

'Penny for them,' said Larter suddenly.

'What?' Looking up from his drink, Umber saw that Sharp had gone—to the loo, presumably.

'Are you getting my old mate into more trouble than he can handle, boy?'

'No more than he is me.'

'That's what I was afraid of. The pair of you egging each other on. There's no telling what you might bring crashing down on your heads.'

'Reckon we should drop it, do you, Bill?'

'Bloody certain you should. But you won't. You've both got the same look in your eye—the damn-the-consequences look. But consequences can be treacherous. You should never damn them till you know what they are.'

'I'll remember that.'

'No you won't.' Larter smiled. 'Not until it's too late, anyway.'

UMBER DWELT on Larter's warning that night, as he tried to sleep on the old man's squeaking sofa. He did not feel a lot better come morning. But his determination was intact. Larter insisted on cooking him a bacon-and-egg breakfast to see him on his way. Sharp was still not up when Umber left.

'Sleeping it off,' was Larter's judgment as he walked him to the door. 'And he's not as young as he used to be,' he added, as Umber stepped out into a dark Ilford morning. 'You should remember that.'

Umber was not as young as he used to be, either. A day's reading in the British Library proved a test for his eyesight as well as his concentration. And it was a sobering reminder of just how much he had forgotten about the subject he had once known so well.

Junius. The tormentor of politicians. Who was he? The editor of the Oxford University Press's *Letters of Junius* provided a list of sixty-one names— essentially the list Umber had set himself to work through for his thesis. Most of them had had a book or pamphlet written in support of their claim. *Junius Discovered. Junius Revealed. Junius Unveiled.* It was a morass as well as a mystery. A researcher could sink without trace in its murky depths.

He left when the library closed, at five o'clock, with a sheaf of photo-copied pages and a bundle of notes. He was mentally drained and in no mood to hear Sharp and Larter describe their afternoon at the football. He drank a couple of pints in the pub opposite the library, then, on a woozy whim, took the tube to Green Park and made his way through the quiet streets of Mayfair to Kingsley House.

It was a five-floor red-brick apartment block, exuding an air of reticent affluence. Quite why Umber had gone there he could not properly have explained. Oliver Hall had said he would fly over on Sunday, so there could be no question of catching him unawares. And yet . . . Umber stood on the other side of the road, wondering if he should try his luck.

In the end, it seemed absurd not to. He climbed the short flight of steps to the gleaming array of bell-pushes and pushed the one for number 58. There was a crackle and a female voice addressed him. 'Yes?'

'Mrs Hall?'

'Yes.'

'Er, my name's David Umber.'

'My husband's expecting you tomorrow. He's not here yet.'

'Tomorrow?' Umber decided to play dumb. 'Oh, I see. I'm sorry. I thought . . . I must have got the day wrong. Can I perhaps . . .?'

'You'd better come up.' The door-release buzzed.

Why Mrs Hall had let him in was a question he found no answer to during the brief lift ride to the third floor. She could easily have sent him packing.

The door of number 58 was ajar, and he stepped inside. The flat was warm and softly lit, with lots of sleek, oversized furniture. Guitar music was playing in the high-ceilinged drawing room and on a long, low table in front of the artfully faked fire were a slew of magazines and a chunky tumbler containing what looked like a very large gin and tonic.

Mrs Hall was a slim, strong-featured, blonde-haired woman in her mid-forties, expensively dressed in a dark red shot-silk suit with high-heeled sandals. She looked mid-forties but could have been older. She was not a woman likely to deny herself whatever it took to maintain her appearance.

'There you are,' she said, her voice poised and neutral. 'I'm Marilyn Hall.' They shook hands. 'Won't you sit down?'

'Thanks.' He sat opposite the sofa where the position of the tumbler suggested she had been sitting.

'Would you like a drink? I'm having a G and T.'

'The same for me would be fine.'

'Great.' She moved to a cabinet in the far corner of the room, poured his drink then returned with it and sat down.

He half-raised the glass and sipped from it. 'It was good of you to see me. I suppose I'm lucky there's anyone here.'

'I've been over doing some shopping. Oliver knows I have to hit Bond Street sooner or later. Jersey may be a tax haven. But fashion? Forget it.'

'Did he tell you why we've arranged to meet?'

'Oh yes. Jane's been on to him. Everyone's in the loop. Radd's murder'—
she smiled—'has really put the cat among the pigeons.'

'You think so?'

'What do you do for a living?' she asked, blithely ignoring his question.

'I'm kind of . . . between livings at the moment.'

'Do you think that's why you've started down this road?' She gazed at him,
defying him to be offended by her candour. 'Too much time on your hands?'

'I don't believe Radd killed your husband's daughters.'

'Somebody did.'

'Does Oliver talk about them much?'

'No.'

'A closed subject, then?'

Marilyn shrugged. 'Isn't that what the past should be?'

'I don't think so, no. Especially when we don't understand it.'

'Ah. I see.' She sipped at her drink. 'But then Oliver tells me you're a historian, so I guess that makes you biased.'

'Not biased. Just inquisitive.'

'Well, enquire away. I can't help you. And you'll get nothing out of
Oliver. Take it from one who knows. Are you in London for long?'

'Not sure.'

'What's in the bag?' She nodded towards his holdall.

'I've been doing some research into eighteenth-century politics.'

'Amazing.'

'But true. Ever hear the name Junius?'

'No.'

'Or Griffin?'

'Some sort of . . . dragon?'

'Some sort, yes.'

'Oliver tells me you're a widower as well as a historian.'

'That's true.'

'Being alone after years of love can't be easy.'

Umber could find no response to that. He was in truth surprised by the
degree to which Marilyn had taken him aback. He swallowed some gin.

'If you are alone . . . that is.'

He managed a smile. 'More or less.'

'Would you like to go to the theatre with me next Thursday? I have a couple of tickets. It's Shakespeare. Your sort of thing, I imagine. Oliver's not going to be able to make it. It seems a pity to waste the seat.'

She was asking him out. It seemed barely credible. But it was true. She was a mature and attractive woman, unafraid to hold his gaze. She knew what she was doing. What she had said merely skimmed the surface of what she meant. An offer of some kind was on the table, and who was running the bigger risk was far from clear. But in that uncertainty, her half-smiling expression implied, lay the object of the exercise.

Umber cleared his throat and swallowed some more gin. 'Which play?'

Marilyn leaned back in the couch. 'Does it matter?' she said softly.

UMBER DECIDED to say nothing to Sharp about Marilyn Hall's theatre invitation. He told himself this was because it was not entirely clear that he had accepted it and, besides, it was even less clear he would still be in London come Thursday. 'Call me on the day,' Marilyn had ambiguously concluded. 'Would you prefer me not to mention your visit to Oliver?'

'Why should I?'

'Oh, just because . . . he might not believe you'd mistaken the day.'

'But won't it be rather awkward for us to pretend we haven't met?'

'Not really. I won't be here, you see.' She had smiled. 'Oliver's choice.'

'Well . . . in that case . . .'

'I'll say nothing.'

'IT WAS a bloody stupid idea to go there in the first place,' Sharp complained when Umber reached Ilford and reported what had happened.

'Maybe,' Umber admitted. 'But, as it turns out, I've got the better of Oliver Hall without him being aware of it. He didn't want us to meet Marilyn, did he? Well, now one of us has.'

'And what have we got out of you meeting her?'

'The knowledge that she and Oliver don't trust each other.'

'We might have been able to work that out anyway. You should be asking yourself whether *you* can trust Marilyn Hall to keep her mouth shut.'

UMBER SPENT most of Sunday sitting at the table in Larter's dining room sifting through the notes and photocopied extracts he had brought back from the library—to little avail. The sixty-plus candidates for Junius's identity resolved themselves to fewer than twenty serious possibilities. Those were the ones Umber had concentrated on for his thesis. Yet there were, he now recalled, objections to all of them.

Umber wrote out his short-listed names on a fresh sheet of paper. He then struck out those names eliminated by strong circumstantial evidence, usually their absence abroad at times when Junius was writing notes to the proprietor of the *Public Advertiser* containing information available only to someone resident in London. Next to go were those who died before Junius wrote his last private letter in January 1773, then those with whom Junius had engaged in private correspondence. The list was shortened to four: Lord Chesterfield, Philip Francis, Lauchlin Macleane and Lord Temple.

Modern historians had settled on Philip Francis, an obscure War Office clerk. His opinions, character and whereabouts fitted Junius like a glove. The handwriting was the problem. Junius wrote fluently and elegantly, while Francis scratched away crabbily all his life. If he had used a disguised hand, it should logically have been inferior to the real thing, not the other way round. Francis seemed too secretive a man to have employed an amanuensis, and nobody could suggest who he might have chosen for the role.

Meanwhile, some graphologists detected a similarity between Junius's handwriting and that of Christabella Dayrolles, wife of Lord Chesterfield's godson, Solomon Dayrolles. Thus, bizarrely, the finger of suspicion swung towards its least credible target—Lord Chesterfield, a septuagenarian, half-blind, stone-deaf and largely bedridden old nobleman who had died two months after the newspaper's receipt of Junius's very last letter.

The name Christabella Dayrolles chimed distantly in Umber's memory. Yes. *She* was the subject he had been working on at Oxford in 1981. He could recall little of what he had learned about her and there was nothing in any of the books he had consulted to assist him. If he still had his boxful of Junius papers, it would be a different matter. But he did not.

'WHAT *DO* you know about her?' Sharp demanded when Umber explained the problem to him during their drive to Mayfair late that afternoon.

'Precious little. Her husband was a diplomat and a favourite of his godfather. Chesterfield's letters to Dayrolles are a treasure trove of information on politics and court life. Mrs Dayrolles was . . . Dayrolles's wife. Mother of his children. Keeper of the domestic flame. Stereotypical eighteenth-century female. Or not. I don't know.'

'But her handwriting resembles Junius's?'

'Yes. Superficially, I seem to remember. But Chesterfield as Junius? I could never buy that.'

'What about her husband, then?'

'Dayrolles? He's never been in the frame.'

'Why not?'

It was a good question. And there was a good answer, he felt certain, though he could not recall what it was. 'I'm going to have to go back into it, George. That's all I can tell you.'

'Well, maybe you won't have to, if Oliver Hall gives us a lead.'

'Yeah,' said Umber halfheartedly. 'Maybe.'

AT 58 KINGSLEY HOUSE, Oliver's presence and Marilyn's absence turned out to constitute more than a simple swap of hosts. The atmosphere was cooler, almost chill. There were fewer lights on. There was no music. The tone of everything was palpably different.

Oliver Hall had less hair than a couple of decades before and it was grey. He had developed a slight stoop, and was wearing razor-creased trousers, cashmere sweater, check shirt. He did not offer them a drink. They had his attention. That was all.

'I never expected to see either of you again,' he said when they had sat down. 'It's doubly surprising to see you together.'

'You've spoken to your former wife about our visit to her?' said Sharp.

'Oh yes. I'm fully apprised.'

'What about Sally's attempt to phone her just before she died?' put in Umber. 'Did Questred tell you about that?'

'You can assume I know everything I need to know.'

'She didn't try to phone you as well, did she?' asked Sharp.

'Not as far as I know. But she might have phoned me, got no answer and failed to leave a message.'

It was a precise and incontrovertible answer. It gave nothing away—except his reluctance to give anything away.

'Has Radd's murder made you doubt his guilt, Mr Hall?' Umber asked.

'No.'

'What about your son?' asked Sharp. 'How does he feel about it?'

'The same as I do, I imagine. We haven't actually discussed the matter. Jeremy clearly isn't concerned about it. Otherwise he'd have contacted me.'

'You don't see a lot of each other, then?'

'As much as we both want, Mr Sharp. Neither more nor less.'

'Relations with a step-parent can be difficult, I'm told. Maybe your remarriage put some distance between you.'

Hall smiled faintly. 'No. It didn't.'

'How does he get on with . . . Mrs Hall?'

'Very well, thank you.'

'There doesn't seem to be much you can tell us.'

'True, I'm afraid. But . . .' Hall spread his hands in a gesture hinting at conciliation. 'I accept your motives are honourable. I believe you're mistaken, though. Radd was responsible for my daughters' deaths. There's nothing any of us can do to bring them back. I've learned to accept that.' He fixed his gaze on Umber. 'Others must learn to accept their own loss. The idea that Sally was murdered . . . It's simply not credible.'

'I believe it,' said Umber, with quiet emphasis.

'So do I,' said Sharp.

'I see.' Hall looked at each of them in turn. 'Well, let me tell you what I have in mind. I have business in the City tomorrow and the day after. I can't get down to Marlborough until Tuesday night. It'll take time to talk all this through with Jane. And with Edmund, of course. We need to discuss your concerns calmly and rationally. If that leads any of us to question the official view of the case, I can promise you our full support in reopening the inquiry.'

'You can?'

'Absolutely.' Hall smiled at him, but the smile did not touch his eyes.

'HE THINKS he's got us where he wants us,' said Sharp as they rode down in the lift.

'And has he?'

'This trip to Marlborough he's oh-so-reasonably agreed to take is just for show. He'll come back after a couple of days and tell us they're all singing from the same hymn sheet: Radd guilty; Radd dead; end of story.'

They reached the van and climbed in. Sharp did not speak again until they were turning into Berkeley Square.

'I don't have to sit around twiddling my thumbs while he plays his little game, Umber. And I don't intend to. I'm going to Jersey.'

'You are?'

'No better time to size up Jeremy Hall than when his father isn't there to interfere.'

'When do we go?'

'*We* don't. *I* do. I'm driving down to Portsmouth tonight. I've already booked the ferry.'

'But . . . you couldn't have known what Oliver Hall was going to say.'

'I could have cancelled if he'd proved more open-minded than I expected. Doubted he would, though. And I was right.'

'What am I supposed to do?'

Sharp braked at traffic lights on Picadilly. 'Go see Sally's therapist. Knuckle down to your research on Mrs Dallyroll. And cover my tracks if Hall or the Questreds get in touch before we're ready for them.'

FOUR

Irritated though he was at Sharp for booking his passage to Jersey without telling him, Umber could not deny that it made sense for one of them to go while Oliver Hall was out of the way. And since he had not been entirely open with Sharp about his dealings with Marilyn Hall, he was in no position to complain.

He spent Monday morning at the British Library, ordering a further batch of books, then working his way through various entries in the *Dictionary of National Biography* in search of background information on the Dayrolles connection.

The known facts were tantalisingly meagre. Solomon Dayrolles's date of birth was unrecorded, but could hardly be later than 1710. His first diplomatic appointment was as secretary to the Ambassador to Vienna from 1727 to 1730. Dayrolles's uncle obtained the position for him through the influence of the young Lord Chesterfield, Solomon's godfather.

Chesterfield was at this period the great wit of Georgian political life. He had been a favourite of George II when the latter was still Prince of Wales, but offended the King after his accession by his attacks on the Prime Minister, Sir Robert Walpole. Chesterfield drifted into the opposition camp and the circles of the new Prince of Wales, George's hated son, Frederick.

In 1751, Dayrolles married the eighteen-year-old Christabella Peterson, daughter of an Irish colonel. The couple had four children. Chesterfield had by then retired from active politics, and his old age was afflicted by tragedy—the sudden death of a beloved son—and illness. When he died, in 1773, his godson-cum-friend was at his bedside.

Solomon Dayrolles died in March 1786, his widow, Christabella, in August 1791. William Cramp, in his book *Junius and His Works Compared with the Character and Writings of the Earl of Chesterfield*, was the first to suggest, in 1851, that Mrs Dayrolles might have written the letters of Junius at Chesterfield's dictation. Cramp's theory was generally ridiculed on account of the Earl's age and infirmity, the similarities between Mrs Dayrolles's handwriting and that of Junius dismissed as insignificant.

But the similarities were too striking to be rejected without further study. Umber could remember thinking that when he had inspected some examples for himself. He had learned what more he could about Christabella Dayrolles, though it had not been much. But where had he learned it *from*?

He read the two columns in the *DNB* entry for Solomon Dayrolles again. Then he recognised a long-forgotten name: The Dayrolles's eldest daughter, also called Christabella, had married the Hon. Townsend Ventry. There were some documents, categorised as the Ventry Papers, lodged in a county records office somewhere. Umber had gone to take a look at them. But where? He recalled an airless Midlands town on a hot afternoon. Derby. Nottingham. Leicester. Somewhere like that.

A glance at the Reading Room clock reminded him that he would be late for his appointment with Claire Wheatley if he did not stir himself. He made a hasty exit and headed for the street.

CLAIRE WHEATLEY shared a smart address in Wimpole Street with an acupuncturist and a reflexologist. The waiting room was empty and the door to the room beyond ajar. Somebody on the other side of it was playing back telephone messages. Umber half pushed, half knocked at the door and went in.

Claire Wheatley was sitting at a desk, with her feet propped on one end, munching a sandwich. Umber did not recognise her. Big-eyed and pixie-faced, she was dressed all in black: zip-fronted top, pleated miniskirt, tights and suede boots. Her spikily cropped hair was black as well. She switched off the answering machine and swung her legs to the floor.

'Sorry,' she said, swallowing a mouthful of sandwich. 'I'd planned to have finished this before you arrived. My noon appointment overran.' She packed the rest of the sandwich back in its wrapper and stood up. 'Do you want to sit down?' She gestured towards a pair of soft leather armchairs as she rounded the desk. 'What about a cup of tea or coffee?'

'I'm fine, thanks.' He lowered himself into one of the armchairs. 'It was good of you to agree to see me.'

Claire nodded thoughtfully, then sat down in the chair opposite him. 'What have you been doing since Sally died, David?'

'Teaching, mostly. In Prague for the last two or three years.'

'Alice seems to think you're out of work. Is that right?'

'Yes and no. Anyway, how I make a living is irrelevant.'

'Not really. You lost your wife five years ago. Now you've lost your job. Sounds like there's a gaping hole where most people your age have a family, a career and a fairly clear idea of the direction they're headed in.'

'A hole you think I'm trying to fill by chasing after Sally's ghost?'

'That's not exactly how I'd put it.'

'How would you put it, then?'

'Are you sure you want to know?'

'I can take it, Claire.' Umber forced a smile.

'OK. You left Sally because you were worn out by her. Maybe you'd have gone back to her eventually. We'll never know, will we? Because Sally's dead. She committed suicide, David. You know it. I know it. Those left behind tend to blame themselves for not doing enough to prevent a suicide. We've both blamed ourselves for not saving Sally. But if she didn't kill herself—well, we wouldn't be to blame, would we? We'd be off the hook.'

'You never suspected she might do away with herself, though, did you?'

'I was aware we were . . . treading a thin line. I thought we were the right side of it. I was wrong.'

'Why do you think she did it?'

'Because she'd spent eighteen years believing that Tamsin Hall wasn't dead, but couldn't go on believing it. Because she'd lost you for the sake of that fantasy. Because, in the end, she'd run out of hope. I'm not going to deny failing her. I should have done more. I should have intervened. But it's not always easy to spot the warning signs. The change in her behaviour was certainly sudden. You've spoken to Alice. You know what I mean.'

'She might have walked out on her appointment with you because she'd suddenly realised you weren't doing anything for her.'

'OK.' Claire smiled weakly. 'I guess I deserved that.' She leaned back in the chair. 'I admit our last meeting went badly.'

'The appointment before the one she broke, you mean?'

'No. I saw Sally the day she died.'

That stopped Umber in his tracks. 'Alice didn't mention that.'

'She doesn't know. I guess I was too ashamed to tell her. That's really why I agreed to see you. Even psychotherapists need to unburden themselves sometimes. And hearing how she was that day . . . may help you understand.'

'Go on.'

'Well, I was worried about her. I couldn't get Sally to speak to me on the phone. So, I went to Hampstead to see her. As it turned out, I spotted Sally sitting in a coffee shop near the tube station. I went in and tried to talk to her. It didn't go well. Truth is, her attitude annoyed me. I asked her about the broken appointment and she just dismissed the subject. Then I spotted the magazine she'd been reading. It was from my waiting room. My PLEASE DO NOT REMOVE sticker was still on the cover. That riled me. I asked if and when she was planning to return it. She got up, threw the magazine at me and walked out. "You don't need to worry about me any more," she shouted. Those were the last words she ever spoke to me.' Claire rubbed her hands together, then parted them in a gesture of helplessness. 'I'm sorry I let her go like that, David. Sorry I didn't . . . save her from herself.'

'Maybe something else really had cropped up. Maybe something else is why she was murdered.'

'The truth about what happened at Avebury?'

'Exactly.'

'Don't you think Oliver Hall would have uncovered that, given the lengths he went to?'

'Sally told you about the private detective he employed? Alan Wisby.'

Claire frowned. 'No. But he came to see me a few months *after* her death. I had no idea he'd been working for Hall from way back. He explained that Oliver Hall wanted to find out why Sally had killed herself in case it had some bearing on his daughters' deaths.'

That meant Oliver Hall had still been on the trail five years ago. Why? He had claimed only yesterday to have accepted Radd's guilt long since. 'What did you tell Wisby?'

'Nothing. He asked a few questions. When he realised he wasn't going to get anywhere, he gave up and left.'

'What sort of questions?'

'He wanted to know what had been on Sally's mind in the months before her death. He quoted a name at me. Asked if Sally had mentioned it. I can't remember it now. Somebody linked with the Avebury case, I suppose.'

'Nevinson?'

'He was the other witness, right? No. That wasn't it.'

'Sharp?'

'The policeman? No.'

Umber hesitated, then threw out one more name, sure in his own mind of the answer Claire would give. 'Griffin?'

'Yes,' she said, confounding him. 'That was it.'

HALF AN HOUR later, Umber was walking fast along South Street. He stood a better chance of finding Oliver Hall at home in the evening, but he could not wait till then. He recited to himself as he went the multiplying significances of what Claire Wheatley had told him. Oliver Hall did not believe Radd had killed his daughters. Wisby had been working for him all these years: probing, enquiring, ever seeking the answer. And the answer had something to do with Griffin.

The warmth had been restored to the flat in Kingsley House. The music was back, more wallpapery this time, soothingly electronic. Marilyn was wearing fluffy mules and a peach-coloured dressing gown, belted at the waist. The material of the gown was soft and clinging.

'This is a surprise,' she said. 'I thought you'd wait till Thursday.'

'I was looking for your husband. Sorry if I disturbed you.'

'That's OK.' She smiled. 'I was just taking a shower. Coffee? Tea? Something stronger?'

'No thanks. I won't stop.'

'That's a pity.'

'When will he be back?'

'Oliver? Hard to say. Six? Seven? I don't know. Do you want to leave a message for him?'

'You could tell him I've found out about Wisby.'

'Who?'

'The private detective he's hired.'

'First I've heard of it. How long has this man been working for Oliver?'

'More than twenty years, on and off.'

'And what's he been investigating? Or is that a stupid question?'

'Anything but, given how certain Oliver was that Radd was guilty.'

'I see,' said Marilyn. 'Well, I'll certainly tell him. Of course, he may deny employing the man.'

'I can prove it. Wisby approached a woman called Claire Wheatley, who was Sally's psychotherapist, on Oliver's behalf.'

'Perhaps Wisby was lying about working for him.'

'Somebody's lying.'

'If it's Oliver, he's not likely to stop now. Are you sure you want me to tell him you know about Wisby?'

Marilyn's casual cynicism regarding her husband's honesty was strangely disarming. 'Whose side are you on, Marilyn?'

'Whose do you think?'

'Not mine.'

'You could be wrong about that. Tell you what. I stand a much better chance than you do of finding out for certain whether Oliver's had this man Wisby on some kind of long-term retainer—and, if so, why. As a matter of fact, I *want* to find out. In case I'm one of the subjects he's been enquiring into. I'll pass on everything I learn to you.'

'Why would you do that?'

'Because I know nothing about this, David. And Oliver isn't supposed to have any secrets from me. If he has, well, I might need an ally.'

'Think you can trust me?'

'Yes.' She smiled, her eyes narrowing slightly. 'Of course I do.'

UMBER FELT both encouraged and disturbed by his visit to Kingsley House. He had a lead, of sorts, and a spy in the enemy camp whose reliability was questionable, to say the least. The Halls were pursuing different and conflicting strategies, for reasons Umber was a long way from understanding. He could not trust Marilyn. But he could not afford to ignore her.

Sensing he would not be able to concentrate on the books he had ordered at the British Library until he had explored at least one other avenue, he headed for Green Park tube station. His destination was Southwark, where Wisby Investigations Ltd operated out of an address in Blackfriars Road. He had learned this much from Claire Wheatley's telephone directory.

Number 171A Blackfriars Road was a first-floor office above a shoe-repair business. A young, yawning Asian woman was the sole occupant. She broke off from typing to tell him, 'They're all out.'

'I'm looking for Alan Wisby.'

'He's retired. Has been for nearly a year now. Monica Wisby's in charge.'

'When will she be back?'

'I don't know. Could be late. Do you want to leave a message?'

'For what it's worth, yeah.'

She grabbed a notepad and pen. 'What's your name?'

'Umber. David Umber. Monica's already—'

'You're David Umber?' She looked surprised. 'Can you prove it?'

Umber took out his wallet and placed his brand-new British Library reader's card on the desk.

The young woman looked at the photograph on it, then up at him. 'Monica said you might turn up, but I wasn't to hand it over or even mention we had it—unless you had some ID.' She opened the desk drawer and took out a sealed buff envelope. 'This is for you.'

His name was printed on the envelope and there was one sheet of paper inside. It was signed at the bottom *A. E. Wisby.*

Dear Mr Umber

Monica apprised me of Sharp's visit to my old place of business. He gave her your name and number for me to contact. I don't trust phones *or* policemen, so I'm willing to talk to you as long as you come alone. I'm on the Kennet and Avon, between Newbury and Kintbury. You'll recognise the boat's name when you see it.

UMBER MADE IT to Paddington in time to catch a crowded five o'clock commuter train that stopped at Kintbury station, which, he learned, was right next to the canal.

The train reached Kintbury at 6.30. The sun had set behind dark clouds, and a still, greying twilight filled the air. Umber lingered on the platform, watching the other passengers who had got off leave the station. The canal was separated from the railway line by the width of the small station car park. The train rumbled off into the dusk. The car park emptied. Umber was alone in the descending silence. He headed for the towpath.

Wisby was more or less certain to be aboard his boat come evening. But it had to be five or six miles to Newbury and it would be pitch-black long before Umber got there. He was pinning his hopes on finding Wisby's boat within the first couple of miles. There was none ahead that he could see, but that was not far, on account of the canal's winding route.

The silence was suddenly broken as a high-speed train roared into view beyond the wood-fringed fields to his left. The brightly lit carriages sped past in a barrage of sound—and were gone. He pressed on.

A few minutes later, rounding the next bend, Umber saw a humpback bridge ahead and the pale line of a track leading up from it across a sloping field on the other side of the canal. And then he saw the dark shape of a boat moored just beyond the bridge. He stepped up the pace.

There was no road in sight. The mooring was quiet and inaccessible. Umber saw no signs of life as he approached the boat. It was smartly painted and well maintained, roped fore and aft to stakes driven into the bank. Its name was lettered boldly on the prow: *Monica*.

Umber stepped into the bow area and voiced a hopeful 'Hello?' But the doors to the cabin were padlocked shut. Wisby was obviously not there.

Then, as he stepped back, the padlock suddenly fell to the deck with a thump. Umber stared at it. The ragged edges of the loop glinted up at him. Someone had cut through the lock, then replaced it loosely on the hasp.

He flicked the hasp back and pulled the doors open. The cabin was in darkness, the twilight seeping through the half-curtained windows scarcely penetrating the deep shadows. He felt for a light switch, but could not find one. His fumblings did chance on a torch, however, hanging just inside the doorway. He unhooked it and switched it on.

The torch beam revealed what seemed at first to be an immaculate interior of polished wood and burnished brass, with nothing out of place. Then the light fell on a slew of papers across the floor, at the foot of a three-drawer metal filing cabinet. Someone had ransacked the cabinet.

Umber was about to step into the cabin when he felt the boat lurch beneath him. As he turned, he saw a gap opening between the boat and the bank. A man in a black track suit was standing on the towpath, staring at him—a man he knew from their encounter in Yeovil as John Walsh.

Umber froze. Walsh must have broken into the boat, failed to find what he had been looking for, then lain in wait for Wisby. But it was not Wisby who had walked into his trap.

Walsh had untied the rope and shoved the boat away from the bank. But the rope at the other end of the vessel was still fastened, causing it to drift out diagonally across the canal. There was already too wide a gap to jump from the bow. Umber would have to reach the stern to get off.

'You shouldn't be here,' Walsh shouted. In the same instant, there were heavy footfalls on the roof of the cabin.

Umber turned just in time to see a burly, camouflage-clad figure looming above him. He glimpsed the blurred arc of a baseball bat swinging towards him and raised his arm to protect himself, the torch still clasped in his hand. The rubber barrel of the torch took the direct force of the blow. Then something else struck the back of his head. And the rest was darkness.

UMBER WAS COLD. God, he was cold, shivering as he woke to a damp patter of rain on his face. Slowly, wincing as a pain throbbed through his head, he pulled himself up into a sitting position.

The night was inkily black. He could see virtually nothing, but knew he was still aboard the *Monica*. The boat was rocking gently beneath him, the cabin doors creaking on their hinges. And there was another sound, of wood thumping dully against wood. The boat must be adrift, he reasoned.

He clambered awkwardly to his feet, his every movement slowed by dizzying pulses of pain. He put his hand behind his head and felt a tender, oozing lump. There was that thumping again. And he could make out the shadow of something beyond and above the cabin. A lock gate, perhaps? Yes. That had to be it. The *Monica* had drifted down to the next lock.

He felt his way round the bulwark to where he had boarded and reached out blindly into the darkness. Nothing. He scrabbled around the deck until he found the broken padlock, tossed this in the direction of where he thought the bank should be and heard it fall to earth rather than into water. He pulled the left-hand cabin door wide open and, grasping its handle, stretched out further into the void, flapping his arm in search of a hold. Still nothing. He slumped back against the door. It was hopeless. He was going to have to phone for assistance. He reached into his pocket for his mobile. Not there. It must have slipped out onto the deck. He lowered himself to his knees and felt around for it in the small bow area. Then he understood. It was not there because Walsh had taken it.

To get off the boat, he was going to have to reach the stern. He could go through the cabin, but the aft door was bound to be locked. There was a ledge either side of the cabin, Umber vaguely recalled, but it was desperately narrow. The roof was a better option. He grasped what felt like a rail fixed to the roof, put one foot on the bulwark and pulled himself up.

In the same instant, the boat bounced against something, pitching Umber forward. His hand slipped from the rail. He lost his balance and fell.

It was the ground he hit, not water. The *Monica* had drifted into the bank. A jarred shoulder and a red mist of pain were worth it to feel grass beneath him. He levered himself slowly upright and blundered forward until he reached the jutting balance beam of the lock gate. He leaned against it and looked at the luminous dial of his wristwatch. It was a few minutes before nine.

The shaly surface of the towpath crunched beneath his feet as he took a few tentative steps away from the beam. Logically, if he kept to the path, with the canal to his right, he would make it to Newbury in the end.

HE NEVER MADE it to Newbury. A slow, stumbling mile or so later, he reached another lock, and a road bridge over the canal. He was feeling worse now, nausea and dizziness sweeping over him ever more frequently. Seeing the lights of a house a short distance along the road, he headed towards it.

The couple whose door Umber knocked at responded with genuine concern, never querying his explanation that he had injured himself in a fall on the towpath. The woman disinfected his wound as best she could, then her husband drove him to hospital. He was swiftly processed through Casualty. Concussion, the doctor told him after stitching the gash at the back of his head, should not be taken lightly. They would have to take him in for observation.

A nurse gave him some painkillers once he was on the ward. Maybe they were more than just painkillers. He certainly knew very little after taking them until morning. Even then, connected thought seemed beyond him. He knew he should feel angry about what had happened, but relief that he was still alive blotted out everything else.

The doctor came to see him around midday with the news that his X-rays had shown no abnormalities. Since he was conscious, coherent and complaining of nothing worse than a headache, he could leave, provided a friend or relative came to pick him up.

This was easier stipulated than accomplished. Larter had no car. Sharp was in Jersey. Umber considered phoning his parents, but soon rejected the idea. In the end, he could think of only one person to ask.

'ARE YOU SURE you're well enough to be discharged?' was Alice's less than encouraging greeting when she arrived several hours later. 'You certainly don't look it. What happened to you?'

'Long story.'

'Yeah? Well, judging by the amount of traffic heading into London on the M4, I'll have plenty of time to hear it. Let's go.'

Umber was happy to tell her the truth in the hope it would persuade her he really was on to something. In that, however, he was to be disappointed.

'Why didn't you tell the police about this?'

'They'd probably have arrested me for breaking into Wisby's boat.'

'Which you didn't do.'

'No, Alice, I didn't.'

'And where is Wisby?'

'Haven't a clue.'

'But you went to the canal basically because he invited you?'

'Yes. You can ask Claire about Wisby. She'll vouch for his existence.'

'Maybe I'll do that.'

'You think I made all this up?'

'I don't know, David. I just don't know.'

IT WAS NEARLY six o'clock by the time Alice delivered him to 45 Bengal Road, Ilford, and Larter was not at home. Umber had little doubt as to where the old man could be found, but Alice, having accepted responsibility for his welfare, insisted on driving him to the Sheepwalk to check on the point.

Larter was installed with a pint at his favourite fireside table. He surprised Umber by appearing pleased to see him, though he added, 'You look like death warmed up.' He volunteered nothing more in Alice's presence, seeming to sense her ingrained suspicion of policemen, even retired ones. She declined a drink and did not linger.

'Do something for me, will you?' she said as Umber walked her out to her car. 'Take more care.'

'Who was she?' Larter demanded as soon as Umber returned to the pub.

'An old friend of my wife's.'

'Did you tell her George was going to Jersey?'

'Of course not.'

'Did you tell anyone?'

'No. Why?'

'George is in trouble.'

'What sort of trouble?'

'The Jersey police stopped him as he was leaving the ferry last night and searched the van. They found a bag of heroin inside each wheel arch.'

'You're joking.'

'Wish I was, boy. The duty solicitor who got his case phoned me a few hours ago. George was up before the magistrates this morning. They remanded him in custody on smuggling charges.

'They fitted him up.'

'Someone did, yeah. Planted the drugs in transit, then tipped off Customs at St Helier. That's how I read it, anyhow. I don't suppose I'd be far off in guessing that whoever that someone was had something to do with whatever scrape you got into last night?'

'No, you wouldn't.'

'I'd better give you the message George's solicitor asked me to pass on to you, then, from George. You're not to go to Jersey under any circumstances.'

'Not go? I can't just . . . abandon him.'

'It's what he's telling you to do. I reckon he thinks it'd be too dangerous.' Larter took a thoughtful sup of beer. 'Of course, George never has been the best judge of what's good for him. So . . .' He looked expectantly at Umber. 'When do you leave?'

FIVE

Umber had never been to Jersey before. The view he had from the taxi during the drive from the airport to St Helier was of an undulating, daffodil-spattered English landscape, with French place names and architectural styles grafted on—a pretty island, and a small one: that had been apparent from the air. Oliver Hall had settled there because of its tax-haven status, but maybe he had found another kind of haven in the process.

The approach to St Helier was along a busy main road round a wide, south-facing bay, with the rooftops of the town, the lofty ramparts of Fort Regent and the piers and derricks of the harbour growing ever closer ahead. Umber had asked to be taken straight to the offices of Le Templier & Burnouf of Hill Street, where he hoped to learn all he could about Sharp's prospects. He had a suspicion they were far from bright.

It was lunchtime. The pavements were crowded, the traffic thick. The taxi stopped and started and eventually reached Umber's destination: a brass-plaqued legal practice in an elegant Georgian building.

Umber had half hoped that Sharp's solicitor, Nigel Burnouf, might agree to see him there and then, but it was not to be. The receptionist told him to come back at two thirty.

He filled the hour and a bit this left him with by booking himself into the nearest hotel—the Pomme d'Or in Liberation Square—and doing a small amount of research on the Halls. Oliver was not listed in the Jersey telephone directory, which came as no surprise. But Jeremy's entry gave an address in Le Quai Bisson, St Aubin, an address he shared with Rollers Sail & Surf School. The map supplied in Umber's room showed St Aubin to be a village a few miles back round the coast. And the timetable in the bus station right opposite the hotel promised a half-hourly service.

Back at Le Templier & Burnouf promptly at two thirty, Umber was sent straight into Nigel Burnouf's office.

He was a plump, placid, middle-aged man with sandy hair, gold-framed spectacles and a reassuring air of unflustered efficiency.

'I was a little surprised when Janet said I was to expect you, Mr Umber,' he said after they had shaken hands and sat down. 'Didn't you get my message?'

'Oh, I got it, yes.'

'And proceeded to ignore it. Well, I confess the possibility you might do so had occurred to me. As I suspect it has to Mr Sharp.'

'I'm here to do whatever it takes to get him out of trouble.'

'That's rather a tall order, I'm afraid. He was caught red-handed.'

'You do understand he was definitely framed, don't you?'

'It's what he tells me. But facts are facts. It would help me if you could suggest who might have framed him—and why.'

'Hasn't George come up with a name?'

'No. Could you enlighten me, perhaps?'

Sharp had said nothing about the Halls. In the circumstances Umber could only follow Sharp's lead. 'There's nothing I can tell you at the moment. I need to make a few enquiries.'

'Thus exposing yourself to those risks Mr Sharp is so anxious you shouldn't run?'

'I'll be careful.'

'Do you want me to tell him that? Or will you do so yourself? I can arrange for you to visit him.'

'I'll hold off on that, thanks. In fact . . .'

'You'd rather he didn't know you were here?'

'Well . . . yes. He'd only worry about me. How is he?'

'Much as you'd expect. His problem is time. It hangs heavy. And is likely to go on doing so. He'll reappear before the magistrates next week, when a further, lengthier remand in custody is more or less inevitable.'

'No chance of bail?'

'Realistically, none. Drug smugglers are notorious for jumping bail.'

'And when will the case come to trial?'

'Not for several months, at least.' Burnouf leaned forward. 'The best way to help your friend in the meantime, Mr Umber, is to let me have any information that's even marginally relevant.'

'I do have something that might help. This.' Umber took a sealed envelope out of his pocket and placed it on Burnouf's desk. 'A statement, I suppose you'd call it. My record of certain recent events not unconnected with what's happened to George. It will give you some material for his defence.'

'You want me to read it?'

'No. Not unless . . . I should happen to meet with a fatal accident. Until then, hold on to the statement for me.'

Burnouf's eyes widened. 'Aren't you being rather melodramatic?'

'I hope so. But I have good reason to doubt it. So just in case . . .'

'I see.' Burnouf picked up the envelope. 'Very well. If those are your instructions.' He took a roll of Sellotape out of his desk drawer, tore off a few strips and stuck them over the flap and seams of the envelope. 'Sign across the seals, would you, Mr Umber?' He proffered a pen. Umber obliged. 'Your receipt.' Burnouf hastily filled in a form and handed it over. 'All done.'

THE NUMBER 15 bus dropped Umber in the centre of St Aubin, a smart, bustling seaside town clustered round a harbour filled with yachts and motorboats clinking at their moorings in the late-afternoon sun. He asked directions of a passer-by and was pointed along the harbourside boulevard to the first turning.

Le Quai Bisson was a narrow side street leading to several old stone warehouses. The doors of Rollers Sail & Surf were firmly closed, the small office to the rear locked. The place had a pre-season look about it, with last year's tide tables still displayed in the office window.

A steep flight of steps led up beside the warehouse to a higher road. Halfway up the steps was the entrance to the flat into which the roof area of the building had been converted. Umber could hear the bass output of an amplifier within. He took an optimistic stab at the bell.

The door opened to a gust of heavy metal and a blank stare from a slightly built young woman dressed in black combat trousers and a purple T-shirt. Dark, straggly hair fell either side of her narrow face, in which a vermilion slash of lipstick was the only trace of colour. The shadows beneath her eyes and the pallor of her skin did not suggest that sailing and surfing were recreations she often indulged in.

'Hi,' she said with a lopsided grin.

'Jeremy in?'

'Not right now. Is this business?'

'Not exactly. He knows me from a long time back. I'm David Umber.'

'Umber?' She looked genuinely incredulous. 'Fuck me. The Shadow Man.'

'What?'

'Never thought you'd show up. Bloody hell. I'm Chantelle, by the way.' The name went some way, Umber supposed, to explain the hint of a French accent. 'Do you want to come in?'

'OK. Thanks.' He stepped into a narrow hallway and was led into a large lounge-diner-bedroom. There were dormer windows to either side and a Catherine-wheel window set in the gable at the front of the warehouse, through which there was a sparkling blue glimpse of the harbour.

'Sorry the place is such a mess. Fancy a tea?'

'Sure.'

'I've just made some.' She stepped into the kitchen to fetch her mug and fill one for him. 'There you go.'

She cleared a drift of magazines and CDs from the couch, so that he could sit down, then plonked herself on the end.

'What's this about Shadow Man?' he asked.

'Oh, it's what Jem calls you. On account of your name. Umber. From the Latin for shadow, isn't it?'

'Yes. It is. But I'm surprised . . . Jem . . . talks about me at all.'

'Are you really surprised? I mean, it was quite a thing, what happened to his sisters. It stays with him. He likes to talk about it sometimes. Can't stop himself, to tell the truth. Not that I want him to.'

'How long have you known him?'

'About six months.' She smiled. 'Best six months of my life.'

'That's nice to hear.'

'Yeah.' She looked bashful. 'So, tell me—' She broke off as the throaty roar of a motorbike engine half-drowned the music. 'Hold on. That sounds like Jem now.' She leaned across the bed for a view through the nearest window. 'Yeah. Thought so.'

A few moments later the front door opened and a tall, broad-shouldered man entered, then froze in midstride at the sight of Umber.

Jeremy Hall was barely recognisable as the small boy Umber had first seen at Avebury twenty-three years previously. He was in his early thirties now, a tanned and muscular figure in red and black motorcycling leathers, his fair hair curlier than in childhood, his eyes a greyer shade of blue. There was certainty and a simmer of anger in his steely gaze.

'Guess who,' chirruped Chantelle.

Jeremy set down his crash helmet and gauntlets on the hall table, then stepped slowly into the room.

Umber rose cautiously from the couch. 'I'm sorry not to have phoned ahead,' he ventured. 'This must be a bit of a shock for you.'

'Aren't you going to say hello, Jemmy?' put in Chantelle. 'It's the—'

'Shadow Man.' Jeremy's voice was cold and hard. 'I know. David Umber.' He nodded. 'I've been expecting him.'

Chantelle blinked in surprise. 'Expecting him? You never said.'

Jeremy took a coin out of his pocket and flicked it onto the bed. 'Do me a favour, sugar. Pop down to the shop and buy an *Evening Post*.'

Chantelle blushed slightly. She picked up the coin and walked out of the room, leaving the two men alone together.

'The old man warned me you might pull something like this.'

'I only want to—'

'Dig up a load of stuff that's best forgotten.'

'It's far from forgotten by you—according to Chantelle.'

'Leave her out of it. Look, there's nothing I can tell you about Sally.'

'I don't know what your father said, but—'

'Here's the deal. The only deal you'll get from me. I'll meet you in St Helier tomorrow afternoon at La Frégate. It's a café on the seafront, shaped like a capsized boat. You can't miss it. Be there at four.'

'All right. But why can't we—?'

'*Shut up.*' Jeremy levelled a threatening finger at Umber. 'We're playing to my rules, not yours, OK. It's tomorrow or nothing.'

'OK.' Umber tried to sound calmer than he felt. Why his visit had so enraged Jeremy he did not understand. But he could imagine that rage tipping over into violence all too easily. 'Tomorrow afternoon it is.'

W HEN U MBER woke the next morning, having slept for ten solid hours, he felt, if not quite his old self, then at least a close approach to it. He stumbled into the bathroom, emerging half an hour later showered, shaved and alert. There was not even the trace of a headache, although the stitches in his wound tugged at his scalp occasionally to remind him of his tangle with Walsh and baseball-bat man.

He pulled back the curtains to confront a wide blue sky across which a strong wind was blowing fluffy bundles of cloud. Only then, with sunlight filling the room, did he notice, as he turned away from the window, the envelope that had been slid beneath his door.

It was blank. Inside was a slim mail-order catalogue, advertising 'Jersey's premier antiquarian and secondhand books dealer'—folded open at the page devoted to the eighteenth century.

Q UIRES , of Halkett Place, St Helier (established 1975, proprietor Vernon Garrard), was clearly the place of first resort for Jersey bibliophiles: a multi-roomed glory hole of Dickens, Scott, Austen, Defoe, Pepys, Shakespeare, *et al*. When Umber arrived midmorning, there were only a couple of other customers, none of them in the main room, where Garrard was conducting a telephone conversation at the cluttered cash desk in the corner.

Umber had no idea who might have slipped Garrard's catalogue under his door, but he knew what he had been supposed to infer. Junius was why he had been sent to Quires. There could be no other reason. Just as there could be no question of ignoring the clue he had been supplied with.

The eighteenth-century shelf was an unremarkable if well-bound selection of Pope, Swift, Hume and Dr Johnson. Umber fingered his way slowly along the spines. Then he heard the telephone go down behind him and the sound of a chair being pushed back. He turned to find Garrard bearing soft-footedly down on him.

A balding, round-shouldered man of sixty or so, Garrard wore the dusty tweed and corduroy uniform of his trade and the resigned expression of one well aware that browsers outnumber serious customers in the secondhand books world by a depressing margin. 'Can I help you?' he enquired.

'I was wondering if you had any editions of the *Letters of Junius*.'

'Junius? No. I'm afraid not. He doesn't crop up very often. I had a nice Junius in a few months back.' He smiled weakly. 'Snapped up, I'm afraid.'

'Was that a first edition?'

'Er, no. Second, as I recall. A two-volume set.'

'The 1773, you mean?'

'Do I? Probably. It sounds as if you'd know better than I would.'

'How was it bound?'

'Handsomely, if slightly unusually. Most Juniuses are in calfskin, but this was vellum.'

'If you don't mind my asking, how did you come by it?'

'Rather oddly, as it happens. I never even knew I had it until a customer asked to buy it. My brother Bernard sometimes minds the shop for me. He must have taken it into stock. We have sellers as well as buyers who call in. Bernard can be infuriatingly neglectful of record-keeping, I'm afraid.'

'So, its origin is a mystery.'

'You could say so, yes.'

'And the person who bought it?'

Unaccountably, Garrard loosed a dry but hearty laugh. His eyes twinkled mischievously. 'Oh dear, oh dear. Here we go again. Your name would be Umber, I assume.'

'What?' Umber stared at the bookseller in astonishment. 'How do you know that?'

'I've been down the Junius road with a Mr Wisby only last week.'

'*Wisby?*'

'Yes. He phoned me this morning and said you might call round. This is an entertaining charade, though a baffling one from my point of view. Still, I've no wish to go on acting as go-between. If I give you his number, I trust that'll be the last I hear of the matter.'

UMBER RANG Wisby from the first call box he came to after leaving Quires. The promptness of Wisby's answer suggested he had been expecting the call.

'Mr Wisby?'

'The very same.' The susurrous voice was unmistakable, even after more than twenty years.

'I thought you didn't trust phones.'

'Needs must. Besides, communicating with you by letter didn't turn out very satisfactorily, did it?'

'What the hell's going on?'

'Not a hundred per cent certain. But I probably know more than you do. If you want to talk about it, join me in Royal Square in ten minutes.'

LESS THAN TEN minutes later, Umber was in a flagstoned piazza overlooked by the handsome nineteenth-century buildings housing Jersey's parliament and principal court. On a bench in the centre of the square, reading a newspaper, was a lean man in a brown raincoat. He had to be Alan Wisby.

He looked much as Umber remembered, though greyer, in skin as well as hair, and perhaps even thinner. There was a grizzled moustache, too, which he might or might not have previously sported. He looked up as Umber approached and nodded an unsmiling greeting. Umber sat down beside him.

'Have you read yesterday's *Jersey Evening Post*, Mr Umber?'

'No.'

'Tiny article on page five took my eye. Drug smuggler caught coming off the ferry from Portsmouth Monday night was up before the beak. Name of Sharp. George Sharp.'

'I'm not here to play games, Mr Wisby.'

'Good. Though I'm told someone's been playing games with *Monica*. My narrowboat, I mean. She was set loose from her mooring on the Kennet and Avon Canal Monday night. Busy old night, Monday, it seems.'

'I went down to Kintbury at *your* invitation. You weren't on the boat. Two people were waiting for you, though.'

'I spotted them earlier in the day and decided to make myself scarce. I didn't set you up, Mr Umber, if that's what you thought.'

'I didn't, actually.'

'Good.'

'They'd broken into the boat and been through your files.'

'They were welcome to. I'd already removed what they were looking for.'

'And what was that?'

'Well, that's the sixty-four-thousand-dollar question, isn't it?'

'Are you going to answer it?'

'I'm going to try. Where shall we begin?'

'Oliver Hall. What's he been paying you to do?'

'Nothing. I took a look at the Avebury case for Hall back in 1982. That was the last time I had any dealings with the man.'

'I know that's not true. You told Claire Wheatley—'

'I lied.' Wisby smiled fleetingly. 'Loose ends have always niggled at me, Mr Umber. When I handed over the day-to-day running of the business to Monica, I revisited a few cases that had left me dissatisfied. Avebury was one of them, and your wife's sudden death brought it to the front of the queue. I thought her psychotherapist likelier to cooperate if I led her to believe I was working for Hall. Didn't get much out of her, though. However, I've made some headway recently. Thanks to Junius.'

'You had a letter too, did you?'

'The same one as Sharp received, I assume. "It is the misfortune of your life that you should never have been acquainted with the truth with respect to the Marlborough murderers." Etcetera, etcetera. Familiar?'

'Word for word.'

'Sharp had you down as prime suspect, I take it.'

'Initially.'

'That's the trouble with policemen. They think in straight lines. Of course, he lacked a crucial piece of information, one I turned up five years ago. The letter brought it centre stage.'

'What might that be?'

'All in good time, Mr Umber. Let's not rush our fences. I was over here last week double-checking a few points. I hadn't planned to do anything on the strength of my conclusions straight away, but the arrival of the heavy mob canalside forced my hand. That's why I'm back. What about you?'

'George was intending to speak to Jeremy Hall. Someone went to considerable lengths to stop him. So, I reckoned I ought to pay Jeremy a call. But how did you know I was on the island?'

'It stood to reason, with Sharp here as well. I tried a few hotels and struck lucky at the Pomme d'Or. Have you seen Jeremy yet?'

'Yesterday afternoon.'

'How was he?'

'Not a happy bunny. Threw me out.'

'Understandable. He's under a lot of pressure. I should know, since I'm the one applying it. That's why I steered you towards Quires. So we could get together before you queered the pitch for me.'

'Who bought the vellum-bound Junius? Was it Jeremy?'

'Yes. I had to pay Garrard over the odds for an unreadable history of Jersey before he'd give me a description of the customer, but there was no doubt who it fitted. My deal now with Jeremy is that he hands over the Junius and in return I don't tell his father he stirred up all this trouble for his family by sending anonymous letters to Sharp and me and God knows who else.'

'Jeremy sent them?'

'I think his purchase of the book proves he did. And the book proves something else—if it's authentic. That's where you come in. You'll be able to say for certain if it's the copy Griffin promised to show you at Avebury.'

'Well, yes, I can. But—'

'How did it get to Jersey, hey?' Wisby turned to look Umber in the eye. 'And what does it mean? I think I know. I think I have it all worked out.'

'Planning to let me in on the secret?'

'Yes—as soon as we have the book.'

'Tell me now.'

Wisby shook his head. 'Too risky. You might try to do your own deal with Jeremy and cut me out. Got a meeting arranged with him, have you?'

'Yes. I have.'

'Where and when?'

'A café on the seafront. La Frégate. Four o'clock.'

'That's where and when *I'm* meeting him.' Wisby laughed. 'Quite a comedian, isn't he? He thinks we're in cahoots. As we are now, I suppose.'

'Are we?'

'Might as well be. Don't you reckon?'

PARTNERING UP with Wisby did not leave Umber with a pleasant taste in the mouth. But he could see, when he reviewed matters back at the hotel, that they stood a better chance of extracting the truth from Jeremy Hall by joining forces. Theirs was only a temporary alliance, Umber told himself. Once they had learned the truth—whatever it was—different rules would apply.

La Frégate was a café housed in an artful representation of the inverted hull of a wooden ship, beached on St Helier's breezy seafront. The chill edge to the breeze had driven its few customers inside, with the solitary exception of Alan Wisby. He was sitting at one of the outdoor tables, hunched over a cigarette and a cup of tea, when Umber arrived. There was nearly a quarter of an hour to go till their appointment with Jeremy Hall, but beating Wisby to any rendezvous was clearly next to impossible.

'Couldn't wait, hey?' said Wisby by way of greeting.

'Like you, it seems.'

'No, no. I got here early for the sea air.'

Umber went into the café and bought a coffee. By the time he came back out, a way to wrong-foot Wisby had presented itself appealingly to his mind.

He sat down and looked at the man. 'You can tell me your theory now.'

'No, no. Not until the books are in our hands.'

508 | ROBERT GODDARD

'It's too late for me to cut my own deal with Jeremy now, isn't it? So there's no need for you to hold out on me.'

Wisby squinted at Umber in the dazzling sunlight. 'No need for me not to, either.'

'Oh, but there is. Particularly if you want to be able to rely on my say-so as to whether the Junius he brings with him is the one Griffin promised to show me at Avebury. And that's central to your theory, isn't it?'

'Yes,' Wisby reluctantly agreed.

'So you need to be certain. Absolutely certain. And for that you need to give me something in advance.'

'Don't you trust me, Mr Umber?'

'Not at all.'

Wisby drew on his cigarette. 'Well, it's good to know where we stand, I suppose.' He sat in thoughtful silence for a moment. 'All right. I'll tell you my theory. Griffin *is* central. Why didn't he turn up at Avebury?'

'I don't know. It's a total mystery.'

'Perhaps not. If he *did* turn up.'

'What do you mean?'

'Donald Collingwood was already dead when I went back over the case five years ago, so I went to see his widow. Seems Collingwood came into money straight after the Miranda Hall inquest. Not a fortune but a tidy sum. He spun his missus a yarn about a lucky bet, but she never believed him. Just like she never believed he drove through Avebury on the 27th of July, 1981.'

'What?'

'Seems there was no reason for him to have been on that road. And yet he came forward three weeks into the inquiry to account for the car that followed the van. Don't you see? He was put up to it. Paid . . . to cover Griffin's tracks.'

'Griffin?'

'He was the car driver, not Collingwood. Griffin saw what happened and, good citizen that he was, set off after the van. Well, I think he caught up with it—or was allowed to, once the driver realised he was being tailed. I think Griffin was murdered to stop him giving the police any evidence.'

'What about a body?'

'I've checked the records carefully. There were no unclaimed corpses within any feasible radius of Avebury in late July of '81. And no missing-person report anywhere for anyone called Griffin.'

'Sounds like you've gone a long way to proving yourself wrong, then.'

'Not if his body was carefully disposed of.'

'Come off it. You're stretching.'

'Wait till you hear what Jeremy Hall has to tell us, Mr Umber. The key is how the book got from Avebury twenty-three years ago to Jersey a few months ago. I reckon—'

'Mr Umber?' Both men turned at the call. 'One of you two Mr Umber?' It was the serving girl leaning out through the door of the café. 'There's someone on the phone for you.'

Umber hurried inside. The girl pointed towards the telephone at one end of the counter. He picked it up. 'Hello?'

'That you, Shadow Man?' Jeremy Hall's voice was slightly slurred, as if he had been drinking.

'Yes. It's me. Why aren't you here?'

'Wisby with you, is he?'

'Yes. As you arranged. I repeat: why aren't you here?'

'I decided we ought to meet somewhere more private, the old man's place. With him and Marilyn away, it's nice and quiet. I'm there now. Wisby knows where it is. Come on over.'

'OK. But, Jeremy, you ought to know Wisby and I aren't—'

'Save it. I don't want to hear. Remember the day we first met?'

'Of course.'

'There was a kestrel above us. I saw it. Turning and turning in the sky. Predator or prey. We're one or the other. You want your Junius, Shadow Man? You come and find him.'

'I SMELL A RAT,' said Wisby as he accelerated his hire car well beyond the sedate island-wide speed limit of forty miles per hour. 'If he's planning to play some kind of trick on us . . .'

'I thought you had him where you wanted him.'

'I do. But despite that he's calling the shots. Which is worrying.'

They turned inland halfway round the bay and headed north along a winding road through a tree-filled valley—Waterworks Valley, according to Wisby, named on account of its several reservoirs. Sunlight sparkled on the still blue water and the bright yellow daffodils in the roadside meadows.

As they rounded a bend, a gated driveway led off to the left, climbing through landscaped grounds towards a large house set among trees. A sign identified it as Eden Holt.

'This is it,' said Wisby. He pulled up in front of the gates, lowered his window and pressed a button set next to an intercom grille on a post. 'Let's see if he's going to let us in.'

He was—without even bothering to confirm it was them. The gates swung slowly open. Wisby drove through.

The house commanded an expansive view of the rolling Jersey country-side. An elegantly meticulous re-creation of a three-storeyed Queen Anne mansion, with porticoed entrance, mullioned windows and high, slender chimneys, its grey stone glistened opulently in the sunshine.

The drive ran between the house and a wide, oval lawn to a triple garage. In front of the garage stood Jeremy's motorbike, propped at an angle, sun-light shimmering on its petrol tank. Wisby stopped short of the balustraded steps that led up to the front door, and they climbed out into crystalline air and suspended silence, which the slamming of the car doors pierced like muffled gunshots. As the two men started up the steps, they saw that the broad, green dolphin-knockered door was ajar. Wisby pushed it open, giving them a view of the hall—a vast chequerboard of black and white marble tiles leading to a curving staircase. Doors stood open to ground-floor rooms on either side. But Jeremy did not step out of any of them.

'Where is he?' muttered Wisby. 'What's he—?'

'Look,' Umber cut in. 'Look, man.'

Umber's gaze had drifted to a console table against the wall. On it was a silver tray bearing two small books, held together by a rubber band. The books' smooth white covers identified their binding as vellum. And the gold-lettering on their spines identified them as unquestionably unique.

'That's them, isn't it?' Wisby asked, glancing at Umber.

Umber nodded. There could be no doubt. There had only ever been one vellum-bound, gilt-titled Junius, specially prepared to the author's specification in 1773. 'At last,' Umber murmured. 'At long— What was that?'

He whirled round at a sound behind him: a sharp, metallic ping. Almost at once, there was a second ping and, this time, he saw what had caused it. A small pebble struck the roof of the car and bounced off.

Umber rushed down the steps onto the driveway and looked up. There were dormer windows set in the grey-slated roof, their lower halves obscured by a parapet running round the edge of the roof. In the centre of the parapet, was a pediment. Jeremy Hall was leaning nonchalantly against its sloping left-hand side.

'Spotted what's waiting for you in the hall, Shadow Man?' he called.

'Yes,' Umber replied.

'Take them. They're yours.'

'We want more than the books,' shouted Wisby as he caught up with Umber. 'You know what my terms are.'

'Oh yes,' Jeremy shouted back. 'I know.'

'Come down. Let's talk. Like we agreed.'

'Like you demanded, you mean. Remember the kestrel, Shadow Man? Predator or prey. We're one or the other. Never both.' He seemed to look beyond them, into the distance. 'There's so much air up here. So much sky. And everything's so very, very simple.'

'Come down,' shouted Wisby.

'All right,' Jeremy responded. 'I will.'

In that second, Umber knew what Jeremy was going to do. Umber stepped forward. And so did Jeremy. Out into the empty air beyond the parapet. Out into a place he could see so clearly. Out—and down.

Umber closed his eyes a fraction of a second before Jeremy hit the ground. When he opened them he knew what he would see. The tide of blood seeping from the smashed body declared the death as an unalterable fact. As it had been for the sister, so it was now for the brother.

Umber thought of Jane Hall, standing in the cemetery above Marlborough, mourning her daughters and comforting herself with the knowledge that at least she still had a living, breathing son. Soon, all too soon, she would have that comfort snatched away from her.

Umber had done nothing to save the daughters. And now his action, for reasons he did not properly understand, had destroyed the son.

'Oh God,' he murmured. 'Oh dear God.'

The car engine burst suddenly into life. Umber looked round and saw Wisby reversing the vehicle away from him. It bumped up onto the lawn, then Wisby slammed it into forward gear, swerved round onto the drive and accelerated towards the gates.

Umber's reactions were addled by shock. He could not comprehend what was happening. Where was Wisby going? What in God's name did he think he was doing?

The probable answer hit Umber like a blow. He ran across the drive and up the steps to the open front door.

In the hall, on the console table, the silver tray stood empty.

SIX

U mber walked south along the Waterworks Valley road through the encroaching dusk. After two or three miles, he reached the village of Millbrook, where there was a call box. He went in, dialled 999 and asked for the police.

'There's been a suicide at Eden Holt, a house in Waterworks Valley,' he said, ignoring requests for his name and location. Then he rang off.

He crossed the road and waited at the bus stop. He knew he was on the route of the half-hourly service to the airport. And he knew for a rock-solid certainty that the airport was where Wisby would have headed, fearing an encounter with Umber if he lingered on the island. He had what he wanted: the vellum-bound Junius. And no doubt he was determined to keep it.

THERE WAS NO SIGN of Wisby in the check-in area at the airport. A word at the information desk revealed that there were several flights to various British destinations he could already have left on. Umber prowled the car park, inspecting lookalike cars until he found one whose rear tyres were smeared with mud and grass from a recent lawn skid. That clinched it. The bird had flown. He suspected that Wisby had intended all along to spring some kind of double-cross as soon as the Junius's authenticity had been confirmed. A glance at the books from ten feet away was hardly sufficient for Umber to do that, but Wisby had clearly decided to settle for it in the suddenly and savagely altered circumstances.

Umber had been so close to laying his hands on the fabled special copy of the 1773 Junius, and to reading what Griffin had described to him twenty-three years previously as an illuminating inscription, that he could scarcely believe he had let the opportunity slip through his fingers.

The galling thought of Wisby studying the inscription over an in-flight drink suddenly alerted Umber to the one question above all he should have put to Vernon Garrard, proprietor of Quires. He rushed back into the terminal building and made for the payphones.

It was past the shop's closing time, but the recorded message gave an out-of-hours number to try. Umber rang it—and Garrard answered.

'David Umber here, Mr Garrard.'

A sigh. 'I rather thought our business was concluded, Mr Umber.'

'There's a question I forgot to ask. What was the inscription in the Junius?'

'Inscription? There wasn't one.'

'No inscription? You're sure?'

'I'm sure there *wasn't*. But as to whether there *had been* . . .'

'What do you mean?'

'The flyleaves had been torn out of both volumes, Mr Umber.'

UMBER BOOKED a seat on a morning flight to Gatwick and took the bus back to St Helier. He should have phoned Larter and warned him of his return, but could not bring himself to, knowing that, if he did, he would have to explain why he was leaving Jersey. It was not as if he had made any progress towards securing Sharp's release from prison.

Jane Questred and Oliver Hall would certainly travel to Jersey as soon as the news of Jeremy's death reached them. Umber must not be there when they arrived. He could not look them in the face and tell them how he had watched, helplessly but culpably, their son's self-destruction. He could not.

IT WAS NEARLY one o'clock the next day when Umber reached Ilford. He checked the Sheepwalk on his way to Bengal Road from the station. Larter was not there. Nor did he seem to be at home. Umber stood on the doorstep, wondering how long the old boy might be gone.

'David!'

He turned and was surprised to see Claire Wheatley standing by a sleek blue TVR on the other side of the street. He hurried across to join her.

'What's brought you all the way out here, Claire?'

'You. I got the address from Alice.' Her tone had an edge of hostility or anxiety—he could not decide which. 'Where have you been since Tuesday?'

'Why do you want to know?'

'Alice told me about picking you up from the hospital, David. And about your run-in with the people who were looking for Wisby. It seems to have sparked something off. Get in the car. I'll tell you on the way.'

'On the way where?'

'Whipps Cross Hospital. According to one of his neighbours, that's where Bill Larter is.'

'Bill's in hospital?'

'The house was burgled last night, apparently. He tackled the burglars and got beaten up.'

Before Umber could articulate a response to Claire's news, she hustled him into the car and drove away. And then she told him the rest of her news.

'The practice was broken into on Wednesday night. The police reckoned the intruders were looking for drugs and didn't have the brains to realise a psychotherapist isn't a psychiatrist. They certainly made a hell of a mess. But I think that was just camouflage. They went through my client files, yet nothing was taken. You know what they were looking for, David . . .'

'Your notes on Sally,' Umber responded glumly.

'Has to be, doesn't it? I destroyed them a year after Sally's death, as it happens, so they went away empty-handed. Last night they tried their luck here. That's three break-ins, counting the raid on Wisby's boat. So what exactly are they after, David?'

'At a guess, I'd say they're trying to figure out how close Sally was to the truth. And whether any of us knows as much as she knew.'

'That's my guess too. I've had to move in with Alice in case they come to my house. My life's been turned upside-down since you called round. The way I see it, you were either followed or you told someone about me—someone you shouldn't have trusted.'

'Marilyn Hall,' he murmured. The sequence of events assembled themselves with sickening logic in Umber's mind. He had mentioned Claire when he had called at Kingsley House. He had mentioned Wisby too. 'I am sorry, Claire. Really. I'm afraid things are worse than you think.'

'How can they be?'

'You'll understand when I tell you what I've been doing since Tuesday.'

CLAIRE HAD PULLED into the car park at Whipps Cross Hospital by the time Umber had finished his account. She turned off the engine and said nothing at first, her gaze unfocused. When eventually she spoke, she was pensive.

'I guess I owe you an apology, David. For denying you were onto something. For insisting Sally couldn't have been murdered.'

'We're even, then. I never intended to drag you into this.'

'No, well, I'm in it now. Go and see your friend, David. I'll wait here.'

Umber had to claim a blood relationship with Larter before he was allowed to see him. The old man was in poor shape, broken ribs having led to a collapsed lung. He had a suction tube in his chest and oxygen on tap to aid his breathing. The sister instructed Umber to keep conversation to a minimum.

'Lucky . . . I didn't have . . . my teeth in,' Larter wheezily joked. 'I'd probably have had them . . . knocked down my throat.'

'Were there two of them, Bill?'

'Yeah. Smug-looking geezer . . . and some bruiser with a baseball bat.'

'Did they say what they were after?'

'Not *what* . . . *Who*.' Larter pointed a shaky finger at Umber. 'Thought I could . . . take them on.' He managed a weak grin. 'Bloody stupid of me.'

'I'm sorry, Bill. This is all getting way out of hand.'

'Yeah.' Another grin. 'Maybe George is better off . . . where he is . . . But don't hold back, son . . . It's too late for that . . . It's them . . . or you.'

Before leaving the hospital, Umber promised Larter he would board up the window that Walsh and baseball-bat man had broken. He had the keys to the house and permission to stay there as long as he needed to. As it turned out, however, Claire had other ideas about his accommodation.

'I've just spoken to Alice. She suggested you stay at her house.'

'Safety in numbers, you mean? All right. If Alice insists.'

'It's more than that. The three of us have to decide what to do for the best.'

AT 45 BENGAL ROAD, Umber found some chipboard and tools in the garden shed, as Larter had said he would. He knocked out the broken glass from the smashed pane in the back door and covered the gap as best he could.

Then he busied himself on the telephone. The one meagre consolation he could take from what had happened in Jersey was that Wisby had got away with less than he must have reckoned on: the inscription had been removed from his stolen Junius. There had to be a reason for that. And Umber's historical training gave him an advantage over Wisby; there was a trail he could follow that might lead to the secret contained in the inscription.

Several phone calls later, he had established that the Ventry Papers were held at the Staffordshire County Record Office. With the weekend looming, he would have to wait until Monday to inspect them.

DUSK HAD GIVEN way to night by the time Umber had made his way by public transport from Ilford to Hampstead.

'Good of you to join us,' was Alice's sarcastic greeting. She had been hitting the gin, to judge by the half-empty tumbler of something with lemon clutched in her hand as she opened the door.

An aroma of fresh paint still lingered in the drawing room. Redecoration was evidently complete. Some platitudinous enthusing over the colour scheme died on Umber's lips. Claire, who was sitting by the fire with a mug of green tea, rolled her eyes at him as Alice pulled round a chair.

'Would you like some tea, David?' Claire asked.

'I expect he'd prefer a beer,' said Alice. 'Help yourself.'

Umber made his way to the kitchen, found a bottle of Grolsch in the fridge and hunted down a glass.

'I'm sorry for dragging you both into this,' he ventured as he rejoined them. 'I never intended to cause you any trouble.'

'What *did* you intend to do?' Alice snapped.

'Learn the truth.' He sat down and countered her glare with a level gaze.

'I'm not going to start believing Sally was murdered just because you've stirred up a hornets' nest. Sally was alone when she died. There was no intruder. No murderer.'

'You can't be absolutely certain of that, Alice,' put in Claire.

Alice tossed her head pettishly. 'Not you too.'

'We need to consider every possibility.'

'OK, then. Consider this. How did the murderer get in?'

'It was a summer's evening. She'd have had the windows open.'

'Yeah. But her windows happened to be on the second floor.'

'He could have swung down from the roof and through the open top half of the sash,' said Umber.

'Who are we talking about here? The SAS?'

'A professional of some kind. That's who we're talking about.'

'I think David's right,' said Claire, calmly but firmly. 'Sally was on to something. And somebody was determined to stop her bringing it into the open. Think about it, Alice. If Sally really was murdered, do you want to let her killers get away with it?'

'Of course not.'

'OK, then. We have two options as I see it. One, tell David to go back to Prague and hope everything blows over. Or two, do all we can to find out what Sally may have uncovered.'

Alice looked sceptically at Claire and Umber in turn. 'You've left it five years too late. If there were any clues, they're long gone.'

'What happened to her possessions?'

'Ask David.'

Umber winced. Alice had urged him to take whatever keepsakes he wanted. But guilt, grief and a secret, simmering anger at Sally for running away from life had deluded him into believing he wanted none. 'I don't know what happened to them,' he said hoarsely.

'Her parents took some stuff,' Alice stated matter-of-factly. 'The rest—clothes and such—went to Oxfam.'

'Were there any papers?' Claire asked. 'Notes? Diaries?'

'I can't say,' Alice replied. 'Whatever there was her parents removed.'

'We'd better contact them, then.' Claire looked at Umber. 'Do you know where they live, David?'

'Unless they've moved, yes. They have a bungalow on the Hampshire coast, near Christchurch.' Umber had few happy memories of his parents-in-law—as few, he suspected, as they had of him. 'There's something you should understand, Claire,' he said hesitantly. 'The Wilkinsons and I, er . . .'

'What he means,' put in Alice, 'is that they hate his guts. They aren't likely to give him the time of day, let alone the chance to root through whatever they have left of Sally's.'

'It's not as bad as that,' Umber protested.

'Alice and I will go to see them without you,' said Claire dispassionately.

'Excuse me?' spluttered Alice.

'Tomorrow,' Claire breezed calmly on. 'I think we can all agree there's no time to be lost.'

CLAIRE AND ALICE set off for Hampshire in Claire's TVR at 10.30 the next morning. There was no guarantee the Wilkinsons would be at home, of course. But the risk of a wasted journey was preferable to the possibility that Reg Wilkinson would forbid them to come if they phoned ahead. Alice predicted that he would not let them past the door, but her pessimism was partly a symptom of her hangover. Claire seemed more confident.

'They'll be happy to talk about Sally. Silence is never golden for bereaved parents.' The professional had spoken.

As far as she and Alice were concerned, Umber was planning to spend the day at the British Library, boning up on Junius. In fact, he had no such intention. Alan Wisby had given him the slip in Jersey; that did not mean he could go on doing so. Umber had no doubt that Wisby would stay well away from *Monica*. But the man had to stay somewhere. And that put another Monica in the frame.

UMBER DID NOT seriously expect to find anyone in the office at 171A Blackfriars Road on a Saturday morning. His ambitions were fixed no higher than extracting a home address or telephone number for Monica Wisby from the shoe-repair man in the ground-floor shop. So he turned the handle of the door leading to the stairs up to the first floor fully expecting to find it locked. But it was not.

A tall, broad-hipped, big-bosomed woman in tight jeans and a clinging sweater was fingering her way through a set of bulging folders in a battered filing cabinet when Umber stepped into the room at the top of the stairs. She had a mane of bottle-blonde hair and a rawboned face.

'Monica Wisby?' he ventured, already certain it was her.

She started violently. 'Who the fuck are you?'

'David Umber.'

'How did you get in?'

'The door was open.'

'Bloody well shouldn't be. We're not open for business.' She hip-barged the drawer of the filing cabinet shut. Then recognition of his name kicked in. 'Hold on. Did you say Umber?'

'Yes. You know. The guy you were holding a letter for last week on your ex-husband's behalf. Where is he? He and I need to meet. Urgently.'

'He obviously doesn't agree. Otherwise you wouldn't be asking me. But you got it spot-on. *Ex*-husband. Alan keeps in touch with me when he wants to. But I've heard nothing from him since he sent me the letter for you. I'm fed up having to explain to his clients that his freelance activities have nothing to do with me. First there was that policeman. And then . . . what's his name?' She grabbed a scrap of paper from the nearest desk. 'Nevinson.'

'What? *Percy* Nevinson?'

'He didn't give me a Christian name. But he's been on several times this week.' She gave Umber the note. *Mr Nevinson called again for Mr Wisby. Please call with any news. 01672 799332.*

'Mind if I use your phone?'

Monica looked as if she wanted to refuse on principle but was unsure what the principle might be. 'Oh, be my guest,' she said.

Umber picked up the telephone and dialled. Abigail Nevinson answered.

'Miss Nevinson? This is David Umber.'

'Mr Umber. What can I do for you?'

'Is Percy there?'

'No. Percy has, er . . . gone away. To one of his ufological conferences.'

'Where's it being held?'

'I'm . . . not sure.'

'How would you get in touch with him in an emergency?'

'I'd have to wait for him to contact me.'

'Is that normal when he goes to one of these things?'

'Well, no. Not really. It's a little . . . concerning, I have to admit. I imagine it's just a weekend event, though. They normally are. Unless . . .'

'What?'

'I've just read about Jeremy Hall in the paper, Mr Umber. I suppose you know what's happened.'

'Yes.'

'You don't think Percy's trip has anything to do with that, do you?'

Umber did think so. In fact, he felt certain of it, though what dealings Nevinson might have had with Wisby were a mystery to him. That applied to a good deal else as well. Every step he took led him further into a labyrinth of lies. For every one he nailed there was another waiting to deceive him.

FROM BLACKFRIARS ROAD he walked aimlessly towards Tate Modern, pausing amid the ambling tourists on the Millennium Bridge to stare downriver and wrestle in his mind with the confusions and contradictions that threatened to swamp him. Nevinson had gone to Jersey. Umber's every instinct told him so. Maybe Umber should follow. But what could he hope to achieve? There was still no trail that promised to lead to the truth.

He ended up walking most of the way back to Hampstead. Physical exhaustion seemed to be the only brake on the enervating whirl of his thoughts. He took a decision of sorts during the long trudge through Finsbury and Camden Town. It involved misleading Claire and Alice, but he reckoned he would be doing them a favour.

THEY HAD RETURNED from Hampshire when he reached 22 Willow Hill.

'Alice is busy upstairs on her computer,' Claire said as she let him in. 'We got back half an hour ago. And we found something.'

A spiral-bound crimson-covered scrapbook was lying on the kitchen table. 'My God,' he said. 'I never thought I'd see that again.'

Sally had amassed a collection of newspaper cuttings relating to Miranda Hall's murder and Tamsin Hall's presumed murder. Triggered by Radd's out-of-the-blue confession, nine years after the event, she had bought a scrap-book and pasted the cuttings into it, along with new ones reporting Radd's trial. The book was a testament to her belief that 'somebody has to keep a proper record in case they fiddle with the facts and hope we won't notice'. It was around then that Umber had begun to understand the intractability of her plight. Time had hardened Sally's wounds, not healed them.

'Morbid reading, isn't it?' said Claire from behind him.

'Yes. And Sally did read it. All too often.'

'Unlike her parents, then. I don't think they'd ever brought themselves to open it. Not her mother, anyway. Reg Wilkinson had a stroke the year after Sally died. He's virtually mute, so there's no way to tell what he might or might not have made of it. Peggy was happy to let us borrow the scrapbook if it helped to make any sense of Sally's death.'

'Can't see how it could do that. There's nothing in these cuttings we don't already know.'

'That's not strictly true, David. Turn to the back of the book.'

Umber did so. A sheet of paper had been slipped inside the cover: a page torn out of a glossy *Hello!* magazine. Under the heading INSIDE STORY was an assortment of paparazzo-snapped celebrities.

'As soon as I saw it I remembered,' said Claire. 'When I had that stupid row with Sally in the coffee shop the day she died, and she threw the maga-zine at me. You remember? I told you about it?'

'Yes.' He looked round and frowned at her.

'Until I saw that, I'd forgotten that before she threw the magazine at me she tore a page out of it.'

'And this is it?'

'Has to be. She must have seen something significant in a month-old copy of *Hello!* in my waiting room. That must be why she walked out. Because what she saw made a counselling session with me suddenly irrelevant.'

Umber looked at the page again and turned it over. More pictures of movie stars out shopping in sunglasses and baseball caps or sunbathing in swimsuits. 'I don't get it,' he said. 'What's significant about any of this?'

Claire flipped the page back over. 'There,' she said, pointing to a spread of three photographs of mixed-doubles tennis, featuring an actor and actress Umber had never heard of on one side of the net, and a tennis player he had heard of, plus girlfriend, on the other. According to the captions, the actor and actress were taking a break from the Cannes Film Festival. The bronzed, raven-haired tennis star entertaining them on a local court was Monaco-based Michel Tinaud, of whom great things were expected at the forthcoming French Open. 'He's why Sally went to Wimbledon that week,' Claire continued. 'Remember what she told Alice? "I don't need a ticket." She wasn't going to watch tennis. She was going to speak to a tennis player.'

'Why?' Umber already knew the answer, but the question was apt nonetheless. He knew. But he did not understand.

'It has to be the girlfriend,' said Claire.

And so it did. Unnamed by *Hello!*, Tinaud's playing companion, who featured in only one picture, had long fair hair tied in a ponytail and was biting her lower lip and wrinkling her brow in concentration.

'Recognise the expression?' Claire turned to a page nearer the front of the scrapbook, where one of the Halls' photographs of Tamsin had been reproduced in a newspaper. The two-year-old Tamsin was wrinkling her brow at the camera and biting her lower lip.

'It's a common expression,' Umber murmured. 'It doesn't mean—'

'Sally saw something. She was the girl's nanny. She knew her as closely as her mother did. Well enough to recognise the child in the woman. The girl on the tennis court looks about twenty to me. The right age.'

'You can't be sure.'

'Sally was sure.'

'Was she?' Umber was playing for time—the time he needed to think. Because he had seen something too. Not a tantalising resemblance to a missing two-year-old girl, but an unmistakable similarity to someone he had met only recently. The hair was a different colour, a different style. But there was no doubt in Umber's mind. Michel Tinaud's girlfriend . . . was Chantelle.

As Umber slipped the *Hello!* page back into the scrapbook and closed it, he saw Alice walk in through the door behind Claire.

'You look like you've seen a ghost,' she said. 'Think you have?'

'Maybe.'

'We reckon Sally was more certain. I've just been catching the latest tennis news on the Web. Tinaud's just gone out of the Nasdaq Open in Miami in the first round. The next big tournament is the Monte Carlo Masters. Home ground for Tinaud. So, I guess he'll already be back there.'

'And you're going to suggest we go see him?'

'I was sceptical about this whole thing, David. You know that. But I'm convinced now. Sally went to Wimbledon the day before she died in order to confront that man. We've got to find out what happened. We have to go.'

'No,' he said quietly.

'What?'

'I thought it all through while you were down in Hampshire. Sally's dead. We can't bring her back to life. All we'll do by chasing after answers to questions no one's forcing us to ask is to put ourselves in unnecessary danger. We have to give it up. I'm going back to Prague. I'm bowing out.'

'You can't.'

'I can. And I will. What's more, I advise you to follow my example.'

'What about George Sharp?'

'I'm not responsible for what happens to George. He dragged me into this. He'll have to drag himself out.'

Alice stared at him with a mixture of surprise and contempt. 'I thought you'd finally found some moral fibre. But no. It was just a passing phase. This is the real you, isn't it? The spineless shit Sally should never have—'

'*Alice.*' Claire glared at her friend, commanding her silence. Then she turned back to Umber. 'You're not serious about this, are you, David? We've just uncovered the biggest clue to what Sally was up to. And you want to walk away from it?'

'Self-preservation, Claire. That's what it comes down to. I'm not going on with this. It's as simple as that.'

'*We'll* go on with it.'

'You shouldn't. You really shouldn't.'

'David, I—'

'You're wasting your breath, Claire,' said Alice. 'Sometimes the wrong thing to do is the only thing to do. Isn't that so, David?'

Umber shrugged.

Alice nodded grimly. Her low opinion of him made the deception all too easy to carry off, Umber realised. She wanted to believe in his loss of nerve too badly to question its genuineness.

IT TOOK UMBER no more than a few minutes to pack his belongings. He hoped to make it out of the house without further debate. But Claire cornered him in the hall.

'How soon are you going back to Prague?' she asked.

'Not sure. Within a couple of days. I . . . thought I'd go and see my parents before I left.'

'I'll give you a lift to the station.'

'No need. I'll take the tube.' He brushed past her to the door and opened it. 'Bye.'

'This isn't goodbye, David.' She followed him out, ostentatiously pulling the door shut behind her. 'We both know that. You've fooled Alice, but you haven't fooled me.'

'I'm not trying to fool anyone.'

'Fine. Have it your way. But I'll go back indoors and persuade Alice to see it *my* way—unless you stop arguing and get in the car.'

Umber stopped arguing. The truth was that Claire left him little choice. A few minutes later, they were heading towards Swiss Cottage in her TVR.

'Let's cut the crap, shall we, David? You took a decision while we were down in Hampshire, but chickening out wasn't it. My guess is you decided to go it alone, probably out of some warped sense of chivalry. You think we'll be safer if you leave us out of whatever it is you're planning to do. I suspect you've worked something out you're not telling us about.'

Umber shook his head. 'You've got it all wrong, Claire.'

'You thought we'd get nothing out of the Wilkinsons. But we came back with a genuine lead. Yet you didn't change your mind. You ploughed straight on with your cover story. That can only be because you already knew about Tinaud and the girl.'

'How could I?'

'I don't know. Unless—' She braked sharply to a halt. A car behind them blared its horn. Claire held up a hand in apology, then pulled into a parking space and turned to stare at Umber. Her eyes were sparkling with the satisfaction of a sudden insight. 'You've seen her, haven't you?'

'Of course not.'

'Look me in the eye and tell me I'm wrong.'

He looked her in the eye. But he said nothing. He knew she would see through any lie he told. She already had.

She turned off the engine, her gaze still fixed on him. Then she said, calmly and quietly, 'There's no guarantee she's still with Tinaud. But Tinaud can tell us what happened when Sally tracked him down. It makes sense to ask him. He may also be able to tell us where the girl is. And he can certainly tell us who he believes her to be. There's every reason to go and see him. And I will. Unless you're prepared to tell me why I shouldn't.'

Umber sighed. 'Look Claire, the reason's obvious. The reason is what happened to Sally when she got too close. I don't want that to happen to you. Or Alice. Sally was my wife. And I was at Avebury when they took Tamsin. I have to take the risks. You don't. I can't let you. Give me a few days, Claire. You can stall Alice that long. A few days is all I ask.'

The pretence was over. Claire dropped Umber at the next tube station. An hour and a half later, he was at Gatwick, buying a ticket for the first flight next morning to Jersey. He booked into the cheapest of the airport hotels for the night.

ON SUNDAY morning, Umber drove a hired Peugeot to St Aubin. All was quiet in Le Quai Bisson. Nothing had outwardly changed at Rollers Sail & Surf. There was no sign of life, nor sound of it. He mounted the steps to the flat and pressed the doorbell. There was no response. He lowered himself onto his haunches and pushed up the flap of the letterbox. Chantelle, he felt certain, was not there. He had come more in hope than expectation, knowing that the only other step open to him—going to Eden Holt to confront Jeremy's parents with his suspicions—was a step into the profoundest unknown.

The purr of a car engine behind and below him seeped into his consciousness. He glanced round to see the driver's door of a sleek navy-blue Mercedes SL open—and Marilyn Hall climb out.

She was dressed in jeans, leather jacket and polo-neck sweater, the unisex look of a piece with the cool, appraising stare she gave him before locking the car and starting up the steps.

'Who did you expect to find here, David. A ghost?'

He nodded. 'In a sense. I was looking for Chantelle.'

'*Who?*'

'You must know about her.'

'No.'

'Really? Why don't you seem surprised to see me, then?'

She frowned at him in apparent puzzlement, then plucked a key out of one of the zip pockets of her jacket. 'We can talk inside.'

She unlocked the door and he followed her in. Already, the flat had an air of desertion about it. The living room was emptier than he remembered.

'Oliver wanted me to pick up a couple of things,' Marilyn explained. 'He hadn't the heart to come himself.' She was sombre and unsmiling, the flirtatiousness buried deep. 'Lucky for you it was me he sent, because I'm the only member of the family who knows you were at Eden Holt when Jeremy died.'

'How did you find out?' he asked, as calmly as he could.

She held his gaze. 'That can wait. Tell me about Chantelle.'

'She was here last week. I thought she was Jeremy's girlfriend.'

'There *was* a girl in Jeremy's life. But they split up more than a year ago. And she wasn't called Chantelle.'

Some instinct held Umber back from telling Marilyn who he believed Chantelle really was. He could not afford to show his hand until he knew what she held in hers.

'I don't see any sign of her, do you?' Marilyn looked around. 'Just Jeremy's bachelor stuff.'

'She must have left as soon as she heard about Jeremy.'

'Why would she do that?' She arched an eyebrow. 'Are you sure Chantelle isn't just a figment of your imagination? Wisby didn't mention her.'

The name took Umber aback. '*Wisby?*'

'That's how I knew you were there when Jeremy threw himself off the roof. Wisby told me. He came up to me yesterday as I was parking my car in St Helier. He'd followed me from Eden Holt, waiting for the chance to speak to me alone, he said. The atmosphere at the house . . . well, you can imagine. Jane's barely coherent. And Oliver's as close to broken as I've seen him. I had to get away. Shopping for essentials was a decent excuse.'

'What happened was Wisby's fault. Did he tell you that?'

'It hardly matters whose fault it was, David. I can tell you who Oliver and Jane will blame if they ever find out you were there.'

'Why haven't they found out?'

'Because Wisby's put me in a difficult position.' Disarmingly, she smiled. 'He's blackmailing me.'

'With what?' But even as he asked, Umber guessed the answer.

'Junius. Your speciality, I believe. The vellum-bound edition.'

'What's that to you?'

'Nothing. But it was in Jeremy's possession, wasn't it? Wisby can prove that. Which as good as proves that Jeremy sent the letters to Wisby and Sharp that stirred all this up. And that he clearly didn't believe Radd was his sisters' murderer. Jeremy's death has been a savage blow to Oliver, and to Jane. If they learn their son didn't trust them . . . well, I'm not sure either of them could cope with that.'

'Wisby's selling the books to you?'

'That's what it comes down to, yes. Without them he can't back up his allegations. And he won't want to anyway. He'll have a turned a big enough profit to keep his mouth shut.'

'He's alleged more than that Jeremy sent the letters, Marilyn, hasn't he?'

'Some crazy stuff about the man who originally owned the books being murdered, you mean? Oh, he fed that into the works as well, yes. I didn't know what to make of it. As far as I can see, though, it would only make everything worse for Oliver. My priority is limiting the damage you and Wisby caused by pressurising Jeremy. I don't want it to get any worse.'

'It's a funny thing, Marilyn.' Umber took a step towards her. 'The more candid you are with me, the more duplicitous I suspect you of being.'

'Duplicitous?' Her eyes twinkled. 'That's a big word for a Sunday morning.'

'How much are you paying Wisby?'

'A hundred thousand.'

Umber gasped. 'That's a hell of a lot of damage limitation.'

'It's loose change, actually. Oliver's always been very generous to me.'

'Is that why you married him?'

'It was a consideration,' she replied, with unblinking coolness. 'Do you want a cut of that generosity, David?'

'What?'

'Finding you here was . . . fortuitous, to say the least. I've been worrying that Wisby might try to trick me into accepting duplicates of the Junius, leaving him free to do what I'll already have paid him not to. He strikes me as the type to want the penny *and* the bun.'

'You want me to authenticate the Junius for you?'

'Yes. In fact, I want you to conduct the exchange for me. Never having to see or speak to Wisby again would suit me rather well.'

'Wouldn't that be a little risky, Marilyn? I might take off with the Junius myself and do my worst with it.'

'And what would your worst be? You're hardly likely to inflict the truth on Oliver and Jane when you come out of it so badly yourself. Besides, the Junius is no use to me. I only want it out of Wisby's hands.'

Umber paused for a momentary show of reflection before he responded. Then he said, 'All right. I'll do it. If you do something for me in return. I want the keys to this place, including those for the office and the boat store.'

She looked long and hard at him 'Why?'

Umber allowed himself a smile. 'And no questions asked.'

'Think Chantelle will come back, do you?'

Umber did not think that. But he did think there might be clues to her whereabouts to be found. 'Like I said, Marilyn. No questions.'

'I can have duplicates of all the keys cut for you tomorrow. You can have them then. The exchange is fixed for noon tomorrow. I can't get the money until the banks open. Do you have a car with you?'

'Yes.'

'All right. You know the Pier Road multistorey in St Helier?'

'Beneath Fort Regent?'

'That's the one. Drive up past it to Mount Bingham. You'll see a small car park with a view of the harbour. I'll meet you there at eleven, deliver the cash and tell you where Wisby will be waiting. He's going to phone me around then with his choice of rendezvous.' She raised her eyebrows. 'He seems to feel the need to behave like some character in a spy novel.'

'Perhaps he doesn't trust you.'

'We'll agree then how to meet up afterwards,' she went on blithely. 'I have to take my own precautions. Oliver's not paying me a lot of attention at the moment. But I can't go missing too often.'

'I'm sorry, you know.' He looked her in the eye, needing to be sure she believed him. 'For what happened to Jeremy. Sorrier than I can say.'

'We're all sorry.' She moved suddenly away and across the room, to the chest of drawers beside the bed, and picked up an expensively chunky wristwatch. 'The Rolex Oliver gave Jeremy for his eighteenth birthday,' she explained. 'One of the things I was sent to collect. He wasn't wearing it, you see. Didn't want to smash it in the fall, I suppose. Which means he'd already made up his mind to kill himself when he left here on Thursday afternoon. You didn't push him off the roof, David. He jumped. You didn't force him to send those letters. He brought it all on himself.'

'What else did you come for?' Umber asked, evading the subject.

'There should be an address book. By the phone maybe? We need it to notify Jeremy's friends.'

Umber stepped over to where the telephone sat amid crooked stacks of CDs in the lee of the hi-fi tower. There was indeed a dogeared address book sitting beneath it. Umber slid it free and handed it to her.

'I've got what I came for. We ought to leave.'

'You go ahead. I'll let myself out.'

'Nice try. But there's no deadlock on the door. I can't leave the flat unsecured. After tomorrow, you can come and go on your own. But you'll have to be careful. If Oliver finds you here he won't be as easily fobbed off as me.'

'I don't think you're easily fobbed off at all, Marilyn. I think you're just tolerant of other people's secretiveness . . . on account of your own.'

'You really know how to sweet-talk a girl, don't you?' She gave him a fleeting, enigmatic little smile. 'Let's go.'

UMBER DID NOT intend to stir far from St Aubin. He had told Marilyn openly that he suspected her of duplicity and it was true. What form it took he had no way of determining, but her ignorance and indifference where Chantelle was concerned could have been feigned. He proposed to keep a close eye on the flat in case anyone tried to conduct a search before he could—or in case, against the odds, Chantelle returned.

He had noticed that there was a small hotel on the harbourside boulevard just beyond the turning into le Quai Bisson. A prowl round past Rollers Sail & Surf revealed there were first-floor rooms at the back of the hotel with a view of the flat. The receptionist, used to people requesting a sea-facing room, had no difficulty accommodating him. He booked himself in.

Then he went along to the supermarket in the centre of town, bought some sandwiches and bottled water and returned to the hotel to keep watch.

He had bought a day-old copy of the *Jersey Evening Post*, too, and, in the privacy of his room, bleakly perused its coverage of the 'Eden Holt Tragedy'. There was a quote from the police, appealing for the anonymous caller who had alerted them to Jeremy's death to come forward.

Nobody went near the flat all day. When nightfall came, Umber relaxed, reasoning that no one would visit the flat once they had to switch on lights, because it would signal their presence to anyone who might be watching.

If anyone was even planning to, of course. *If* there was anything to find. *If* . . . But ifs were all he had to bet on.

NEXT MORNING at 10.30, Umber set off for St Helier. He spotted Marilyn's Mercedes in the car park at the top of Mount Bingham as he crested the rise from Pier Road. As he pulled in beside it, he saw she was speaking to someone on her mobile, so he sat where he was, looking down at the docks and the ferry terminal spread out below him, at Elizabeth Castle and the causeway linking it to the shore, exposed by the retreating tide.

'Penny for them,' said Marilyn as she pulled open the passenger door and slipped in beside him. 'Well, rather more than a penny, actually.'

Resting on her knees was a black leather briefcase. She plucked off her sunglasses and looked at him. 'This is the money.' She snapped open the case to reveal neatly stacked wads of twenty-pound notes. 'Bank of England issue, as Wisby specified.' Then she closed it again. 'And here are the keys.' She handed him an assortment of Yales and mortises held on a ring.

'Thanks.'

'You're to meet our man at La Rocque. It's a village on the coast about five miles east of here.'

'I've got a map. I'll find the place easily enough.'

'There are parking spaces by the harbour just after you pass the Martello tower. He'll be waiting for you there.'

'Does he know *who* he'll be waiting for?'

'I told him I was sending someone.'

'It could be quite a shock for him, then.'

'I imagine the contents of the case will help him get over it.'

'And afterwards? You'll want to see what you've got for your money.'

'Oliver is taking Jane to see the undertaker at three o'clock. My presence is not required. I'll meet you at the flat then.' Marilyn slid the briefcase across to him. 'In case you need it, good luck.'

'Thanks. I'll see you later, Marilyn.'

'Right,' she said, smiling tightly. Then she climbed swiftly out of the car.

UMBER FOLLOWED the coast road out through St Helier's straggling eastern suburbs. The weather was a mixture of winter grimness and spring cheer—ambiguous, uncertain, on the cusp of the seasons.

As he neared Le Hocq, he pulled in and waited. When only five minutes remained till Marilyn's noon appointment with Wisby, he drove on.

It was barely another mile to La Rocque. He slowed as he passed its Martello tower, scanning the arc of parking spaces facing the harbour. He was looking for a hire car, and he saw one almost immediately, his eye drawn to the H-prefixed numberplate. There was a single occupant, staring straight ahead at the harbour. The profile was Wisby's.

He pulled in to the left of the car and looked round, meeting Wisby's gaze, in which there was not the merest flinch of surprise, though a surprise it must have been—and a big one.

Umber climbed out, carrying the briefcase. He opened the passenger door of the other car and eased himself in beside Wisby.

'Mr Umber,' Wisby said neutrally. 'We meet again.'

'Not in your game plan, I dare say.'

'No. But I wasn't to know you'd got into bed with Marilyn Hall, was I?' Umber refused to be provoked. 'She thought you might try to trick her.'

'Sorry I left you in the lurch at Eden Holt the other day, by the way. It was nothing personal.'

'Did you really do all this just for a fat payoff?'

'No. But I've decided to settle for one. You too, I imagine. What have you gone for? Cash or kind?'

'Where are the books?'

'Ah. Is that it? A late revival of your historical career. I might have a minor disappointment for you on that front.'

'I know the flyleaves are missing, Wisby. I checked with Garrard, like you should have.'

'I should. You're right. But you said yourself the vellum-bound 1773 edition is unique. Even without the flyleaves, it proves my case. A case Marilyn Hall can't afford to let me go public with.'

'Exploiting the Hall family's grief is beneath contempt.'

'That's what you think I'm doing, is it? How much do you know about Marilyn Hall, I wonder? Less than me, I suspect. I've done my research, you see.' Wisby smiled thinly. 'Like you should have.'

'And what have you learned?'

'Enough to make me worry I may have settled for too modest a sum.'

'Are you going to tell me what you're getting at?'

'No.' Wisby squinted at the ocean. 'You'll find out in your own good time.'

'Where are the books?' snapped Umber, losing patience.

'You can have them when I have the money.'

Umber flipped up the lid of the briefcase, giving his companion a clear view of the contents. There was a gleam of satisfaction in Wisby's eyes. He reached out for the case. But Umber held on. 'The books.'

'They're in the glove compartment. In front of you.'

Umber stretched one hand forward to open the compartment. Its door flopped down. And there were the books, vellum-bound and gilt-edged, the spines facing him. He angled his head to read the gold-lettered titles. Not *Junius's Letters I* and *II*, like every other edition, but simply: JUNIUS 1 and 2.

'The money, Mr Umber,' said Wisby. 'If you please.'

Umber surrendered the case and took the books out of the glove box. It was strange to lay his hands at long last on the prize Griffin had promised to deliver to him at Avebury twenty-three years previously.

He opened the first volume. A few jagged scraps close to the binding were all that remained of the flyleaf, but the title page was untouched. The name of Junius appeared at the top in bold Gothic capitals. Umber's gaze shifted to the bottom: 'Printed for Henry Sampson Woodfall, MDCCLXXIII'. The date was right. It *was* Junius's personal copy.

He looked round at Wisby, who was checking the money.

'It seems to be all here,' said Wisby, with a flicker of a smile, snapping the briefcase shut. 'Why were the flyleaves removed, do you think?'

'You tell me.'

'It's obvious, isn't it? To break the evidential link with Griffin. Without them they're just another copy of Junius's letters.'

'Not quite.'

'No. But they'd seem so, other than to an expert. And having removed the flyleaves, where better to lose the books than in an antiquarian bookshop? I doubt that Garrard's scatterbrained brother bought them. I suspect they were simply slipped onto the shelf. Not by Jeremy, obviously. Perhaps by someone who was trying to keep them *from* Jeremy. By implication someone Jeremy knew. Someone . . . close to him.'

The man's logic was as seductive as it was disturbing. But Umber had no intention of acknowledging as much. 'Are we done?'

Wisby nodded. 'I believe we are.'

SEVEN

Umber reached St Aubin with more than an hour to spare before his appointment with Marilyn. He parked the car at his hotel, headed round to le Quai Bisson and let himself into the flat.

Everything was as it had been the previous day. Since Umber did not really know what he was looking for, he could devise no subtler method of searching than moving everything to see what might be concealed by cushions, magazines, books, CDs and the like. Nothing, was the answer.

He decided to try his luck in the Rollers Sail & Surf office. Hurrying down to it, he found the right key after a couple of tries and went in. It was a cramped, single-windowed room, furnished with a desk, swivel chair, filing cabinet and cupboard. A communicating door leading into the boat store stood half open, explaining the salt-tinged mustiness that filled the air.

Umber decided to start with the filing cabinet. He walked over to it and pulled the top drawer open.

Whether he heard something first or merely sensed movement behind him he could not have said. Perhaps the breath Chantelle took as she lunged across the room at him, knife in hand, was sharp enough to be audible.

He threw himself to one side. The blade of the knife struck the metal-work of the drawer at an angle but with enough force to dent it. He heard her cry out 'Shit!' in pain at the jarring of her wrist. The knife fell from her hand and clattered to the floor. Umber looked into Chantelle's eyes. Fear and hatred and desperation burned back at him.

'You bastard!' she screamed. She stooped for the knife.

His foot got there first, stamping down hard across the handle. She grabbed his ankle and tried to pull him off, but she was no match for him. He grasped her waist and swung her round into the angle of filing cabinet and wall, where he pinned her by his own weight.

'Let go of me,' she shouted, flailing at him with her fists.

He caught her wrists and forced her arms back above her head. Their faces were no more than a couple of inches apart now. 'Listen to me, Chantelle,' he shouted. 'I know who you are. But I've told no one. No one.'

'I don't care who you've told. I just want to make you suffer for what you did to Jem. You boxed him into a corner. You left him no way out.' She closed her eyes. Tears flowed down her cheeks.

'Wisby was the one threatening him, Chantelle. Not me.'

She reopened her eyes and stared at him through her tears. 'You're lying. Wisby and you are in it together. Jem said so.'

'I know he thought that and I understand why. But he was wrong. And I can prove it. Wisby's gone. Left the island. He wouldn't have gone if he knew about you. But he doesn't. I give you my word, Chantelle. Trust me. Please.'

Her arms slackened. Her expression altered fractionally. 'Give me one good reason why I should.'

'Because I'm your only hope.'

'You haven't told anyone about me?'

'I told Marilyn I'd met Jeremy's girlfriend here. A girlfriend she knew nothing about. But I didn't tell her what I really think you and Jeremy were to each other.'

Chantelle swallowed. 'What d'you think we were?'

'Brother and sister,' Umber whispered. Then he stepped back, releasing her wrists. Her arms fell to her sides.

She stared at him, barely blinking. A frozen moment passed. Then she said, 'How did you rumble me?'

'I didn't. Sally did. My wife. She left a clue. I only came across it recently. A magazine cutting.'

Chantelle closed her eyes and sighed. 'That fucking magazine. Changed my life. My whole life.'

'Why don't you—?'

Chantelle's eyes flashed open, wide and alarmed, at the sound of a car drawing near. Umber grabbed her and hurried her into the boat store.

'Don't worry,' he whispered. 'It's Marilyn. She's come to see me. She'll go up to the flat. I'll follow and speak to her there. Just wait here, will you?'

'OK,' said Chantelle in a quavering voice.

'I'll be as quick as I can. Just stay still and silent.' He squeezed her shoulder, then slipped out through the office.

And there he stopped. The car was not Marilyn's. It was a charcoal-grey BMW. And Umber would have sworn he had seen it before—in Yeovil.

Thoughts tumbled through his brain. It was Walsh's car. Which meant it was Walsh, not Marilyn, waiting for him in the flat. Which meant Umber had clearly been set up. But he had no choice but to climb the stairs to the flat and go in. If Walsh came down, he would find Chantelle.

Umber shut the office door and ran up the steps. A few seconds later, he was in the flat. But the main room was empty.

'Umber!' came Walsh's voice from the kitchen. Umber turned.

Walsh was leaning against the fridge, arms folded. 'I was just going to come and look for you. Thanks for saving me the effort.'

'What are you doing here?'

'Marilyn sent me.' Walsh smiled his gleaming smile. 'Well, that's not strictly true. *I* sent *her* yesterday. And now I've come myself.'

'What do you want?'

'These, obviously.' Walsh gestured at the Juniuses on the worktop where Umber had left them. 'For starters. The main course is Chantelle. What do you know about her, Umber? What have you found out?'

'Nothing.'

'Let me explain the situation to you.' Walsh glanced at his watch. 'Wisby will have been picked up at the airport by now. By the police, acting on a tip-off. The serial numbers of the notes you gave him match those on a van-load of cash stolen from Securicor in Essex six months ago. Wisby will have a lot of explaining to do. As will the man videoed delivering the money to him at La Rocque earlier today. If and when the film comes to the attention of the police, that is. You catch my drift?'

'I catch it.'

'So, what can you tell me about Chantelle?'

'Like I said: nothing.'

Walsh took two slow steps towards Umber. 'You know who she is, Umber. You've worked it out. And according to what you told Marilyn, you've recently met her. Well, I'd like to meet her too. Very much. So would one or two other people I know. Can you arrange that?'

'No. I can't. I wouldn't know how to.'

'I find that hard to believe.'

The next thing Umber knew was that his face was pressed against the frame of the door to the main room, his right arm doubled up behind him several degrees beyond its natural limit.

'I'd be happy to reopen those stitches I can see in the back of your head with a few taps against this doorpost,' Walsh rasped in his ear. 'More than happy. So, I suggest you start talking. You're going to—'

'*Stop!*' It was Chantelle's voice. 'Let go of him.'

Umber could not see her, but he glimpsed her shadow in the hallway.

'Happy to.' Walsh released Umber's arm. 'Now you're here.'

Umber turned in time to see Chantelle advancing towards Walsh, her right arm tucked behind her, and guessed what she was about to do.

'Good to see you again, Cherie,' said Walsh. 'It's been far too—'

The blade plunged into his stomach. He rocked on his feet, clutching at her as the knife tore through his flesh and innards and the fabric of his shirt, blood spilling between them.

He lolled forward against her. His weight pushed her back. The knife came out of him. There was yet more blood. He dropped to his knees, then fell sideways into the kitchen doorway.

He moaned and pressed his right hand to his stomach. His body slackened. He twitched twice. And then he was still.

'WHAT ARE WE GOING to do, Shadow Man?' Chantelle's voice was tremulous and plaintive. But the 'we' was important. Umber had asked her to trust him. And now it seemed she did.

They were sitting on the bed, facing the Catherine-wheel window. Umber had covered Walsh's body as best he could with the hall rug. Chantelle had removed her blood-smeared T-shirt and trousers and was now enveloped in Jeremy's dressing gown, but bloodstains remained on the trainers she would at some point have to put back on.

'We can't stay here,' he said, forcing his brain to reason its way through the shock of what had happened. 'They'll come looking for him sooner or later. And you know who *they* are, don't you, Chantelle? Or should I call you Cherie?'

'Chantelle's my name now. And I don't know who they are. Or *what* they are. The people my parents work for, I mean. My foster parents, I ought to call them. My *false* parents. That man . . .' She gestured towards the door.

'Walsh?'

She shook her head. 'Waldron. Eddie Waldron. Uncle Eddie, he wanted me to call him. But I never did. I was always frightened of him. He'd have forced you to tell on me. When I saw his car . . . ' Her head sank. 'I knew it was him or me. I thought, finish Uncle Eddie this time, girl. Stop him ever hurting you again.'

There were questions—a host of them—Umber longed to put to her. But they would have to wait. The need now was to act. 'My car's just round the corner. We'll walk to it and drive away.'

'What about Eddie?'

'We leave him here. I'm betting those who find him won't want to set the police on us. On you, anyway.'

'I can't walk down the street looking like this.'

'Could you put on some of Jeremy's clothes?'

'I suppose.'

'Do that. And fast. We should go as soon as we can.'

Leaving her to it, Umber hurried out into the hall. Taking a deep breath, he pulled the rug clear of the body of the man he now knew as Eddie Waldron. He unclipped the small bunch of keys he had seen hanging from one of Waldron's belt-loops. The remote for the BMW was among them.

He stepped gingerly into the kitchen, keeping clear of the pool of blood, and hunted down a tea towel, Sellotape and a roll of black plastic rubbish sacks. He took these out into the hall, wrapped the knife in the tea towel, put the bundle inside one of the rubbish sacks, folded it over and taped down the ends. Then he returned to the kitchen to collect the Juniuses.

'I'm ready,' said Chantelle. She was wearing jeans baggy enough to cover all but the toes of her bloodstained trainers, even though they were rolled up several inches at the ankle, and a navy-blue sweater that hung to just above her knees. Umber saw her glance fall to Waldron's feet protruding from the rug. 'Christ,' she murmured. 'I really did it, didn't I?'

'Don't think about it,' said Umber. 'We're leaving now. Put your clothes in this.' He peeled off a second rubbish sack and tossed it to her, then moved to the front door and edged it open. There was neither sight nor sound of movement. He signalled to Chantelle. 'Come on. Go down to the office and wait there. I'm going to check his car. Then we'll go.'

Chantelle nodded and headed past him. Umber followed. As he descended the steps, he flicked the remote at the BMW. The door locks released. He glanced into the car, but could not see what he was looking for. He strode round to the boot and opened it. Inside was a smart-looking camcorder, nestling in a shoulder bag. And there, to his astonishment, was a white cardboard box fastened with string. The word *JUNIUS* stared at him in his own, long-ago handwriting. He shook his head and smiled.

'What is it?' called Chantelle from the doorway of the office.

'Something I never expected to see again.'

She hurried over. Umber handed her the Juniuses, then hauled the box out, wedging the black plastic bundle under the string, and hoisted the camcorder bag onto his shoulder. 'I'll explain later. Let's get moving.'

They loaded everything they were carrying into the boot of Umber's hire car, then he went into the hotel and checked out.

'Where have you been staying?' Umber asked Chantelle.

'A small hotel on the other side of St Helier.'

'Right. We'll pick up your stuff, pay your bill and make for the airport.

'We're leaving Jersey?'

'The sooner the better.'

Umber's every instinct told him they would be safer off the island. What they were going to do back in England he had no idea.

'Where did you grow up, Chantelle?' he asked as they headed round the coast road towards St Helier.

'South Africa. Hong Kong. Gibraltar. We moved about. My parents—'

She broke off. 'Roy and Jean Hedgecoe. That's what they're called. Not Dad and Mum to me any more. Roy was in import-export, whatever that meant. He had business with strange people.'

'Any brothers or sisters?'

'No. Just me. When I was sixteen, we moved to Monaco. A reward, I guess. For looking after me so carefully. We lived high there.'

'And you met Michel Tinaud?'

'Yeah. He thought he was God's gift. So did I. I was pretty stupid back then. I had no idea what was really going on. I was a different person. Some other girl they'd brought me up to be. I was crazy about Michel. I went to Paris with him. Then Wimbledon. That's when everything changed. I know you want me to tell you what happened when Sally tracked me down. But can I tell you later? I just . . . don't want to talk about it right now.'

'OK.'

'But I *will* talk about it.' She glanced at him. 'I promise.'

THEY ENTERED St Helier and drove through the Fort Regent tunnel, then followed the main road out to the east until Chantelle pointed out the Hotel Talana ahead of them. Umber pulled into the car park at the rear and Chantelle went in to pack her few belongings and check out.

While she was gone, Umber fetched the camcorder from the boot. He unloaded the cassette, dropped it onto the ground and stamped on it several times. He dragged the tape out of the wreckage, shoved it into his pocket for later destruction and got back into the car. At least he did not have to worry about being fitted up as Wisby's accomplice now, though there was no telling what Wisby would say about him to the police. After all, Wisby had no way of knowing that Umber was not party to the plot against him. His best hope of persuading the police to believe that he had been framed was to tell at least some of the truth about his reasons for visiting Jersey and to finger Umber as a treacherous accomplice. He could not prove that Umber had played any part in blackmailing Jeremy Hall, but he *could* prove that Umber had been working with George Sharp, another self-proclaimed victim of a frame-up. If the police then learned that there had been a killing at Jeremy's flat, they would eventually go to see Sharp's solicitor. Burnouf would probably be sufficiently alarmed to give them sight of the statement in which Umber had made it very clear that he was in Jersey to extract information from Jeremy Hall by whatever means he could devise.

Umber glanced at his watch. It was nearly six o'clock. By the time he got there, it would be too late for conducting business at Le Templier & Burnouf, so either he would have to leave the statement where it was . . . or he would not be leaving Jersey as soon as he wanted to.

UMBER TRIED to persuade Chantelle to fly home without him, but to no avail. Then he tried to persuade her to eat something, but she insisted she was not hungry and in truth he had no appetite himself. After booking into the Prince of Wales, the hotel overlooking the beach at Grève de Lecq on Jersey's north coast, they walked down to the shore and watched the sea crash in, the surf a ghostly grey rim to the blackness of the night-time ocean.

'You saw me that day, didn't you, Shadow Man? The day my first life ended. The life I don't even remember. You were at Avebury on July the 27th, 1981.'

'Me and a few others, yes.'

'But most of them are dead, aren't they? My sister. My brother. Your wife. All gone now.'

'What about the day your second life ended, Chantelle? Can you bear to tell me about that?'

'Reckon I've got to.'

'It'd be good if you wanted to.'

'I do.' She shivered. 'Let's go inside.'

There was a trayful of paraphernalia for making tea and coffee in Umber's room. He turned the radiator up to maximum while the kettle was boiling, then sat on the bed. Chantelle took the only chair, which she dragged close to the radiator. She looked drained and haunted and, somewhere deep inside, damaged. She sat hunched in the chair, holding her mug of coffee in both hands, her voice barely above a whisper.

'I suppose I knew from my early teens that there was something iffy about the way Roy made a living. And about the people he did business with. I never asked. That wasn't encouraged. I was spoiled rotten and I liked it. We had it soft in Monte Carlo. Big duplex looking straight out onto the Med. Everything I wanted. Except . . . background. There was no family. No grandparents, aunts, uncles and cousins like my friends had. Unless you counted Uncle Eddie, which you can bet I didn't. Only children of dead only children. That was Roy and Jean's story. And they were sticking to it.

'It didn't bother me, anyway. I was having too much fun. After I finished school, they wanted me to go to university and I thought, great, that'll be in

England. But no. They didn't want that. Easy to see why, now. At the time, I thought they were just being overprotective. They were keen on Nice, so I could come home at weekends. We argued. In the end, I went nowhere. That pissed them off. I went with boys they didn't approve off. That pissed them off some more. Then I met Michel and it was, like, all is forgiven. He was perfect as far as they were concerned.

'Then came the Wimbledon trip. They couldn't really object after going such a bundle on him. So what did they do? They came with us. Michel had rented a flat near the club and I stayed with him there. Roy and Jean booked themselves into a plush hotel. I thought that they were just using my trip as an excuse to visit London. We saw some of the sights together while Michel was busy practising. Though now, when I look back, I see what they really did was . . . mind me. Make sure that whatever they couldn't help worrying *might* happen *didn't* happen.

'But it happened anyway. Despite them. It was June the 23rd, 1999. Michel was still at the club; I'd gone back to the flat. Hadn't been there more than a few minutes when Sally arrived. She'd followed me from the club, she said. She told me who she was. Then she told me who I was.

'I thought she was mad. Michel thought the same when he arrived. More or less threw her out. Told me to forget about her. She was a crazy woman trying to get to him through me. Typical of him to decide it was all about *him*. We rowed. I went for a walk to clear my head. I didn't believe Sally. But I didn't exactly *dis*believe her either, even then. What she'd said made a horrible kind of sense. It wasn't something I could just ignore.

'Sally was waiting for me at the corner of the street, as I suppose I'd half hoped she would be. I walked with her to Southfields tube station, listening as she talked. I made a deal with her. I'd think about what she'd said. I'd ask my "parents" some questions. I'd meet her on Friday morning, to talk some more. We agreed the boating lake in Wimbledon Park as a rendezvous. She kissed me and went into the station. And I never saw her again.

'I never got the chance to put any questions to Roy and Jean. Michel had called them and they were at the flat when I got back. Why had I let her in? Why had I talked to her? I was gobsmacked. It was like I'd done something wrong, *really* wrong. They were taking me back to Monte Carlo right away, they said. Michel sided with them, said he couldn't concentrate on his tennis with so much going on. I saw through him that night, but I didn't bother to argue. I could tell it was a waste of breath.

'Roy and Jean went back to their hotel, saying they'd collect me in the morning. I decided there and then I wasn't going to be collected. I started another row with Michel, knowing he'd react by storming out. He was a pretty predictable kind of guy. Once he was out of the way, I packed a rucksack and left. I walked all the way into the centre of London. It was a warm night. I remember sitting on the Embankment at dawn thinking: You've done it now, girl, you really have. I wasn't short of money, of course. I bought breakfast, tried to stop feeling sorry for myself and asked a policeman where I could look up back copies of national newspapers.

'I ended up spending most of the day in the Newspaper Library at Colindale. As soon as I saw one of the photographs of Tamsin Hall, I knew. Sally had told me the truth. I read every report there was on the case. I stayed there till closing time, then spent that night at a hotel. Early next morning, I went back to Wimbledon. It was risky, of course. But I had to see Sally again. I had to tell her I believed her and ask her what to do next. I waited for her in the park for hours. She never turned up, obviously. She was already dead by then. I found that out from the paper the next morning.

'They'd killed her. I was certain of that. Not Roy and Jean. But whoever was behind the whole thing. They'd ordered her death like they'd ordered Tamsin's abduction—*my* abduction. I still don't know who gave the order. And why. And back then I didn't even want to find out. I was so frightened. There was no one I could trust.

'So I ran. For years. India. Hawaii. South America. All over. A guy I met in Nepal fixed me up with a fake French passport and I became Chantelle Fontanet. But sooner or later, pretending you don't care what the truth is about your life doesn't cut it any more. Last summer, I came face to face with the realisation that I had to try to find the answers to all the questions.

'Sally had told me that Oliver and Jane were divorced. She'd also told me that Jeremy was living with his father here in Jersey. I felt sure Jeremy had to be innocent. He was only ten years old at the time, after all. I reckoned he was the one member of the family I might be able to trust. *Might.* I came to Jersey and tracked him down to St Aubin, watched him going out with his sailing classes. I hung around, working up the courage to approach him.

'As it turned out, *he* approached *me*. He'd noticed the attention I was paying him and one day demanded to know what I was up to. I ummed and ahhed a bit. And then—what would you call it? Sibling instinct? I don't know. But he recognised me. "It's you, isn't it?" he said. "You've come back."

'Jem was on pretty poor terms with Oliver by then. He didn't quite trust him any more. Or Marilyn. Things had never been the same since Radd's confession, he said. There was no good reason to believe Radd was telling the truth. But they did. The way he saw it, my turning up was his reward for keeping the faith. He was . . . exultant. High on the joy of it. So was I.

'Those first few months were just the absolute best. We rented a flat in St Malo, as it seemed safer to spend most of our time together in France. Once the sailing season was over, I had Jem to myself. We were careful. I dyed my hair. And we never used mobiles. Jem taught me to stop doing that thing with my lower lip that had caught Sally's eye in *Hello!* People must have taken us for boyfriend and girlfriend, I suppose.'

'But there were still those questions, niggling away at us. It seemed worse for Jem than for me. Our parents were two people I'd never known. But he'd loved and trusted them implicitly. He needed to know the truth more than I did. He couldn't let it go. It was Marilyn he was most suspicious of. She was spending more and more time in London. She and Oliver were virtually separated. When I described Eddie Waldron to Jem, he thought it sounded like a man he'd once seen Marilyn with in St Helier. She came over for Christmas. Jem was expected to spend the holiday at Eden Holt, and it would have looked odd if he'd refused, so off he went. He got into a row with them about Radd—and asked Marilyn a lot of pointed questions about how she and Oliver had met.

'He got more of a reaction than he'd bargained for. On New Year's Eve, when he was shopping in St Helier, he spotted Marilyn hurrying out of a bank with a brown-paper parcel in her hand, looking furtive. He followed her into Royal Square, where she sat down on a bench and unwrapped the parcel. Inside were two small antique books. Well, Marilyn's no book collector, is she? Jem was suspicious. Specially when she tore the front page out of each of the books and folded them away in her handbag. Then she put the books into a carrier bag and headed off.

'Jem followed her to Quires, in Halkett Place. He watched her through the window and saw her slip the books onto the shelf. Then she left. Jem went into the shop and took a look at the books. When he saw what they were, he knew he had to buy them. They were evidence. Evidence that Marilyn was keen to get off her hands. Jem had got hold of a transcript of the original inquest, so he knew what you'd told the coroner about Griffin and the special edition of the Junius letters. And there they were. Minus the flyleaves. The fact that Marilyn had torn them out clinched it for him. His probing over Christmas had panicked her. Maybe she'd meant to get rid of the books for years but hadn't bothered to till then.

'The Junius letters were clearly the key to it all, but Jem didn't really understand why. He couldn't get the idea out of his head of using them in some way to expose the truth. Eventually, he decided to construct a message out of words and phrases in the letters and send it to three people outside the family who he hoped could be goaded into going back into the case. Sharp. Wisby. And Hollins—the policeman who put Radd away. Looks like Hollins ignored the letter. But Sharp and Wisby rose to the bait.

'Jem didn't kill himself because he was afraid you'd expose his campaign to his parents, y'know. He did it to shield me. He was spooked by the ruthlessness of whoever's behind all this. He felt guilty for stirring up trouble for me. He didn't quite believe they'd killed Sally. But when they killed Radd? Then he believed. He didn't know where they'd stop. He wanted the truth to come out. All he got for his pains was unwelcome attention from you and Wisby. You meeting me was the last straw, I reckon. So he sent me to St Malo, knowing he never would meet up with me there. And then he went to finish it with you and Wisby the only way he could.

'I'm alone now, like I guess I always have been. I don't know what to do. I can't hide; I can't show myself. I want justice for Jem. And for myself. I want everyone to face the truth. And I want to know what the truth is.'

Chantelle was so clearly exhausted when she went back to her room that Umber hoped she would sleep for the rest of the night. He held out no such hope for himself. He lay on his bed, not even bothering to undress, staring into the darkness above his head.

He rose at dawn and slipped out of the hotel, carrying the knife in its bundle of black plastic. He fetched the bag containing Chantelle's blood-stained clothes from the car and followed the coast path as it climbed a hill to the west. He had to cut through a small copse and a bank of bracken beyond to reach the edge of the cliff. He tossed the bag and the bundle over. They fell among rocks and foaming sea, lost to the eye almost at once.

THE NEXT MORNING they left Grève de Lecq and headed back to St Helier, so that Umber could retrieve his statement from Burnouf. The danger of discovery, Umber assured Chantelle, was minimal. It was just too soon for the police to have thought of contacting Burnouf. And Waldron's associates had no reason to. It was a simple errand, swiftly and easily accomplished. Nothing would go wrong. That did not stop him telling Chantelle what to do if something *did* go wrong, however. They sat in the car in the Pier Road multistorey, facing a concrete wall, as nine o'clock ticked round.

'If I'm not back by ten, leave without me. Take the Juniuses with you and get off the island. Go to London. Phone this woman.' He passed her Claire Wheatley's card. 'Claire was Sally's psychotherapist. You can trust her. Tell her everything. She'll know what to do for the best.'

'But you *will* be back by ten, won't you?'

'I fully intend to be.'

'So, no need to worry, then.'

'None at all. I'll see you soon.' He gave her a parting smile and climbed out of the car.

THE RECEPTIONIST at Le Templier & Burnouf was sorting through the post when Umber arrived, and took a while to absorb the message that he wanted the envelope he had left with Burnouf and he wanted it now. She rang Burnouf on the internal line and he agreed to spare Umber five minutes.

The ever placid solicitor was still on the phone, instructing the receptionist to fetch the envelope from the safe, when Umber hurried into his office.

'Thank you, Janet.' Burnouf rang off. 'Good morning, Mr Umber. Bright and early, I see.'

'Sorry to burst in on you. I, er . . . well, there's been a . . .'

'Promising development? You left your statement as a precaution, so I understood. Retrieving it suggests precautions are no longer necessary.'

'I've . . . changed my mind about it. I'm allowed to do that, aren't I?'

'Of course. It's just . . .' Burnouf frowned. 'Mr Sharp reappears before the magistrates this morning. I tried to reach you at the Pomme d'Or to discuss his prospects, but they said you'd checked out.'

Umber smiled weakly. 'I found somewhere cheaper.'

'Should I still say nothing to him about your activities on his behalf?'

'I'll leave that for you to decide.'

'Really? You seem, if I may—' There was a tap at the door. The receptionist came in with the taped and sealed envelope. 'Thank you, Janet.'

'There's the receipt,' said Umber, whipping it out of his pocket and placing it on the desk. 'May I?' He held out his hand.

'By all means.' Burnouf passed him the envelope. 'There's space on the receipt for you to confirm retrieval. He proffered a pen. Umber signed. 'Leaving Jersey, Mr Umber?'

'Did I say I was?'

'No. It's just . . . an impression I have.'

'Thanks for this,' Umber said stiffly. 'I've got to go. I'll be in touch.' He turned and made for the door, but before he reached it something stopped him. He looked back at Burnouf. 'Perhaps you could pass a message to George for me after all. Tell him . . . it isn't over.'

UMBER HURRIED out of Le Templier and Burnouf and started back the way he had come, his thoughts fixed on getting himself and Chantelle off Jersey as quickly as possible. He glanced at his watch. It had just turned half past nine; he was comfortably on schedule. His gaze returned to the street ahead.

And he found himself looking into the eyes of Percy Nevinson.

'David! Well, well, well.' Nevinson beamed at him. 'How very nice to see you. And how very unexpected.'

Umber's heart sank. 'Percy, I—'

'I assume we're bound for the same destination this morning.'

'Where might that be, Percy?'

'The magistrates' court.' Nevinson winked. 'Mr Sharp's hearing. It should prove interesting, I think. Of course, you may be able to tell me how he finds himself in such a position. Why don't we grab a cup of coffee? '

'Sorry. I'm in a rush. Can't stop.'

'Well, I'll walk with you and we can talk as we go. You see, I can hardly believe Mr Sharp's predicament is unconnected with the latest tragedy to strike the Hall family. Jeremy Hall's suicide is what prompted me to come to Jersey. I imagine you can tell me a good deal about that, if you've a mind to.'

'But I don't have a mind to, Percy. That's the point. Now I—'

The events of the next few seconds were compressed into a bewildering jumble in Umber's mind. A white Transit van appeared suddenly, bounced up onto the pavement and lurched to a halt a few inches from him, the side-door sliding open fast as it did so. He was grabbed from behind by someone on the pavement, the envelope plucked from his hand. A second figure grasped his shoulders. Then he was hoisted into the van.

He was face down on an oily blanket covering the floor as the door slammed shut. There was a shout of '*Go!*' then the van surged forward.

His head was yanked up. A blindfold was slung across his eyes, a strip of duct tape slapped across his mouth. His hands were crushed together behind his back, then cords twined round his wrists and tightened. He tried to struggle up, but a boot descended heavily on his neck.

Then came a rasping voice close to his ear. 'Lie still or we'll break every fucking bone in your body.'

THEY WERE on the road for about half an hour, Umber estimated. His shock faded slightly, but his fear only increased. What they meant to do with him he did not know. The only consolation he had was that they had struck too soon. He might have led them to Chantelle if they had held off.

Eventually, the van came to a halt. The side door slid open, and he was pulled upright and bundled into the open air. 'Start walking,' came the instruction. He was frogmarched forward for about twenty yards. Then: 'Get in the car.' He was pushed through an open car doorway, a hand pressing down his head to clear the frame. The door clunked shut behind him.

He could smell new leather and a residue of cigar smoke, and sensed there was someone beside him. He heard an envelope being torn open, a rustling of paper. A few minutes of silence followed. Then the man beside him spoke in a soft, moist, sticky tone, as if he was sucking a toffee.

'Listen carefully, Mr Umber. I'm going to offer you a deal. We want Cherie. Or Chantelle, as I gather she calls herself now. And we believe you can find her for us. There's a time limit, naturally—three days. I'm going to put a card in your pocket.' Umber felt something being slipped into his shirt pocket. 'There's a phone number on it. Ring us by noon on Friday with details of where and when we can collect the girl. In return, we'll arrange for a reliable witness to tell the police he saw the drugs being planted on Sharp's van and we'll refrain from sending them this incriminating document you've kindly supplied us with. We cleaned up after you at the flat in St Aublin, but there's a body waiting to be found in an abandoned car at Noirmont Point which fingerprints and DNA would tie you to for certain *if* the police were pointed in the right direction. Wisby's likely to throw all sorts of accusations your way. You need to be in a position to refute them. But I don't need to spell it out for you, do I? You're an intelligent man. You can see there's no choice. So, just nod your head to confirm we have a deal. That's all you have to do. That and deliver the girl, of course.' There was a pause. 'Well?'

A moment slowly passed. Then Umber nodded.

'Thank you, Mr Umber. Its a pleasure doing business with you.'

UMBER'S CAPTORS led him back to the van and it set off once more. When it came to a halt, the side door was slid open and Umber was hauled through the doorway and onto his feet. His hands were untied, the door slid shut behind him and the van pulled away. By the time he had removed the blindfold and let his eyes adjust to the light, the van was out of sight. He was standing by a five-bar gate into a field, on the other side of which a herd of Jersey cattle were grazing contentedly. One of them cast him a mildly curious glance.

Umber started walking in the direction the van had taken, reasoning fuzzily that a main road was likely to be closer ahead than behind. His throat was dry, his lips were sore from the tape, his eyes ached from constriction by the blindfold and the back of his head was throbbing. But none of these discomforts had the merit of taking his mind off the deal he had notionally struck.

Within three days, he was required to betray Chantelle to her pursuers, something he had no intention of doing. But what was he to do instead?

A forty-minute hike through a maze of lanes took Umber to the village of Maufant, where he had to wait half an hour for a bus back to St Helier.

It was gone one o'clock by the time he was delivered to Liberation Square. He hurried up Pier Road to the multistorey, hoping he would find the hire car gone—and Chantelle with it.

The car was where he had parked it, but Chantelle was not there. The car was unlocked, the key still in the ignition. He opened the boot. Her bag had gone, along with the Juniuses. His bag and the box of Junius-related papers remained. Umber had to assume that Chantelle would leave Jersey and make for London, so he decided to call Claire and forewarn her.

But all he got on her practice number was the answering machine. And her mobile was switched off. He got no response from Alice's home number either. He went back to the car and headed for the airport.

There was no queue at the BA desk and the woman on duty was chatting with a female colleague as he approached. One of them had a newspaper open in her hands. The name 'Jeremy Hall' reached Umber's ears an instant before they noticed him. He peeled off to inspect a rack of leaflets, remaining within earshot as their conversation continued.

'The coffin was on the one-thirty flight. His mother was aboard. I saw her in the club lounge. Like a ghost, she was. So pale.'

'Was the father with her?'

'There was a man. But he didn't look like this picture of Oliver Hall.'

'The second husband, then. It must be dreadful for all of them. '

Umber had heard enough. He interrupted and booked himself onto the 5.30 flight. His eye strayed to the newspaper they had been reading. He could see the headline: MURDERED GIRLS' BROTHER TO BE BURIED IN ENGLAND. Was it possible that Chantelle had been on the same flight as her mother— and her dead brother? He felt sick at the thought.

After checking in his box of notes as hold luggage, he made for the pay-phones and called Claire again. It was the same story: recorded messages at the practice and Alice's house, and Claire's mobile was still switched off.

Nor did the story change when he tried again at Gatwick, after a short but anxious flight. Umber's only recourse now was to head for Hampstead and hope to find Claire and Alice in. The box he was carrying seemed to weigh more every time he picked it up, so after the Gatwick Express had delivered him to Victoria, he took a taxi.

It was gone eight thirty when the taxi pulled up outside 22 Willow Hill. The hall light was on, but the ground and first-floor rooms were in darkness. Claire's TVR was not parked nearby. The auguries were far from good. Umber thought he had wheedled an undertaking out of Claire to dissuade Alice from going to Monte Carlo to grill Michel Tinaud. But it was begin-ning to look as if they had both overestimated her powers of dissuasion.

The lights *were* on in the top-floor flat, which was occupied, Alice had mentioned, by an articled clerk called Piers. Umber clambered out of the taxi and pressed the bell next to the neatly printed label: PIERS BURTON.

Just as he was about to give the bell a second prod, the door opened. A curly-haired young man in fogeyish casual wear regarded him through owlish, black-framed glasses and ventured a wary hello.

'Piers, right?'

'Yes. I—'

'I'm David. I'm, er . . . a friend of Alice's.'

'Alice isn't here. There was a note waiting for me when I got home this evening. She's taken off with her friend Claire. The note didn't say where.'

'Did it say for how long?'

'Open-ended, apparently. A few days. A week. She wasn't sure.'

'Right.' Monte Carlo it had to be. Claire's mobile had probably been switched off during the flight. If Chantelle had tried to contact her, she would not have succeeded. The fail-safe Umber had supplied her with had proved to be useless. 'Well, thanks.'

'No problem.'

FAST RUNNING OUT of options, Umber booked himself in at a hotel near Euston Station for the night. He thought about trying Claire's mobile again, then thought better of it for reasons that had begun to take shape in his mind.

He did some more thinking in a large and noisy pub a few doors along from the hotel. If Claire and Alice were intent on confronting Tinaud, it might be better, in fact, if they knew as little as possible about his errant former girlfriend's whereabouts. But that conclusion left Umber alone and resourceless. If he was no better placed come Friday, the roof would fall in on all of them. He had to seize the initiative. But how?

Quite suddenly, around the time a tsunami of cheers burst over him following a goal in the football match splashed across the pub's widescreen TV, the glimmer of an answer came to him. And with it a sliver of hope.

Junius held the key. Chantelle had said as much and maybe she was right. Wisby believed that Griffin had been done away with by Tamsin's abductors, that his special edition of Junius's letters had ended up in the hands of Marilyn Hall. Did that make her one of the abductors? If so, it was a chink in the armour of whoever she had been acting for—the juicy-voiced man in the car, for one. If Umber could pin Griffin's murder on her, it would give him a bargaining chip. It was a tall order. It required him to trace the previously untraceable Griffin. And that brought him back to the hunt for Junius.

EIGHT

Opening the Junius box returned Umber, for the duration of a sleepless night, to his past, before Avebury. His life had been so simple then, so unfettered. A sense of that freedom reached him from every eagerly scribbled note, every neatly labelled batch of papers. They were the work of a younger, sharper-brained man, a man who believed academic zeal was the surest way to prise a secret from its history.

Separate bundles of notes and photocopied documents recalled to Umber the effort he had devoted to each line of research. THE HIGHGATE SOURCE. Examination of postmarks revealed that a significant number of the Junius letters were dispatched to the *Public Advertiser* by penny post from the Highgate Village post office. Which of the candidates lived in Highgate or had friends or relatives who lived there? THE COURIER QUESTION. Junius began a letter to Henry Woodfall on 18 January 1772 with the statement: 'The gentleman who transacts the conveyancing part of our correspondence tells me there was much difficulty last night'. Woodfall's letters to Junius were always left at prearranged coffee-house drops around the Strand. Did Junius always use the same courier for their collection? If so, was there any evidence as to his identity? THE AMANUENSES . . . Ah yes. This was the point Umber's researches had arrived at towards the end of the Trinity term of 1981. And there was a clutch of papers labelled *Christabella Dayrolles*. He sifted through them in search of the notes he knew he must have made during his inspection of the Ventry Papers, likely repository of any clue that Christabella Dayrolles had written the letters at Junius's dictation.

Umber had evidently examined all there was to be examined on the uncelebrated doings of the wife of Lord Chesterfield's godson. But this amounted to very little. If Christabella Dayrolles *was* Junius's amanuensis, he had chosen wisely. Her discretion alone had survived her. For the Ventry Papers, Umber had written the briefest of notes: *16/7/81. Ventry Papers. Prob a dead end, but worth checking Kew ref in sister's letter to Mrs V of 19 Oct 1791.*

What was the Kew reference? The note did not say. Umber had intended to follow it up long before there was any danger of forgetting it. But eleven days after his visit to the Staffordshire County Record Office, something had happened to put such matters out of his mind. Until now. He had to go to Stafford and nail down the reference. It might be a waste of precious time, but he could not know that without going.

HE CAUGHT an early train from Euston the next morning and was in Stafford by nine o'clock.

The staff at the County Record Office were soothingly efficient. The Ventry Papers were in his hands within half an hour. They had been bound in several marbled leather volumes by a Ventry of the Edwardian period, who had added a comprehensive table of contents. Umber steered a straight course through boundary disputes, rent-rolls and local hunt politics to the letter of 19 October 1791, written by Christabella Ventry's younger sister, Mary Croft, from London. She dwelt on family affairs that would be known to both parties. There were several references to their 'dear departed mother' (Christabella Dayrolles), who had died two months previously. And then came the reference to Kew.

*The depth of feeling expressed by so many since Mother's passing is a
testament to the nobility and generosity of her character. I was more
affected than I can say to receive a letter this week past from her dear
and troubled friend at Kew, who confesses himself sorely afflicted by
the loss of her counsel and acquaintanceship.*

That was it. It amounted to hardly anything. Yet there was just enough, in
the description of the friend as dear and troubled, in the mention of their
mother's role as his adviser, in the way Mary Croft avoided naming him, to
draw Umber in. There was no easy way to follow it up, however, Umber
admitted to himself as he sat aboard the lunchtime train back to London. An
unnamed man living in Kew two centuries before was effectively untraceable.
Umber would have to search for him by exploring any connections with Kew
that he could find in the affairs of Lord Chesterfield and Solomon Dayrolles.

Such researches could last for weeks, if not months. Umber had two
days. It was, quite simply, a hopeless task.

When Umber got off the train at Euston, he did not know what to do or
where to go. Largely by inertia, it seemed to him, he drifted down into the
Underground station, and bought a ticket to Kew.

On the tube, he tried to apply his mind to the problem like the historian
he had once been. What did he know about eighteenth-century Kew?

It was a place with royal connections. George II, when still Prince of
Wales, lived at Richmond Lodge, which he retained when he became king.
His son Frederick, the next Prince of Wales, settled with his wife Augusta at
Kew House, just to the north. After Frederick's death in 1751, Princess
Augusta pursued his ambition to transform the estate into the famous
botanical gardens. Frederick's son, the future George III, grew up at Kew
under the combined influence of his widowed mother and her trusted
adviser, the Earl of Bute. Junius reserved a particular venom for both parties, insinuating that they were lovers.

As soon as he left Kew Gardens station, Umber wandered into a bookshop that caught his eye and bought a pocket history of the area: *The Story
of Kew*. He leafed through it over a cup of coffee in a café, lingering on the
chapters devoted to the Georgian period. Then he left the café and headed
towards Kew Green. A map of 1800 reproduced in *The Story of Kew*
showed the whole area east of the Botanical Gardens as fields. There were
only two small areas of housing: one centred on the Green, at the northern

end of the Gardens, the other lining the opposite bank of the Thames either side of Kew Bridge. Logically, Christabella's mystery friend had to have lived in one of these locations.

It could not have been the Green, Umber sensed as he prowled across it, scanning the elegant Palladian frontages of the surrounding houses. In 1791, they would have been the residences of princes and princesses. Surely, Christabella's friend could not have dwelt among them. To fit Umber's hazy image of him, he needed to be an observer from a safe distance.

Umber crossed Kew Bridge and turned right along Strand-on-the-Green, a riverside path running east round a curve of the Thames, past well-kept fishermen's cottages and gentlemen's villas from the eighteenth century. This, he reckoned, was more like it. Humbler than Kew Green, but still smart enough, and within easy reach. It was only a hunch, of course. He was in no position to back it up. There was simply not enough—

He came to a sudden halt and stared at the building in front of him. It was a small, yellow-brick cottage squeezed between two grander residences. The front door was undersized, accessed by a short flight of steps, and above and to one side of it was a stone-carved likeness of a mythical beast, acting as a lampholder. The creature had the wings and head of an eagle, set on the body of a lion. It was a griffin.

Deciding to let chance and circumstance take their course, Umber pressed the bell, staring into the stone eye of the griffin as he did so.

'Good afternoon.' The door had been opened by a tall man of sixty or so with wavy grey hair and a ruggedly handsome face. The guernsey he was wearing gave him a maritime air, suggesting his stooped posture had been acquired from long acquaintance with cramped ships' cabins, his squinting gaze from the scanning of many horizons. 'Can I help you?'

'I . . .' Umber did not know what to say, or at any rate how to begin to say it. 'I'm looking for . . . a Mr Griffin.'

The man smiled. 'Well, you've found him.'

UMBER SAT in the small, spruce drawing room and explained himself as best he could. He had got no further than the bizarre truth that he had come in search of someone he had been due to meet twenty-three years previously, when his host, who had introduced himself as Philip Griffin, interrupted.

'Sounds as if you're talking about my brother Henry, Mr Umber. Before we go any further, I ought to tell you that 1981 was the last year anyone ever saw or heard of him. I was out of the country at the time. I didn't find out that Henry had gone missing till I got back here thirteen years later. So, when and where did you have this appointment with him?'

'Avebury. July the 27th, 1981.'

'Avebury? 1981?' Griffin's brow furrowed. 'Haven't I read something recently about a murder at Avebury in 1981?' He snapped his fingers. 'That's right. The bloke they got for it was murdered in prison a couple of weeks ago. What's Henry got to do with all this?'

Umber answered as fully as he could. He emphasised that his theory about what had happened to Henry Griffin was just that: a theory.

'I'm sorry to be the bearer of bad news, Mr Griffin,' he concluded. 'I suppose you must have hoped he was still alive somewhere.'

'It's OK. I wrote Henry off a long time ago. He and I didn't really see eye to eye. That was one of the reasons I left Father and him to it after Mother died, and took myself off round the world. I lost touch with them, and didn't come back for nearly twenty years. When I did, I found Father going gaga with this house collapsing around his ears—and no trace of Henry. The neighbours said it was the summer of '81 when Henry vanished. So, it sounds as if your theory fits the facts, doesn't it?'

'Yes. I suppose it does.'

'And it also sounds as if Henry died trying to be a good citizen, which is some consolation. But you haven't mentioned the reason for your appointment with Henry.'

'Ah. Well, I was at Oxford, studying for a PhD. Your brother phoned me out of the blue, saying he had a pair of books relevant to the subject of my thesis which he was sure would interest me. We agreed to meet at Avebury so that I could take a look at them.'

'What books were these?'

'A special edition of the letters of Junius.'

'Junius?' Griffin's expression suggested surprise rather than incomprehension. 'Well, well, well.'

'You've heard of him?'

'Oh yes. Growing up in this house, you could hardly fail to. The Griffin family legend, we'd better call it. Junius . . . and our claim to the throne.'

'What?'

'Laughable, isn't it? But Henry believed it. So did Father.' Griffin smiled ruefully. 'Don't worry. I'm not about to serve a writ on the Queen and demand the keys to Buckingham Palace. But it's entertaining stuff in its way. Want me to fill you in on it?'

'Yes, please.'

'Well, before I do, let's get back to these books. How special were they?'

'Very. A uniquely bound copy of the letters printed for Junius's own use.'

'I see. Which means it ties in with something Father said a couple of times. He called Henry a thief, but he never said what he was supposed to have stolen. Father must have kept the books hidden away. And Henry must have found them.' Griffin rose to his feet. 'Wait here, would you? There's something I want to show you.'

Close to ten minutes passed, during which the sounds of drawers being opened and closed in an upper room reached Umber's ears intermittently. Then Griffin returned, clutching a stapled sheaf of papers.

'There was a lot of Henry's stuff left here when Father died. I kept this, if only because it's as handy an account of the family legend as you could ask for. As you'll see, Henry hoped to get it published. But it wasn't to be.' He passed the papers to Umber. 'Take your time. I'll make some tea.'

Umber was alone again. He looked at the papers in his hand. The top sheet was a rejection letter to Henry from the editor of *History Today*, dated April 16, 1980, referring to an article that Henry had submitted, entitled 'Junius, the Royal Family and the Griffins of Kew'. The editor described the piece as 'diverting', but crushingly added, 'I am sorry to say that you provide no supporting evidence for any of your extraordinary assertions.' The typed article was attached. Umber settled down to read it.

My family has lived in Kew for nearly two hundred years. Strangely, the founder of our family was a man none of us is related to. This man, Frederick Lewis Griffin, is historically very important, though history has nothing to say about him.

Frederick Griffin was born in Covent Garden, London, on 29 June 1732. He was an illegitimate son of Frederick, Prince of Wales, by the actress Sarah Webster. His mother gave him the surname Griffin because the Prince had been known, in his childhood in Hanover, as '*Der Grief*'—the Griffin, a beast he was supposed to resemble.

The Prince paid Sarah Webster a generous allowance for his son's upbringing, continuing to do so after his marriage to Princess Augusta of Saxe-Gotha in 1736. When Sarah Webster died, in 1740,

the Prince arranged for his friend the Earl of Chesterfield to look
after the boy, who was given an excellent education.

Frederick Griffin was an undergraduate at Oxford when the Prince
died suddenly on March 20, 1751, aged 44. Princess Augusta
immediately cancelled the allowance paid to him and he was forced
to leave Oxford. Lord Chesterfield obtained a position for him in the
East India Company, and he spent the next ten or twelve years in
India, returning to England in the mid-1760s a moderately wealthy
man. He bought a small house at Strand-under-Green (now Strand-
on-the-Green) and lived there for the rest of his life.

It has always been believed in my family that he chose to live at
Strand-under-Green because of its proximity to the royal residences
of Kew Palace and Richmond Lodge. He had heard the rumour that
Princess Augusta had murdered his father, because he had discovered
her long-standing affair with the Earl of Bute. He had heard another
rumour concerning his half-brother, King George III, who had by
now succeeded to the throne. This was that George, while still Prince
of Wales, had secretly married Hannah Lightfoot, a Quaker, and had
a son by her, known as George Rex. Once on the throne, George had
put Hannah aside and contracted a politically more expedient
marriage to Princess Charlotte Sophia of Mecklenburg-Strelitz.

Frederick Griffin was appalled by such conduct and began a
letter-writing campaign under the name of Junius, protesting at
corruption in the high offices of government. Princess Augusta, 'the
odious hypocrite', as Junius called her, came in for particularly
harsh criticism. The letters, which appeared in the *Public Advertiser*
for three years, came to an abrupt end early in 1772, when Princess
Augusta's death deprived Junius of his principal target.

Frederick Griffin at some point befriended the young George Rex,
who was later appointed Notary Public to the Governor of Cape
Colony in South Africa. This appointment was subject to two
conditions: firstly that he should never return to England; secondly
that he should never marry. The intention was obviously to ensure
that his claim to the throne died with him. He abided by these
conditions to the extent that he remained in South Africa until his
death in 1839 and left no legitimate issue there.

We must now move forward to the famous theft of the parish

records at St Anne's Church, Kew, during the night of February 22/23, 1845. This has never been satisfactorily explained, although it has often been alleged that the Royal Family required the removal of the record of a marriage or baptism that they found embarrassing.

It has always been believed in my family that the theft was organised at the behest of Prince Albert to nullify a potential threat to the legitimacy of Queen Victoria's claim to the throne: the threat was posed by the fact that George Rex married a local woman called Mary Ann Leavers at St Anne's Church on 30 December 1796. Frederick Griffin was one of the witnesses.

When George Rex's marriage became known to the King, he took steps to have the couple separated and banished his son to South Africa. What George Rex did not know when he took ship for Cape Town in 1797, however, was that his wife was pregnant. A son, John, was born on January 3, 1798. His mother did not survive the birth. Honouring a promise given to her, Frederick Griffin became the boy's guardian and sought to protect his identity by conferring his own surname upon him.

Frederick Griffin died on August 25, 1815, aged 83. The written record of the burial was stolen from St Anne's Church, Kew, in 1845, along with the record of his ward's baptism.

John Griffin, rightful heir to the throne of England, led a quiet and private life and died on October 8, 1870, aged 72. He was my great-great-grandfather.

Philip Griffin had brought in the promised tea by the time Umber had finished reading. 'What do you think of it?' he asked.

'It could all be true. The Hannah Lightfoot–George Rex story is semi-official history these days. Your family legend accounts for the theft of the registers, but unfortunately there's no supporting evidence.'

'Could the special edition Junius have changed that?'

'It depends on the inscription. Your brother described it as illuminating. I suppose he was hoping my work on Junius would beef up his case. The Chesterfield connection certainly ties in with some leads I was following.'

'Father always said something called the Royal Marriages Act meant the Griffins' claim to the throne failed on technical grounds.'

'It's a good point. Since the Act was passed—in 1772—members of the Royal Family have needed the monarch's consent before they can marry. In which case, George Rex's marriage to Mary Ann Leavers doesn't count.'

'Something and nothing, then?'

'I wouldn't say that. It's a humdinger of a story. If I'd been able to dig up some hard evidence, it might have turned my file-and-forget thesis on Junius into a best-selling book. With your brother as co-author.'

Griffin smiled. 'Henry would have liked that.'

'So would I.' A thought suddenly struck Umber. 'What sort of car did your brother drive, Mr Griffin—the one he was travelling in to Avebury?'

'I don't know. He used to run a . . .' Griffin struggled with his memory for a moment. 'Triumph Herald estate. Yes, that's right.'

'What colour was it?' Umber asked, replaying in his mind's eye the glimpse he had had of the car that had followed the van out of Avebury that day in July 1981, past the small, broken body of Miranda Hall.

'Dark green.'

'Of course.' Dark green it was. Dark green it had to be.

DUSK WAS coming on when Umber left Strand-on-the-Green and wandered back towards Kew. He was more or less at the halfway point of the three days he had been given to find Chantelle and hand her over. He had traced Henry Griffin. He had learned what Griffin had meant to tell him at Avebury. And he had established Griffin's murder by Tamsin Hall's abductors as a virtual certainty. But none of that made any difference. Nor did the strange tale of the Griffins of Kew, which would once have delighted and fascinated him. It was no help in his predicament. It left him powerless to defy those who required an answer of him by noon on Friday.

Alcohol put Umber to sleep that night back at the hotel. He woke, dry-throated and gritty-eyed, with the stitches in his head tugging sharply at his scalp. Dawn was edging its grey fingers between the curtains of his room, and the traffic on Euston Road was only just beginning to thicken. He stared out at it as he sipped a black coffee, wondering what to do.

The answer came to him in the shower. Failing to contact Claire, Chantelle would have sought some other way out of the waking nightmare her life had become. It was quite possible she had flown to England on the same plane as her dead brother and the mother who thought she was dead too. Even if she had not, their destination must have drawn her as well. Home. The place where it all began. The unremembered start of her journey. There was nowhere else she was likelier to have gone.

Before setting off, Umber tried Claire's mobile. And this time there was an answer.

'Hello.' Her voice sounded as if she had just woken up.

'Claire. It's me. David.'

'David. Where are you?'

'London. Sorry if I woke you. I thought you'd already be up. You're an hour on in Monaco, aren't you?

'You must have been out to Hampstead, if you know where we are.'

'I thought you were going to wait until you'd heard from me, Claire.'

'For a few days. That's what we agreed. And that's as long as I *could* wait. Alice would have gone without me otherwise.'

'Have you spoken to Tinaud?'

'Not yet. His PA's blocking us. I haven't pushed it. I've been hoping you'd call and say there was no need. *Is* that what you're going to say?'

'In a sense. I'm in over my head, Claire. I know too much. I don't want to put you in the same position. Don't speak to Tinaud. And don't come back to London until you've heard from me again.'

'*What?* What's happening, David?'

'Trust me in this. You'll learn nothing from Tinaud I don't already know. But speaking to him may get you the attention of some very dangerous people. Don't do it. And don't come back here. At least for a few days.'

'You're going to have to—'

'Goodbye, Claire.' He put the phone down, certain, because he had withheld his number, that she would not be able to call him back.

HE SKIPPED breakfast, checked out of the hotel, took a cab to Liverpool Street Station and boarded a train for Ilford. The only place he could think of to store his box of Junius Papers was 45 Bengal Road. He planned to leave a note for Larter, then head west.

But his plan had taken no account of the pressure on beds in the National Health Service. Larter had been patched up and sent home. He was moving gingerly around the kitchen, preparing a bacon-and-egg start to the day, when Umber let himself in.

'Where have you been hiding yourself?' was the old man's wheezily barbed greeting. 'And what's in that bloody box?'

'Some old research papers of mine. I was hoping you could hold on to them for me. No one's going to come after them. I promise.'

'Better hadn't.' Larter hoiked an old cricket bat out from beside the fridge. 'I'll be ready for them this time.'

'Remember the one you called a smug-looking geezer?'

'What about him?'

'He won't be coming. I can tell you that for a fact.'

He eyed Umber suspiciously. 'Do I want to know how you can be so sure?'

'No, Bill. You don't.'

'Spoke to George yesterday. Said he'd had a . . . message from you. "It isn't over." Right?'

'Right.'

'How long before it is?'

'Not long at all. One way or the other.'

'Shall I put in an extra rasher for you?' Larter gestured at the frying pan with his spatula.

'Can't stop. But I'll be in touch.' Umber dropped the spare set of keys Larter had given him on the table. 'Thanks, Bill.'

'Don't mention it. And good luck, son.'

DOOR TO DOOR from 45 Bengal Road to the Royal Berkshire Hospital in Reading took Umber nearly two hours. Time was sliding through his fingers like sand. If the stitches in his head had not been causing him such discomfort, he would probably have given the out-patients' clinic a miss, but, as the whims of the NHS would have it, he did not have to wait long for the stitches to be removed and felt instantly better for it.

By one thirty he was clambering off a bus in Marlborough High Street. His first port of call was WH Smith, where he grabbed a copy of the local weekly newspaper. He was still in the queue, waiting to pay for it, when he found what he was looking for among the funeral notices.

HALL, Jeremy. Died tragically in Jersey, Thursday, March 25, aged
33. Dearest son of Jane and Oliver. A service of celebration for his
life will be held at Holy Cross Church, Ramsbury, on Friday, April 2,
at 11 a.m., followed by interment at Marlborough Cemetery at noon.
Family flowers only.

Umber reread the notice after he left the shop. It had to be a coincidence. But it did not feel like one. Jeremy Hall was due to be buried on the day and at the hour of the deadline Umber had been set for handing over Chantelle.

UMBER ENTERED the Kennet Valley Wine Company little expecting to find Edmund Questred manning the till. In truth, he was faintly surprised to find the shop open at all. But Questred had found a stand-in—a plump, bespectacled, middle-aged woman with an engaging smile.

'Good afternoon,' she said. 'Can I help you?'

'I'm looking for Mr Questred.'

'I'm afraid he's not in today. There's been a family bereavement.'

'I know. A terrible business. Do you happen to know which undertaker is handling the funeral? I, er . . .'

'*Umber.*' The office door beyond the counter opened by a foot or so and Edmund Questred stared out. 'Come in here.' He glanced at the woman. 'It's OK, Pam. We know each other.'

Umber edged round the counter and moved through into the office. Questred closed the door behind him.

'What are you doing here?' Questred looked and sounded too tired to summon up much in the way of overt hostility. 'And why do you want to know which undertaker we're using?'

The answer was that Chantelle might want to see Jeremy one last time before the funeral. But it was not an answer Umber could afford to give. 'I'm not sure. Just trying to draw something out, I suppose.'

'Haven't you the decency to drop all this now Jeremy's dead?'

'It's not a question of decency. But I'm sorry about Jeremy. Truly.'

'You're not planning to show up at the funeral, are you?'

'Would it be so awful if I did?'

Questred shook his head, as if despairing of Umber's insensitivity altogether. 'You have no idea, do you? Jane's lost three children. *Three.* Jeremy's suicide has brought back the grief of Tamsin and Miranda's deaths as well. If it weren't for Katy, I'm not sure Jane would be able to get through this. Seeing you won't help. I'm absolutely sure of that.'

Umber looked Questred in the eye. 'All I can say is . . . she won't see me unless I feel she has to.'

'Don't make tomorrow any more difficult than it has to be, Umber. Please don't do that to her.'

'I won't.'

'Is that a promise?'

'Yes.' It was one promise Umber was sure he could keep, if only because the events of tomorrow were so comprehensively beyond his control. 'It is.'

UMBER HEADED ALONG the High Street to the Ivy House Hotel, where he booked himself in for the night. Before going to his room, he borrowed the local Yellow Pages and hunted down the addresses of Marlborough undertakers. There were only two, so it seemed easier to walk round than phone ahead. As it happened, the first one he tried, a short walk away at the eastern end of town, was the firm handling the Jeremy Hall funeral.

He had harboured no wish to view the deceased, but felt bound to ask if he could do so, if only to camouflage his curiosity about who else had been to the chapel of rest for the same reason. The receptionist had been well schooled in the arts of discretion, however. She was giving nothing away, other than that he was the first person from outside the family to make such a request—which happened to be exactly what he wanted to know. So much for his hunch that Chantelle would not be able to stay away. Unless, of course, she had claimed to be a relative. A cousin perhaps.

He did not linger by the coffin. He prowled the room for a few minutes, just long enough to suggest that he was a sincere mourner, then hurried out.

The cemetery was his next destination. Men were at work digging the grave, not far from Miranda Hall's, where Jeremy Hall would be laid to rest tomorrow. There was a good chance Chantelle would go there.

But there was no sign of her. She could have been and gone, of course. She might be planning to visit later. Or she might be determined to stay away. She might be miles away. In a part of his mind, Umber hoped she was. But in another part, the part where hope held no sway, he knew she was not.

He walked out along the Ridgeway, then on across the downs towards Avebury. The afternoon began to fade into evening. The light was pearly grey, the air cool but barely moving. Once he saw a large bird that could have been a kestrel, hovering away to the north. But he could not be sure. He pressed on through the broad, rolling landscape.

He had acknowledged the probable futility of his journey long before he reached Avebury. The simple truth was that even if he was right about the places Chantelle would feel drawn to, he had no way of calculating when or even if she would actually visit them. If he found her, it would be pure luck.

Cresting the last hillock before the henge came into view, he half expected he *would* see her, walking slowly along one of the banks, head bowed, lost in thought. But she was not there. Umber walked most of the way round the northeastern bank, from which he had a clear view of the Cove. No one was loitering by the Adam and Eve stones.

He finished up in the high street of the village with nothing to show for his efforts, and headed towards the Red Lion. Chantelle might be waiting till dusk to put in an appearance, he told himself. He would wait at the pub, as he had waited before.

But someone had got there before him. As Umber rounded the front of the pub, he saw a figure seated at one of the tables, muffled up against the encroaching chill, anorak collar turned up, Tilley hat brim turned down.

'Good evening, David,' said Percy Nevinson. 'Thank goodness you've arrived. It's getting decidedly nippy out here.'

'Percy.' There had been a risk of bumping into Nevinson. Umber had realised that. But the pub was not the man's natural territory. It was clear that this encounter, unlike their last, was not a product of chance.

'Shall we go inside? Perhaps I could buy you a drink?'

'All right.' Umber struggled to recover himself. If Chantelle did turn up, the last person he wanted for company was Nevinson. Getting rid of the man would be next to impossible, however. Maybe it was safer for them to be inside the Red Lion than out. 'Let's do that.'

The bar was quiet. Nevinson bought Umber a pint, and a half for himself. They sat at a table by the window, Umber taking the chair facing it, so that he had a view of the road and the stones of the henge's southern inner circle.

Nevinson took off his hat, smiling at Umber with irritating mildness. 'When Abigail came back from Marlborough this afternoon, she told me she'd spotted you from the bus. I felt sure you'd come out here sooner or later if I waited long enough. Our last meeting was . . . rudely interrupted. It's good to have this opportunity to take up where we left off.'

'Look, Percy, I—'

'It's no good claiming to be in a hurry this time, David. The last bus to Marlborough left at six fifteen. Even if you phoned for a taxi now, we'd have at least twenty minutes to chat.'

'All right. Let's chat.' Umber smiled grimly and flung himself into an attempt to lead the discussion, since discussion there clearly had to be. 'Talking of Abigail, did you tell her why you went to Jersey? Or are you sticking to the ufological-conference line?'

Nevinson pursed his lips. 'A white lie to spare my sister's feelings, nothing more. Naturally, I've . . . come clean since returning home.'

'*Completely* clean, Percy? Did you mention hiring Wisby?'

Nevinson grimaced. 'That would only have confused her.'

'Why *did* you hire him?'

'I didn't. Not really. I asked him to share his findings with me, that's all. Which he never did, beyond what he judged sufficient to extract an exorbitant fee from me.'

'Slippery character, Wisby.'

'Indeed.'

'What about standing idly by while I was grabbed off the street by a couple of heavies in St Helier? As a law-abiding citizen, shouldn't you have phoned the police? You'd witnessed a kidnapping, after all.'

'In a sense, I *did* consult the police. A policeman, that is.' Nevinson's grin broadened. 'Well, a *retired* policeman. I spoke to Mr Sharp at the magistrates' court. Well, in a park *near* the magistrates' court, to be strictly accurate.'

'How come? He's in custody.'

'Not since Tuesday. He was granted bail, you see.'

'*What?*'

'Bail. In consideration of his status as a retired police officer, apparently. A thousand pounds and the surrender of his passport.' Nevinson's grin acquired a sickly thinness. 'I'm rather surprised you didn't know.'

Nevinson's surprise was nothing compared with Umber's. Larter had not breathed a word about this. Yet he must have been aware of it. For some reason, he and Sharp had decided to keep Umber in the dark. 'Are you sure about this, Percy?'

'How could I not be? I was there when the magistrates said their piece.'

'And what did George say when you talked?'

'Well, he was surprised to see me, naturally. But he rapidly deduced that news of Jeremy Hall's death had brought me to the island. He was very interested by what I had to tell him about you. And about Wisby, of course. It was at his request that I took the matter of your apparent kidnapping no further. He said he'd deal with it. I confess I'm not entirely clear what he meant by that.'

Neither was Umber. What in God's name was Sharp up to? How had he wangled bail, which Burnouf had said was next to impossible? And where had he been since?

'Wisby was up before the magistrates himself on Tuesday,' Nevinson went on. 'Caught trying to leave Jersey in possession of stolen money, apparently. No bail for him, of course. I think Mr Sharp meant to visit him before leaving Jersey himself.'

'He said he was going to visit Wisby?'

'Not in so many words.'

'And what about leaving Jersey?'

'I took it as read. Why would he stay when the next stage in the Hall family drama is about to unfold here in Wiltshire? Lack of a passport is no bar to travelling from Jersey to England, after all. I'm surprised he hasn't been in touch with you. Why would he be avoiding you, I wonder?'

'I'm wondering the same myself.'

'Could it be that Wisby has told him something that causes him to doubt your loyalty? If so, he may suspect you weren't really kidnapped at all. Or that you subsequently struck some kind of deal to secure your release.'

'Well, take it from me it wasn't a put-up job. And I've done no deals.'

'I'm happy to take your word on both scores, David. Despite all the evidence to the contrary—your current state of unfettered liberty for a start. Which I note you've conspicuously failed to explain.'

'Now just a—'

'None of my business, I'm sure. We must all shift for ourselves in this world. It was only a matter of time, after all.'

'What was?'

'Your removal from the chessboard.' Nevinson leaned forward, fixing Umber with a stare and lowering his voice. 'The powers that be have decreed that there can be no queening of pawns in this game.'

THE ONLY WAY to shake off Nevinson, it became clear, was to return to Marlborough. But Umber had to endure a further twenty minutes of the man until a taxi arrived. He stopped listening once Nevinson had veered off onto his favourite topic: the role of the intelligence community in stifling research into the Martian origins of the stone circles and avenues scattered around Avebury. Umber's mind filled instead with doubts and questions concerning Sharp's activities since Tuesday. He began to suspect that Nevinson was right. Sharp had concluded he could no longer be trusted. That was why he had sworn Larter to secrecy about his release. Umber's unannounced visit to Ilford, none the worse for his supposed kidnapping, must have seemed like confirmation of his treachery.

He had lied to Nevinson in one crucial regard. He *had* done a deal, albeit one he did not intend to fulfil. There *were* good reasons to believe he might have gone over to the opposition—whoever the opposition might be. He could not prove his good faith. He could only demonstrate it. But as long as Chantelle continued to elude him, there was no way he could do that.

During the taxi ride back to Marlborough, a suspicion somehow more disturbing even than the possibility that Sharp had written him off as a traitor formed in Umber's mind. Maybe Sharp was the one who had done the deal. Maybe his release on bail had been a quid pro quo. If so, Umber was more isolated than ever and the danger to Chantelle was all the greater.

NINE

The taxi dropped Umber outside the Ivy House, but he did not go in. Instead, he walked along the high street to the Green Dragon and took the edge off his anxiety with a couple of pints and double whisky chasers. It was gone ten o'clock when he made his woozy way back to the hotel. He had no plan now beyond a few hours' sleep.

'Message for you,' said the receptionist, handing him a note along with his key. 'Could you phone this number? Urgent, apparently.'

Umber stared at the piece of paper in his hand. A mobile number was written on it. And that was all. 'There's no name,' he blearily objected.

'He didn't leave one. Declined to, actually. I did ask.'

'Old? Young?'

'Not young. Polite. But . . . edgy. You know? Definitely edgy.'

Umber dialled the number from the phone in his room. It was answered before the second ring.

'That you, Umber?'

It was not the voice Umber had expected to hear. He had convinced himself that the message was from Sharp.

'Know who this is?'

'Of course.'

'We need to meet. Tonight.'

'Why?'

'Want the truth? The whole truth? And a way out of it?'

'Yes.'

'Then don't argue. I'll pick you up at midnight in front of the Town Hall.'

The line went dead.

Umber put the phone down, his mind struggling with the implications of what had just happened. It was too alluring to be anything but a trap. But he would go. He could not resist the bait.

MARLBOROUGH was quiet, the high street largely empty. Umber was early. He waited, sitting on the steps that led up to the Town Hall entrance.

Shortly after St Mary's Church clock struck twelve, a gleaming blue-black Bentley purred round the sharp bend to Umber's left and pulled in. Oliver Hall nodded at him through the driver's window, then jerked his head towards the passenger's door. Umber stood up, walked round and climbed in.

'You came, then.' Hall's face was sallow in the filtered amber lamplight, his eyes weary, his mouth set in a grim, charcoal-shadowed line.

'I said I would.'

'You *said* you'd wait to hear from me before visiting Jeremy. You didn't, though, did you?'

'Sharp's arrest forced my hand.'

'Did it really?'

'Yes. It really did.'

'Let's go.' Hall swung the car round into Kingsbury Street and headed up the hill Umber had climbed earlier on his way to the cemetery.

'How did you know where to find me?' he asked.

'Edmund told me you were in Marlborough. It was a fair bet you'd stay at the Ivy House again.'

'Where are you staying?'

'Worried about how close Marilyn is, are you, Umber?'

'Should I be?'

'No. She's still in London. I'm here alone.' Hall followed the road round to the right at the top of the hill and took another right onto the main road.

'Where are we going?'

'Savernake Forest. Where my ex-wife has convinced herself Radd buried Tamsin. No possibility of interruption there. No prying eyes or ears.'

The road curved as it climbed Postern Hill. At the top, Umber knew, Savernake began. Several square miles of heavily wooded land in which bodies could plausibly be buried—and secrets likewise.

'Jane believes our three children are all dead now, Umber. Do you believe that?'

'Do *you?*'

They drove in silence, the unanswered cross-questions contending in the darkness between them. The car's headlamps arced across the screen of trees ahead of them, then Hall said, with quiet emphasis, 'Of course not.'

Umber was at first too dumbstruck to respond. 'You mean . . .?'

'Tamsin is Cherie . . . is Chantelle. That's what I mean. You know it. And I've always known it.'

'You've *known*? All along?'

'Oh yes. Sometimes I've envied Jane her certainty. The simplicity of her grief. The finality of it. Tamsin dead rather than taken.' Hall sighed. 'But only sometimes.' He pulled in off the road. The cones of light from the head-lamps tunnelled ahead of them along a track leading into the woods. Hall drove slowly over the rough surface. 'Let's get clear of the road,' he said.

Fifty yards or so sufficed. At that point Hall steered into the side of the track and stopped. He turned off the engine and the lights. Darkness closed around them like a hood. Then Umber saw the glow of the dashboard lighter. Hall lit a cigar, then lowered the window. The damp night air drifted in, thinning the pungent smoke.

'What now?' Umber asked.

'I talk. And you listen.' Hall drew on the cigar. 'I've always done my best for my children, Umber. You may find that assertion ironic in the light of what you know. But it's true. I've done everything in my power to protect them.

'I'm going to tell you a story—the story of my life. It begins—and I sup-pose it ends—with money. The making of it. The multiplying of it. And the spending of it. I don't do much of the last. No need, really, with Marilyn on hand. And the first isn't strictly my line. But the second? I'm a past master at that. The keeping, the concealing and the breeding of wealth. That's my speciality. You could call it a gift. I don't, though. I understand all too clearly now how big a curse it can be. Because of the sort of people it's brought me into contact with.

'My career in banking was entirely above board until I met . . . let's call him Smith. I suspect you may have met him recently yourself, in Jersey. You may also have seen his oversized yacht moored in St Helier Harbour. I believed that Smith was a bona fide businessman. Likewise the friends he recommended me to. Later, I realised they were all criminals. I could have stopped acting for them at that point. But I didn't. The commission they paid was generous. And there was a thrill, I don't deny, to working for them.

Plus a good many fringe benefits. They were difficult people to say no to.

'Smith's consortium was powerful, with interests and associates around the world. But they were also invisible. And they wanted to stay that way. They had money to invest. Lots of it. More than they could handle. Which is where I came in. I made their money work for them—discreetly.

'I also laundered it, of course. The profits they made through me left no trail that could be followed to their doors. But I don't have to involve myself much in that kind of activity any more. After a certain point, which we passed long ago, the process becomes self-replicating. The system takes over. And it's a good system. Foolproof. I should know. I designed it.

'The crimes these people made their lavish livings out of were as vile as you can imagine. They wore smart suits. They spoke softly. But that was merely the side they chose to show me. I persuaded myself I deserved the considerable rewards that working for them brought me. I set up my own business and became wealthy in my own right. I maintained a notional presence in conventional banking, but it was only cover for my activities on behalf of the consortium. I was *their* banker exclusively. I loved my work.

'I don't any more. I haven't for many years. I still act for them, of course. It's not the sort of job you can resign from. But I would if could. Like a shot. What it boils down to is this. They decided that I knew too many of their secrets. I was their one potential weakness—an unacceptable risk, but also indispensable. They needed a way to guarantee my loyalty absolutely. And they found such a way: the theft of my youngest child. To ensure the safety of my other two children, and in return for evidence of Tamsin's continued well-being, I would serve them unquestioningly. And so I did. Ironically, Miranda's death, which formed no part of their plan, rendered it even more effective. I only had Jeremy left then to fear for. And my fear was all the greater as a result. Carrying that secret dread around with me destroyed my marriage. But what could I do? Tamsin's life would have been forfeit—as well as Jeremy's—if I'd told anyone the truth.

'The flaw in any plan, of course, is the unpredictability of events. Griffin saw what happened and followed the van. He had to be disposed of. But then someone else had to be found to account for the car you saw driving past the pub. And Miranda's death raised the stakes. The planned abduction became a callous murder. Worse, it was an unsolved murder, which meant it didn't fade from the public mind. So then I was required to hire Wisby to give the impression that I was doing everything in my power to crack the case. And eventually it was decided that someone had to be found to admit he'd killed both girls. Step forward Brian Radd. As a sex offender, he needed the kind of protection in prison only someone like Smith could arrange for him. In return he was willing to confess to anything.

'Then there was Tamsin herself—Cherie, Chantelle—growing to rebellious adulthood. And Sally, always looking for the girl she believed was still alive—and finding her, by chance, in the pages of a magazine. They killed Sally, dressing it up to look like suicide. The man you know as Walsh was good at that kind of thing. Cherie gave Walsh the slip, though, became Chantelle and eventually, last year, contacted Jeremy. Well, you know about that. Stirring up all the secrets. And someone must have tipped off the consortium about Sharp's intention to question Radd. Taking him out was an overdue precaution on their part. But it didn't work, did it? In the end, there were too many hatches to batten down. Jeremy's death has made them doubt my reliability. I just don't have enough to lose any more. But I'm untouchable. I've wrapped up their investments so tightly they know they can't unravel them without me.

'I'm glad to be paying them back in some small measure for the hell they've forced me to live through these past twenty-three years. Recently I've discovered that it was even worse than I thought. I never doubted that Marilyn was a gold-digger. I was happy to overlook that for the fun she brought back into my life. But now I realise she was one of them all along, steered into my path after Jane and I split up. Her possession of the Junius letters proves that. She was there when they grabbed Griffin, took the books from his car and hid them. Why? As ammunition to use against the consortium if the need ever arose. That would be my guess. When Jeremy started pressurising her, she panicked and tried to get rid of them. But she kept the flyleaves. That was a big mistake. I found them, you see.

'I spoke to Tamsin on the telephone earlier today. Chantelle, I should say. But she'll always be Tamsin to me. She sounded desperate. Well, she must have been, mustn't she, to phone me, of all people? We agreed to meet tomorrow morning. I agreed to tell her the truth about her life.

'I've had Sharp on to me as well. He hasn't worked everything out yet, but he's getting close. I fixed his release on bail, just to show Smith and his friends that they couldn't always have things their own way. I didn't tell Sharp that, of course. Nor did I disabuse him of the notion he seems to have got into his head that you've been nobbled.

'Tomorrow promises to be a busy day. The burial of a son. The resurrection of a daughter. And then . . . the sky falls in. That's what it would mean, Umber. If Tamsin returns to life, twenty-three years' worth of lies collapses around her. Then Smith would need a firebreak between the consortium and me. To create it, he'd have to kill me. And Tamsin too. Plus you, of course. I mention that in case you need an incentive to do what I'm going to ask you to do. It truly is a matter of life and death.

'I want you to meet Tamsin tomorrow morning and tell her what's happened. I want you to persuade her to turn her back on all this. I want you to take her away. I have a letter for you to deliver to a man called Ives. He has an office in Zürich. Ives has access to funds held on my behalf and can arrange new identities for both of you. With his help, you can disappear. It's an escape route I devised for my own use a long time ago. But now I realise that escape is simply not possible for me. The consortium would never stop looking for me, because they couldn't afford to. In the end, they'd hunt me down.

'They'll decide, however reluctantly, to let you and Tamsin go, because they'll need to lie low. They'll have their money, after all. I've seen to that. Sharp's continued probing will force Smith to be careful, and the suspicion that I've passed the missing flyleaves on to you will prompt Marilyn to urge caution. My guess is that they'll arrange for the case against Sharp to be dropped. Maybe the case against Wisby as well.

'This is the deal, Umber. Tamsin says she'll be at Pewsey railway station when the seven twenty-four for London leaves in the morning. There'll be quite a few commuters at the station. Maybe she wants witnesses to our reunion. Maybe she doesn't trust me. I could hardly blame her if she didn't. I used to catch the first train up to London from Pewsey every weekday, you know, in those halcyon days before July the 27th, 1981. She's hardly likely to know that, of course. But I think of it a lot.

'I've booked the pair of you on a noon flight from Heathrow to Zürich. Take this envelope. The tickets are inside. It also contains the letter to Ives and the Junius flyleaves. Be sure Tamsin understands why you have to go. If I met her tomorrow, I wouldn't have the strength of mind to go through with this. This is her only hope. And she's the only child I have left.

'This is the only way out, Umber. I have a gun under my seat. When you've gone, I'll put it to my head and pull the trigger. I've got a note to leave on the dashboard. It'll make the coroner's job very easy. Smith and his friends won't have to worry about me any more. And that means they won't have to worry about Tamsin. Or you. Provided you're never heard of again.

'I don't know what Tamsin's planning in the morning. A graveside confrontation with her mother, perhaps? It mustn't happen. She trusts you. Talk her out of it. Take her in out of the storm, Umber. Do that for me. End this. Now. It's time you left. I've said enough. There's no need for you to say anything. Just take the envelope and go.'

THE 7.24 to Paddington was on time, according to the information screen. But as yet there was nothing to see beyond the illusory convergence of the silvery-grey lines of rail in the misty distance.

David Umber was there, as Oliver Hall had told him to be. He was standing on the footbridge, short of sleep and ragged of nerve. His thoughts were clear, taut, stretched thin by doubt and anxiety. He had resolved to do what Hall had beseeched him to do. But if Chantelle did not step off the London train, his resolution would count for nothing.

The escape route that Hall had mapped out for him was a flight into exile, a fresh start with a heavy price. A long time would have to pass before he could risk contacting his parents. His friends in Prague and elsewhere would be lost to him. But he would go on living. Not so Oliver Hall. The sound of the gunshot that had ended his life still echoed in Umber's memory. The sound—and the long, vast silence of the forest that had engulfed it.

He tensed. There was the train, materialising in the distance as a dark, growing shape. He picked up his bag and headed for the steps leading down to the platform. By the time he reached it, the waiting passengers were edging forward. Umber threaded his way among them.

Then the carriages were rolling past, slowing as they went. Umber shrank back, scanning the windows for a glimpse of Chantelle. He heard himself muttering 'Please, God, let her be aboard.'

The train came to a halt. The doors opened. Looking towards the front of the train, Umber saw no one get off except the guard. He turned to look the other way. And there she was. He stepped out of her line of sight, into the gateway next to the station building, resisting the urge to run towards her for fear she would take fright and jump back on the train. He could see her gazing nervously past him along the platform, her grip on the rucksack hoisted on her shoulder visibly tightening. She was braced for a first sight of her father.

The last of the train doors slammed shut. The guard blew his whistle. Chantelle glanced over her shoulder to check there was no one waiting at the end of the platform behind her. The train began to move. She glanced back. And Umber stepped into view.

She gaped at him, open-mouthed and wordless, as the train accelerated past them, the draught blowing her hair across her face.

'Shadow Man,' was all Chantelle could find to say in the end.

'Your father isn't coming, Chantelle.' Umber stepped cautiously towards her. 'He sent me.'

'You didn't come back to the car. I thought I'd lost you.'

'So did I.'

'But you're all right?'

'I'm fine.'

'Where's my father?'

'Come and sit down.' He pointed to a bench a little way along the platform behind him. 'There's a lot I have to tell you.'

THE NEXT TRAIN to London was due in an hour. Until then they sat on a bench and Umber told Chantelle all that had happened to him since their parting in Jersey. She wept, shedding tears for a man she could not remember: her father, who had ruined her life but was offering her another to take its place. She was weeping for her mother who, though still alive, was as good as dead to her. She was weeping for the unfairness of it all.

'I was giving in to all kinds of fantasies on the way here,' Chantelle said when he had finished. 'My father turning out to be a nice guy despite everything. Taking me to meet my mother and making everything all right again. I saw my mother on the flight from Jersey, would you believe? But I couldn't speak to her. I could still speak to her today, though, couldn't I? At the church. She'll be there, in just a few hours, to say goodbye to Jem. And I could be there too. But if I am . . .' She thumbed the tears away from her eyes and gazed imploringly at Umber. 'What my father planned for us, will it work?'

'I think so, yes.'

'They have to bury Jem without me?'

'Yes.'

'How long before we have to go?'

Umber glanced at his watch. 'Half an hour. Till the London train gets in. It stops at Reading. We can take the coach from there to Heathrow.'

'I think I'll stretch my legs. I . . . need some space. Y'know?'

'I know.'

She rose and walked away, along the platform. Umber wondered what she was thinking. They were, in many ways, strangers to each other. That would change, though. It was bound to, in the days and weeks—and months and years—that lay ahead of them.

Claire, Alice, George Sharp: they would not understand. It was, ironically, essential they should not. It was vital that his conduct should be a mystery to them, vital that he should never explain.

'I guess that makes us even, Sal,' he murmured. 'Now we're both destined to be misjudged.'

The zip on Chantelle's rucksack was not fully closed. Through the gap Umber could see the pale vellum spines of the Juniuses that she had kept safe for him. The sudden need for certainty came over him. He tugged the zip another few inches and lifted the volumes out. They were tied together with pink ribbon. Chantelle must have bought it specially. He smiled at the thought as he placed the two volumes on the bench beside him, opened his holdall and pulled out the envelope that Oliver Hall had given him. He raised its flap and delicately removed the missing flyleaves. He opened the first volume of the Junius and matched the jagged left-hand edge of one flyleaf to the dogtooth fragments held by the book's binding. The match was perfect. He gazed in wonderment at the inscription, unable to imagine how different his life would have been if he had seen this twenty-three years ago. Both flyleaves were inscribed *Frederick L. Griffin, Strand-under-Green, March 1773*, but one bore an additional inscription, in the same hand. Junius's 'gentleman who transacts the conveyancing part of our correspondence' had been identified at last. Umber chuckled at the irony of it and glanced along the platform, eager to show Chantelle this final confirmation of what he could still scarcely believe.

She was looking in his direction, but did not seem to notice his signal. Then he realised she was looking past him, focusing on something she could see down the line. He turned to see for himself.

It was an approaching train, speeding towards them. It could not be the London train. It was far too early, and it was travelling too fast to stop.

He looked back at Chantelle. In that instant, fear gripped him. She was standing at the very edge of the platform. Her face was a mask of concentration, her eyes staring, her brain judging distance and speed.

Umber sprang up from the bench and started running towards her. The train's horn blared. The noise of it grew. Umber's feet pounded the concrete as he ran, his lungs straining. He had never run faster in his life. But the distance he had to cover was too great. 'Don't!' he shouted.

The dark blur of the locomotive swept past Umber. In the shrinking instant before Chantelle jumped into its path, he closed his eyes.

The train was gone. Noise and motion were spent. The present was a frozen moment. Umber opened his eyes and looked up.

Chantelle was crouching on the platform, her hands held over her mouth, looking straight at him. She had not jumped.

Umber stared disbelievingly at her. Then he felt his lips curling into a broad, spontaneous grin. 'Chantelle,' he said, shaking his head in relief. 'I thought you were going to jump.'

'I know.' Something between a sob and a gasp came over her. She squeezed her eyes shut. 'So did I.'

Umber moved across to her. Clasping her beneath the arms, he pulled her gently to her feet, then led her back towards the bench.

'Are you OK?' he asked banally, when they were sitting down again.

'Reckon so.' Chantelle pulled a tissue out of her pocket and dabbed her eyes. 'Now I know I can't do it. I guess I'm just not the type.' She forced a smile. 'In the split-second when I so nearly went through with it, suddenly, I wanted to live. Like never before.'

'Thank God for that.'

'Looks like you're stuck with me now.'

'That won't be a problem.'

'Don't be too sure. I can be a real pain sometimes.'

'That's all right. So can I.'

She sighed and looked down. 'What's that?' She pointed to a small piece of paper lying at their feet. 'Is it what I think it is?'

Umber nodded and picked it up. 'I was going to show it to you just now.'

'What does it say?'

'OK.' Umber cleared his throat. 'The initial inscription reads: *Frederick L. Griffin, Strand-under-Green, March 1773*. That's the same on both flyleaves. But on this one, from the first volume, it continues underneath, in the same hand, though written many years later, I assume: *For my ward, John Griffin, in memory of those two of Junius's most trusted friends and assistants who predeceased him: Mrs Solomon Dayrolles, his loyal amanuensis; and Mr Robert Umber, his valiant courier.*

'What does it mean?'

'It means that Frederick Griffin came into possession of the book in March 1773, which we know is when it was sent to Junius. Then, towards the end of his life, Griffin passed the book on to his ward, dedicating it to the memory of two people who had helped Junius in his letter-writing campaign.'

'So . . . Frederick Griffin was Junius?'

'Looks like it.'

'One of his helpers has your surname.'

'Yes.' Umber smiled. 'So he does. An ancestor, I imagine.'

'But . . . how can that be?'

How indeed? Umber truly had no answer to give.

'David?'

It was, he realised with a shock, the first time Chantelle had ever addressed him by name. Something had changed between them. He was the Shadow Man no longer.

IT IS A LITTLE after noon on the first Friday of April, 2004. Sunlight and shadow feint and dodge between the standing stones at Avebury. A short, tubby, middle-aged man dressed for hiking moves at a slow, reflective pace across the northern inner circle of the henge. He stares thoughtfully at the pair of stones known as Adam and Eve as he passes them, but does not stop.

A few miles to the east, at Marlborough Cemetery, a burial is in progress. The mourners are gathered at the graveside, heads bowed as the priest recites the prayer of committal. His words carry across this other expanse of standing stones. 'Forasmuch as it hath pleased Almighty God . . .'

Some miles to the south, a police cordon has been slung across the start of a track through Savernake Forest. Two cars with Wiltshire Constabulary badges on their doors have pulled onto the grass verge of the main road. Three emergency vehicles have drawn up along the track itself behind a parked Bentley, which men in white overalls are inspecting.

Many miles to the south, off Jersey, a telephone is ringing in the master cabin of a vast, sleek-lined private cruiser as it noses out from St Helier Harbour into the sea lane. And soon it will be answered.

But not before British Airways Flight 714 to Zürich has lifted off the runway at Heathrow Airport and soared into the sky.

It began at Avebury. But it did not end there.

ROBERT GODDARD

Home: Winchester
Former career: civil servant
Unfulfilled ambition: to be good at cricket

Robert Goddard was once quoted as saying that his mind is always churning over story ideas, to the point that even pondering the consequences of ordering a scone or a tea cake in a café can be enough to set him off. 'I do find it difficult to stop my mind browsing possible plots,' he confirms. 'It's what my brain does naturally when not focusing on anything else in particular. Ideas come from all manner of sources, some historical, some not. I try to find those that will work for a book.'

For his most recent novel, inspiration came from the atmosphere of Avebury in Wiltshire, and its ancient standing stones. 'I always wanted to use it for the start of a story, and it just seemed so right for *Sight Unseen*.' Also woven into the plot is the mystery surrounding 'Junius', an eighteenth-century commentator on political life whom Goddard had read about when he was a history undergraduate at Cambridge. 'I didn't study Junius, although I did study eighteenth-century politics. He just stuck in my mind as being someone I wanted to know more about, and eventually the idea for a book based around him came to me. To be honest, it's a puzzle to me that anyone would not want to study the past. It is, after all, the only way to explain the present.'

It's difficult to imagine the ceaselessly inventive Goddard doing anything other than write. And it is no surprise that teaching, which he tried for a time, didn't suit him. 'Teaching practice alone was enough to convince me that there had to be a less stressful way to use my interest in history.' He drifted into a clerical job with Devon County Council, which lasted nine years and had just two benefits: it introduced him to his wife, Vaunda; and it left him the mental energy to develop his writing in the evenings, which led to his first book, *Past Caring*, being published in 1987. His insatiable curiosity about the past has served him well, so far providing him with material for a remarkable total of seventeen novels.

And how does he unwind? 'Walking is ideal relaxation. Having said that, it is also ideal for dreaming up story lines and untangling plots . . .'